OXFORD ENGLISH NOVELS

General Editor: JAMES KINSLEY

The Adventures of

RODERICK RANDOM

TOBIAS SMOLLETT

The Adventures of
RODERICK RANDOM

Edited with an Introduction by
PAUL-GABRIEL BOUCÉ

Oxford New York Toronto Melbourne
OXFORD UNIVERSITY PRESS
1979

Oxford University Press, Walton Street, Oxford OX2 6DP

OXFORD LONDON GLASGOW
NEW YORK TORONTO MELBOURNE WELLINGTON
KUALA LUMPUR SINGAPORE JAKARTA HONG KONG TOKYO
DELHI BOMBAY CALCUTTA MADRAS KARACHI
NAIROBI DAR ES SALAAM CAPE TOWN

Introduction, Notes, Bibliography, and Chronology
© *Oxford University Press 1979*

British Library Cataloguing in Publication Data
Smollett, Tobias
    [Roderick Random]. The adventures of Roderick
Random.—(Oxford English novels).
I. Title   II. Adventures of Roderick Random
III. Boucé, Paul-Gabriel   IV. Series
823'.6   PR3694.R6   78-41108

ISBN 0-19-255370-4

*Printed in Great Britain by
Western Printing Services Ltd, Bristol*

CONTENTS

ACKNOWLEDGEMENTS   xvii

INTRODUCTION   xix

NOTE ON THE TEXT   xxxvi

SELECT BIBLIOGRAPHY   xxxvii

A CHRONOLOGY OF TOBIAS GEORGE SMOLLETT   xli

Preface   xliii

Apologue   xlvii

I. *Of my birth and parentage*   I

II. *I grow up—am hated by my relations—sent to school—neglected by my grandfather—maltreated by my master—seasoned to adversity —form cabals against the pedant—debarred access to my grandfather—hunted by his heir—demolish the teeth of his tutor*   4

III. *My mother's brother arrives—relieves me—a description of him— goes along with me to the house of my grandfather—is encountered by his dogs—defeats them after a bloody engagement—is admitted to the old gentleman—a dialogue between them*   8

IV. *My grandfather makes his will—our second visit—he dies—his will is read in presence of all his living descendants—the disappointment of my female cousins—my uncle's behaviour*   12

V. *The schoolmaster uses me barbarously—I form a project of revenge, in which I am assisted by my uncle—I leave the village—am settled at the university by his generosity*   15

VI. *I make great progress in my studies—am caressed by every body— my female cousins take notice of me—I reject their invitation— they are incensed and conspire against me—I am left destitute by a misfortune that befals my uncle—Gawky's treachery—my revenge*   19

VII. *I am entertained by Mr. Crab—a description of him—I acquire the art of surgery—consult Crab's disposition—become necessary to him—an accident happens—he advises me to launch out into the world—assists me with money—I set out for London*   25

Contents

VIII. *I arrive at Newcastle—meet with my old school-fellow Strap— we determine to walk in company to London—set out on our journey—put up at a solitary ale-house—are disturbed by a strange adventure in the night* 31

IX. *We proceed on our journey—are overtaken by a highwayman who fires at Strap, is prevented from shooting me by a company of horsemen, who ride in pursuit of him—Strap is put to bed at an inn—Adventures at that inn* 37

X. *The highwayman is taken—we are detained as evidences against him —proceed to the next village—he escapes—we arrive at another inn, where we go to bed—in the night we are awaked by a dreadful adventure—next night we lodge at the house of a school-master— our treatment there* 42

XI. *We descry the waggon—get into it—arrive at an inn—our fellow- travellers described—a mistake is committed by Strap, which pro- duces strange things* 47

XII. *Captain Weazel challenges Strap, who declines the combat—an affair between the captain and me—the usurer is fain to give miss Jenny five guineas for a release—we are in danger of losing a meal —the behaviour of Weazel, Jenny, and Joey on that occasion—an account of Captain Weazel and his lady—the captain's courage tried—Isaac's mirth at the captain's expence* 53

XIII. *Strap and I are terrified by an apparition—Strap's conjec- ture—the mystery explained by Joey, we arrive at London—our dress and appearance described—we are insulted in the street—an adventure in the ale-house—we are imposed upon by a waggish footman—set to rights by a tobacconist—take lodgings—dive for a dinner—an accident at our ordinary* 60

XIV. *We visit Strap's friend—a description of him—his advice—we go to Mr. Cringer's house—are denied admittance—an accident befals Strap—his behaviour thereupon—an extraordinary adven- ture occurs, in the course of which I lose all my money* 66

XV. *Strap moralizes—presents his purse to me—we inform our landlord of my misfortune, who unravels the mystery—I present myself to Cringer—he recommends and turns me over to Mr. Staytape—I become acquainted with a fellow dependant, who explains the characters of Cringer and Staytape—and informs me of the method to be pursued at the Navy-Office, and Surgeon's-hall—Strap is employed* 72

Contents

XVI. *My new acquaintance breaks an appointment—I proceed by myself to the Navy-Office—address myself to a person there, who assists me with his advice—I write to the board—they grant me a letter to the Surgeons at the hall—I am informed of the beau's name and character—I find him—he makes me his confident in an amour—desires me to pawn my linen, for his occasions—I recover what I lent him—some curious observations of Strap on that occasion—his vanity*   77

XVII. *I go to Surgeon's hall, where I meet with Mr. Jackson—I am examined—a fierce dispute arises between two of the examiners—Jackson disguises himself to attract respect—is detected—in hazard of being sent to Bridewell—he treats us at a tavern—carries us to a night-house, a troublesome adventure there—we are committed to the Round-house—carried before a justice—his behaviour*   85

XVIII. *I carry my qualifications to the Navy-Office—the nature of it—the behaviour of the s—t—y——Strap's concern for my absence—a battle between him and a blacksmith—the troublesome consequences of it—his harrangue to me—his friend the school-master recommends me to a French apothecary, who entertains me as a journeyman*   92

XIX. *The characters of Mr. Lavement, his wife and daughter—some anecdotes of the family—the mother and daughter rivals—I am guilty of a mistake that gives me present satisfaction, but is attended with troublesome consequences*   98

XX. *I am assaulted and dangerously wounded—I suspect Odonnel, and am confirmed in my opinion—I concert a scheme of revenge, and put it in execution—Odonnel robs his own servant, and disappears—I make my addresses to a lady, and am miraculously delivered from her snare*   104

XXI. *Squire Gawky comes to lodge with my master—is involved in a troublesome affair, out of which he is extricated by me—he marries my master's daughter—they conspire against me—I am found guilty of theft—discharged—deserted by my friends—I hire a room in St. Giles's where, by accident, I find the lady to whom I made my addresses, in a miserable condition——I relieve her*   109

XXII. *The history of Miss Williams*   117

XXIII. *She is interrupted by a bailif, who arrests, and carries her to the Marshalsea—I accompany her—bring witnesses to prove she is not the same person named in the writ—the bailif is fain to give her a present, and discharge her—we shift our lodging—she*

*resumes her story and ends it—my reflections thereupon—she
makes me acquainted with the progress of a common woman of the
town—resolves to quit that way of life*   127

XXIV. *I am reduced to great misery—assaulted on Tower-hill by a
press-gang, who put me on board a tender—my usage there—my
arrival on board of the Thunder man of war, where I am put in
irons, and afterwards released by the good offices of Mr. Thomson,
who recommends me as assistant to the surgeon—he relates his own
story, and makes me acquainted with the characters of the captain,
surgeon, and first mate*   138

XXV. *The behaviour of Mr. Morgan—his pride, displeasure and
generosity—the œconomy of our mess described—Thomson's further friendship—the nature of my duty explained——the situation
of the sick*   145

XXVI. *A disagreeable accident happens to me in the discharge of my
office—Morgan's nose is offended—a dialogue between him and the
ship's steward—upon examination, I find more causes of complaint
than one—my hair is cut off—Morgan's cookery—The manner of
sleeping on board——I am waked in the night by a dreadful noise*   150

XXVII. *I acquire the friendship of the surgeon, who procures a warrant
for me, and makes me a present of cloaths—a battle between a midshipman and me—the surgeon leaves the ship—the captain comes
on board with another surgeon—a dialogue between the captain and
Morgan—the sick are ordered to be brought upon the quarter-deck
and examined—the consequences of that order—a madman accuses
Morgan, and is set at liberty by command of the captain, whom he
instantly attacks and pummels without mercy*   154

XXVIII. *The captain enraged, threatens to put the madman to death
with his own hand—is diverted from that resolution by the arguments and persuasion of the first lieutenant and surgeon—we set
sail for St. Helens, join the fleet under the command of Sir
C—n—r O—le, and proceed for the West-Indies—are overtaken
by a terrible tempest—my friend Jack Rattlin has his leg broke by a
fall from the main-yard—the behaviour of doctor Mackshane—
Jack opposes the amputation of his limb, in which he is seconded by
Morgan and me, who undertake the cure, and perform it successfully*   161

XXIX. *Mackshane's malice—I am taken up and imprisoned for a spy—
Morgan meets with the same fate—Thomson is tampered with to
turn evidence against us——disdains the proposal, and is mal-*

Contents

treated for his integrity—Morgan is released to assist the surgeon
during an engagement with some French ships of war—I remain
fettered on the poop, exposed to the enemy's shot, and grow
delirious with fear—am comforted after the battle by Morgan, who
speaks freely of the captain; is over-heard by the centinel, who
informs against him, and again imprisoned——Thomson grows
desperate, and nothwithstanding the remonstrances of Morgan and
me, goes over-board in the night   165

XXX. We lament over the fate of our companion—the captain offers
his liberty, which he refuses to accept—we are brought before him
and examined—Morgan is sent back to custody, whither also I am
remanded after a curious trial   170

XXXI. I discover a subornation against me, by means of a quarrel
between two of the evidences; in consequence of which, I am set at
liberty, and prevail upon Morgan to accept of his freedom on the
same terms—Mackshane's malice—we arrive at Jamaica, from
whence in a short time we beat up to Hispaniola in conjunction
with the West-Indian squadron—we take in water, sail again, and
arrive at Carthagena—reflections on our conduct there   177

XXXII. Our land forces being disembarked, erect a faschine battery—
our ship is ordered with four more, to batter the fort of Bocca
Chica—Mackshane's cowardice—the chaplain's phrenzy—honest
Rattlin loses one hand—his heroism, and reflections on the
battle—Crampley's behaviour to me during the heat of the fight   180

XXXIII. A breach being made in the walls, our soldiers give the assault,
take the place without opposition—our sailors at the same time
become masters of all the other strengths near Bocca Chica, and
take possession of the harbour—the good consequences of this
success—we move nearer the town—find two forts deserted, and
the channel blocked up with sunk vessels; which however, we find
means to clear—land our soldiers at La Quinta—repulse a body of
militia—attack the castle of St. Lazar, and are forced to retreat
with great loss—the remains of our army are re-embarked—an
effort of the admiral to take the town—the œconomy of our
expedition described   184

XXXIV. An epidemic fever rages among us—we abandon our conquests
—I am seized with the distemper; write a petition to the captain,
which is rejected—I am in danger of suffocation through the malice
of Crampley; and relieved by a serjeant—my fever encreases—
the chaplain wants to confess me—I obtain a favourable crisis—
Morgan's affection for me proved—the behaviour of Mackshane

Contents

and Crampley towards me—Captain Oakhum is removed into
another ship with his beloved doctor—our new captain described—
an adventure of Morgan   189

XXXV. *Captain Whiffle sends for me—his situation described—his surgeon arrives, prescribes for him, and puts him to bed—a bed is put
up for Mr. Simper contiguous to the state-room, which, with other
parts of the captain's behaviour, gives the ship's company a very
unfavourable idea of their commander—I am detained in the West-
Indies, by the admiral, and go on board the Lizard sloop of war, in
quality of surgeon's mate, where I make myself known to the surgeon, who treats me very kindly—I go on shore, sell my ticket,
purchase necessaries, and at my return on board, am surprized at
the sight of Crampley, who is appointed lieutenant of the sloop—
we sail on a cruize—take a prize, in which I arrive at port
Morant, under the command of my mess-mate, with whom I live in
great harmony*   197

XXXVI. *A strange adventure—in consequence of which I am extremely
happy—Crampley does me ill offices with the captain: but his
malice is defeated by the good-nature and friendship of the surgeon
—we return to Port Royal—our captain gets the command of a
larger ship, and is succeeded by an old man—Brayl is provided
for—we receive orders to sail for England*   201

XXXVII. *We depart for Europe—a misunderstanding arises between
the captain and surgeon, through the scandalous aspersions of
Crampley—the captain dies—Crampley tyrannizes over the surgeon, who falls a victim to his cruelty—I am also ill used—the
ship strikes—the behaviour of Crampley and the seamen on that
occasion—I get on shore, challenge the captain to single combat—
am treacherously knocked down, wounded and robbed*   207

XXXVIII. *I get up, and crawl into a barn, where I am in danger of
perishing thro' the fear of the country people—their inhumanity—
I am succoured by a reputed witch—her story—her advice—she
recommends me as a valet to a single lady, whose character she
explains*   211

XXXIX. *My reception by that lady—I become enamoured of Narcissa
—recount the particulars of my last misfortune—acquire the good
opinion of my mistress—an account of the young 'Squire—I am
made acquainted with more particulars of Narcissa's situation
—conceive a mortal hatred against Sir Timothy—I examine my
lady's library and performances—her extravagant behaviour*   217

Contents

XL. *She is surprized at my learning—communicates her performances to me—I impart some of mine to her—am mortified at her faint praise—Narcissa approves of my production—I gain an involuntary conquest over the cook-wench and dairy-maid—their mutual resentment and insinuations—the jealousy of their lovers* 223

XLI. *Narcissa being in danger from the brutality of Sir Timothy, is rescued by me, who revenge myself on my rival—I declare my passion, and retreat to the sea-side—I am surrounded by smugglers, and carried to Buloign—I find my uncle lieutenant Bowling, in great distress, and relieve him—our conversation* 228

XLII. *He takes his passage in a Cutter for Deal—we are accosted by a Priest, who proves to be a Scottishman—his professions of friendship—he is affronted by the lieutenant, who afterwards appeases him by submission—my uncle embarks—I am introduced by the priest to a capuchin, in whose company I set out for Paris—the character of my fellow-traveller—an adventure on the road—I am shocked at his behaviour* 236

XLIII. *We lodge at a house near Amiens, where I am robbed by the capuchin, who escapes while I am asleep—I go to Noyons in search of him, but without success—I make my condition known to several people, but find no relief—I grow desperate—join a company of soldiers—inlist in the regiment of Picardy—we are ordered into Germany—I find the fatigues of the march almost intolerable—quarrel with my comerade, in a dispute upon politicks—he challenges me into the field, wounds and disarms me* 242

XLIV. *The Gascon does not use his victory with all the moderation that might have been expected—In order to be revenged I learn the science of Defence—we join Marechal Duc de Noailles—are engaged with the allies at Dettingen, and put to flight—the behaviour of the French soldiers on that occasion—I industriously seek another combat with the old Gascon, and vanquish him in my turn—our regiment is put into winter-quarters at Rheims, where I find my friend Strap—our recognition—he supplies me with money, and procures my discharge—we take a trip to Paris; from whence we set out for London by the way of Flanders, where we safely arrive* 247

XLV. *I enquire about my uncle, and understand he has gone to sea—take lodgings at Charing-cross—go to the Play, where I meet with an adventure—I go to an ordinary; the guests described—become acquainted with Medlar and doctor Wagtail* 257

Contents

XLVI. *Wagtail introduces me to a set of fine gentlemen, with whom I spend the evening at a tavern—our conversation—the characters of my new companions——the doctor is roasted—the issue of our debauch*   269

XLVII. *Strap communicates to me a conquest he had made on a chandler's widow—finds himself miserably mistaken—I go to the opera —admire Melinda—am cautioned by Banter—go to the assembly at Hampstead—dance with that young lady—receive an insolent message from Bragwell, whose mettle is soon cooled—am in favour with my mistress, whom I visit next day; and am bubbled out of eighteen guineas at cards—Strap triumphs at my success, but is astonished at my expence—Banter comes to my lodging, is very sarcastic at my expence, and borrows five guineas from me, as a proof of his friendship*   278

XLVIII. *We repair to the coffee-house, where we overhear a curious dispute between Wagtail and Medlar, which is referred to our decision—the doctor gives us an account of his experiment—Medlar is roasted by Banter at the ordinary—the old gentleman's advice to me*   286

XLIX. *I receive a challenge—the consequences of it—the quarrel being made up, I am put in arrest, by the care and affection of Strap— but immediately released upon explaining my affair—the behaviour of Mr. Oregan and his two friends—I visit Melinda, whom I divert with an account of the duel—I propose marriage—she refers the matter to her mother, of whom I make a solemn demand of her daughter—the old lady's behaviour—I am discarded, resent their disdain*   290

L. *I long to be revenged on Melinda—apply to Banter for his assistance —he contrives a scheme for that purpose, which is put in execution with great success—I make an attempt on the heart of Miss Gripewell, but am disappointed—I grow melancholy at my disappointment, and have recourse to the bottle—receive a billet doux—am ravished with the contents—find myself involved in an intrigue, which I imagined would make my fortune—am confounded at my mistake, which banishes all thoughts of matrimony*   297

LI. *I cultivate an acquaintance with two noblemen—am introduced to Earl Strutwell—his kind promise and invitation—the behaviour of his porter and lacquey—he receives me with an appearance of uncommon affection—undertakes to speak in my behalf to the minister—informs me of his success, and wishes me joy—introduces a conversation about Petronius Arbiter—falls in love with my*

Contents

watch, which I press upon him—I make a present of a diamond
ring to Lord Stradle—impart my good fortune to Strap, and
Banter, who disabuses me, to my utter mortification   306

LII. I attempt to recover my watch and jewel, but to no purpose—
resolve to revenge myself on Strutwell by my importunity—am
reduced to my last guinea—obliged to inform Strap of my necessity,
who is almost distracted with the news—but nevertheless obliged to
pawn my best sword for present subsistence—that small supply being
near exhausted, I am almost stupified with my misfortunes—go to
the gaming table, by the advice of Banter, and come off with unexpected success—Strap's extacy—Mrs. Gawkey waits upon me,
professes remorse for her perfidy, and implores my assistance—I do
myself a piece of justice by her means, and afterwards reconcile her
to her father   313

LIII. I purchase new cloaths—reprimand Strutwell and Straddle—
Banter proposes another matrimonial scheme—I accept of his
terms—set out for Bath in a stage-coach, with the young lady and
her mother—the behaviour of an officer and lawyer, our fellow
travellers, described—a smart dialogue between my mistress and
the captain   321

LIV. Day breaking, I have the pleasure of viewing the person of miss
Snapper, whom I had not seen before—the soldier is witty upon me
—is offended, talks much of his valour—is reprimanded by a grave
gentlewoman—we are alarmed with the cry of highwaymen—I get
out of the coach, and stand on my defence—they ride off without
having attacked us—I pursue them—one of them is thrown from
his horse and taken—I return to the coach—am complimented by
Miss Snapper—the captain's behaviour on this occasion—the
prude reproaches me in a soliloquy—I upbraid her in the same
manner—the behaviour of Mrs. Snapper at breakfast, disobliges
me—the lawyer is witty upon the officer, who threatens him   326

LV. I resolve to ingratiate myself with the mother, and am favoured by
accident—the precise lady finds her husband, and quits the coach—
the captain is disappointed of his dinner—we arrive at Bath—I
accompany Miss Snapper to the Long-Room, where she is attacked
by beau N—h, and turns the laugh against him—I make love to
her and receive a check—I squire her to an assembly, where I am
blest with a sight of my dear Narcissa, which discomposes me so
much, that Miss Snapper, observing my disorder, is at pains to
discover the cause—is picqued at the occasion, and in our way
home, pays me a sarcastic compliment—I am met by Miss

Contents

Williams, who is maid and confidante of Narcissa—she acquaints
me with her lady's regard for me while under the disguise of a servant, and describes the transports of Narcissa on seeing me at the
assembly in the character of a gentleman—I am surprized with an
account of her aunt's marriage, and make an appointment to meet
Miss Williams next day   333

LVI. I become acquainted with Narcissa's brother, who invites me to his
house—where I am introduced to that adorable creature—after
dinner, the Squire retires to take his nap—Freeman guessing the
situation of my thoughts, withdraws likewise on pretence of
business—I declare my passion for Narcissa—am well received—
charmed with her conversation—the Squire detains us to supper—I
elude his design by a stratagem, and get home sober   341

LVII. Miss Williams informs me of Narcissa's approbation of my flame
—I appease the Squire—write to my mistress, am blessed with an
answer—beg leave of her brother to dance with her at a ball; obtain
his consent and her's—enjoy a private conversation with her—am
perplexed with reflections—have the honour of appearing her
partner at the ball—we are complimented by a certain nobleman—
he discovers some symptoms of passion for Narcissa—I am stung
with jealousy—Narcissa alarmed, retires—I observe Melinda in
the company—the Squire is captivated by her beauty   349

LVIII. Tortured with jealousy, I go home and abuse Strap——receive a
message from Narcissa, in consequence of which I hasten to her
apartment, where her endearing assurances banish all my doubts
and apprehensions—in my retreat I discover somebody in the dark,
whom, suspecting to be a spy, I resolve to kill: but to my great surprize, am convinced of his being no other than Strap—Melinda
slanders me—I become acquainted with Lord Quiverwit, who
endeavours to sound me with regard to Narcissa—the Squire is
introduced to his lordship, and grows cold towards me——I learn
from my confidante, that this nobleman professes honourable love
to my mistress, who continues faithful to me, nothwithstanding the
scandalous report she has heard to my prejudice—I am mortified
with an assurance that her whole fortune depends upon the pleasure
of her brother—Mr. Freeman condoles me on the decline of my
character, which I vindicate so much to his satisfaction, that he
undertakes to combat fame in my behalf   356

LIX. I receive an extraordinary message at the door of the Long Room,
which I however enter, and affront the Squire, who threatens to
take the law of me—I rebuke Melinda for her malice—she weeps

Contents

with vexation—Lord Quiverwit is severe upon me—I retort his
sarcasm—am received with the utmost tenderness by Narcissa,
who desires to hear the story of my life—we vow eternal constancy to one another—I retire—am waked by a messenger, who
brings a challenge from Quiverwit, whom I meet, engage, and
vanquish   361

LX. I am visited by Freeman, with whom I appear in publick, and am
caressed—I am sent for by Lord Quiverwit, whose presence I quit
in a passion—Narcissa is carried off by her brother—I intend to
pursue him, and am dissuaded by my friend—I engage in play, and
lose all my money—set out for London—try my fortune at the
gaming-table, without success—receive a letter from Narcissa—
bilk my taylor   366

LXI. I am arrested—carried to the Marshalsea—find my old acquaintance beau Jackson in that jail—he informs me of his adventures—
Strap arrives, and with difficulty is comforted—Jackson introduces
me to a poet—I admire his conversation and capacity—am deeply
affected with my misfortune—Strap hires himself as a journeyman-
barber   372

LXII. I read Melopoyn's tragedy, and conceive a vast opinion of his
genius—he recounts his adventures   378

LXIII. The continuation and conclusion of Mr. Melopyn's story   386

LXIV. I am seized with a deep melancholy, and become a sloven—I am
relieved by my uncle—he prevails upon me to engage with his
owners, as surgeon of the ship which he commands—he makes me a
considerable present—entertains Strap as his steward—I take
leave of my friends, and go on board—the ship arrives at the
Downs   396

LXV. I set out for Sussex—consult Mrs. Sagely—atchieve an interview
with Narcissa—return to the ship—we get clear of the channel—I
learn our destination—we are chaced by a large ship—the company
are dismayed, and encouraged by the captain's speech—our pursuer happens to be an English man of war—we arrive on the coast
of New Guinea, purchase 400 negroes, sail for Paraguay, get safe
into the river of Plate and sell our cargo to great advantage   403

LXVI. I am invited to the Villa of a Spanish Don, where we meet with
an English gentleman, and make a very interesting discovery—we
leave Buenos Ayres, and arrive at Jamaica   410

Contents

LXVII. *I visit my old friend Thomson—we set sail for Europe, meet with an odd adventure—arrive in England—I ride across the country from Portsmouth to Sussex—converse with Mrs. Sagely, who informs me of Narcissa's being in London—in consequence of this intelligence, I proceed to Canterbury—meet with my old friend Morgan—arrive at London—visit Narcissa—introduce my father to her—he is charmed with her good sense and beauty—we come to a determination of demanding her brother's consent to our marriage*   418

LXVIII. *My father makes a present to Narcissa—the letter is dispatched to her brother—I appear among my acquaintance—Banter's behaviour—the Squire refuses his consent—my uncle comes to town—approves of my choice—I am married—we meet the Squire and his lady at the play—our acquaintance is courted*   426

LXIX. *My father intends to revisit the place of his nativity—we propose to accompany him—my uncle renews his will in my favour, determines to go to sea again—we set out for Edinburgh—purchase our paternal estate—proceed to it—halt at the town where I was educated—take up my bond to Crab—the behaviour of Potion and his wife, and of my female cousins—our reception at the estate—Strap marries Miss Williams, and is settled by my father to his own satisfaction—I am more and more happy*   432

NOTES   436

ACKNOWLEDGEMENTS

It is a pleasure to acknowledge my indebtedness to all my Smollett-ian predecessors, especially that genuine friend and scholar, the late Lewis M. Knapp, to whose memory I wish to dedicate the present volume. My most grateful thanks go to Wolfson College, Cambridge, for its friendly hospitality; to the staffs of the Rare Books Room, University Library, Cambridge, and of the Sterling Library, University of London, for their unfailing and courteous help. Dr Hugh Plommer and Madame Françoise Chevassus were my learned mentors in Latin and Greek. Professors D. E. Evans, R. H. Greenwood, Cecil Price, David Thomas, and Mr Tomos Roberts of Bangor unravelled the mysteries of eighteenth-century Welsh toponymy. Mr R. J. Roberts, Keeper of Printed Books, Bodleian Library, kindly provided a photocopy of the 'Apologue'. Brigadier Peter Young, and my French colleagues Professors Michel Perrin, Georges Lamoine, and Madame Brigitte Mitchell offered valuable suggestions. Last but not least, I express my gratitude to Professor James Kinsley for his cheerful encouragements, and also for his sorely tried editorial patience.

INTRODUCTION

As the very selective bibliography which follows will amply show, much has already been written about Tobias Smollett's personality and fiction. There is little reason to believe that the renewal of interest, which originated in the United States about 1925, will cease suddenly. Smollett, a notoriously fiery-tempered Scotsman and an apt illustration of the 'perfervidum ingenium Scotorum', forever ready to blow his Caledonian top, even when he should have known better as a canny Scot naturally inclined to weigh the pros and cons before launching into action, was an angry young man of the 1740s. Although he belonged to a good family, he had no personal fortune at his disposal, and like many another enterprising Scotsman in the eighteenth century, he had to fend for himself in a world which was not precisely friendly to the droves of northerners flocking south. Samuel Johnson's sneeringly arch remark to Mr Ogilvie, a native of Scotland, on 6 July 1763, is an apt summary of the more or less patent hostility felt and expressed by many Englishmen then: 'the noblest prospect which a Scotchman ever sees, is the high road that leads him to England'! This was somewhat uncharitable, as the 'great Cham'—a literary nickname Smollett coined in a letter to John Wilkes (16 March 1759)—must have forgotten by 1763 that he himself with his pupil David Garrick had left Lichfield, Staffordshire, for London in 1737.

Smollett, after attending Glasgow University for some years without taking any degree, interrupted his apprenticeship with two well-known local surgeons, William Stirling and John Gordon, and left for London some time after June 1739. As L. M. Knapp[1] has ably demonstrated in his standard biography, young Smollett's situation should, most emphatically, not be confused with Roderick's, the eponymous hero of his first novel published in 1748. Although Smollett's ready cash must have been relatively limited, he was no 'friendless orphan', as he described poor Roderick in the Preface. Probably the most accurate assessment of the newly arrived aspiring author's situation in London, is to be found in the 'Memoirs' published by his friend and biographer John Moore, in the 1797 edition

[1] L. M. Knapp (see Select Bibliography), pp. 24-7. Henceforth referred to as Knapp.

of Smollett's works: 'He set out accordingly with a small sum of money and a very large assortment of letters of recommendation: whether his relations intended to compensate for the scantiness of the one by their profusion in the other, is uncertain; but he has been often heard to declare, that their liberality in the last article was prodigious.' (I, cxv). A caveat to readers of Smollett's *Roderick Random* still tempted to stumble into the ever-gaping trap of facile bio-criticism is therefore not out of order here. As I have tried to show in my *Novels of Tobias Smollett* (1976), nothing has been more damaging to Smollett's literary reputation than the obstinately perverse assimilation of his person with his fictional personae, especially his first hero Roderick Random, and with the cantankerous Welsh squire Matt Bramble, a type of *bourru bienfaisant*, or in other words, a misanthrope with a heart of gold, doing good by stealth, in his last, and probably most successful novel, *The Expedition of Humphry Clinker* (1771). Critics would loop the fictional loop all too easily, from the boisterous, if not roisterous young blade 'on the make' in London, to the kindly, if choleric grumbling squire, who by the end of the epistolary novel is seen to have mellowed into a decent paternal and avuncular figure. Roderick is no more Smollett's autobiographical portrait than Matt Bramble: both are fictive creations of his literary talent, endowed with an entirely autonomous life of their own. This tendency to view Smollett's personality—human and literary—in the light of his fictional characters may be called 'inverted autobiography'.[1]

This is not to say, of course, that there are no links between Smollett's actual 'lived' experiences and his first novel *Roderick Random*, which is obviously a young man's novel, still fresh from his fast-moving personal experiences, such as his departure from Scotland in 1739; his startled discovery of the fascinating kaleidoscope of glittering life in the metropolis; the abortive struggles of a dour young author to have his unfortunate tragedy *The Regicide* staged in London; the unbelievably harsh, even nightmarish world of the Navy on board the *Chichester* during the ill-fated and extravagantly costly (both in good guineas, but even more so in callously cheap human lives) expedition to Cartagena in the West Indies (1740–1); his quick wooing and winning of a Jamaican beauty and heiress, Anne Lassells; his return to England and his efforts to set up as a

[1] See my *Novels of Tobias Smollett*, pp. 40–67, 'Autobiography and the Novels'.

surgeon in London. Meanwhile he maintained a fervent interest in literature, as is shown by his lyric—which appeared in slightly altered form in *Roderick Random*—'A New Song' (1745), his 'Tears of Scotland'—a poem composed after the Jacobites were defeated at Culloden on 16 April 1746, throbbing with sorrow and tightly controlled patriotic fervour for his 'hapless Caledonia'—and finally by his vitriolic Popean verse satires, *Advice* (1746) and its companion poem, *Reproof* (1747). Although little or nothing is known about Smollett's life from his return to England about February 1742 to mid-1744, it is in no way exaggerated to advance that young Smollett's life between his departure from Glasgow in 1739 to the publication of his first novel in January 1748 had been exceptionally fast-paced and fruitful in character-moulding experiences. By 1747 or 1748, he had even sired a daughter, Elizabeth, whose untimely death in April 1763 dealt Smollett and his wife a crushing emotional blow, from which the fond father probably never quite recovered.

This rapid sketch of Smollett's manifold activities before the publication of *Roderick Random* would be incomplete without some mention again of his continued and well-nigh obsessive efforts to get *The Regicide* produced in London. Smollett, like Johnson in 1737 with his *Irene*, left Scotland with his much cherished tragedy in his pocket. Between 1739 and 1749, when at long last the poor tragic brainchild of Smollett was published by subscription, *The Regicide* became a sort of dramatic and psychological millstone round his neck. Some of the bitterness and harshness of the author's lasting resentment may be felt still glowing in the self-vindicating preface of the play, and certainly in the pathetic story of Melopoyn's disappointments and rebuffs in Chapters LXII and LXIII of *Roderick Random*. But Melopoyn should nevertheless not be viewed as the autobiographical representation of Smollett the young thwarted playwright. At best, or worst, Melopoyn is a fictive *doppelgänger*, stemming from Smollett's gnawing artistic frustration, but no factually faithful specular image.

In the span of nine years, Smollett had amassed enough factual, psychological, and ethical experience (especially as a surgeon's second mate during the Cartagena expedition) on which to draw for the rest of his writing life. It certainly stood him in good stead, particularly for the raw material of *Roderick Random* and *Peregrine Pickle* (1751). But leading a fairly adventurous life is not tantamount to becoming the author of celebrated novels of adventure. Throughout the eighteenth century, and well into the nineteenth, at a time when British power was seeking 'vi et armis' to expand its economic dominion over distant lands and seas, thousands of men led much more adventurous lives than Smollett, who after his *Wanderjahre* became perforce very much of an overworked stay-at-home, heaping upon himself incredibly heavy burdens of financially necessary translations, compilations, or literary journalism. Smollett did not revisit his native Scotland until 1753, and afterwards travelled there on two occasions only, in 1760 and in 1766. He made the Grand Tour only belatedly in 1763–5, at a time when he was morally battered and physically sick, as the all too often querulous tone of the opening letters in his *Travels through France and Italy* (1766) makes stridently clear. He had already been on the Continent some time before 1744, and in 1749.

He spent the summer of 1750 in Paris, travelled again to the Continent in the summer of 1759, but always on fairly brief visits, curtailed by the chronically low state of his finances. It was a grim irony that Smollett, the ardent patriot viscerally attached to his homeland, should have been, in a touristic way, the discoverer of Nice and the French Riviera during his frantic search for health in 1763–5, and also that he should have died in Leghorn (17 September 1771), where he had been residing for two years after leaving England in the autumn of 1768, thousands of miles away from his English and Scottish friends, amongst Italians for whom he displayed little understanding or fondness, at least in his *Travels through France and Italy*. Neither the spirit of peripatetic adventures, nor the Romantic lure of Mediterranean climes, had induced Smollett to expatriate himself. But Smelfungus, as Sterne somewhat unfairly nicknamed Smollett in *A Sentimental Journey* (1768), ran a losing unSternean race with consumptive death, reaching its eschatological close with the tranquil fortitude of a genuine adventurer who knows that the game is up. Famous dying words tend to be notoriously apocryphal. Smollett—unlike Voltaire on his deathbed in 1778, who is reported to have exclaimed as a lamp flared up, 'Les flammes! Déjà!'— according to one of his nineteenth-century biographers, Oliphant Smeaton (*Tobias Smollett*, Edinburgh, 1897) displayed no such fear, but departed for his last adventure to 'The undiscover'd country from whose bourn / No traveller returns' with the following words of stoical appeasement to his wife: 'All is well, my dear.'

.   .   .

Unlike Richardson and Fielding, whose literary reputations were already well established by 1747–8, Smollett was but another struggling tiro who had published nothing apart from one song and three poems, for whose critical reception we have to rely on his word only. Not without some understandable authorial pride, he wrote to his Scottish friend Alexander Carlyle in 1747 that *Advice* and *Reproof* had 'made some Noise here, and a Ballad set to Musick under the name of the Tears of Scotland, a Performance very well received at London, as I hope it will be in your Country which gave Rise to it'.[1] Again, the only source of information concerning the composition of his *The Adventures of Roderick Random*—to give the book its full title—is to be found in Smollett's correspondence with Carlyle, in a letter written probably in December 1747:

Since I wrote my last Letter to you, I have finished a Romance in two small Volumes, called the Adventures of Roderick Random, which will be published in a Fortnight. It is intended as a Satire on Mankind, and by the Reception it has met with in private from the best Judges here I have reason to believe it will succeed very well. As I have long ago disposed of the Copy, I know not what Method the Booksellers will follow in the Sale of it, but I believe some Hundreds will be sent to Scotland. If you shall light on it, read it with Candour, and report me and my Cause aright.[2]

The novel was duly advertised in several London newspapers, for instance the *General Evening Post* (15–17 December 1747): 'Next Month will be publish'd in two neat pocket-volumes (Price bound 6s.) The Adventures of Roderick Random ... Printed for J. Osborn in Pater-noster-row.' Another advertisement in the same newspaper appeared in the issue for 7–9 January, announcing the date of forthcoming publication as 21 January 1748. As an entry for January 1748 in the printer William Strahan's main ledger (now in the British Library) shows, 2,000 copies were issued anonymously, certainly a large order for a first novel by an unknown author, especially when compared with the 3,000 copies—also printed by Strahan, for Millar—of Fielding's first edition of *Joseph Andrews* (1742). As L. M. Knapp was the first to discover in 1932,[3] some 6,500 copies of

---

[1] Knapp, *Letters* (see Select Bibliography), p. 5. Hereafter referred to as *Letters*.

[2] Ibid., pp. 6–7.

[3] See Knapp, pp. 94–5. See also O. M. Brack and J. B. Davis's 1970 article, and A. H. Smith's invaluable London Ph.D. thesis, 1976, cited in the Select Bibliography.

Introduction

Roderick Random came off Strahan's presses from January 1748 to November 1749. A second edition with frontispieces by Hayman and Grignion was quick to follow in April 1748, then a third in January 1750, and a fourth—the last one Smollett is known to have revised himself, and to which he added the 'Apologue' included in the present volume—printed by August 1754, but postdated 1755 for the usual commercial reasons, as actual publication had been delayed until the autumn of 1754. By 1770, *Roderick Random* had reached its eighth London edition. There is no doubt that 'the success of *Roderick Random* was immediate, impressive, and prolonged'.[1]

The printed critical data concerning the book's reception are relatively scarce, and it would be pointless to reproduce here the scanty relevant material gleaned by F. W. Boege and L. M. Knapp, who have had to rely mostly on passing references and allusions in private letters. Of more interest are the young successful author's reactions, as expressed in another letter to his friend Carlyle (7 June 1748). There Smollett unashamedly basks in his recent literary fame, as his authorship was not kept secret for long in London, although as late as 1752 Lady Mary Wortley Montagu in a letter from abroad to her daughter the Countess of Bute still thought *Roderick Random* had been written by Fielding. Two main points emerge from Smollett's triumphant letter. First, with an oblique, if somewhat touchingly naïve, outburst of authorial vanity, he seeks to excuse 'several inaccuracies in the Stile' by coyly discovering to his friend 'that the whole was begun and finished in the Compass of Eight months, during which time several Intervals happened of one, two, three and four Weeks, wherein I did not set pen to paper, so that a little Incorrectness may be excused'. This is certainly a sly bid for 'puff oblique'! Secondly, Smollett expresses grave, and apparently sincere, concern at the unpleasant and unfortunate tendency to view *Roderick Random* as more or less autobiographical, with the twofold consequence that he was assimilated with his eponymous hero, and that many people, such as his old schoolmaster, John Love, thought that they were the thinly disguised models for most of his vitriolic satirical portraits. Much of the subsequent critical misinterpretation of Smollett's first novel and later fiction stems from this curiously perverse disregard of his solemn caveat:

[1] Knapp, p. 94.

Introduction

I shall take this Opportunity therefore of declaring to you, in all the sincerity of the most unreserved Friendship, that no Person living is aimed at in all the first part of the Book; that is, while the scene lies in Scotland and that (the account of the Expedition to Carthagene excepted) the *whole* is not so much a Representation of my Life as of that of many other needy Scotch Surgeons whom I have known either personaly or by Report.[1]

In a century notorious for libels and libel suits, Smollett, in spite of his lashing satirical propensities, no doubt felt he had to be careful: a resolution he did not always manage to keep up, since he was to attack most virulently Admiral Knowles in the May 1758 issue of his *Critical Review*, with the smarting result that he was heavily fined and sentenced to three months' imprisonment in the King's Bench Prison (Nov. 1760–Feb. 1761). On two separate occasions again, Smollett tried desperately to clear his book from the disastrous implications of persistent autobiographical misreading. To the fourth edition of 1755, as already stated, he felt it necessary to affix the monitory pictorial 'Apologue', whose final paragraph is noteworthy for its archly serious tone. Then, as late as 1763, in a reply to an admiring American reader's 'fan letter' he again most solemnly affirmed:

The only Similitude between the Circumstances of my own Fortune and those I have attributed to Roderick Random consists in my being born of a reputable Family in Scotland, in my being bred a Surgeon, and having served as a Surgeon's mate on board a man of war during the Expedition to Carthagene. The low Situations in which I have exhibited Roderick I never experienced in my own Person.[2]

At the age of twenty-seven, in about six months of actual work, Smollett had written a highly successful novel of about 220,000 words, a feat of literary rapidity he was to renew again in 1755–7, when, according to his biographer John Moore, he composed over 2,600 quarto pages of his *Complete History of England* (1757–8) in fourteen months. The penurious young Scot 'on the make' in the literary London of the late 1740s had undoubtedly managed to launch himself on its treacherous waters not with a whimper but a bang.

The critical appreciation of *Roderick Random* has all too often been marred by an insidious, and pernicious quasi-automatic labelling as 'realistic'. This supposes that the novelist does little but hold up a mirror to the external world, in which reality obligingly

[1] *Letters*, p. 8.   [2] *Letters*, p. 112.

reflects itself, or to use an anachronic simile, the novelist is but a photographer and his work but a photographic plate on which the external world prints itself. This presupposition rests on the wide-spread concept of literature as a form of cognitive mimesis, more or less skilfully achieved according to each writer's particular sensibility and literary talent. Mimesis also supposes, in a most un-Heraclitean way, that 'reality' is a static, amorphous 'given', while it is, in fact, a constantly shifting sensuous construct, at the mobile intersection of a writer's individual perception and of a changing external world. In other words, the novel does not passively reflect a reality that would be given once and for all, but it seeks to *discover* it, through the sensuous apprehension of writers. A typical mimetic assessment of Smollett is Thackeray's in his *English Humourists* (1853): 'He did not invent much, as I fancy, but had the keenest perceptive faculty, and described what he saw with wonderful relish and delightful broad humour.' What Thackeray, although an acutely percipient critic at times, failed to see is that fiction is but the illusion of an illusion, or in keeping with the word's etymology, 'a skilful lie'. From the preceding concept of fiction, not as a mirror but as an individual (re)discovery of a dynamic reality, it follows that each novel is stamped and hallmarked by its character of fictive *uniqueness*, although some general patterns in the private adventures, in the psychological and ethical reactions of the heroes, may be traced. Furthermore, critical attention has been focused for too long exclusively on the binary relationship of the novelist to his finished literary product, without paying due attention to the ever-present 'reader over the shoulder', a discovery that Sterne was probably the first to exploit to its dazzlingly capricious full, in that intemporally most modern of books, *Tristram Shandy*. It is true also that long before John Preston in his *The Created Self* (1970), or Wolfgang Iser in *The Implied Reader* (1974) brilliantly sought to determine the reader's role in fiction, some eighteenth-century critics had perceived the part played by the anonymous but forever active reader. In Lyttelton's *Dialogues of the Dead* (1760), in Dialogue XXVIII, actually composed by Mrs Elizabeth Montagu, the bookseller objects to Plutarch's somewhat indignant moralistic and didactic contentions: 'Our readers must be amused, flattered, soothed; such adventures must be offered to them as they would like to have a share in.'

From the foregoing considerations, the basic ambiguity of all novels of adventure may be deduced. Such fiction is ambiguous because it is ambivalent, being structurally turned both toward the external physical world as apprehended by the author's specific perception, and toward that virtual world of the archreader who demands—as the Augustan age was, after the manner of Horace, keenly aware—to be entertained *and* morally instructed. This is what Cedric Watts has most aptly called the 'Janiform novel': 'As Janus is the two-headed god, a Janiform novel is a two-faced novel: morally it seems to be centrally or importantly paradoxical or self-contradictory.'[1] There is no doubt that *Roderick Random* is very much of an unintentionally Janiform novel, in which the young author, himself both repelled and fascinated by the rampant corruption and violence of the contemporary scene, despite his careful but conventional show of scrupulous moral didacticism, actually displays nearly constant duplicity and moral paradoxicality because, more or less consciously, he relies on what Cedric Watts (p. 41) calls 'the reader's imaginative complicity', not only with corrupt characters, but also with the fascinating spectacle of evil at work either in such microcosms as the closed world of the *Thunder*, or the macrocosms of whole nations engaging in absurdly bloody wars (for instance the expedition to Cartagena and the battle of Dettingen). It is also obvious that the 'Janiformity' of *Roderick Random* is technically enhanced by Smollett's use of the pseudo-autobiographical mode. The first person narrative makes it all the easier for the reader to identify vicariously with the hero, so that his comfortable armchair passivity is deftly seduced into a gratifying temporary illusion of almost godlike energy and invulnerability. Roderick goes through enough adventures to knock flat on their backs as many real-life heroes as the proverbial cat has lives. Roderick's toughness, buttressed by patience in adversity and also by that most powerful craving for revenge which pervades the novel, his dashing gusto for life, its hard knocks, bad bruises, but also for its carnal and financial sweets, make of Smollett's first hero a true archetypal figure of the Ulysses-type.

Much of the body-and-mind-shattering violence, for which Smollett has been so often blamed as a 'coarse' or, in eighteenth-century critical parlance, 'low' author, can be explained, if not entirely condoned, by the essential 'Janiformity' of his fiction, also

[1] Cedric Watts, 'Janiform Novels', *English*, xxiv, Summer 1975, no. 119, 40–9. Quotation, p. 40.

to be detected in his later novels, especially *Peregrine Pickle* (1751), and *Ferdinand Count Fathom* (1753). A case in point is Smollett's recurrent fascination with money, and to a lesser extent, sex, which must both rank very high in the hierarchy of archcorrupters. Without stressing the obvious autobiographical undertones, it is noteworthy that Smollett from the very beginning of his career expresses his haunting and harrowing concern about money. The poet in *Advice* (1746) is battling against poverty: 'From the pale hag, O! could I once break loose; / Divorc'd, all hell should not re-tie the noose!' (ll. 4–5), while in *Reproof* (1747) he flays various usurers, capitalists, financiers, and profiteers. Probably too little attention has been paid to the epigraph, taken from Horace's *Satires*, II.v (*Et genus et virtus nisi cum re vilior alga est*—see Notes), which appeared on the title-page of *Roderick Random*. The line is spoken by Ulysses, who finds himself destitute before going back to Ithaca. He is seeking advice from the seer Tiresias on how to repair the depredations caused by the riotous living of Penelope's suitors. The seer obliges with a series of wordly-wise pragmatic tips of more than dubious morality, including the ways and means of turning into a successful will-hunter. The satirical intent, although implicit, is obvious enough, and poor Ulysses returning penniless from his adventurous wanderings is little more than the stock-figure of the *adversarius*, whose apparently innocent questions and qualms afford ample scope for Tiresias's satirical pseudo-advice, a technique Smollett used in *Advice* and *Reproof*. Ulysses-Roderick is soon made to realize that money lies at the root of all his troubles, and Tiresias-Smollett harps on the theme from the very beginning to the very end of the novel.

In the opening lines of the novel it is striking how money asserts its baneful influence at once. The harsh old judge has 'a singular aversion' for beggars, he rejects his son for marrying privately 'a poor relation', and the pregnant mother in order to know the significance of a dream concerning her future offspring 'at last consulted a Highland seer, whose favourable interpretation he [Roderick's father] would have secured beforehand by a bribe, but found him incorruptible'. Roderick's childhood and schooling is marked by the callous financial neglect with which his grandfather the judge treats him, before disappointing his expectations, as well as his more clamorous female cousins', in a testament that leaves the totality of his fortune to a favourite grandson. From then on, nearly in every chapter, money—usually the dire lack of it—will rear its ugly head, or the frantic, nearly obsessive quest for it, by means fair or foul. When Roderick, after a particularly penurious stretch in the French army, does come into some money thanks to the providential legacy his long-lost friend Strap has received (Chapter XLIV), as his store is quickly squandered away in fashionable London, he soon turns fortune-hunter (Chapter LIII) and woos the deformed Miss Snapper more for her bulging bags of guineas than for her gibbous protuberances. Even Roderick's supposedly romantic passion for the beautiful, if somewhat unreal Narcissa, is not devoid of financial connotations. A measure of his more mature and disinterested love will be his readiness to marry Narcissa, by the end of the novel, without her fortune ('Sans dot!'), which her brute of a brother unlawfully withholds from her. But in the very last lines of the novel, the reader is relieved to learn that, after a lawsuit, Roderick will 'certainly recover' his wife's fortune, a piece of intelligence confirmed in *Peregrine Pickle*, Chapter XXXVIII (see Notes).

After all these variations on the power of money, which are barely sketched here, the last three chapters of *Roderick Random* could be viewed as a grand finale of financial felicity (this being the symbolically meaningful last word of the novel). Thomson, another long-lost friend, not knowing Roderick's recent affluence due both to his trading venture (gold and slaves) and the 'cognitio' of his long-disappeared *and* rich father, is ready to help his old friend financially, while the two former messmates gloat over the fate of their old tyrannical commander, Oakhum, who is dead after having embezzled some of the *Thunder*'s prize money. Likewise, his cruel sycophant, Doctor Mackshane, is suitably punished by the retributive justice of a money-minded Providence, and now lies in prison, a destitute wretch, whom the two friends take ambiguous and furtive pleasure in relieving: 'ten pistoles', such is Roderick's delicious self-righteous generosity. Money is no longer an agent of corruption, but one of reward. Even the kindly Mrs Sagely receives a gift of thirty guineas, accompanied by the resolve of paying her an annuity to the same amount. Morgan, the friendly, if somewhat fiery-tempered Welsh surgeon's mate of the *Thunder*, is discovered by Roderick, settled in Canterbury as a well-to-do apothecary, where he 'married an apothecary's widow with whom he now enjoyed a pretty good sum of money'. By the end of the same Chapter LXVII, Roderick receives £15,000 from his father, which added to his own £3,000, make him a rich gentleman indeed, while at the beginning of the following chapter, Narcissa receives an appreciative £500 from her future father-in-law. Old friends or enemies turn up, in a predictable way, and the end of the novel could be caricatured as a sort of fictional auditing of accounts, where old debts of gratitude are paid off, but old scores of hostility or resentment are settled as well, and with a vengeance. Banter, the coffee-house wit, asks for ten guineas, gets twenty and some apparently well-meaning advice to boot, which he is perhaps sensible enough to reject. Orson Topehall, Narcissa's brother, in his boorish letter to Roderick's father, simply refuses to believe that Don Rodriguez is a man of property. On the contrary, the ever generous Lieutenant Bowling promises to give two thousand guineas to Roderick's and Narcissa's first child. Suitably enough, in Chapter LXIX, the fox-hunting heir of the old judge has squandered his estate, so that Roderick's father can buy it back, thus retrieving his paternal estate. The Potions, who had let down Roderick when he was poor, get snubbed for their (lack of) pains, as well as one of Roderick's female cousins, who had also been unkind to him formerly: her husband has already spent her fortune. One can almost hear an authorial *sotto voce* 'Serves her right too', a kind of rough retributive justice, not totally devoid of *schadenfreude*, in spite of the cosy moral righteousness, implicitly shared by the reader.

Here Smollett touches one of the archetypal mainsprings of fiction. Beyond the slightly ridiculous financial prize-giving of a typically conventional ending, where the 'goodies' are suitably rewarded, and the 'baddies' no less adequately punished, he plays ambiguously and not unskilfully on the perennial fascination of evil on the one hand, and on a firmly grounded, if banal, inner certainty that the just will eventually triumph on the other. In Smollett's own words, taken from the morally bellicose Preface of *Roderick Random*, 'modest merit struggling with every difficulty to which a friendless orphan is exposed, from his own want of experience, as well as from the selfishness, envy, malice, and base indifference of mankind' will finally prevail and be rewarded accordingly. The long-thwarted just may even indulge in the luxurious thrill of charitable forgiveness. The now bankrupt fox-hunting cousin of Roderick is promised a commission in the army by Don Rodriguez who will purchase it. Miss Williams, the former prostitute—whose woeful tale is told during an appropriate stasis in the action (Chapters XXII–XXIII)—and the already reformed companion of Narcissa, is married off to Strap, who receives £500 from the ever generous and bountiful Don Rodriguez. Once more, blasé modern critics, who find such a conventional happy ending—complete with a return to the 'good life' of the country as in all four other novels of Smollett's—ludicrous and improbable, should search beyond the stylized ethics of the coda. These same critics fail to see that such a happy ending as that of *Roderick Random*, beyond its apparent conventionality, 'represents a degree of wish fulfilment . . . [and] provides a way in which the author can thumb his nose at the spite and malice of those who hinder a young man's getting on in the world', to borrow the thoughtful analysis of David Daiches's 'Smollett Reconsidered'.[1] The author of *Roderick Random*, although this judgement will sound paradoxical, thus displays his own brand of moral optimism, by seeking to reconcile in his 'Janiform' novel the harsh world of violence with the somewhat gauche, but deeply yearned for, coexisting world of sensibility.

Nowhere is this more evident than in Smollett's treatment of sex, a notoriously difficult subject for an author with a strict Scottish Presbyterian upbringing. Samuel Johnson, in his well-known *Rambler* no. 4 of 31 March 1750, holds that the purpose of modern 'romances' is

to teach the Means of avoiding the Snares which are laid by Treachery for Innocence, without infusing any Wish for that Superiority with which the Betrayer flatters his Vanity; to give the Power of counteracting Fraud, without the Temptation to practise it; to initiate Youth by mock Encounters in the Art of necessary Defence, and to increase Prudence without impairing Virtue.

A noble finality indeed, also expressed in an equally apotropaic manner by Smollett in his 'Dedication' of *Ferdinand Count Fathom* (1753), where he declares that his purpose is to set up his evil hero 'as a beacon for the benefit of the unexperienced and unwary, who from the perusal of these memoirs, may learn to avoid the manifold snares with which they are continually surrounded in the paths of life'. But in the fictional description of sexual activities, this moralistic high-mindedness is apt to become a flimsy, soon-forgotten pretext, as for instance in John Cleland's *Memoirs of a Woman of Pleasure* (1748–9)—better known as *Fanny Hill*—or in de Sade's

[1] See Select Bibliography. Quotation from p. 118.

Justine ou les malheurs de la vertu (1791). The hypnotic fascination of sexual evil soon transforms the reader—'Hypocrite lecteur,— mon semblable,—mon frère!', as Baudelaire puts it—into a fictional accomplice and a willing voyeur. Roderick, in modern parlance, would certainly be called 'phallocratic', and a 'male chauvinist pig'. From his first ancillary amours (with Crab's servant maid in Chapter VII,) it is obvious that he is a natural adept of the 'double standard', whereby buxom wenches may be slept with in garrets in order to gratify what he calls his 'amorous complexion' (Chapter VI), while such fine ladies as his beloved Narcissa should keep chaste until their wedding night.

Roderick's strong sexual lusts lead him into various scrapes, somewhat complacently described: the night house scene in Chapter XVII, where 'nothing would serve [him] but a wench'; the furtive intercourse with Lavement's daughter, made doubly delicious by the hot spice of mistaken identity and resentment, in Chapter XIX; the grotesque tryst with the amorous old hag of seventy, Miss Withers, who belongs to the same caricatural family of senile lust as Fielding's Slipslop, in Chapter L. But the acme of hypocritical ambiguity is reached in Chapter XLII, when Roderick is travelling in Northern France with a bawdy Capuchin monk. After having dined well at a peasant's house near Abbeville, two of his comely daughters creep into the barn where they lodge for the night, and make a frank offer of their sexual services. The incident would be fairly banal, if at the time Roderick had not already met Narcissa, and fallen deeply in love with her: 'In vain did my reason suggest the respect I owed to my dear mistress Narcissa; the idea of that lovely charmer, rather increased than allayed the ferment of my spirits; and the young Paisanne had no reason to complain of my remembrances.' Instead of being shocked at his own lecherous infidelity, Roderick finds it more convenient and morally comfortable to reproach the monk with his cynical philandering. . . . But morality, under the guise of a subtly ironical retributive justice, is apparently safeguarded: the monk robs Roderick of all his cash, and thus punishes him in the following chapter. Also ambiguous is the barely controlled erotic frenzy of Roderick as he rushes into the nuptial chamber, and finds his chaste blushing Narcissa 'a feast, a thousand times more delicious than my most sanguine hope presaged!' (Chapter LXVIII). The use of gastronomic vocabulary ('feast', 'delicious') connotes the reification of Narcissa into a mere tasty morsel, an oral metaphor Smollett often uses in such circumstances. Renaldo, in Chapter LXVI of *Ferdinand Count Fathom*, also behaves like a ravenous beast: 'and like a lion rushing on his prey, approached the nuptial bed, where Serafina, surrounded by all the graces of beauty, softness, sentiment, and truth, lay trembling as a victim at the altar. . . .' Foreshadows of de Sade, Freud, D. H. Lawrence, and Henry Miller already? Hardly, but there is ample evidence that beneath the apparently straightforward, rumbustious treatment of sex in *Roderick Random*, lurks a pervasive ambiguity inherent in the 'Janiform' structure of the novel.

Roderick Random should be read neither as unadulterated reportage nor as a pontificating ethical hornbook. It remains, first and foremost, a most enjoyable and laughable book, very much an antisplenetic novel. Dr George Cheyne, Smollett's fellow-Scotsman, would have approved of it in his *English Malady* (1733), where he prescribed that 'Reading must be light, entertaining, and diverting, as well as Food.' As his father notices in Chapter LXVI, Roderick's adventures had been the most profitable school of adversity, which 'enlarged the understanding, improved the heart, steeled the constitution, and qualified a young man for all the duties and enjoyments of life, much better than any education which affluence could bestow'. But such continual adventures would soon grow monotonous, if their narration and dramatic suspense were not broken and relieved by Smollett's powerful *vis comica*. It has long been fashionable for critics to purse their thin academic lips at Smollett's supposed coarseness and indecency. In his long article 'Beef and Bouillon . . .', G. S. Rousseau quotes 'a distinguished eighteenth-century scholar'—who prefers to remain anonymous—and who writes in a private letter:

I cannot read Smollett anymore. . . . For no reason at all people are hurt and humiliated, even skinned; even those who help him to perpetrate fun. Jokes about hunchbacked people and lame matrons. Pissing for no reason at all. . . . Can you really call him a novelist of amusement? Can you honestly say there is one moment of pleasure in the whole of Smollett?[1]

Our distinguished critic must have suffered from a surfeit of William Burroughs, or he must have forgotten the anti-splenetic advice of William Stukeley, who in his treatise *Of the Spleen* (1723)

[1] See Select Bibliography, G. S. Rousseau, 1977, pp. 14–15.

held the commonsensical, but often disregarded, view that 'The wheels of life grow rusty without continual motion, and death is no other than a cessation of motion.' Matthew Bramble, somewhat like Sterne on the last page of *Tristram Shandy*, bk IV, realized by the end of *Humphry Clinker* that 'we should sometimes increase the motion of the machine, to *unclog the wheels of life*; and now and then take a plunge amidst the waves of excess, in order to case-harden the constitution'. There is no better tonic and adjuvant for promoting the vigorous circulation of the animal spirits dear to Rabelais, than a good laugh, even a horse-laugh. It is strange that the same critics, who out of fashionable hyper-intellectuality are ready to enthuse over the cinematographic gags of Mack Sennett, Buster Keaton, Laurel and Hardy, or Charlie Chaplin, should frown and raise sternly reproving eyebrows at Smollett's occasional chamber-pot humour. Would such critics answer the barbed definition given by Goldsmith in Letter XIII of *The Citizen of the World* (1762): 'a set of men called answerers of books, who take upon them to watch the republic of letters, and distribute reputation by the sheet; they somewhat resemble the eunuchs in a seraglio, who are incapable of giving pleasure themselves, and hinder those that would'?

There is in British literature a streak of earthy demotic fun from Chaucer and Dunbar to Swift, Smollett, and Sterne, which managed to survive, in a more or less clandestine way, in spite of the dictates or puritanism, or later, of Victorian prudery. Such refined critics have probably never heard of the gales of guffaws raised by the late Max Miller's *Blue Book*, or of the rough and ready humour of the Scottish comedian Billy Connolly. Yes, there *are* gags galore in *Roderick Random*, and even more so in *Peregrine Pickle*. Yes, Strap gets pissed upon in Chapter XIV, or rather receives 'the unsavoury deluge' discharged from a chamber-pot, an incident not infrequent in the less sanitation-minded London or Edinburgh of the eighteenth century. The anonymous critic quoted by G. S. Rousseau fails to remember that this urinous ordeal by proxy—Roderick escapes unscathed—is symbolic of the two raw young Scotsmen's initiation into the hellish metropolis. As Strap sums up their first eventful forty-eight hours in London: 'We have been jeered, reproached, buffeted, pissed upon, and at last stript of our money; and I suppose by and by we shall be stript of our skins' (Chapter XV), with the conclusion that 'surely the devil had set up his throne in London', an observation Strap reiterates in Chapter XVIII:

Introduction

'London is the devil's drawing room.' Although some of Smollett's comic scenes in *Roderick Random* rely perhaps a bit too heavily on what Bergson in *Le Rire* (1900) defined as 'du mécanique plaqué sur du vivant'—for instance, when in Chapter XIII Strap tumbles headlong into the ordinary with disastrous consequences, or in Chapter XXI when Gawky and Lavement in their fright of an irate Roderick trip each other downstairs—as early as this first novel there are promising signs of a more sophisticated type of comic.[1] In Chapter XVI Beau Jackson receives a dysorthographic love-letter from a common Drury Lane strumpet, which is the direct, if still awkward, forerunner of the sparkling polysemous verbal juggling displayed in the unforgettable letters of Tabitha Bramble and her maid Win Jenkins in *Humphry Clinker*.

Finally, *Roderick Random* and the rest of Smollett's fiction should be enjoyed—as Damian Grant has vigorously contended in his *Tobias Smollett: A Study in Style* (1977)—for their sheer stylistic gusto, breathtaking energy, and splendid evocative power. What could be more memorable than the savage vignettes, etched with caricatural vitriol, of the rotund and carbuncular Crab (Chapter VII), of the Jewish usurer Isaac Rapine, and of the grasshopper-like Captain Weazel (Chapter XI)? Unfortunately, Smollett's heroines, especially Narcissa, are depicted in a flat conventional way, which gives them little or no lifelike reality. *Roderick Random* is very much of a man's book, written mostly with men in mind—but not exclusively so, as the love-interest was obviously meant to catch and hold the female readers' attention. But all the same, in *Roderick Random* the rough, but enjoyable give and take of the gun-room or wardroom, the barbed banter of the coffee-house, the playhouse, and gambling den are never far away. A man's world then, not unlike Kipling's at times, with its brief flashes of material glory, and blissful ecstasy, also with its bleak and dreary struggles, stupid and costly blunders, but with the ever present, deep-rooted urge to reach happiness. It is a strangely human, and, in its own unsophisticated way, humane book, for which an alternative epigraph could be borrowed from Smollett's *Reproof*: 'I pity and defy.'

P.-G. B.

[1] For a complete study of the 'Structures of the Comic', see my *Novels of T. Smollett*, pp. 302–42.

NOTE ON THE TEXT

The present text follows the first edition (1748) catalogued as C.95.aa.10 in the British Library: signatures I 9 of volume I and E 4 of volume II are cancels (see A. H. Smith's study listed in the Select Bibliography). No attempt has been made to modernize Smollett's spelling, apart from eliminating the long 's' and correcting obvious typographical errors. The important 'Apologue' is taken from the fourth edition (1755) in the Bodleian Library (Vet.A5.f. 2857–8).

SELECT BIBLIOGRAPHY

BIBLIOGRAPHY (Textual and Critical): L. M. Knapp, 'Smollett's Works as Printed by William Strahan', *The Library*, xiii (1932), [282]–91; D. M. Korte, *An Annotated Bibliography of Smollett Scholarship* (1969); O. M. Brack and J. B. Davis, 'Smollett's Revisions of *Roderick Random*', *The Papers of the Bibliographical Society of America*, 64 (1970), 295–311; *NCBEL*, ii, ed. G. Watson (1971), cols. 962–70; A. H. Smith, 'A Duplicate Setting in the Second Edition of Smollett's *Roderick Random*', *The Library*, xxviii (1973), [309]–18; *Tobias Smollett: An Excerpt from the General Catalogue of Printed Books* (British Museum Publications Limited, 1974), 28 cols.; L. M. Knapp, 'Smollett', in *The English Novel* (1974), ed. A. E. Dyson, pp. [112]–27; G. Sutherland, 'Illustrated Editions of Tobias Smollett's Novels: A Checklist and Commentary', Edinburgh Ph.D. thesis, 1974; R. C. Cole, 'Smollett and the Eighteenth-Century Irish Book Trade', *Papers of the Bibliographical Society of America*, 69 (1975), 345–63; A. H. Smith, 'The Printing and Publication of Early Editions of the Novels of Tobias George Smollett', London University Ph.D. thesis in librarianship, 1976, an admirable work of reference; F. Cordasco, *Tobias George Smollett: A Bibliographical Guide* (1978).

GENERAL WORKS ON SMOLLETT

BIOGRAPHY: L. M. Knapp, *Tobias Smollett: Doctor of Men and Manners* (1949); *The Letters of Tobias Smollett*, ed. L. M. Knapp (1970).
MODERN STUDIES (in chronological order): H. S. Buck, *A Study in Smollett, chiefly 'Peregrine Pickle'* (1925); A. Whitridge, *Tobias Smollett: A Study of his Miscellaneous Works* [1925]; H. S. Buck, *Smollett as Poet* (1927); E. Joliat, *Smollett et la France* (1935); C. E. Jones, *Smollett Studies* (1942); L. L. Martz, *The Later Career of Tobias Smollett* (1942); G. M. Kahrl, *Tobias Smollett, Traveler-Novelist* (1945); F. W. Boege, *Smollett's Reputation as a Novelist* (1947); L. Brander, *Tobias Smollett* (1951); A. D. McKillop, 'Tobias Smollett', in *The Early Masters of English Fiction* (1956), pp. 147–81; M. Orowitz, 'Smollett and the Art of Caricature', *Spectrum*, ii (1958), [155]–67; A. B. Strauss, 'On Smollett's Language', in *English Institute Essays, 1958* (1959), pp. 25–54; M. A. Goldberg, *Smollett and the Scottish School* (1959); R. Paulson, 'Satire in the Early Novels of Smollett', *JEGP*, lix (1960), 381–402; W. B. Piper, 'The Large Diffused Picture of Life in Smollett's Early Novels', *Studies in Philology*, lx (1963), 45–56; R. Alter, 'The Picaroon as Fortune's Plaything', in *Rogue's Progress* (1964), pp. 58–79; D. J. Bruce, *Radical Doctor Smollett* (1964); A. Parreaux, *Smollett's London* (1965); H. R. Steeves, *Before Jane Austen: The Shaping of The English Novel* (1965), see ch. viii 'Sad Dogs and Saints: Tobias Smollett', pp. 131–59; L. M. Knapp, 'Early Scottish Attitudes towards Tobias Smollett', *Philological Quarterly*, xlv (1966), 262–9; T. Bloch, 'Smollett's Quest for Form', *Modern Philology*, lxv (1967), 103–13; R. Giddings, *The Tradition of Smollett*

(1967); R. Paulson, 'Smollett: The Satirist as a Character Type', ch. 5 in his *Satire and the Novel in Eighteenth-Century England* (1967), pp. 165-218; P. Stevick, 'Stylistic Energy in the Early Smollett', *Studies in Philology*, lxiv (1967), pp. 712-19; R. D. Spector, *Tobias Smollett* (1968); A. Cozza, *Tobias Smollett* (1970); P. G. Boucé, *Les Romans de Smollett* (1971), published in English as *The Novels of Tobias Smollett* (1976), slightly abridged, revised, and with a bibliography updated to mid-1975; G. S. Rousseau and P. G. Boucé, eds., *Tobias Smollett: Bicentennial Essays Presented to Lewis M. Knapp* (1971); G. S. Rousseau, 'Smollett and the Picaresque: Some Questions about a Label', *Studies in Burke and his Time*, xii (1971), 1886-904; P. G. Boucé, 'Smollett's Pseudo-Picaresque: A Response to Rousseau's "Smollett and the Picaresque" ', *Studies in Burke and his Time*, xiv (1972), 73-9; A. Ross, 'The Show of Violence in Smollett's Novels', *Yearbook of English Studies*, 77 (1972), 118-29; J. M. Warner, 'Smollett's Development as a Novelist', *Novel*, v (1972), 148-61; D. Brooks, *Number and Pattern in the Eighteenth-Century Novel* (1973), see chs. vi and vii, pp. 123-59, which deal with Smollett's novels; J. M. Warner, 'The Interpolated Narratives in the Fiction of Fielding and Smollett: An Epistemological View', *Studies in the Novel*, v (1973), 271-83; D. Daiches, 'Smollett Reconsidered', in *Miscellanea Anglo-Americana: Festschrift für Helmut Viebrock* (1974), pp. 109-36; S. Auty, *The Comic Spirit of Eighteenth-Century Novels* (1975), see ch. iv, 'Smollett and Sterne and Animal Spirits', pp. 103-79; T. R. Preston, *Not in Timon's Manner: Feeling, Misanthropy, and Satire in Eighteenth-Century England* (1975), see ch. 4, 'Tobias Smollett—A Risible Misanthrope', pp. 69-120; M. Rosenblum, 'Smollett as Conservative Satirist', *ELH*, 42 (1975), 556-79; J. C. Beasley, 'Romance and the "New" Novels of Richardson, Fielding and Smollett', *Studies in English Literature*, xvi, 437-50; G. S. Rousseau, 'Beef and Bouillon: A Voice for Tobias Smollett, with Comments on his Life, Works and Modern Critics', *The British Studies Monitor*, vii, Winter 1977, [4]-56; D. Grant, *Tobias Smollett: A Study in Style* (1977), a vigorous and perceptive analysis; J. Sekora, *Luxury: The Concept in Western Thought, Eden to Smollett* (1977).

EDITIONS OF *RODERICK RANDOM*

First published on 21 January 1748 (see my Introduction to the present volume). Smollett corrected and revised the next three London editions of 1748, 1750, and 1755. The second edition appeared with frontispieces by F. Hayman and C. Grignion. By 1770 *Roderick Random* had reached its eighth London edition, the last to be published in Smollett's lifetime: for more details see G. Sutherland's and A. H. Smith's Ph.D. theses listed above in the Bibliography. Numerous piracies were published in Dublin (1748-9, 1755, 1762, 1768, 1770, etc.), but also in London (1748, 1770?, 1775, 1779, 1780) and in Edinburgh (1778, 1784, 1791), both within and outside the copyright restriction period. The 1792 London edition, published by C. Lowndes—in the Harvard and Princeton libraries—is notable for its six folio coloured plates drawn by Thos. Rowlandson. *Roderick Random* has been included in all the collected editions of Smollett's works, from the first one, published in Dublin (1775-6), to the Shakespeare Head edition of Smollett's novels (Oxford, 1925-6): see the list in *NCBEL*. It was translated into German (1754), French (1761), Russian (1788), Danish (1802), Dutch (1805), and Swedish (1824).

Select Bibliography

SPECIAL STUDIES OF *RODERICK RANDOM*

Nearly all the modern studies listed above deal with *Roderick Random* at varying length. The closest analysis of the novel's structure will be found in my *Novels of Tobias Smollett* (1976), pp. 100–24. Also of direct relevance to the study of *Roderick Random* are the following articles and essays: H. S. Buck, 'A *Roderick Random* Play, 1748', *MLN*, xliii (1928), 111–12; L. M. Knapp, 'Smollett's Verses and their Musical Settings', *MLN*, xlvi (1931), 224–32; A. Lawrence, 'L'influence de Lesage sur Smollett', *Revue de Littérature Comparée*, xii (1932), 533–45; L. M. Knapp, 'The Naval Scenes in *Roderick Random*', *PMLA*, xlix (1934), 593–8; O. E. Deutsch, 'Poetry Preserved in Music: Bibliographical Notes on Smollett and Oswald, Handel, and Haydn', *MLN*, lxiii (1948), 73–88; J. Dobson, 'Smollett the Surgeon', *Annals of the Royal College of Surgeons*, xx (1957), 260–4 (gives the exact date of Smollett's examination at Barber-Surgeons' Hall, 4 Dec. 1739, and the names of his examiners); M. C. Battestin, 'On the Contemporary Reputations of *Pamela, Joseph Andrews*, and *Roderick Random:* Remarks by an "Oxford Scholar", 1748', *Notes and Queries*, xv (1968), 450–2; J. B. Davis, '*The Adventures of Roderick Random*, by T. G. Smollett. A Critical Edition: Edited and with an Introduction', University of Virginia, Ph.D. thesis, 1969; G. N. Underwood, 'Linguistic Realism in *Roderick Random*', *JEGP*, lxix (1970), 32–40 (should be corrected and completed by T. K. Pratt's article listed below); A. G. Fredman, 'The Picaresque in Decline: Smollett's First Novel', in *English Writers of the Eighteenth Century* (1971), ed. J. H. Middendorf, pp. [189]–207, a sensible view of a much-debated problem; F. McCombie, 'The Strange Distemper of Narcissa's Aunt', *Notes and Queries*, xviii (1971), 55–6, should be completed by J. F. Sena's article *infra*; G. Graband, *et al.*, 'Quantitative Methoden zur Stilanalyse von Texten: T. G. Smollett, *Roderick Random* (1748) und *Humphry Clinker* (1771)', *Mitteilungen der Technischen Universität Carolo-Wilhelmina zu Braunschweig*, vii (1972) [six unnumbered pages]; T. K. Pratt, 'Linguistics, Criticism, and Smollett's *Roderick Random*', *University of Toronto Quarterly*, xlii (1972), 26–39; N. C. Starr, 'Smollett's Sailors', *The American Neptune*, xxxii (1972), 81–99; T. K. Pratt, 'A Study of the Language in Tobias Smollett's *Roderick Random*', London University Ph.D. thesis, 1975, a thorough and detailed study (649 pp.), which proved a great help during the preparation of this volume; J. F. Sena, 'Smollett's Portrait of Narcissa's Aunt: The Genesis of an "Original"', *English Language Notes*, xiv (1977), 270–5; R. Bjornson, *The Picaresque Hero in European Fiction* (1977), see ch. 11. 'The Picaresque Hero as Young Nobleman: Victimization and Vindication in Smollett's *Roderick Random*', pp. 228–45, an enthusiastic, but most questionable, assessment of the picaresque elements in *Roderick Random*; I. C. Ross, 'Language, Structure and Vision in Smollett's *Roderick Random*', *Études Anglaises*, xxxi (1978), 52–63. An edition of *Roderick Random*, with full textual and critical apparatus by O. M. Brack and J. B. Davis is in active preparation, and will be published by the Delaware University Press.

A CHRONOLOGY OF
TOBIAS GEORGE SMOLLETT

1721 (19 March)	Baptized in the parish church of Cardross, Dumbartonshire, Scotland
Dates uncertain	Attends Dumbarton Grammar School, and Glasgow University
1735 (c. November)	Works in a dispensatory in Glasgow
1736 (30 May)	Begins five years' apprenticeship to William Stirling and John Gordon, Glasgow surgeons
1739 (after June)	Goes to London; passes his examination at Barber-Surgeons' Hall, 4 December
1740 (10 March)	Receives his warrant as surgeon's second mate in the Navy; begins service in the *Chichester* (3 April); sails to Jamaica (26 Oct.–10 Jan. 1741) in the Cartagena expedition
1741 (September)	Back in England
1741–4	Movements uncertain; may have returned to West Indies; marries Anne Lassells (probably c. 1743), heiress daughter of a Jamaica planter
1744 (May)	Practises as a surgeon in London
1746	Writes 'The Tears of Scotland'
1746 (September)	*Advice*, a verse satire
1747 (January)	*Reproof*, a sequel to *Advice*
1747–8	Prepares translation of Lesage's *Gil Blas*, published Oct. 1748
1748 (c. 21 January)	*The Adventures of Roderick Random*
1749 (June)	*The Regicide* published after nearly 10 years of frustrating struggles to get it produced on the stage
1749 (c. September)	Tours Flanders, Holland, and part of France, Paris probably included
1750 (Summer)	Visits Paris and the Low Countries
1751 (February)	*The Adventures of Peregrine Pickle*
1752 (January)	*Habbakuk Hilding*, a virulent attack on Fielding, probably by Smollett
1752 (March)	*An Essay on the External Use of Water*
1753 (February)	*The Adventures of Ferdinand Count Fathom*; c. June–November, visits Scotland for the first time in 15 years
1754 (August)	Fourth edition of *Roderick Random*, dated 1755, set up and printed, with 'Apologue'
1755 (February)	*Don Quixote*, a translation begun c. 1748
1755–7	Working on *A Complete History of England*, published 1757–8

A Chronology of Tobias George Smollett

1756 (March)	In collaboration with 3 others, launches the *Critical Review*, and serves as an editor and reviewer until 1763
1756 (April)	Edition of *A Compendium of Authentic and Entertaining Voyages*
1757 (January, February, April, May)	*The Reprisal*, a farce in two acts, performed at the Theatre Royal in Drury Lane; published 1 Feb. 1757
1758 (March)	Second edition of *Peregrine Pickle*, revised and altered
1758 (May)	Savage attack against Admiral Knowles in the *Critical Review*
1760 (January)	Begins publication of *The British Magazine*, where *The Adventures of Sir Launcelot Greaves* appear serially from Jan. 1760 to Dec. 1761
1760 (November to late February 1761)	In the King's Bench Prison for libel of Admiral Knowles
1760–5	Writing the *Continuation of the Complete History of England*
1761–5	Joint editor of the *Works of Voltaire*
1762 (29 May to 12 February 1763)	Edits the weekly *Briton* in support of Lord Bute
1762	Health deteriorates; seeks appointment abroad in a warm climate
1763 (3 April)	Only child, Elizabeth, dies, aged 15
1763 (June)	With wife and friends, leaves for France and Italy; resides in Nice from Nov. 1763 to April 1765
1765 (July)	Returns to England
1766 (May)	*Travels through France and Italy*
1766 (May–August)	Travels to Scotland, then returns to Bath and London
1768	Completes *The Present State of All Nations* begun in 1760
1768 (Autumn)	Leaves for Italy. Finally settles near Leghorn
1769 (April)	*The History and Adventures of an Atom*, a political satire, most probably by Smollett
1771 (June)	*The Expedition of Humphry Clinker*
1771 (17 September)	Dies at Il Giardino, a villa on the side of Monte Nero in Antignano, near Leghorn. Buried in the English cemetery in Leghorn
1773	*Ode to Independence*, composed in 1766, published posthumously
1776	Translation of Fénelon's *Adventures of Telemachus* published posthumously

PREFACE

OF all kinds of satire, there is none so entertaining, and universally improving, as that which is introduced, as it were, occasionally, in the course of an interesting story, which brings every incident home to life; and by representing familiar scenes in an uncommon and amusing point of view, invests them with all the graces of novelty, while nature is appealed to in every particular.

The reader gratifies his curiosity, in pursuing the adventures of a person in whose favour he is prepossessed; he espouses his cause, he sympathizes with him in distress, his indignation is heated against the authors of his calamity; the humane passions are inflamed; the contrast between dejected virtue, and insulting vice, appears with greater aggravation, and every impression having a double force on the imagination, the memory retains the circumstance, and the heart improves by the example. The attention is not tired with a bare Catalogue of characters, but agreeably diverted with all the variety of invention; and the vicissitudes of life appear in their peculiar circumstances, opening an ample field for wit and humour.

Romance, no doubt, owes its origin to ignorance, vanity and superstition. In the dark ages of the world, when a man had rendered himself famous for wisdom or valour, his family and adherents availed themselves of his superior qualities, magnified his virtues, and represented his character and person as sacred and supernatural. The vulgar easily swallowed the bait, implored his protection, and yielded the tribute of homage and praise even to adoration; his exploits were handed down to posterity with a thousand exaggerations; they were repeated as incitements to virtue; divine honours were paid, and altars erected to his memory, for the encouragement of those who attempted to imitate his example; and hence arose the heathen mythology, which is no other than a collection of extravagant Romances.——As learning advanced, and genius received cultivation, these stories were embellished with the graces of poetry, that they might the better recommend themselves to the attention; they were sung in publick, at festivals, for the instruction and delight of the audience; and rehearsed before battle, as incentives to deeds of glory. Thus tragedy and the epic muse were born, and, in the progress of taste, arrived at perfection.——It is no wonder, that the ancients could not relish a fable in prose, after they had seen so many remarkable events celebrated in verse, by their best poets; we therefore, find no romance among them, during the æra of their excellence, unless the Cyropædia of Zenophon[1] may be so called; and it was not till arts and sciences began to revive, after the irruption of the Barbarians into Europe, that any thing of this kind appeared. But when the minds of men were debauched by the imposition of priest-craft to the most absurd pitch of credulity; the authors of romance arose, and losing sight of probability, filled their performances with the most monstrous hyperboles. If they could not equal the ancient poets in point of genius, they were resolved to excel them in fiction, and apply to the wonder rather than the judgment of their readers. Accordingly they brought negromancy to their aid, and instead of supporting the character of their heroes, by dignity of sentiment and practice, distinguished them by their bodily strength, activity and extravagance of behaviour. Although nothing could be more ludicrous and unnatural than the figures they drew, they did not want patrons and admirers, and the world actually began to be infected with the spirit of knight-errantry, when Cervantes, by an inimitable piece of ridicule,[2] reformed the taste of mankind, representing chivalry in the right point of view, and converting romance to purposes far more useful and entertaining, by making it assume the sock, and point out the follies of ordinary life.

The same method has been practised by other Spanish and French authors, and by none more successfully than by Monsieur Le Sage, who in his adventures of Gil Blas,[3] has described the knavery and foibles of life, with infinite humour and sagacity.—The following sheets I have modelled on his plan, taking the liberty, however, to differ from him in the execution, where I thought his particular situations were uncommon, extravagant, or peculiar to the country in which the scene is laid.——The disgraces of Gil Blas, are for the most part, such as rather excite mirth than compassion; he himself laughs at them; and his transitions from distress to happiness, or at least ease, are so sudden, that neither the reader has time to pity him, nor himself to be acquainted with affliction.—This conduct, in my opinion, not only deviates from probability, but prevents that generous indignation, which ought to animate the reader, against the sordid and vicious disposition of the world.

I have attempted to represent modest merit struggling with every difficulty to which a friendless orphan is exposed, from his own want of experience, as well as from the selfishness, envy, malice, and base indifference of mankind.—To secure a favourable pre-possession, I have allowed him the advantages of birth and educa-tion, which in the series of his misfortunes, will, I hope, engage the ingenuous more warmly in his behalf; and though I foresee, that some people will be offended at the mean scenes in which he is in-volved, I persuade myself the judicious will not only perceive the necessity of describing those situations to which he must of course be confined, in his low estate; but also find entertainment in view-ing those parts of life, where the humours and passions are undis-guised by affectation, ceremony, or education; and the whimsical peculiarities of disposition appear as nature has implanted them.—But I believe I need not trouble myself in vindicating a practice authorized by the best writers in this way, some of whom I have already named.

Every intelligent reader will, at first sight, perceive I have not deviated from nature, in the facts, which are all true in the main, although the circumstances are altered and disguised to avoid personal satire.[1]

It now remains, to give my reasons for making the chief person-age of this work a North-Briton; which are chiefly these: I could at a small expence bestow on him such education as I thought the dignity of his birth and character required, which could not possibly be obtained in England, by such slender means as the nature of my plan would afford. In the next place, I could represent simplicity of manners in a remote part of the kingdom, with more propriety, than in any place near the capital; and lastly, the disposition of the Scots, addicted to travelling, justifies my conduct in deriving an adventurer from that country.

Preface

That the delicate reader may not be offended at the unmeaning oaths which proceed from the mouths of some persons in these memoirs, I beg leave to premise, that I imagined nothing could more effectually expose the absurdity of such miserable expletives, than a natural and verbal representation of the discourse with which they are commonly interlarded.

APOLOGUE

A Young painter indulging a vein of pleasantry, sketched a kind of conversation-piece, representing a bear, an owl, a monkey, and an ass; and to render it more striking, humorous and moral, distinguished every figure by some emblem of human life.

Bruin was exhibited in the garb and attitude of an old, toothless, drunken soldier; the owl perched upon the handle of a coffee-pot, with spectacle on nose, seemed to contemplate a news paper; and the ass, ornamented with a huge tye-wig, (which, however, could not conceal his long ears) sat for his picture to the monkey, who appeared with the implements of painting. This whimsical groupe afforded some mirth, and met with general approbation, until some mischievous wag hinted that the whole was a lampoon upon the friends of the performer: an insinuation which was no sooner circulated, than those very people who applauded it before, began to be alarmed, and even to fancy themselves signified by the several figures of the piece.

Among others, a worthy personage in years, who had served in the army with reputation, being incensed at the supposed outrage, repaired to the lodgings of the painter, and finding him at home, 'Heark ye, Mr. Monkey, said he, I have a good mind to convince you that tho' the bear has lost his teeth, he retains his paws, and that he is not so drunk but he can perceive your impertinence—'Sblood! sir, that toothless jaw is a damned scandalous libel—but, don't you imagine me so chopfallen as not to be able to chew the cud of resentment.'——Here he was interrupted by the arrival of a learned physician, who advancing to the culprit with fury in his aspect, exclaimed, 'Suppose the augmentation of the ass's ears should prove the diminution of the baboon's—nay, seek not to prevaricate, for by the beard of Æsculapius! there is not one hair in this periwig that will not stand up in judgment to convict thee of personal abuse—Do but observe, captain, how this pitiful little fellow has copied the very curls—the colour, indeed, is different, but then the form and foretop are quite similar.'—While he thus remonstrated in a strain of vociferation, a venerable senator entered, and waddling up to the delinquent, 'Jackanapes! cried he, I will now let thee see, I can read something else than a news paper, and that, without the help of spectacles—here is your own note of hand, sirrah, for money which if I had not advanced, you yourself would have resembled an owl, in not daring to shew your face by day, you ungrateful, slanderous knave!'

In vain the astonished painter declared that he had no intention to give offence, or to characterize particular persons: they affirmed the resemblance was too palpable to be overlooked, they taxed him with insolence, malice, and ingratitude; and their clamours being overheard by the public, the captain was a bear, the doctor an ass, and the senator an owl to his dying day.

Christian reader, I beseech thee, in the bowels of the Lord, remember this example while thou art employed in the perusal of the following sheets; and seek not to appropriate to thyself that which equally belongs to five hundred different people. If thou should'st meet with a character that reflects thee in some ungracious particular, keep thy own counsel; consider that one feature makes not a face, and that tho' thou art, perhaps, distinguished by a bottle nose, twenty of thy neighbours may be in the same predicament.

CHAPTER I

Of my birth and parentage

I WAS born in the northern part of this united kingdom in the house of my grandfather, a gentleman of considerable fortune and influence, who had on many occasions signalized himself in behalf of his country; and was remarkable for his abilities in the law, which he exercised with great success, in quality of a judge, particularly against beggars, for whom he had a singular aversion.

My father, his youngest son, fell in love with a poor relation, who lived with the old gentleman, and performed the office of house-keeper; whom he privately espoused; of which marriage I am the first fruit.—During her pregnancy, a dream discomposed my mother so much, that my father, tired with her importunity, at last consulted a seer, whose favourable interpretation he would have secured before-hand by a bribe, but found him incorruptible. She dreamed, she was delivered of a tennis-ball,[1] which the devil (who to her great surprize, acted the part of a midwife) struck so forcibly with a racket, that it disappeared in an instant; and she was for some time inconsolable for the loss of her off-spring; when all of a sudden, she beheld it return with equal violence, and earth itself beneath her feet, whence immediately sprung up a goodly tree covered with blossoms, the scent of which operated so strongly on her nerves that she awoke.—The attentive sage, after some deliberation, assured my parents, that their first-born would be a great traveller, that he would undergo many dangers and difficulties, and at last return to his native land, where he would flourish with great reputation and happiness.—How truly this was foretold, will appear in the sequel. —It was not long before some officious person informed my grand-father of familiarities that passed between his son and house-keeper, which alarmed him so much, that, a few days after, he told my father it was high time for him to enter into the holy state of matrimony, and that he had provided a match for him, to which he could in justice have no objections. My father, finding it would be

I

impossible to conceal his situation much longer, frankly owned what he had done, and excused himself for not having asked the consent of his father, by saying, he knew it would be to no purpose; and that, had his inclination been known, my grandfather might have taken such measures as would have effectually put the gratification of it out of his power: he added, that no exception could be made to his wife's virtue, birth, beauty, and good sense, and as for fortune, it was beneath his consideration.—The old gentleman, who kept all his passions (except one) in excellent order, heard him to an end with great temper; and then calmly asked, how he proposed to maintain himself and spouse?—He replied he could be in no danger of wanting, while his father's tenderness remained, which he and his wife would always cherish with the utmost veneration; that he was persuaded his allowance would be suitable to the dignity and circumstances of his family, and the provision already made to his brothers and sisters, who were happily settled under his protection. —Your brothers and sisters, said my grandfather, did not think it beneath them to consult me in an affair of such importance as matrimony; neither (I suppose) would you have omitted that piece of duty, had you not some secret fund in reserve, to the comforts of which I leave you, with a desire that you will this night, seek out another habitation for yourself and wife, whither in a short time, I will send you an account of the expence I have been at in your education, with a view of being reimbursed.—Sir, you have made the grand tour—you are a polite gentleman—a very pretty gentleman— I wish you a great deal of joy, and am your very humble servant. So saying, he left my father in a situation easily imagined. However, he did not long hesitate; for being perfectly well acquainted with his father's disposition, he did not doubt that he was glad of this pretence to get rid of him; and as his resolves were invariable like the laws of the Medes and Persians,[1] he knew it would be to no purpose to attempt him by prayers and intreaties; so without any farther application, he betook himself with his disconsolate bedfellow, to a farm-house, where an old servant of his mother dwelt; there they remained some time in a situation but ill adapted to the elegance of their desires and tenderness of their love; which nevertheless, my father endured, rather than supplicate an unnatural and inflexible parent: but my mother, foreseeing the inconveniencies she would be exposed to, if she must be delivered in this place (and her pregnancy was very far advanced) without communicating her design to her husband, went in disguise to the house of my grandfather, hoping that her tears and condition would move him to compassion, and reconcile him to an event which could not otherwise be amended.—She found means to deceive the servants, and was introduced as an unfortunate lady, who wanted to complain of some matrimonial grievances, it being my grandfather's particular province to decide in all cases of scandal. She was accordingly admitted into his presence, where discovering herself, she fell at his feet, and in the most affecting manner, implored his forgiveness; at the same time, representing the danger that threatned not only her life, but that of his own grandchild which was about to see the light.—He told her, he was sorry that the indiscretion of her and his son had compelled him to make a vow, which put it out of his power to give them any assistance—That he had already imparted his thoughts on that subject to her husband, and was surprised that they should disturb his peace with any further importunity.—This said, he retired.—The violence of my mother's affliction had such an effect on her constitution, that she was immediately seized with the pains of childbed; and had not an old maid-servant to whom she was very dear, afforded her pity and assistance, at the hazard of incurring my grandfather's displeasure, she and the innocent fruit of her womb must have fallen miserable victims to his rigour and inhumanity. —By the friendship of this poor woman, she was carried up to a garret, and immediately delivered of a man-child, the story of whose unfortunate birth, he himself now relates.—My father being informed of what had happened, flew to the embraces of his darling spouse, and while he loaded his off-spring with paternal caresses, could not forbear shedding a flood of tears, on beholding the dear partner of his heart (for whose ease he would have sacrificed the treasures of the east) stretched upon a flock-bed,[1] in a miserable apartment, unable to protect her from the inclemencies of the weather.—It is not to be supposed that the old gentleman was ignorant of what passed, tho' he affected to know nothing of the matter, and pretended to be very much surprized, when the son of his deceased eldest son, a pert boy, who lived with him as his heir apparent, acquainted him with the affair; he determined therefore to preserve no medium, but immediately (on the third day after her delivery) sent her a peremptory order to begone, and turned off the servant who had preserved her life. This behaviour so exasperated my father, that he had recourse to the most dreadful imprecations, and on his bare knees implored that heaven would renounce him, if ever he should forget or forgive the barbarity of his sire.—The injuries which this unhappy mother received from her removal in such circumstances, and the want of necessaries where she lodged, together with her grief and anxiety of mind, soon threw her into a languishing disorder which put an end to her life. My father, who loved her tenderly, was so affected with her death, that he remained six weeks deprived of his senses; during which time, the people where he lodged, carried the infant to the old man, who relented so far, on hearing the melancholy story of his daughter-in-law's death, and the deplorable condition of his son, that he sent the child to nurse, and ordered my father to be carried home to his house, where he soon recovered the use of his reason.—Whether this hard-hearted judge felt any remose for his cruel treatment of his son and daughter; or (which is more probable) was afraid his character would suffer in the neighbourhood; he professed great sorrow for his conduct to my father, whose delirium was succeeded by a profound melancholy and reserve. At length he disappeared, and not-withstanding all imaginable inquiry, could never be heard of, which confirmed most people in the opinion of his having made away with himself in a fit of despair.—How I understood the particulars of my birth, will appear in the course of these memoirs.

CHAPTER II

*I grow up—am hated by my relations—sent to school—
neglected by my grandfather—maltreated by my master—
seasoned to adversity—form cabals against the pedant—
debarred access to my grandfather—hunted by his heir
—demolish the teeth of his tutor*

THERE were not wanting some, who suspected my uncles of being concerned in my father's fate, on the supposition that they would all share in the patrimony destined for him: and this conjecture seemed supported by reflecting, that in all his calamities they never discovered the least inclination to serve him; but, on the contrary, by all the artifices in their power, fed his father's resentment, and

strengthened his resolution of leaving him to misery and want.—
But people of judgment treated this insinuation as an idle chimera;
because had my relations been so wicked as to consult their interest
by committing such an atrocious crime, the fate of my father
would have extended to me too, whose life was another obstacle to
their expectation.—Mean while, I grew apace, and as I strongly resembled my father, who was the darling of the tenants, I wanted
nothing which their indigent circumstances could afford: but their
favour was a weak resource against the jealous enmity of my cousins;
who, the more my infancy promised, conceived the more implacable
hatred against me; and before I was six years of age, had so effectually blockaded my grandfather, that I never saw him but by stealth;
when I sometimes made up to his chair as he sat to view his labour-
ers in the field: on which occasions, he would stroak my head, bid
me be a good boy, and promise he would take care of me.—I was
soon after sent to school at a village hard by, of which he had been
dictator time out of mind: but as he neither paid for my board, nor
supplied me with clothes, books, and other necessaries I required,
my condition was very ragged and contemptible, and the school-
master, who through fear of my grandfather taught me *gratis*, gave
himself no concern about the progress I made under his instruction.
—In spite of all these difficulties and disgraces, I became a good
proficient in the Latin tongue; and as soon as I could write tolerably, pestered my grandfather with letters to such a degree, that he
sent for my master, and chid him severely for bestowing such pains
on my education, telling him, that if ever I should be brought to the
gallows for forgery, which he had taught me to commit, my blood
should lie on his head.—The pedant, who dreaded nothing more
than the displeasure of his patron, assured his honour that the boy's
ability was more owing to his own genius and application, than to
any instruction or encouragement he received; that, although he
could not divest him of the knowledge he had already imbibed,
unless he would impower him to disable his fingers, he should endeavour, with G—d's help, to prevent his future improvement.
And indeed, he punctually performed what he had undertaken: for,
on pretence that I had wrote impertinent letters to my grandfather,
he caused a board to be made with five holes in it, through which
he thrust the fingers and thumb of my right hand, and fastened it
by whip-cord to my wrist, in such a manner, that I was effectually
debarr'd the use of my pen. But this restraint I was freed from in a

few days, by an accident which happened in a quarrel between me and another boy, who taking upon him to insult my poverty, I was so incensed at this ungenerous reproach, that with one stroke of my machine, I cut him to the skull, to the great terror of myself and school-fellows, who left him bleeding on the ground, and ran to inform the master of what had happened. I was so severely punished for this trespass, that, were I to live to the age of Methusalem,[1] the impression it made on me would not be effaced; no more than the antipathy and horror I conceived for the merciless tyrant who inflicted it. The contempt which my appearance naturally produced, in all who saw me, the continual wants I was exposed to, and my own haughty disposition, impatient of affronts, involved me in a thousand troublesome adventures, by which I was at length enured to adversity, and emboldened to undertakings far above my years. I was often inhumanly scourged for crimes I did not commit, because having the character of a vagabond in the village, every piece of mischief whose author lay unknown, was charged upon me.—I have been found guilty of robbing orchards I never entered, of killing cats I never hurted, of stealing gingerbread I never touched, and of abusing old women I never saw.—Nay, a stammering carpenter had eloquence enough to persuade my master, that I fired a pistol loaded with small shot, into his window; though my landlady and the whole family bore witness, that I was a-bed fast asleep at the time when this outrage was committed.—I was flogged for having narrowly escaped drowning, by the sinking of a ferry-boat in which I was passenger.—Another time for having recovered of a bruise occasioned by a horse and cart running over me.—A third time, for being bit by a baker's dog.—In short, whether I was guilty or unfortunate, the vengeance and sympathy of this arbitrary pedagogue were the same. Far from being subdued by this infernal usage, my indignation triumphed over that slavish awe which had hitherto enforced my obedience; and the more my years and knowledge increased, the more I perceived the injustice and barbarity of his behaviour. By the help of an uncommon genius, and the advice and direction of our usher, who had served my father in his travels, I made a surprising progress in the classicks, writing and arithmetick; so that before I was twelve years old, I was confessedly the best scholar in the school: This qualification, together with a boldness of temper, and strength of make, which had subjected almost all my cotemporaries, gave me such influence over them, that I began to form cabals against my persecutor; and was in hopes of being able to bid him defiance in a very short time.—Being at the head of a faction consisting of thirty boys, most of them of my own age, I was determined to put their mettal to trial, that I might know how far they were to be depended upon, before I put my grand scheme in execution: with this view we attacked a body of stout apprentices, who had taken possession of a part of the ground allotted to us, for the scene of our diversions; and who were then playing at nine-pins on the spot: but I had the mortification to see my adherents routed in an instant, and a leg of one of them broke in his flight by the bowl, which one of our adversaries had detached in pursuit of us.— This discomfiture did not hinder us from engaging them afterwards, in frequent skirmishes which we maintained by throwing stones at a distance, wherein I received many wounds, the scars of which still remain. Our enemies were so harassed and interrupted by these alarms, that they at last abandoned their conquest, and left us to the peaceable enjoyment of our own territories.—It would be end-less to enumerate the exploits we performed in the course of this confederacy, which became the terror of the whole village; inso-much, that when different interests divided it, one of the parties commonly courted the assistance of Roderick Random (by which name I was known)[1] to cast the balance, and keep the opposite faction in awe.—Meanwhile, I took the advantage of every play-day, to present myself before my grandfather, to whom I seldom found access, by reason of his being so closely besieged by a numer-ous family of his female grandchildren, who, though they perpetu-ally quarrelled among themselves, never failed to join against me, as the common enemy of all. His heir, who was about the age of eighteen, minded nothing but fox-hunting, and indeed was quali-fied for nothing else, notwithstanding his grandfather's indulgence, in entertaining a tutor for him at home; who at the same time per-formed the office of parish clerk. This young Acteon,[2] who inherited his grandfather's antipathy to every thing in distress, never set eyes on me, without uncoupling his beagles, and hunting me into some cottage or other, whither I generally fled for shelter. In this christian amusement, he was encouraged by his preceptor, who, no doubt, took such opportunities to ingratiate himself with the rising sun, observing that the old gentleman, according to course of nature, had not long to live, being already on the verge of fourscore. —The behaviour of this rascally sycophant incensed me so much, that one day, when I was beleagued by him and his hounds into a farmer's house, where I had found protection, I took aim at him (being an excellent marksman) with a large pebble, which struck out four of his foreteeth, and effectually incapacitated him for doing the office of a clerk ever after.

CHAPTER III

My mother's brother arrives—relieves me—a description of him—goes along with me to the house of my grandfather —is encountered by his dogs—defeats them after a bloody engagement—is admitted to the old gentleman—a dialogue between them

ABOUT this time, my mother's only brother, who had been long abroad, lieutenant of a man of war, arrived in his own country; where being informed of my condition, he came to see me, and out of his slender finances, not only supplied me with what necessaries I wanted for the present, but resolved not to leave the country, until he had prevailed on my grandfather to settle something handsome for the future. This was a task to which he was by no means equal, being entirely ignorant not only of the judge's disposition, but also unacquainted with the ways of men in general, to which his education on board had kept him an utter stranger.—He was a strong built man, somewhat bandy-legged, with a neck like that of a bull, and a face which (you might easily perceive) had withstood the most obstinate assaults of the weather.—His dress consisted of a soldier's coat altered for him by the ship's taylor, a stripped flannel jacket, a pair of red breeches japanned with pitch, clean grey worsted stockings, large silver buckles that covered three-fourths of his shoes, a silver-laced hat whose crown over-looked the brims about an inch and a half, a black bob wig in the buckle, a check shirt, a silk handkerchief, an hanger with a brass handle girded to his thigh by a tarnished laced belt, and a good oak plant under his arm.—Thus equipt, he set out with me (who by his bounty made a very decent appearance) for my grandfather's house, where we were saluted by Jowler and Cæsar, whom my cousin, young master, had let loose at our approach. Being well acquainted with the inveteracy

8

Chapter III

of these curs, I was about to betake myself to my heels, when my
uncle seizing me with one hand, brandished his cudgel with the
other, and at one blow laid Cæsar sprawling on the ground: but
finding himself attacked at the same time in the rear by Jowler, and
fearing Cæsar might recover, he drew his hanger, wheel'd about,
and by a lucky stroke, severed Jowler's head from his body.—By
this time, the young fox-hunter and three servants armed with
pitch-forks and flails were come to the assistance of the dogs, whom
they found breathless upon the field. My cousin was so provoked
at the death of his favourites, that he ordered his attendants to advance, and take vengeance on their executioner, whom he loaded
with all the curses and reproaches his anger could suggest.—Upon
which my uncle stepped forwards with an undaunted air, at the
sight of whose bloody weapon, his antagonists fell back with precipitation; when he accosted their leader thus:—'Lookée, brother,
your dogs having boarded me without provocation, what I did was
in my own defence.—So you had best be civil, and let us shoot a-
head, clear of you.' Whether the young 'squire misinterpreted my
uncle's desire of peace, or was enraged at the fate of his hounds
beyond his usual pitch of resolution, I know not; but he snatched a
flail from one of his followers, and came up with a shew of assaulting the lieutenant, who putting himself into a posture of defence,
proceeded thus:——'Lookée, you lubberly son of a w—e, if you
come athwart me, 'ware your gingerbread-work.[1]—I'll be foul of
your quarter, d—n me.' This declaration followed by a flourish of
his hanger, seemed to check the progress of the young gentleman's
choler, who, upon turning about, perceived his attendants had slunk
into the house, shut the gate, and left him to decide the contention
by himself.—Here a parley ensued, which was introduced by my
cousin's asking, 'Who the d—l are you?—What do you want?—
Some scoundrel of a seaman (I suppose) who has deserted and
turned thief.—But don't think you shall escape, sirrah,—I'll have
you hanged, you dog,—I will.—Your blood shall pay for that of my
two hounds, you ragamuffin.—I would not have parted with them
to save your whole generation from the gallows, you ruffian, you.'
——'None of your jaw, you swab,[2]—none of your jaw (replied my
uncle) else I shall trim your laced jacket for you—I shall rub you
down with an oaken towel,[3] my boy—I shall.'——So saying, he
sheathed his hanger and grasped his cudgel. Mean-while the people
of the house being alarm'd, one of my female cousins opened a

9

window, and asked what was the matter?—'The matter! (answered the lieutenant) no great matter, young woman.—I have business with the old gentleman, and this spark, belike, won't allow me to come along side of him, that's all.'—After a few minutes pause, we were admitted, and conducted to my grandfather's chamber, through a lane of my relations, who honoured me with very significant looks, as I passed along.—When we came into the judge's presence, my uncle, after two or three sea-bows, expressed himself in this manner: —'Your servant, your servant.—What chear, father? what chear? —I suppose you don't know me—may hap you don't.—My name is Tom Bowling,[1]—and this here boy, you look as if you did not know him neither,—'tis like you mayn't.—He's new-rigged, i' faith;— his cloth don't shake in the wind so much as it wont to do.—'Tis my nephew, d'ye see, Roderick Random,—your own flesh and blood, old gentleman, don't lag a stern, you dog, don't (pulling me forward).' My grandfather (who was laid up with the gout) re- ceived this relation, after his long absence, with that civility and coldness which was peculiar to him; told him he was glad to see him, and desired him to sit down.—'Thank ye, thank ye, sir, I had as lief stand, (said my uncle) for my own part, I desire nothing of you; but if you have any conscience at all, do something for this poor boy, who has been used at a very unchristian rate.—Un- christian do I call it?—I am sure the Moors in Barbary, have more humanity than to leave their little ones to misery and want.—I would fain know, why my sister's son is more neglected than that there Fair-weather Jack, (pointing to the young 'squire, who with the rest of my cousins, had followed us into the room.) Is he not as near a-kin to you as the other?—Is not he much handsomer and better built than that great chucklehead?—Come, come, consider, old gentleman, you are going in a short time, to give an account of your evil actions.—Remember the wrongs you did his father; and make all the satisfaction in your power, before it be too late.—The least thing you can do, is to settle his father's portion on him.'— The young ladies, who thought themselves too much concerned, to contain themselves any longer, set up their throats altogether against my protector, who stopped his ears with his fingers, and cried out, that all the devils in hell had broke loose upon him.—'Scurvy companion,—sawcy tarpawlin,—rude, impertinent fellow, did he think to prescribe to grandpapa.—His sister's brat had been too well taken care of,—Grandpapa was too just not to make a difference between an unnatural rebellious son, and his dutiful loving children who took his advice 'in all things;' and such expressions, were levelled against him with great violence; until the judge at length commanded silence.—He calmly rebuked my uncle for his unmannerly behaviour, which he said he would excuse on account of his education: he told him he had been very kind to the boy, whom he had kept at school seven or eight years, although he was informed he made no progress in his learning; but was addicted to all manner of vice, which he the rather believed, because he himself was witness to a barbarous piece of mischief he had committed on the jaws of his chaplain.—But however, he would see what the lad was fit for, and bind him apprentice to some honest tradesman or other, provided he would mend his manners, and behave for the future, as became him.—The honest tar (whose pride and indignation boiled within him) answered my grandfather; that it was true he had sent him to school, but it had cost him nothing, for he had never been at one shilling expence, to furnish him with food, raiment, books, or other necessaries; so, that it was not to be much wondered at, if the boy made small progress; and yet, whoever told him so, was guilty of a damn'd lie, for he was allowed by those who understood those matters, to be the best scholar of his age, in all the country; the truth of which he would maintain, by laying a wager of his whole half year's pay on the boy's head;—(with these words he pulled out his purse, and challenged the company.)— Neither is he addicted to vice, as you affirm, but very much exposed to ill usage, by your neglect, on which occasions, d'ye see, he never fails to shew his spirit, which has been misrepresented to you.—As for what happened to your chaplain, I am only sorry, that he did not knock out the scoundrel's brains, instead of his teeth.—By the Lord, if ever I come up with him, he had better be in Greenland,— that's all.—Thank you for your courteous offer, of binding the lad apprentice to a tradesman, I suppose you would make a taylor of him[1]—would you?—I had rather see him hang'd, d'ye see.—Come along, Rory, I perceive how the land lies, my boy,—let's tack about, i' faith,—while I have a shilling thou shan't want a tester.[2] B'wye, old gentleman, you're bound for the other world, but I believe damnably ill provided for the voyage.—Thus ended our visit, and we returned to the village, my uncle muttering curses all the way against the old shark and the young fry that surrounded him.

CHAPTER IV

My grandfather makes his will.—Our second visit—he dies—his will is read in presence of all his living descendants—the disappointment of my female cousins— my uncle's behaviour

A FEW weeks after our first visit, we were informed that the old judge, after a fit of thoughtfulness, which lasted three days, had sent for a notary and made his will; that the distemper had mounted from his legs to his stomach, and being conscious of his approaching end, he had desired to see all his descendants without exception. —In obedience to this summons, my uncle set out with me a second time, to receive the last benediction of my grandfather; often repeating by the road, 'Ey, ey, we have brought up the old hulk at last.[1]—You shall see,—you shall see the effect of my admonition.' —When we entered his chamber, which was crowded with his relations, we advanced to the bed-side, where we found him in his last agonies, supported by two of his grand-daughters, who sat on each side of him, sobbing most piteously, and wiping away the froth and slaver as it gathered on his lips, which they frequently kissed with a shew of great anguish and affection.—I know not whether or not he perceived my uncle, who approached him with these words, 'What! he's not a weigh.[2] How fare ye,—how fare ye, old gentleman?—Lord have mercy upon your poor sinful soul.'—But the dying man turned his sunken eyes towards us,—when my uncle went on.—'Here's poor Rory come to see you before you die and receive your blessing.—What man! don't despair,—you have been a great sinner, 'tis true,—what then? There's a righteous judge above,—isn't there? He minds me no more than a porpuss[3]— Yes, yes, he's a going,—the land crabs will have him, I see that;— his anchor's a peak,[4] i' faith!'—This homely consolation scandalized the company so much, and especially the parson, who probably thought his province invaded, that we were obliged to retire into another room, where in a few minutes, we were convinced of my grandfather's decease, by a dismal yell uttered by the young ladies in his apartment; whither we immediately hastened, and found his heir, who had retired a little before, into a closet under pretence of giving vent to his sorrow, asking, with a countenance beslubbered with tears, if his grandpapa was certainly dead?—'Dead! (says my uncle, looking at the body) ay, ay, I'll warrant him as dead as a herring.——Odd's fish! now my dream is out for all the world.—I thought I stood upon the Fore-castle, and saw a parcel of carrion crows foul of[1] a dead shark that floated alongside, and the devil perching on our sprit-sailyard,[2] in the likeness of a blue bear—who, d'ye see, jumped over-board upon the carcase, and carried it to the bottom in his claws.'—'Out upon thee, reprobate (cries the parson) out upon thee, blasphemous wretch!—Dost thou think his honour's soul is in the possession of Satan?'—The clamour immediately arose, and my poor uncle, who was shouldered from one corner of the room to the other, was obliged to lug out in his own defence, and swear he would turn out for no man, till such time as he knew who had a title to send him a-drift.——'None of your tricks upon travellers (said he;) may hap, old buff has left my kinsman here, his heir;—If he has, it will be the better for his miserable soul.—Odd's bob! I'd desire no better news.—I'd soon make a clear ship, I warrant you.'—To avoid any farther disturbance, one of my grandfather's executors, who was present, assured Mr. Bowling, that his nephew should have all manner of justice; that a day should be appointed, after the funeral, for examining the papers of the deceased, in presence of all his relations; till such time every desk and cabinet in the house should remain close sealed; and that he was very welcome to be witness of this ceremony, which was immediately performed to his satisfaction.—In the mean time, orders were given to provide mourning for all the relations, in which number I was included: but my uncle would not suffer me to accept of it, until I should be assured whether or no I had reason to honour his memory so far.—During this interval, the conjectures of people, with regard to the old gentleman's will, were various: as it was well known, he had, besides his landed estate, which was worth 700 *l. per annum*, six or seven thousand pounds at interest. Some imagined, that the whole real estate (which he had greatly improved) would go to the young man whom he always entertained as his heir; and that the money would be equally divided between my female cousins (five in number) and me.—Others were of opinion, that as the rest of his children had been already provided for, he would only bequeath two or three hundred pounds to each of his grand-daughters, and leave the bulk of the

sum to me, to atone for his unnatural usage towards my father.——
At length the important hour arrived, and the will was produced in
the midst of the expectants, whose looks and gestures formed a
groupe that would have been very entertaining to an unconcerned
spectator.—But the reader can scarce conceive the astonishment
and mortification that appeared, when an attorney pronounced
aloud, the young 'squire sole heir of all his grandfather's estate
personal and real.—My uncle, who had listened with great attention, sucking the head of his cudgel all the while, accompanied
these words of the attorney with a stare, and *whew*, that alarmed the
whole assembly. The eldest and pertest of my female competitors,
who had been always very officious about my grandfather's person,
enquired with a faultering accent, and visage as yellow as an orange,
'if there were no legacies?' she was answered, 'none at all.'—
Upon which she fainted away.—The rest, whose expectations
(perhaps) were not so sanguine, supported their disappointment
with more resolution; though not without giving evident marks of
indignation, and grief at least as genuine as that which appeared in
them at the old gentleman's death. My conductor, after having
kicked with his heel for some time against the wainscot, began: 'So
there's no legacy, friend, ha!—here's an old Succubus;—but somebody's soul howls for it, d—n me!'—The parson of the parish, who
was one of the executors, and had acted as ghostly director of the
old man, no sooner heard this, than he cried out, 'Avaunt, unchristian reveler! avaunt! wilt thou not allow the soul of his honour
to rest in the grave till the resurrection?'—But this zealous pastor
did not find himself so warmly seconded, as formerly, by the young
ladies, who now joined my uncle against him, and accused him of
having acted the part of a busy-body with their grandpapa, whose
ears he had most certainly abused by false stories to their prejudice,
or else he would not have neglected them, in such an unnatural
manner.—The young 'squire was much diverted with this scene,
and whispered to my uncle, that if he had not murdered his dogs,
he would have shewn him glorious fun, by hunting a black badger[1]
(so he term'd the clergyman).—The surly lieutenant, who was not
in an humour to relish this amusement, replied, 'you and your dogs
may be damned.—I suppose you'll find them with your old dad, in
the latitude of hell.—Come, Rory—about ship, my lad, we must
steer another course, I think.'—and away we went.

CHAPTER V

The School-master uses me barbarously.—I form a project of revenge, in which I am assisted by my uncle.——I leave the village——am settled at an university by his generosity

ON our way back to the village, my uncle spoke not a word during the space of a whole hour, but whistled with great vehemence, the tune of, *Why should we quarrel for riches,*[1] *&'c.* his visage being contracted all the while into a most formidable frown. At length his pace was increased to such a degree, that I was often left behind a considerable way, which when he perceived, he would wait for me; and when I was almost up with him, call out in a surly tone, 'Bear a hand,[2] damme!—must I bring to[3] every minute for you, you lazy dog.'—Then laying hold of me by the arm, haul me along, until his good nature (of which he had a good share) and reflection, getting the better of his passion, he would say, 'Come, my boy, don't be cast down,—the old rascal is in hell,—that's some satisfaction;— you shall go to sea with me, my lad.—*A light heart and a thin pair of breeches, goes thro' the world, brave boys*; as the song goes—eh!'— Though this proposal did not at all suit my inclination, I was afraid of discovering my aversion to it, lest I should disoblige the only friend I had in the world; and he was so much a seaman, that he never dreamt I could have any objection to his design; conse- quently, gave himself no trouble in consulting my approbation. But this resolution was soon dropt, at the advice of our usher, who assured Mr. Bowling, it would be a thousand pities to baulk my genius, which would certainly, one day, make my fortune on shore, provided it received due cultivation.—Upon which, this generous tar determined (though he could ill afford it) to give me university education; and accordingly settled my board and other expences, at a town not many miles distant,[4] famous for its colleges, whither we repaired in a short time.—But before the day of our departure, the school-master, who no longer had the fear of my grandfather before his eyes, laid aside all decency and restraint, and not only abused me in the grossest language his rancour could suggest, as a wicked profligate, dull, beggarly miscrant, whom he had taught out of charity; but also inveighed in the most bitter manner against the memory of the judge (who by the bye had procured that settlement for him) hinting, in pretty plain terms, that the old gentleman's soul was damn'd to all eternity, for his injustice in neglecting to pay for my learning.—This brutal behaviour, added to the sufferings I had formerly undergone, made me think it high time to be revenged of this insolent pedagogue. Having consulted my adherents, I found them all staunch in their promises to stand by me; and our scheme was this:—In the afternoon preceeding the day of departure for the university, I was to take the advantage of the usher's going out to make water (which he regularly did at four o'clock) and shut the great door, that he might not come to the assistance of his superior. This being done, the assault was to be begun, by my advancing to the master and spitting in his face. I was to be seconded by two of the strongest boys in the school, who were devoted to me; their business was to join me in dragging the tyrant to a bench, over which he was to be laid, and his bare posteriors heartily flogged with his own birch, which we proposed to wrest from him in the struggle; but if we should find him too many for us all three, we were to demand the assistance of our competitors, who should be ready to reinforce us, or oppose any thing that might be undertaken by the rest of the boys for the master's relief. One of my principal assistants was called Jeremy Gawky,[1] son and heir of a wealthy gentleman in the neighbourhood; and the name of the other, Hugh Strap,[2] the cadet of a family which had given shoemakers to the village time out of mind.—I had once saved Gawky's life, by plunging into a river where he was on the point of being drowned, and by the help of swimming, dragging him ashore; I had often rescued him from the clutches of those whom his insufferable arrogance had provoked, to a resentment he was not able to sustain;—and I had many times saved his reputation and posteriors, by performing his exercises at school; so that it is not to be wondered at, if he had a particular regard for me and my interests. The attachment of Strap, flowed from a voluntary, disinterested inclination, which had manifested itself on many occasions in my behalf, having once rendered me the same service as I had afforded to Gawky, by saving my life at the risk of his own; and often fathered offences I had committed, for which he suffered severely, rather than I should feel the weight of the punishment I deserved.—These two champions were the more willing to engage in this enterprize, as they intended to leave the school next day, as well as I; the first being ordered by his father to return into the country, and the other being bound apprentice to a barber, at a market town not far off.

In the mean time, my uncle being informed of my master's behaviour to me, was enraged beyond all composition, and vowed revenge so heartily, that I could not refrain from telling him the scheme I had concerted, which he heard with great satisfaction, at every sentence squirting out a mouthful of spittle, tinctured with tobacco, of which he constantly chewed a large quid.—At last, pulling up his breeches, he cried, 'No, no, Z—ds! that won't do neither,——howsomever, 'tis a bold undertaking, my lad,—that I must say, i' faith!—but lookée, lookée, how dost propose to get clear off?—won't the enemy give chace, my boy?—ay, ay, that he will, I warrant—and alarm the whole coast—ah! G—d help thee, more sail than ballast, Rory.—Let me alone for that—leave the whole to me—I'll shew him the foretop-sail,[1] I will.—If so be that your ship-mates are jolly boys, and won't flinch, you shall see, you shall see; egad, I'll play him a salt-water trick—I'll bring him to the gang-way, and anoint him with a cat and nine tails,—he shall have a round dozen doubled, my lad, he shall—and be left lashed, to his meditations.'—We were very proud of our associate, who immediately went to work, and prepared the instrument of his revenge with great skill and expedition; after which, he ordered our baggage to be packed up and sent off, a day before our attempt, and got horses ready to be mounted, as soon as the affair should be over. At length the hour arrived, when our auxiliary, seizing the opportunity of the usher's absence, bolted in, secured the door, and immediately laid hold of the pedant by his collar, who bawled out 'Murder! Thieves!' —with the voice of a stentor. Though I trembled all over like an aspen-leaf, I knew there was no time to be lost, and accordingly got up, and summoned our associates to my assistance. Strap without any hesitation obeyed the signal, and seeing me leap upon the master's back, ran immediately to one of his legs, which pulling with all his force, this dreadful adversary was soon humbled to the ground; upon which Gawky, who had hitherto remained in his place, under the influence of an universal trepidation, hastened to the scene of action, and insulted the fallen tyrant with a loud huzza, in which the whole school joined.—This noise alarmed the usher, who finding himself shut out, endeavoured, partly by threats, and partly by entreaties, to procure admission.—My uncle bid him have a little patience, and he would let him in presently; but if he

17

pretended to move from that place, it should fare the worse with the son of a b—ch his superior, on whom he intended only to bestow a little wholesome chastisement, for his barbarous usage of Rory, 'to which (said he) you are no stranger.'—By this time we had dragged the criminal to a post, to which Bowling tied him with a rope he had provided on purpose, after having fastened his hands behind his back, pulled down his breeches, and tucked up his garments and shirt, as far as they would go.—In this ludicrous posture he stood (to the no small entertainment of the boys, who crowded about him, and shouted with great exultation at the novelty of the sight) venting bitter imprecations against the lieutenant, and reproaching his scholars with treachery and rebellion: when the usher was admitted, whom my uncle accosted in this manner: 'Harkée, Mr. Syntax, I believe you are an honest man, d'ye see—and I have a respect for you—but for all that, we must for our own security (d'ye see) belay you for a short time.'—With these words, he pulled out some fathoms of cord, which the honest man no sooner saw, than he protested with great earnestness, that he would allow no violence to be offered to him, at the same time accusing me of perfidy and ingratitude. But Bowling representing, that it was in vain to resist, and that he did not mean to use him with violence and indecency; but only to hinder him from raising the hue and cry against us, before we should be out of their power; he allowed himself to be bound to his own desk, where he sat a spectator of the punishment inflicted on his principal. My uncle having upbraided this arbitrary wretch with his inhumanity to me, told him, that he proposed to give him a little discipline for the good of his soul: which he immediately put in practice, with great vigour and dexterity. This smart application to the pedant's withered posteriors, gave him such exquisite pain, that he roared like a mad bull, danced, cursed, blasphemed, and acted to the life, the part of a frantick bedlamite. When the lieutenant thought himself sufficiently revenged, he took his leave of him in these words, 'Now, friend, you'll remember me the longest day you have to live—I have given you a lesson, that will let you know what flogging is, and teach you to have more sympathy for the future—shout, boys, shout.'—This ceremony was no sooner over, than my uncle proposed they should quit the school, and convoy their old comrade Rory to a public house, about a mile from the village, where he would treat them all.—This offer being joyfully embraced, he addressed himself to Mr. Syntax, and begged

him to accompany us, which he refused with great disdain, telling
my benefactor, that he was not the man he took him to be.—'Well,
well, old surly (replied my uncle, shaking his hand) thou art an
honest fellow notwithstanding; and if ever I have the command of
a ship, thou shalt be school master, i' faith.' So saying, he dismissed
the boys, and locking the door, left the two preceptors to console
one another; while we moved forwards on our journey, attended by
a numerous retinue, whom he treated according to his promise.—
We parted with many tears, and lay that night at an inn on the road,
about ten miles short of the town where I was to remain, at which
we arrived next day, and I found I had no cause to complain of the
accommodations provided for me; being boarded at the house of
an apothecary, who had married a distant relation of my mother.
In a few days after, my uncle set out for his ship, after having
settled the necessary funds for my maintenance and education.

CHAPTER VI

*I make great progress in my studies——am caressed by
every body——my female cousins take notice of me——I reject
their invitation——they are incensed and conspire against
me——I am left destitute by a misfortune that befals my
uncle—Gawky's treachery——my revenge*

As I was now capable of reflection, I began to consider my precarious situation; that I was utterly abandoned by those whose duty
it was to protect me; and that my sole dependance was on the generosity of one man, who was not only exposed by his profession, to
continual dangers, which might one day deprive me of him for
ever; but also (no doubt) subject to those vicissitudes of disposition,
which a change of fortune usually creates; or, which a better
acquaintance with the world might produce:—for I always ascribed his benevolence to the dictates of a heart as yet undebauched
by a commerce with mankind.—Alarmed at these considerations, I
resolved to apply myself with great care to my studies, and enjoy
the opportunity in my power: This I did with such success, that
in the space of three years, I understood Greek very well, was

pretty far advanced in the mathematics, and no stranger to moral and natural philosophy: logick I made no account of; but above all things, I valued myself on my taste in the *Belle Lettre*, and a talent for poetry, which had already produced some morceaus, that brought me a great deal of reputation. These qualifications added to a good face and shape, acquired the esteem and acquaintance of the most considerable people in town, and I had the satisfaction to find myself in some degree of favour with the ladies; an intoxicating piece of good fortune, to one of my amorous complexion ! which I obtained, or at least preserved, by gratifying their propensity to scandal, in lampooning their rivals.——Two of my female cousins lived in this place, with their mother, after the death of their father, who left his whole fortune (which was considerable) equally divided between them; so that if they were not the most beautiful, they were at least the richest toasts in town; and received daily the addresses of all the beaux and cavaliers of the country.——Although I had hitherto been looked upon by them with the most supercilious contempt, which I endeavoured to return by the most perfect neglect, my character now attracted their notice so much, that I was given to understand, I might be honoured with their acquaintance, if I pleased.—The reader will easily perceive, that this condescension either flowed from the hope of making my poetical capacity subservient to their malice, or at least of screening themselves from the lash of my resentment, which they effectually provoked.—I enjoyed this triumph with great rapture; and not only rejected their offer with disdain, but, in all my performances, whether satire or panegyric, industriously avoided mentioning their names, even while I celebrated those of their intimates, which mortified their pride exceedingly, and incensed them to such a degree, that they rendered themselves universally ridiculous in satisfying their resentment against me.—The first stroke of their revenge consisted in their hiring a poor collegian to write verses against me, the subject of which was my own poverty, and the catastrophe of my unhappy parents; but besides the badness of the composition (of which they themselves were ashamed) they did not find their account in endeavouring to reproach me with those misfortunes, which they and their relations had intailed upon me; and which consequently, reflected much more dishonour on themselves, than on me, who was the innocent victim of their barbarity and avarice.—Finding this plan miscarry, they found means to irritate a young gentleman against me, by telling him I had lampooned his mistress; and so effectually succeeded in the quality of incendiaries, that this enraged lover determined to seize me next night, as I returned to my lodgings from a friend's house that I frequented; with this view, he waited in the street, attended by two of his companions, to whom he had imparted his design of carrying me down to the river, in which he proposed to have me heartily ducked, notwithstanding the severity of the weather, it being then about the middle of December.—But this stratagem did not succeed; for, being apprised of their ambush, I got home another way, and by the help of my landlord's apprentice, emptied a close stool out of the garret window, which did great execution upon them; and next day, occasioned so much mirth at their expence, that they found themselves under a necessity of leaving the town, until the adventure should be entirely forgotten.——My cousins (though twice baffled in their expectation) did not however, desist from persecuting me, who had now enraged them beyond a possibility of forgiveness, by detecting their malice, and preventing its effects: neither would I have found them more humane, had I patiently submitted to their rancour, and bore without murmuring the rigour of their unreasonable hate; for, I have found by experience, that though small favours may be acknowledged, and slight injuries atoned, there is no wretch so ungrateful as he, whom you have most generously obliged; and no enemy so implacable, as those who have done you most wrong.—These good-natured creatures, therefore, had recourse to a scheme which conspired with a piece of bad news I soon after received, to give them all the satisfaction they desired: this plan was to debauch the faith of my companion and confident, and prevail on him to betray the trust I reposed in him, by imparting to them the particulars of my small amours, which they published with such exaggerations, that I suffered very much in the opinion of every body, and was utterly discarded, by the dear creatures whose names had been called in question.—While I was busied in tracing out the author of this treachery, that I might not only be revenged on him, but also vindicate my character to my friends; I one day, perceived the looks of my landlady so altered, when I went home to dinner, that upon enquiring into the cause, she screwed up her mouth, and fixing her eyes on the ground, told me her husband had received a letter from Mr. Bowling, with one enclosed for me—she was very sorry for what had happened, both for my sake, and his own.——People should be more cautious of their conduct—she was always afraid his brutal behaviour would bring him into some misfortune or other.—As for her part, she would be very ready to befriend me; but she had a small family of her own to maintain.—The world would do nothing for her if she should come to want—charity begins at home.—She wished I had been bound to some substantial handicraft, such as a weaver or shoemaker, rather than loiter away my time in learning foolish nonsense that would never bring me in a penny—but some folks are wise, and some are otherwise.——I was listening to this mysterious discourse, with great amazement, when her husband entered, and without speaking a syllable, put both the letters into my hand. —I received them trembling, and read what follows:

To ROGER POTION

SIR,
'This is to let you know that I have quitted the Thunder man of war; being obliged to sheer off, for killing my captain, which I did fairly on the beach, at Cape Tiberoon,[1] in the island of Hispaniola;[2] having received his fire, and returned it, which went through his body:—and I would serve the best man so that ever stept between stem and stern, if so be that he struck me, as captain Oakhum,[3] did. I am (thank God) safe among the French, who are very civil, thof I don't understand their lingo,—and I hope to be restored in a little time, for all the great friends and parliamentary interest of the captain, for I have sent home to my landlord in Deal,[4] an account of the whole affair, with our bearings and distances while we were engaged, whereby I have desired him to lay it before his majesty, who (G—d bless him) will not suffer an honest tar to be wronged. —My love to your spouse, and am

> *Your loving friend,*
> *and servant to command,*
> *while*

THOMAS BOWLING

Chapter VI

To RODERICK RANDOM

DEAR RORY,

'Don't be grieved at my misfortune—but mind your book, my lad. I have got no money to send you; but what of that?—Mr. Potion will take care of you, for the love he bears to me; and let you want for nothing, and it shall go hard, but I will see him one day repaid. —No more at present, but rests

Your dutiful uncle
and servant, till death,
THOMAS BOWLING

This letter (which with the other was dated from Port Louis in Hispaniola) was no sooner read, than the apothecary shaking his head, began:——'I have a very great regard for Mr. Bowling, that's certain,—and could be well content——but times are very hard.—There's no such thing as money to be got—I believe 'tis all vanished under-ground, for my part.—Besides, I have been out of pocket already, having entertained you since the beginning of this month, without receiving a six-pence,—and G—d knows if ever I shall;—for I believe it will go hard with your uncle.—And more than that, I was thinking of giving you warning, for I want your apartment for a new 'prentice, whom I expect from the country every hour.—So, I desire you will this week provide yourself with another lodging.'——The indignation which this harangue inspired, gave me spirits to support my reverse of fortune; and to tell him, I despised his mean, selfish disposition so much, that I would rather starve than be beholden to him for one single meal. Upon which, out of my pocket-money, I paid him to the last farthing of what I owed, and assured him, I would not sleep another night under his roof.—This said, I sallied out, in a transport of rage and sorrow, without knowing whither, to fly for shelter, having not one friend in the world capable of relieving me, and only three shillings in my purse.—After giving way for a few minutes to the dictates of my rage, I went and hired a small bed-room at the rate of one shilling and six-pence *per* week, which I was obliged to pay *per-*advance, before the landlord would receive me; hither I removed my luggage; and next morning got up, with a view of craving the advice and assistance of a person who had on all occasions, loaded

23

me with caresses, and made frequent offers of friendship, while I was under no necessity of accepting them.—He received me with his wonted affability, and insisted on my breakfasting with him, which I did not think fit to refuse.—But when I communicated the occasion of my visit, he appeared so disconcerted, that I concluded him wonderfully affected with the misery of my condition, and looked upon him as a man of the most extensive sympathy and benevolence.—He did not leave me long under this mistake; for recovering himself out of his confusion, he told me, he was grieved at my misfortune, and desired to know what had passed between my landlord Mr. Potion and me. Whereupon I recounted the conversation; and when I repeated the answer I made to his ungenerous remonstrance with regard to my leaving his house, this pretended friend affected a stare, and exclaimed, 'Is it possible you could behave so ill to the man who had treated you so kindly all along?'—— My surprise at hearing this, was not at all affected, whatever his might be; and I gave him to understand, with some warmth, that I did not imagine he would so unreasonably espouse the cause of a scoundrel, who ought to be expelled from every social community. —This heat of mine, gave him all the advantage he desired over me, and our discourse (after much altercation) concluded in his desiring never to see me again in that place; to which I yielded my consent, assuring him, that had I been as well acquainted with his principles formerly as I was now, he never should have had an opportunity to make that request.—And thus we parted.

On my return, I met my old comrade 'squire Gawky, whom his father had sent, some time ago, to town, for his improvement in writing, dancing, fencing; and to see the world. As I had lived with him, since his arrival, on the footing of our old intimacy, I made no scruple of informing him of the lowness of my circumstances, and asking a small supply of money, to answer my present expence; upon which he pulled out an handful of half-pence with a shilling or two among them, and swore that was all he had to keep his pocket till next quarter day; having lost the greatest part of his allowance the night before at billiards. Though this might very well be true, I was extremely mortified at his indifference; for he neither discovered any sympathy for my mishap, nor desire of alleviating my distress; and accordingly, I left him without uttering one word. But when I afterwards understood, that he was the person who had formerly betrayed me to the malice of my cousins, to whom likewise he had carried the tidings of my forlorn situation, which afforded them great matter of triumph and exultation, I determined with myself to call him to a severe account; for which purpose, I borrowed a sword, and wrote a challenge, desiring him to meet me at a certain time and place, that I might have an opportunity of punishing his perfidy, at the expence of his blood.—He accepted the invitation, and I betook myself to the field, though not without feeling considerable repugnance to the combat, which frequently attacked me in cold sweats by the way;—but the desire of revenge, the shame of retracting, and hope of conquest, conspired to repel these unmanly symptoms of fear; and I appeared on the plain with a good grace: there I waited an hour beyond the time appointed, and was not ill pleased to find he had no mind to meet me; because now I should have an opportunity of exposing his cowardice, displaying my own courage, and of beating him soundly wheresoever I should find him, without any dread of the consequence.—Elevated with these suggestions, which entirely banished all thoughts of my deplorable condition, I went directly to Gawky's lodgings, where I was informed of his precipitate retreat, he having set out for the country in less than an hour after he had received my billet.—Whereupon, I was vain enough to have the whole story inserted in the news, although I was fain to sell a gold-laced hat to my landlord, for less than half-price, to defray the expence, and contribute to my subsistence.

CHAPTER VII

I am entertained by Mr. Crab——a description of him——I acquire the art of surgery——consult Crab's disposition—— become necessary to him—an accident happens—he advises me to launch out into the world——assists me with money ——I set out for London

THE fumes of my resentment being dissipated, as well as the vanity of my success, I found myself deserted to all the horrors of extreme want, and avoided by mankind as a creature of a different species, or rather as a solitary being, no ways comprehended within the scheme or protection of providence. My despair had rendered me almost quite stupified, when I was one day told, that a gentleman desired to see me, at a certain publick house, whither immediately I repaired; and was introduced to one Mr. Launcelot Crab[1] a surgeon in town, who was engaged with two more, in drinking a liquor called *pop-in*, composed by tossing a quartern of brandy into a quart of small beer.—Before I relate the occasion of this message, I believe it will not be disagreeable to the reader, if I describe the gentleman who sent for me, and mention some circumstances of his character and conduct, which may illustrate what follows, and account for his behaviour to me.

This member of the faculty was aged fifty, about five foot high, and ten round the belly; his face was capacious as a full moon, and much of the complexion of a mulberry: his nose resembling a powder-horn, was swelled to an enormous size, and studded all over with carbuncles; and his little grey eyes reflected the rays in such an oblique manner, that while he looked a person full in the face, one would have imagined he was admiring the buckle of his shoe.——He had long entertained an implacable resentment against Potion, who, tho' a younger practitioner, had engrossed more business than he, and once had the assurance to perform a cure, whereby he disappointed and disgraced the prognostic of the said Crab.—This quarrel, which was at one time upon the point of being made up, by the interposition and mediation of friends, had been lately inflamed beyond a possibility of reconciliation by the respective wives of the opponents, who, chancing to meet at a christening, disagreed about precedence, proceeded from invectives to blows, and were with great difficulty, by the gossips, prevented from converting the occasion of joy, into a scene of blood.

The difference between these rivals was in the height of rancour, when I was sent for by Crab, who received me as civilly as I could have expected from one of his disposition; and after desiring me to sit, enquired into the particulars of my leaving the house of Potion; which when I had related, he said with a malicious grin,—'Here's a sneaking dog!—I always thought him a fellow without a soul, d—n me!—a canting scoundrel, who has crept into business by his hypocrisy, and kissing the a—se of every body.'——'Ay, ay, (says another) one might see with half an eye, that the rascal has no honesty in him, by his going so regularly to church.' This sentence was confirmed by the third, who assured his companions, that

Potion was never known to be disguised in liquor but once, at a meeting of the godly, where he had distinguished himself by an *extempore* prayer an hour long.—After this preamble, Crab addressed himself to me in these words, 'Well, my lad, I have heard a good character of you, and I'll do for you.——You may send your things to my house when you please.——I have given orders for your reception.——Z—ds! what does the booby stare at?—If you have no mind to embrace my courteous offer, you may let it alone and be d—n'd.'——I answered with a submissive bow, that I was far from rejecting his friendly offer, of which I would immediately avail myself, as soon as he should inform me, on what footing I should be entertained.——'What footing (d—n my blood, cried he) d'ye expect to have a footman and couple of horses kept for you?'—No, Sir (I replied) my expectations are not quite so sanguine.—That I may be as little burthensome as possible, I would willingly serve in your shop, by which means I may save you the expence of a journey-man, or porter at least, for I understand a little pharmacy, having employed some of my leisure hours in the practice of that art, while I lived with Mr. Potion: neither am I altogether ignorant of surgery, which I have studied with great pleasure and application.—'O ho! you did (says Crab). Gentlemen, here is a compleat artist!——Studied surgery! what? in books I suppose.—I shall have you disputing with me, one of these days, on points of my profession.—You can already account for muscular motion (I warrant) and explain the mystery of the brain and nerves —ha!—You are too learned for me, d—n me.—But let's hear no more of this stuff,—can you bleed and give a clyster, spread a plaister and prepare a potion? answer me to that.'—Upon my answering him in the affirmative, he shook his head, telling me, he believed he should have little good of me, for all my promises;— but however, he would take me in for the sake of charity.—I was accordingly that very night admitted to his house, and had an apartment assigned to me in the garret, which I was fain to put up with, notwithstanding the mortification my pride suffered in this change of circumstances. I was soon convinced of the real motives which induced Crab to receive me in this manner: for besides the gratification of his revenge, in exposing the selfishness of his antagonist, in opposition to his own generosity, which was all affectation, he had occasion for a young man who understood something of the profession, to fill up the place of his eldest apprentice, lately dead, not without violent suspicion of foul play from his master's brutality.—The knowledge of this, together with his daily behaviour to his wife, and the young apprentice, did not at all contribute to my enjoying my new situation with ease; however, as I did not perceive how I could bestow myself to better advantage, I resolved to study Crab's temper with all the application, and manage it with all the address I was master of.—And it was not long before I found out a strange peculiarity of humour, which governed his behaviour towards all his dependants.—I observed when he was pleased, he was such a niggard of his satisfaction, that if his wife or servants betrayed the least symptom of participation, he was offended to an insupportable degree of choler and fury, the effects of which they seldom failed to feel.—And when his indignation was roused, submission and soothing always exasperated it beyond the bounds of reason and humanity.—I therefore pursued a contrary plan; and one day, when he honoured me with the names of ignorant whelp and lazy ragamuffin—I boldly replied, I was neither ignorant nor lazy, since I both understood, and performed my business as well as he could do for his soul: neither was it just to call me ragamuffin, for I had a whole coat on my back, and was descended from a better family than any he could boast an alliance with. He gave tokens of great amazement at this assurance of mine, and shook his cane over my head, regarding me all the time with a countenance truly diabolical. Although I was terribly startled at his menacing looks and posture, I yet had reflection enough left, to convince me, I had gone too far to retract, and that this was the critical minute which must decide my future lot, in his service; whereupon I snatched up the pestle of a mortar, and swore if he offered to strike me without cause, I would see whether his scull or my weapon was hardest.—He continued silent for some time, and at last broke forth into these ejaculations,—'This is fine usage from a servant to a master,——very fine!——damnation!——but, no matter, you shall pay for this, you dog, you shall.——I'll do your business——yes, yes, I'll teach you to lift your hand against me.'— So saying, he retired and left me under dreadful apprehensions, which vanished intirely at our next meeting, when he behaved with unusual complacency, and treated me with a glass of punch after dinner.—By this conduct, I got the ascendency over him in a short time, and became so necessary to him, in managing his business while he was engaged at the bottle, that fortune began to wear a kinder aspect with regard to me; and I consoled myself for the disregard of my former acquaintance, with the knowledge I daily imbibed, by a close application to the duties of my employment, in which I succeeded beyond my own expectation.—I was on very good terms with my master's wife, whose esteem I acquired and cultivated, by representing Mrs. Potion in the most ridiculous lights my satirical talents could invent, as well as by rendering her some christian offices, when she had been too familiar with the dram bottle, to which she had often times recourse for consolation, under the affliction she suffered from a barbarous husband.—In this manner I lived, without hearing the least tidings of my uncle, for the space of two years, during which time I kept little or no company, being neither in a humour to relish, nor in a capacity to maintain much acquaintance: for the Nabal[1] my master allowed me no wages; and the small perquisites of my station scarce supplied me with the common necessaries of life.—I was no longer, a pert, unthinking coxcomb, giddy with popular applause, and elevated with the extravagance of hope; my misfortunes had taught me how little the caresses of the world during a man's prosperity, are to be valued by him; and how seriously and expeditiously he ought to set himself about making himself independent of them. My present appearance, therefore, was the least of my care, which was wholly engrossed in laying up a stock of instruction that might secure me against the caprice of fortune for the future. I became such a sloven, and contracted such an air of austerity, that every body pronounced me crest-fallen; and Gawky returned to town without running any risk from my resentment, which was by this time pretty much cooled, and restrained by prudential reasons, so effectually, that I never so much as thought of obtaining satisfaction for the injuries he had done me.—When I deemed myself sufficiently master of my business, I began to cast about for an opportunity of launching into the world, in hopes of finding some provision, that might make amends for the difficulties I had undergone: but, as this could not be effected without a small sum of money to equip me for the field, I was in the utmost perplexity how to raise it, well knowing, that Crab, for his own sake, would never put me in a condition to leave him, when his interest was so much concerned in my stay.—But a small accident, which happened about this time, determined him in my favour. This was no other than the pregnancy of his maid servant, who declared her situation to me, assuring me at the same time, that I was the occasion of it. Although I had no reason to question the truth of this imputation, I was not ignorant of the familiarities which had passed between her master and her; of which availing myself, I represented to her the folly of laying the burthen at my door, when she might dispose of it to much greater advantage with Mr. Crab: She listened to my advice, and next day acquainted him with the pretended success of their mutual endeavour.——He was far from being over-joyed at this proof of his vigour, which he foresaw might have very troublesome consequences; not that he dreaded any domestic grumblings and reproaches from his wife, whom he kept in perfect subjection; but because he knew it would furnish his rival Potion with a handle for insulting and undermining his reputation, there being no scandal equal to that of uncleanness, in the opinion of those who inhabit that part of the island where he lived.—He therefore took a resolution worthy of himself, which was, to persuade the girl, that she was not with child, but only afflicted with a disorder incident to young women, which he could easily remove: with this view (as he pretended) he prescribed for her such medicines, as he thought would infallibly procure abortion; but in this he was disappointed, for the maid being advertised by me of his design, and at the same time well satisfied with her own condition, absolutely refused to follow his directions; and threatned to publish her situation to the world, if he did not immediately take some method of providing for the important occasion, which she expected in a few months.—It was not long before I guessed the result of his deliberation, by his addressing himself to me (one day) in this manner: 'I am surprised, that a young fellow like you, discovers no inclination to push his fortune in the world.—By G—d, before I was of your age, I was broiling on the coast of Guinea.—Damme! what's to hinder you from profiting by the war, which will certainly be declared in a short time against Spain?[1]—You may easily get on board of a king's ship in quality of a surgeon's mate, where you will certainly see a great deal of practice, and stand a good chance of getting prize money.'—I laid hold of this declaration, which I had long wished for, and assured him I would follow his advice with pleasure, if it was in my power; but that it was impossible for me, to embrace an opportunity of that kind, having no friend to advance a little money, to supply me with what necessaries I should want, and defray the expences of my journey to London.—He told me, that few neces-

saries were required; and as for the expence of my journey, he
would lend me money, not only for that purpose, but also to maintain me comfortably in London, until I should procure a warrant
for my provision aboard ship.—I gave him a thousand thanks for
his obliging offer (although I was very well apprized of his motive,
which was to make his chamber-maid lay the child to me after I
was gone; and accordingly set out in a few weeks for London; my
whole fortune[1] consisting of one suit of cloaths, half a dozen
ruffled shirts, as many plain, two pair worsted stockings, as many
thread; a case of pocket instruments, a small edition of Horace,
Wiseman's surgery,[2] and ten guineas in cash; for which Crab took
my bond, bearing 5 *per cent.*[3] interest; at the same time giving me a
letter to the member of parliament for our town, which he said
would do my business.

CHAPTER VIII

I arrive at Newcastle——meet with my old school-fellow Strap
——we determine to walk in company to London—set out
on our journey——put up at a solitary ale-house——are
disturbed by a strange adventure in the night

THERE is no such convenience as a waggon in this country, and my
finances were too weak to support the expence of hiring a horse;
I determined therefore to set out with the carriers, who transport
goods from one place to another on horse-back, this I accordingly
put in execution, on the first day of November 1739, sitting upon
a pack-saddle between two baskets; one of which contained my
goods in a knapsack. But by the time we arrived at Newcastle upon
Tyne, I was so fatigued with the tediousness of the carriage, and
benumbed with the coldness of the weather, that I resolved to
travel the rest of my journey on foot, rather than proceed in such a
disagreeable manner.

The hostler of the inn at which we put up, understanding I was
bound for London, advised me to take my passage in a collier,
which would be both cheap and expeditious, and withal much
easier than to walk upwards of three hundred miles through deep
roads, in the winter time; which he believed I had not strength

enough to perform.—I was almost persuaded to take his advice, when, one day, stepping into a barber's shop to be shaved, the young man, while he lathered my face, accosted me thus: 'Sir, I presume you are a Scotchman.' To which I answered in the affirmative.—'Pray (continued he) of what part of Scotland?'—I no sooner told him, than he discovered great emotion, and not confining his operation to my chin and upper lip, besmeared my whole face with great agitation.—At which I was so offended, that starting up, I asked him what the d—l he meant by using me so?—He begged pardon, telling me his joy in meeting with a countryman, had occasioned some confusion in him; and craved my name.—But when I declared my name was Random he exclaimed in a rapture, 'How! Rory Random?' The same, I replied, looking at him with astonishment; 'What, cried he, don't you know your old school-fellow, Hugh Strap?' At that instant recollecting his face, I flew into his arms, and in the transport of my joy, gave him back one half of the suds he had so lavishly bestowed on my countenance; so that we made a very ludicrous appearance, and furnished a great deal of mirth to his master and shop-mates, who were witnesses of this scene.—When our mutual caresses were over, I sat down again to be shaved, but the poor fellow's nerves were so discomposed by this unexpected meeting, that his hand could scarcely hold the razor, with which (nevertheless) he found means to cut me in three places, in as many strokes. His master, perceiving his disorder, bid another supply his place; and after the operation was performed, gave Strap leave to pass the rest of the day with me.—We retired immediately to my lodgings, where calling for some beer, I desired to be informed of his adventures, which contained nothing more, than that his master dying before his time was out, he had come to Newcastle about a year ago, in expectation of journey-work, along with three young fellows of his acquaintance who worked in the keels;[1] that he had the good fortune of being employed by a very civil master, with whom he intended to stay till the spring, at which time he proposed to go to London, where he did not doubt of finding encouragement.—When I communicated to him my situation and design, he did not approve of my taking a passage by sea, by reason of the danger of a winter voyage, which is very hazardous along that coast, as well as the precariousness of the wind, which might possibly detain me a great while, to the no small detriment of my fortune: whereas, if I would venture by land, he would bear me company, carry my baggage as well as his own, all the way; and if we should find ourselves fatigued, it would be no hard matter for us to find on the road, either return-horses or waggons, of which we might take the opportunity for a very trifling expence.—I was so ravished at this proposal, that I embraced him affectionately, and assured him he might command my purse to the last farthing; but he gave me to understand, he had saved money sufficient to answer his own occasions; and that he had a friend in London, who would soon introduce him into business, in that capital; and might possibly have it in his power to serve me likewise.

Having concerted our plan and settled our affairs that night, we departed next morning, by daybreak, armed with a good cudgel each, my companion being charged with the furniture of us both, crammed into one knapsack, which he carried after the manner of soldiers on a march; and our money sewed between the lining and wastband of our breeches, except some loose silver for our immediate expence on the road.—We travelled all day at a round pace, but being ignorant of the proper stages, we were benighted at a good distance from any inn, which compelled us to take up our lodging at a small hedge ale-house, that stood by itself on a by road, about half a mile from the high way: There we found a pedlar of our own country, in whose company we regaled ourselves with bacon and eggs and a glass of good ale, before a comfortable fire, conversing all the while very sociably with the landlord and his daughter, an hale buxome lass, who entertained us with great good humour, and in whose affection I was vain enough to believe I had made some progress.—About eight a clock, we were all three, at our own desire, shewn into an apartment, where were two beds, in one of which Strap and I betook ourselves to rest, and the pedlar occupied the other, though not before he had prayed a considerable time *extempore*; searched into every corner of the room, and fastened the door on the inside with a strong iron screw, which he carried about with him for that use.—I slept very sound till midnight, when I was disturbed by a violent motion of the bed, which shook under me with a continual tremor.—Alarmed at this phœnomenon, I jogged my companion, whom to my no small amazement, I found drenched in sweat, and quaking through every limb; he told me with a low faultering voice, that we were undone; for there was a bloody highwayman loaded with pistols, in the next room; then, bidding me make as little noise as possible, he directed me to a small chink in the board partition, through which I could see a thick set brawny fellow, with a fierce countenance, sitting at a table in company with our young landlady, having a bottle of ale and a brace of pistols before them.——I listened with great attention, and heard him say in a terrible tone: 'D—n that son of a b—h, Smack the coachman!——he has served me a fine trick, indeed!——but d—tion seize me, if I don't make him repent it!—I'll teach the scoundrel to give intelligence to others, while he is under articles with me.'——Our landlady endeavoured to appease this exasperated robber, by saying, that he might possibly be mistaken in Smack, who perhaps kept no correspondence with the other gentleman that robbed his coach,—and that if an accident had disappointed him to day, he might soon find opportunities enough to atone for his lost trouble.——'I'll tell thee what, my dear Bett (replied he) I never had, nor never will, while my name is Rifle,[1] have such a glorious booty as I missed to-day.—Z—ds! there was 400 *l.* in cash to recruit men for the king's service, besides the jewels, watches, swords, and money belonging to the passengers;—had it been my fortune to have got clear off with so much treasure, I would have purchased a commission in the army, and made you an officer's lady, you jade, I would.'——'Well, well (cries Betty) we must trust to providence for that;—but did you find nothing worth taking, which escaped the other adventurer?'——Not much, faith (said the lover;) I gleaned a few things,—such as a pair of pops, silver-mounted (here they are) I took them loaded out of the pockets of the captain who had the charge of the money, together with a gold watch, which he had concealed in his breeches.—I likewise found ten Portugal pieces in the shoes of a quaker, whom the spirit moved to revile me with great bitterness and devotion; but what I value myself mostly for, is this here purchase, a gold snuff-box, my girl, with a young gentleman's picture on the inside of the lid: which I untied out of the tail of a pretty lady's smock.'——Here, as the devil would have it, the pedlar snored so loud, that the highwayman snatching his pistols, started up, crying, 'Hell and d—n—n! I am betrayed,—who's that in the next room?' Mrs. Betty told him, he need not be uneasy, there were only three poor wearied travellers, who, mistaking the road, had taken up their lodging there, and were asleep long ago.—'Travellers! says he, spies, you b—ch! but no matter—by G—d, I'll send them all to hell in an instant.'—

Chapter VIII

He accordingly run towards our door; when his sweetheart interposing, assured him, there was only a couple of poor young Scotchmen, who were too raw and ignorant to give him the least cause of
suspicion; and the third was a Presbyterian pedlar of the same nation,
who had often lodged in the house before.—This declaration satisfied the thief, who swore he was glad there was a pedlar there, for he
wanted some linen.—Then in a jovial manner, he put about the
glass,[1] mingling his discourse to Betty, with caresses and familiarities,
that spoke him very happy in his amours. During that part of the
conversation which regarded us, Strap had crept under the bed,
where he lay without sense or motion, so that it was with great
difficulty I persuaded him our danger was over, and prevailed on
him to wake the pedlar, and inform him of what we had seen and
heard.—This itinerant merchant no sooner felt somebody shaking
him by the shoulder, than he started up, calling as loud as he
could,——'Thieves, thieves!—L—d have mercy on us.' Rifle,
alarmed at this exclamation, jumped up, cocked one of his pistols,
and turned towards the door to kill the first man who should enter;
for he verily believed himself beset; when his Dulcinea,[2] after an
immoderate fit of laughter, persuaded him, that the poor pedlar
dreaming of thieves, had only cried out in his sleep.—Meanwhile
my comrade had undeceived our fellow-lodger, and informed him
of his reason for disturbing him; upon which, getting up softly he
peeped through the hole, and was so terrified with what he saw,
that, falling down on his bare knees, he put up a long petition to
heaven, to deliver him from the hands of that ruffian, and promised
never to defraud a customer for the future of the value of a half-
penny, provided he might be rescued from his present distress.——
Whether or not this disburthening his conscience afforded him any
ease, I know not; but he slipt into bed again and lay very quiet until
the robber and his mistress were asleep, which he understood by
their snoring in concert; then, rising softly, he untied a rope that
was round his pack, and making it fast to one end of it, opened the
window with as little noise as possible, and lowered his goods into
the yard with great dexterity; which having done, he moved gently
to our bedside, and bid us farewel, telling us, that as we run no risk,
we might take our rest with great confidence, and in the morning
assure the landlord that we knew nothing of his escape: then
shaking us by the hands, and wishing us all manner of success, he
let himself drop from the window without any danger to the ground,

which was not above one yard from his feet as he hung on the outside. Although I did not think proper to accompany him in his flight, I was not at all free from apprehension, when I reflected on what might be the effects of the highwayman's disappointment, who certainly intended to make free with the pedlar's ware. Neither was my companion at more ease in his mind, but on the contrary so possessed with the dreadful idea of Rifle, that he solicited me strongly to follow our countryman's example, and so elude the fatal resentment of that terrible adventurer, who would certainly wreak his vengeance on us, as accomplices of the pedlar's elopement.— But I represented to him, the danger of giving Rifle cause to think we knew his profession, by putting him in mind, that if ever he should meet us again on the road (which was far from being impossible) he would look upon us as dangerous acquaintance, and find it his interest to put us out of the way.—I told him withal, the confidence I had in Betty's good-nature; in which he acquiesced, and during the remaining part of the night, we concerted a proper method of behaviour, to render us unsuspected in the morning.

It was no sooner day, than Betty, entering our chamber, and perceiving the window open, cried out, 'Ods bobs![1] Sure you Scotchmen must have hot constitutions, to lie all night with the window open in such cold weather!'—I feigned to start out of sleep, and withdrawing the curtain, called, 'What's the matter?' When she shewed me, I affected surprize, and said, 'Bless me! the window was shut when we went to bed.'—'I'll be hanged, said she, if Sawny Waddle the pedlar has not got up in a dream and done it, for I heard him very obstropulous[2] in his sleep.—Sure I put a chamberpot under his bed.'—With these words she advanced to the bed in which he lay, and finding the sheets cold, she exclaimed, 'Good lack a daisy! the rogue is fled!'—'Fled (cried I, with a feigned amazement) G—d forbid!—Sure he has not robbed us.'—Then springing up, I laid hold of my breeches, and emptied all my loose money into my hand; which having reckoned, I said, Heaven be praised our money is all safe.—Strap, look to the knapsack.—He did so, and found all was right.—Upon which, we asked with seeming concern, if he had stole nothing belonging to the house.—'No, no, replied she, he has stole nothing but his reckoning;' which, it seems this pious pedlar had forgot to discharge in the midst of his devotion.—Betty, after a moment's pause withdrew, and immediately we could hear her waken Rifle, who no sooner heard of Waddle's flight, than he jumped out of bed and dressed, venting a thousand execrations, and vowing to murder the pedlar if ever he could set his eyes on him again; 'For, said he, the scoundrel has by this time raised the hue and cry against me.'—Having dressed himself in a hurry, he mounted his horse, and for that time rid us of his company and a thousand fears that were the consequence of it.—While we were at breakfast, Betty endeavoured by all the cunning she was mistress of, to learn whether or no we suspected our fellow-lodger, whom we saw take horse; but as we were on our guard, we answered her sly questions with a simplicity she could not distrust; when all of a sudden, we heard the trampling of a horse's feet at the door. This noise alarmed Strap so much, whose imagination was wholly engrossed by the image of Rifle, that with a countenance as pale as milk, he cried out, 'O Lord! there's the highwayman returned!'— Our landlady startled at these words, said, 'What highwayman, young man?—Do you think any highwaymen harbour here?'— Though I was very much disconcerted at this piece of indiscretion in Strap, I had presence of mind enough to tell her, we had met a horse-man the day before, whom Strap had foolishly supposed to be a highwayman, because he rode with pistols; and that he was terrified at the sound of a horse's feet ever since.—She forced a smile at the ignorance and timorousness of my comrade; but I could perceive, (not without great concern) that this account was not at all satisfactory to her.

CHAPTER IX

We proceed on our journey—are overtaken by an
highwayman who fires at Strap, is prevented from shooting
me by a company of horsemen, who ride in pursuit of him—
Strap is put to bed at an inn—Adventures at that inn

AFTER having paid our score, and taken leave of our hostess, who embraced me tenderly at parting, we proceeded on our journey, blessing our selves that we had come off so well. We had not walked about five miles, when we observed a man on horse-back galloping after us, whom we in a short time recognized to be no other than this formidable hero who had already given us so much vexation.—

He stopped hard by me, and asked if I knew who he was?—My astonishment had disconcerted me so much, that I did not hear his question, which he repeated with a volley of oaths and threats; but I remained as mute as before.—Strap seeing my discomposure, fell upon his knees in the mud, uttering with a lamentable voice, these words: 'For Ch—ist's sake, have mercy upon us, Mr. Rifle, we know you very well.'—'O ho! cried the thief, you do!—but by G—d, you never shall be evidence against me in this world, you dog!'——So saying, he drew a pistol, and fired it at the unfortunate shaver, who fell flat upon the ground without speaking one word.— My comrade's fate, and my own situation, rivetted me to the place where I stood, deprived of all sense and reflection; so that I did not make the least attempt either to run away, or deprecate the wrath of this barbarian, who snapped a second pistol at me; but before he had time to prime again, perceived a company of horse-men coming up; whereupon he rode off, and left me standing motionless as a statue, in which posture I was found by those whose appearance had saved my life.—This company, which consisted of three men in livery, well armed, was headed by an officer, who (as I afterwards learned) was the person from whom Rifle had taken the pocket pistols the day before; and who, making known his misfortune to a nobleman he met on the road, assuring him, his non-resistance was altogether owing to his consideration for the ladies in the coach, procured the assistance of his Lordship's servants to go in quest of the plunderer.—This holiday captain scampered up to me with great address, and asked who fired the pistol which he had heard.—As I had not yet recovered my reason, he, before I could answer, observed a body lying on the ground: at which sight, his colour vanished, and he pronounced with a faultering tongue, 'Gentlemen, here's murder committed! Let us alight.'—'No, no, said one of his followers, let us rather pursue the murderer.—Which way went he, young man?'—By this time, I had recollected myself so far as to tell them he could not be a quarter of a mile before them; and beg one of them to assist me in conveying the corps of my friend to the next house, in order to its being interred.—The captain foreseeing that in case he pursued, he must soon come to action, began to curb his horse, and give him the spur at the same time, which made the creature rear up and snort in such a manner, that he called out, his horse was frightened and would not proceed; at the same time wheeling him round and round, stroking his neck, whistling and

wheedling him with 'Sirrah, sirrah—gently, gently, &c.'—'Z—ds!
(cries one of the servants) sure my Lord's Sorrel is not resty!'[1]—
With these words, he bestowed a lash on his buttocks, and Sorrel
disdaining the rein, sprung forward with the captain at a pace that
would have soon brought him up with the robber, had not the girth
(happily for him) given way, by which means he landed in the dirt;
and two of his attendants continued their pursuit, without minding
his situation in the least.—Mean while one of the three who remained at my desire, turning the Body of Strap to one side, in order
to see the wound which had killed him, found him still warm and
breathing; whereupon I immediately let him blood, and saw him,
with inexpressible joy, recover; having received no other wound
than what his fear inflicted.——Having got him upon his legs, we
walked together to an inn, about half a mile from the place, where
Strap being not quite recovered, went to bed; and in a little time
after, the third servant returned with the captain's horse and furniture, leaving himself to crawl after as well as he could. This Gentleman of the sword upon his arrival, complained grievously of the
bruise occasioned by his fall; and on the recommendation of the
servant, who warranted my ability, I was employed to bleed him,
for which he rewarded me with half a crown.

The time between this and dinner, I passed in observing a game
at cards, between two farmers, an exciseman, and a young fellow in
a rusty gown and cassock, who, as I afterwards understood, was
curate of a neighbouring parish.——It was easy to perceive that
the match was not equal; the two farmers being partners, having to
do with a couple of sharpers, who stript them of all their cash in a
very short time.—But what surprised me very much, was to hear
this clergyman reply to one of the countrymen who seemed to
suspect foul play, in these words: 'D—n me, friend, d'ye question
my honour?'—I did not at all wonder to find a cheat in canonicals,
this being an animal frequent in my own country; but I was scandalized at the indecency of his behaviour, which appeared in the oaths
he swore, and the baudy songs which he sung.——At last, to make
amends, in some sort, for the damage he had done the unwary
boors, he pulled out a fiddle from the lining of his gown, and
promising to treat them with a dinner, began to play most melo-
diously, singing all the while in concert.—This good humour of the
parson inspired the company with so much glee, that the farmers
soon forgot their losses, and all hands went to dancing in the yard.

While we were agreeably amused in this manner, our musician spying a horseman riding towards the inn, stopt all of a sudden, crying out, 'Gad so! gentlemen, I beg your pardon, there's our dog of a doctor coming into the inn.'—And immediately concealed his instrument, and ran towards the gate, where he took hold of the vicar's bridle, and helped him off, enquiring very cordially into the state of his health.—This rosy son of the church (who might be about the age of fifty) having alighted, and entrusted the curate with his horse, stalked with great solemnity into the kitchen, where, sitting down by the fire, he called for a bottle of ale and a pipe; scarce deigning an answer to the submissive questions of some present who knew him, about the welfare of his family.—While he indulged himself in this state, amidst a profound silence, the curate approaching him with great reverence, asked if he would not be pleased to honour us with his company at dinner? To which he answered in the negative, saying, he had been to visit 'squire Bumpkin, who had drank himself into a high fever at the last assizes; and that he had, on leaving his own house, told Betty he should dine at home.—Accordingly, when he had made an end of his bottle and pipe, he got up and moved towards the door with the same dignity as when he entered; where his journeyman stood ready with his nag.—He had no sooner mounted, than this facetious person, coming into the kitchen, began in this manner: 'There the old rascal goes, and the D—l go with him.—You see how the world wags,[1] gentlemen.——By G—d, this rogue of a vicar does not deserve to live;—and yet he has two livings worth 400 *l. per annum*, while poor I am fain to do all his drudgery, and ride twenty miles every Sunday to preach, for what? why truly, for 20 *l.* a year.[2]—I scorn to boast of my own qualifications, but—comparisons, you know, are odious.—I should be glad to know how this swag-bellied doctor deserves to be more at ease than me.—He can loll in his elbow chair at home, indulge himself in the best of victuals and wine, and enjoy the conversation of Betty, his house-keeper.—— You understand me, gentlemen.—Betty is the doctor's poor kins-woman, and a pretty girl she is;—but no matter for that;—ay, and a dutiful girl to her parents, whom she goes to see regularly every year, though I must own I could never learn in what county they live.—My service t'ye gentlemen.'——By this time dinner being ready, I waked my companion, and we eat all together with great chearfulness and satisfaction. When our meal was ended, and every

40

man's share of the reckoning adjusted, the curate went out on
pretence of some necessary occasion, and mounting his horse, left
the two farmers to satisfy the host in the best manner they could.—
We were no sooner informed of this piece of finesse, then the exciseman who had been silent hitherto, began with a malicious grin,
'Ay, ay, this is an old trick of Shufle,[1]—I could not help smiling,
when he talked of treating.—You must know, this is a very curious
fellow.—He picked up some scraps of learning while he served
young lord Trifle at the university.—But what he most excells in,
is pimping.—No man knows his talents better than I, for I was
valet de chambre to 'squire Tattle, an intimate companion of
Shuffle's lord.—He got himself into a scrape, by pawning some of
his lordship's cloaths, on which account he was turned away; but
as he was acquainted with some particular circumstances of my
lord's conduct, he did not care to exasperate him too much, and so
made interest for his receiving orders, and afterwards recommended
him to the curacy which he now enjoys.—However, the fellow
cannot be too much admired for his dexterity in making a comfortable livelihood, in spite of such a small allowance.——You hear he
plays a good stick, and is really diverting company—this makes
him agreeable wherever he goes;—and as for playing at cards, there
is not a man within three counties a match for him;—the truth is,
he is a damnable cheat, and can shift a card with such address, that
it is impossible to discover him.'—At this he was interrupted by
one of the farmers, who asked him, why he had not justice enough
to acquaint them with these particulars before they engaged in
play?—The exciseman replied without any hesitation, that it was
none of his business to intermeddle between man and man; besides,
he did not know they were ignorant of Shuffle's character, which
was notorious to the whole country.—This did not satisfy the
other, who taxed him with abetting and assisting the curate's
knavery, and insisting on having his share of the winning returned;
which the exciseman as positively refused, affirming, that whatever
slights Shuffle might practise on other occasions, he was very certain, that he had play'd on the square with them, and would answer
it before any bench in christendom; so saying, he got up, and having
paid his reckoning, sneaked off. The landlord thrusting his neck
into the passage, to see if he was gone, shook his head, saying, 'Ah!
Lord help us! if every sinner was to have his deserts.—Well, we
victuallers must not disoblige the excisemen.[2]—But, I know what,

—if parson Shuffle and he were weighed together, a straw thrown into either scale would make the balance kick the beam.—But, masters, this is under the rose,[1] continued Boniface[2] with a whisper.'

CHAPTER X

The highwayman is taken—we are detained as evidences against him—proceed to the next village—he escapes—we arrive at another inn, where we go to bed—in the night we are awaked by a dreadful adventure—next night we lodge at the house of a school-master—our treatment there

STRAP and I were about to depart on our journey, when we perceived a croud on the road, coming towards us, shouting and hollowing all the way. As it approached, we could discern a man on horse-back in the middle, with his hands tied behind him, whom we soon knew to be Rifle.—This highwayman not being so well mounted as the two servants who went in pursuit of him, was soon overtaken, and after having discharged his pistols, made prisoner without any further opposition. They were carrying him in triumph, amidst the acclamations of the country people, to a justice of peace in a neighbouring village, but stopt at our inn to join their companion and take refreshment. When Rifle was dismounted, and placed in the yard, within a circle of peasants armed with pitchforks, I was amazed to see what a pitiful dejected fellow he now appeared, who had but a few hours ago, filled me with so much terror and confusion.—My companion was so much encouraged by this alteration in his appearance, that going up to the thief, he presented his clenched fists to his nose, and declared, that he would either cudgel or box with the prisoner for a guinea, which he immediately produced; and began to strip—but was dissuaded from this adventure by me, who represented to him the folly of the undertaking, as Rifle was now in the hands of justice, which would, no doubt, give us all satisfaction enough.—But what made me repent of our impertinent curiosity, was our being detained by the captors, as evidence against him, when we were just going to set forward. However, there was no remedy; we were obliged to comply, and accordingly joined in the cavalcade, which luckily took the same road that we proposed.—About the twilight we arrived at the place of our destination, but as the justice was gone to visit a gentleman in the country, with whom he would probably stay all night, the robber was confined in an empty garret three stories high, from which it seemed impossible for him to escape: this, nevertheless, was the case; for next morning, when they went up stairs, to bring him before the justice, the bird was flown, having got out at the window upon the leads, from whence he continued his rout along the tops of the adjoining houses, and got into another garret window, where he sculked, until the family were asleep, at which time he ventured down stairs, and let himself out by the street door, which was found open. This event was a great disappointment to those that apprehended him, who were flushed with hopes of the reward; but gave me great joy, as I was permitted now to continue my journey without any further molestation.—Resolving to make up for the small progress we had hitherto made, we this day travelled with great vigour, and before night got to a market-town twenty miles from the place from whence we set out in the morning, without meeting any adventure worth notice.——Here having taken up our lodging at an inn, I found myself so fatigued, that I began to despair of performing our journey on foot, and desired Strap to enquire if there was any waggon, return-horses, or other cheap carriage in this place, to depart for London to-morrow or next day.—He was informed, that the waggon from Newcastle for London had halted here two nights ago, and that it would be an easy matter to overtake it, if not the next day, at farthest the day after the next.—This piece of news gave us some satisfaction, and after making a hearty supper on hashed mutton, we were shewn to our room, which contained two beds, the one allotted for us, and the other for a very honest gentleman, who, we were told, was then drinking below. Though we could have very well dispensed with his company, we were glad to submit to this disposition, as there was not another bed empty in the house; and accordingly went to rest, after having secured our baggage under the bolster. About two or three a-clock in the morning, I was waked out of a very profound sleep, by a dreadful noise in the chamber, which did not fail to throw me into an agony of consternation, when I heard these words pronounced with a terrible voice.—'Blood and wounds! run the halbert into the guts of him that's next you, and I'll blow the other's brains out presently.'—This dreadful salutation had no sooner reached the ears of Strap, than starting out of bed, he run against some body in the dark, and overturned him in an instant, at the same time bawling out, 'Fire! murder! fire!' which in a moment alarmed the whole house, and filled our chamber with a crowd of naked people. —When lights were brought, the occasion of all this disturbance soon appeared; which was no other than our fellow lodger, whom we found lying on the floor scratching his head, with a look testifying the utmost astonishment, at the concourse of apparitions that surrounded him.—This honest gentleman was, it seems, a recruiting serjeant, who having listed two country fellows over-night, dreamed they had mutinied, and threatened to murder him and the drummer who was along him.—This made such an impression on his imagination, that he got up in his sleep, and expressed himself as above.—When our apprehension of danger vanished, the company beheld one another with great surprize and mirth; but what attracted the notice of every one, was our landlady with nothing on but her shift and a large pair of buckskin breeches with the backside before, which she had slipt on in the hurry, and her husband with her petticoat about his shoulders: one had wrapt himself in a blanket, another was covered with a sheet, and the drummer who had given his only shirt to be washed, appeared in *querpo*[1] with the bolster rolled about his middle.——When this affair was discussed, every body retired to his own apartment, the serjeant slipt into bed, and my companion and I slept without any further disturbance till the morning, when we got up, went to breakfast, paid our reckoning, and set forward in expectation of overtaking the waggon; in which, however, we were disappointed that day. As we exerted ourselves more than usual, I found myself quite spent with fatigue, when we entered a small village in the twilight. We enquired for a publick house, and were directed to one of a very sorry appearance. At our entrance the landlord,[2] who seemed to be a venerable old man, with long grey hair, rose from a table placed by a large fire in a very neat paved kitchin, and with a chearful countenance accosted us in these words: '*Salvete Pueri—ingredimini.*'[3]—I was not a little pleased to hear our host speak Latin, because I was in hopes of recommending myself to him by my knowledge in that language; I therefore answered with hesitation,—*Dissolve frigus, ligna super foco.—large reponens.*[4]—I had no sooner pronounced these words, than the old gentleman running towards me, shook me by the hand, crying, '—*Fili mi dilectissime! unde venis!—a superis, ni fallor?*'[5]—in short, finding we were both read in the classicks, he did not know how to testify his regard, but ordered his daughter, a jolly rosy-cheeked damsel, who was his sole domestic, to bring us a bottle of his *quadrimum.*—repeating from Horace at the same time, '—*Deprome quadrimum sabinâ, O Thaliarche, merum diotâ.*'[1] This *quadrimum* was excellent ale of his own brewing, of which he told us he had always an *amphora* four years old, for the use of himself and friends. —In the course of our conversation, which was interlarded with scraps of Latin, we understood that this facetious person was a school-master, whose income being small, he was fain to keep a glass of good liquor for the entertainment of passengers, by which he made shift to make the two ends of the year meet.—'I am this day, said he, the happiest old fellow in his majesty's dominions.— My wife, rest her soul, is in heaven. My daughter is to be married next week;—but the two chief pleasures of my life are these (pointing to the bottle and a large edition of Horace that lay on the table). I am old, 'tis true,—what then? the more reason I should enjoy the small share of life that remains, as my friend Flaccus advises:—— *Tu ne quæsieris scire (nefas.) Quem, mihi quem tibi finem dii dederint* ——*Carpe diem quam minimum credula postero.*'[2]—As he was very inquisitive about our affairs, we made no scruple of acquainting him with our situation, which when he had learned, he enriched us with advices how to behave in the world, telling us that he was no stranger to the deceits of mankind.—In the mean time he ordered his daughter to lay a fowl to the fire for supper, for he was resolved this night to regale his friends——*permittens divis cætera.*[3]—While our entertainment was preparing, our host recounted the adventures of his own life, which, as they contain nothing remarkable, I forbear to rehearse. When we had fared sumptuously and drank several bottles of his *quadrimum,* I expressed a desire of going to rest, which was with some difficulty complied with, after he had informed us that we should overtake the waggon by noon next day; and that there was room enough in it for half a dozen, there being only four passengers as yet in that convenience.—Before my comrade and I fell asleep we had some conversation about the good humour of our landlord, which gave Strap such an idea of his benevolence, that he was positive we should pay nothing for our lodging and entertainment.—'Don't you observe, said he, that he has conceived a particular affection for us,—nay, even treated us at supper with extraordinary fare, which, to be sure, we should not of

ourselves, have called for?'—I was partly of Strap's opinion; but
the experience I had of the world made me suspend my belief till
to-morrow morning, when, getting up betimes, we breakfasted with
our host and his daughter, on hasty-pudding and ale, and desired
to know what we had to pay.—'Biddy will let you know, gentlemen,
said he, for I never mind these matters.—Money-matters are beneath the concern of one who lives on the Horatian plan.—*Cre-
scentem sequitur cura pecuniam.*'[1] Mean while Biddy having consulted a slate that hung in a corner, told us, our reckoning came to
8s. 7d.——'Eight shillings and seven pence! cried Strap, 'tis impossible—you must be mistaken, young woman.'—'Reckon again,
child, (says her father, very deliberately) perhaps you have mis-
counted.'—'No indeed, father, (she replied) I know my business
better.'—I could contain my indignation no longer, but said it was
a very unconscionable bill, and demanded to know the particulars;
upon which the old man got up, muttering 'Ay, ay, let us see the
particulars,—that's but reasonable.'—And taking pen, ink, and
paper, wrote the following

Items:	*s.*	*d.*
To bread and beer	0	6
To a fowl and sausages	2	6
To four bottles *quadrim.*	2	0
To fire and tobacco	0	7
To lodging	2	0
To breakfast	1	0
	8	7

As he had not the appearance of a common publican, and had
raised a sort of veneration in me by his demeanor the preceding
night, it was not in my power to upbraid him as he deserved;
therefore I contented myself with saying, I was sure he did not
learn to be an extortioner from Horace. He answered, 'I was a but
young man and did not know the world, or I would not tax him
with extortion, whose only aim was to live *contentus parvo,*[2] and
keep off *importuna pauperies.*'[3]—My fellow-traveller could not so
easily put up with this imposition; but swore he should either take
one third of the money, or go without.——While we were engaged
in this dispute, I perceived the daughter go out, and conjecturing
the occasion, immediately paid the exorbitant demand, which was

no sooner done, than Biddy returned with two stout fellows, who came in on pretence of taking their morning draught; but in reality to frighten us into compliance.—Just as we departed, Strap, who was half distracted on account of this piece of expence, went up to the school-master, and grinning in his face, pronounced with great emphasis: '*Semper avarus eget.*'[1]——To which the pedant replied, with a malicious smile;—'*Animum rege, qui, nisi paret, imperat.*'[2]

CHAPTER XI

We descry the waggon——get into it——arrive at an inn——
our fellow travellers described——a mistake is committed by
Strap, which produces strange things

WE travelled half a mile without exchanging one word; my thoughts being engrossed by the knavery of the world, to which I must be daily exposed; and the contemplation of my finances, which began sensibly to diminish.—At length Strap, who could hold no longer, addressed me thus:—'Well, fools and their money are soon parted. —If my advice had been taken, that old skin-flint should have been damn'd before he had got more than the third of his demand.—'Tis a sure sign you came easily by your money, when you squander it away in this manner.—Ah! God help you, how many bristly beards must I have mowed before I earned 4 shillings and three pence halfpenny, which is all thrown to the dogs?—How many days have I sat weaving hair, till my toes were numbed by the cold, my fingers cramp'd, and my nose as blue as the sign of the periwig that hung over the door?—What the devil was you afraid of? I would have engaged to box with any one of those fellows who came in, for a guinea.—I'm sure I have beat stouter men than either of them.' ——And indeed, my companion would have fought any body, when his life was in no danger; but he had a mortal aversion to fire arms and all instruments of death. In order to appease him, I assured him, no part of this extraordinary expence should fall upon his shoulders; at which he was affronted, and told me, he would have me to know, that although he was a poor barber's boy, he had a soul to spend his money with the best 'squire of the land.—Having walked all day at a great pace, without halting for a refreshment, we descried towards the evening, to our inexpressible joy, the waggon about a quarter of a mile before us; and by that time we came up with it, were both of us so weary, that I verily believe it would have been impracticable for us to have walked one mile further.——We therefore bargained with the driver, whose name was Joey, to give us a cast to the next stage for a shilling; at which place we would meet the master of the waggon, with whom we might agree for the rest of the journey.

Accordingly the convenience stopt, and Joey having placed the ladder, Strap (being loaded with our baggage) mounted first; but just as he was getting in, a tremendous voice assailed his ears in these words: 'God's fury! there shall no passengers come here.'— The poor shaver was so disconcerted at this exclamation, which both he and I imagined proceeded from the mouth of a giant, that he descended with great velocity, and a countenance as white as paper.——Joey perceiving our astonishment, called with an arch sneer, 'Waunds, captain! whay woan't yau sooffer the poor waggon-eer to meake a penny?—Coom, coom, young man, get oop, get oop,—never moind the coptain,—I'se not afear'd of the coptain.'— This was not encouragement sufficient to Strap, who could not be prevailed upon to venture up again; upon which I attempted, though not without a quaking heart, when I heard the same voice muttering like distant thunder: 'By G—d I won't be used so, d—n—n seize me if I am!'—However I crept in, and by accident got an empty place in the straw, which I immediately took posses-sion of, without being able to discern the faces of my fellow-travellers in the dark. Strap following with the knapsack on his back, chanced to take the other side, and by a jolt of the carriage, pitched directly upon the stomach of the captain, who bellowed out in a most dreadful manner: 'Blood and thunder! where's my sword?'—At these words, my frighted comrade started up, and at one spring, bounced against me with such force, that I thought the supposed son of Anak[1] intended to smother me.—In the mean time a female voice cried out, 'Bless me! what is the matter, my dear?' 'The matter, replied the captain, damn my blood! my guts are almost squeezed out by that Scotchman's hump.' Strap trembling all the while at my back, asked him pardon, and laid the blame of what had happened upon the jolting of the waggon.—The woman who spoke before, went on: 'Ay, ay, my dear, it is our own fault— we may thank ourselves for all the inconveniences we meet with.—

I thank God, I never travelled so before,—I'm sure if my lady or Sir John was to know where we are, they would not sleep this night for vexation.—I wish to God we had writ for the chariot,—I know we shall never be forgiven.' 'Come, come, my dear (replied the captain) it don't signify fretting now,—we shall laugh it over as a frolick.—I hope you will not suffer in your health.—I shall make my lord very merry with our adventures in the *Diligence*.'[1]—This discourse gave me such a high notion of the captain and his lady, that I durst not venture to join in the conversation; but immediately after, another female voice begins: 'Some people give themselves a great many needless airs——better folks than any here have travelled in waggons before now.——Some of us have rode in coaches and chariots with three footmen behind them, without making so much fuss about it.—What then? we are now all upon a footing, therefore let us be sociable and merry.—What do you say, Isaac? Is'n't this a good motion, you doting rogue?—Speak, you old *cent. per cent.*[2] fornicator.——What desperate debt are you thinking of? What mortgage are you planning? Well, Isaac, positively you shall never gain my favour, till you turn over a new leaf; grow honest, and live like a gentleman.——In the mean time, give me a kiss, you old fumbler.'[3]—These words, accompanied with a hearty smack, enlivened the person to whom they were addressed, to such a degree, that he cried in transport, tho' with a quavering voice, 'Ah! you wanton baggage—upon my credit, you are a waggish girl, he, he, he.'—This laugh introduced a fit of coughing, which almost suffocated the poor usurer (such, we afterwards found, was the profession of this our fellow-traveller).—About this time, I fell asleep, and enjoyed a comfortable nap till such time as we arrived at the inn where we put up.—Here, having got out of the waggon first, I had an opportunity of viewing the passengers in order as they entered.—The first who appeared was a brisk airy girl, about twenty years old, with a silver-laced hat on her head, instead of a cap, a blue stuff riding suit trimmed with silver, very much tarnished, and a whip in her hand.—After her, came limping, an old man with a worsted night-cap, buttoned under his chin, and a broad brimmed hat slouched over it, an old rusty blue cloak tied about his neck, under which appeared a brown surtout, that covered a threadbare coat and waste-coat, and, as we afterwards discerned, a dirty flannel jacket.—His eyes were hollow, bleared and gummy; his face was shrivelled into a thousand wrinkles, his gums were destitute of teeth, his nose sharp and drooping, his chin peeked and prominent, so that when he mumped[1] or spoke, they approached one another like a pair of nut-crackers; he supported himself on an ivory-headed cane, and his whole figure was a just emblem of winter, famine and avarice.—But how was I surprized when I beheld the formidable captain leading in his wife; in the shape of a little, thin creature, about the age of forty, with a long, withered visage, very much resembling that of a baboon, through the upper part of which, two little grey eyes peeped: He wore his own hair in a queue that reached to his rump, which immoderate length, I suppose, was the occasion of a baldness that appeared on the crown of his head, when he deigned to take off his hat, which was very much of the size and cock of Pistol's.[2]—Having laid aside his great coat, I could not help admiring the extraordinary make of this man of war: He was about five foot and three inches high, sixteen inches of which went to his face and long scraggy neck; his thighs were about six inches in length, his legs resembling spindles or drum-sticks, two feet and an half, and his body, which put me in mind of extension without substance,[3] engrossed the remainder;— so that on the whole, he appeared like a spider or grasshopper erect,—and was almost a *vox & preterea nihil*.[4]—His dress consisted in a frock of what is called bear-skin,[5] the skirts of which were about half a foot long, an Hussar waistcoat, scarlet breeches reaching half way down his thigh, worsted stockings rolled up almost to his groin, and shoes with wooden heels at least two inches high; he carried a sword very near as long as himself in one hand, and in the other conducted his lady, who seemed to be a woman of his own age, and still retained some remains of an agreeable person; but so ridiculously affected, that had I then known as much of the world as I do now, I might have easily perceived in her, the deplorable vanity and second-hand airs of a lady's woman.—We were all assembled in the kitchen, when captain Weazel (for that was his name) desired a room with a fire for himself and spouse; and told the landlord, they would sup by themselves.—The inn-keeper replied, that he could not afford them a room by themselves; and as for supping, he had prepared victuals for the passengers in the waggon without respect of persons, but if he could prevail on the rest to let him have his choice in a separate manner, with all his heart: This was no sooner said, than all of us declared against the proposal, and miss Jenny (our other female passenger) observed, that if captain Weazel and his lady had a mind to sup by themselves, they might wait until we should have done.——At this, the captain put on a martial frown and looked very big, without speaking; while his yoke-fellow, with a disdainful toss of her nose, muttered something about 'Creature;'[1]—which miss Jenny over-hearing, stept up to her, saying, 'None of your names, good Mrs. Abigail;—creature quotha,—I'll assure you,—No such creature as you neither—no ten pound sneaker—no quality coupler.'[2]—Here the captain interposed with a 'Damme, madam, what d'ye mean by that?'——'Damn you, sir, who are you? (replied miss Jenny) who made you a captain, you pitiful, trencher-scraping, pimping curler?—'Sdeath! the army is come to a fine pass, when such fellows as you get commissions.—What, I suppose you think I don't know you?—By G—d, you and your helpmate are well met,—a cast-off mistress, and a bald *valet de chambre* are well yoked together.' 'Blood and wounds! (cried Weazel) d'ye question the honour of my wife, madam?—Hell and damnation! No man in England durst say so much.—I would flea[3] him, carbonado him! Fury and destruction! I would have his liver for my supper.'—So saying, he drew his sword, and flourished with it, to the great terror of Strap: while miss Jenny snapping her fingers, told him, she did not value his resentment a f—t.—In the midst of this quarrel, the master of the waggon alighted, who understanding the cause of it, and fearing the captain and his lady would take so much umbrage, as to leave his carriage, was at great pains to have every thing made up, which he at last accomplished, and we sat down to supper all together. At bedtime we were shewn to our apartments. The old usurer, Strap and I, were conducted to one room; the captain, his wife, and miss Jenny to another.——About midnight, my companion's bowels being disordered, he got up, in order to go backward; in his return, mistaking one door for another, he entered Weazel's chamber, and without any hesitation went to bed to his wife, who was fast asleep; the captain being at another end of the room, groping for some empty vessel, his own chamber-pot being leaky: As he did not perceive Strap coming in, he went toward his own bed, after having found a convenience; but no sooner did he feel a rough head with a cotton night-cap on it, than it came into his mind, that he was got to miss Jenny's bed instead of his own, and that the head he felt, was that of some gallant, with whom she had made an assignation.—Full of this conjecture, and scandalized at the prostitution

51

of his apartment, he snatched up the vessel he had just before filled, and emptied it at once on the astonished barber and his own wife, who waking at that instant, broke forth into lamentable cries, which not only alarmed the husband beyond measure, but frightened poor Strap almost out of his senses; for he verily believed himself bewitched; especially when the incensed captain seized him by the throat, with a volley of oaths, asking him how he durst have the presumption to attempt the chastity of his wife.—Poor Strap was so amazed and confounded, that he could say nothing, but,—'I take God to witness she's a virgin for me.'—Mrs. Weazel enraged to find herself in such a pickle, through the precipitation of her husband, got up in her shift, and with the heel of her shoe, which she found at the bed-side, belaboured the captain's bald pate, till he cried 'Murder.'—'I'll teach you to empty your stink-pots on me, (cried she) you pitiful, hop o' my thumb[1] coxcomb.—What? I warrant you're jealous, you man of lath.[2]——Was it for this I condescended to take you to my bed, you poor, withered, sapless twig?'——The noise occasioned by this adventure, had brought the master of the waggon and me to the door, where we overheard all that passed, with great satisfaction. In the mean time we were alarmed with the cry of 'Rape! Murder! Rape!' which miss Jenny pronounced with great vociferation.—'O! you vile, abominable old villain, (said she) would you rob me of my virtue?—But I'll be revenged of you, you old goat! I will!——help! for heaven's sake! help!—I shall be ravished! ruined! help!'——Some servants of the inn hearing this cry, came running up stairs with lights, and such weapons as chance afforded; when we beheld a very diverting scene.—In one corner stood the poor captain shivering in his shirt, which was all torn to rags: with a woful visage, scratched all over by his wife, who had by this time wrapt the covering about her, and sat crying on the side of her bed.—In the other end, lay the old usurer sprawling on miss Jenny's bed, with nothing on him but his flannel jacket over his shirt, and his tawny meagre limbs exposed to the air; while she held him fast by the two ears, and loaded him with execrations.——When we asked what was the matter, she affected to weep, and told us, she was afraid that wicked rogue had ruined her in her sleep, and bid us take notice of what we saw, for she intended to make use of our evidence against him.—The poor wretch looked like one more dead than alive, and begged for Christ's sake to be released; which was no sooner done, than he protested she was no woman, but a devil incarnate—that she had first seduced his flesh to rebel, and then betrayed him.—'Yes, cockatrice[1] (continued he, with a faulter-ing voice) thou knowest thou did'st spread this snare for me—but thou shalt not succeed—for I will hang myself before thou shalt get a farthing of me.'—So saying, he crawled to his own bed, groaning all the way.—We then advanced to the captain, who told us, 'Gentlemen, here has been a damn'd mistake; but I'll be revenged on him who was the occasion of it.——That Scotchman who carries the knapsack shall not breathe this vital air another day, if my name be Weazel.—My dear, I ask you ten thousand pardons; you are sensible I could mean no harm to you.'——'I know not what you meant (replied she, sobbing) but I know I have got enough to send me to my grave.'—At length they were reconciled.—The wife was complimented with a share of miss Jenny's bed (her own being overflowed) and the master of the waggon invited Weazel to sleep the remaining part of the night with him. I retired to mine, where I found Strap mortally afraid, he having got away in the dark, while the captain and his lady were at logger-heads.

CHAPTER XII

Captain Weazel challenges Strap, who declines the combat
—an affair between the captain and me——the usurer is fain
to give miss Jenny five guineas for a release——we are in
danger of losing a meal——the behaviour of Weazel, Jenny,
and Joey on that occasion—an account of captain Weazel
and his lady—the captain's courage tried—Isaac's mirth
at the captain's expence

NEXT morning, I agreed to give the master of the waggon ten shillings for my passage to London, provided Strap should be allowed to take my place when I should be disposed to walk.—At the same time I desired him to appease the incensed captain, who by this time had got into the kitchen, with a drawn sword in his hand, and threatned with many oaths, to sacrifice the villain, who at-tempted to violate his bed; but it was to no purpose for the master to explain the mistake, and assure him of the poor lad's innocence,

who stood trembling behind me all the while: the more submission
that appeared in Strap, the more implacable seemed the resentment of Weazel, who swore he must either fight him, or he would
instantly put him to death.—I was extremely provoked at this insolence, and told him, it could not be supposed that a poor barber lad
would engage a man of the sword at his own weapon; but I was persuaded he would wrestle or box with him.—To which proposal
Strap immediately gave assent, by saying, he would box with him
for a guinea.—Weazel replied with a look of disdain, it was beneath
any gentleman of his character to fight like a porter, or even to put
himself on a footing, in any respect, with such a fellow as Strap.—
'Ods bodikins![1] (cries Joey) sure coptain, yaw wauld not coommit
moorder! Here's a poor lad that is willing to make attoonement for
his offence; and an that woant't satisfie yaw, offers to fight yaw
fairly.—An yaw woan't box, I dare say, he will coodgel with yaw.—
Woan't yaw, my lad?'—Strap, after some hesitation, answered,
'Ye—yes, I'll cudgel with him.'—But this expedient being also rejected by the captain, I began to smell his character, and tipping
Strap the wink, told the company, that I had always heard it said,
the person who receives a challenge should have the choice of the
weapons; this therefore being the rule in point of honour, I would
venture to promise on the head of my companion, that he would
even fight captain Weazel at sharps; but it should be with such
sharps as Strap was best acquainted with, namely razors.—At my
mentioning razors, I could perceive the captain's colour to change,
while Strap pulling me by the sleeve, whispered with great eagerness;—'No, no, no; for the love of God, don't make any such
bargain.'——At length, Weazel recovered himself, turned towards
me, and with a ferocious countenance, asked, 'Who the devil are
you?—will you fight me?' With these words, putting himself in a
posture, I was grievously alarmed at seeing the point of a sword
within half a foot of my breast; and springing to one side, snatched
a spit that stood in the chimney corner, with which I kept my
formidable adversary at bay, who made a great many half longes,
skipping backward every time, till at last I got him pinned up in a
corner, to the no small diversion of the company. While he was in
this situation, his wife entered, and seeing her husband in these
dangerous circumstances, uttered a dreadful scream, and swooned:
Upon this, Weazel demanded a cessation, which was immediately
granted; and after his lady had recovered, was contented with the

submission of Strap, who falling on his knees before him, protested the innocence of his intention, and asked pardon for the mistake he had committed. This affair being ended without bloodshed, we went to breakfast, but missed two of our company, to wit, miss Jenny and the usurer. As for the first, Mrs. Weazel informed us, that she had kept her awake all night with her groans; and that when she got up this morning, miss Jenny was so much indisposed, that she could not proceed on her journey.—At this moment, a message came from her to the master of the waggon, who immediately went into her chamber, followed by us all.—She told him in a lamentable tone, that she was afraid of a miscarriage owing to the fright she received last night, from the brutality of Isaac; and as the event was uncertain, desired the usurer might be detained to answer for the consequence.—Accordingly this ancient Tarquin[1] was found in the waggon, whither he had retired to avoid the shame of last night's disgrace; and brought by force into her presence.—He no sooner appeared, than she began to weep and sigh most piteously, and told us, if she died, she would leave her blood upon the head of that ravisher.——Poor Isaac, turning up his eyes and hands to heaven, prayed that God would deliver him from the machinations of that Jezabel; and assured us with tears in his eyes, that his being found in bed with her, was the result of her own invitation.—The waggoner understanding the case, advised Isaac to make it up, by giving her a sum of money, to which he replied with great vehemence, 'A sum of money!—a halter for the cockatrice!'—'O! 'tis very well, (said miss Jenny) I see it is in vain to attempt that flinty heart of his, by fair means.—Joey, be so good as to go to the Justice, and tell him there is a sick person here, who wants to see him on an affair of consequence.'—At the name of justice, Isaac trembling like an aspen-leaf, and bidding Joey stay, asked with a faultering voice, 'what she would have?' She told him, that as he had not perpetrated his wicked purpose, she would be satisfied with a small matter.— And though the damage she might sustain in her health, might be irreparable, she would give him a release for an hundred guineas.— 'An hundred guineas! (cried he in an extasy) an hundred furies!— Where should a poor old wretch like me, have an hundred guineas? if I had so much money, d'ye think I would be found travelling in a waggon, at this season of the year?'—'Come, come, (replied Jenny) None of your miserly artifice here.—You think I don't know Isaac Rapine the money-broker in the Minories.[2]—Ah! you old rogue! many a pawn have you had from me and my acquaintance which was never redeemed.'—Isaac finding it was in vain to disguise himself, offered twenty shillings for a discharge, which she absolutely refused under fifty pounds: At last, however, she was brought down to five, which he paid with great reluctancy, rather than be prosecuted for a rape.—After which this sick person made shift to get into the waggon, and we set forwards in great tranquillity, Strap being accommodated with Joey's horse, the driver himself chusing to walk.—This morning and forenoon we were entertained with an account of the valour of captain Weazel, who told us of his having once knocked down a soldier that made game of him; of tweaking a drawer by the nose, who found fault with his picking his teeth with a fork; and of his sending a challenge to a cheese-monger, who had the presumption to be his rival,——for the truth of which he appealed to his wife.——She confirmed whatever he said, and observed such a thing happened that day, 'I received a love-letter from 'squire Gobble;[1]——and don't you remember, my dear, I was prodigiously sick that very night with eating ortolans,[2] when my lord Diddle[3] took notice of my complexion's being altered, and my lady was so alarmed, that she had well nigh fainted.' —Yes, my dear, (replied the captain) you know, my lord said to me, with a sneer,'—'Billy, Mrs. Weazel is certainly breeding.'—'And I answered cavalierly, My lord, I wish I could return the compliment. —Upon which the whole company broke out into an immoderate fit of laughter; and my lord, who loves a repartée dearly, came round and bussed me.'——We travelled in this manner five days, without interruption or meeting any thing worth notice: Miss Jenny (who soon recovered her spirits) entertaining us every day with diverting songs, of which she could sing a great number; and rallying her old gallant, who notwithstanding could never be reconciled to her.—On the sixth day, while we were about to sit down to dinner, the innkeeper came and told us, that three gentlemen just arrived, had ordered the victuals to be carried to their apartment, altho' he had informed them that they were bespoke by the passengers in the waggon. To which they had replied, 'The passengers in the waggon might be damn'd—their betters must be served before them,—they supposed it would be no hardship on such travellers to dine upon bread and cheese for one day.'—This was a terrible disappointment to us all; and we laid our heads together how to remedy it; when miss Jenny proposed that captain Weazel, being by profession a soldier, ought in this case to protect and prevent us from being insulted.—But the captain excused himself, saying, he would not for the world be known to have travelled in a waggon; swearing at the same time, that could he appear with honour, they should eat his sword sooner than his provision.—Upon this declaration, miss Jenny snatching his sword, drew it, and run immediately to the kitchin, where she threatned to put the cook to death, if he did not send the victuals into our chamber immediately.—The noise she made, brought the three strangers down, one of whom no sooner perceived her, than he cried out, 'Ha! Jenny Ramper![1] what the devil brought thee hither?'——'My dear Jack Rattle! (replied she, running into his arms) is it you?—Then Weazel may go to hell for a dinner—I shall dine with you.'—They consented to this, with a great deal of joy; and we were on the point of being reduced to a very uncomfortable meal, when Joey understanding the whole affair, entered the kitchin with a pitchfork in his hand, swore he would be the death of any man who should pretend to seize the victuals prepared for the waggon.——This menace had like to have produced fatal consequences; the three strangers drawing their swords, and being joined by their servants, and we ranging ourselves on the side of Joey; when the landlord interposing, offered to part with his own dinner to keep the peace, which was accepted by the strangers; and we sat down at table without any further molestation.—In the afternoon, I chose to walk along with Joey, and Strap took my place.—Having entered into conversation with this driver, I soon found him to be a merry, facetious, good-natured fellow, and withal very arch: He informed me, that miss Jenny was a common girl upon the town, who falling into company with a recruiting officer, he carried her down in the stage-coach from London to Newcastle, where he had been arrested for debt, and was now in prison; upon which she was fain to return to her former way of life, in the manner we found her.—He told me likewise, that one of the gentlemen's servants, whom we left at the inn, having accidentally seen Weazel, immediately knew him, and acquainted Joey with some particulars of his character, as follows: That he had served my lord Frizzle in quality of *valet de chambre* many years; while he lived separate from his lady: But upon their reconciliation, she expressly insisted upon Weazel's being turned off, as well as the woman he kept: whereupon his lordship, to get rid of them both with a good grace, proposed that he should marry his mistress, and he would procure a commission for him in the army; this expedient was agreed to, and Weazel is now, by his lordship's interest, ensign in ——'s regiment. I found he and I had the same sentiments with regard to Weazel's courage, which we resolved to put to the trial, by alarming the passengers with the cry of, 'an highway man!' as soon as we should discover an horseman appear. This we put in practice towards the dusk, when we descried a man on horseback approaching us. Joey had no sooner intimated to the people in the waggon, that he was afraid we should be all robbed, than a general consternation arose: Strap jumped out of the waggon and hid himself behind a hedge. The usurer put forth ejaculations, and made a rustling among the straw, which made us conjecture he had hid something under it. Mrs. Weazel wringing her hands, uttered lamentable cries; and the captain, to our great amazement, began to snore; but this artifice did not succeed; for miss Jenny, shaking him by the shoulder, bawl'd out, ''Sdeath! captain, is this a time to snore, when we are going to be robbed?— Get up for shame, and behave like a soldier and a man of honour.'— Weazel pretended to be in a great passion for being disturbed, and swore he would have his nap out if all the highwaymen in England surrounded him.——'D—n my blood! what are you afraid of (continued he;') at the same time trembling with such agitation, that the whole carriage shook.—This singular piece of behaviour incensed miss Ramper so much, that she cried out, 'D—n your pitiful soul, you are as arrant a poltroon as ever was drummed out of a regiment.—Stop the waggon, Joey—let me get out, and by G—d, if I have rhetorick enough, the thief shall not only take your purse, but your skin also.'—So saying, she leapt out with great agility.—By this time the horseman came up with us, and happened to be a gentleman's servant well known to Joey, who communicated our scheme, and desired him to carry it on a little further, by going up to the waggon, and questioning those within it.—The stranger consenting for the sake of diversion, approached it, and in a terrible tone, demanded, 'Who have you got here?'—Isaac replied with a lamentable voice, 'Here is a poor miserable sinner, who has got a small family to maintain, and nothing in the world wherewithal, but these fifteen shillings, which if you rob me of, we must all starve together.'—'Who's that sobbing in the other corner?' (said the supposed highwayman). 'A poor unfortunate woman, (answered Mrs. Weazel) upon whom I beg you for Christ's sake, to have com-

passion.'—'Are you maid or wife?' (said he)—'Wife to my sorrow,'
(cried she).—'Who, or where is your husband?' (continued he).—
'My husband, (replied Mrs. Weazel) is an officer in the army, and
was left sick at the last inn where we dined.'—'You must be mistaken, madam, (said he) for I myself saw him get into the waggon
this afternoon;—But pray what smell is that? Sure your lap-dog
has befoul'd himself;—let me catch hold of the nasty cur, I'll teach
him better manners.'—Here he laid hold of one of Weazel's legs,
and pulled him from under his wife's petticoats where he had concealed himself. The poor trembling captain being detected in this
inglorious situation, rubbed his eyes, and affecting to wake out of
sleep, cried, 'What's the matter?—What's the matter?'—'The
matter is not much, (answered the horseman) I only called in, to
enquire after your health, and so adieu, most noble captain.'—
Having said this, he clapped spurs to his horse, and was out of sight
in a moment.—It was some time before Weazel could recollect
himself, but at length, re-assuming the big look, he said, 'Damn the
fellow! why did he ride away, before I had time to ask how his lord
and lady do?—Don't you remember Tom, my dear?' addressing
himself to his wife.—'Yes, (replied she) I think I do remember
something of the fellow,—but you know I seldom converse with
people of his station.'—'Hoy day! (cried Joey) so yaw knaw the
young mon, captain?'—'Know him, (said Weazel) many a time has
he filled a glass of Burgundy for me, at my lord Trippit's table.'—
'And what may his neame be, coptain,' (said Joey). 'His name!—
his name (replied Weazel) is Tom Rinser.'—'Waunds! (cried Joey)
a has changed his true neame then! for I'se lay any wager he was
christened John Trotter.'—This observation raised the laugh
against the captain, who seemed very much disconcerted; when
Isaac broke silence, and said, 'It was no matter who or what he was,
since he had not proved the robber we suspected.—And that we
ought to bless God for our narrow escape.'—'Bless God, (said
Weazel) bless the devil! for what? had he been a highwayman, I
should have eat his blood, body and guts, before he had robbed me,
or any one in this *Diligence*.'—'Ha, ha, ha! (cried miss Jenny) I believe you will eat all you kill indeed, captain.'—The usurer was so
pleased at the event of this adventure, that he could not refrain from
being severe, and took notice that captain Weazel seemed to be a
good Christian, for he had armed himself with patience and resignation, instead of carnal weapons; and worked out his salvation with

fear and trembling.—This piece of satire occasioned a great deal of mirth at Weazel's expence, who muttered a great many oaths, and threatned to cut Isaac's throat;—which the usurer taking hold of, said, 'Gentlemen and ladies, I take you all to witness, that my life is in danger from this bloody-minded officer.—I'll have him bound over to the peace.'[1] This second sneer, procured another laugh against him, and he remained crest-fallen during the remaining part of our journey.

CHAPTER XIII

Strap and I are terrified by an apparition—Strap's conjecture——the mystery explained by Joey——we arrive at London——our dress and appearance described—we are insulted in the street——an adventure in the ale-house—we are imposed upon by a waggish footman—set to rights by a tobacconist—take lodgings—dive for a dinner—an accident at our ordinary

WE arrived at our inn, supped and went to bed; but Strap's distemper continuing, he was obliged to get up in the middle of the night, and taking the candle in his hand, which he had left burning for the purpose, he went down to the house of office; whence in a short time he returned in a great hurry, with his hair standing on end, and a look betokening horror and astonishment. Without speaking a word, he set down the light, and jumped into bed behind me, where he lay and trembled with great violence.—When I asked him what was the matter? he replied, with a broken accent, 'God have mercy on us! I have seen the devil.'—Though my prejudice was not quite so strong as his, I was not a little alarmed at this exclamation, and much more so, when I heard the sound of bells approaching our chamber, and felt my bedfellow cling close to me, uttering these words, 'Christ have mercy upon us! there he comes.'—At that instant, a monstrous overgrown raven entered our chamber, with bells at its feet, and made directly towards our bed.—As this creature is reckoned in our country, a common vehicle for the devil and witches to play their pranks in, I verily believed we were haunted; and in a violent fright, shrunk my head under the bed-cloaths.—This terrible apparition leapt upon the bed, and after giving us several severe dabbs with its beak through the blankets, hopped away, and vanished. Strap and I recommended ourselves to the protection of heaven with great devotion, and when we no longer heard the noise, ventured to peep up and take breath.—But we had not been long freed from this phantom, when another appeared, that had well nigh deprived us both of our senses. We perceived an old man enter the room, with a long white beard that reached to his middle; there was a certain wild peculiarity in his eyes and countenance, that did not savour of this world: and his dress consisted of a brown stuff coat, buttoned behind, and at the wrists, and an odd-fashioned cap of the same stuff upon his head.—I was so amazed that I had not power to move my eyes from such a ghastly object, but lay motionless, and saw him come streight up to me: when he got to the bed, he wrung his hands, and cried with a voice that did not seem to belong to a human creature, 'Where is Ralph?' I made no reply; upon which, he repeated in an accent still more preternatural; 'Where is Ralpho?'——He had no sooner pronounced these words, than I heard the sound of the bells at a distance; which the apparition having listened to, tript away, and left me almost petrified with fear. It was a good while before I could recover myself so far as to speak: and when at length I turned about to Strap, I found him in a fit, which, however, did not last long.—When he came to himself, I asked his opinion of what had happened; and he assured me, that the first must certainly be the soul of some person damned, which appeared by the chains about its legs (for his fears had magnified the creature to the bigness of a horse, and the sound of small morris bells to the clanking of massy chains)—As for the old man, he took it to be the spirit of somebody murdered long ago in this place, which had power granted it to torment the assassin in the shape of a raven, and that Ralpho was the name of the said murderer.—Although I had not much faith in his interpretation, I was too much troubled to enjoy any sleep; and in all my future adventures, never passed a night so ill.——In the morning, Strap imparted the whole affair to Joey, who after an immoderate fit of laughter, explained the matter, by telling him that the old man was the landlord's father, who had turned idiot some years ago, and diverted himself with a tame raven, which, it seems, had hopped away from his apartment in the night, and induced him to follow it to our chamber, where he had inquired after it, under the name of Ralpho.

Nothing remarkable happened during the remaining part of our journey, which continued six or seven days longer: At length we entered the great city, and lodged all night at the inn, where the waggon halted.—Next morning, all the passengers parted different ways; while my companion and I sallied out to enquire for the member of parliament to whom I had a letter of recommendation from Mr. Crab. As we had discharged our lodging at the inn, Strap took up our baggage, and marched behind me in the street with the knapsack on his back, as usual, so that we made a very whimsical appearance.—I had dressed myself to the greatest advantage; that is, put on a clean ruffled shirt, my best thread stockings, my hair (which was of the deepest red) hung down upon my shoulders, as lank and streight as a pound of candles; and the skirts of my coat reached to the middle of my leg; my waistcoat and breeches were of the same piece, and cut in the same taste; my hat very much resembled a Barber's bason in the shallowness of the crown and narrowness of the brims. Strap was habited in a much less aukward manner than me; but a short crop eared wig that very much resembled Scrub's in the play,[1] and the knapsack on his back, added to what is called a queer phiz, occasioned by a long chin, an hook nose, and high cheek bones, rendered him on the whole a very fit subject of mirth and pleasantry. As we walked along, Strap, at my desire, enquired of a carman whom we met, whereabouts Mr. Cringer lived;—and was answered by a stare accompanied with the word, 'Anan!'[2] Upon which I came up in order to explain the question, but had the misfortune to be unintelligible likewise, the carman damning us for a lousy Scotch guard, and whipping up his horses with a 'Gee ho!' which nettled me to the quick, and roused the indignation of Strap so far, that after the fellow was gone a good way, he told me he would fight him for a farthing.—While we were deliberating what was next to be done, an hackney coachman driving softly along, and perceiving us standing by the kennel, came up close to us, and calling, 'A coach, master!' by a dexterous management of the reins, made his horses stumble in the wet, and bedaub us all over with mud.—After which, he drove on, applauding himself with a hearty laugh, in which several people joined, to my great mortification; but one more compassionate than the rest seeing us strangers, advised me to go into an ale-house, and dry myself. I thanked him for his advice, which I immediately complied with; and going into the house he pointed out, called for a pot of beer, and sat down by the fire in a public room, where we cleaned ourselves as well as we could—In the mean time, a wag who sat in a box, smoking his pipe, understanding by our dialect who we were, came up to me, and, with a very grave countenance, asked me, how long I had been caught? As I did not know the meaning of his question, I made no answer; and he went on, saying, it could not be a great while, for my tail was not yet cut; at the same time taking hold of my hair, and tipping the wink to the rest of the company, which seemed highly entertained with his wit.—I was incensed at this usage, but afraid of resenting it, because I happened to be in a strange place, and perceived the person who spoke to me, was a brawny fellow, for whom I was by no means a match. However, Strap having either more courage or less caution, could not put up with the insults that I suffered; but told him with a peremptory tone, 'He was an uncivil fellow, for making so free with his betters.'—Whereupon, the wit going toward him, asked, 'What he had got in his knapsack?' Is it oat-meal or brimstone,[1] Sawney? (said he) seizing him by the chin, which he shook to the inexpressible diversion of all present.—My companion feeling himself assaulted in such an opprobrious manner, disengaged himself in a trice, and lent his antagonist such a box on the ear, as made him stagger to the other side of the room; and in a moment, a ring was formed for the combatants.[2]—Seeing Strap beginning to strip, and my blood being heated with indignation, which banished all other thoughts, I undressed myself to the skin in an instant, and declared, that as the affront that occasioned the quarrel was offered to me, I would fight it out myself; upon which one or two cried out, 'That's a brave Scotch boy; you shall have fair play, by G—d.' This gave me fresh spirits, and going up to my adversary, who by his pale countenance, did not seem much inclined to the battle, I struck him so hard on the stomach that he reeled over a bench, and fell to the ground. Here I attempted to get a-top of him in order to improve my success, according to the manner of my own country; but was restrained by the spectators, one of whom endeavoured to raise up my opponent, but in vain; for he protested he would not fight, not being quite recovered of a late illness.—I was very well pleased with this excuse, and immediately dressed myself, having acquired the good opinion of the company for my bravery, as did also my comrade Strap, who shook me by the hand and wished me joy of the victory.—After having drank our pot, and dried our cloaths, we enquired of the landlord if he knew Mr. Cringer[1] the member of parliament, and were amazed at his replying in the negative; for we imagined, he must be every bit as conspicuous here, as in the borough he represented; but he told us we might possibly hear of him as we passed along.—Whereupon we betook ourselves to the street, where, seeing a footman standing at a door, we made up to him, and asked if he knew where our patron lived.—This member of the party-coloured fraternity,[2] surveying us both very minutely, said he knew Mr. Cringer very well, and bid us turn down the first street on our left, then turn to the right, and then to the left again, after which we would observe a lane, through which we must pass, and at the other end we should find an alley that leads to another street, where we should see the sign of the thistle and three pedlars, and there he lodged.—We thanked him for his information, and went forwards, Strap telling me, that he knew this person to be an honest friendly man by his countenance, before he opened his mouth; in which opinion I acquiesced, ascribing his good manners to the company he daily saw in the house where he served.—We followed his directions punctually, in turning to the left and to the right, and to the left again; but instead of seeing a lane before us, we found ourselves at the side of the river, which perplexed us not a little; and my fellow-traveller ventured to pronounce, that we had certainly missed our way.—By this time we were pretty much fatigued with our walk, and not knowing how to proceed, I went into a small snuff-shop hard by, encouraged by the sign of the high-lander, where I found, to my inexpressible satisfaction, the shop-keeper my countryman.—He was no sooner informed of our pere-grination, and the directions we had received from the footman, than he informed us we had been imposed upon, telling us, that Mr. Cringer lived in the other end of the town; and that it would be to no purpose for us to go thither to-day, for by that time he was gone to the House.—I then asked him if he could recommend us to a lodging, which he readily did, by giving us a line to one of his acquaintance who kept a chandler's shop not far from St. Martin's Lane;[3] here we hired a bed-room, up two pair of stairs, at the rate of 2s. *per* week, so very small, that when the bed was let down, we were obliged to carry out every other piece of furniture that be-longed to the apartment, and use the bedstead by way of chairs.—

Chapter XIII

About dinner-time, our landlord asked us how we proposed to live, to which we answered, that we would be directed by him.—'Well then (says he) there are two ways of eating in this town, for people of your condition; the one more creditable and expensive than the other: the first, is to dine at an eating-house frequented by well dressed people only, and the other is called diving, practised by those who are either obliged or inclined to live frugally.'—I gave him to understand that provided the last was not infamous, it would suit much better with our circumstances than the other.—'Infamous (cried he) God forbid, there are many creditable people, and rich people, ay and fine people, that dive every day.—I have seen many a pretty gentleman bedaubed all over with lace, dine in that manner, very comfortably for three pence half-penny, and go afterwards to the coffee-house, where he made a figure with the best lord in the land;—but your own eyes shall bear witness.—I will go along with you to-day and introduce you.'—He accordingly carried us to a certain lane, where stopping, he bid us observe him, and do as he did, and walking a few paces, dived into a cellar and disappeared in an instant.—I followed his example, and descended very successfully, where I found myself in the middle of a cook's shop, almost suffocated with the steams of boil'd beef, and surrounded by a company consisting chiefly of hackney-coachmen, chairmen, draymen, and a few footmen out of place or on board wages; who sat eating shin of beef, tripe, cow-heel or sausages, at separate boards, covered with cloths, which turned my stomach.— While I stood in amaze, undetermined whether to sit down or walk upwards again, Strap, in his descent missing one of the steps, tumbled headlong into this infernal ordinary, and overturned the cook as she was carrying the porringer of soup to one of the guests: In her fall, she dashed the whole mess against the legs of a drummer belonging to the foot guards, who happened to be in her way, and scalded him so miserably, that he started up, and danced up and down, uttering a volley of execrations that made my hair stand on end. While he entertained the company in this manner, with an eloquence peculiar to himself, the cook got up, and after a hearty curse on the poor author of this mischance, who lay under the table scratching his rump with a woful countenance, emptied a salt-seller in her hand, and stripping down the patient's stocking which brought the skin along with it, applied the contents to the sore.— This poultice was scarce laid on, when the drummer, who had

65

begun to abate of his exclamation, broke forth into such a hideous yell, as made the whole company tremble; then seizing a pewter pint-pot that stood by him, squeezed the sides of it together, as if it had been made of pliant leather, grinding his teeth at the same time with a most horrible grin. Guessing the cause of this violent transport, I bid the woman wash off the salt, and bathe the part with oil, which she did, and procured him immediate ease. But here another difficulty occurred, which was no other than the landlady's insisting on his paying for the pot he had rendered useless; he swore he would pay for nothing but what he had eat, and bid her be thankful for his moderation, or else he would prosecute her for damages.—Strap foreseeing it would all land at him, promised to satisfy the cook, and called for a dram of gin to treat the drummer with, which entirely appeased him, and composed all animosities. After this our landlord and we sat down at a board, and dined upon shin of beef most deliciously; our reckoning amounting to two pence halfpenny each, bread and small beer included.

CHAPTER XIV

We visit Strap's friend——a description of him——his advice——we go to Mr. Cringer's house——are denied admittance——an accident befals Strap——his behaviour thereupon——an extraordinary adventure occurs, in the course of which I lose all my money

IN the afternoon, my companion proposed to call at his friend's house, which, we were informed, was in the neighbourhood, whither we accordingly went, and were so lucky as to find him at home. This gentleman, who had come from Scotland three or four years ago, kept a school in town, where he taught the Latin, French and Italian languages; but what he chiefly professed was the pronounciation of the English tongue, after a method more speedy and uncommon than any practised heretofore; and indeed if his scholars spoke like their master, the latter part of his undertaking was certainly performed to a tittle; for although I could easily understand every word of what I had heard hitherto since I entered England, three parts in four of his dialect were as unintelligible to me, as if he had spoke in Arabick or Irish.——He was a middle-sized man, and stooped very much, though not above the age of forty; his face was very much pitted with the small-pox, his eyes blear'd, and his mouth extended from ear to ear.—He was dressed in a night-gown of plaid, fastened about his middle with a serjeant's old sash, and a tie-perriwig with a fore-top three inches high, in the fashion of king Charles the second's reign.—After he had received Strap (who was related to him) very courteously, he enquired of him, who I was; and being informed, took me by the hand, telling me, he was at school with my father.—When he understood my situation, he assured me that he would do me all the service in his power, both by his advice and otherwise; and while he spoke these words, he eyed me with great attention, walking round me several times, and muttering, 'O Ch—st! O Ch—st! fat a saight is here?'—I soon guessed the reason of his ejaculation, and said, 'I suppose, sir, you are not pleased with my dress.'—'Dress, (answered he) you may caal it fat you please, in your country, but I vaw to Gad, 'tis a masquerade here.—No christian will admit such a figure into his hawse.—Upon my conscience! I wonder the dogs did not hunt you.—Did you pass through St. James's market?[1]— God bless my eye-saight! you look like a cousin-german of Ouran Outang.'—I began to be a little serious at this discourse, and asked him, if he thought I should obtain entrance tomorrow at the house of Mr. Cringer, on whom I chiefly depended, for an introduction into business.—'Mr. Cringer, Mr. Cringer (replied he, scratching his cheek) may be a very honest gentleman—I know nothing to the contrary; but is your sole dependance upon him?—Who recommended you to him?'——I pulled out Mr. Crab's letter, and told him the foundation of my hopes; at which he stared at me, and repeated, 'O Ch—st!'—I began to conceive bad omens from this behaviour of his, and begged he would assist me with his advice; which he promised to do very frankly; and as a specimen, directed us to a perriwig ware-house, in the neighbourhood, in order to be accommodated; laying strong injunctions on me not to appear before Mr. Cringer, till I had parted with these carroty locks, which (he said) were sufficient to beget an antipathy against me, in all mankind.—And as we were going to pursue this advice, he called me back, and bid me be sure to deliver my letter into Mr. Cringer's own hand.—As we walked along, Strap triumphed greatly in our reception with his friend, who (it seems) had assured him, he would in a day or two provide for him, with some good master; and 'now (says he) you shall see how I will fit you with a wig——There's ne'er a barber in London (and that's a bold word) can palm a rotten caul,[1] or a penny-weight of dead hair[2] upon me.'—And indeed this zealous adherent did wrangle so long with the merchant, that he was desired twenty times to leave the shop, and see if he could get one cheaper elsewhere. At length I made choice of a good handsome bob,[3] for which I paid fifteen shillings; and returned to our lodging, where Strap, in a moment, rid me of that hair which had given the school-master so much offence.

We got up next day betimes, having been informed that Mr. Cringer gave audience by candle-light to all his dependants, he himself being obliged to attend the levee of my lord Terrier, at break of day; because his lordship made one at the minister's between eight and nine a-clock.—When we came to Mr. Cringer's door, Strap, to give me an instance of his politeness, run to the knocker, which he employed so loud and so long, that he alarmed the whole street; and a window opening up two pair of stairs in the next house, a chamber-pot was discharged upon him so successfully, that the poor barber was wet to the skin, while I, being luckily at some distance, escaped the unsavoury deluge.—In the mean time, a footman opening the door, and seeing no body in the street but us, asked with a stern countenance, if it was I who made such a damned noise, and what I wanted.—I told him I had business with his master, whom I desired to see.—Upon which, he clapt the door in my face, telling me, I must learn better manners before I could have access to his master. Vexed at this disappointment, I turned my resentment against Strap, whom I sharply reprimanded for his presumption; but he not in the least regarding what I said, wrung the urine out of his perriwig, and lifting up a large stone, flung it with such force against the street-door of that house from whence he had been bedewed, that the lock giving way, it flew wide open, and he took to his heels, leaving me to follow him as I could.—Indeed there was no time for deliberation; I therefore pursued him with all the speed I could exert, until we found ourselves, about the dawn, in a street we did not know. Here as we wandered along, gaping about, a very decent sort of a man, passing by me, stopped of a sudden, and took up something, which having examined, he turned, and presented it to me with these words, 'Sir, you have dropt half a crown.'[1]—I was not a little surprized at this instance of honesty, and told him, it did not belong to me; but he bid me recollect and see if all my money was safe, upon which I pulled out my purse (for I had bought one since I came to town) and reckoning my money in my hand, which was now reduced to five guineas, seven shillings and two pence, I assured him I had lost nothing.—'Well then, (says he) so much the better,—this is Godsend—and as you two were present when I picked it up, you are entitled to equal shares with me.'—I was astonished at these words, and looked upon this person to be a prodigy of integrity, but absolutely refused any part of the sum.—'Come, gentlemen, (said he) you are too modest.—I see you are strangers—but you shall give me leave to treat you with a whet this cold raw morning.' —I would have declined this invitation, but Strap whispered to me, that the gentleman would be affronted, and I complied.— 'Where shall we go? (said the stranger) I am quite ignorant of this part of the town.'—I informed him that we were in the same situation: Upon which he proposed to go into the first public house we should find open. As we walked together, he began in this manner: 'I find by your tongues you are come from Scotland, gentlemen.— My grandmother by the father's side was of your country, which has prepossessed me so much in its favour, that I never meet a Scotchman but my heart warms.—The Scots are a very brave people.—There is scarce a great family in the kingdom, that cannot boast of some exploits performed by its ancestors many hundred years ago.——There's your Douglasses, Gordons, Campbels, Hamiltons.—We have no such ancient families here in England.— Then you are all very well educated.—I have known a pedlar talk in Greek and Hebrew, as well as if they had been his mother tongue.—And for honesty—I once had a servant, his name was Gregory Macgregor, I would have trusted him with untold gold.'— This eulogium on my native country, gained my affection so strongly, that I believe I could have gone to death to serve the author; and Strap's eyes swam in tears. At length, as we passed through a dark narrow lane, we perceived a public house, which we entered; and found a man sitting by the fire, smoking a pipe with a pint of purl[2] before him.—Our new acquaintance asked us, if ever we had drank egg flip;[3] to which we answering in the negative, he assured us of a regale, and ordered a quart to be prepared, calling for pipes and tobacco at the same time. We found this composition very palatable, and drank heartily; the conversation (which was introduced by the gentleman) turning upon the snares that young unexperienced people are exposed to in this metropolis.—He described a thousand cheats that are daily practised upon the ignorant and unwary; and warned us of them with so much good-nature and concern, that we blessed the opportunity which threw us into his way.—After we had put the cann about[1] for some time, our new friend began to yawn, telling us he had been up all night with a sick person; and proposed we should have recourse to some diversion to keep him awake.—'Suppose (said he) we should take a hand at whist for pastime.—But let me see, that won't do, there's only three of us; and I cannot play at any other game.—The truth is, I seldom or never play, but out of complaisance, or at such a time as this, when I am in danger of falling asleep.'——Although I had no great inclination for gaming, I felt no aversion to pass an hour or two at cards with a friend; and knowing that Strap understood as much of the matter as I, made no scruple of saying, 'I wish we could find a fourth hand.'—While we were in this perplexity, the person, whom we found at our entrance, overhearing our discourse, took the pipe from his mouth very gravely, and accosted us thus: 'Gentlemen, my pipe is out, you see, (shaking the ashes into the fire) and rather than you should be baulked, I don't care if I take a hand with you, for a trifle,—but remember I won't play for any thing of consequence.'—We accepted his profer with pleasure; and having cut for partners, it fell to my lot to play with him, against our friend and Strap, for three pence a game.——We were so successful, that in a short time I was half a crown gainer; when the gentleman whom we had met in the street observing he had no luck to-day, proposed to leave off, or change partners.—By this time I was inflamed with my good fortune, and the expectation of improving it, as I perceived the two strangers plaid but indifferently: therefore I voted for giving him his revenge, with which he complied after some intreaty, and cutting again, Strap and I (to our mutual satisfaction) happened to be partners.—My good fortune attended me still, and in less than an hour, we had got thirty shillings of their money; for as they lost, they grew the keener and doubled stakes every time. At last the inconstant goddess began to veer about, and we were very soon stript of all our gains, and about forty shillings of our own money. This mortified me extremely, and had a visible effect on the muscles of Strap's face, which lengthened apace; but our

antagonists perceiving our condition, kindly permitted us to retrieve our loss, and console ourselves with a new acquisition.—
Then my companion wisely suggested it was time to begone; upon
which, the person who had joined us in the house began to curse
the cards; and muttered that we were indebted to fortune only for
what we had got, no part of our success being owing to our good
play.—This insinuation nettled me so much, that I challenged him
to continue the game for a crown; and he was with difficulty persuaded to accept the invitation.—This contest ended in less than an
hour, to my inexpressible affliction, who lost every shilling of my
own money, Strap absolutely refusing to supply me with a six-
pence.—The gentleman, at whose request we had come in, perceiving by my disconsolate looks the situation of my heart, which
well nigh bursted with grief and resentment, when the other
stranger got up, and went away with my money; began in this
manner: 'I am truly afflicted at your bad luck, and would willingly
repair it, was it in my power.—But what in the name of goodness
could provoke you to tempt your fate so long? It is always a maxim
with gamesters to pursue success as far as it will go, and to stop
whenever fortune shifts about.—You are a young man, and your
passions too impetuous; you must learn to govern them better:—
However, there is no experience like that which is bought; you will
be the better for this the longest day you have to live.—As for the
fellow who has got your money, I don't half like him. Did not you
observe me tip you the wink, to leave off in time?'—I answered,
No. 'No, (continued he) you was too eager to mind any thing but
the game.—But, harkee, (said he, in a whisper) are you satisfied of
that young man's honesty? his looks are a little suspicious;—but
I may be mistaken;—he made a great many grimaces while he
stood behind you;—this is a very wicked town.'—I told him I was
very well convinced of my comrade's integrity, and that the grimaces
he mentioned were doubtless owing to his anxiety at my loss.——
'O ho! if that be the case, I ask his pardon.—Landlord, see what's
to pay.'—The reckoning came to eighteen pence, which having
discharged, the gentleman shook us both by the hand, and saying
he should be very glad to see us again, departed.

CHAPTER XV

*Strap moralizes—presents his purse to me—we inform our
landlord of my misfortune, who unravels the mystery——I
present myself to Cringer—he recommends and turns me
over to Mr. Staytape——I become acquainted with a
fellow-dependant, who explains the characters of Cringer and
Staytape——and informs me of the method to be pursued at
the Navy-Office and Surgeon's-hall—Strap is employed*

In our way to our lodging, after a profound silence on both sides,
Strap with a hideous groan observed, that we had brought our pigs
to a fine market. To this I made no reply, and he went on: 'God
send us well out of this place, we have not been in London eight and
forty hours, and I believe we have met with eight and forty thousand
misfortunes.—We have been jeered, reproached, buffetted, pissed
upon, and at last stript of our money; and I suppose by and by we
shall be stript of our skins.—Indeed, as to the money part of it,
that was owing to our own folly; Solomon says, *Bray a fool in a
mortar, and he will never be wise.*[1] Ah! God help us, an ounce of
prudence is worth a pound of gold.' This was no time for him to
tamper with my disposition, already mad with my loss, and inflamed with resentment against him, who had refused me a little
money to attempt to retrieve it. I therefore, turned towards him
with a stern countenance, and asked him, 'Who he called fool!'
Being altogether unaccustomed with such looks from me, he stood
still and stared in my face for some time; then, with some confusion,
uttered 'Fool!—I called no body fool but myself;—I am sure, I am
the greatest fool of the two, for being so much concerned at other
people's misfortunes;—but *Nemo omnibus horis sapit.*[2]—that's all—
that's all.'—Upon which a silence ensued that brought us to our
lodging, where I threw myself into the bed in an agony of despair,
resolving to perish for want, rather than apply to my companion
or any other body for relief; but Strap, who knew my temper, and
whose heart bled within him at my distress, after some pause, came
to the bed-side, and putting a leather purse into my hand, burst
into tears, crying, 'I know what you think: but I scorn your
thoughts.—There's all I have in the world, take it, and I'll perhaps

get more for you before that be done—if not, I'll beg for you, steal for you, go through the wide world with you, and starve with you, for though I be a poor cobler's son, I am no scout.'[1]—I was so touched with the generous passion of this poor creature, that I could not refrain from weeping also, and we mingled our tears together for some time.—Upon examining the purse, I found in it two half guineas and half a crown, which I would have returned to him, saying, he knew better than I how to manage it; but he absolutely refused my proposal, and told me, it was more reasonable and decent that he should depend upon me who was a gentleman, than that I should be controuled by him.

After this friendly contest was over, and our minds more at ease, we informed our landlord of what had happened to us, taking care to conceal the extremity to which we were reduced: He no sooner heard the story, than he assured us we had been grievously imposed upon by a couple of sharpers, who were associates; and that this polite, honest, friendly, humane person, who had treated us so civilly, was no other than a rascally money-dropper, who made it his business to decoy strangers in that manner, to one of his own haunts, where an accomplice or two was always waiting to assist in pillaging the prey they had run down.—Here the good man recounted a great many stories of people who had been reduced, cheated, pilfered, beat,——nay, even murdered by such villains. I was confounded at the artifice and wickedness of mankind, and Strap lifting up his eyes and hands to heaven, prayed that God would deliver him from scenes of such iniquity; for surely the devil had set up his throne in London.—Our landlord being curious to know what reception we had met with at Mr. Cringer's, we acquainted him with the particulars, at which he shook his head, and told us, we had not gone the right way to work; that there was nothing to be done with a m—b—r of p—m—t without a bribe; that the servant was commonly infected with the master's disease, and expected to be paid for his work, as well as his betters.—He therefore advised me to give the footman a shilling the next time I desired admittance to my patron, or else I should scarce find an opportunity to deliver my letter. Accordingly, next morning, when the door was opened, I slipt a shilling into his hand, and told him I had a letter for his master.—I found the good effects of my liberality; for the fellow let me in immediately, and taking the letter out of my hand, desired me to wait in a kind of passage, for an answer.

In this place I continued standing three quarters of an hour, during which time I saw a great many young fellows, whom I formerly knew in Scotland, pass and repass, with an air of familiarity in their way to and from the audience chamber: while I was fain to stand shivering in the cold, and turn my back to them, that they might not perceive the lowness of my condition.—At length, Mr. Cringer came out to see a young gentleman to the door, who was no other than 'squire Gawky, dressed in a very gay suit of cloaths: At parting Mr. Cringer shook him by the hand, and told him he hoped to have the pleasure of his company at dinner. Then turning about towards me, asked what were my commands: when he understood I was the person who had brought the letter from Mr. Crab, he affected to recollect my name, which however, he pretended he could not do, till he had consulted the letter again; to save him that trouble, I told him my name was Random.——Upon which he went on, 'Ay, ay, Random, Random, Random——I think I remember the name;' and very well he might, for this very individual Mr. Cringer had many a time rode before my grandfather's cloak-bag, in quality of footman.——'Well, (says he) you propose to go on board a man of war, as surgeon's mate.' To which I replied by a low bow. 'I believe it will be a difficult matter (continued he) to procure a warrant, there being already such a swarm of Scotch surgeons at the Navy-Office,[1] in expectation of the next vacancy, that the commissioners are afraid of being torn in pieces, and have actually applied for a guard to protect them.—However, some ships will soon be put in commission, and then we shall see what's to be done.'—So saying, he left me, exceedingly mortified at the different reception Mr. Gawky and I had met with from this upstart, proud, mean member, who (I imagined) would have thought it an happiness to have it in his power to be grateful for the obligations he owed to my family.

At my return, I was surprized with the agreeable news of Strap's being employed on the recommendation of his friend the school-master, by a perriwig-maker in the neighbourhood, who allowed him five shillings *per* week, besides bed and board.—I continued to dance attendance every other morning at the levée of Mr. Cringer, during a fortnight, in which time I became acquainted with a young fellow of my own country and profession, who also depended on the member's interest; but was treated with much more respect than I, both by the servants and master, being often admitted into a parlour, where there was a fire, for the convenience of the better sort of those who waited for him.—Thither I was never permitted to penetrate on account of my appearance, which was not at all fashionable; but was obliged to stand blowing my fingers in a cold lobby, and take the first opportunity of Mr. Cringer's going to the door, to speak with him.—One day, while I enjoyed this occasion, a person was introduced, whom Mr. Cringer no sooner saw, then running towards him, he saluted him with a bow to the very ground, and afterwards shaking him by the hand with great heartiness and familiarity, called him his good friend, and asked very kindly how Mrs. Staytape,[1] and the young ladies did; then, after a whisper which continued some minutes, wherein I over-heard the word *Honour* repeated several times with great emphasis, Mr. Cringer introduced me to this gentleman, as to a person whose advice and assistance I might depend upon, and having given me his direction, followed me to the door, where he told me, I needed not give myself the trouble to call at his house any more, for Mr. Staytape would do my business for me. At that instant my fellow dependant coming out after me, over-heard the discourse of Mr. Cringer, and making up to me in the street, accosted me very civilly, which I looked upon as no small honour, considering the figure he made; for he was dressed in a blue frock with a gold button, a green silk waistcoat trimmed with gold, black velvet breeches, white silk stockings, silver buckles, a gold-laced hat, a spencer wig,[2] and a silver hilted hanger, with a fine clouded cane[3] in his hand.—'I perceive (says he) you are but lately come from Scotland:—pray what may your business with Mr. Cringer be?—I suppose it is no secret—and I may possibly give you some advice that will be serviceable; for I have been surgeon's second mate on board of a seventy-gun ship, and consequently know a good deal of the world.'—I made no scruple to disclose my situation, which when he had learned, he shook his head, and told me he had been pretty much in the same circumstances about a year ago; that he had relied on Cringer's promises so long, that his money (which was considerable) as well as his credit, was quite exhausted; and when he wrote to his relations for a fresh supply, instead of money, he received nothing but reproaches, and the epithets of idle, debauched fellow: That after he had waited at the Navy-Office many months for a warrant, to no purpose, he was fain to pawn some of his cloaths, which raised him a small sum, wherewith

75

he bribed the s—t—y, who soon procured a warrant for him, notwithstanding he had affirmed the same day, that there was not one vacancy.—That he had gone on board, where he remained nine months; at the end of which the ship was put out of commission, and the company to be paid off in Broad-street[1] the very next day. —That his relations being reconcil'd to him, had charg'd him to pay his devoirs regularly to Mr. Cringer, who had informed them by letter, that his interest alone had procured the warrant; in obedience to which command, he came to his levee every morning as I saw, though he looked upon him to be a very pitiful scoundrel. —In conclusion, he asked me if I had yet passed at Surgeon's-Hall?[2] To which I answered, I did not so much as know it was necessary.—'Necessary! (cried he) O lord, O lord! I find I must instruct you—come along with me, and I'll give you some information about that matter.'—So saying, he carried me into an alehouse, where he called for some beer and bread and cheese, on which we breakfasted. While we sat in this place, he told me I must first go to the Navy-Office, and write to the board, desiring them to order a letter for me to the Surgeon's-Hall, that I may be examined touching my skill in surgery: That the Surgeons, after having examined me, would give me my qualification sealed up in form of a letter directed to the commissioners, which qualification I must deliver to the secretary of the board, who would open it in my presence, and read the contents. After which, I must employ my interest to be provided for as soon as possible.—That the expence of his qualification for second mate of a third rate,[3] amounted to thirteen shillings, exclusive of the warrant, which cost him half a guinea and half a crown, besides the present to the secretary, which consisted of a three pound twelve piece.—This calculation was like a thunder-bolt to me, whose whole fortune did not amount to twelve shillings—I accordingly made him acquainted with this part of my distress, after having thanked him for his information and advice.—He condoled with me on this occasion; but bid me be of good chear, for he had conceived a friendship for me, and would make all things easy.—'Tis true he was run out at present, but to-morrow or next day, he was certain of receiving a considerable sum; of which he would lend me what would be sufficient to answer my exigences. This frank declaration pleased me so much, that I pulled out my purse and emptied it before him, begging him to take what he pleased for pocket expence until he should receive his own money.—With a good deal of pressing he was prevailed upon to take five shillings, telling me that he might have what money he pleased at any time, for the trouble of going into the city; but as he had met with me, he would defer his going thither till to-morrow, when I should go along with him, and he would put me in a way of acting for myself, without a servile dependance on that rascal Cringer, much less on the lousy taylor to whom I heard him turn you over.——'How (cried I) is Mr. Staytape a taylor?'—'No less, I'll assure you (answer'd he) and I confess, more likely to serve you than the member: For provided you can entertain him with politics and conundrums, you may have credit with him for as many and as rich cloaths as you please.'—I told him, I was utterly ignorant of both, and so incens'd at Cringer's usage, that I would never set my foot within his door again.—After a good deal more conversation, my new acquaintance and I parted, having made an appointment to meet next day at the same place, in order to set out for the city.— I went immediately to Strap, and related every thing which had happen'd, but he did not at all approve of my being so forward to lend money to a stranger, especially as we had been already so much impos'd upon by appearances. 'However, (said he) if you are sure he is a Scotchman, I believe you are safe.'

CHAPTER XVI

My new acquaintance breaks an appointment—I proceed,
by myself, to the Navy-Office—address myself to a Person
there, who assists me with his advice—I write to the board
—they grant me a letter to the Surgeons at the Hall—I am
inform'd of the beau's name and character—I find him—
he makes me his confident in an amour—desires me to pawn
my linen, for his occasions—I recover what I lent him
—some curious observations of Strap on that occasion—
his vanity

IN the morning I got up and went to the place of rendezvous, where I waited two hours in vain; and was so exasperated against him for breaking his appointment, that I set out for the city by myself, in hopes of finding the villain, and being reveng'd on him for his perfidy.—At length I found myself at the Navy-Office, which I entered, and saw crowds of young fellows walking below; many of whom made no better appearance than myself—I consulted the physiognomy of each, and at last made up to one whose counten- ance I lik'd; and ask'd, if he could instruct me in the form of the letter which was to be sent to the board, to obtain an order for examination: He answered me in broad Scotch, that he would shew me the copy of what he had wrote for himself, by the direction of another who knew the form: And accordingly pulled it out of his pocket for my perusal; and told me, that if I was expeditious, I might send it in to the board before dinner, for they did no business in the afternoon. He then went with me to a coffee-house hard by, where I wrote the letter, which was immediately delivered to the messenger; who told me, I might expect an order to-morrow about the same time.—Having transacted this piece of business, my mind was a good deal compos'd; and as I had met with so much civility from this stranger, I desired further acquaintance with him, fully resolved however, not to be deceived by him so much to my preju- dice as I had been by the beau—He agreed to dine with me at the cook's shop which I frequented; and on our way thither, carried me to 'Change,[1] where I was in some hopes of finding Mr. Jackson (for that was the name of the person who had broke his appointment)— I sought him there to no purpose, and on our way to the other end of the town, imparted to my companion his behaviour towards me: Upon which, he gave me to understand, that he was no stranger to the name of beau Jackson (so he was called at the Navy-Office) altho' he did not know him personally; that he had the character of a good-natur'd careless fellow, who made no scruple of borrowing from any body that would lend; that most people who knew him, believed he had a good enough principle at the bottom; but his extravagance was such, he would probably never have it in his power to manifest the honesty of his intention.—This account made me sweat for my five shillings, which I nevertheless did not alto- gether despair of recovering, provided I could find out the debtor.— This young man likewise added another circumstance of 'Squire Jackson's history, which was, that being destitute of all means to equip him for sea, when he receiv'd his last warrant, he had been recommended to a person who lent him a little money, after he had signed a will and power, entitling that person to lift his wages when they should become due, as also to inherit his effects in case of his

78

death.—That he was still under the tutorage and direction of that gentleman, who advanced him small sums from time to time upon this security, at the rate of 50 *per cent*. But at present his credit was very low, because his funds would do little more than pay what he had already receiv'd; this moderate interest included.—After the stranger (whose name was Thomson) had entertain'd me with this account of Jackson, he inform'd me, that he himself had passed for a third mate of a third rate, about four months ago; since which time, he had constantly attended at the Navy-Office, in hopes of a warrant, having been assur'd from the beginning, both by a Scotch member and one of the commissioners to whom the member recommended him, that he should be put into the first vacancy; notwithstanding which promise, he had had the mortification to see six or seven appointed in the same station almost every week—that now being utterly impoverish'd, his sole hope consisted in the promise of a friend lately come to town, to lend him a small matter, for a present to the s—t—y; without which he was persuaded he might wait a thousand years to no purpose.—I conceived a mighty liking for this young fellow, which (I believe) proceeded from the similitude of our fortunes: We spent the whole day together; and as he lived at Wapping,[1] I desir'd him to take a share of my bed.—Next day we returned to the Navy-Office, where, after being called before the board and question'd about the place of my nativity and education, they order'd a letter to be made out for me, which, upon paying half a crown to the clerk, I receiv'd, and deliver'd into the hands of the clerk at Surgeon's-Hall, together with a shilling for his trouble in registering my name.—By this time my whole stock was diminished to two shillings, and I saw not the least prospect of relief, even for present subsistence, much less to enable me to pay the fees at Surgeon's-Hall for my examination, which was to happen in a fortnight.—In this state of perplexity, I consulted Strap, who assured me, he would pawn everything he had in the world, even to his razors, before I should want: but this I absolutely rejected, telling him, I would a thousand times rather list for a soldier, of which I had some thoughts, than be any longer a burthen to him.— At the word soldier, he grew pale as death, and begged on his knees, I would think no more of that scheme. 'God preserve us all in our right wits! (cried he) would you turn soldier, and perhaps be sent abroad against the Spaniards, where you must stand and be shot at like a woodcock?—Heaven keep cold lead out of my carcass! and

et me die in a bed like a christian, as all my fore-fathers have done.
—What signifies all the riches and honours of this life, if one enjoys
not content—And in the next, there is no respect of persons.
Better be a poor honest Barber with a good conscience, and time to
repent of my sins upon my death bed, than be cut off (God bless us)
by a musket shot, as it were in the very flower of one's age, in the
pursuit of riches and fame.—What signifies riches (my dear friend!)
do they not make unto themselves wings, as the wise-man saith;[1]
and does not Horace observe, "*Non domus aut fundus, non æris
acervus aut auri Ægroto domini deduxit corpore febrem, non animo
curas.*"[2]—I could moreover mention many other sayings in contempt of riches, both from the bible and other good books; but as I
know you are not very fond of these things, I shall only assure you,
that if you take on to be a soldier, I will do the same; and then if
we should both be slain, you will not only have your own blood to
answer for, but mine also: And peradventure the lives of all those
whom we shall kill in battle.—Therefore I pray you, consider
whether you will sit down contented with small things, and share
the fruits of my industry in peace, 'till providence shall send better
tidings; or by your despair, plunge both our souls and bodies into
everlasting perdition, which God of his infinite mercy forbid.'—I
could not help smiling at this harangue, which was delivered with
great earnestness, the tears standing in his eyes all the time; and
promised to do nothing of that sort without his consent and concurrence.—He was much comforted with this declaration; and told
me, in a few days he should receive a week's wages which should be
at my service, but advised me in the mean time, to go in quest of
Jackson, and recover, if possible, what he had borrow'd of me.—I
accordingly trudg'd about from one end of the town to the other, for
several days, without being able to learn any thing certain concerning him: And, one day, being extreamly hungry and allur'd by the
steams that regal'd my nostrils from a boiling cellar, I went down
with an intention to gratify my appetite with two-penny worth of
beef; when, to my no small surprize, I found Mr. Jackson sitting at
dinner with a footman.—He no sooner perceiv'd me than he got up,
and shook me by the hand, saying, 'He was glad to see me, for he
intended to have call'd at my lodgings in the afternoon.'—I was so
well pleas'd with this rencounter, and the apologies he made for not
keeping his appointment, that I forgot my resentment, and sat
down to dinner, with the happy expectation of not only recovering

my own money before we should part, but also reaping the benefit of his promise to lend me wherewithal to pass examination; and this my sanguine complexion suggested, notwithstanding the account Thompson gave me of him, ought to have taught me better.— When we had feasted sumptuously, he took his leave of the footman, and adjourned with me to an ale-house hard by, where after shaking me by the hand again, he began thus, 'I suppose you think me a sad dog, Mr. Random, and I do confess that appearances are against me —but I dare say you will forgive me when I tell you, my not coming at the time appointed, was owing to a peremptory message, I receiv'd from a certain lady, whom—harkee (but this is a great secret) I am to marry very soon—You think this strange perhaps, but it is not less true for all that—a five thousand pounder, I'll assure you, besides expectations—For my own part, devil take me if I know what any woman can see engaging about me—but a whim you know,——and then one would not baulk one's good fortune— You saw that footman who din'd with us—he's one of the honestest fellows that ever wore livery—You must know, it was by his means, I was introduced to her, for he made me first acquainted with her woman, who is his mistress—ay, many a crown has he and his sweet-heart had of my money—but what of that! things are now brought to a bearing.—I have—(come a little this way) I have propos'd marriage, and the day is fix'd—she's a charming creature! and writes like an angel—O lord! she can repeat all the English tragedies as well as e'er a player in Drury-Lane;[1] and indeed is so fond of plays, that to be near the stage, she has taken lodgings in a court hard by the theatre—But you shall see—you shall see—here's the last letter she sent me.'—With these words he put it into my hand, and I read (to the best of my remembrance) as follows:

'Dire creatur,
As you are the animable hopjack of my contempleshons, your ay-dear is constantanously skimming before my kimmerical fansie, when morfeus sheds illeusinary puppies upon the I's of dreeming mortels; and when lustroos febus shines from his kotidian throne: Wheerpon, I shall consceif old whorie time has lost his pinners, as also cubit his harrows, until thou enjoy sweet slumbrs in the love-sick harrums of thy faithful to commend 'till death.

'Vinegar-yard Droory lane,[2]   'CLAYRENDER'[3]
    January 12th.'

While I was reading, he seemed to be in an extasy, rubbing his hands, and bursting out into fits of laughter; at last he caught hold of my hand, and squeezing it, cried out, 'There is stile for you! what do you think of this billet doux?' I answer'd, 'It might be sublime for aught I knew, for it was altogether above my comprehension.'—'O ho! (said he) I believe it is—both tender and sublime—she's a divine creature! and so doats upon me!——Let me see—what shall I do with this money, when I have once got it into my hands?—In the first place I shall do for you—I'm a man of few words—but, say no more—that's determin'd—Whether would you advise me to purchase some post, by which I may rise in the state; or lay out my wife's fortune in land, and retire to the country at once?' I gave my opinion without hesitation, that he could not do better than buy an estate and improve it; especially since he had already seen so much of the world. Then I launch'd out into the praises of a country life, as describ'd by the poets whose works I had read— He seem'd to relish my advice, but withal told me, that although he had seen a great deal of the world both at land and sea, having cruiz'd three whole months in the Channel, yet he should not be satisfied until he had visited France, which he propos'd to do before he should settle; and to carry his wife along with him.—I had nothing to object to his proposal; and ask'd him, how soon he hop'd to be happy.—'As to that (replied he) nothing obstructs my happiness, but the want of a little ready cash—for you must know, my friend in the city has gone out of town for a week or two; and I unfortunately missed my pay at Broad-street, by being detain'd too long by the dear charmer—but there will be a recal at Chatham[1] next week, whither the ship's books are sent, and I have commission'd a friend in that place to receive the money.'—'If that be all (said I) there's no great harm in deferring your marriage a few days.' —'Yes, faith! but there is (replied he) you don't know how many rivals I have, who would take all advantages against me—I would not baulk the impatience of her passion for the world—the least appearance of coldness and indifference would ruin all: and such offers don't occur every day.' I acquiesc'd in this observation, and enquir'd how he intended to proceed: At this he rubb'd his chin, and said, 'Why, truly I must be oblig'd to some friend or other—do you know nobody that would lend me a small sum for a day or two?'—I assur'd him, I was such an utter stranger in London, that

Chapter XVI

I did not believe I could borrow a guinea, if my life depended upon it.—'No (said he) that's hard—that's hard—I wish I had any thing to pawn upon my soul! you have got excellent linen (feeling the sleeve of my shirt) how many shirts of that kind have you got?'—I answer'd, 'six ruffled and six plain.'—At which he testified great surprize, and swore that no gentleman ought to have more than four —'How many d'ye think I have got (continued he;) but this and another as I hope to be sav'd!—I dare say we shall be able to raise a good sum out of your superfluity—let me see—let me see—each of these shirts are worth eighteen shillings at a moderate computation—now suppose we pawn them for half price—eight times eight is sixty-four, that's three pound four—z—ds! it will do—give me your hand.'—'Softly, softly, Mr. Jackson (said I) don't dispose of my linen without my consent: first pay me the crown you owe me, and then we shall talk of other matters.'—He protested he had not above one shilling in his pocket, but that he would pay me out of the first money raised from the shirts—This piece of assurance incensed me so much, that I swore I would not part with him until I had received satisfaction for what I had lent him, and as for the shirts I would not pawn one of them to save him from the gallows. ——At this expression he laughed aloud, and then complained, it was damned hard, that I should refuse him a trifle, that would infallibly enable him not only to make his own fortune, but mine also.—'You talk of pawning my shirts (said I) what would you think of selling this hanger, Mr. Jackson? I believe it would fetch a good round sum.'——'No, hang it (said he) I can't appear decently, without my hanger, or by G—d it should go.'—However, seeing me inflexible with regard to my linen, he at length unbuckled his hanger, and shewing me the sign of three blue balls, desired me to carry it thither and pawn it for two guineas.—This office I would by no means have performed, had I seen any likelihood of having my money otherwise; but not willing, out of a piece of false delicacy, to neglect the only opportunity I should, perhaps, ever had, I ventured into a pawn-broker's shop, where I demanded two guineas on the pledge, in the name of Thomas Williams.—'Two guineas, (said the pawn-broker, looking at the hanger) this piece of goods has been here several times before, for thirty shillings; however, since I believe the gentleman to whom it belongs will redeem it, he shall have what he wants;' and accordingly he paid me the money, which I carried to the house where I had left Jackson , and calling for change, I counted out to him seven and thirty shillings, reserving the other five for myself.—After looking at the money some time, he said, 'D—n it! it don't signify—this won't do my business; so you may as well take half a guinea or a whole one, as the five shillings you have kept.'—I thanked him kindly, but refused to accept of any more than was my due, because I had no prospect of repaying it.—Upon which he stared in my face, and told me, I was excessively raw, or I would not talk in that manner.— 'Blood! (cried he) I have a very bad opinion of a young fellow who won't borrow of his friend, when he's in want—'tis the sign of a sneaking spirit.—Come, come, Random, give me back the five shillings, and take this half guinea, and if ever you are able to pay me, I believe you will; if not, d—n me, if ever I ask it.'—When I reflected on my present necessity, I suffered myself to be persuaded, and after making my acknowledgments to Mr. Jackson, who offered to treat me with a play, I returned to my lodgings with a much better opinion of this gentleman than I had in the morning: and at night, imparted my day's adventure to Strap, who rejoiced at my good luck, saying, 'I told you, if he was a Scotchman you was safe enough—and who knows but this marriage may make us all.— You have heard, I suppose, as how a countryman of ours, a journeyman baker, run away with a great lady of this town, and now keeps his coach—Ecod![1] I say nothing; but yesterday morning as I was shaving a gentleman at his own house, there was a young lady in the room—a fine buxom wench, i' faith! and she threw so many sheep's eyes[2] at a certain person, whom I shall not name, that my heart went knock, knock, knock, like a fulling mill,[3] and my hand sh— sh— shook so much that I sliced a piece of skin off the gentleman's nose; whereby he swore a deadly oath, and was going to horsewhip me, when she prevented him, and made my peace.—*Omen haud malum!*[4] Is not a journeyman barber as good as a journeyman baker? The only difference is, the baker uses flour for the belly, and the barber uses it for the head: and as the head is a more noble member than the belly, so is a barber more noble than a baker—for what's the belly without the head?—Besides, I am told he could neither read nor write; now you know I can do both: And moreover speak Latin.—But I will say no more, for I despise vanity—nothing is more vain than vanity.'—With these words he pulled out of his pocket a wax candle's end, which he applied to his forehead; and upon examination, I found he had combed his own hair over the toupee of his wig, and was indeed in his whole dress become a very smart shaver.[1]—I congratulated him on his prospect with a satirical smile, which he understood very well; and shaking his head, observed I had very little faith, but the truth would come to light in spite of my incredulity.

CHAPTER XVII

I go to Surgeon's-hall, where I meet with Mr. Jackson——
I am examined——a fierce dispute arises between two of the
examiners——Jackson disguises himself to attract respect——
is detected——in hazard of being sent to Bridewell——he treats
us at a tavern——carries us to a night-house a troublesome
adventure there——we are committed to the Round house——
carried before a justice——his behaviour

WITH the assistance of this faithful adherent, who gave me almost all the money he earned, I preserved my half guinea entire, till the day of examination, when I went with a trembling heart to Surgeon's-hall, in order to undergo that ceremony.—Among a croud of young fellows who walked in the outward hall, I perceived Mr. Jackson, to whom I immediately went up, and enquiring into the state of his amour, understood it was still undetermined by reason of his friend's absence, and the delay of the recal at Chatham, which put it out of his power to bring it to a conclusion.—I then asked what his business was in this place; to which he replied, he was resolved to have two strings to his bow, that in case the one failed he might use the other; and with this view, he was to pass that night for a higher qualification.—At that instant a young fellow came out from the place of examination, with a pale countenance, his lip quivering, and his looks as wild as if he had seen a ghost.—He no sooner appeared, than we all flocked about him with the utmost eagerness to know what reception he had met with; which (after some pause) he described, recounting all the questions they had asked, with the answers he made. In this manner, we obliged no less than twelve to recapitulate, which, now the danger was past, they did with pleasure, before it fell to my lot: At length the beadle called my name, with a voice that made me tremble, as much as if it had been the last trumpet: However, there was no remedy, I was conducted into a large hall, where I saw about a dozen of grim faces sitting at a long table.[1] One of whom bid me come forward in such an imperious tone, that I was actually for a minute or two bereft of my senses.—The first question he put to me was, 'Where was you born?' To which I answered, In Scotland.—'In Scotland (said he) I know that very well—we have scarce any other countrymen to examine here—you Scotchmen have overspread us of late as the locusts did Egypt:[2]—I ask you in what part of Scotland was you born?'—I named the place of my nativity, which he had never before heard of: He then proceeded to interrogate me about my age, the town where I served my time, with the term of my apprenticeship; and when I had informed him that I served three years only, he fell into a violent passion; swore it was a shame and a scandal to send such raw boys into the world as surgeons; that it was great presumption in me, and an affront upon the English, to pretend to sufficient skill in my business, having served so short a time, when every apprentice in England was bound seven years at least; —that my friends had done better if they had made me a weaver or shoemaker, but their pride would have me a gentleman (he supposed) at any rate, and their poverty could not afford the necessary education.—This exordium did not at all contribute to the recovery of my spirits, but on the contrary, reduced me to such a situation that I was scarce able to stand; which being perceived by a plump gentleman, who sat opposite to me, with a skull before him, he said Mr. Snarler was too severe upon the young man; and turning towards me, told me, I need not be afraid, for no body would do me any harm; then bidding me take time to recollect myself, he examined me touching the operation of the trepan,[3] and was very well satisfied with my answers.—The next person who questioned me was a wag, who began by asking me if I had ever seen amputation performed; to which I replying in the affirmative, he shook his head and said, 'What! upon a dead subject, I suppose? If (continued he) during an engagement at sea, a man should be brought to you with his head shot off, how would you behave?'—After some hesitation, I owned, such a case had never come under my observation; neither did I remember to have seen any method of cure proposed for such an accident, in any of the systems of surgery I had perused. Whether it was owing to the simplicity of my answer, or the archness of the question, I know not, but every member at the board deigned to smile, except Mr. Snarler, who seemed to have very little of the *animal risibile* in his constitution.—The facetious member, encouraged by the success of his last joke, went on thus: 'Suppose you was called to a patient of a plethoric habit,[1] who had been bruised by a fall, what would you do?' I answered, I would bleed him immediately. 'What, (said he) before you tied up his arm?'—But this stroke of wit not answering his expectation, he desired me to advance to the gentleman who sat next him; and who with a pert air, asked what method of cure I would follow in wounds of the intestines.—I repeated the method of cure as it is prescribed by the best chirurgical writers; which he heard to an end, and then said with a supercilious smile. 'So, you think with such treatment the patient might recover?'—I told him I saw nothing to make me think otherwise.—'That may be (resumed he) I won't answer for your foresight;—but did you ever know a case of this kind succeed?' I acknowledged I did not; and was about to tell him I had never seen a wounded intestine; but he stopt me, by saying with some precipitation, 'Nor never will.—I affirm, that all wounds of the intestines, whether great or small, are mortal.'—'Pardon me, brother (says the fat gentleman) there is very good authority'——Here he was interrupted by the other, with 'Sir, excuse me, I despise all authority.—*Nullius in verba*.[2]—I stand upon my own bottom.'[3]— 'But Sir, Sir, (replied his antagonist) the reason of the thing shews' —'A fig for reason (cried this sufficient member) I laugh at reason, give me ocular demonstration.'—The corpulent gentleman began to wax warm, and observed that no man acquainted with the anatomy of the parts, would advance such an extravagant assertion.— This *inuendo* enraged the other so much, that he started up, and in a furious tone exclaimed: 'What Sir! do you question my knowledge in anatomy?'—By this time, all the examiners had espoused the opinion of one or other of the disputants, and raised their voices all together, when the chairman commanded silence and ordered me to withdraw. In less than a quarter of an hour, I was called in again, and received my qualification sealed up, and was ordered to pay five shillings.—I laid down my half-guinea upon the table, and stood some time, until one of them bid me begone; to this I replied, I will, when I have got my change; upon which another threw me five shillings and six-pence, saying, I would not be a true Scotchman if I went away without my change. I was afterwards obliged to give three shillings and six-pence to the beadles, and a shilling to an old woman who swept the hall: This disbursement sunk my finances to thirteen pence half-penny, with which I was sneaking off, when Jackson perceiving it, came up to me, and begged I would tarry for him and he would accompany me to the other end of the town, as soon as his examination should be over. I could not refuse this to a person that was so much my friend; but I was astonished at the change of his dress, which was varied in half an hour from what I have already described, to a very grotesque fashion.——His head was covered with an old smoaked tye-wig[1] that did not boast one crooked hair, and a slouched hat over it, which would have very well become a chimney-sweeper or a dust-man;—his neck was adorned with a black crape, the ends of which he had twisted, and fixed in the button-hole of a shabby great coat that wrapped up his whole body; his white silk stockings were converted into black worsted hose; and his countenance was rendered venerable by wrinkles, and a beard of his own painting.——When I expressed my surprize at this metamorphosis, he laughed, and told me, it was done by the advice and assistance of a friend who lived over the way, and would certainly produce something very much to his advantage; for it gave him the appearance of age, which never fails of attracting respect. I applauded his sagacity, and waited with impatience, for the effects of it. At length he was called in, but whether the odness of his appearance excited a curiosity more than usual in the board, or his behaviour was not suitable to his figure, I know not, he was discovered to be an impostor, and put into the hands of the beadle, in order to be sent to Bridewell.[2] So that instead of seeing him come out with a chearful countenance, and a surgeon's qualification in his hand, I perceived him led through the outward hall as a prisoner; and was very much alarmed and anxious to know the occasion; when he called with a lamentable voice and piteous aspect, to me, and some others who knew him; 'For God's sake, gentlemen, bear witness that I am the same individual John Jackson, who served as surgeon's second mate on board the Elizabeth, or else I shall go to Bridewell.'—It would have been impossible for the most austere hermit that ever lived, to have refrained from laughing at his appearance and address; we therefore indulged ourselves a good while at his expence, and afterwards pleaded his cause so effectually with the beadle, who was gratified with half a crown, that the prisoner was dismissed; and in a few moments resumed his former gaiety;—swearing, since the board had refused his money, he would spend it every shilling before he went to bed in treating his friends; at the same time inviting us all to favour him with our company.—It was now ten o'clock at night, and as I had a great way to walk in a town where I was a stranger, I was prevailed upon to be of their party, in hopes he would afterwards accompany me to my lodgings, which he faithfully promised. —He carried us to his friend's house, who kept a tavern over the way, where we remained drinking punch, until the liquor mounted up to our heads, and made us all extremely frolicksome: I, in particular was so much elevated, that nothing would serve me but a wench, at which Jackson expressed much joy, and assured me I should have my desire before we parted.—Accordingly, when he had paid the reckoning we sallied out, roaring and singing; and were conducted by our leader to a place of nocturnal entertainment, where I immediately attached myself to a fair one, with whom I proposed to spend the remaining part of the night; but she not relishing my appearance, refused to grant my request before I had made her an acknowledgment, which not suiting my circumstances we broke off our correspondence, to my no small mortification and resentment, because I thought the mercenary creature had not done justice to my merit.—In the mean time, Mr. Jackson's dress had attracted the inclinations and assiduities of two or three nymphs, who loaded him with caresses, in return for the arrack punch[1] with which he treated them; till at length, notwithstanding the sprightly sallies of these charmers, sleep began to exert his power over us all: and our conductor called, 'To pay.' When the bill was brought, which amounted to twelve shillings, he put his hand in his pocket, but might have saved himself the trouble, for his purse was gone.— This accident disconcerted him a good deal at first, but after some recollection he seized the two Dulcineas, who sat by him, one in each hand; and swore if they did not immediately restore his money, he would charge a constable with them.—The good lady at the bar seeing what passed, whispered something to the drawer, who went out; and then with great composure, asked what was the matter?— Jackson told her he was robbed, and if she refused him satisfaction, he would have her and her whores committed to Bridewell.——— 'Robbed (cried she) robbed, in my house! gentlemen and ladies I take you all to witness, this person has scandalized my reputation.' —At that instant, seeing the constable and watch enter, she went on,

'What! you must not only endeavour by your false aspersions to ruin my character; but even commit an assault against my family? Mr. Constable, I charge you with this uncivil person, who has been guilty of a riot here, I shall take care and bring an action against him for defamation.'—While I was reflecting on this melancholy event, which had made me quite sober, the lady whose favours I had solicited, being piqued at some repartee that passed between us, cried, 'They are all concerned;' and desired the constable to take us all into custody, which was performed instantly, to the utter astonishment and despair of us all, except Jackson, who having been often in such scrapes was very little concerned, and charged the constable in his turn, with the landlady and her whole bevy: Upon which we were carried all together prisoners to the round-house;[1] where Jackson (after a word of comfort to us) informed the constable of his being robbed, to which he said he would swear next morning before the justice.—'Ay, ay, (says the bawd) we shall see whose oath will most signify.'—In a little time the constable calling Jackson into another room, spoke to him thus: 'I perceive that you and your company are strangers, and am very sorry for your being involved in such an ugly business as this is. I have known this woman a great while; she has kept a notorious house in the neighbourhood these many years; and although often complained of as a nuisance, still escapes thro' her interest with the J—t—ces, to whom she and all of her employment, pay contribution quarterly for protection.—As she charged me with you first, her complaint will have the preference, and she can procure evidence to swear whatever she shall please to desire them. So that, unless you make it up before morning, you and your companions may think yourselves happily quit for a month's hard labour in Bridewell.—Nay, if she should swear a robbery or assault against you, you will be committed to Newgate,[2] and tried next sessions at the Old-Baily[3] for your life.' This last piece of information had such an effect upon Jackson, that he agreed to make it up, provided his money might be restored: The constable told him, that instead of restoring what they had stol'n, he was pretty certain, it would cost him some more before they would come to any composition.—But however, he had compassion on him, and would, if he pleased, sound them about a mutual release.—The unfortunate beau thanked him for his friendship, and returned to us, where he acquainted us with the substance of his dialogue; while the constable desiring to speak in

90

private with our adversary, carried her into the next room, and
pleaded our cause so effectually, that she condescended to make him
umpire: He accordingly proposed an arbitration, to which we gave
our assent; and he fined each party in three shillings to be laid out
in a bowl of punch, wherein we drowned all animosities, to the inexpressible joy of my two late acquaintances and me, who had been
in the state of the damned ever since Jackson mentioned Bridewell
and Newgate.—By the time we had finished our bowl, to which, by
the by, I had contributed my last shilling, it was morning; and I
proposed to move homeward, when the constable gave me to understand, he could discharge no prisoners but by order of the justice,
before whom we must appear.—This renewed my regret, and I
cursed the hour in which I had yielded to Jackson's invitation.—
About nine a-clock we were escorted to the house of a certain
justice not many miles distant from Covent-Garden;[1] who no
sooner saw the constable enter with a train of prisoners at his
heels, than he saluted him as follows: 'So, Mr. Constable, you are a
diligent man—what den of rogues have you been scouring?' Then
looking at us, who appeared with a dejected air, he continued, 'Ay,
ay, thieves, I see—old offenders—O your humble servant, Mrs.
Harridan![2] I suppose these fellows have been taken robbing your
house—yes, yes, here's an old acquaintance of mine—you have used
expedition (said he to me) in returning from transportation; but we
shall save you that trouble for the future—the surgeons will fetch
you from your next transportation at their expence.'[3] I assured his
worship he was mistaken in me, for he had never seen me in his life
before.—To this he replied, 'How, you impudent rascal, dare you
say so to my face? Do you think I am to be imposed upon by that
northern accent which you have assumed? but it shan't avail you—
you shall find me too far north for you.[4]—Here, clerk, write this
fellow's *mittimus*[5]—His name is Patrick Gaghagan.'—Here Mr.
Jackson interposed, and told him, I was a Scotchman lately come
to town, descended of a good family, and that my name was Random.—The justice looked upon this declaration as an outrage
against his memory, on which he valued himself much; and strutting
up to Jackson, with a fierce countenance, put his hands in his sides,
and said, 'Who are you, Sir?—Do you give me the lie?—Take
notice, gentlemen, here's a fellow who affronts me upon the bench
—but I'll lay you fast, sirrah, I will—for notwithstanding your
laced jacket, I believe you are a notorious felon.'—My friend was so

much abashed at this menace, which was thundered out with great vociferation, that he changed colour, and remained speechless—This his worship took for a symptom of guilt, and to compleat the discovery continued his threats.——'Now, I am convinced you are a thief,—your face discovers it—you tremble all over—your conscience won't lie still—you will be hang'd, sirrah (raising his voice) you will be hanged, and happy had it been for the world, as well as your own miserable soul, if you had been detected and cut off in the beginning of your career.—Come hither, clerk, and take this man's confession.'—I was in an agony of consternation, when the constable going into another room with his worship, acquainted him with the truth of the story: upon which he returned with a smiling countenance, and addressing himself to us all, said, it was always his way to terrify young people, when they came before him, that his threats might make a strong impression on their minds, and deterr them from engaging in scenes of riot and debauchery which commonly ended before the judge.—Thus having cloaked his own want of discernment, under the disguise of paternal care, we were dismissed, and I found myself as much lightened as if a mountain had been lifted from off my breast.

CHAPTER XVIII

*I carry my qualifications to the Navy-Office—the nature of it
—the behaviour of the s—t—y——Strap's concern for
my absence——a battle betwixt him and a blacksmith——the
troublesome consequences of it——his harangue to me——his
friend the school-master recommends me to a French
apothecary, who entertains me as a journeyman*

I WOULD willingly have gone home to sleep, but was told by my companions, that we must deliver our letters of qualification at the Navy-Office before one a-clock; upon which we repaired thither, and gave them to the s—t—y, who opened and read them, and I was mightily pleased to find myself qualified for second mate of a third rate. When he had stuck them all together on a file, one of our company asked if there were any vacancies; to which he answered,

No. Then I ventured to enquire if any ships were to be put in commission soon.—At which he surveyed me with a look of ineffable contempt, and pushing us out of his office, locked the door without deigning us one word.—We went down stairs and conferred together on our expectations, when I understood that each of them had been recommended to one or other of the commissioners; and each of them promised the first vacancy that should fall; but that none of them relied solely upon that interest, without a present to the s—t—y, with whom the c—mm—rs went snacks.[1]— For which reason each had provided a small purse; and I was asked what I proposed to give?—This was a vexatious question to me, who (so far from being in a capacity to gratify a ravenous s—t—y) had not wherewithal to buy me a dinner.—I therefore answered, I had not determined yet what to give; and sneaked off towards my own lodging, cursing my fate all the way, and inveighing with much bitterness against the barbarity of my grandfather, and the sordid avarice of my relations, who left me a prey to contempt and indigence.—Full of these disagreeable reflections, I arrived at the house where I lodged, and relieved my landlord from great anxiety on my account; for this honest man believed I had met with some dismal accident, and that he should never see me again.—Strap, who had been to see me in the morning, understanding I had been abroad all night, was almost distracted, and after having obtained leave of his master, had gone in quest of me, though he was even more ignorant of the town than I. Not being willing to inform my landlord of my adventure, I told him, I had met an acquaintance at Surgeon's-hall, with whom I spent the evening and night, but being very much infested by bugs, I had not slept much, and therefore intended to take a little repose; so saying, I went to bed and desired to be awakened if Strap happened to come while I should be asleep.—— I was accordingly roused by my friend himself, who entered my chamber about three a-clock in the afternoon; and presented a figure to my eyes, that I could scarce believe real.—In short, this affectionate shaver, setting out towards Surgeon's-hall, had enquired for me there to no purpose; from thence he found his way to the Navy-Office, where he could hear no tidings of me, because I was unknown to every body then present; he afterwards went upon Change in hopes of seeing me upon the Scotch walk;[2] but without any success: At last, being almost in dispair of finding me, he resolved to ask every body he met in the street, if perchance any one could give him information about me: and actually put his resolution in practice, in spite of the scoffs, curses and reproaches with which he was answered; until a blacksmith's 'prentice, seeing him stop a porter with a burden on his back, and hearing his question, for which he received a hearty curse, called to him, and asked if the person he enquired after was not a Scotchman?—Strap replied with great eagerness, 'Yes, and had on a brown coat with long skirts.'—'The same (said the blacksmith) I saw him pass about an hour ago.'—'Did you so? (cried Strap, rubbing his hands) Odd! I am very glad of that—which way went he?'—'Towards Tyburn in a cart,[1] (said he) if you make good speed, you may get thither time enough to see him hanged.'—This piece of wit incensed my friend to such a degree, that he called the blacksmith scoundrel, and protested he would fight him for half a farthing.—'No, no, (said the other, stripping) I'll have none of your money—you Scotchmen seldom carry any about you—but I'll fight you for love.'—There was a ring immediately formed by the mob; and Strap finding he could not get off honourably without fighting, at the same time burning with resentment against his adversary, quitted his cloaths to the care of the multitude, and the battle began with great violence on the side of Strap, who in a few minutes exhausted his breath and spirits on his patient antagonist, who sustained the assault with great coolness, till finding the barber quite spent, he returned the blows he had lent him, with such interest, that Strap, after having received three falls on the hard stones, gave out, and allowed the blacksmith to be the better man.—The victory being thus decided, it was proposed to adjourn to a cellar hard by and drink friends.— But when my friend began to gather up his cloaths, he perceived that some honest person or other had made free with his shirt, neckcloath, hat and wig, which were carried off; and probably his coat and waistcoat would have met with the same fate, had they been worth the stealing.—It was in vain for him to make a noise, which only yielded mirth to the spectators; he was fain to get off in this manner, which he accomplished with much difficulty, and appeared before me, all besmeared with blood and dirt.—Notwithstanding this misfortune, such was his transport at finding me safe and sound, that he had almost stifled and stunk me to death with his embraces.—After he had cleaned himself and put on one of my shirts, and a woolen night-cape instead of hat and wig; I recounted to him the particulars of my night's campaign, which filled him

with admiration, and made him repeat with great energy an observation which was often in his mouth, *viz*. 'London is the devil's
drawing room.'—As neither of us had dined, he desired me to get
up, and the milk-woman coming round at that instant, he went
down stairs and brought up a quart, with a penny brick,[1] on which
we made a comfortable meal. He then shared his money with me,
which amounted to eighteen-pence, and left me, with an intention to borrow an old wig and hat of his friend the school-
master.

He was no sooner gone, than I began to consider my situation
with great uneasiness, and revolved all the schemes my imagination
could suggest, in order to chuse and pursue some one that would
procure me bread; for it is impossible to express the pangs I felt,
when I reflected on the miserable dependance in which I lived, at
the expence of a poor barber's boy.—My pride took the alarm,
and having no hopes of succeeding at the Navy-Office, I came to a
resolution of enlisting in the foot guards next day, *coute qui coute*.[2]
—This extravagant design, by flattering my disposition, gave great
satisfaction, and I was charging the enemy at the head of my own
regiment, when Strap's return interrupted my reverie.—The
school-master had made him a present of the tye-wig which he wore
when I was introduced to him, together with an old hat, whose
brims would have overshadowed a Colossus.—Though Strap had
ventured to wear them in the dusk, he did not chuse to entertain
the mob by day; therefore went to work immediately and reduced
them both to a moderate size. While he was employed in this
manner, he addressed me thus:—'To be sure, Mr. Random, you
are born a gentleman, and have a great deal of learning—and indeed
look like a gentleman, for as to person you may hold up your head
with the best of them.—On the other hand, I am a poor, but
honest cobler's son—my mother was as industrious a woman as ever
broke bread, 'till such time as she took to drinking, which you very
well know—but every body has failings—*humanum est errare*.[3]—
Now for myself I am a poor journeyman barber, tolerably well made,
and understand some Latin, and have a smattering of Greek—but
what of that? perhaps I might also say that I know a little of the
world—but that is not to the purpose—though you be gentle and I
simple, it does not follow but that I who am simple may do a good
office to you who are gentle.—Now this is the case—my kinsman the
school-master—perhaps you did not know, how nearly he is related

to me—I'll satisfy you in that presently—his mother and my grandfather's sister's nephew—no, that's not it—my grandfather's brother's daughter—rabbit it![1] I have forgot the degree—but this I know, he and I are cousins seven times removed.'—My impatience to know the good office he had done me, got the better of my temper, and I interrupted him at this place, with, 'D—n your relation and pedigree,—if the school-master or you can be of any advantage to me, why don't you tell it, without all this preamble.'—When I pronounced these words with some vehemence, Strap looked at me for some time with a grave countenance, and then went on: 'Surely, our pedigree is not to be d—n'd, because it is not so noble as yours. —I am very sorry to see such an alteration in your temper of late— you was always fiery, but now you are grown as crabbed as old Periwinkle the drunken tinker, on whom you and I (God forgive us) plaid so many unlucky tricks, while we were at school;—but I will no longer detain you in suspence, because (doubtless) nothing is more uneasy than doubt—*dubio procul dubio nil dubius*.[2]—My friend, or relation, or which you will, or both, the school-master, being informed of the regard I have for you—for you may be sure, I did not fail to let him know your good qualities—by the by, he has undertaken to teach you the pronounciation of the English-tongue, without which (he says) you will be unfit for business in this country.—I say, my relation has spoke in your behalf to a French apothecary who wants a journeyman; and on his recommendation, you may have fifteen pounds *per* year, bed and board, whenever you please.'——I was too much interested in this piece of news to entertain it with indifference; but jumping up, I insisted on Strap's accompanying me immediately to the house of his friend, that I might not lose this opportunity through the least delay or neglect on my part.—We were informed that the school-master was in company at a public house in the neighbourhood, whither we repaired, and found him drinking with the very individual apothecary in question. When he was called to the door at our desire, and observed my impatience, he broke out in his usual term of admiration: 'O Ch—st! I suppose when you heard of this offer, you did not take leisure enough to come down stairs, but leapt out of the window; did you overturn no porter nor oyster-woman in your way?—It was a mercy of God you did not knock your brains out against some post in your career.—O' my conscience! I believe had I been in the inmost recesses of my habitation,—the very *penetralia*,[3]—even in bed with my wife; your eagerness would have surmounted bolts, bars, decency and every thing.—The den of Cacus, or *Sancti sanctorum*[1] could not have hid me from you. But come along, the gentleman of whom I spoke is in the house, I will present you to him forthwith.' —When I entered the room, I perceived four or five people smoaking, one of whom the school-master accosted thus:—'Mr. Lavement,[2] here is the young man of whom I spoke to you.'—The apothecary, who was a little old withered man, with a forehead about an inch high, a nose turned up at the end, large cheek bones that helped to form a pit for his little grey eyes, a great bag of loose skin hanging down on each side in wrinkles, like the alforjas[3] of a baboon; and a mouth so accustomed to that contraction which produces grinning, that he could not pronounce a syllable without discovering the remains of his teeth, which consisted of four yellow fangs, not improperly by anatomists, called *canine*.—This person (I say) after having eyed me sometime; said, 'Oho, 'tis ver well, Mons. Concordance;—yong man, you are ver welcome, take one coup of bierre.—and come to mine house to-marrow morning, Mons. Concordance vil shew you de way.'[4]—Upon this I made my bow, and as I went out of the room, could hear him say, *Ma foy! c'est un beau garçon, c'est un galliard.*[5]—As I had by my own application while I served Crab, acquired the French tongue well enough to read authors written in that language, and understand any thing that occurred in conversation, I determined to pretend ignorance to my new master, that he and his family, whom I supposed to be of the same country, not being on the reserve before me, might possibly discover something in discourse, which would either yield me amusement or advantage.—Next morning Mr. Concordance carried me to the apothecary's house, where the bargain was made, and orders given to provide an apartment for me immediately.— But before I entered upon business, the school-master recommended me to his taylor who gave me credit for a suit of cloaths to be paid out of the first moiety of my wages, and they were begun that very day; he afterwards accommodated me with a new hat, on the same terms; so that in a few days, I hoped to make a very fashionable appearance.—In the mean time, Strap conveyed my baggage to the place allotted for me, which was a back room up two pair of stairs, furnished with a pallet for me to lie upon, a chair without a back, an earthen chamber-pot without a handle, a bottle by way of candlestick, and a triangular piece of glass instead of a mirrour; the rest of

97

its ornaments having been lately removed to one of the garrets, for the convenience of the servant of an Irish captain, who lodged in the first floor.

CHAPTER XIX

The characters of Mr. Lavement, his wife and daughter——
some anecdotes of the family——the mother and daughter
rivals——I am guilty of a mistake that gives me present
satisfaction, but is attended with troublesome consequences

NEXT day, while I was at work in the shop, a bouncing damsel well dressed came in, on pretence of finding a vial for some use or other; and taking an opportunity when she thought I did not mind her, of observing me narrowly, went away with a silent look of disdain—I easily guessed her sentiments, and my pride took the resolution of entertaining the same indifference and neglect towards her—At dinner, the maids with whom I dined in the kitchen, gave me to understand that this was my master's only daughter, who would have a very handsome fortune, on account of which, and her beauty, a great many young gentlemen made their addresses to her—that she had been twice on the brink of marriage, but disappointed by the stinginess of her father, who refused to part with a shilling as long as he should live—for which reason the young lady did not behave to her father with all the filial veneration that might be expected: In particular, she harbour'd the most perfect hatred for his countrymen, in which disposition her mother join'd, who was an English woman; and by the hints they dropp'd, I learn'd the grey mare was the better horse[1]—that she was a matron of a high spirit, which was often manifested at the expence of her dependants: That she lov'd diversions; and look'd upon miss as her rival in all parties; which was indeed the true cause of her disappointments; for had the mother been hearty in her interest, the father would not have ventur'd to refuse her demands.—Over and above this intelligence, I of myself, soon made more discoveries; Mr. Lavement's significant grins at his wife, while she look'd another way, convinc'd me that he was not at all content with his lot: And his behaviour in presence of the captain, made me believe his chief torment was jealousy.—As for my own part, I was consider'd in no other light than that of a menial servant, and had been already six days in the house without being honour'd with one word from either mother or daughter, the latter (as I understood from the maids) having at table one day, expressed some surprize that her papa should entertain such an aukward, mean-looking journeyman.—I was nettled at this piece of information, and next sunday, (it being my turn to take my diversion) dressed myself in my new cloaths to the greatest advantage, and, vanity apart, made no contemptible figure.—After having spent most part of the day in company with Strap and some of his acquaintance, I came home in the afternoon, and was let in by miss, who not knowing me, dropt a low courtesy as I advanced, which I returned with a profound bow, and shut the door—By that time I had turn'd about, she had perceiv'd her mistake, and chang'd colour, but did not withdraw. The passage being narrow, I could not get away without jostling her; so, I was forc'd to remain where I was, with my eyes fix'd on the ground, and my face glowing with blushes—At length her vanity coming to her assistance, she went away tittering, and I could hear her pronounce the word 'creature:' From this day forward, she came into the shop fifty times every day, upon various pretences, and put in practice so many ridiculous airs, that I could easily perceive her opinion of me was chang'd, and that she did not think me altogether an unworthy conquest—But my heart was so steel'd against her charms by pride and resentment, which were two chief ingredients in my disposition, that I remain'd insensible to all her arts; and notwithstanding some advances she made, could not be prevail'd upon to yield her the least attention— This neglect soon banish'd all the favourable impressions she felt for me, and the rage of a slighted woman took place in her heart; which she manifested not only in all the suggestions her malice could invent to my prejudice with her father, but also in procuring for me such servile employments, as she hoped, would sufficiently humble my spirit. One day in particular, she order'd me to brush my master's coat, but I refusing, a smart dialogue ensued, which ended in her bursting into tears of rage; when her mother interposing, and examining into the merits of the cause, determin'd it in my favour; and this good office I ow'd not to any esteem or consideration she had for me, but solely to the desire of mortifying her daughter, who on this occasion observ'd, that let people be never so much in the right, there were some folks who would never do them justice; but to be sure, they had their reason for it, which some people were not ignorant of, although they despised their little arts.—This insinuation of some people and some folks, put me upon observing the behaviour of my mistress more narrowly for the future; and it was not long before I had reason to believe that she look'd upon her daughter as a rival in the affections of captain Odonnell, who lodged in the house.—In the mean time my industry and knowledge gain'd me the good will of my master, who would often say in French, '*Mardy!*[1] *c'est un bon Garçon.*' He had a great deal of business; but as he was mostly employ'd among his fellow refugees,[2] his profits were small.—However, his expence for medicines was not great, he being the most expert man at a succedaneum,[3] of any apothecary in London, so that I have been sometimes amaz'd to see him without the least hesitation, make up a physician's prescription, though he had not in his shop one medicine mention'd in it.—Oyster-shells he could convert into crab's eyes;[4] common oil into oil of sweet almonds; syrup of sugar into balsamic syrup;[5] Thames water into aqua cinnamomi;[6] turpentine into capivi;[7] and a hundred more costly preparations were produc'd in an instant, from the cheapest and coursest drugs of the *materia medica*: And when any common thing was order'd for a patient, he always took care to disguise it in colour or taste, or both, in such a manner, as that it could not possibly be known.—For which purpose, cochineal[8] and oil of cloves were of great service among many nostrums[9] which he possess'd; there was one for the venereal disease, that brought him a good deal of money; and this he conceal'd so artfully from me, that I could never learn its composition: But during the eight months I stay'd in his service, he was so unfortunate in the use of it, that three parts in four of those who took it, were fain to confirm the cure with a salivation[10] under the direction of another doctor.—This bad success, in all appearance, attach'd him the more to his specifick; and before I left him, I may venture to say, he would have sooner renounc'd the Trinity (notwithstanding his being a good Huegonot) than his confidence in the never-failing power of this remedy.—Mr. Lavement had attempted more than once, to introduce a vegetable diet[11] into his family, by launching out into the praise of it, and decrying the use of flesh, both as a Physician and Philosopher; but all his rhetoric could not make one proselyte to his opinion, and even the wife of his bosom declared against the proposal.—Whether it was owing to the little regard she paid to her husband's admonition in this particular, or to the natural warmth of her constitution, I know not; but this lady's passions became every day more and more violent, till at last she look'd upon decency as an unnecessary restraint; and one afternoon when her husband was abroad, and her daughter visiting, order'd me to call a hackney coach, in which she and the captain drove off towards Covent-Garden.—Miss came home in the evening, and supping at her usual hour, went to bed. About eleven a clock my master enter'd, and ask'd if his wife was gone to sleep: Upon which I told him, my mistress went out in the afternoon, and was not yet return'd.—This was like a clap of thunder to the poor Apothecary, who starting back, cried '*Mort de ma vie!*'[1] vat you tell a me?—My wife not, at home!'—At that instant a patient's servant arriv'd with a prescription for a draught, which my master taking, went into the shop to make it up himself.—While he rubb'd the ingredients in a glass mortar, he enquir'd of me, whether or no his wife went out alone; and no sooner heard that she was in company with the captain, than with one blow he split the mortar into a thousand pieces, and grinning like the head of a bass viol,[2] exclaim'd, 'Ah traitresse!'[3]—It would have been impossible for me to have preserv'd my gravity a minute longer, when I was happily reliev'd by a rap at the door, which I open'd, and perceiv'd my mistress coming out of a coach; she flounc'd immediately into the shop, and addressed her husband thus: 'I suppose you thought I was lost, my dear—Captain Odonnell has been so good as to treat me with a play.'—'Play—play (replied he) Oho! yes by gar, I believe ver prettie play.'—'Bless me! (she said) what's the matter?' —'Vat de matter? (cried he, forgetting all his former complaisance) by gar, you be one damn dog's wife—ventre bleu![4] me vill show you vat it is to put one horn upon mine head. Pardieu! le capitaine Odonnell be one.'—Here the captain, who had been all the while at the door discharging the coach, entering, said with a terrible voice, 'D—mme! what am I?'—Mr. Lavement changing his tone, immediately saluted him with, '*Oh serviteur monsieur le capitaine, vous etes un galant homme—ma femme est fort obligée.*'[5]—Then turning about towards me, pronounc'd with a low voice, '*Et diablement obligeante sans doute.*'—'Harkee, Mr. Lavement, (said the captain) I am a man of honour, and I believe you are too much of a gentleman to be offended at the civility I shew your wife.'——This declaration had such an effect on the apothecary, that he resum'd

all the politeness of a Frenchman; and with the utmost prostration
of compliment, assur'd the captain that he was perfectly satisfied
with the honour he had done his wife.—Matters being thus compos'd, every body went to rest.—Next day I perceiv'd thro' a glass
door that open'd from the shop into a parlour, the captain talking
earnestly to miss, who heard him with a look that expressed anger
mingled with scorn; which however he at last found means to
mollify, and seal'd his reconciliation with a kiss.—This soon convinc'd me of the occasion of the quarrel; but notwithstanding all
my vigilance, I could never discover any other commerce between
them.—In the mean while, I had reason to believe I had inspir'd
one of the maids with tender sentiments for me; and one night when
I thought every other person in the house asleep, I took the opportunity of the other maid's absence (for she had got leave to go and
visit her sick father who liv'd at Richmond)[1] to avail myself of my
conquest: Accordingly I got up, and (naked as I was) explor'd my
way in the dark, to the garret where she lay.—I was ravish'd to find
the door open, and moved softly to her bed-side, transported with
the hope of compleating my wishes.—But what horrors of jealousy
and disappointment did I feel, when I found her asleep, fast locked
in the arms of a man, whom I easily guessed to be no other than the
captain's servant! I was upon the point of doing some rash thing,
when the noise of a rat scratching behind the wainscoat, put me to
flight, and I was fain to get back to my own bed in safety.—Whether
this alarm had disorder'd my mind, or that I was led astray by the
power of destiny, I know not; but instead of turning to the left
when I descended to the second story, I persu'd the contrary
course, and mistook the young lady's bed-chamber for my own. I
did not perceive my mistake before I had run against the bed posts;
and then it was not in my power to retreat undiscover'd: for the
nymph being awake, felt my approach, and with a soft voice, bid
me make less noise lest the Scotch-booby in the next room should
over-hear us. This hint was sufficient to inform me of the nature of
the assignation; and as my passions, at any time high, were then in
a state of exaltation, I was resolved to profit by my good fortune.—
Without any more ceremony therefore, I made bold to slip into bed
to this charmer, who gave me as favourable a reception as I could
desire.—Our conversation was very sparing on my part, but she upbraided the person whom I represented, with his jealousy of me,
whom she handled so roughly, that my resentment had well nigh

occasion'd a discovery more than once; but I was consoled for her hatred of me, by understanding from her own mouth, that it was now high time to salve her reputation by matrimony; for she had reason to fear she could not much longer conceal the effects of their mutual intercourse.—While I was meditating an answer to this proposal, I heard a noise in my room, like something heavy falling down upon the floor: Upon which, I started up, and creeping to the door of my chamber, observ'd by moon-light, the shadow of a man groping his way out; whereupon, I retir'd to one side to let him pass, and saw him go down stairs as expeditiously as he could.—It was an easy matter to divine that this was the captain, who having over-slept himself, had got up at last to keep his assignation; and finding my door open, had enter'd into my apartment instead of that of his mistress, where I supplied his place.—But finding his mistake, by falling over my chair, was afraid the noise might alarm the family, and for that reason made off, delaying the gratification of his desire till another opportunity.—By this time, I was satisfied; and instead of returning to the place from whence I came, retreated to my own castle, which I fortified by bolting the door; and in the congratulation of my own happiness fell asleep.—But the truth of this adventure could not be long conceal'd from my young mistress, who next day came to an eclaircisement with the captain, upon his lamenting his last night's disappointment, and begging pardon for the noise he had made.—Their mutual chagrin, when they came to the knowledge of what had happen'd, may be easily conjectur'd, though each had a peculiar grief unfelt by the other; for she was conscious of having not only betray'd to me the secrets of her commerce with him; but also, of having incensed me by the freedoms she had taken with my name, beyond a hope of reconciliation.—On the other hand, his jealousy suggested, that her sorrow was all artifice; and that I had supplied his place with her own privity and consent.—That such was the situation of their thoughts, will appear in the sequel—for that very day she came into the shop where I was alone, and fixing her eyes, swimming in tears, upon me, sigh'd most piteously: But I was proof against her distress, by recollecting the epithets with which she had honour'd me the night before; and believing that the good reception I enjoy'd was destin'd for another. I therefore took no notice of her affliction; and she had the mortification to find her disdain return'd four-fold.—However, from thenceforward she thought proper to use me with more complaisance than usual, knowing that it was in my power at any time to publish her shame.—By these means my life became much more agreeable (though I never could prevail upon myself to repeat my nocturnal visit) and as I every day improv'd in my knowledge of the town, I shook off my aukward air by degrees, and acquir'd the character of a polite journeyman apothecary.

CHAPTER XX

I am assaulted and dangerously wounded—I suspect Odonnell, and am confirmed in my opinion—I concert a scheme of revenge, and put it in execution—Odonnell robs his own servant, and disappears—I make my addresses to a lady, and am miraculously deliver'd from her snare

ONE night about twelve a clock, as I return'd from visiting a patient at Chelsea,[1] I receiv'd a blow on my head from an unseen hand, that stretch'd me senseless on the ground; and was left for dead, with three stabs of a sword in my body.—The groans I utter'd when I recover'd the use of my reason, alarm'd the people of a solitary ale-house, that stood near the spot where I lay, and they were humane enough to take me in, and send for a surgeon who dressed my wounds, and assur'd me they were not mortal. One of them penetrated through the skin and muscles of one side of my belly, in such a manner, that (doubtless) the assassin imagin'd he had run me through the entrails.—The second slanted along one of my ribs, and the last, which was intended for the *Coup de Grace*, being directed to my heart, the sword snapt upon my breast bone, and the point remain'd sticking in the skin.—When I reflected upon this event, I could not persuade myself, that I had been assaulted by a common footpad; because it is not usual for such people to murder those they rob, especially when they meet with no resistance; and I found my money and every thing else about me (but my carcase) safe. I concluded therefore, that I must either have been mistaken for another, or oblig'd to the private resentment of some secret enemy for what had happened; and as I could remember nobody who had the least cause of complaint against me, except

Chapter XX

captain Odonnell and my master's daughter, my suspicion settled
upon them, though I took care to conceal it, that I might the sooner
arrive at confirmation.—With this view, I went home in a chair
about ten a clock in the morning; and as the chairmen supported
me into the house, met the captain in the passage; who no sooner
saw me, than he started back, and gave evident signs of guilty confusion, which he would have accounted for from the surprize
occasion'd by seeing me in such a condition.—My master having
heard my story, condoled me with a good deal of sympathy, and
when he understood my wounds were not dangerous, order'd me
to be carried up stairs to bed; though not without some opposition
from his wife, who was of opinion, it would be better for me to go
to an hospital, where I should be more carefully attended.—My
meditation was employ'd in concerting with myself some method of
revenge against 'Squire Odonnell and his enamorata, whom I
looked upon as the authors of my misfortune; when miss (who was
not at home at my arrival) entered my chamber; and saying, she
was sorry for the accident that had befallen me, asked me if I
suspected any body to be the assassin: Upon which I fixed my eyes
stedfastly upon her, and answer'd, 'Yes.'—She discover'd no symptom of confusion; but replied hastily, 'If that be the case, why
don't you take out a warrant to have him apprehended?—It will
cost but a trifle—if you have no money, I'll lend you.'—This
frankness not only cur'd me of my suspicion with respect to her;
but even stagger'd my belief in regard to the captain, of whose
guilt I resolv'd to have farther proofs, before I enterpriz'd any
thing in the way of revenge.—I thanked her kindly for her generous
offer; which however I had no occasion to accept, being determin'd
to do nothing rashly: For though I could plainly perceive the person who attacked me, to be a soldier whose face I thought was
familiar to me, I could not swear with a safe conscience to any
particular man; and granting I could, my prosecution of him would
not much avail.—This I pretended, lest the captain hearing from
her, that I knew the person who wounded me, might think proper
to withdraw before I could be in a condition to requite him.—In
two days I was up, and able to do a little business, so that Mr.
Lavement made shift to carry on his practice, without hiring
another journeyman in my room.—The first thing I attempted
towards a certain discovery of my secret enemy, was to get into
Odonnell's apartment, while he was abroad in an undress, and

105

examine his sword, the point of which being broke off, I applied the fragment that was found sticking in my body; and found it answer'd the fractur'd part exactly.—There was now no room left for doubt; and all that remain'd, was to fix upon a scheme of revenge, which almost solely engrossed my thoughts during the space of eight nights and days.—Sometimes I was tempted to fall upon him in the same manner as he had practised upon me, and kill him outright.—But this my honour oppos'd, as a piece of barbarous cowardice, in which he was not to be imitated.—At other times, I entertain'd thoughts of demanding satisfaction in an honourable way; but was diverted from this undertaking, by considering the uncertainty of the event, and the nature of the injury he had done me, which did not intitle him to such easy terms.—At last I determin'd to pursue a middle course; and actually put my design in execution after this manner.—Having secured the assistance of Strap and two of his acquaintance whom he could depend upon; we provided ourselves in disguises, and I caused the following letter to be deliver'd to him by one of our associates in livery, one Sunday evening.

Sir,
'If I may be allowed to judge from appearance, it will not be disagreeable to you, to hear that my husband is sent for to Bagshot[1] to visit a patient, and will not return till to-morrow night; so that if you have any thing to propose to me (as your behaviour on many occasions has seemed to insinuate) you will do well to embrace the present opportunity of seeing

Yours, &c.

This letter was signed with the name of an apothecary's wife, who lived in Chelsea, of whom I had heard Odonnell was an admirer.—Every thing succeeded to our wish.—The amorous hero hastened towards the place of assignation; and was encountered by us in the very place where he had assaulted me.—We rushed upon him all at once, secured his sword, stript off his cloaths even to the skin, which we scourged with nettles till he was blistered from head to foot, notwithstanding all the eloquence of his tears and supplications. When I was satisfied with the stripes I had bestowed, we carried off his cloaths, which we hid in a hedge near the place, and left him stark naked, to find his way home in the best manner he could, while I took care to be there before him.—I afterwards understood that in his way to the lodgings of a friend, who lived in the skirts of the town, he was picked up by the watch, who carried him to the Round-house, from whence he sent for cloaths to his lodgings; and next morning arrived at the door in a chair, wrapt up in a blanket he had borrowed; for his body was so sore and swelled that he could not bear to be confined in his wearing apparel.—He was treated with the utmost tenderness by my mistress and her daughter, who vied one with the other in their care and attendance of him; but Lavement himself could not forbear expressing his joy, by several malicious grins, while he ordered me to prepare an unguent to anoint him with.—As to myself, no body can doubt my gratification, when I had every day an opportunity of seeing my revenge protracted on the body of my adversary, by the sores and ulcers I had been the cause of; and indeed I not only enjoyed the satisfaction of having flead[1] him alive, but another also which I had not foreseen.—The story of his being attacked and stript in such a place, having been inserted in the news, gave information to those who found his cloaths next day, whither to bring them; and accordingly he retrieved every thing he had lost, except a few letters, among which was that which I had wrote to him in the name of the apothecary's wife.—This and the others, which (it seems) were all on the subject of love, (for this Hibernian hero was one of those people who are called fortune-hunters) fell into the hands of a certain female author, famous for the scandal she has published; who, after having embellished them with some ornaments of her own invention, gave them to the town in print.—I was very much shocked on reflecting, that I might possibly be the occasion of a whole family's unhappiness, on account of the letter I had written; but was eased of that apprehension, when I understood that the Chelsea apothecary had commenced a law-suit against the printer for defamation; and looked upon the whole as a piece of forgery, committed by the author, who had disappeared.—But whatever might be his opinion of the matter, our two ladies seemed to entertain a different idea of it; for, as soon as the pamphlet appeared, I could perceive their care of their patient considerably diminish, until at last it ended in total neglect.—It was impossible for him to be ignorant of this change, any more than of the occasion of it; but as he was conscious to himself of having deserved worse than contempt at their hands, he was glad to come off so cheaply, and contented himself with muttering curses and threats against the apothecary, who (as he imagined) having got an inkling of the appointment with his wife, had taken revenge of him in the manner described. —By that time he had got a new scarf skin,[1] his character was become so notorious, that he thought it high time for him to decamp; which he performed one night without beat of drum, after having robbed his own servant of every thing that belonged to him except the cloaths he had on his back.—A few days after he disappeared, Mr. Lavement, for his own security, took into custody a large old trunk which he had left; and as it was very heavy, made no question of the contents being sufficient to indemnify him for what Odonnel owed in lodging.—But a month being elapsed without hearing any tidings of this adventurer; and my master being impatient to know what the trunk contained; he ordered me to break it open in his presence, which I performed with the pestle of our great mortar, and discovered, to his inexpressible astonishment and mortification, a heap of stones.

About this time, my friend Strap informed me of an offer he had to go abroad with a gentleman in quality of *valet de chambre*, and at the same time assured me, that whatever advantage he might propose to himself from this prospect, he could not bear the thoughts of parting from me; so much was he attached to my fortune.—In spite of all the obligations I owed this poor honest fellow, ingratitude is so natural to the heart of man, that I began to be tired of his acquaintance; and now, that I had contracted other friendships which appeared more creditable, I was even ashamed to see a journeyman barber enquiring after me with the familiarity of a companion.—I therefore, on pretence of consulting his welfare, insisted upon his accepting the proposal, which he at last determined to embrace, with great reluctance, and in a few days took his leave of me, shedding a flood of tears, which I could not behold without emotion.—I now began to look upon myself as a gentleman in reality; learned to dance of a Frenchman whom I had cured of a fashionable distemper; frequented plays during the holidays; became the oracle of an ale-house, where every dispute was referred to my decision; and at length contracted an acquaintance with a young lady, who found means to make a conquest of my heart, and upon whom I prevailed, after much attendance and solicitation, to give me a promise of marriage.—As this beautiful creature passed for a rich heiress, I blessed my good fortune, and was actually on

Chapter XX

the point of crowning all my wishes, by matrimony; when one morning, I went to her lodgings, and her maid being abroad, took the privilege of a bridegroom to enter her chamber, where to my utter confusion I found her in bed with a man.—Heaven gave me patience and presence of mind enough to withdraw immediately; and I thanked my stars a thousand times for a happy discovery, by which I resolved to profit so much, as to abandon all thoughts of marriage for the future.

CHAPTER XXI

Squire Gawky comes to lodge with my master——is involved in a troublesome affair, out of which he is extricated by me ——he marries my master's daughter——they conspire against me——I am found guilty of theft——discharged—deserted by my friends——I hire a room in St. Giles's—where, by accident, I find the lady to whom I made my addresses, in a miserable condition——I relieve her

WHILE I enjoyed myself at large in this temper of mind, Mr. Lavement let his first floor to my countryman and acquaintance 'Squire Gawky, who by this time had got a lieutenancy in the army, and such a martial ferocity in his appearance, that I was afraid he would remember what had happened between us in Scotland, and atone for his breach of appointment then, by his punctuality now; but whether he had actually forgot me, or was willing to make me believe so, he betrayed not the least symptom of recognition at sight of me, and I remained quite cured of my apprehension; though I had occasion not long after to be convinced, that howsoever his externals might be altered, he was at bottom the same individual Gawky whom I have already described.—For coming home late one night from the house of a patient, I heard a noise in the street, and as I approached, perceived two gentlemen in custody of three watchmen. The prisoners, who seemed to be miserably disfigured with dirt, complained bitterly of the loss of their hats and wigs; and one of them, whom by his tongue I knew to be a Scotchman, lamented most piteously, offering a guinea for his liberty, which the watchman refused, alledging that one of his companions was wounded grievously, and that he must stand to the consequence. —My prejudice in favour of my native country was so strong, that I could not bear to see any body belonging to it in distress, and therefore, with one blow of my faithful cudgel, knocked down the watchman who had hold of the person for whom I was chiefly concerned.—He no sooner found himself disengaged, than he betook himself to his heels, and left me to maintain the dispute as I should think proper; and indeed I came off but scurvily, for before I could avail myself of my speed, I received a blow on the eye, from one of the other two, that had well nigh deprived me of the use of that organ; however, I made shift to get home, where I was informed of captain[1] Gawky's being robb'd and abused by a company of foot-pads; and was ordered by my master to prepare emollient glyster and paregorick[2] draught, in order to allay and compose the ferment of his spirits, occasioned by the barbarous treatment he had undergone, while he took twelve ounces of blood from him immediately.—When I enquired into the particulars of this adventure, and understood by the servant, that he came in just before me, without hat and wig, I made no scruple of believing him to be the person I had released, and was confirmed in that belief upon hearing his voice, to which (before that event) I had been so long a stranger. My eye being considerably swelled and inflamed, I could not reflect upon my enterprise without cursing my own folly, and even resolving to declare the truth of the whole story, in order to be revenged on the cowardly wretch, for whom I had suffered: Accordingly, next day, after he had told, in presence of my master, his wife and daughter, who came to visit him, a thousand lies concerning the prowess he had shewn in making his escape, I ventured to explain the mystery, and calling in the evidence of my contused eye, upbraided him with cowardice and ingratitude.— Gawky was so astonished at this discourse, that he could not answer one word; and the rest of the company stared at one another; till at length my mistress repremanded me for my insolent behaviour, and threatened to turn me away for my presumption.—Upon which, Gawky (having recollected himself) observed, as the young man might have mistaken another person for him, he could forgive his insinuations, more especially as he seemed to have suffered for his civility; but advised me to be more certain in my conjectures for the future, before I ventured to publish them to the prejudice of any man.—Miss applauded the captain's generosity in pardoning one who had so villainously aspersed him, and I began to imagine her praise was not at all disinterested.—But the apothecary, who perhaps had more penetration, or less partiality than his wife and daughter, differed from them in his sentiments of the matter, and expressed himself to me in the shop in this manner: 'Ah mon pauvre Roderique! you ave more of de veracité dan of de prudence —bot mine vife and dater be diablement sage, and Mons. le capitaine un fanfaron, pardieu!'[1]—This elogium on his wife and daughter, though meant ironically by him, was nevertheless literally just; for by espousing the cause of Gawky, the one obliged a valuable lodger, and the other acquired a husband at a juncture, when one was absolutely necessary; for the young lady finding the effects of her correspondence with Odonnel becoming plainer and plainer every day, insinuated herself so artfully into the affection of this new lodger, that in less than a fortnight, on pretence of going to a play, they drove away together to the Fleet, where they were coupled;[2] from thence removed to a bagnio,[3] where the marriage was consummated; and in the morning came home, where they asked her father's and mother's blessing.—The prudent parents, notwithstanding the precipitation with which it was carried on, did not think fit to refuse their approbation; for the apothecary was not ill pleased to find his daughter married to a young man of a good prospect, who had not mentioned to him one syllable on the article of her dowry; and his wife was rejoiced at being rid of a rival in her gallants, and a spy upon her pleasures.—Nor was I without self-enjoyment at this event, when I reflected upon the revenge I had unwittingly taken upon my enemy, in making him a cuckold by anticipation.—But I little dreamed what a storm of mischief was brewing against me, whilst I thus indulged myself.—Whatever face Gawkey put on the matter, my discovery of the adventure before related, and the reproaches I vented against him, had stung him to the soul, and cherished the seeds of emnity so strongly in his breast, that he (it seems) imparted his indignation to his wife, who being as desirous as he to compass the ruin of one that not only slighted her caresses, but was able on any occasion to discover particulars not at all advantageous to her character, readily joined in a conspiracy against me, which (had it taken effect as they expected) would infallibly have brought me to an ignominious death.

My master having several times missed large quantities of medicines of which I could give no account, at last lost all patience, and in plain terms taxed me with having embezzled them for my own use. As I could only oppose my single asseveration to this suspicion, he told me one day, 'By gar, your vord not be give me de satisfaction—me find necessaire to chercher for my medicine, pardonnez moy—il faut chercher—me demand le clef of your coffre a cette heure.'—Then raising his voice to conceal the fright he was in, lest I should make any opposition, he went on, 'Oui, foutre, I charge you rendrer le clef of your coffre—moi—si, moi qui vous parle.'— I was fired with so much resentment and disdain at this accusation, that I burst into tears, which he took for a sign of guilt; and pulling out my key, told him he might satisfy himself immediately, though he would not find it so easy to satisfy me for the injury my reputation had suffered from his unjust suspicion.—He took the key and mounted up to my chamber, attended by the whole family; saying, 'He bien, nous verrons—nous verrons.'—But what was my horror and amazement, when opening my chest, I saw them pull out an handful of the very things that were missing, and heard him pronounce, 'Ah ha! vous etes bien venues—mardie, Mons. Roderique, you be fort innocent!'—I had not power to utter one word in my own vindication, but stood motionless and silent, while every body present made their respective remarks on what appeared against me.—The servants said, they were sorry for my misfortune, and went away repeating, 'Who would have thought it!' My mistress took occasion from this to rail against the practice of employing strangers in general; and Mrs. Gawky, after having observed that she never had a good opinion of my fidelity, proposed to have me carried before the justice and committed to Newgate immediately. Her husband was actually upon the stairs in his way for a constable, when Mr. Lavement, knowing the cost and trouble of a prosecution to which he must bind himself, and at the same time dreading lest some particulars of my confession might affect his practice, called out, 'Restez mon fils! restez, it be veritablement one grand crime wich dis pauvre diable have committed—bot peutetre de good God give him de penitence, and me vil not have upon mine head de blood of one sinner.'—The captain and his lady used all the christian arguments their zeal could suggest, to prevail on the apothecary to pursue me to destruction, and represented the injustice he did to the community of which he was a member, in letting a villain escape, who would not fail of doing more mischief in the world, when he should reflect on his coming off so easily now;—but their eloquence made no impression on my master, who turning to me, said, 'Go, miserable, go from mine house, quick, quick—and make reparation for your *mauvaise* actions.'—By this time my indignation had roused me from the stupefaction in which I had hitherto remained, and I began in this manner: 'Sir, appearances, I own, condemn me; but you are imposed upon as much as I am abused—I have fallen a sacrifice to the rancour of that scoundrel (pointing to Gawky) who has found means to convey your goods hither, that the detection of them might blast my reputation, and accomplish my destruction.—His hatred of me is owing to a consciousness of having wronged me in my own country; for which he in a cowardly manner refused me the satisfaction of a gentleman; —he knows moreover, that I am no stranger to his dastardly behaviour in this town, which I have recounted before;—and he is unwilling that such a testimony of his ingratitude and pusilanimity should live upon the earth; for this reason he is guilty of the most infernal malice to bring about my ruin.—And I am afraid, madam, (turning to Mrs. Gawky) you have too easily entered into the sentiments of your husband—I have often found you my enemy; and am well acquainted with the occasion of your being so, which I don't at present think proper to declare;—but I would not advise you, for your own sake, to drive me to extremity.' This address enraged her so much, that with a face as red as scarlet, and the eyes of a fury, she strutted up to me, and putting her hands in her sides, spit in my face, saying, I was a scandalous villain, but she defied my malice; and that unless her papa would prosecute me like a thief as I was, she would not stay another night under his roof.—At the same time, Gawky assuming a big look, told me, he scorned what lies I could invent against him; but that if I pretended to asperse his wife, he would put me to death, by G—d.—To this I answered, 'I wish to God I could meet with thee in a desart, that I might have an opportunity of revenging thy perfidy towards me, and rid the world of such a rascal—What hinders me this moment (said I, seizing an old bottle that stood by) from doing myself that justice?' I had no sooner armed myself in this manner, than Gawky and his father-in-law retired in such a hurry, that the one overturned the other, and rolled together down stairs; while my mistress swooned away with fear; and her daughter asked if I intended to murder her.——I gave her to understand that nothing was farther from my intention; that I would leave her to the stings of her own conscience;

but was firmly resolved to slit her husband's nose, whenever fortune should offer a convenient opportunity.—Then going down stairs, I met Lavement coming up trembling with the pestle in his hand, and Gawky behind armed with his sword pushing him forward.—I demanded a parley, and having assured them of my pacific disposition; Gawky exclaimed, 'Ah! villain! you have killed my dear wife.'—And the apothecary cried, 'Ah! coquin![1] vere is my child?'—'The lady (said I) is above stairs, unhurt by me, and will a few months hence (I believe) reward your concern.'—Here she called to them herself, and desired they would let the wretch go, and trouble themselves no farther about him.—To which her father consented, observing nevertheless, that my conversation was fort mystérieux.—Finding it impossible to vindicate my innocence, I left the house immediately, and went to the schoolmaster, with an intention of clearing myself to him, and asking his advice with regard to my future conduct; but to my inexpressible vexation, was told he was gone to the country, where he would stay two or three days.—I returned with a design of consulting some acquaintance I had acquired in my master's neighbourhood; but my story had taken air, through the officiousness of the servants, and not one of my friends would vouchsafe me a hearing.—Thus I found myself, by the iniquity of mankind, in a much more deplorable condition than ever: for though I had been formerly as poor, my reputation was without blemish, and my health unimpaired till now;—but at present my good name was lost, my money gone, my friends were alienated, my body infected by a distemper contracted in the course of an amour; and my faithful Strap, who alone could yield me pity and assistance, absent I knew not where.

The first resolution I could take in this melancholy conjuncture, was to remove my cloaths to the house of the person with whom I had formerly lodg'd; there I remained two days, in hopes of getting another place, by the interest of Mr. Concordance, to whom I made no doubt of being able to vindicate my character;—but in this I reckoned without my host, for Lavement took care to be beforehand with me, and when I attempted to explain the whole affair to the schoolmaster, I found him so prepossessed against me, that he would scarce hear me to an end; but when I had finished my justification, shook his head, and beginning with his usual exclamation, 'O Ch—st! said, that won't go down with me.—I am very sorry I should have the misfortune of being concerned in the affair, but however shall be more cautious for the future—I will trust no man from henceforward—no, not my father who begat me—nor the brother who lay with me in my mother's womb—should the genius of truth appear I would question its veracity; and if Daniel[1] would rise from the dead I should think him an impostor.'—I told him, that one day, it was possible, he might be convinced of the injury I had suffered, and repent of his premature determination.—To which he answered the proof of my innocence would make his bowels vibrate with joy; 'but till that shall happen (continued he) I must beg to have no manner of connection with you—my reputation is at stake—O my good God! I shall be looked upon as your accomplice and abettor—people will say Jonathan Wild[2] was but a type of me—boys will hoot at me as I pass along; and the cinder wenches[3] belch forth reproaches wafted in a gale impregnated with gin—I shall be notorious—the very butt of slander, and cloaca of infamy.'—I was not in an humour to relish the climax of expressions upon which this gentleman valued himself in all his discourses; but without any ceremony took my leave, cursed with every sentiment of horror, which my situation could suggest.—I considered, however, in the intervals of my despondence, that I must in some shape suit my expence to my calamitous circumstances, and with that view hired an apartment in a garret near St. Giles's,[4] at the rate of nine pence *per* week.—In this place I resolved to perform my own cure, having first pawned three shirts to purchase medicines and support for the occasion.

One day when I sat in this solitary retreat, musing upon the unhappiness of my fate, I was alarmed by a groan that issued from a chamber contiguous to mine, into which I immediately run, and found a woman stretched on a miserable truckle bed, without any visible signs of life. Having applied a smelling bottle to her nose, the blood began to revisit her cheeks, and she opened her eyes; but, good heaven! what were the emotions of my soul, when I discovered her to be the same individual lady, who had triumphed over my heart, and to whose fate I had almost been inseparably joined! Her deplorable situation filled my breast with compassion, and every tender idea reviving in my imagination, I flew into her embrace; she knew me immediately, and straining me gently in her arms, shed a torrent of tears, which I could not help encreasing: At length, casting a languishing look at me, she pronounced with a feeble voice, 'Dear Mr. Random, I do not deserve this concern at your hands——I am a vile creature, who had a base design upon your person——suffer me to expiate that and all my other crimes by a miserable death, which will not fail to overtake me in a few hours.' —I encouraged her as much as I could, told her I forgave all the injury she had designed for me; and that although my circumstances were extremely low, I would share my last farthing with her. —In the mean time, begged to know the immediate cause of that fit from which she had just recovered, and I would endeavour by my skill to prevent any more such attacks.—She seemed very much affected with what I said, took my hand and pressed it to her lips, saying, 'You are too generous! I wish I could live to express my gratitude—but alas! I perish for want.'—Then shutting her eyes, relapsed into another swoon.—Such extremity of distress must have waked the most obdurate heart to sympathy and compassion: What effect then must it have on mine, that was naturally prone to every tender passion? I ran down stairs and sent my landlady to a chymist's shop for some cinnamon-water, while I returning to this unfortunate creature's chamber, used all the means in my power to bring her to herself, which with much difficulty I accomplished, and made her drink a glass of the cordial to recruit her spirits; then I prepared a little mulled red wine and a toast, which having taken, she found herself thoroughly revived, and informed me, that she had not tasted food for eight and forty hours before.—As I was impatient to know the occasion and nature of her calamity, she gave me to understand that she was a woman of the town by profession —that in the course of her adventures, she found herself dangerously infected with a distemper to which all of her class are particularly subject;—that her malady gaining ground every day, she was become loathsome to herself as well as to every one else, when she resolved to retire to some obscure corner, where she might be cured with as little noise and expence as possible;—that she had accordingly chosen this place of retreat, and put herself into the hands of an advertising doctor, who having fleeced her of all the money she had, or could procure, left her three days ago in a worse condition than that in which he found her;—that except the cloaths on her back, she had pawned or sold every thing that belonged to her, to satisfy that rapacious quack, and quiet the clamour of her landlady, who still persisted in her threats to turn her out into the street.—After having moralized upon these particulars, I proposed that she should lodge in the same room with me, which would save some money; and assured her I would myself undertake her cure as well as my own, during which she should partake of all the conveniences I could afford to myself.—She embraced my offer with unfeigned acknowledgment, and I began to put it in practice immediately.—I found to my great satisfaction, in her, not only an agreeable companion, whose conversation greatly alleviated my chagrin, but also a careful nurse, who served me with the utmost fidelity and affection. One day, while I testified my surprise that a woman of her beauty, good sense, and education (for she had a large portion of each) could be reduced to such an infamous and miserable way of life as that of a prostitute; she answered with a sigh, 'These very advantages were the cause of my undoing.'— This remarkable reply inflamed my curiosity to such a degree, that I begged she would favour me with the particulars of her story, and she complied in these words.

CHAPTER XXII

The history of Miss WILLIAMS

My father was an eminent merchant in the city, who having, in the course of trade, suffered very considerable losses, retired in his old age with his wife to a small estate in the country, which he had purchased with the remains of his fortune.—At that time I being but eight years of age, was left in town for the convenience of education; boarded with an aunt, who was a rigid Presbyterian, and who confined me so closely to what she called the duties of religion, that in time I grew weary of her doctrines, and by degrees conceived an aversion for the good books she daily recommended to my perusal. As I increased in age, and appeared with a person not disagreeable, I contracted a good deal of acquaintance among my own sex; one of whom, after having lamented the restraint I was under from the narrowness of my aunt's sentiments, told me, I must now throw off the prejudices of opinion imbibed under her influence and example, and learn to think for myself;—for which purpose she advised me to read Shaftsbury,[1] Tindal,[2] Hobbs,[3] and all the books that are remarkable for their deviation from the old way of thinking, and by comparing one with another, I would soon be able to form a system of my own.—I followed her advice, and whether it was owing to my prepossession against what I had formerly read, or the clearness of argument in these my new instructors, I know not, but I studied them with pleasure, and in a short time became a professed Free-thinker. Proud of my new improvement, I argued in all companies, and that with such success, that I soon acquired the reputation of a philosopher, and few people durst undertake me in a dispute.—I grew vain upon my good fortune, and at length pretended to make my aunt a proselyte to my opinion; but she no sooner perceived my drift, than taking the alarm, she wrote to my father an account of my heresy, and conjured him, as he tendered the good of my soul, to remove me immediately from the dangerous place where I had contracted such sinful principles: Accordingly, my father ordered me into the country, where I arrived in the fifteenth year of my age, and by his command, gave him a detail of all the articles of my faith, which he did not find so unreasonable as they had been re-presented.—Finding myself suddenly deprived of the company and pleasures of the town, I grew melancholy, and it was some time before I could relish my situation.—But solitude became every day more and more familiar to me, and I consoled myself in my retreat with the enjoyment of a good library, at such times as were not em-ployed in the management of the family, (for my mother had been dead three years) in visiting, or some other party of rural diversion. ——Having more imagination than judgment, I addicted myself too much to poetry and romance; and in short was looked upon as a very extraordinary person by every body in the country where I resided.——I had one evening strayed with a book in my hand, into a wood that bordered on the high road, at a little distance from my father's house; when a certain drunken 'squire, riding by, per-ceived me, and crying, 'Z—ds! there's a charming creature!' alighted in a moment, catched me in his arms, and treated me so rudely, that I shrieked as loud as I could, and in the mean time opposed his violence with all the strength that rage and resentment could inspire.—During this struggle, another horseman came up, who seeing a lady so unworthily used, dismounted and flew to my assistance.—My ravisher, mad with disappointment, or provoked with the reproaches of the other gentleman, quitted me, and run-ning to his horse, drew a pistol from the saddle and fired it at my protector, who happily receiving no damage, went up, and with the butt end of his whip, laid him prostrate on the ground, before he could use the other, which his antagonist immediately seized, and clapping to the 'squire's breast, threatned to put him to death for his cowardice and treachery: Upon this I interposed and begged his life, which was granted to my request, after he had asked pardon, and swore his intention was only to obtain a kiss.—However, my defender thought proper to unload the other pistol, and throw away the flints, before he gave him his liberty.—This courteous stranger conducted me home, where my father having learned the signal service he had done me, loaded him with caresses, and insisted on his lodging that night at our house.—If the obligation he had conferred upon me justly inspired me with sentiments of gratitude, his appearance and conversation seemed to intitle him to somewhat more.—He was about the age of two and twenty, among the tallest of the middle-size; had chestnut coloured hair which he wore tied up in a ribbon; a high polished fore-head, a nose inclining to the aqualine, lively blue eyes, red pouting lips, teeth as white as snow, and a certain openness of countenance,—but what need I describe any more particulars of his person? I hope you will do me the justice to believe I do not flatter, when I say he was the exact resemblance of you; and if I had not been well acquainted with his family and pedigree, I should have made no scruple of concluding him your brother.—He spoke little, and seemed to have no reserve, for what he said was ingenuous, sensible, and uncommon.—In short (said she, bursting into tears) he was formed for the ruin of our sex.—His behaviour was modest and respectful, but his looks were so significant that I could easily observe, he secretly blessed the occasion that introduced him to my acquaintance.—We learned from his discourse that he was eldest son of a wealthy gentleman in the neighbourhood, to whose name we were no strangers; that he had been to visit an acquaintance in the country, from whose house he was returning home, when my shrieks brought him to my rescue.—All night long my imagination formed a thousand ridiculous expectations: There was so much of knight-errantry in this gentleman's coming to the relief of a damsel in distress, with whom he immediately became enamoured, that all I had read of love and chivalry recurred to my fancy, and I looked upon myself as a princess in some region of romance, who being delivered from the power of a brutal giant or satyr by a generous Oroondates,[1] was bound in gratitude, as well as led by inclination, to yield up my affections to him without reserve. In vain did I endeavour to chastise these foolish conceits by reflexions more reasonable and severe: The amusing images took full possession of my mind, and my dreams represented my hero sighing at my feet, in the language of a despairing lover.—Next morning after breakfast he took his leave, when my father begged the favour of a further acquaintance with him; to which he replied by a compliment to him, and a look to me so full of eloquence and tenderness, that my whole soul received the soft impression.—In a short time he repeated his visit; and as a recital of the particular steps he pursued to ruin me, would be too tedious and impertinent, let it suffice to say, he made it his business to insinuate himself into my esteem, by convincing me of his own good sense, and at the same time flattering my understanding: This he performed in the most artful manner, by seeming to contradict me often through misapprehension, that I might have an opportunity of clearing myself, the more to my own honour.——Having thus secured my good opinion, he began to give me some tokens of a particular passion founded on a veneration for the qualities of my mind, and as an accidental ornament, admir'd the beauties of my person; till at length, being fully persuaded of his conquest, he chose a proper season for the theme, and disclos'd his love in terms so ardent and sincere, that it was impossible for me to disguise the sentiments of my heart, and he received my approbation with the most lively transport. After this mutual declaration, we contrived to meet more frequently, which we did in private interviews, where we enjoy'd the conversation of one another, in all the elevation of fancy and impatience of hope, that reciprocal adoration can inspire.—He professed his honourable intentions, of which I made no question, lamented the avaritious disposition of his father, who had destin'd him for the arms of another, and vowed eternal fidelity with such an appearance of candour and devotion, that I became a dupe to his deceit, and in an evil hour crowned his eager desire with full possession.—Cursed be the day on which I gave away my innocence and peace, for a momentary gratification which has entailed upon me such misery and horror! cursed be my beauty that first attracted the attention of the seducer! cursed be my education, that by refining my sentiments, made my heart the more susceptible! cursed be my good sense that fixed me to one object, and taught me the preference I enjoyed was but my due! Had I been ugly, no body would have tempted me; had I been ignorant, the charms of my person would not have atoned for the coarseness of my conversation; had I been giddy, my vanity would have divided my inclinations, and my ideas would have been so diffused, that I should never have listened to the enchantments of one alone.

But to return to my unfortunate story; we gave a loose to guilty pleasure, which for some months banished every other concern.— But by degrees, his visits became less frequent, and his behaviour less warm: I perceived his coldness, my heart took the alarm, my tears reproached him, and I insisted upon the performance of his promise to espouse me, that whatever should happen, my reputation might be safe: He seemed to acquiesce in my proposal, and left me on pretence of finding a proper clergyman to unite us in the bands of wedlock.—But alas! the Inconstant had no intention to return: I waited a whole week with the utmost impatience; sometimes doubting his honour, at other times inventing excuses for him, and condemning myself for harbouring the least suspicion of his faith.—At length, I understood from a gentleman who dined at our house, that this perfidious wretch was on the point of setting out for London with his bride, to buy cloaths for their approaching nuptials.—This information distracted me! the more so, as I found myself some months gone with child, and reflected, that it would be impossible to conceal my disgrace, which would not only ruin the character I had acquired in the country, but also bring the grey hairs of an indulgent parent with sorrow to the grave. Rage took possession of my soul; I denounced a thousand imprecations, and formed as many schemes of revenge against the traitor who had undone me! then my resentment would subside to silent sorrow: I recalled the tranquility I had lost, I wept over my infatuation, and sometimes a ray of hope would intervene, and for a moment cheer my drooping heart; I would revolve all the favourable circumstances of his character, repeat the vows he made, ascribe his absence to the vigilance of a suspicious father, who compelled him to a match his soul abhorred, and comfort myself with the expectation of seeing him before the thing should be brought to any terms of agreement.—But how vain was my imagination? The villain left me without remorse, and in a few days the news of his marriage spread all over the country.—My horror was then inconceivable! and had not the desire of revenge diverted the resolution, I should infallibly have put an end to my miserable life.—My father observed the symptoms of my despair; and though I have good reason to believe, he guessed the cause, was at a great deal of pains to seem ignorant of my affliction, while he endeavoured with paternal fondness to alleviate my distress. I saw his concern, which increased my anguish, and raised my fury against the author of my calamity, to an implacable degree. Having furnished myself with a little money, I made an elopement from this unhappy parent in the night-time, and about break of day, arrived at a small town from whence a stage-coach set out for London, in which I embarked, and next day alighted in town; the spirit of revenge having supported me all the way against every other reflection.—My first care was to hire a lodging, in which I kept myself very retired, having assumed a feigned name, that my character and situation might be the better concealed.—It was not long before I found out the house of my ravisher, whither I immediately repaired in a transport of rage, determined to act some desperate deed for the satisfaction of my despair, though the hurry of my spirits would not permit me to concert or resolve upon a particular plan. When I demanded admission to Lothario[1] (so let me call him) I was desired to send up my name and business; but this I refused, telling the porter I had business for his master's private ear: Upon which I was conducted into a parlour until he should be informed of my request.——There I remained about a quarter of an hour, when a servant entered and told me his master was engaged with company, and begged to be excused at that time.—My temper could hold out no longer: I pulled a poignard from my bosom where I had concealed it, and rushing out, flew up stairs like a fury, exclaiming, 'Where is this perfidious villain! could I once plunge this dagger into his false heart, I would then die satisfied.'—The noise I made alarmed not only the servants, but the company also, who hearing my threats, came forwards to the stair-case to see what was the matter. By this time I was seized, disarmed, and with-held by two footmen; in this situation I felt the most exquisite torture in beholding my undoer approach with his young wife; I could not endure the sight, was deprived of my senses, and fell into a severe fit, during which I know not how I was treated; but when I recovered the use of reflection, found myself on a bed in a paultry apartment, where I was attended by an old woman, who asked a thousand impertinent questions relating to my condition; and informed me that my behaviour had thrown the whole family into confusion; that Lothario affirmed I was mad, and pretended to

Chapter XXII

have me sent to Bedlam,[1] but my lady persuaded herself there was more in my conduct than he cared should be known, and had taken to her bed on bare suspicion, having first ordered that I should be narrowly looked to.—I heard all she said without making any other reply, than desiring she would do me the favour to call a chair; but this (she told me) could not be done without her master's consent, which, however, was easily procured, and I was conveyed to my own lodging in a state of mind that baffles all description. The agitation of my thoughts produced a fever, which brought on a miscarriage; and I believe it is well for my conscience that heaven thus disposed of my burden; for let me own to you with penitence and horror, if I had brought a living child into the world, my frenzy would have prompted me to sacrifice the little innocent to my resentment of the wrongs done me by the father.

After this event my rage abated, and my hate became more deliberate and calm; when one day, my landlady informed me that there was a gentleman below who desired to see me, having something of consequence to impart, which he was sure would contribute to my peace of mind.—I was exceedingly alarmed at this declaration, which I attempted to interpret a thousand ways; and before I came to any determination he entered my room, with an apology for intruding upon me against my knowledge or consent.—I surveyed him some time, but could not remember to have seen him before; then with a faultering accent, demanded what was his business with me?—Upon which, he desired I would give him a particular audience, and he did not doubt of communicating something that would conduce to my satisfaction and repose. As I thought myself sufficiently guarded against any violence, I granted his request, and bid the woman withdraw.—The stranger then advancing, gave me to understand that he was well acquainted with the particulars of my story, having been informed of them from Lothario's own mouth—that from the time he knew my misfortunes, he had entertained a detestation for the author of them; which had of late been increased and inflamed to a desire of revenge, by a piece of dishonourable conduct towards him—that hearing of my melancholy situation, he had come with an intention of offering his assistance and comfort, and was ready to espouse my quarrel and forthwith take vengeance on my seducer, provided I would grant him one consideration, which (he hoped) I should see no reason to refuse.——Had all the artifice of hell been employed in composing a persuasive, it could not have had a more instantaneous or favourable effect than this discourse had upon me.—I was transported with a delirium of gloomy joy; I hugged my companion in my arms, and vowed that if he would make good his promise, my soul and body should be at his disposal.—The contract was made; he devoted himself to my revenge, undertook to murder Lothario that very night, and to bring me an account of his death before morning.—Accordingly, about two of the clock, he was introduced to my chamber, and assured me my perfidious lover was no more; that although he was not entitled to such an honourable proceeding, he had fairly challenged him to the field, where he upbraided him with his treachery towards me, for whom (he told him) his sword was drawn, and after a few passes, left him weltering in his blood.—I was so savaged by my wrongs, that I delighted in the recital of this adventure, made him repeat the particulars, feasted my eyes with the blood that remained on his cloaths and sword, and yielded up my body as a recompence for the service he had done me. My imagination was so engrossed by these ideas, that in my sleep I dreamed Lothario appeared before me, pale, mangled and bloody, blamed my rashness, protested his innocence, and pleaded his own cause so pathetically, that I was convinced of his fidelity, and waked in a fit of horror and remorse.—My bed-fellow endeavoured to sooth, console, and persuade me that I had but barely done justice to myself.—I dropt asleep again, and the same apparition recurred to my fancy.—In short, I passed the night in great misery, and looked upon my avenger with such abhorrence, that in the morning, perceiving my aversion, he insinuated there was still a possibility of Lothario's recovery; it was true, he left him wounded on the ground, but not quite dead; and perhaps his hurts might not be mortal.—At these words I started up, bid him fly for intelligence, and if he could not bring me tidings of Lothario's safety, at least consult his own and never return, for I was resolved to surrender myself to justice, and declare all that I knew of the affair, that, if possible, I might expiate my own guilt, by incurring the rigours of a sincere repentance and ignominious death.—He very cooly represented the unreasonableness of my prejudice against him, who had done nothing but what his love of me inspired, and honour justified; —that now he had at the risk of his life, been subservient to my revenge, I was about to discard him as an infamous agent occasionally necessary: and that even if he should be so lucky as to bring news of Lothario's safety, it was probable my former resentment might revive, and I would upbraid him with having failed in his undertaking.—I assured him that, on the contrary, he would be dearer to me than ever, as I should be convinced he acted more on the principles of a man of honour, than on those of a mercenary assassin, and scorned to take away the life of an adversary (how inveterate soever) which fortune had put in his power.—'Well then, madam, (said he) whatever may have happened, I shall find it no difficult matter to satisfy you in that.'—And took his leave, in order to enquire into the consequences of his duel.—I was now more sensible than ever of the degrees of guilt and misery; all the affliction I had suffered hitherto was owing to my own credulity and weakness, and my conscience could only accuse me of venal crimes; but now that I looked upon myself as a murderer, it is impossible to express the terrors of my imagination, which was incessantly haunted by the image of the deceased, and my bosom stung with the most exquisite agonies, of which I saw no end.—At length, Horatio[1] (for so I shall call my keeper) returned, and telling me I had nothing to fear, delivered into my hands a billet containing these words.

MADAM,
'As I understand it is of consequence to your peace, I take this liberty to inform you, that the wounds I received from Horatio are not mortal. This satisfaction my humanity could not deny even to a person who has endeavoured to disturb the repose, as well destroy the life of

Lothario.'

Being well acquainted with his hand, I had no reason to suspect an imposition in this letter, which I read over and over with a transport of joy, and caressed Horatio so much, that he appeared the happiest man alive. Thus was I won from despair by the menaces of a greater misfortune than that which depressed me.—Griefs are like usurpers, the most powerful deposes all the rest—But my raptures were not lasting—that very letter which in a manner reestablished my tranquility, in a little time banished my peace.— His unjust reproaches, while they waked my resentment, recalled my former happiness, and filled my soul with rage and sorrow.— Horatio, perceiving the situation of my mind, endeavoured to divert my chagrin, by treating me with all the amusements and entertainments of the town. I was gratified with every indulgence I could desire; introduced into the company of other kept-mistresses, by whom an uncommon deference was paid me; and I began to lose all remembrance of my former condition, when an accident brought it back to my view with all its interesting circumstances.—Diverting myself one day with some news papers, which I had not before perused, the following advertisement attracted my attention.

'WHEREAS a young gentlewoman disappeared from her father's house, in the county of ——, about the end of September, on account (as is supposed) of some uneasiness of mind, and has not been as yet heard of; whoever will give an information about her, to Mr. —— of Gray's-Inn,[1] shall be handsomely rewarded; or if she will return to the arms of her disconsolate parent, she will be received with the utmost tenderness, whatever reasons she may have to think otherwise, and may be the means of prolonging the life of a father, already weighed down almost to the grave with age and sorrow.'

This pathetic remonstrance had such an effect on me, that I was fully resolved to return like the prodigal son, and implore the forgiveness of him who gave me life; but alas! upon inquiry, I found he had paid his debt to nature a month before, lamenting my absence to his last hour, having left his fortune to a stranger as a mark of his resentment of my unkind and undutiful behaviour.—Penetrated with remorse on this occasion, I sunk into the most profound melancholy, and considered myself as the immediate cause of his death.—I lost all relish for company, and indeed most of my acquaintances no sooner perceived my change of temper, than they abandoned me. Horatio, disgusted at my insensibility, or (which is more probable) cloyed with possession, became colder and colder every day, till at last he left me altogether, without making any apology for his conduct; or securing me against the miseries of want, as a man of honour ought to have done, considering the share he had in my ruin; for I afterwards learned that the quarrel between Lothario and him, was a story trumped up to rid the one of my importunities, and give the other the enjoyment of my person, which, it seems, he lusted after, upon seeing me at the house of my seducer.—Reduced to this extremity, I cursed my own simplicity, uttered horrid imprecations against the treachery of Horatio; and as I became every day more and more familiarized to the loss of innocence, resolved to be revenged on the sex in general, by practising their own arts upon themselves.—Nor was an opportunity long wanting: An old gentlewoman, under pretence of sympathizing, visited me, and after having condoled with me on my misfortunes, and professed a disinterested friendship, began to display the art of her occupation, in encomiums on my beauty, and invectives against the wretch who had forsaken me; insinuating withal that it would be my own fault if I did not still make my fortune by the extraordinary qualifications with which nature had endowed me.—I soon understood her drift, and gave her such encouragement to explain herself, that we came to an agreement immediately to divide the profits of my prostitution, accruing from such gallants as she should introduce to my acquaintance. The first stroke of my dissimulation, was practised upon a certain J—ge, to whom I was recommended by this matron, as an innocent creature just arrived from the country; he was so transported with my appearance and feigned simplicity, that he paid a hundred guineas for the possession of me for one night only, during which I behaved in such a manner, as to make him perfectly well-pleased with his purchase.

CHAPTER XXIII

She is interrupted by a bailif,[1] *who arrests, and carries her to the Marshalsea——I accompany her——bring witnesses to prove she is not the same person named in the writ——the bailif is fain to give her a present, and discharge her——we shift our lodging——she resumes her story and ends it——my reflections thereupon——she makes me acquainted with the progress of a common woman of the town— resolves to quit that way of life*

HER story was here interrupted by a rap at the door, which I no sooner opened, than three or four terrible fellows rushed in, one of whom accosted my fellow lodger thus:——'Madam, your servant— you must do me the favour to come along with me—I have got a writ against you.'—While the bailif (for so he was) spoke thus, his

followers surrounded the prisoner, and began to handle her very
roughly.—This treatment incensed me so much, that I snatched up
the poker, and would certainly have used it in defence of the lady,
without any regard to the strength and number of her adversaries,
had not she begged me with a composure of countenance, for which
I could not account, to use no violence in her behalf, which could
be of no service to her, but might be very detrimental to myself.—
Then turning to the leader of this formidable troop, she desired to
see the warrant, and having perused it, said with a faultering voice,
'I am not the person whose name is here mentioned; arrest me at
your peril.'—'Ay, ay, Madam, (replied the catch-pole)[1] we shall
prove your identity.—In the mean time, whether will you be
pleased to be carried to my house or to Jail?'[2]—'If I must be confined (said she) I would rather have your house for a prison than a
common Jail.'—'Well, well, (answered he) if you have money
enough in your pocket, you shall be entertained like a princess.'—
But when she acquainted him with her poverty, he swore he never
gave credit, and ordered one of his myrmidons[3] to call a coach to
carry her to the Marshalsea[4] at once.—While this was a doing she
took me aside, and bid me be under no concern on her account, for
she knew how to extricate herself from this difficulty very soon, and
perhaps gain something by the occasion.—Although her discourse
was a mystery to me, I was very well pleased with her assurance, and
when the coach came to the door, offered to accompany her to
prison, to which, after much intreaty, she consented.—When we
arrived at the gate of the Marshalsea, our conductor alighted, and
having demanded entrance, presented the writ to the turnkey, who
no sooner perceived the name of Elizabeth Cary, than he cried,
'Ah ha! my old acquaintance Bett! I'm glad to see thee with all my
heart.'—So saying he opened the coach door, and helped her to dis-
mount; but when he observed her face, he started back, saying,
'Z—ds! who have we got here?'—The bailif, alarmed at this interrogation, cried with some emotion, 'Who the devil should it be, but
the prisoner Elizabeth Cary?' The turnkey replied, 'That Elizabeth
Cary!—I'll be damned if that's Elizabeth Cary, more than my
grandmother.—D—n my blood, I know Bett Cary as well as if I
had made her.'——Here the lady thought fit to interpose, and tell
the catchpole, if he had taken her word for it at first, he might have
saved himself and her a great deal of trouble.—'It may be so
(answered he) but by G—d, I'll have further evidence that you are

not the person before you and I part.'—'Yes, yes, (said she) you shall have further evidence to your cost.'—Upon this we adjourned into the lodge, and called for a bottle of wine, where my companion wrote a direction to two of her acquaintance, and begged the favour of me to go to their lodgings, and request them to come to her immediately: I found them together at a house in Bridges's street,[1] Drury-lane, and as they were luckily unengaged, they set out with me in a hackney-coach without hesitation, after I had related the circumstances of the affair, which flattered them with hopes of seeing a bailif trounced; for there is an antipathy as natural between the whores and bailifs, as that subsisting between mice and cats.—Accordingly, when they entered the lodge, they embraced the prisoner very affectionately by the name of Nancy Williams; and asked how long she had been nabb'd, and for what?—On hearing the particulars of her adventure repeated, they offered to swear before a justice of peace that she was not the person mentioned in the writ, whom, it seems, they all knew; but the bailif, who by this time was convinced of his mistake, told them he would not put them to that trouble.—'Ladies (said he) there's no harm done— you shall give me leave to treat you with another bottle, and then we'll part friends.'—This proposal was not at all relished by the sisterhood; and miss Williams told him: Sure he did not imagine her such a fool as to be satisfied with a paultry glass of sour wine.— Here the turnkey interrupted her, by affirming with an oath, that the wine was as good as ever was tipped over tongue.—'Well (continued she) that may be—but was it the best of champaign, it is no recompence for the damage I have suffered both in character and health, by being wrongfully dragged to jail—At this rate no innocent person is safe, since any officer of justice, out of malice, private pique, or mistake, may injure and oppress the subject with impunity —but, thank heaven, I live under the protection of laws that will not suffer such insults to pass unpunished, and I know very well how to procure redress.'—Mr. Vulture (for that was the bailif's name) finding he had to deal with one who would not be imposed upon, began to look very sullen and perplexed, and leaning his fore-head on his hand, entered into a deliberation with himself, which lasted a few minutes, and then broke out in a volley of dreadful curses against the old b—ch our landlady (as he called her) for having misinformed him.—After much wrangling and swearing, the matter was referred to the decision of the turnkey, who calling for the other bottle, mulcted[1] the bailif in all the liquor that had been drank, coach-hire, and a couple of guineas for the use of the plaintif.—The money was immediately deposited; miss Williams gratified the two evidences with one half, and putting the other in her pocket drove home with me, leaving the catchpole grumbling over his loss, yet pleased in the main, for having so cheaply got clear of a business that might have cost him ten times the sum, and his place to boot.——This guinea was a very seasonable relief to us, who were reduced to great necessity, six of my shirts and almost all my cloaths, except those on my back, being either pawned or sold for our maintenance before this happened.—As we resented the behaviour of our land-lady, our first care was to provide ourselves with another lodging, whither we removed next day, with an intention to keep ourselves as retired as possible until our cure should be compleated.—When we were fixed in our new habitation, I intreated her to finish the story of her Life, which she pursued in this manner:

The success of our experiment on the J—ge, encouraged us to practice the same deceit on others, and my virginity was five times sold to good purpose; but this harvest lasted not long, my character taking air, and my directress deserting me for some new game. Whereupon I took lodgings near Charing cross,[2] at two guineas *per* week, and began to entertain company in a public manner:—But my income being too small to defray my expence, I was obliged to retrench, and enter into articles with the porters of certain taverns, who undertook to find employment enough for me, provided I would share my profits with them.—Accordingly, I was almost every night engaged with company, among whom I was exposed to every mortification, danger and abuse that flow from drunkenness, brutality and disease.—How miserable is the condition of a courte-zan, whose business it is to sooth, suffer, and obey the dictates of rage, insolence and lust!—As my spirit was not sufficiently humbled to the will, nor my temper calculated for the conversation of my gallants, it was impossible for me to overcome an aversion I felt for my profession, which manifested itself in a settled gloom on my countenance, and disgusted these sons of mirth and riot so much, that I was frequently used in a shocking manner, and kicked down stairs with disgrace.—The messengers seeing me disagreeable to their benefactors and employers, seldom troubled me with a call, and I began to find myself almost totally neglected. To contribute towards my support, I was fain to sell my watch, rings, trinkets, with the best part of my cloaths; and I was one evening musing by myself, on the misery before me, when I received a message from a bagnio, whither I repaired in a chair, and was introduced to a gentleman dressed like an officer, with whom I supped *tête à tête*, in a sumptuous manner, and after drinking a hearty glass of champaign, went to bed.—In the morning when I awoke I found my gallant had got up, and drawing aside the curtain, could not perceive him in the room; this gave me some uneasiness, but as he might have retired on some necessary occasion, I waited a full hour for his return; and then in the greatest perplexity got up, and rung the bell.—When the waiter came to the door, he found it locked, and desired admittance, which I granted, after observing with great surprize that the key remained on the inside, as when we went to bed.—I no sooner enquired for the captain, than the fellow staring with a distracted look, cried, 'How, madam! is he not a-bed?' And when he was satisfied as to that, run into a closet adjoining to the chamber, the window of which he found open.—Through this the adventurer had got upon a wall, from whence he dropped down into a court and escaped; leaving me to be answerable, not only for the reckoning, but also for a large silver tankard and posset-bowl,[1] which he had carried off with him.—It is impossible to describe the consternation I was under, when I saw myself detained as a thief's accomplice (for I was looked upon in that light) and carried before a justice, who mistaking my confusion for a sign of guilt, committed me after a short examination to Bridewell, having advised me, as the only means to save my life, to turn evidence, and impeach my confederate.—I now concluded, the vengeance of heaven had overtaken me, and that I must soon finish my career by an ignominious death.—This reflection sunk so deep into my soul, that I was for some days deprived of my reason, and actually believed myself in hell, tormented by fiends: Indeed, there needs not a very extravagant imagination to form that conjecture; for of all the scenes on earth, that of Bridewell approaches nearest the idea I had always entertained of the infernal regions.—Here I saw nothing but rage, anguish and impiety; and heard nothing but groans, curses and blasphemy.—In the midst of this hellish crew, I was subjected to the tyranny of a barbarian, who imposed upon me tasks that I could not possibly perform, and then punished my incapacity with the utmost rigour and inhumanity. I was often whipt into a swoon, and lashed out of it, during which miserable intervals, I was robbed by my fellow-prisoners of every thing about me, even to my cape, shoes and stockings: I was not only destitute of necessaries, but even of food, so that my wretchedness was extreme. Not one of my acquaintance to whom I imparted my situation, would grant me the least succour or regard, on pretence of my being committed for theft; and my landlord refused to part with some of my own cloaths which I sent for, because I was indebted to him for a week's lodging.—Overwhelmed with calamity, I grew desperate, and resolved to put an end to my grievances and life together; for this purpose I got up in the middle of the night, when I thought every body round me asleep, and fixing one end of my handkerchief to a large hook in the ceiling, that supported the scales on which the hemp is weighed, I stood upon a chair and making a noose on the other end, put my neck into it, with an intention to hang myself, but before I could adjust the knot, I was surprised and prevented by two women who had been awake all the while, and suspected my design.—In the morning my attempt was published among the prisoners, and punished with thirty stripes, the pain of which co-operating with my disappointment and disgrace, bereft me of my senses and threw me into an extasy of madness, wherein I tore the flesh from my bones with my teeth, and dashed my head against the pavement.—So that they were obliged to set a watch over me, to restrain me from doing further mischief to myself and others.— This fit of phrenzy continued three days, at the end of which I grew calm and sullen; but as the desire of making away with myself still remained, I came to a determination of starving myself to death, and with that view refused all sustenance. Whether it was owing to the want of opposition, or to the weakness of nature, I know not, but on the second day of my fast, I found my resolution considerably impaired, and the calls of hunger almost insupportable.—At this critical conjuncture a lady was brought into the prison, with whom I had contracted an acquaintance while I lived with Horatio; she was then on the same footing as I was, but afterwards quarreling with her gallant, and not finding another to her mind, altered her scheme of life, and set up a coffee-house among the hundreds of Drury,[1] where she entertained gentlemen with claret, arrack and the choice of half a dozen damsels, who lived in her house. This serviceable matron, having neglected to gratify a certain j—ce for the connivance she enjoyed, was indicted at the quarter sessions, in consequence of which her bevy was dispersed and herself committed to Bridewell.—She had not been long there, before she learned my disaster, and coming up to me, after a compliment of condolance, enquired into the particulars of my fate: While we were engaged in discourse together, the master coming up, told me that the fellow on whose account I had suffered was taken, that he had confessed the theft, and cleared me of any concern in the affair; for which reason he, the master, had orders to discharge me, and that I was from that moment free. This piece of news soon banished all thoughts of death, and had such an instantaneous effect on my countenance, that Mrs. Coupler (the lady then present) hoping to find her account in me, very generously offered to furnish me with what necessaries I wanted, and take me into her own house, as soon as she could compromise matters with the j—ces.—The conditions of her offer, were, that I should pay three guineas weekly for my board, and a reasonable consideration besides for the use of such cloaths and ornaments as she should supply me with, to be deducted from the first profits of my embraces.—These were hard terms; but not to be rejected by one who was turned out helpless and naked into the wide world, without a friend to pity or assist her.—I therefore embraced her proposal, and she being bailed in a few hours, took me home with her in a coach. As I was by this time conscious of having formerly disgusted my admirers by my reserved and haughty behaviour, I now endeavoured to conquer that disposition, and the sudden change of my fortune giving me a flow of spirits, I appeared in the most winning and gay manner I could assume. Having the advantage of a good voice and education over most of my rivals, I exerted my talents to the uttermost, and soon became the favourite with all company.—This success alarmed the pride and jealousy of Mrs. Coupler, who could not bear the thoughts of being eclipsed: She therefore made a merit of her envy, and whispered about among her customers that I was unsound.[1]—There needed no more to ruin my reputation and blast my prosperity; every body shunned me with marks of aversion and disdain, and in a very short time I was as solitary as ever. Want of gallants was attended with want of money to satisfy my malicious landlady, who having purposely given me credit to the amount of eleven pounds, took out a writ against me, and I was arrested in her own house.—Though the room was crouded with people, when the bailif entered, not one of them had compassion enough to attempt to molify my prosecutrix, far less to pay the debt; they even laughed at my tears, and one of them bid me be of good cheer, for I should not want admirers in Newgate. At that instant a sea lieutenant came in, and seeing my plight, began to enquire into the circumstances of my misfortune, when this wit advised him to keep clear of me, for I was a fire-ship.[1]—'A fire-ship! (replied the sailor) more like a poor galley in distress that has been boarded by such a fire-ship as you; if so be that be the case, she stands in more need of assistance.— Harkee, my girl, how far have you over-run the constable?'—I told him that the debt amounted to eleven pounds, besides the expence of the writ.—'An that be all (said he) you shan't go to the bilboes this bout.'[2]—And taking out his purse, paid the money, discharged the bailif, and telling me, I had got into the wrong port, advised me to seek out a more convenient harbour, where I could be safely hove down,[3] for which purpose he made me a present of five guineas more.—I was so touched with this singular piece of generosity, that for some time I had not power to thank him.— However, as soon as I had recollected myself, I begged the favour of him to go with me to the next tavern, where I explained the nature of my disaster, and convinced him of the falsehood of what was reported to my prejudice so effectually, that he from that moment attached himself to me, and we lived in great harmony together, until he was obliged to go to sea, where he perished in a storm.

Having lost my benefactor, and almost consumed the remains of his bounty, I saw myself in danger of relapsing into my former necessity, and began to be very uneasy at the prospect of bailifs and jails;—when one of the sisterhood, a little stale, advised me to take lodgings in a part of the town where I was unknown, and pass for an heiress, which might entrap some body to be my husband, who would possibly be able to allow me an handsome maintenance, or at worst screen me from the dread and danger of a prison, by becoming liable for whatever debts I should contract.—I approved of this scheme, towards the execution of which my companion clubbed her wardrobe, and undertook to live with me in quality of my maid; with the proviso, that she should be reimbursed and handsomely considered out of the profits of my success.—She was immediately detached to look out for a convenient place, and that very day hired a genteel apartment in Park-street,[4] whither I moved in a coach loaded with her baggage and my own.—I made my first appearance in a blue riding-habit trimmed with silver; and my maid acted her part so artfully, that in a day or two, my fame was spread all over the neighbourhood, and I was said to be a rich heiress just arrived from the country.—This report brought a swarm of gay young fellows about me; but I soon found them out to be all indigent adventurers like myself, who crouded to me like crows to a carrion, with a view of preying upon my fortune.—I maintained, however, the appearance of wealth as long as possible, in hopes of gaining some admirer more for my purpose; and at length, I attracted the regard of one who would have satisfied my wishes, and managed matters so well, that a day was actually fixed for our nuptials: In the interim, he begged leave to introduce an intimate friend to me, which request as I could not refuse, I had the extreme mortification and surprize, to see next night, in that friend, my old keeper Horatio, who no sooner beheld me than he changed colour; but had presence of mind enough to advance and salute me, bidding me (with a low voice) be under no apprehension, for he would not expose me.—In spite of this assurance, I could not recover myself so far, as to entertain them, but withdrew to my chamber on pretence of a severe head-ach, to the no small concern of my adorer, who took his leave in the tenderest manner, and went off with his friend.

Having imparted my situation to my companion, she found it high time for us to decamp, and that without any noise, because we were not only indebted to our landlady, but also to several tradesmen in the neighbourhood.—Our retreat (therefore) was concerted and executed in this manner: Having packed up all our cloaths and moveables in small parcels, she (on pretence of fetching cordials for me) carried them at several times, to the house of an acquaintance, where she likewise procured a lodging, to which we retired, in the middle of the night, opening the street door, when every other body in the house was asleep.—I was now obliged to aim at lower game, and accordingly spread my nets among trades people; but found them all too phlegmatic or cautious for my art and attractions; till at last I became acquainted with you, on whom I practised all my dexterity; not that I believed you had any fortune or expectation of one, but that I might transfer the burthen of such debts as I had incurred or could contract, from myself to another, and at the same time, avenge myself of your sex, by rendering miserable, one who bore such resemblance to the wretch who ruined me;—but heaven preserved you from my snares, by the discovery you made, which was owing to the negligence of my maid in leaving the chamber-door unlocked, when she went to buy sugar for breakfast.—The person in bed with me, was a gentleman whom I had allured the night before, as he walked homeward pretty much elevated with liquor; for by this time, my condition was so low, that I was forced to turn out, in the twilight, to the streets in hopes of prey.—When I found myself detected and forsaken by you, I was fain to move my lodging and dwell two pair of stairs higher than before: My companion being disappointed in her expectations, left me, to trade upon her own bottom,[1] and I had no other resource, than to venture forth like the owls, in the dark, to pick up a precarious and uncomfortable subsistence. I have often sauntered between Ludgate-hill and Charing-cross,[2] a whole winter-night, exposed not only to the inclemency of the weather, but like-wise to the rage of hunger and thirst, without being so happy as to meet with one cully,[3] then creep up to my garret in a deplorable, draggled condition, sneak to bed, and try to bury my appetite and sorrows in sleep.—When I lighted on some rake or tradesman reeling home drunk, I frequently suffered the most brutal treatment, in spite of which I was obliged to affect gaiety and good humour, tho' my soul was stung with resentment and disdain, and my heart loaded with grief and affliction.—In the course of these nocturnal adventures, I was infected with the disease, that in a short time render'd me the object of my own abhorrence, and drove me to the retreat, where your benevolence rescued me from the jaws of death.

So much candour and good sense appeared in this lady's narration, that I made no scruple of believing every syllable of what she said; and expressed my astonishment at the variety of miseries she had undergone, in so little time; for all her misfortunes had happened within the compass of two years.—I compared her situation with my own, and found it a thousand times more wretched: I had endured hardships, 'tis true; my whole life had been a series of such, and when I looked forward, the prospect was not much bettered—but then, they were become habitual to me, and consequently, I could bear them with less difficulty—If one scheme of life should not succeed, I could have recourse to another, and so to a third, veering about to a thousand different shifts, according to the emergencies of my fate, without forfeiting the dignity of my character, beyond a power of retrieving it, or subjecting myself wholly to the caprice and barbarity of the world. On the other hand, she had known and relished the sweets of prosperity, she had been brought up under the wings of an indulgent parent, in all the delicacies to which her sex and rank entitled her; and without any extravagance of hope, entertained herself with the view of uninterrupted happiness thro' the whole scene of life—How fatal then, how tormenting, how intolerable must her reverse of fortune be! a reverse, that not only robbs her of these external comforts, and plunges her into all the miseries of want, but also murthers her peace of mind, and entails upon her the curse of eternal infamy!— Of all professions I pronounced that of a courtezan the most deplorable, and her of all courtezans the most unhappy.—She allowed my observation to be just in the main, but at the same time, affirmed, that notwithstanding the disgraces which had fallen to her share, she had not been so unlucky in the condition of a prostitute as many others of the same community.—'I have often seen (said she) while I strolled about the streets at mid-night, a number of naked wretches reduced to rags and filth, huddled together like swine, in the corner of a dark alley; some of whom, but eighteen months before, I had known the favourites of the town, rolling in affluence, and glittering in all the pomp of equipage and dress.'— And indeed the gradation is easily conceived; the most fashionable woman of the town is as liable to contagion, as one in a much humbler sphere; she infects her admirers, her situation is publick, she is avoided, neglected, unable to support her usual appearance, which however she strives to maintain as long as possible; her credit fails, she is obliged to retrench and become a night-walker, her malady gains ground, she tampers with her constitution and ruins it; her complexion fades, she grown nauseous to every body, finds herself reduced to a starving condition, is tempted to pick pockets, is detected, committed to Newgate, where she remains in a miserable condition, 'till she is discharged because the plaintiff appears not to prosecute her. No body will afford her lodging, the symptoms of her distemper are grown outrageous, she sues to be admitted into an hospital, where she is cured at the expence of her nose;[1] she is turned out naked into the streets, depends upon the addresses of the canaille, is fain to allay the rage of hunger and cold with gin, degenerates into a state of brutal insensibility, rots and dies upon a dunghill.—Miserable wretch that I am! perhaps the same horrors are decreed for me!—'No (cried she after some pause)

137

I shall never live to such extremity of distress! my own hand shall open a way for my deliverance, before I arrive at that forlorn period!'——Her condition filled me with sympathy and compassion. I revered her qualifications, looked upon her as unfortunate, no criminal; and attended her with such care and success, that in less than two months, her health, as well as my own, was perfectly re-established.——As we often conferred upon our mutual affairs, and interchanged advice; a thousand different projects were formed which upon further canvassing appeared impracticable.—We would have gladly gone to service; but who would take us in without recommendation? At length an expedient occurred to her, of which she intended to lay hold; and this was, to procure with the first money she should earn, the homely garb of a country wench, go to some village at a good distance from town, and come up in a waggon as a fresh girl for service,[1] by which means, she might be provided for in a manner much more suitable to her inclination, than her present way of life.

CHAPTER XXIV

I am reduced to great misery—assaulted on Tower-hill by a press-gang, who put me on board a tender—my usage there —my arrival on board of the Thunder man of war, where I am put in irons, and afterwards released by the good offices of Mr. Thomson, who recommends me as assistant to the surgeon—he relates his own story, and makes me acquainted with the characters of the captain, surgeon, and first mate

I APPLAUDED the resolution of Miss Williams, who a few days after, was hired in quality of bar-keeper, by one of the ladies who had witnessed in her behalf at the Marshalsea; and who since that time had got credit with a wine merchant, whose favourite she was, to set up a convenient house of her own.—Thither my fellow lodger repaired, after having taken leave of me, with a torrent of tears, and a thousand protestations of eternal gratitude; assuring me, she would remain in this new situation no longer than till she should pick up money sufficient to put her other design in execution.

As for my own part, I saw no resource but the army or navy, between which I hesitated so long, that I found myself reduced to a starving condition.—My spirit began to accommodate itself to my beggarly fate, and I became so mean, as to go down towards Wapping, with an intention to enquire for an old school-fellow of mine, who (I understood) had got the command of a small coasting vessel, then in the river, and implore his assistance.—But my destiny prevented this abject piece of behaviour; for as I crossed Tower-wharf,[1] a squat tawny fellow, with a hanger by his side, and a cudgel in his hand, came up to me, calling, 'Yo, ho! brother, you must come along with me.'—As I did not like his appearance, instead of answering his salutation, I quickened my pace in hopes of ridding myself of his company; which he perceiving, whistled aloud, and immediately another sailor appeared before me, who laid hold of me by the collar and began to drag me along.—Not being of a humour to relish such treatment, I disengaged myself of the assailant, and with one blow of my cudgel, laid him motionless on the ground: and perceiving myself surrounded in a trice, by ten or a dozen more, exerted myself with such dexterity and success, that some of my opponents were fain to attack me with drawn cutlasses; and after an obstinate engagement, in which I received a large wound on the head, and another on my left cheek, I was disarmed, taken prisoner, and carried on board a pressing tender;[2] where, after being pinioned like a malefactor, I was thrust down into the hold, among a parcel of miserable wretches, the sight of whom well nigh distracted me.—As the commanding officer had not humanity enough to order my wounds to be dressed, and I could not use my own hands, I desired one of my fellow-captives who was unfettered, to take a handkerchief out of my pocket and tie it round my head to stop the bleeding. He pulled out my handkerchief ('tis true) but instead of applying it to the use for which I designed it, went to the grating of the hatchway, and with astonishing composure, sold it before my face to a bum-boat-woman* then on board, for a quart of gin, with which he treated his companions, regardless of my circumstance and intreaties.

I complained bitterly of this robbery, to the midshipman on deck, telling him at the same time, that unless my hurts were

---

*A bum-boat-woman, is one who sells bread, cheese, greens, liquor, and fresh provision to the sailors, in a small boat that lies along-side of the ship.

dressed, I should bleed to death. But compassion was a weakness of which no man could justly accuse this person, who squirting a mouthful of dissolved tobacco upon me, through the gratings, told me, 'I was a mutinous dog, and that I might die and be damned.'—Finding there was no other remedy, I appealed to patience, and laid up this usage in my memory, to be recalled at a fitter season.—In the mean time, loss of blood, vexation and want of food, contributed, with the noisome stench of the place, to throw me into a swoon; out of which I was recovered by a tweak of the nose, administered by the tar who stood centinel over us, who at the same time regaled me with a draught of flip,[1] and comforted me with the hopes of being put on board of the Thunder next day, where I would be freed from handcuffs, and cured of my wounds by the doctor.—I no sooner heard him name the Thunder, than I asked, if he had belonged to that ship long; and he giving me to understand, he had belonged to her five years, I enquired if he knew lieutenant Bowling?—'Know lieutenant Bowling (said he)—odds my life! and that I do;—and a good seaman he is, as ever stept upon forecastle, —and a brave fellow as ever crackt bisket;—none of your Guinea pigs,[2]—nor your fresh-water, wishy washy, fair-weather fowls.—Many a taught[3] gale of wind has honest Tom Bowling and I weathered together.—Here's his health with all my heart, whereever he is, a-loft or a-low—in heaven or in hell—all's one for that—he needs not be ashamed to shew himself.'—I was so much affected with this elogium, that I could not refrain from telling him, I was lieutenant Bowling's kinsman; at which he expressed an inclination to serve me, and when he was relieved brought some cold boiled beef in a platter and biscuit, on which we supped plentifully, and afterwards drank another can of flip together. While we were thus engaged, he recounted a great many exploits of my uncle, who (I found) was very much beloved by the ship's company, and pitied for the misfortune that happened to him in Hispaniola, which I was very glad to be informed was not so great as I imagined; for captain Oakhum had recovered of his wounds, and actually at that time, commanded the ship. Having by accident, in my pocket my uncle's letter written from Port Louis, I gave it my benefactor (whose name was Jack Rattlin)[4] for his perusal; but honest Jack told me frankly, he could not read, and desired to know the contents, which I immediately communicated: When he heard that part of it, in which, he says, he had wrote to his landlord in Deal; he cried,

'Body o' me! that was old Ben Block,[1]—he was dead before the letter came to hand.—Ey, ey, had Ben been alive, lieutenant Bowling would have had no occasion to sculk so long.—Honest Ben was the first man that taught him to hand, reef and steer.[2]—Well, well, we must all die, that's certain,—we must all come to port sooner or later,—at sea or on shore; we must be fast moored one day,—death's like the best bower anchor,[3] as the saying is, it will bring us all up.'[4]—I could not but signify my approbation of the justness of Jack's reflections; and enquired into the occasion of the quarrel between captain Oakhum and my uncle, which he explained in this manner.——'Captain Oakhum, to be sure, is a good man enough,—besides, he's my commander;—but what's that to me!—I do my duty, and value no man's anger of a rope's end.—Now the report goes, as how he is a lord's, or baron knight's brother, where-by (d'ye see me)[5] he carries a strait arm,[6] and keeps a loof from his officers, thof, may hap, they may be as good men in the main as he. Now we lying at anchor in Tuberoon bay, lieutenant Bowling had the middle watch, and as he always kept a good-look out, he made (d'ye see) three lights in the offing, whereby he run down to the great cabbin for orders, and found the captain asleep;—whereupon he waked him, which put him in a main high passion, and he swore woundily at the lieutenant, and called him lousy Scotch son of a whore, (for I being then centinel in the steerage,[7] heard all) and swab and swabbard, whereby the lieutenant returned the salute, and they jawed together fore and aft[8] a good spell, till at last the captain turned out, and laying hold of a rattan, came athwart Mr. Bowling's quarter; whereby he told the captain, that if he was not his commander, he would heave him over-board, and demanded satisfaction a-shore, whereby in the morning watch, the captain went ashore in the pinnace,[9] and afterwards the lieutenant carried the cutter[10] a-shore; and so they, leaving the boats crews on their oars, went away together; and so (d'ye see) in less than a quarter of an hour we heard firing, whereby we made for the place, and found the captain lying wounded on the beach, and so brought him on board to the doctor, who cured him in less than six weeks. But the lieutenant clapt on all the sail he could bear, and had got far enough a-head before we knew any thing of the matter; so that we could never after get sight of him, for which we were not sorry, because the captain was mainly wroth, and would certainly have done him a mischief;—for he afterwards caused him to be run on the ships

141

books,[1] whereby he lost all his pay, and if he should be taken, would be tried as a deserter.'

This account of the captain's behaviour gave me no advantageous idea of his character; and I could not help lamenting my own fate, that had subjected me to such a commander. However, making a virtue of necessity, I put a good face on the matter, and next day was with the other pressed men put on board of the Thunder lying at the Nore.[2]—When we came along-side, the mate who guarded us thither, ordered my hand-cuffs to be taken off, that I might get on board the easier; which being perceived by some of the company who stood upon the gangboards[3] to see us enter, one of them called to Jack Rattlin, who was busied in doing this friendly office for me; 'Hey, Jack, what Newgate galley have you boarded in the river as you came along? Have we not thieves enow among us already?' Another observing my wounds, which still remained exposed to the air, told me, my seams were uncaulked, and that I must be new payed.[4]—A third, seeing my hair clotted together with blood, as it were, into distinct cords, took notice, that my bows were manned with the red ropes,[5] instead of my side.—A fourth asked me, if I could not keep my yards square without iron braces? and in short, a thousand witticisms of the same nature, were passed upon me, before I could get up the ship's side.—After we had been all entered upon the books, I enquired at one of my ship-mates where the surgeon was, that I might have my wounds dressed, and had actually got as far as the middle deck (for our ship carried eighty guns) in my way to the cock-pit,[6] when I was met by the same midshipman who had used me so barbarously in the tender: He seeing me free from my chains, asked, with an insolent air, who had released me? To this I foolishly answered, with a countenance that too plainly declared the state of my thoughts; 'Whoever did it, I am persuaded did not consult you in the affair.'—I had no sooner uttered these words, than he cried, 'D—n you, you saucy son of a b—ch, I'll teach you to talk so to your officer.'—So saying, he bestowed on me several severe stripes, with a supple Jack[7] he had in his hand; and going to the commanding officer, made such a report of me, that I was immediately put in irons by the master at arms,[8] and a centinel placed over me.—Honest Rattlin, as soon as he heard of my condition, came to me, and administered all the consolation he could, and then went to the surgeon in my behalf, who sent one of his mates to dress my wounds. This mate

was no other than my old friend Thomson, with whom I became acquainted at the Navy-Office, as before mentioned. If I
knew him at first sight, it was not so easy for him to recognize
me, disfigured with blood and dirt, and altered by the misery I had
undergone.—Unknown as I was to him, he surveyed me with looks
of compassion, and handled my sores with great tenderness. When
he had applied what he thought proper, and was about to leave me,
I asked him if my misfortunes had disguised me so much, that he
could not recollect my face? Upon this he observed me with great
earnestness for some time, and at length, protested he could not
recollect one feature of my countenance.—To keep him no longer
in suspense, I told him my name; which when he heard, he embraced me with affection, and professed his sorrow in seeing me in
such a disagreeable situation. I made him acquainted with my story,
and when he heard how inhumanly I had been used in the tender,
he left me abruptly, assuring me, I should see him again soon. I had
scarce time to wonder at his sudden departure, when the master at
arms came to the place of my confinement, and bid me follow him
to the quarter-deck,[1] where I was examined by the first lieutenant,
who commanded the ship in the absence of the captain, touching
the treatment I had received in the tender from my friend the midshipman, who was present to confront me.—I recounted the particulars of his behaviour to me, not only in the tender, but since my
being on board the ship, part of which being proved by the evidence
of Jack Rattlin and others, who had no great devotion for my
oppressor, I was discharged from confinement to make way for
him, who was delivered to the master at arms to take his turn in the
Bilboes.—And this was not the only satisfaction I enjoyed, for I
was, at the request of the surgeon, exempted from all other duty,
than that of assisting his mates in making and administring medicines to the sick.—This good office I owed to the friendship of Mr.
Thomson, who had represented me in such a favourable light to the
surgeon, that he demanded me of the lieutenant, to supply the
place of his third mate, who was lately dead.—When I had obtained
this favour, my friend Thomson carried me down to the cock-pit,
which is the place allotted for the habitation of the surgeon's
mates: And when he had shewn me their birth (as he called it) I was
filled with astonishment and horror.—We descended by divers
ladders to a space as dark as a dungeon, which I understood was
immersed several feet under water, being immediately above the

hold: I had no sooner approached this dismal gulph, than my nose was saluted with an intolerable stench of putrified cheese, and rancid butter,[1] that issued from an apartment at the foot of the ladder, resembling a chandler's shop, where, by the faint glimmering of a candle, I could perceive a man with a pale meagre countenance, sitting behind a kind of desk, having spectacles on his nose, and a pen in his hand.—This (I learned of Mr. Thomson) was the ship's steward, who sat there to distribute provision to the several messes, and to mark what each received.—He therefore presented my name to him, and desired I might be entered in his mess; then taking a light in his hand, conducted me to the place of his residence, which was a square of about six feet, surrounded with the medicine chest, that of the first mate, his own, and a board by way of table fastened to the mizen-mast; it was also enclosed with canvas nailed round to the beams of the ship, to screen us from the cold, as well as the view of the midshipmen and quarter-masters, who lodged within the cable tiers[2] on each side of us: In this gloomy mansion, he entertained me with some cold salt pork, which he brought from a sort of locker, fixed above the table; and calling for the boy of the mess, sent him for a can of beer, of which he made excellent flip to crown the banquet.—By this time I began to recover my spirits, which had been exceedingly depressed with the appearance of every thing about me, and could no longer refrain from asking the particulars of Mr. Thomson's fortune, since I had seen him in London.——He told me, that being disappointed in his expectations of borrowing money to gratify the rapacious s—t—ry at the Navy-Office, he found himself utterly unable to subsist any longer in town, and had actually offered his service, in quality of mate, to the surgeon of a merchant's ship bound to Guinea[3] on the slaving trade; when one morning, a young fellow, of whom he had some acquaintance, came to his lodgings, and informed him, that he had seen a warrant made out in his name at the Navy-Office, for surgeon's second mate of a third rate: This unexpected piece of good news he could scarcely believe to be true; more especially, as he had been found qualified at Surgeon's-hall for third mate only; but that he might not be wanting to himself, he went thither to be assured, and actually found it so: Whereupon, demanding his warrant, it was delivered to him, and the oaths administered immediately.—That very afternoon, he went to Gravesend in the tilt-boat,[4] from whence he took a place in the tide-coach for Rochester;[5] next morning got on board

the Thunder, for which he was appointed, then lying in the harbour
at Chatham; and the same day was mustered by the clerk of the
checque.[1]—And well it was for him, that such expedition was used;
for in less then twelve hours after his arrival, another William
Thomson came on board, affirming that he was the person for whom
the warrant was expedited, and that the other was an impostor.—
My friend was grievously alarmed at this accident; the more so, as
his namesake had very much the advantage over him, both in
assurance and dress.—However, to acquit himself of the suspicion
of imposture, he produced several letters written from Scotland to
him in that name, and recollecting that his indentures were in his
box on board, he brought them up, and convinced all present, that
he had not assumed a name which did not belong to him.—His
competitor enraged, that they should hesitate in doing him justice
(for to be sure, the warrant had been designed for him) behaved
with so much indecent heat, that the commanding officer, (who was
the same gentleman I had seen) and the surgeon, were offended at
his presumption, and making a point of it with their friends in town,
in less than a week got the first confirmed in his station.—'I have
been on board (said he) ever since, and as this way of life is become
familiar to me, have no cause to complain of my situation.—The
surgeon is a good-natured indolent man; the first mate (who is now
on shore on duty) is indeed a little proud and cholerick, as all
Welchmen are, but in the main, a friendly honest fellow.—The
lieutenants I have no concern with; and as for the captain, he is too
much of a gentleman to know a surgeon's mate, even by sight.'

CHAPTER XXV

*The behaviour of Mr. Morgan—his pride, displeasure and
generosity—the œconomy of our mess described—Thomson's
further friendship—the nature of my duty explained——
the situation of the sick*

WHILE he was thus discoursing to me, we heard a voice on the
cockpit ladder, pronounce with great vehemence, in a strange
dialect, 'The devil and his dam blow me from the top of Mounchdenny,[2] if I go to him before there is something in my belly;—let

his nose be as yellow as a saffron, or as plue as a pell (look you) or as green as a leek, 'tis all one.'—To this somebody answered, 'So it seems my poor mess-mate must part his cable for want of a little assistance.—His fore-top-sail is loose already; and besides, the doctor ordered you to overhaul him;—but I see, you don't mind what your master says.'—Here he was interrupted with, 'Splutter and oons! you lousy tog, who do you call my master? get you gone to the doctor, and tell him my birth, and my education, and my abilities; and moreover, my behaviour is as good as his, or any gentleman's (no disparagement to him) in the whole world—Got pless my soul! does he think, or conceive, or imagine, that I am a horse, or an ass, or a goat, to trudge backwards and forwards, and upwards and downwards, and by sea and by land, at his will and pleasures?—Go your ways, you rapscallion, and tell doctor Atkins,[1] that I desire and request, that he will give a look upon the tying man, and order something for him, if he be dead or alive, and I will see him take it by and by, when my craving stomach is satisfied, look you.'—At this the other went away, saying, that if they would serve him so, when he was a dying, by G—d, he'd be foul of them in the other world.—Here Mr. Thomson let me know that the person we heard, was Mr. Morgan[2] the first mate, who was just come on board from the hospital, where he had been with sick people.—At the same time, I saw him come into the birth.—He was a short thick man, with a face garnished with pimples, a snub nose turned up at the end, an excessive wide mouth, and little fiery eyes, surrounded with skin puckered up in innumerable wrinkles.—My friend immediately made him acquainted with my case; when he regarded me with a very lofty look, but without speaking, set down a bundle he had in his hand, and approached the cupboard, which when he had opened, he exclaimed in a great passion, 'Cot is my life! all the pork is gone, as I am a christian!' Thomson then gave him to understand, that as I had been brought on board half famished, he could do no less than entertain me with what was in the locker; and the rather, as he had bid the steward enter me in the mess.—Whether this disappointment made Mr. Morgan more peevish than usual, or he really thought himself too little regarded by his fellow-mate, I know not, but after some pause, he went on in this manner—'Mr. Thomson, perhaps you do not use me with all the good manners, and complaisance, and respect (look you) that becomes you, because you have not vouchsafed to advise with me

in this affair.—I have, in my time (look you) been a man of some
weight, and substance, and consideration, and have kept house and
home, and paid scot and lot, and the king's taxes; ay, and maintained
a family to boot.—And moreover, also, I am your senior, and your
elder, and your petter, Mr. Thomson.'—'My elder I'll allow you to
be, but not my better (cried Thomson, with some heat.)'—'Cot is
my saviour, and witness too (said Morgan, with great vehemence)
that I am more elder, and therefore more petter by many years than
you.'—Fearing this dispute might be attended with some bad consequence, I interposed, and told Mr. Morgan, I was very sorry for
having been the occasion of any difference between him and the
second mate; and that rather than cause the least breach in their
good understanding, I would eat my allowance by myself, or seek
admission into some other company.—But Thomson with more
spirit than discretion (as I thought) insisted upon my remaining
where he had appointed me; and observed that no man possessed
of generosity and compassion, would have any objection to it, considering my birth and talents, and the misfortunes I had of late so
unjustly undergone.—This was touching Mr. Morgan on the right
key, who protested with great earnestness, that he had no objection
to my being received in the mess; but only complained, that the
ceremony of asking his consent was not observed. 'As for a shentleman in distress (said he, shaking me by the hand) I lofe him as I
lofe my own powels: For Got help me! I have had vexations
enough upon my own pack.'—And as I afterwards learned, in so
saying he spoke no more than what was true; for he had been once
settled in a very good situation in Glamorganshire, and was ruined
by being security for an acquaintance.—All differences being composed, he untied his bundle, which consisted of three bunches of
onions, and a great lump of Cheshire cheese wrapt up in a handkerchief; and taking some biscuit from the cupboard, fell to with a
keen appetite, inviting us to a share of the repast.—When he had
fed heartily on this homely fare, he filled a large cup made of a
cocoa-nut shell, with brandy, and drinking it off, told us, 'Prandy
was the best menstruum[1] for onion and sheese.'—His hunger being
appeased, he began to shew a great deal of good humour; and being
inquisitive about my birth, no sooner understood that I was descended of a good family, then he discovered a particular good-will
to me on that account, deducing his own pedigree in a direct line
from the famous Caractacus[2] king of the Britons, who was first the

prisoner and afterwards the friend of Claudius Cæsar.—Perceiving how much I was reduced in point of linnen, he made me a present of two good ruffled shirts, which with two of check Mr. Thomson gave me, enabled me to appear with decency.—Mean while the sailor, whom Mr. Morgan had sent to the doctor, brought a prescription for his mess-mate, which when Mr. Welchman had read, he got up to prepare it, and asked if the man was 'Tead or alive.' ——'Dead! (replied Jack) if he was dead he would have no occasion for doctor's stuff.—No, thank God, death has'n't as yet boarded him, but they have been yard arm and yard arm these three glasses.'[1] —'Are his eyes open? (continued the mate.)'——'His starboard eye (said the sailor) is open, but fast jamm'd in his head; and the haulyards of his under jaw are given way.'——'Passion of my heart! (cried Morgan) the man is as pad as one would desire in a summer's day!—Did you feel his pulses? To this, the other replied with 'Anan?'—Upon which this Cambro Briton,[2] with great earnestness and humanity, ordered the tar to run to his mess-mate and keep him alive till he should come with the medicine, 'and then (said he) you shall peradventure, pehold what you shall see.'—The poor fellow with great simplicity ran to the place where the sick man lay, but in less than a minute, returned with a woful countenance, and told us his comrade had struck.[3] Morgan hearing this, exclaimed, 'Mercy upon my salfation! why did you not stop him till I came?'— 'Stop him (said the other) I hailed him several times, but he was too far on his way, and the enemy had got possession of his close quarters;[4] so that he did not mind me.'—'Well, well, (said he) we all owe heaven a Teath.—Go your ways, you ragamuffin, and take an example and a warning, look you, and repent of your misteets.'— So saying, he pushed the seaman out of the birth.

While he entertained us with reflections suitable to this event, we heard the boatswain pipe to dinner; and immediately the boy belonging to our mess, run to the locker, from whence he carried off a large wooden platter, and in a few minutes, returned with it full of boiled peas, crying, 'Scaldings,'[5] all the way as he came.—The cloaths, consisting of a piece of an old sail, was instantly laid, covered with three plates, which by the colour, I could with difficulty discern to be metal, and as many spoons of the same composition, two of which were curtailed in the handles, and the other in the lip. Mr. Morgan himself enriched this mess with a lump of salt butter, scooped from an old gallipot,[6] and a handful of onions shorn, with some pounded pepper.—I was not very much tempted with the appearance of this dish, of which, nevertheless, my mess-mates eat heartily, advising me to follow their example, as it was banyan day,[1] and we could have no meat till next noon.—But I had already laid in sufficient for the occasion; and therefore desired to be excused; expressing a curiosity to know the meaning of banyan day.—They told me, that on Mondays, Wednesdays and Fridays, the ship's company had no allowance of meat, and that these meagre days were called banyan days, the reason of which they did not know; but I have since learned they take their de-nomination from a sect of devotees in some parts of the East Indies, who never taste flesh.

After dinner, Thomson led me round the ship, shewed me the different parts, described their uses, and as far as he could, made me acquainted with the particulars of the discipline and œconomy practised on board.—He then demanded of the boatswain, an hammock for me, which was slung in a very neat manner by my friend Jack Rattlin; and as I had no bed-cloaths, procured credit for me with the purser, for a matrass and two blankets.—At seven a-clock in the evening, Morgan visited the sick, and having ordered what was proper for each, I assisted Thomson in making up his prescriptions: But when I followed him with the medicines into the sick birth or hospital, and observed the situation of the patients, I was much less surprised to find people die on board, than astonished to find any body recover.—Here I saw about fifty miserable distempered wretches, suspended in rows, so huddled one upon another, that not more than fourteen inches[2] of space was allotted for each with his bed and bedding; and deprived of the light of the day, as well as of fresh air; breathing nothing but a noisome atmosphere of the morbid steams exhaling from their own excrements and diseased bodies, devoured with vermin hatched in the filth that surrounded them, and destitute of every convenience necessary for people in that helpless condition.

CHAPTER XXVI

A disagreeable accident happens to me in the discharge of my office——Morgan's nose is offended——a dialogue between him and the ship's steward——upon examination, I find more causes of complaint than one——my hair is cut off——Morgan's Cookery—the manner of sleeping on board—I am waked in the night by a dreadful noise

I COULD not comprehend how it was possible for the attendants to come near those who hung on the inside towards the sides of the ship, in order to assist them, as they seemed barricadoed by those who lay on the outside, and entirely out of reach of all visitation.— Much less could I conjecture how my friend Thomson would be able to administer clysters, that were ordered for some in that situation.—When I saw him thrust his wig in his pocket, and strip himself to his waistcoat in a moment, then creep on all fours, under the hammocks of the sick, and forcing up his bare pate between two, kept them asunder with one shoulder, until he had done his duty.— Eager to learn the service, I desired he would give me leave to perform the next operation of that kind; he consenting, I undressed myself after his example, and crawling along, the ship happened to roll, which alarmed me; I laid hold of the first thing that came within my grasp, with such violence, that I overturned it, and soon found by the smell that issued upon me, I had not unlocked a box of the most delicious perfume; it was well for me that my nostrils was none of the most delicate, else I know not how I might have been affected by this vapour, which diffused itself all over the ship to the utter discomposure of every body who tarried on the same deck;—neither was the consequence of this disgrace confined to my sense of smelling only, for I felt my misfortune more ways than one. That I might not, however, appear altogether disconcerted in this my *coup d'essai*, I got up, and pushing my head with great force between two hammocks, towards the middle, where the greatest resistance was, I made an opening indeed, but not understanding the knack of dexterously turning my shoulder to maintain my advantage, I had the mortification to find myself stuck up as it were in a pillory, and the weight of three or four people bearing on each side of my neck, so that I was in danger of strangulation.—While I remained in this defenceless posture, one of the sick men, rendered peevish by his distemper, was so enraged at the smell I had occasioned, and the rude shock he had received from me in my elevation, that with many bitter reproaches, he seized me by the nose, which he tweaked so unmercifully that I roared with anguish. Thomson perceiving my condition, ordered one of the waiters to my assistance, who with much difficulty disengaged me from this embarras, and hindered me from taking vengeance of the sick man, whose indisposition would not have screened him from the effects of my indignation.

After having made an end of our ministry for that time, we descended to the cockpit, my friend comforting me for what had happened, with a homely proverb, which I do not chuse to repeat.[1] —When we had got half way down the ladder, Mr. Morgan, before he saw us, having intelligence by his nose, of the approach of something extraordinary, cried, 'Cot have mercy upon my senses! I pelieve the enemy has poarded us in a stink-pot!' Then directing his discourse to the steward, from whom he imagined the odour proceeded, he reprimanded him severely for the freedoms he took among gentlemen of birth, threatned to smoak him like a padger with sulphur, if ever he should presume to offend his neighbours with such smells, for the future: The steward, conscious of his own innocence, replied with some warmth, 'I know of no smells but those of your own making.'—This repartee introduced a smart dialogue, in which the Welchman undertook to prove, that though the stench he complained of, did not flow from the steward's own body, he was nevertheless the author of it, by serving out damaged provisions to the ship's company; and in particular, putrified cheese, from the use of which only, he affirmed, such unsavoury steams could arise.—Then he launched out into praises of good cheese, of which he gave the analysis; explained the different kinds of that commodity, with the methods practised to make and preserve it; and concluded with observing, that in yielding good cheese, the county of Glamorgan might vie with Cheshire itself, and was much superior to it in the produce of goats and putter.—I gathered from this conversation, that if I went into the birth in my present pickle, I should be no welcome guest, and therefore desired Mr. Thomson to go before, and represent my calamity; at which the first mate expressing some concern, went upon deck immediately, taking his way through the cable tire, and by the main hatchway, to avoid encountering with me; desiring me to clean myself as soon as possible, for he intended to regale himself with a dish of salmagundy and a pipe.—Accordingly, I set about this disagreeable business, and soon found I had more causes of complaint than I at first imagined: For I perceived some guests had honoured me with their company, whose visit I did not at all think seasonable; neither did they seem inclined to leave me in a hurry, being in possession of my chief quarters, where they fed without reserve at the expence of my blood.—But considering it would be much easier to extirpate this ferocious colony in the infancy of their settlement, than after they should be multiplied and naturalized to the soil, I took the advice of my friend, who, to prevent such misfortunes, went always closs shaved, and made the boy of our mess cut off my hair, which had been growing since I left the service of Lavement. The second mate lent me an old bob wig to supply the loss of that covering. This affair being ended, and every thing adjusted in the best manner my circumstances would permit, the descendant of Caractacus returned, and ordering the boy to bring a piece of salt beef from the brine, cut off a slice and mixed it with an equal quantity of onions, which seasoning with a moderate proportion of pepper and salt, he brought it into a consistence with oil and vinegar.—Then tasting the dish, assured us, it was the best salmagundie, that ever he made, and recommended it to our palate with such heartiness, that I could not help doing honour to his preparation. But I had no sooner swallowed a mouthful, than I thought my entrails were scorched, and endeavoured with a deluge of small beer, to allay the heat it occasioned.——Supper being over, Mr. Morgan having smoaked a couple of pipes, and supplied the moisture he had expended with as many cans of flip, of which we all partook, a certain yawning began to admonish me, that it was high time to repair by sleep the injury I had suffered from want of rest the preceeding night; which being perceived by my companions, whose time of repose was by this time arrived, they proposed we should turn in, or in other words, go to bed. Our hammocks, which hung parallel to one another, on the outside of our birth, were immediately unlashed, and I beheld each of my mess-mates spring with great agility into his respective nest, where they seemed to lie concealed, very much at their ease.—But it was some time before I could prevail upon myself to trust my carcase at such a distance from the ground, in a narrow bag, out of which, I imagined, I should be apt, on the least motion in my sleep, to tumble down at the hazard of breaking my bones. I suffered myself, however, to be persuaded, and taking a leap to get in, threw myself quite over, with such violence, that had I not luckily got hold of Thomson's hammock, I should have pitched upon my head on the other side, and in all likelihood fractured my scull.—After some fruitless efforts, I succeeded at last; but the apprehension of the jeopardy in which I believed myself, withstood all the attacks of sleep, till towards the morning-watch, when in spite of my fears, I was over-powered with slumber: tho' I did not long enjoy this comfortable situation; being arroused with a noise so loud and shrill, that I thought the drums of my ears were burst by it; this was followed by a dreadful summons pronounced by a hoarse voice, which I could not understand. While I was debating with myself whether or not I should wake my companion, and enquire into the occasion of this disturbance, I was informed by one of the quarter-masters, who passed by me with a lanthorn in his hand, that the noise which alarmed me, was occasioned by the boatswain's mates who called up the larboard watch, and that I must lay my account with such interruption every morning at the same hour.—Being now more assured of my safety, I addressed myself again to rest, and slept till eight a-clock, when getting up, and breakfasting with my comrades, on biscuit and brandy, the sick were visited and assisted as before; after which my good friend Thomson explained and performed another piece of duty, to which I was a stranger.—At a certain hour in the morning, the boy of the mess went round all the decks, ringing a small hand-bell, and in rhimes composed for the occasion, inviting all those who had sores to repair before the mast, where one of the doctor's mates attended, with applications to dress them.

CHAPTER XXVII

I acquire the friendship of the surgeon, who procures a warrant for me, and makes me a present of cloaths——a battle between a midshipman and me——the surgeon leaves the ship ——the captain comes on board with another surgeon——a dialogue between the captain and Morgan——the sick are ordered to be brought upon the quarter-deck and examined—— the consequences of that order——a madman accuses Morgan, and is set at liberty by command of the captain, whom he instantly attacks and pummels without mercy

WHILE I was busied with my friend in this practice, the doctor chanced to pass by the place where we were, and stopping to observe me, appeared very well satisfied with my method of application; and afterwards sent for me to his cabbin, where, having examined me touching my skill in surgery, and the particulars of my fortune, interested himself so far in my behalf, as to promise his assistance in procuring a warrant for me, seeing I had been already found qualified at Surgeon's hall, for the station I now filled on board; and this he the more cordially engaged in, when he understood I was nephew to lieutenant Bowling, for whom he expressed a particular regard.—In the mean time, I could learn from his discourse, that he did not intend to go to sea again with captain Oakhum, having, as he thought, been indifferently used by him during the last voyage.

While I lived tollerably easy, in expectation of preferment, I was not altogether without mortifications, which I not only suffered from the rude insults of the sailors, and petty officers, among whom I was known by the name of *Loblolly Boy*;[1] but also from the disposition of Morgan, who, though friendly in the main, was often very troublesome with his pride, which expected a good deal of submission from me, and delighted in recapitulating the favours I had received at his hands.

About six weeks after my arrival on board, the surgeon bidding me follow him into his cabbin, presented a warrant to me, by which I was appointed surgeon's third mate on board the Thunder.—This

Chapter XXVII

he had procured by his interest at the Navy-Office; as also another
for himself, by virtue of which he was removed into a second rate.
I acknowledged his kindness in the strongest terms my gratitude
could suggest, and professed my sorrow at the prospect of losing
such a valuable friend, to whom I hoped to have recommended myself still further, by my respectful and diligent behaviour.—But his
generosity rested not here;—for, before he left the ship, he made me
a present of a chest and some cloaths, that enabled me to support
the rank to which he had raised me.—I found my spirit revive with
my good fortune; and now I was an officer, resolved to maintain the
dignity of my station, against all opposition or affronts; nor was it
long before I had occasion to exert my resolution; my old enemy
the midshipman (whose name was Crampley) entertaining an implacable animosity against me, for the disgrace he had suffered on
my account, had since that time taken all opportunities of reviling
and ridiculing me, when I was not intitled to retort his bad usage.
—And even after I had been rated on the books, and mustered
as surgeon's mate, did not think fit to restrain his insolence.—In
particular, being one day present, while I dressed a wound in a
sailor's leg, he began to sing a song, which I thought highly injurious to the honour of my country, and therefore signified my
resentment, by observing, that the Scots always laid their account
in finding enemies among the ignorant, insignificant and malicious.
—This unexpected piece of assurance enraged him to such a
degree, that he lent me a blow on the face, which I verily thought
had demolished my cheekbone; I was not slow in returning the
obligation, and the affair began to be very serious, when by accident
Mr. Morgan, and one of the master's mates, coming that way,
interposed, and inquiring into the cause, endeavoured to promote a
reconciliation; but finding us both exasperated to the uttermost, and
bent against accommodation, they advised us, either to leave our
difference undecided till we should have an opportunity of ter-
minating it on shore, like gentlemen, or else chuse a proper place
on board, and bring it to an issue by boxing. This last expedient was
greedily embraced; and being forthwith conducted to the ground
proposed, we stript in a moment, and began a very furious contest,
in which I soon found myself inferior to my antagonist, not so much
in strength and agility, as in skill, which he had acquired in the
school at Hockley in the Hole,[1] and Tottenham-Court.[2]—Many
cross-buttocks[3] did I sustain, and pegs[4] on the stomach without

number, till at last, my breath being quite gone, as well as my vigour wasted, I grew desperate, and collecting all my spirits in one effort, threw in at once head, hands, and feet with such violence, that I drove my antagonist three paces backward into the main hatch-way, down which he fell, and pitching upon his head and right shoulder, remained without sense and motion.—Morgan looking down, and seeing him lie in that condition, cried, 'Upon my conscience, as I am a Christian sinner (look you) I believe his pattles are all ofer; but I take you all to witness that there was no treachery in the case, and that he has suffered by the chance of war.'
——So saying, he descended to the deck below, to examine into the situation of my adversary; and left me very little pleased with my victory, as I found myself not only terribly bruised, but likewise in danger of being called to account for the death of Crampley: But this fear vanished when my fellow-mate, having by bleeding him in the juglar, brought him to himself, and assured himself of the state of his body, called up to me, to be under no concern, for the midshipman had received no other damage than as pretty a luxation of the *os humeri*,[1] as one would desire to see on a summer's day.—Upon this information, I crawled down to the cockpit, and acquainted Thomson with the affair, who, providing himself with bandages, &c. necessary for the occasion, went up to assist Mr. Morgan in the reduction of the dislocation.—When this was successfully performed, they wished me joy of the event of the combat; and the Welchman, after observing, that in all likelihood, the ancient Scots and Britons were the same people, bid me 'Praise Cot for putting mettle in my pelly, and strength in my limbs to support it.'—I acquired such reputation by this recounter (which lasted twenty minutes) that every body became more cautious in his behaviour towards me; though Crampley with his arm in a sling, talked very high, and threatened to seize the first opportunity of retrieving on shore, the honour he had lost by an accident, from which I could justly claim no merit.

About this time, captain Oakhum, having received sailing orders, came on board, and brought along with him a surgeon of his own country, who soon made us sensible of the loss we suffered in the departure of doctor Atkins; being grossly ignorant, and intolerably assuming, false, vindictive, and unforgiving; a merciless tyrant to his inferiors, an abject sycophant to those above him. In the morning after the captain came on board, our first mate, according to custom, went to wait on him with a sick list, which when this grim commander had perused, he cried with a stern countenance, 'Blood and oons![1] sixty-one sick people on board of my ship!—Harkee you, sir, I'll have no sick in my ship, by G—d.' The Welchman replied, he should be very glad to find no sick people on board; but while it was otherwise, he did no more than his duty in presenting him with a list.—'You and your list may be d—n'd, (said the captain, throwing it at him) I say, there shall be no sick in this ship while I have the command of her.'—Mr. Morgan being nettled at this treatment, told him, his indignation ought to be directed to Got Almighty, who visited his people with distempers, and not to him, who contributed all in his power towards their cure. The Bashaw[2] not being used to such behaviour in any of his officers, was enraged to fury at this satirical insinuation, and stamping with his foot, called him insolent scoundrel, threatning to have him pinioned to the deck, if he should presume to utter another syllable. But the blood of Caractacus being thoroughly heated, disdained to be restricted by such a command, and began to manifest itself in, 'Captain Oakhum, I am a shentleman of birth and parentage (look you) and peradventure, I am moreover ——.' Here his harrangue was broke off by the captain's steward, who being Morgan's countryman, hurried him out of the cabbin before he had time to exasperate his master to a greater degree, which would certainly have been the case; for the indignant Welchman, could hardly be hindered by his friend's arguments and intreaties, from re-entering the presence chamber, and defying captain Oakhum to his teeth.— He was, however, appeased at length, and came down to the birth, where finding Thomson and me at work preparing medicines, he bid us leave off our lapour and go to play, for the captain, by his sole word and power and command, had driven sickness a pegging to the tevil, and there was no more malady on poard. So saying, he drank off a gill of brandy, sighed grievously three times, poured forth an ejaculation of 'Got pless my heart, liver, and lungs!' and then began to sing a Welch song with great earnestness of visage, voice and gesture.—I could not conceive the meaning of this singular phænomenon, and saw by the looks of Thomson, who at the same time, shook his head, that he suspected poor Cadwallader's brains were unsettled. He perceiving our amazement, told us, he would explain the mystery; but at the same time, bid us take notice, that he had lived poy, patchelor, married man and widower, almost forty years, and in all that time, there was no man nor mother's son in the whole world, who durst use him so ill as captain Oakhum had done. Then he acquainted us with the dialogue that passed between them, as I have already related it; and had no sooner finished this narration, than he received a message from the surgeon, to bring the sick-list to the quarter-deck, for the captain had ordered all the patients thither to be reviewed.—This inhuman order shocked us extremely, as we knew it would be impossible to carry some of them on the deck, without imminent danger of their lives; but as we likewise knew it would be to no purpose for us to remonstrate against it, we repaired to the quarter-deck in a body, to see the extraordinary muster; Morgan observing by the way, that the captain was going to send to the other world, a great many evidences to testify against himself. When we appeared upon deck, the captain bid the doctor, who stood bowing at his right hand, look at these lazy, lubberly sons of bitches, who were good for nothing on board, but to eat the king's provision, and encourage idleness in the skulkers.—The surgeon grinned approbation, and taking the list, began to examine the complaints of each as they could crawl to the place appointed.—The first who came under his cognizance, was a poor fellow just freed of a fever, which had weakened him so much, that he could hardly stand.—Mr. Mackshane (for that was the doctor's name) having felt his pulse, protested he was as well as any man in the world; and the captain delivered him over to the boatswain's mate, with orders that he should receive a round dozen at the gangway immediately, for counterfeiting himself sick when he was not;—but before the discipline could be executed, the man dropt down on the deck, and had well nigh perished under the hands of the executioner.—The next patient to be considered, laboured under a quartan ague,[1] and being then, in his interval of health, discovered no other symptoms of distemper, than a pale meagre countenance, and emaciated body; upon which, he was declared fit for duty, and turned over to the boatswain;—but being resolved to disgrace the doctor, died upon the forecastle next day, during his cold fit.—The third complained of a pleuretic stitch,[2] and spitting of blood, for which doctor Mackshane prescribed exercise at the pump to promote expectoration; but whether this was improper for one in his situation, or that it was used to excess, I know not, but in less than half an hour, he was suffocated with a deluge of blood that issued from his lungs.—A fourth, with much difficulty climbed to the quarter-deck, being loaded with a monstrous ascites[1] or dropsy, that invaded his chest so much, he could scarce fetch his breath; but his disease being interpreted into fat, occasioned by idleness and excess of eating, he was ordered, with a view to promote perspiration and enlarge his chest, to go aloft immediately: It was in vain for this unwieldy wretch, to alledge his utter incapacity, the boatswain's driver[2] was commanded to whip him up with a cat and nine tails: The smart of this application made him exert himself so much, that he actually arrived at the foot-hook-shrouds,[3] but when the enormous weight of his body had nothing else to support it than his weakened arms, either out of spite or necessity, he quitted his hold, and plumped into the sea, where he must have been drowned, had not a sailor who was in a boat along-side, saved his life, by keeping him afloat, till he was hoisted on board by a tackle—It would be tedious and disagreeable to describe the fate of every miserable object that suffered by the inhumanity and ignorance of the captain and surgeon, who so wantonly sacrificed the lives of their fellow-creatures. Many were brought up in the height of fevers, and rendered delirious by the injuries they suffered in the way.—Some gave up the ghost in the presence of their inspectors; and others, who were ordered to their duty, languished a few days at work, among their fellows, and then departed without any ceremony.—On the whole, the number of sick was reduced to less than a dozen; and the authors of this reduction were applauding themselves for the service they had done to their king and country, when the boatswain's mate informed his honour, that there was a man below lashed to his hammock by the direction of the doctor's mate, and that he begged hard to be released; affirming, he had been so maltreated only for a grudge Mr. Morgan bore to him, and that he was as much in his senses as any man aboard.—The captain hearing this, darted a severe look at the Welchman, and ordered the man to be brought up immediately: Upon which, Morgan protested with great fervency, that the person in question was as mad as a March-hare; and begged for the love of Got, they would at least keep his arms pinioned during his examination, to prevent him from doing mischief.—This request the commander granted for his own sake, and the patient was produced, who insisted upon his being in his right wits with such calmness and strength of argument, that every body present was inclined to believe him, except Morgan, who affirmed there was no trusting to appearances; for he himself had been so much imposed upon by his behaviour two days before, that he had actually unbound him with his own hands, and had well nigh been murdered for his pains: this was confirmed by the evidence of one of the waiters, who declared, he had pulled this patient from the doctor's mate, whom he had gotten down and almost strangled.—To this the man answered, that the witness was a creature of Morgan's, and was suborned to give his testimony against him by the malice of the mate, whom the defendant had affronted, by discovering to the people on board, that Mr. Morgan's wife kept a gin-shop in Rag Fair.[1]—This anecdote produced a laugh at the expence of the Welchman, who shaking his head with some emotion, said, 'Ay, ay, 'tis no matter,— God knows, 'tis an arrant falshood.'—Captain Oakhum, without any further hesitation, ordered the fellow to be unfettered; at the same time, threatening to make Morgan exchange situations with him for his spite; but the Briton no sooner heard the decision in favour of the madman, than he got up the mizzen-shrouds, crying to Thomson and me to get out of his reach, for we should see him play the tevil with a vengeance. We did not think fit to disregard this caution, and accordingly got up on the poop, whence we beheld the maniac (as soon as he was released) fly at the captain like a fury, crying, 'I'll let you know, you scoundrel, that I am commander of this vessel'—and pummel him without mercy. The surgeon, who went to the assistance of his patron, shared the same fate; and it was with the utmost difficulty, that he was mastered at last, after having done great execution among those who opposed him.

CHAPTER XXVIII

*The captain enraged, threatens to put the madman to death
with his own hand——is diverted from that resolution by the
arguments and persuasion of the first lieutenant and surgeon
——we set sail for St. Helens, join the fleet under the command
of Sir C——n——r O—le,[1] and proceed for the West-
Indies—are overtaken by a terrible tempest—my friend
Jack Rattlin has his leg broke by a fall from the main-
yard—the behaviour of doctor Mackshane——Jack opposes
the amputation of his limb, in which he is seconded by Morgan
and me, who undertake the cure, and perform it successfully*

THE captain was carried into his cabbin, so enraged with the treatment he had received, that he ordered the fellow to be brought
before him, that he might have the pleasure of pistoling him with
his own hand; and would certainly have satisfied his revenge in this
manner, had not the first lieutenant remonstrated against it, by
observing that in all appearance, the fellow was not mad but
desperate; that he had been hired by some enemy of the captain to
assassinate him, and therefore ought to be kept in irons till he could
be brought to a court-martial, which, no doubt, would sift the
affair to the bottom, by which, important discoveries might be
made, and then sentence the criminal to a death adequate to his
demerits.—This suggestion, improbable as it was, had the desired
effect upon the captain, being exactly calculated for the meridian of
his intellects; more especially, as doctor Mackshane espoused this
opinion, in consequence of his previous declaration that the man was
not mad.—Morgan finding there was no more damage done, could
not help discovering by his countenance, the pleasure he enjoyed
on this occasion; and while he bathed the doctor's face with an
embrocation, ventured to ask him, Whether he thought there were
more fools or madmen on board? But he would have been wiser in
containing this sally, which his patient carefully laid up in his
memory, to be taken notice of at a more fit season.—Mean while we
weighed anchor, and on our way to the Downs,[2] the madman, who
was treated as a prisoner, took an opportunity, while the centinel
attended him at the head,[3] to leap over-board, and frustrate the

revenge of the captain.—We staid not long at the Downs, but took the benefit of the first easterly wind to go round to Spithead;[1] where having received on board provisions for six months, we sailed from St. Helens,[2] in the grand fleet bound for the West-Indies on the ever memorable expedition of Carthagena.[3]

It was not without great mortification, I saw myself on the point of being transported to such a distant and unhealthy climate, destitute of every convenience that could render such a voyage supportable; and under the dominion of an arbitrary tyrant, whose command was almost intolerable: However, as these complaints were common to a great many on board, I resolved to submit patiently to my fate, and contrive to make myself as easy as the nature of the case would allow.—We got out of the channel with a prosperous breeze, which died away, leaving us becalmed about fifty leagues to the westward of the Lizard:[4] But this state of inaction did not last long; for next night our main-top-sail was split by the wind, which in the morning encreased to a hurricane.—I was wakened by a most horrible din, occasioned by the play of the gun carriages upon the decks above, the creaking of cabins, the howling of the wind through the shrouds, the confused noise of the ship's crew, the pipes of the boatswain and his mates, the trumpets[5] of the lieutenants, and the clanking of the chain-pumps.[6]—Morgan, who had never been at sea before, turned out in a great hurry, crying, 'Got have mercy and compassion upon us! I believe we have got upon the confines of Lucifer and the d—ned!'—while poor Thomson lay quaking in his hammock, putting up petitions to heaven for our safety.—I got out of bed[7] and joined the Welchman, with whom (after having fortified ourselves with brandy) I went above; but if my sense of hearing was startled before, how must my sight be appalled in beholding the effects of the storm? The sea was swelled into billows mountain-high, on the top of which our ship sometimes hung, as if it was about to be precipitated to the abyss below! Sometimes we sunk between two waves that rose on each side higher than our topmast head,[8] and threatned by dashing together, to overwhelm us in a moment! Of all our fleet, consisting of a hundred and fifty sail, scarce twelve appeared, and these driving under their bare poles, at the mercy of the tempest. At length the masts of one of them gave way, and tumbled over-board with a hideous crash! Nor was the prospect in our own ship much more agreeable;—a number of officers and sailors run backward and forward with distraction in their looks, hollowing to one another, and unknowing what they should attend to first. Some clung to the yards, endeavouring to unbend the sails that were split into a thousand pieces flapping in the wind; others tried to furl those which were yet whole, while the masts, at every pitch, bent and quivered like twigs, as if they would have shivered into innumerable splinters!—While I considered this scene with equal terror and astonishment, one of the main-braces broke, by the shock whereof two sailors were flung from the yard's arm into the sea, where they perished, and poor Jack Rattlin thrown down upon the deck, at the expence of a broken leg. Morgan and I ran immediately to his assistance, and found a splinter of the shin-bone thrust by the violence of the fall through the skin: As this was a case of too great consequence to be treated without the authority of the doctor, I went down to his cabin, to inform him of the accident, as well as to bring up dressings, which we always kept ready prepared.—I entered his apartment without any ceremony, and by the glimmering of a lamp, perceived him on his knees, before something that very much resembled a crucifix; but this I will not insist upon, that I may not seem too much a slave to common report, which indeed assisted my conjecture on this occasion, by representing doctor Mackshane as a member of the church of Rome.—Be this as it will, he got up in a sort of confusion, occasioned (I suppose) by his being disturbed in his devotion, and in a trice, snatched the object of my suspicion from my sight.—After making an apology for my intrusion, I acquainted him with the situation of Rattlin, but could by no means prevail upon him to visit him on deck where he lay; he bid me desire the boatswain to order some of the men to carry him down to the cockpit, and in the mean time he would direct Thomson in getting ready the dressings.—When I signified to the boatswain the doctor's desire, he swore a terrible oath, that he could not spare one man from the deck, because he expected the masts would go by the board every minute.—This piece of information did not at all contribute to my peace of mind; however, as my friend Rattlin complained very much, with the assistance of Morgan, I supported him to the lower deck, whither Mr. Mackshane, after much intreaty, ventured to come, attended by Thomson with a boxful of dressings, and his own servant, who carried a whole set of capital instruments.—He examined the fracture and the wound, and concluding from a livid colour extending itself upon the limb, that a

mortification would ensue, resolved to amputate the leg immediately.
—This was a dreadful sentence to the patient, who recruiting himself with a quid of tobacco, pronounced with a woful countenance,
'What! is there no remedy, doctor? must I be dock'd?[1] can't you
splice it?'—'Assuredly, doctor Mackshane (said the first mate) with
submission, and deference, and veneration to your superior abilities,
and opportunities, and stations (look you) I do apprehend, and conjecture, and aver, that there is no occasion nor necessity to smite off
this poor man's leg.'—'God almighty bless you, dear Welchman!
(cried Rattlin) may you have fair wind and weather wheresoever
you're bound, and come to an anchor in the road of heaven[2] at last.'
—Mackshane, very much incensed at his mate's differing in opinion
from him so openly, answered, that he was not bound to give an
account of his practice to him; and in a peremptory tone, ordered
him to apply the tourniquet.—At the sight of which, Jack starting
up, cried, 'Avast, avast! d—n my heart, if you clap your nippers on
me, till I know wherefore!—Mr. Random, won't you lend a hand
towards saving of my precious limb? Odd's heart, if lieutenant
Bowling was here, he would not suffer Jack Rattlin's leg to be
chopped off like a piece of old junk.'[3]—This pathetic address to me,
joined to my inclination to serve my honest friend, and the reasons
I had to believe there was no danger in delaying the amputation,
induced me to declare myself of the first mate's opinion, and affirm
that the preternatural colour of the skin, was owing to an inflam-
mation occasioned by a contusion, and common in all such cases,
without any indication of an approaching gangrene. Morgan, who
had a great opinion of my skill, manifestly exulted in my fellowship, and asked Thomson's sentiments of the matter, in hopes of
strengthening our association with him too; but he being of a meek
disposition, and either dreading the enmity of the surgeon, or
speaking the dictates of his own judgment, in a modest manner, espoused the opinion of Mackshane, who by this time, having consulted with himself, determined to act in such a manner, as to
screen himself from censure; and at the same time revenge himself
on us, for our arrogance in contradicting him.—With this view, he
demanded to know if we would undertake to cure the leg at our
peril; that is, be answerable for the consequence.—To this Morgan
replied, that the lives of his creatures are in the hands of Got alone;
and it would be great presumption in him to undertake for an event
that was in the power of his maker, no more than the doctor could

promise to cure all the sick to whom he administered his assistance; but if the patient would put himself under our direction, we would do our endeavour to bring his distemper to a favourable issue, to which, at present, we saw no obstruction.—I signified my concurrence; and Rattlin was so over-joyed, that shaking us both by the hands, he swore no body else should touch him, and if he died, his blood should be upon his own head.—Mr. Mackshane, flattering himself with the prospect of our miscarriage, went away, and left us to manage it as we should think proper; accordingly, having sawed off part of the splinter that stuck through the skin, we reduced the fracture, dressed the wound, applied the eighteen-tailed bandage, and put the leg in a box, *secundum artem.*[1]—Every thing succeeded according to our wish, and we had the satisfaction, of not only preserving the poor fellow's leg, but likewise of rendering the doctor contemptible among the ship's company, who had all their eyes on us during the course of this cure, which was compleated in six weeks.

CHAPTER XXIX

Mackshane's malice——I am taken up and imprisoned for a spy——Morgan meets with the same fate—Thomson is tampered with to turn evidence against us——disdains the proposal, and is maltreated for his integrity——Morgan is released to assist the surgeon during an engagement with some French ships of war——I remain fettered on the poop, exposed to the enemy's shot, and grow delirious with fear—— am comforted after the battle by Morgan, who speaks freely of the captain; is over-heard by the centinel, who informs against him, and again imprisoned—Thomson grows desperate, and notwithstanding the remonstrances of Morgan and me, goes over-board in the night

IN the mean time, the storm subsided into a brisk gale, that carried us into the warm latitudes, where the weather became intolerable and the crew very sickly.—The doctor left nothing unattempted towards the completion of his vengeance against the Welchman and me. He went among the sick under pretence of enquiring into their grievances, with a view of picking up complaints to our prejudice; but finding himself frustrated in that expectation, by the good-will we had procured from the patients by our diligence and humanity, he took the resolution of listening to our conversation, by hiding himself behind the canvas that surrounded our birth; here too he was detected by the boy of our mess, who acquainted us with this piece of behaviour, and one night, while we were picking a large bone of salt-beef, Morgan discerned something stir against our hangings, which immediately interpreting to be the doctor, he tipt me the wink, and pointed to the place, where I could evidently perceive some body standing; upon which, I snatched up the bone, and levelled it with all my force at him, saying, 'Whoever you are, take that for your curiosity.'—It had the desired effect, for we heard the listener tumble down, and afterwards crawl to his own cabbin.—I applauded myself much for this feat, which turned out one of the most unlucky exploits of my life, Mackshane from that night marking me out for destruction.—About a week thereafter, as I was going my rounds among the sick, I was taken prisoner, and carried to the poop by the master at arms, where I was loaded with irons, and stapled to the deck, on pretence that I was a spy on board, and had conspired against the captain's life.—How ridiculous soever this imputation was, I did not fail to suffer by it all the rigour that could be shewn to the worst of criminals, being exposed in this miserable condition to the scorching heat of the sun by day, and the unwholesome damps by night, during the space of twelve days, in which time I was neither brought to trial, nor examined touching the probability of my charge.—I had no sooner recovered the use of my reflection, which had been quite overthrown by this accident, than I sent for Thomson, who, after condoling with me on the occasion, hinted to me, that I owed this misfortune to the hatred of the doctor, who had given in an information against me to the captain, in consequence of which I was arrested, and all my papers seized.—While I was cursing my capricious fate, I saw Morgan ascend the poop, guarded by two corporals, who made him sit down by me, that he might be pinioned in the same machine.— Notwithstanding my situation, I could scarce refrain from laughing at the countenance of my fellow prisoner, who, without speaking one word, allowed his feet to be inclosed in the rings provided for that purpose; but when they pretended to fasten him on his back, he grew outragious, and drawing a large couteau from his side-pocket, threatened to rip up the belly of the first man who should approach him, in order to treat him in such an unworthy manner.—They were preparing to use him very roughly, when the lieutenant on the quarter-deck, called up to them to let him remain as he was.—He then crept towards me, and taking me by the hand, bid me 'put my trust in Got.'—And looking at Thomson, who sat by us trembling, with a pale visage, told him, there were two more rings for his feet, and he should be glad to find him in such good company.——But it was not the intention of our adversary to include the second mate in our fate: Him he excepted to be his drudge in attending the sick, and is possible, his evidence against us: With this view he sounded him afar off, but finding his integrity incorruptible, he harrassed him so much out of spite, that in a short time this mild creature grew weary of his life.

While I and my fellow-prisoner comforted each other in our tribulation, the admiral discovered four sail of ships to leeward, and made signal for our ship and four more to chace: Hereupon, every thing was cleared for an engagement, and Mackshane foreseeing he would have occasion for more assistants than one, obtained Morgan's liberty; while I was left in this deplorable posture to the chance of battle.—It was almost dark when we came up with the sternmost chace, which we hailed, and enquired who they were; they gave us to understand they were French men of war, upon which captain Oakhum commanded them to send their boat on board of him; but they refused, telling him, if he had any business with them, to come on board of their ship: He then threatned to pour in a broad-side upon them, which they promised to return.—Both sides were as good as their word, and the engagement began with great fury.—The reader may guess how I passed my time, lying in this helpless situation, amidst the terrors of a sea-fight; expecting every moment to be cut asunder or dashed in pieces by the enemy's shot! I endeavoured to compose myself as much as possible, by reflecting that I was not a whit more exposed than those who were stationed about me; but when I beheld them employed without intermission, in annoying the foe, and encouraged by the society and behaviour of one another, I could easily perceive a wide difference between their condition and mine: However, I concealed my agitation as well as I could, till the head of the officer of Marines, who stood near me, being shot off, bounced from the deck athwart my face, leaving me well-nigh blinded with brains.—I could contain myself no longer, but began to bellow with all the strength of my lungs; when a drummer coming towards me, asked if I was wounded; and before I could answer, received a great shot in his belly which tore out his intrails, and he fell flat on my breast.—This accident entirely bereft me of all discretion: I redoubled my cries, which were drowned in the noise of the battle; and finding myself disregarded, lost all patience and became frantick; vented my rage in oaths and execrations, till my spirits being quite exhausted, I remained quiet and insensible of the load that oppressed me.—The engagement lasted till broad day, when captain Oakhum, finding he was like to gain neither honour nor advantage by the affair, pretended to be undeceived by seeing their colours; and hailing the ship with whom he had fought all night, protested be believed them Spaniards, and the guns being silenced on each side, ordered the barge to be hoisted out, and went on board of the French commodore.—Our loss amounted to ten killed and eighteen wounded, most part of whom afterwards died.—My fellow-mates had no sooner dispatched their business in the cockpit, than full of friendly concern, they came to visit me.—Morgan ascending first, and seeing my face almost covered with brains and blood, concluded I was no longer a man for this world; and calling to Thomson with great emotion, bid him come up and take his last farewel of his comrade and countryman, who was posting to a petter place, where there were no Mackshanes nor Oakhums to asperse and torment him.—'No (said he, taking me by the hand) you are going to a country where there is more respect shewn to unfortunate shentlemen, and where you will have the satisfaction of peholding your adversaries tossing upon pillows of purning primstone.'—Thomson alarmed at this apostrophe, made haste to the place where I lay, and sitting down by me, with tears in his eyes, enquired into the nature of my calamity.—By this time I had recollected myself so far as to be able to converse rationally with my friends, whom, to their great satisfaction, I immediately undeceived with regard to their apprehension of my being mortally wounded.—After I had got myself disengaged from the carnage in which I wallowed, and partaken of a refreshment which my friends brought along with them, we entered into discourse upon the hardships we sustained, and spoke very freely of the authors of our misery; which being overheard by the centinel who guarded me, he was no sooner relieved, than he reported to the captain every syllable of our conversation, according to the orders he had received: The effects of this soon appeared in the arrival of the master at arms, who replaced Morgan in his former station; and gave the second mate a caution to keep a strict guard over his tongue, if he did not chuse to accompany us in our confinement.—Thomson foreseeing that the whole slavery of attending and dressing the sick and wounded, must now fall upon his shoulders, as well as the ill usage of Mackshane, grew desperate at the prospect, and though I never heard him swear before, imprecated dreadful curses on the heads of his oppressors, declaring, that he would rather quit life altogether, than be much longer under the power of such barbarians.—I was not a little startled at his vivacity, and endeavoured to alleviate his complaints, by representing the subject of my own, with as much aggravation as it would bear, by which comparison he might see the balance of misfortune lay on my side, and take an example from me of fortitude and submission, till such time as we could procure redress, which (I hoped) was not far off, considering, that we should probably be in a harbour in less than three days, where we should have an opportunity of preferring our complaints to the admiral.—The Welchman joined in my remonstrances, and was at great pains to demonstrate, that it was every man's duty as well as interest to resign himself to the divine will, and look upon himself as a centinel upon duty, who is by no means at liberty to leave his post before he is relieved.—Thomson listened attentively to what we said, and at last, shedding a flood of tears, shook his head, and left us, without making any reply.—About eleven at night, he came to see us again, with a settled gloom on his countenance, and gave us to understand, that he had undergone excessive toil since he saw us, and in recompence, had been grossly abused by the doctor, who taxed him with being confederate with us, in a design of taking away his life and that of the captain. After some time spent in mutual exhortation, he got up, and squeezing me by the hand with an uncommon fervour, cried, 'God bless you both,' and left us to wonder at his singular manner of parting with us, which did not fail to make an impression on us both.

Next morning, when the hour of visitation came round, this unhappy young man was a missing, and after strick search, supposed to have gone over-board in the night; which was certainly the case.

CHAPTER XXX

We lament over the fate of our companion——the captain offers Morgan his liberty, which he refuses to accept——we are brought before him and examined——Morgan is sent back to custody, whither also I am remanded after a curious trial

THE news of this event affected my fellow-prisoner and me extremely, as our unfortunate companion had justly acquired by his amiable disposition, the love and esteem of us both; and the more we regretted his untimely fate, the greater horror we conceived for the villain who was undoubtedly the occasion of it.—This abandoned miscreant did not discover the least symptom of concern for Thomson's death, although he must be conscious to himself, of having driven him by ill usage to that fatal resolution; but desired the captain to set Morgan at liberty again to look after the patients. Accordingly, one of the corporals was sent up to unfetter him; when he protested he would not be released until he should know for what he was confined; nor would he be a tennis-ball, nor a shittle-cock,[1] nor a trudge, nor a scullion to any captain under the sun.—Oakhum finding him obstinate, and fearing it would not be in his power to exercise his tyranny much longer with impunity, was willing to shew some appearance of justice, and therefore ordered us both to be brought before him, on the quarter-deck, where he sat in state, with his clerk on one side, and his counsellor Mackshane on the other.—When we approached, he honoured us with this salutation: 'So, gentlemen, d—n my blood! many a captain in the navy would have ordered you both to be tucked up to the yard's arm, without either judge or jury, for the crimes you have been guilty of; but d—n my blood, I have too much good nature, in allowing such dogs as you to make your defence.'—'Captain Oaghum, (said my fellow-sufferer) certainly it is in your power (Got help the while) to tuck us all up at your will, and desire, and pleasures.—And perhaps it would be petter for some of us to be tucked up, than undergo the miseries to which we have been exposed.—So may the farmer hang his kids for his diversion, and amusement, and mirth; but there is such a thing as justice, if not upon earth, surely in heaven, that will punish with fire and prim-

stone all those who take away the lives of innocent people out of
wantonness and parparity (look you.)—In the mean time, I shall be
glad to know the crimes laid to my charge, and see the person who
accuses me.'—'That you shall (said the captain) here doctor, what
have you to say?'—Mackshane stepping forward, hemmed a good
while, in order to clear his throat, and before he began, Morgan
accosted him thus: 'Doctor Mackshane, look in my face—look in the
face of an honest man, who abhorrs a false-witness as he abhorrs the
tevil, and Got be judge between you and me.'—The doctor not
minding this conjuration, made the following speech, as near as I
can remember:—'I'll tell you what, Mr. Morgan, to be sure what
you say is just, in regard to an honest man; and if so be it appears as
how you are an honest man, then it is my opinion, that you deserve
to be acquitted, in relation to that there affair; for I tell you what,
captain Oakhum is resolved for to do every body justice.—As for
my own part, all that I have to alledge, is that I have been informed,
you have spoken disrespectful words against your captain, who to
be sure, is the most honourable and generous commander in the
king's service, without asparagement or acceptation of man, woman
or child.'—Having uttered this elegant harrangue, on which he
seemed to plume himself, Morgan replied, 'I do partly guess, and
conceive, and understand your meaning, which I wish could be
more explicite: But however, I do suppose, I am not to be condemned upon bare hear-say; or if I am convicted of speaking dis-
respectfully of captain Oakhum, I hope there is no treason in my
words.'—'But there's mutiny; by G—d, and that's death by the
articles of war (cried Oakhum.)—In the mean time, let the witnesses be called.'——Hereupon Mackshane's servant appeared, and
the boy of our mess, whom they had seduced and tutored for the
purpose.—The first declared, that Morgan, as he descended the
cockpit ladder, one day, cursed the captain and called him a savage
beast, saying, he ought to be hunted down as an enemy to mankind.
—'This (said the clerk) is a strong presumption of a design formed
against the captain's life.—For why? It presupposes malice afore-
thought, and a criminal intention *a priori*.'—'Right (said the captain
to this miserable grub, who had been an attorney's boy) you shall
have law enough, here's Cook and Littlejohn for it.'[1] This evidence
was confirmed by the boy, who affirmed, he heard the first mate say,
that the captain had no more bowels than a bear, and the surgeon
had no more brains than an ass.—Then the centinel who heard our

discourse on the poop was examined, and informed the court that
the Welchman assured me, that captain Oakhum and doctor
Mackshane would toss upon billows of burning brimstone in hell
for their barbarity.—The clerk observed, that here was an evident
prejudication, which confirmed the former suspicion of a conspiracy against the life of captain Oakhum; for, because, how could
Morgan so positively pronounce that the captain and surgeon
would be damned, unless he had intention to make away with them
before they could have time to repent?—This sage explanation had
great weight with our noble commander, who exclaimed, 'What
have you to say to this, Taffy? you seem to be taken all a-back,
brother, hah!'—Morgan was too much of a gentleman to disown
the text, although he absolutely denied the truth of the comment:
Upon which the captain, strutting up to him, with a ferocious
countenance, said, 'So, Mr. Son-of-a-b—ch, you confess you
honoured me with the names of bear and beast, and pronounced my
damnation! D—n my heart! I have a good mind to have you
brought to a court-martial and hanged, you dog.'—Here Mackshane having occasion for an assistant, interposed, and begged the
captain to pardon Mr. Morgan, with his wonted goodness, upon
condition that he the delinquent should make such submission as
the nature of his misdemeanour demanded.—Upon which the
Cambro-Briton, who on this occasion, would have made no submission to the Great Mogul,[1] surrounded with his guards, thanked
the doctor for his mediation, and acknowledged himself in the wrong
for having called the image of Got, a beast, 'but (said he) I spoke by
metaphor, and parable, and comparison, and types; as we signify
meekness by a lamb, letchery by a goat, and craftiness by a fox; so
we liken ignorance to an ass, and brutality to a bear, and fury to a
tyger;—therefore I made these similies to express my sentiments
(look you) and what I said, before Got, I will not unsay before man
nor peast neither.'—Oakhum was so provoked at this insolence (as
he termed it) that he ordered him forthwith to be carried to the
place of his confinement, and his clerk to proceed in the examination
of me.—The first question put to me, was touching the place of my
nativity, which I declared to be the north of Scotland. 'The north
of Ireland more liker (cried the captain) but we shall bring you up
presently.'—He then asked what religion I professed; and when I
answered, 'The protestant,' swore I was as arrant a Roman as ever
went to mass.—'Come, come, clerk (continued he) catechise him a

little on this subject.'—But before I relate the particulars of the clerk's enquiries, it will not be amiss to inform the reader that our commander himself was a Hibernian, and, if not shrewdly belied, a Roman Catholick to boot.——'You say you are a protestant (said the clerk) make the sign of the cross with your fingers, so, and swear upon it, to that affirmation.'—When I was about to perform this ceremony, the captain cried with some emotion, 'No, no, damme! I'll have no profanation neither.—But go on with your interrogations.'——Well then (proceeded my examiner) how many sacraments are there?'—To which I replied, 'Two.'—'What are they? (said he.)' I answered, 'Baptism and the Lord's Supper.'—'And so you would explode confirmation and marriage altogether? (said Oakhum) I thought this fellow was a rank Roman.'—The clerk, though he was bred under an attorney, could not refrain from blushing at this blunder,[1] which he endeavoured to conceal, by observing, that these decoys would not do with me who seemed to be an old offender.—He went on, with asking if I believed in transubstantiation;[2] but I treated the notion of the real presence with such disrespect that his patron was scandalized at my impiety, and commanded him to proceed to the plot. Whereupon this miserable pettifogger told me, there was great reason to suspect me of being a spy on board; and that I had entered into a conspiracy with Thomson and others not yet detected, against the life of captain Oakhum. —To support which accusation, they adduced the testimony of our boy, who declared he had often heard the deceased Thomson and me whispering together, and could distinguish the words, 'Oakhum, rascal, poison, pistol,' by which it appeared, we did intend to use sinister means to accomplish his destruction. That the death of Thomson seemed to confirm this conjecture, who, either feeling the stings of remorse, for being engaged in such a horrid confederacy, or fearing a discovery, by which he must have infallibly suffered an ignominious death, had put a fatal period to his own existence.— But what established the truth of the whole, was a book in cypher found among my papers, which exactly tallied with one found in his chest, after his disappearance: This, he observed, was a presumption very near proof positive, and would determine any jury in christendom to find me guilty.—In my own defence, I alledged that I had been dragged on board at first very much against my inclination, as I could prove by the evidence of some people now in the ship; consequently could have no design of becoming spy at that time; and ever since had been entirely out of the reach of any correspondence that could justly intail that suspicion upon me;—and as for conspiring against my captain's life, it could not be supposed that any man in his right wits would harbour the least thought of such an undertaking, which he could not possibly perform without certain infamy and ruin to himself, even if he had all the inclination in the world.—That allowing the boy's evidence to be true (which I affirmed was false and malicious) nothing conclusive could be gathered from a few incoherent words: Neither was the fate of Mr. Thomson a circumstance more favourable for the charge; for I had in my pocket, a letter which too well explained that mystery, in a very different manner from that which was supposed: With these words I produced the following letter, which Jack Rattlin brought to me the very day after Thomson disappeared; and told me it was committed to his care by the deceased, who made him promise not to deliver it sooner. The clerk taking it out of my hand, read aloud the contents, which were these:

DEAR FRIEND,

I am so much oppressed with the fatigue I daily and nightly undergo, and the barbarous usage of doctor Mackshane, who is bent on your destruction, as well as mine, that I am resolved to free myself from this miserable life, and before you receive this, shall be no more. I could have wished to die in your good opinion, which I am afraid I shall forfeit by the last act of my life; but if you cannot acquit me, I know you will at least preserve some regard for the memory of an unfortunate young man who loved you.—I recommend it to you, to beware of Mackshane, whose revenge is implacable.—I wish all prosperity to you and Mr. Morgan, to whom pray offer my last respects, and beg to be remembered as your unhappy friend and countryman.

WILLIAM THOMSON.

This letter was no sooner read, than Mackshane, in a transport of rage, snatched it out of the clerk's hands, and tore it into a thousand pieces, saying, it was a villainous forgery, contrived and executed by myself.—The captain and clerk declared themselves of the same opinion, notwithstanding I insisted on having the remains of it compared to other writings of Thomson, which they had in possession; and I was ordered to answer the last article of my accusation, namely, the book of cyphers found among my papers.—'That is

Chapter XXX

easily done (said I.) What you are pleased to call cyphers, are no other than the Greek characters, in which, for my amusement, I kept a diary of every thing remarkable that has occurred to my observation since the beginning of the voyage, till the day on which I was put in irons; and the same method, was practised by Mr. Thomson who copied mine.'—'A very likely story! (cried Mackshane) what occasion was there for using Greek characters, if you were not afraid of discovering what you had wrote?—but, what d'ye talk of Greek characters?—D'ye think I am so ignorant of the Greek language, as not to distinguish its letters from these, which are no more Greek than Chinese? No, no, I will not give up my knowledge of the Greek for you, nor none that ever came from your country.' So saying, with an unparalleled effronterie, he repeated some gibberish, which by the sound seemed to be Irish, and made it pass for Greek with the captain, who looking at me with a contemptible sneer, exclaimed, 'Ah ha! have you caught a tartar?'[1] I could not help smiling at the consummate assurance of this Hibernian, and offered to refer the dispute to any body on board, who understood the Greek alphabet: Upon which Morgan was brought back, and being made acquainted with the affair, took the book and read a whole page in English, without hesitation, deciding the controversy in my favour.—The doctor was so far from being out of countenance at this, that he affirmed Morgan was in the secret, and repeated from his own invention.—Oakhum said, 'Ay, ay, I see they are both in a story,' and dismissed my fellow-mate to his cock-loft,[2] although I proposed that he and I should read and translate separately, any chapter or verse in the Greek-testament in his possession, by which it would appear whether we or the surgeon spoke truth.—Not being endued with eloquence enough to convince the captain that there could be no juggle nor confederacy in this expedient, I begged to be examined by some unconcerned person on board, who understood Greek: Accordingly the whole ship's company, officers and all, were called upon deck, among whom it was proclaimed, that if any of them could speak Greek, he or they so qualified, should ascend the quarter-deck immediately.—After some pause two fore-mast-men came up and professed their skill in that language, which (they said) they acquired during several voyages to the Levant, among the Greeks of the Morea. The captain exulted much in this declaration, and put my journal-book into the hands of one of them, who candidly owned he could neither read nor write; the other acknowledged the same degree of ignorance, but pretended to speak the Greek lingo with any man on board; and addressing himself to me, pronounced some sentences of a barbarous corrupted language, which I did not understand.—I asserted that the modern Greek was as different from that spoke and written by the ancients, as the English used now from the old Saxon spoke in the time of Hengist,[1] and as I had only learned the true original tongue, in which Homer, Pindar, the evangelists and other Great men of antiquity wrote, it could not be supposed that I should know any thing of an imperfect Gothic dialect that rose on the ruins of the former, and scarce retained any traces of the old expression.—But if doctor Mackshane, who pretended to be master of the Greek language, could maintain a conversation with these seamen, I would retract what I had said, and be content to suffer any punishment he should think proper to inflict.—I had no sooner uttered these words, than the surgeon knowing one of the fellows to be his countryman, accosted him in Irish, and was answered in the same brogue; then a dialogue ensued between them, which they affirmed to be Greek, after having secured the secrecy of the other tar, who had his cue in the language of the Morea from his companion, before they would venture to assert such an intrepid falshood.—'I thought (said Oakhum) we should discover the imposture at last,—Let the rascal be carried back to his confinement.—I find he must dangle.'—Having nothing further to urge in my own behalf, before a court so prejudiced with spite, and fortified with ignorance against truth, I suffered myself to be reconducted peaceably to my fellow-prisoner, who hearing the particulars of my trial, lifted up his hands and eyes to heaven, and uttered a dreadful groan; and not daring to disburthen his thoughts to me by speech, lest he might be overheard by the centinel, burst forth into a Welch song, which he accompanied with a thousand contortions of face and violent gestures of body.

CHAPTER XXXI

I discover a subornation against me, by means of a quarrel between two of the evidences; in consequence of which, I am set at liberty, and prevail upon Morgan to accept of his freedom on the same terms——Mackshane's malice——we arrive at Jamaica, from whence in a short time we beat up to Hispaniola, in conjunction with the West-Indian squadron ——we take in water, sail again, and arrive at Carthagena ——reflections on our conduct there

MEAN while, a quarrel happening between the two modern Greeks, the one to be revenged of the other, came and discovered to us the mystery of Mackshane's dialogue, as I have explained it above. This detection coming to the ears of the doctor, who was sensible that (now we were in sight of Jamaica) we should have an opportunity of clearing ourselves before a court-martial, and at the same time, of making his malice and ignorance conspicuous, he interceeded for us with the captain so effectually, that in a few hours we were set at liberty, and ordered to return to our duty.—This was a happy event for me, my whole body being blistered by the sun, and my limbs benumbed for want of motion: But I could not persuade the Welchman to accept of this indulgence, he persisting in his obstinacy to remain in irons until he should be discharged by a court-martial, which he believed would also do him justice on his enemies; at length, I represented to him the precarious issue of a trial, the power and interest of his adversaries, and flattered his revenge with the hope of wreaking his resentment with his own hands upon Mackshane after our return to England: This last argument had more weight with him than all the rest, and prevailed upon him to repair with me to the cockpit, which I no sooner entered, than the idea of my departed friend presented itself to my remembrance, and filled my eyes with tears.—We discharged from our mess the boy who had acted so perfidiously, notwithstanding his tears, intreaties, and professions of penitence for what he had done; but not before he had confessed that the surgeon had bribed him to give evidence against us, with a pair of stockings and a couple of old check shirts, which his servant had since plundered him of.

The keys of our chests and lockers being sent to us by the doctor, we detained the messenger until we had examined the contents; and my fellow-mate finding all his Cheshire cheese consumed to a crust, his brandy exhausted, and his onions gone, was seized with a fit of choler, which he discharged on Mackshane's man in oaths and execrations, threatning to prosecute him as a thief.—The fellow swore in his turn that he never had the keys in his possession till that time, when he received them from his master, with orders to deliver them to us.—'As Got is my judge (cried Morgan) and my salfation, and my witness, whosoever has pilfered my provisions, is a lousy, beggarly, rascally knave! and by the soul of my grandsire! I will impeach, and accuse, and indict him of a roppery, if I did but know who he is.'—Had this happened at sea where we could not repair the loss, in all probability, this descendant of Cadwallader would have lost his wits entirely: but when I observed, how easy it would be to make up for this paultry misfortune, he became more calm, and reconciled himself to the occasion.—A little while after, the surgeon came into the birth, under pretence of taking something out of the medicine-chest, and with a smiling aspect, wished us joy of our deliverance, which (he said) he had been at great pains to obtain of the captain, who was very justly incensed at our behaviour; but he (the doctor) had passed his word for our conduct in time to come, and he hoped we should give him no cause to repent of his kindness.—He expected (no doubt) an acknowledgment from us for this pretended piece of service, as well as a general amnesty of what was past; but he had to do with people who were not quite so apt to forgive injuries as he imagined, or to forget that if our deliverance was owing to his mediation, our calamity was occasioned by his malice; I therefore sat silent while my companion answered, 'Ay, ay, 'tis no matter—Got knows the heart—there is a time for all things, as the wise man[1] saith, there is a time for throwing away stones, and a time to gather them up again.'—He seemed to be disconcerted at this reply, and went away in a pet, muttering something about 'Ingratitude' and 'Fellows,' which we did not think fit to take any notice of.

Our fleet having joined another that waited for us, lay at anchor about a month in the harbour of Port-Royal in Jamaica, during which time something of consequence was certainly transacted, notwithstanding the insinuations of some who affirmed we had no business at all in that place—that in order to take the advantage of the season proper for our enterprize, the West-Indian squadron, which had previous notice of our coming, ought to have joined us at the west end of Hispaniola with necessary stores and refreshments, from whence we could have sailed directly to Carthagena, before the enemy could put themselves in a good posture of defence, or indeed have an inkling of our design. Be this as it will, we sailed from Jamaica, and in ten days or a fortnight, beat up against the wind as far as the isle of Vache,[1] with an intention, as was said, to attack the French fleet, then supposed to be lying near that place; but before we arrived they had sailed for Europe, having first dispatched an advice-boat to Carthagena with an account of our being in these seas, as also of our strength and destination.—We loitered here some days longer, taking in wood, and brackish water, in the use whereof, however, our admiral seemed to consult the health of the men, by restricting each to a quart a day.——At length we set sail, and arrived in a bay to the windward of Carthagena, where we came to an anchor, and lay at our ease ten days longer.—Here again, certain malicious people take occasion to blame the conduct of their superiors, by saying, this was not only throwing away time, which was very precious considering the approach of the rainy season, but also giving the Spaniards time to recollect themselves, and recover from the consternation they were thrown into at the approach of an English fleet, at least three times as numerous as ever appeared in that part of the world before. But if I might be allowed to give my opinion of the matter, I would ascribe this delay to the generosity of our chiefs, who scorned to take any advantage that fortune might give them, even over an enemy. At last, however, we weighed, and anchored again somewhat nearer the harbour's mouth, where we made shift to land our marines, who encamped on the beach, in despite of the enemy's shot, which knocked a good many of them on the head.—This piece of conduct in chusing a camp under the walls of an enemy's fortification, which I believe never happened before, was practised, I presume, with a view of accustoming the soldiers to stand fire, who were not as yet much used to discipline, most of them having been taken from the plough-tail a few months before.—This again has furnished matter for censure against the Ministry, for sending a few raw recruits on such an important enterprize, while so many veteran regiments lay inactive at home: But surely our governours had their reasons for so doing, which possibly may be disclosed with other secrets of the deep. Perhaps they were loth to risk their best troops on such desperate service; or, may be the colonels and field officers of the old corps, who, generally speaking, enjoyed their commissions as sinecures or pensions, for some domestick services rendered to the court, refused to embark in such a dangerous and precarious undertaking; for which, no doubt, they are to be much commended.

CHAPTER XXXII

Our land forces being disembarked, erect a faschine battery
—our ship is ordered with four more, to batter the fort of
Bocca Chica——Mackshane's cowardice——the chaplain's
phrenzy——honest Rattlin loses one hand—his heroism and
reflections on the battle——Crampley's behaviour to me
during the heat of the fight

OUR forces being landed and stationed as I have already mentioned, set about erecting a faschine battery[1] to cannonade the principal fort of the enemy, and in something more than three weeks, it was ready to open. That we might do the Spaniards as much honour as possible, it was determined in a council of war, that five of our largest ships should attack the fort on one side, while the battery plyed it on the other, strengthened with two mortars, and twenty-four cohorns.[2]

Accordingly, the signal for our ship to engage, among others, was hoisted, we being advertised the night before, to make every thing clear for that purpose: and in so doing, a difference happened between captain Oakhum and his well-beloved cousin and counsellor Mackshane, which had well nigh terminated in an open rupture.— The doctor, who had imagined there was no more danger of being hurt by the enemy's shot in the cockpit than in the center of the earth, was lately informed that a surgeon's mate had been killed in that place, by a cannon-ball from two small forts, that were destroyed before the disembarkation of our soldiers; and therefore insisted upon having a platform raised for the convenience of the sick and wounded, in the after-hold, where he deemed himself more secure than on the deck above.—The captain, offended at this extraordinary proposal, accused him of pusilanimity, and told him there was no room in the hold for such an occasion; or if there was, he could not expect to be indulged more than the rest of the surgeons of the navy, who used the cockpit for that purpose: Fear rendering Mackshane obstinate, he persisted in his demand, and shewed his instructions,[1] by which it was authorised: The captain swore these instructions were dictated by a parcel of lazy poltroons who were never at sea; but was obliged to comply, and sent for the carpenter to give him orders about it: But before any such measure could be taken, our signal was thrown out, and the doctor compelled to trust his carcase in the cockpit, where Morgan and I were busy in putting our instruments and dressings in order.

Our ship, with the others destined for this service, immediately weighed, and in less than half an hour came to an anchor before the castle of Bocca Chica, with a spring upon our cable.[2]—The cannonading (which indeed was terrible!) began. The surgeon, after having crossed himself, fell flat on the deck; and the chaplain and purser, who were stationed with us, in quality of assistants, followed his example, while the Welchman and I sat upon a chest looking at one another with great discomposure, scarce able to refrain from the like prostration.—And that the reader may know, it was not a common occasion that alarmed us thus, I must inform him of the particulars of this dreadful din that astonished us. The fire of the Spaniards proceeded from Bocca Chica mounting eighty-four great guns, beside a mortar and small arms; from fort St. Joseph, mounting thirty-six; from two faschine batteries, mounting twenty; and from four men of war, mounting sixty-four guns each.—This was answered by us, from our land battery, mounting twenty-one cannon; our bomb battery, mounting two mortars, and twenty-four cohorns, and five men of war, two of eighty, and three of seventy guns, which fired without intermission. —We had not been many minutes engaged, when one of the sailors brought another on his back to the cockpit, where he tossed him down like a bag of oats, and pulling out his pouch, put a large chew of tobacco in his mouth, without speaking a word; Morgan immediately examined the condition of the wounded man, and cried, 'As I shall answer now, the man is as tead as my great-grandfather.'—'Dead (said his comrade) he may be dead now, for ought I know, but I'll be d—mn'd if he was not alive when I took him up.'—So saying, he was about to return to his quarters, when

I bid him carry the body along with him and throw it over board.
——'D—n the body! (said he) I think 'tis fair enough if I take care of
my own.'——My fellow-mate snatching up the amputation knife,
pursued him half-way up the cockpit ladder, crying, 'You lousy
rascal, is this the church-yard, or the charnel-house, or the sepulchre, or the Golgotha of the ship?'—but was stopt in his carreer by
one calling, 'Yo ho, avast there—scaldings.'—'Scaldings! (answered
Morgan) Got knows 'tis hot enough indeed:—who are you?'—
'Here's one (replied the voice.') and I immediately knew it to be
that of my honest friend Jack Rattlin, who coming towards me,
told me, with great deliberation, he was come to be dock'd at last,
and discovered the remains of one hand which had been shattered
to pieces with grape shot.—I lamented with unfeigned sorrow his
misfortune, which he bore with heroic courage, observing, that
every shot had its commission: It was well it did not take him in the
head; or if it had, what then? he should have died bravely, fighting
for his king and country: Death was a debt which every man owed,
and must pay now as well as another time.—I was much pleased and
edified with the maxims of this sea-philosopher, who endured the
amputation of his left hand without shrinking; the operation being
performed (at his request) by me, after Mackshane, who was with
difficulty prevailed to lift his head from the deck, had declared there
was a necessity for his losing the limb.—While I was employed in
dressing the stump, I asked Jack's opinion of the battle, who
shaking his head, frankly told me, he believed we should do no
good; 'For why, because instead of dropping anchor close under
shore, where we should have had to deal with one corner of Bocca
Chica only, we had opened the harbour, and exposed ourselves to
the whole fire of the enemy from their shipping and fort St. Joseph,
as well as from the castle we intended to cannonade; that besides,
we lay at too great a distance to damage the walls, and three parts
in four of our shot did not take place; for there was scarce any body
on board, who understood the pointing of a gun.—Ah! God help
us! (continued he) if your kinsman lieutenant Bowling had been
here, we should have had other-guess-work.'—By this time our
patients had increased to such a degree, that we did not know which
to begin with; and the first mate plainly told the surgeon, that if he
did not get up immediately, and perform his duty, he would complain of his behaviour to the admiral, and make application for his
warrant.—This effectually roused Mackshane, who was never deaf

to an argument in which he thought his interest was concerned; he therefore rose up, and in order to strengthen his resolution, had recourse more than once to a case-bottle of rum which he freely communicated to the chaplain and purser, who had as much need of such extraordinary inspiration as himself: Being thus supported, he went to work, and arms and legs were hewed down without mercy.—The fumes of the liquor mounting into the parson's brain, conspired with his former agitation of spirits, to make him quite delirious; he stript himself to the skin, and besmearing his body with blood, could scarce be with-held from running upon deck in that condition. Jack Rattlin, scandalized at this deportment, endeavoured to allay his transports with reason; but finding all he said ineffectual, and great confusion occasioned by his frolicks, he knocked him down with his right hand, and by threats kept him quiet in that state of humiliation.—But it was not in the power of rum to elevate the purser, who sat on the floor wringing his hands, and cursing the hour in which he left his peaceable profession of a brewer in Rochester, to engage in such a life of terror and disquiet. —While we diverted ourselves at the expence of this poor devil, a shot happened to take us between wind and water, and its course being through the purser's store-room, made a terrible havock and noise among the jars and bottles in its way, and disconcerted Mackshane so much, that he dropt his scalpel, and falling down on his knees, pronounced his *Pater-noster* aloud; the purser fell backward and lay without sense or motion; and the chaplain grew so outrageous, that Rattlin with one hand, could not keep him under; so that we were obliged to confine him in the surgeon's cabbin, where he was no doubt guilty of a thousand extravagancies.—Much about this time, my old antagonist Crampley came down, with express orders (as he said) to bring me up to the quarter-deck, to dress a slight wound the captain had received by a splinter. His reason for honouring me in particular with this piece of service, being that in case I should be killed or disabled by the way, my death or mutilation would be of less consequence to the ship's company, than that of the doctor or his first mate.—At another time, perhaps, I might have disputed this order, to which I was not bound to pay the least regard; but as I thought my reputation depended upon my compliance, I was resolved to convince my rival that I was no more afraid than he, to expose myself to danger.—With this view, I provided myself with dressings, and followed him immediately to the quarter-deck, through a most infernal scene of slaughter, fire, smoak, and uproar! Captain Oakhum, who leaned against the mizen mast, no sooner saw me approach in my shirt, with the sleeves tucked up to my arm-pits, and my hands dyed with blood, than he signified his displeasure by a frown, and asked why the doctor himself did not come? I told him Crampley had singled me out, as if by his express command; at which he seemed surprized, and threatened to punish the midshipman for his presumption, after the engagement: In the mean time, I was sent back to my station, and ordered to tell Mackshane, that the captain expected him immediately.—I got safe back and delivered up my commission to the doctor, who flatly refused to quit the post assigned to him by his instructions. Hereupon, Morgan, who (I believe) was jealous of my reputation for courage, undertook the affair, and ascended with great intrepidity.——The captain finding the surgeon obstinate, suffered himself to be dressed, and swore he would confine Mackshane as soon as that service should be over.

CHAPTER XXXIII

A breach being made in the walls, our soldiers give the assault, take the place without opposition——our sailors at the same time become masters of all the other strengths near Bocca Chica, and take possession of the harbour—the good consequence of this success——we move nearer the town—— find two forts deserted, and the channel blocked up with sunk vessels; which however, we find means to clear——land our soldiers at La Quinta——repulse a body of militia—— attack the castle of St. Lazar, and are forced to retreat with great loss——the remains of our army are re-imbarked—— an effort of the admiral to take the Town—the œconomy of our expedition described

HAVING cannonaded the fort, during the space of four hours, we were all ordered to slip our cables, and sheer off;[1] but next day the engagement was renewed, and continued from the morning till the afternoon, when the enemy's fire from Bocca Chica slackened, and towards evening was quite silenced.—A breach being made on the other side, by our land-battery, large enough to admit a middle sized baboon, provided he could find means to climb up to it; our general proposed to give the assault that very night, and actually ordered a detachment on that duty: Providence stood our friend upon this occasion, and put it into the hearts of the Spaniards to abandon the fort, which might have been maintained by resolute men, to the day of judgment against all the force we could exert in the attack.—And while our soldiers took possession of the enemy's ramparts, without resistance, the same good luck attended a body of sailors, who made themselves masters of fort St. Joseph, the faschine batteries, and one Spanish man of war; the other three being burnt or sunk by the foe, that they might not fall into our hands.—The taking of these forts, in the strength of which the Spaniards chiefly confided, made us masters of the outward harbour, and occasioned great joy among us; as we laid our accounts with finding little or no opposition from the town: And indeed, if a few great ships had sailed up immediately, before they had recovered from the confusion and despair that our unexpected success had produced among them, it is not impossible that we might have finished the affair to our satisfaction, without any more blood-shed: but this our Heroes disdained, as a barbarous insult over the enemy's distress; and gave them all the respite they could desire, in order to recollect themselves.—In the mean time, Mackshane taking the advantage of this general exultation, waited on our captain, and pleaded his own cause so effectually, that he was re-established in his good graces; and as for Crampley, there was no more notice taken of his behaviour towards me, during the action.—But of all the consequences of the victory, none was more grateful than plenty of fresh water, after we had languished five weeks on the allowance of a purser's quart[1] *per diem* for each man, in the Torrid Zone, where the sun was vertical, and the expence of bodily fluid so great, that a gallon of liquor could scarce supply the waste of twenty-four hours; especially, as our provision consisted of putrid salt beef, to which the sailors gave the name of Irish horse; salt pork of New England, which though neither fish nor flesh, favoured of both; bread from the same country, every biscuit whereof, like a piece of clock work, moved by its own internal impulse, occasioned by the myriads of insects that dwelt within it; and butter served out by the gill, that tasted like train-oil thickened with salt. Instead of small-beer, each man was allowed three half quarterns of brandy or rum, which was distributed every morning, diluted with a certain quantity of his water, without either sugar or fruit to render it palatable, for which reason this composition, was by the sailors not unaptly stiled *Necessity*.[1] Nor was this limitation of simple element owing to a scarcity of it on board, there being at this time water enough in the ship for a voyage of six months, at the rate of half a gallon *per* day to each man: But this fast must (I suppose) have been injoined by way of pennance on the ship's company for their sins; or rather with a view to mortify them into a contempt of life, that they might thereby become more resolute and regardless of danger. How simply then do those people argue, who ascribe the great mortality[2] among us, to our bad provision and want of water; and affirm, that a great many valuable lives might have been saved, if the useless transports had been employed in fetching fresh stock, turtle, fruit, and other refreshments, from Jamaica and other adjacent islands, for the use of the army and fleet! seeing, it is to be hoped, that those who died went to a better place, and those who survived were the more easily maintained.—After all, a sufficient number remained to fall before the walls of St. Lazar, where they behaved like their own country mastifs,[3] which shut their eyes, run into the jaws of a bear, and have their heads crushed for their valour.

But to return to my narration: After having put garrisons into the forts we had taken, and re-imbarked our soldiers and artillery, which detained us more than a week, we ventured up to the mouth of the inner harbour, guarded by a large fortification on one side, and a small redoubt on the other, both of which were deserted before our approach, and the entrance of the harbour blocked up by several old galleons that the enemy had sunk in the channel.—We made shift, however, to open a passage for some ships of war, that favoured the second landing of our troops at a place called La Quinta, not far from the town, where, after a faint resistance from a body of Spaniards, who opposed their disembarkation, they encamped with a design of besieging the castle of St. Lazar, which overlooked and commanded the city: Whether our renowned general had no body in his army who knew how to approach it in form, or that he trusted intirely to the fame of his arms, I shall not determine; but certain it is, a resolution was taken in a council of war, to attack the place with musquetry only, which was put in execution, and succeeded accordingly; the enemy giving them such an hearty reception, that the greatest part of the detachment took up their everlasting residence on the spot.—Our chief not relishing this kind of complaisance in the Spaniards, was wise enough to retreat on board with the remains of his army, which, from eight thousand able men landed on the beach near Bocca Chica, was now reduced to fifteen hundred fit for service.—The sick and wounded were squeezed into certain vessels, which thence obtained the name of hospital ships, though methinks they scarce deserved such a creditable title, seeing none of them could boast of either surgeon, nurse or cook; and the space between decks was so confined, that the miserable patients had not room to sit upright in their beds. Their wounds and stumps being neglected, contracted filth and putrefaction, and millions of maggots were hatched amid the corruption of their sores. This inhuman disregard was imputed to the scarcity of surgeons; though it is well known, that every great ship in the fleet could have spared one at least for this duty, which would have been more than sufficient to remove this shocking inconvenience: But, perhaps, the general[1] was too much of a gentleman to ask a favour of this kind from his fellow-chief,[2] who on the other hand, would not derogate so far from his own dignity, as to offer such assistance unasked; for I may venture to affirm, that by this time, the Dæmon of discord with her sooty wings, had breathed her influence upon our counsels; and it might be said of these great men, (I hope they will pardon the comparison) as of Cæsar and Pompey, the one could not brook a superior, and the other was impatient of an equal:[3] So that between the pride of one, and insolence of another, the enterprize miscarried, according to the proverb, 'Between two stools the backside falls to the ground.'— Not that I would be thought to liken any publick concern to that opprobrious part of the human body, although I might with truth assert, if I durst use such a vulgar idiom, that the nation did hang an a—se[4] at its disappointment on this occasion; neither would I presume to compare the capacity of our heroic leaders to any such wooden convenience as a joint-stool or a close-stool;[5] but only signify by this simile, the mistake the people committed in trusting to the union of two instruments that were never joined.

A day or two after the attempt on St. Lazar, the admiral ordered one of the Spanish men of war we had taken,[6] to be mounted with sixteen guns, and manned with detachments from our great ships, in order to batter the town; accordingly, she was towed into the inner harbour in the night-time, and moored within half a mile of the walls, against which she began to fire at day-break; and continued about four hours exposed to the opposition of at least forty pieces of cannon, which at length obliged our men to set her on fire, and get off as well as they could, in their boats.—This piece of conduct afforded matter of speculation to all the wits, either in the army or the navy, who were at last fain to acknowledge it a stroke of policy above their comprehension.—Some entertained such an irreverent opinion of the admiral's understanding, as to think he expected the town would surrender to his floating battery of sixteen guns: Others imagined his sole intention was to try the enemy's strength, by which he would be able to compute the number of great ships that would be necessary to bring the Spaniards to a capitulation: But this last conjecture soon appeared groundless, in as much as no ships of any kind whatever were afterwards employed on that service.—A third sort swore, that no other cause could be assigned for this undertaking, than that which induced Don Quixote to attack the windmill.[1] A fourth class (and that the most numerous, though without doubt, composed of the sanguine and malicious) plainly taxed this commander with want of honesty as well as sense; and alledged that he ought to have sacrificed private pique to the interest of his country; that where the lives of so many brave fellow citizens were concerned, he ought to have concurred with the general, without being sollicited or even desired, towards their preservation and advantage; that if his arguments could not dissuade him from a desperate enterprize, it was his duty to render it as practicable as possible, without running extreme hazard; that this could have been done, with a good prospect of success, by ordering five or six large ships to batter the town while the land forces stormed the castle, by this means, a considerable diversion would have been made in favour of those troops, who in their march to the assault and in the retreat, suffered much more from the town than from the castle; that the inhabitants seeing themselves vigorously attacked on all hands, would have been divided, distracted and confused, and in all probability, unable to resist the assailants.—— But all these suggestions surely proceed from ignorance and malevolence, or else the admiral would not have found it such an easy matter, at his return to England, to justify his conduct to a ministry at once so upright and discerning.—True it is, that those who undertook to vindicate him on the spot, asserted, there was not water enough for our great ships near the town; tho' this was a little unfortunately urged, because there happened to be pilots in the fleet perfectly well acquainted with the soundings of the harbour, who affirmed there was water enough for five eighty gun ships to lye a-breast in, almost up at the very walls.—The disappointments we suffered, occasioned an universal dejection, which was not at all alleviated by the objects that daily and hourly entertained our eyes, nor by the prospect of what must inevitably happen, if we remained much longer in this place.—Such was the œconomy in some ships, that, rather than be at the trouble of interring the dead, their commanders ordered their men to throw the bodies overboard, many without either ballast or winding-sheet; so that numbers of human carcasses floated in the harbour, until they were devoured by sharks and carrion crows; which afforded no agreeable spectacle to those who survived.—At the same time the wet season began, during which, a deluge of rain falls from the rising to the setting of the sun, without intermission; and that no sooner ceases, than it begins to thunder and lighten with such continual flashing, that one can see to read a very small print by the illumination.

CHAPTER XXXIV

*An epidemick fever rages among us———we abandon our
conquests———I am seized with the distemper; write a petition
to the captain, which is rejected———I am in danger of
suffocation through the malice of Crampley; and relieved by
a serjeant———my fever increases———the chaplain wants to
confess me———I obtain a favourable crisis—Morgan's affection
for me proved—the behaviour of Mackshane and Crampley
towards me———Captain Oakhum is removed into another ship
with his beloved doctor—our new captain described—an
adventure of Morgan*

THE change of the atmosphere, occasioned by this phœnomenon, conspired with the stench that surrounded us, the heat of the climate, our own constitutions impoverished by bad provision, and our despair, to introduce the bilious fever[1] among us, which raged with such violence that three fourths of those whom it invaded, died in a deplorable manner; the colour of their skin, being by the extreme putrefaction of their juices, changed into that of soot.

Our conductors finding things in this situation, perceived it was high time to relinquish our conquests, which we did, after having rendered their artillery useless and blown up their walls with gunpowder.—Just as we sailed from Bocca Chica on our return to Jamaica, I found myself threatened with the symptoms of this terrible distemper; and knowing very well that I stood no chance for my life, if I should be obliged to lie in the cockpit, which by this time, was grown intolerable even to people in health, by reason of the heat and unwholesome smell of decayed provision;[1] I wrote a petition to the captain representing my case, and humbly imploring his permission to lie among the soldiers in the middle-deck, for the benefit of the air: But I might have spared myself the trouble; for this humane commander refused my request, and ordered me to continue in the place allotted for the surgeon's mates, or else be contented to lie in the hospital, which, by the bye, was three degrees more offensive and more suffocating than our own birth below.—Another in my condition, perhaps, would have submitted to his fate, and died in a pet; but I could not brook the thought of perishing so pitifully, after I had weathered so many gales of hard fortune: I therefore, without minding Oakhum's injunction, prevailed upon the soldiers (whose good-will I had acquired) to admit my hammock among them; and actually congratulated myself upon my comfortable situation, which Crampley no sooner understood, than he signified to the captain, my contempt of his orders; and was invested with power to turn me down again into my proper habitation.—This barbarous piece of revenge, incensed me so much against the author, that I vowed, with bitter imprecations, to call him to a severe account, if ever it should be in my power; and the agitation of my spirits increased my fever to a violent degree.—While I lay gasping for breath in this infernal abode, I was visited by a serjeant, the bones of whose nose I had reduced and set to rights, after they had been demolished by a splinter during our last engagement: He being informed of my condition, offered me the use of his birth in the middle-deck, which was inclosed with canvas and well-aired by a port-hole that remained open within it.—I embraced this proposal with joy, and was immediately conducted to the place, where I was treated, while my illness lasted, with the utmost tenderness and care by his grateful halberdier, who had no other bed for himself than a hen-coop, during the whole passage.— Here I lay and enjoyed the breeze, notwithstanding of which, my malady gained ground, and at length my life was despaired of, though I never lost hopes of recovery, even when I had the mortification to see, from my cabbin window, six or seven thrown overboard every day, who died of the same distemper. This confidence, I am persuaded, conduced a good deal to the preservation of my life, especially, when joined to another resolution I took at the beginning, namely, to refuse all medicine,[1] which I could not help thinking co-operated with the disease, and instead of resisting putrefaction, promoted a total degeneracy of the vital fluid.—When my friend Morgan, therefore, brought his diaphoretic boluses,[2] I put them in my mouth, 'tis true, but without any intention of swallowing them; and when he went away, spit them out, and washed my mouth with water-gruel: I seemingly complied in this manner, that I might not affront the blood of Caractacus, by a refusal which might have intimated a diffidence of his physical capacity; for he acted as my physician; doctor Mackshane never once enquiring about me, or even knowing where I was.—When my distemper was at the height, Morgan thought my case desperate, and after having applied a blister to the nape of my neck, squeezed my hand, bidding me, with a woful countenance, recommend myself to Got and my reteemer; then taking his leave, desired the chaplain to come and administer some spiritual consolation to me; but before he arrived, I had made shift to rid myself of the troublesome application the Welchman had bestowed on my back.—The parson having felt my pulse, enquired into the nature of my complaints, hemmed a little, and began thus: 'Mr. Random, God out of his infinite mercy hath been pleased to visit you with a dreadful distemper, the issue of which no man knows.—You may be permitted to recover, and live many days on the face of the earth: and, which is more probable, you may be taken away and cut off in the flower of your youth: It is incumbent on you, therefore, to prepare for the great change, by repenting sincerely of your sins; of this there cannot be a greater sign, than an ingen'ous confession, which I conjure you to make, without hesitation or mental reservation; and when I am convinced of your sincerity, I will then give you such comfort as the situation of your soul will admit of. Without doubt, you have been guilty of numberless transgressions, to which youth is subject, as swearing, drunkenness, whoredom, and adultery; tell me therefore, without reserve, the particulars of each, especially of the last, that I may be acquainted with the true state of your conscience: For no physician will prescribe for his patient until he knows the circumstances of his disease.' As I was not under any apprehensions of death, I could not help smiling at the doctor's inquisitive remonstrance, which I told him savoured more of the Roman than of the Protestant church, in recommending auricular confession, a thing, in my opinion, not at all necessary to salvation, and which, for that reason, I declined.—This reply disconcerted him a little; however, he explained away his meaning, in making learned distinctions between what was absolutely necessary, and what was only convenient; then proceeded to ask what religion I professed: I answered, that I had not as yet considered the difference of religions, consequently had not fixed on any one in particular, but that I was bred a Presbyterian.—At this word the chaplain discovered great astonishment, and said, he could not comprehend how a Presbyterian was entitled to any post under the English government.[1]—Then he asked if I had ever received the Sacrament, or taken the oaths; to which I replying in the negative, he held up his hands, assured me he could do me no service, wished I might not be in a state of reprobation; and returned to his mess-mates, who were making merry in the ward-room, round a table well stored with bumbo* and wine.— This insinuation, terrible as it was, had not such an effect upon me, as the fever, which, soon after he had left me, grew outragious; I began to see strange chimeras, and concluded myself on the point of becoming delirious: But before that happened, was in great danger of suffocation, upon which I started up in a kind of frantic fit, with an intention to plunge myself into the sea, and as my friend the serjeant was not present, would certainly have cooled myself to some purpose, had I not perceived a moisture upon my thigh, as I endeavoured to get out of my hammock: The appearance of this revived my hopes, and I had reflection and resolution enough to take the advantage of this favourable symptom, by tearing the shirt from my body and the sheets from my bed, and wrapping myself in a thick blanket, in which inclosure, for about a quarter of an hour, I felt the pains of hell; but it was not long before I was recompensed for my suffering by a profuse sweat, that bursting from the whole surface of my skin, in less than two hours, relieved me from

*Bumbo is a liquor composed of rum, sugar, water and nutmeg.

all my complaints, except that of weakness; and left me as hungry as a kite.—I enjoyed a very comfortable nap, after which I was regaling myself with the agreeable reverie of my future happiness, when I heard Morgan, on the outside of the curtain, ask the serjeant, if I was still alive? 'Alive! (cried the other) God forbid he should be otherwise! he has lain quiet these five hours, and I do not chuse to disturb him, for sleep will do him great service.'—'Ay, (said my fellow-mate) he sleeps so sound, (look you) that he will never waken till the great trump plows.—Got be merciful to his soul.—He has paid his debt, like an honest man.—Ay, and moreover, he is at rest from all persecutions, and troubles, and afflictions, of which, Got knows, and I know, he had his own share.—Ochree![1] Ochree! he was a promising youth indeed!'—So saying, he groaned grievously, and began to whine in such a manner, as persuaded me he had a real friendship for me.—The serjeant, alarmed at his words, came into the birth, and while he looked upon me, I smiled, and tipt him the wink; he immediately guessed my meaning, and remained silent, which confirmed Morgan in his opinion of my being dead; whereupon he approached with tears in his eyes, in order to indulge his grief with a sight of the object: And I counterfeited death so well, by fixing my eyes, and droping my under-jaw, that he said, 'There he lies, no petter than a lump of clay, Got help me.' And observed by the distortion of my face, that I must have had a strong sturggle. I should not have been able to contain myself much longer, when he began to perform the last duty of a friend, in closing my eyes and my mouth; upon which, I suddenly snapped at his fingers, and discomposed him so much, that he started back, turned pale as ashes, and stared like the picture of horror! Although I could not help laughing at his appearance, I was concerned for his situation, and stretched out my hand, telling him, I hoped to live and eat some salmagundy of his making in England.—It was some time before he could recollect himself so far as to feel my pulse, and enquire into the particulars of my disease: But when he found I had enjoyed a favourable crisis, he congratulated me upon my good fortune; not failing to ascribe it, under Got, to the blister he had applied to my back, at his last visit; which, by the bye, said he, must now be removed and dressed: He was actually going to fetch dressings, when I feigning astonishment, said, 'Bless me! sure you never applied a blister to me—there is nothing on my back, I assure you.'—Of this he could not be convinced till he had examined, and then endeavoured to conceal his confusion, by expressing his surprize in finding the skin untouched, and the plaister missing.—In order to excuse myself for paying so little regard to his prescription, I pretended to have been insensible when it was put on, and to have pulled it off afterwards, in a fit of delirium. This apology satisfied my friend, who on this occasion abated a good deal of his stiffness in regard to punctilios; and as we were now safely arrived at Jamaica, where I had the benefit of fresh provision, and other refreshments, I recovered strength every day, and in a short time, my health and vigour were perfectly re-established.—When I got up at first, and was just able to crawl about the deck, with a staff in my hand, I met doctor Mackshane, who passed by me with a disdainful look, and did not vouchsafe to honour me with one word: After him came Crampley, who strutting up to me, with a fierce countenance, pronounced, 'Here's fine discipline on board, when such lazy sculking sons of b—ches as you, are allowed, on pretence of sickness, to lollop at your ease, while your betters are kept to hard duty!'—The sight and behaviour of this malicious scoundrel, enraged me so much, that I could scarce refrain from laying my cudgel across his pate; but when I considered my present feebleness, and the enemies I had in the ship, who wanted only a pretence to ruin me, I restrained my passion, and contented myself with telling him, I had not forgot his insolence and malice, and that I hoped we should meet one day on shore.—At this he grinned, shook his fist at me, and swore he longed for nothing more than such an opportunity.

Mean while, our ship was ordered to be heaved down, victualled and watered, for her return to England; and our captain, for some reason or other, not thinking it convenient for him to revisit his native country at this time, exchanged with a gentleman, who on the other hand, wished for nothing so much, as to be safe without the tropick; all his care and tenderness of himself, being insufficient to preserve his complexion from the injuries of the sun and weather.

Our tyrant having left the ship, and carried his favourite Mackshane along with him, to my inexpressible satisfaction; our new commander came on board, in a ten-oar'd barge, overshadowed with a vast umbrella, and appeared in everything quite the reverse of Oakhum, being a tall, thin, young man, dressed in this manner; a white hat garnished with a red feather, adorned his head, from whence his hair flowed down upon his shoulders, in ringlets tied behind with a ribbon.—His coat, consisting of pink-coloured silk, lined with white, by the elegance of the cut retired backward, as it were, to discover a white sattin waistcoat embroidered with gold, unbuttoned at the upper part, to display a broch set with garnets, that glittered in the breast of his shirt, which was of the finest cambrick, edged with right mechlin.[1] The knees of his crimson velvet breeches scarce descended so low as to meet his silk stockings, which rose without spot or wrinkle on his meagre legs, from shoes of blue Meroquin,[2] studded with diamond buckles, that flamed forth rivals to the sun! A steel-hilted sword, inlaid with figures of gold, and decked with a knot of ribbon[3] which fell down in a rich tossle,[4] equipped his side; and an amber-headed cane hung dangling from his wrist:—But the most remarkable parts of his furniture were, a mask on his face, and white gloves on his hands, which did not seem to be put on with an intention to be pulled off occasionally, but were fixed with a ring set with a ruby on the little finger of one hand, and by one set with a topaz on that of the other.——In this garb, captain Whiffle,[5] for that was his name, took possession of the ship, surrounded with a crowd of attendants, all of whom, in their different degrees, seemed to be of their patron's disposition; and the air was so impregnated with perfumes, that one may venture to affirm the clime of Arabia Fœlix[6] was not half so sweet-scented.—My fellow-mate, observing no surgeon among his train, thought he had found an occasion too favourable for himself to be neglected; and remembring the old proverb, 'Spare to speak, and spare to speed,' resolved to sollicit the new captain's interest immediately, before any other surgeon could be appointed for the ship.—With this view he repaired to the cabbin, in his ordinary dress, consisting of a check-shirt and trousers, a brown linen waistcoat, and a night-cap of the same, neither very clean, which for his further misfortune, happened to smell strong of tobacco.—Entering without any ceremony, into this sacred place, he found captain Whiffle reposing upon a couch, with a wrapper of fine chintz about his body, and a muslin cape bordered with lace upon his head; and after several low conge's, began in this manner:——'Sir, I hope you will forgive, and excuse, and pardon the presumption of one who has not the honour of being known unto you, but who is, nevertheless, a shentleman porn and pred, and moreover has had misfortunes, Got help me, in the world.'—Here he was interrupted by the captain, who at first sight of him had started up with great amazement at the novelty of the apparition; and having recollected himself, pronounced, with a look and tone signifying disdain, curiosity and surprize, 'Zauns!¹ who art thou?'——'I am surgeon's first mate on board of this ship (replied Morgan) and I most vehemently desire and beseech you with all submission, to be pleased to condescend and vouchsafe to enquire into my character, and my pehaviour, and my deserts, which, under Got, I hope, will entitle me to the vacancy of surgeon.'—As he proceeded in his speech, he continued advancing towards the captain, whose nostrils were no sooner saluted with the aromatick flavour that exhaled from him, than he cried with great emotion, 'Heaven preserve me! I am suffocated!—Fellow, Fellow, away with thee!—Curse thee, fellow! get thee gone,—I shall be stunk to death!'—At the noise of his outcries, his servants run into his apartment, and he accosted them thus; 'Villains! cut-throats! traitors! I am betrayed! I am sacrificed!—— Will you not carry that monster away? or must I be stifled with the stench of him? oh! oh!'—With these interjections, he sunk down upon his settee in a fit; his *valet de chambre* plied him with a smelling-bottle, one footman chafed his temples with Hungary water,² another sprinkled the floor with spirits of lavender, and a third pushed Morgan out of the cabbin; who coming to the place where I was, sat down with a demure countenance, and, according to his custom, when he received any indignity which he durst not revenge, began to sing a Welch ditty.—I guessed he was under some agitation of spirits, and desired to know the cause; but instead of answering me directly, he asked with great emotion, if I thought him a monster and a stinkard? 'A monster and a stinkard (said I, with some surprize) did any body call you so?'—'Got is my judge (replied he) captain Fifle did call me both; ay, and all the water in the Tawy³ will not wash it out of my remembrance.—I do affirm, and avouch, and maintain, with my soul, and my pody, and my plood, look you, that I have no smells about me, but such as a christian ought to have, except the effluvia of topacco, which is a cephalic,⁴ odoriferous, aromatick herb, and he is a son of a mountain-goat who says otherwise.—As for my being a monster, let that be as it is; I am as Got was pleased to create me, which, peradventure, is more than I shall aver of him who gave me that title; for I will proclaim it before the world, that he is disguised and transfigured, and transmographied with affectation and whimsies; and that he is more like a papoon than one of the human race.'

CHAPTER XXXV

Captain Whiffle sends for me——his situation described——his surgeon arrives, prescribes for him, and puts him to bed—a bed is put up for Mr. Simper contiguous to the state-room, which, with other parts of the captain's behaviour, gives the ship's company a very unfavourable idea of their commander —I am detained in the West-Indies, by the admiral, and go on board of the Lizard sloop of war, in quality of surgeon's mate, where I make myself known to the Surgeon, who treats me very kindly——I go on shore, sell my ticket, purchase necessaries, and at my return on board, am surprized at the sight of Crampley, who is appointed lieutenant of the sloop—— we sail on a cruize——take a prize, in which I arrive at Port Morant, under the command of my mess mate, with whom I live in great harmony

HE was going on, with an elogium upon the captain, when I received a message to clean myself, and go up to the great cabbin, which I immediately performed, sweetening myself with rose-water from the medicine-chest. When I entered the room, I was ordered to stand by the door, until captain Whiffle had reconnoitred me at a distance, with a spy-glass, who having consulted one sense in this manner, bid me advance gradually, that his nose might have intelligence, before it could be much offended: I therefore approached with great caution and success, and he was pleased to say, 'Ay, this creature is tolerable.'—I found him lolling on his couch with a languishing air, his head supported by his *valet de chambre*, who from time to time applied a smelling-bottle to his nose.— 'Vergette,[1] (said he, in a squeaking tone) dost thou think this wretch (meaning me) will do me no injury? may I venture to submit my arm to him?'—'Pon my vord, (replied the valet) I do tink dat dere be great occasion for your honour losing one small quantite of blodt; and the yong mun ave qulque chose of de bonne mine.'— 'Well then (said his master) I think I must venture.'—Then addressing himself to me, 'Hast thou ever blooded any body but brutes?— But I need not ask thee, for thou wilt tell me a most damnable lie.'

—'Brutes, Sir, (answered I, pulling down his glove in order to feel his pulse) I never meddle with brutes.'—'What the devil art thou about? (cried he) dost thou intend to twist off my hand? Gad's curse! my arm is benumbed up to the very shoulder! Heaven have mercy upon me! must I perish under the hands of savages? What an unfortunate dog was I to come on board without my own surgeon, Mr. Simper.'—I craved pardon for having handled him so roughly, and with the utmost care and tenderness tied up his arm with a fillet of silk. While I was feeling for the vein, he desired to know how much blood I intended to take from him, and when I answered, 'Not above twelve ounces,' started up with a look full of horror, and bid me begone, swearing I had a design upon his life. —Vergette appeased him with some difficulty, and opening a bureau, took out a pair of scales, in one of which was placed a small cup; and putting them into my hand, told me, the captain never lost above an ounce and three drachms at one time.—While I prepared for this important evacuation, there came into the cabbin, a young man, gayly dressed, of a very delicate complexion, with a kind of languid smile on his face, which seemed to have been rendered habitual, by a long course of affectation.—The captain no sooner perceived him, than rising hastily, he flew into his arms, crying, 'O! my dear Simper! I am excessively disordered! I have been betrayed, frighted, murdered by the negligence of my servants, who suffered a beast, a mule, a bear to surprize me, and stink me into convulsions with the fumes of tobacco.'—Simper, who by this time, I found, was obliged to art for the clearness of his complexion, assumed an air of softness and sympathy, and lamented with many tender expressions of sorrow, the sad accident that had thrown him into that condition; then feeling his patient's pulse on the outside of his glove, gave it as his opinion, that his disorder was entirely nervous, and that some drops of tincture of castor[1] and liquid laudanum, would be of more service to him than bleeding, by bridling the inordinate sallies of his spirits, and composing the fermentation of his bile proceeding therefrom.—I was therefore sent to prepare this prescription, which was administered in a glass of sack-posset,[2] after the captain had been put to bed, and orders sent to the officers on the quarter-deck, to let no body walk on that side under which he lay.

While the captain enjoyed his repose, the doctor watched over him, and indeed became so necessary, that a cabin was made for

Chapter XXXV

him contiguous to the state-room, where Whiffle slept; that he might be at hand in case of accidents in the night.—Next day, our commander being happily recovered, gave orders, that none of the lieutenants should appear upon deck, without a wig, sword, and ruffles; nor any midshipman, or other petty officer, be seen with a check shirt or dirty linen.—He also prohibited any person whatever, except Simper and his own servants, from coming into the great cabbin, without first sending in to obtain leave.—These singular regulations did not prepossess the ship's company in his favour; but on the contrary, gave scandal an opportunity to be very busy with his character, and accuse him of maintaining a correspondence with his surgeon, not fit to be named.

In a few weeks, our ship was under sailing orders, and I was in hopes of re-visiting my native country in a very short time, when the admiral's surgeon came on board, and sending for Morgan and me to the quarter-deck, gave me to understand, there was a great scarcity of surgeons in the West-Indies, that he was commanded to detain one mate out of every great ship that was bound for England; and desired us to agree among ourselves, before the next day at that hour, which of us should stay behind.——We were thunder-struck at this proposal, and stared at one another some time, without speaking; at length the Welchman broke silence, and offered to re-main in the West-Indies, provided the admiral would give him a surgeon's warrant immediately: But he was told there was no want of chief surgeons, and that he must be contented with the station of mate, till he should be further provided for in due course: Where-upon Morgan flatly refused to quit the ship for which the commis-sioners of the navy had appointed him; and the other told him as plainly, that if we could not determine the affair by ourselves before tomorrow morning, he must cast lots, and abide by his chance.—When I recalled to my remembrance the miseries I had undergone in England, where I had not one friend to promote my interest, or favour my advancement in the navy, and at the same time, reflected on the present dearth of surgeons in the West-Indies, and the un-healthiness of the climate, which every day, almost, reduced the number, I could not help thinking my success would be much more certain and expeditious, by staying where I was, than by returning to Europe.—I therefore resolved to comply with a good grace, and next day, when we were ordered to throw dice, told Morgan, he needed not trouble himself, for I would voluntarily submit to the admiral's pleasure.—This frank declaration was commended by the gentleman, who assured me, it should not fare the worse with me for my resignation: Indeed he was as good as his word, and that very afternoon, procured a warrant, appointing me surgeon's mate of the Lizzard sloop of war, which put me on a footing with every first mate in the service.[1]

My ticket[2] being made out, I put my chest and bedding on board a canoe that was alongside, and having shook hands with my trusty friend the serjeant, and honest Jack Rattlin, who was bound for Greenwich-hospital,[3] I took my leave of Morgan with many tears, after we had exchanged our sleeve-buttons as remembrances of each other.—Having presented my new warrant to the captain of the Lizard, I enquired for the doctor, whom I no sooner saw, than I recollected him to be one of those young fellows with whom I had been committed to the round-house, during our frolick with Jackson, as I have related before.—He received me with a good deal of courtesy, and when I put him in mind of our former acquaintance, expressed great joy in seeing me again, and recommended me to an exceeding good mess, composed of the gunner and the master's mate.—As there was not one sick person in the ship, I got leave to go ashore, next day, with the gunner, who recommended me to a Jew, that bought my ticket, at the rate of 40 *per cent.* discount; and having furnished myself with what necessaries I wanted, returned on board in the evening, and to my great surprize, found my old antagonist Crampley walking upon deck.—Tho' I did not fear his enmity, I was shocked at his appearance, and communicated my sentiments on that subject to Mr. Tomlins, the surgeon, who told me, that Crampley, by the dint of some friends about the admiral, had procured a commission constituting him lieutenant on board the Lizzard: and advised me, now he was my superior officer, to behave with some respect towards him, or else he would find a thousand opportunities of using me ill.—This advice was a bitter potion to me, whom pride and resentment had rendered utterly incapable of the least submission to, or even of reconciliation with the wretch, who had, on many occasions, treated me so inhumanly: However, I resolved to have as little connexion as possible with him, and to ingratiate myself as much as I could with the rest of the officers, whose friendship might be a bulwark to defend me from the attempts of his malice.

In less than a week we sailed on a cruize, and having got round the east end of the island, had the good fortune to take a Spanish Barcolongo,[1] with her prize, which was an English ship bound for Bristol, that sailed from Jamaica a fortnight before, without convoy. All the prisoners who were well, were put on shore on the north-side of the island; the prizes were manned with Englishmen, and the command of the Barcolongo, given to my friend the master's mate, with orders to carry them into Port Morant,[2] and there to remain until the Lizzard's cruize should be ended, at which time she would touch at the same place in her way to Port-Royal.[3]—With him I was sent to attend the wounded Spaniards as well as Englishmen, who amounted to sixteen, and to take care of them on shore, in a house that was to be hired as an hospital.—This destination gave me a great deal of pleasure, as I would, for some time, be freed from the arrogance of Crampley, whose inveteracy against me had already broke out on two or three occasions, since he was become a lieutenant.—My mess-mate, who very much resembled my uncle, both in figure and disposition, treated me on board of the prize, with the utmost civility and confidence; and among other favours, made me a present of a silver hilted hanger, and a pair of pistols mounted with the same metal, which fell to his share in plundering the enemy.—We arrived safely at Morant, and going ashore, pitched upon an empty store-house, which we hired for the reception of the wounded, who were brought to it next day, with beds and other necessaries; and four of the ship's company appointed to attend them, and obey me.

CHAPTER XXXVI

A strange adventure—in consequence of which I am extremely happy——Crampley does me ill offices with the captain: But his malice is defeated by the good-nature and friendship of the surgeon——we return to Port-Royal——our captain gets the command of a larger ship, and is succeeded by an old man——Brayl is provided for——we receive orders to sail for England

WHEN my patients were all in a fair way, my companion and commander, whose name was Brayl,[4] carried me up the country to the house of a rich planter, with whom he was acquainted; where we were sumptuously entertained, and in the evening set out on our return to the ship. When we had walked about a mile by moon-light, we perceived a horseman behind us, who coming up, wished us *good even*, and asked which way we went: His voice, which was quite familiar to me, no sooner struck my ear, than, in spite of all my resolution and reflection, my hair bristled up, and I was seized with a violent fit of trembling, which Brayl mis-interpreting, bid me be under no concern, for he would stand by me.—I told him, he was mistaken in the cause of my disorder; and addressing my-self to the person on horse-back, said, 'I could have sworn by your voice, that you was a dear friend of mine, if I had not been certain of his death.'—To this, after some pause, he replied, 'There are many voices as well as faces that resemble one another; but pray, what was your friend's name?' I satisfied him in that particular, and gave a short detail of the melancholy fate of Thomson, not without many sighs and some tears. A silence ensued which lasted some minutes, and then the conversation turned on indifferent subjects, till we arrived at a house on the road, where the horseman alighted, and begged with so much earnestness, that we would go in and drink a bowl of punch with him, that we could not resist.—But if I was alarmed at his voice, what must my amazement be, when I discovered by the light, the very person of my lamented friend! Perceiving my confusion, which was extreme, he clasped me in his arms and bedewed my face with tears.—It was some time ere I re-covered the use of my reason, overpowered with this event, and longer still before I could speak. So that all I was capable of, was to return his embraces, and to mingle the overflowings of my joy with his; while honest Brayl, affected with the scene, wept as fast as either of us, and signified his participation of our happiness, by hugging us both, and capering about the room like a mad-man.—At length I retrieved the use of my tongue, and cried, 'Is it possible, can you be my friend Thomson? No certainly, alas! he was drowned! and I am now under the deception of a dream!'—Then I relapsed into tears.—He was at great pains to convince me of his being the individual person whom I regretted, and bidding me sit down and compose myself, promised to explain his sudden dis-appearance from the Thunder, and to account for his being at present in the land of the living.—This he acquitted himself of, after I had drank a glass of punch, and recollected myself; by informing us, that with a determination to rid himself of a miserable existence, he had gone in the night-time to the head, while the ship was on her way, from whence he slipped down, as softly as he could by the bows, into the sea, where, after he was heartily ducked, he began to repent of his precipitation, and as he could swim very well, kept himself above water, in hopes of being taken up by some of the ships astern;—that in this situation, he hailed a large vessel and begged to be taken in, but was answered, that she was a heavy sailor, and therefore they did not chuse to lose time, by bringing to; however, they threw an old chest over-board, for his convenience, and told him, that some of the ships a-stern would certainly save him;—that no other vessel came within sight or cry of him, for the space of three hours, during which time he had the mortification of finding himself in the middle of the ocean alone, without support or resting-place, but what a few crazy boards afforded; till at last, he discerned a small sloop steering towards him, upon which he set up his throat, and had the good fortune to be heard and rescued from the dreary waste, by their boat, which was hoisted out on purpose. —'I was no sooner brought on board (continued he) than I fainted; and when I recovered my senses, found myself in bed, regaled with a most noisome smell of onions and cheese, which made me think at first, that I was in my own hammock, along-side of honest Morgan, and that all which had passed was no more than a dream. —Upon enquiry I understood that I was on board of a schooner belonging to Rhode Island, bound for Jamaica, with a cargo of geese, pigs, onions, and cheese; and that the master's name was Robertson, by birth a North Briton, whom I knew at first sight to be an old school-fellow of mine.—When I discovered myself to him, he was transported with surprize and joy, and begged to know the occasion of my misfortune, which I did not think fit to disclose, because I knew his notions with regard to religion, were very severe and confined; therefore contented myself with telling him, I fell over-board by accident; but made no scruple of explaining the nature of my disagreeable station, and of acquainting him with my determined purpose never to return to the Thunder man of war.' —'Although he was not of my opinion in that particular, knowing that I must lose my cloaths, and what pay was due to me, unless I went back to my duty; yet, when I described the circumstances of the hellish life I led, under the tyrannic sway of Oakhum and Mackshane; and among other grievances, hinted a dissatisfaction at the irreligious deportment of my ship-mates, and the want of the true Presbyterian gospel doctrine; he changed his sentiments, and conjured me with great vehemence and zeal to lay aside all thoughts of rising in the navy; and that he might shew how much he had my interest at heart, undertook to provide for me in some shape or other, before he should leave Jamaica.—This he performed to my heart's desire, by recommending me to a gentleman of fortune, with whom I have lived ever since, in quality of surgeon and overseer to his plantations.—He and his lady are now at Kingston, so that I am, for the present, master of this house, to which from my soul, I bid you welcome, and hope you will favour me with your company during the remaining part of the night.'—I needed not a second invitation; but Mr. Brayl, who was a diligent and excellent officer, could not be persuaded to sleep out of the ship: However, he supped with us, and after having drank a chearful glass, set out for the vessel, which was not above three miles from the place, escorted by a couple of stout Negroes, whom Mr. Thomson ordered to conduct him.——Never were two friends more happy in the conversation of one another than we, for the time it lasted: I related to him the particulars of our attempt upon Carthagena, of which he had heard but an imperfect account; and he gratified me with a narration of every little incident of his life since we parted.—He assured me, it was with the utmost reluctance, he could resist his inclination of coming down to Port-Royal to see Morgan and me, of whom he had heard no tidings since the day of our separation; but that he was restrained by the fear of being detained as a deserter.—He told me, that when he heard my voice in the dark, he was almost as much surprized as I was at seeing him afterwards; and in the confidence of friendship, disclosed a passion he entertained for the only daughter of the gentleman with whom he lived, who, by his description, was a very amiable young lady, and did not disdain his addresses; that he was very much favoured by her parents, and did not despair of obtaining their consent to the match, which would at once render him independent of the world.—I congratulated him on his good fortune, which he protested should never make him forget his friend; and towards morning we betook ourselves to rest.

Next day he accompanied me to the ship, where Mr. Brayl entertained him at dinner, and having spent the afternoon together, he took his leave of us in the evening, after he had forced upon me ten pistoles,[1] as a small token of his affection.—In short, while we staid here, we saw one another every day, and generally eat at the same table, which was plentifully supplied by him, with all kinds of poultry, butcher's meat, oranges, limes, lemons, pine-aples, Madeira-wine, and excellent rum; so that this small interval of ten days, was by far the most agreeable period of my life.

At length, the Lizzard arrived; and as my patients were all fit for duty, they and I were ordered on board of her, where I understood from Mr. Tomlins, that there was a dryness[1] between the lieutenant and him, on my account; that rancorous villain having taken the opportunity of my absence, to fill the captain's ears with a thousand scandalous stories, to my prejudice; among other things affirming, that I had been once transported for theft, and that when I was in the Thunder man of war I had been whipt for the same crime.— The surgeon, on the other hand, having heard my whole story from my own mouth, defended me strenuously, and in the course of that good-natured office, recounted all the instances of Crampley's malice against me, while I remained on board of that ship.—Which declaration, while it satisfied the captain of my innocence, made the lieutenant as much my defender's enemy as mine. This infernal be-haviour of Crampley, with regard to me, added such fuel to my former resentment, that at certain times, I was quite beside myself with the desire of revenge, and was even tempted to pistol him on the quarter-deck, though an infamous death must inevitably have been my reward.—But the surgeon, who was my confident, argued against such a desperate action so effectually, that I stifled the flame which consumed me for the present, and resolved to wait a more convenient opportunity.—In the mean time, that Mr. Tomlins might be the more convinced of the wrongs I suffered by this fellow's slander, I begged he would go and visit Mr. Thomson, whose wonderful escape I had made him acquainted with, and enquire of him into the particulars of my conduct, while he was my fellow-mate. This the surgeon complied with, more through curi-osity to see a person whose fate had been so extraordinary, than to confirm his good opinion of me, which, he assured me, was already firmly established.—He therefore set out for the dwelling-place of my friend, with a letter of introduction from me; and being re-ceived with all the civility and kindness I expected, returned to the ship, not only satisfied with my character, beyond the power of doubt or insinuation, but also charmed with the affability and conversation of Thomson, who loaded him and me with presents of fresh stock, liquors and fruit. As he would not venture to come and see us on board, lest Crampley should know and detain him, when the time of our departure approached, I obtained leave to go and bid him farewell.—After we had vowed an everlasting friendship, he pressed upon me a purse with four double dubloons,[1] which I refused as long as I could, without giving umbrage; and having cordially embraced each other, I returned on board, where I found a small box, with a letter directed for me, to the care of Mr. Tomlins.—Knowing the superscription to be of Thomson's handwriting, I opened it with some surprize, and learned that this generous friend, not contented with loading me with the presents already mentioned, had sent for my use and acceptance, half a dozen fine shirts, and as many linnen waistcoats and caps, with twelve pair of new thread-stockings.——Being thus provided with money, and all necessaries for the comfort of life, I began to look upon myself as a gentleman of some consequence, and felt my pride dilate apace.

Next day we sailed for Port-Royal, where we arrived safely with our prizes; and as there was nothing to do on board, I went ashore, and having purchased a laced waistcoat, with some other cloaths at a vendue,[2] made a swaggering figure for some days, among the taverns, where I ventured to play a little at hazard,[3] and came off with fifty pistoles in my pocket. Mean while our captain was promoted to a ship of twenty guns, and the command of the Lizzard given to a man turned of fourscore, who had been lieutenant since the reign of king William[4] to this time, and notwithstanding his long service, would have probably died in that station, had he not employed some prize-money he had lately received, to make interest with his superiors. My friend Brayl was also made an officer about the same time, after he had served in quality of midshipman and mate five and twenty years. Soon after these alterations, the admiral pitched upon our ship to carry home dispatches for the ministry; accordingly we set sail for England, having first scrubbed her bottom,[5] and taken in provision and water for the occasion.

CHAPTER XXXVII

We depart for Europe——a misunderstanding arises between
the captain and surgeon, through the scandalous aspersions
of Crampley——the captain dies—Crampley tyrannizes over
the surgeon, who falls a victim to his cruelty——I am also ill
used——the ship strikes—the behaviour of Crampley and the
seamen on that occasion.——I get on shore, challenge the
captain to single combat——am treacherously knocked
down, wounded and robbed

Now that I could return to my native country in a creditable way,
I felt excessive pleasure in finding myself out of sight of that fatal
island, which has been the grave of so many Europeans; and as I was
accommodated with every thing to render the passage agreeable, I
resolved to enjoy myself as much as the insolence of Crampley
would permit.—This insidious slanderer had found means already
to cause a misunderstanding between the surgeon and captain, who
by his age and infirmities was rendered intolerably peevish, his disposition having also been sowred by a long course of disappointments, and had a particular aversion to all young men, especially to
surgeons, whom he considered as unnecessary animals on board of a
ship.—In consequence of these sentiments, he never consulted the
doctor, notwithstanding his being seized with a violent fit of the
gout and gravel,[1] but applied to a cask of Holland-gin, which was
his sovereign prescription against all distempers: But whether he
was at this time too sparing, or took an overdose of his cordial,
certain it is, he departed in the night, without any ceremony, which
indeed was a thing he always despised, and was found stiff, next
morning, to the no small satisfaction of Crampley, who succeeded
to the command of the vessel.—For that very reason, Mr. Tomlins
and I had no cause to rejoice at this event, fearing that the tyranny
of our new commander would now be as unlimited as his power.—
The first day of his command justified our apprehension: For on
pretence that the decks were too much crowded, he ordered the
surgeon's hen-coops, with all his fowls, to be thrown over-board;
and at the same time, prohibited him and me from appearing on the
quarter-deck. Mr. Tomlins could not help complaining of these

injuries, and in the course of his expostulation dropped some hasty words, of which Crampley taking hold, confined him to his cabbin, where, in a few days, for want of air, he was attacked by a fever, which soon put an end to his life, after having made his will, by which he bequeathed all his estate, personal and real, to his sister; and left to me his watch and instruments, as remembrances of his friendship.—I was penetrated with grief on this melancholy occasion! the more because there was no body on board, to whom I could communicate my griefs, or of whom I could receive the least consolation or advice.—Crampley was so far from discovering the least remorse for his barbarity, at the news of the surgeon's death, that he insulted his memory in the most abusive manner, and affirmed he had poisoned himself out of pure fear, dreading to be brought to a court-martial for mutiny; for which reason, he would not suffer the service of the dead to be read over his body before it was thrown over-board.

Nothing but a speedy deliverance could have supported me under the brutal sway of this bashaw; who to render my life the more irksome, signified to my mess-mates, a desire that I should be expelled from their society.—This was no sooner hinted, than they granted his request; and I was fain to eat in a solitary manner by myself during the rest of the passage, which however soon drew to a period.

We had been seven weeks at sea, when the gunner told the captain, that by his reckoning we must be in soundings,[1] and desired he would order the lead to be heaved.—Crampley swore, he did not know how to keep the ship's way, for we were not within a hundred leagues of soundings, and therefore he would not give himself the trouble to cast the lead.—Accordingly, we continued our course all that afternoon and night, without shortening sail, although the gunner pretented to discover Scilly light;[2] and next morning protested in form against the captain's conduct; for which he was put in confinement.—We discovered no land all that day, and Crampley was still so infatuated as to neglect sounding: But at three o'clock in the morning, the ship struck, and remained fast on a sand bank. This accident alarmed the whole crew; the boat was immediately hoisted out, but as we could not discern which way the shore lay, we were obliged to wait for day-light. In the mean time, the wind increased, and the waves beat against the sloop with such violence, that we expected she would have gone to pieces. The gunner was released and consulted: He advised the captain to cut away the

mast, in order to lighten her; this was performed without success:
The sailors seeing things in a desperate situation, according to
custom,[1] broke up the chests belonging to the officers, dressed
themselves in their cloaths, drank their liquors without ceremony;
and drunkenness, tumult, and confusion ensued.—In the midst of
this uproar, I went below to secure my own effects; and found the
carpenter's mate hewing down the purser's cabbin with his hatchet,
whistling all the while, with great composure. When I asked his
intention in so doing, he replied very calmly, 'I only want to taste
the purser's rum, that's all, master.'—At that instant the purser
coming down, and seeing his effects going to wreck, complained
bitterly of the injustice done to him, and asked the fellow what
occasion he had for liquor, when in all likelihood he would be in
eternity in a few minutes. 'All's one for that (said the plunderer)
let us live while we can.'—'Miserable wretch that thou art! (cried
the purser) what must be thy lot in the other world, if thou diest in
the commission of robbery?'——'Why, hell, I suppose, (replied the
other, with great deliberation,)' while the purser fell on his knees
and begged of heaven that we might not all perish for the sake of one
Jonas.[2]——During this dialogue, I cloathed myself in my best
apparel, girded on my hanger, stuck my pistols loaded in my belt,
disposed of all my valuable moveables about my person, and came
upon deck, with a resolution of taking the first opportunity to get
on shore, which, when the day broke, appeared at the distance of
three miles a-head.—Crampley finding his efforts to get the ship off
ineffectual, determined to consult his own safety, by going into the
boat, which he had no sooner done, than the ship's company
followed so fast, that she would have sunk along-side, had not some
one wiser than the rest cut the rope and put off.—But before this
happened, I had made several attempts to get in, and was always
baulked by the captain, who was so eager in excluding me, that he
did not mind the endeavours of any other body.—Enraged at this
inhuman partiality, and seeing the rope cut, I pulled one of my
pistols from my belt, and cocking it, swore I would shoot any man
who should presume to obstruct my entrance. So saying, I leaped
with my full exertion, and got on board of the boat with the loss of
the skin of one of my shins.—I chanced in my descent to overturn
Crampley, who no sooner got up than he struck at me several times
with a cutlass, and ordered the men to throw me overboard; but
they were too anxious about their own safety to mind what he said.—

Though the boat was very deeply loaded, and the sea terribly high, we made shift to get upon dry land in less than an hour after we parted from the sloop.—As soon as I set foot on *terra firma*, my indignation, which had boiled so long within me, broke out against Crampley, whom I immediately challenged to single combat, presenting my pistols, that he might take his choice: He took one without hesitation, and before I could cock the other fired in my face throwing the pistol after the shot.—I felt myself stunned, and imagining the bullet had entered my brain, discharged mine as quick as possible, that I might not die unrevenged; then flying upon my antagonist, knocked out several of his fore-teeth with the but-end of the piece; and would certainly have made an end of him with that instrument, had he not disengaged himself, and seized his cutlass, which he had given to his servant when he received the pistol. Seeing him armed in this manner, I drew my hanger, and having flung my pistol at his head, closed with him in a transport of fury, and thrust my weapon into his mouth, which it enlarged on one side to his ear.—Whether the smart of this wound disconcerted him, or the unevenness of the ground made him reel, I know not, but he staggered some paces back: I followed close, and with one stroke cut the tendons of the back of his hand, upon which his cutlass dropt, and he remained defenceless.—I know not with what cruelty my rage might have inspired me, if I had not at that instant, been felled to the ground by a blow on the back part of my head, which deprived me of all sensation.—When I received the use of my understanding, I found myself alone in a desolate place, stript of my cloaths, money, watch, buckles, and every thing but my shoes, stockings, breeches, and shirt.—What a discovery must this be to me, who but an hour before, was worth sixty guineas in cash! I cursed the hour of my birth, the parents that gave me being, the sea that did not swallow me up, the poignard of the enemy, which could not find the way to my heart, the villainy of those who had left me in that miserable condition, and in the exstacy of despair, resolved to lie still where I was and perish.

CHAPTER XXXVIII

*I get up, and crawl into a barn, where I am in danger of
perishing thro' the fear of the country people——their
inhumanity——I am succoured by a reputed witch——her story
——her advice——she recommends me as a valet to a single
lady, whose character she explains*

But as I lay ruminating, my passion insensibly abated; I considered
my situation in quite another light from that in which it appeared to
me at first, and the result of my deliberation was to get up if I
could, and crawl to the next inhabited place for assistance.—With
some difficulty I got upon my legs, and having examined my body,
found I had received no other injury than two large contused wounds,
one on the fore and another on the hinder part of my head; which
seemed to be occasioned by the same weapon; namely, the butt-end
of a pistol. I looked towards the sea, but could discern no remains of
the ship; which made me conclude she had gone to pieces, and that
those who remained in her had perished: But, as I afterwards
learned, the gunner, who had more sagacity than Crampley, observing that it was flood when we left her, and that she would
possibly float at high-water, made no noise about getting on shore,
but continued on deck, in hopes of bringing her safe into some
harbour, after the commander had deserted her, for which he expected, no doubt, to be handsomely rewarded.—This he accordingly
performed, and was promised great things by the admiralty for
saving his Majesty's ship; but I never heard he reaped the fruits of
his expectation.—As for my own part, I directed my course towards a small cottage I perceived, and in the road picked up a seaman's old jacket, which I suppose the thief who dressed himself in
my cloaths, had thrown away; this was a very comfortable acquisition to me, who was almost stiff with cold: I therefore put it on, and
as my natural heat revived, my wounds, which had left off bleeding,
burst out afresh; so that finding myself excessively exhausted, I
was about to lie down in the fields, when I discovered a barn on my
left hand, within a few yards of me; thither I made shift to stagger,
and finding the door open, went in, but saw no body; upon which
I threw myself upon a truss of straw, hoping to be soon relieved by

some person or other.—I had not lain here many minutes, when I saw a country-man come in with a pitch-fork in his hand, which he was upon the point of thrusting into the straw that concealed me, and in all probability would have done my business, had I not uttered a dreadful groan, after having essayed in vain to speak.— This melancholy note alarmed the clown, who started back, and discovering a body all besmeared with blood, stood trembling, with the pitch-fork extended before him, his hair erect, his eyes staring, his nostrils dilated, and his mouth wide open.—At another time, I should have been much diverted with this figure, which preserved the same attitude very near a quarter of an hour, during which time I made many unsuccessful efforts to implore his compassion and assistance; but my tongue failed me, and my language was only a repetition of groans: At length an old man arrived, who seeing the other in such a posture, cried, 'Mercy upon en! the leaad's bewitch'd!—why Dick, beest thou besayd thyself?'[1]—Dick, without moving his eyes from the object that terrified him, replied, 'O vather! vather! here be either the devil or a dead mon: I doan't know which o'en, but a groans woundily.'—The father, whose eyesight was none of the best, pulled out his spectacles, and having applied them to his nose, reconnoitred me over his son's shoulder: But no sooner did he behold me, than he was seized with a fit of shaking, even more violent than Dick's, and with a broken accent addressed me thus: 'In the name of the Vather, Zun, and Holy Ghosty, I charge you an you been Satan to begone to the Red-Zea; but an you be a moordered mon, speak, that you may have a christom[2] burial.'—As I was not in a condition to satisfy him in this particular, he repeated his conjuration to no purpose; and they continued a good while in the agonies of fear.—At length the father proposed, that the son should draw nearer and take a more distinct view of the apparition; but Dick was of opinion that his father should advance first, as being an old man past his labour, and if he received any mischief, the loss would be the smaller; whereas he himself might escape, and be useful in his generation.—This prudential reason had no effect upon the senior, who still kept Dick between me and him.—In the mean time I endeavoured to raise one hand as a signal of distress, but had only strength sufficient to cause a rustling among the straw, which discomposed the young peasant so much, that he sprung out at the door, and overthrew his father in his flight.—The old gentleman would not spend time in getting up, but crawled backwards like a crab, with great speed, till he had got over the threshold, mumbling exorcisms all the way.—I was exceedingly mortified to find myself in danger of perishing through the ignorance and cowardice of these clowns; and felt my spirits decay apace, when an old woman entered the barn, followed by the two fugitives, and with great intrepidity advanced to the place where I lay, saying, 'If it be the devil I fearen not, and for a dead mon a can do us no harm.'—When she saw my condition, she cried 'Here be no devil, but in youren fool's head.—Here be a poor miserable wretch, bleeding to death, and if he dies, we must be at the charge of burying him; therefore Dick, go vetch the old wheel-barrow and puten in, and carry him to good-man Hodge's[1] back-door, he is more eable than we to lay out money upon poor vagrants.'——Her advice was taken, and immediately put in execution: I was rolled to the other farmer's door, where I was tumbled out like a heap of dung; and would certainly have fallen a prey to the hogs, if my groans had not disturbed the family, and brought some of them out to view my situation.—But Hodge resembled the Jew more than the good Samaritan,[2] and ordered me to be carried to the house of the parson, whose business it was to practise as well as to preach charity: observing that it was sufficient for him to pay his *quota* toward the maintenance of the poor belonging to his own parish.— When I was set down at the vicar's gate, he fell into a mighty passion, and threatned to excommunicate him who sent as well as those who brought me, unless they would move me immediately to another place.—About this time I fainted with the fatigue I had undergone, and afterwards understood that I was bandied from door to door through a whole village, no body having humanity enough to administer the least relief to me, until an old woman, who was suspected of witchcraft by the neighbourhood, hearing of my distress, received me into her house, and having dressed my wounds, brought me to myself with cordials of her own preparing. —I was treated with great care and tenderness by this grave matron, who, after I had recovered some strength, desired to know the particulars of my last disaster.——This piece of satisfaction I could not refuse to one who had saved my life, therefore related all my adventures without exaggeration or reserve. She seemed surprised at the vicissitudes I had undergone, and drew a happy presage of my future life, from my past sufferings, then launched out into the praise of adversity with so much ardour and good sense, that I concluded she was a person who had seen better days, and conceived a longing desire to hear her story.—She perceived my drift by some words I dropped, and smiling, told me, there was nothing either entertaining or extraordinary in the course of her fortune; but however, she would communicate it to me, in consideration of the confidence I had reposed in her.—'It is of little consequence (said she) to tell the names of my parents, who are dead many years ago: let it suffice to assure you, they were wealthy, and had no other child than me, so that I was looked upon as heiress to a considerable estate, and tiezed[1] with addresses on that account. Among the number of my admirers, there was a young gentleman of no fortune, whose sole dependence was on his promotion in the army, in which at that time he bore a lieutenant's commission.—I conceived an affection for this amiable officer, which in a short time encreased to a violent passion, and, without entering into minute circumstances, married him privately.—We had not enjoyed one another long, in stolen interviews, when he was ordered with his regiment to Flanders; but before he set out, it was agreed between us, that he should declare our marriage to my father by letter, and implore his pardon for the step we had taken without his approbation.—This was done while I was abroad visiting, and just as I was about to return home, I received a letter from my father, importing, that since I had acted so undutifully and meanly, as to marry a beggar, without his privity or consent, to the disgrace of his family, as well as the disappointment of his hopes, he renounced me to the miserable fate I had entailed upon myself, and charged me never to set foot within his doors again.—This rigid sentence was confirmed by my mother, who, in a postscript, gave me to understand that her sentiments were exactly conformable to those of my father, and that I might save myself the trouble of making any applications, for her resolution was unalterable.—Thunderstruck with my evil fortune, I called a coach and drove to my husband's lodgings, where I found him waiting the event of his letter.—Though he could easily divine by my looks, the issue of his declaration, he read with great steadiness the epistle I had received; and with a smile full of tenderness, which I shall never forget, embraced me, saying, *I believe the good lady your mother might have spared herself the trouble of the last part of her postscript.—Well, my dear Betty, you must lay aside all thoughts of a coach, till I can procure the command of a regiment.*——Thus unconcerned behaviour, while

Chapter XXXVIII

it enabled me to support my reverse of fortune, at the same time endeared him to me the more, by convincing me of his disinterested views in espousing me.—I was next day boarded in company with the wife of another officer, who had long been friend and confident of my husband, at a village not far from London, where they parted with us in the most melting manner, went to Flanders, and were killed in sight of one another at the battle of the Wood.[1] Why should I tire you with a description of our unutterable sorrow at the fatal news of this event, the remembrance of which now fills my aged eyes with tears! When our grief subsided a little, and reflection came to our aid, we found ourselves deserted by the whole world, and in danger of perishing for want: Whereupon we made application for the pension, and were put upon the list. Then vowing eternal friendship, sold our jewels and superfluous cloaths, retired to this place (which is in the county of Sussex) bought this little house, where we lived many years in a solitary manner, indulging our mutual sorrow, 'till it pleased heaven to call away my companion, two years ago; since which time I have lingered out an unhappy being, in hopes of a speedy dissolution, when I promise myself the eternal reward of all my cares.—In the mean time, (continued she) I must inform you of the character I bear among my neighbours. ——My conversation being different from that of the inhabitants of the village, my recluse way of life, my skill in curing distempers, which I acquired from books since I settled here, and lastly, my age, have made the common people look upon me as something pre- ternatural, and I am actually at this hour believed to be a witch. The parson of the parish, whose acquaintance I have not been at much pains to cultivate, taking umbrage at my supposed disrespect, has contributed not a little towards the confirmation of this opinion, by dropping certain hints to my prejudice, among the vulgar, who are also very much scandalized at my entertaining this poor tabby cat with the collar about her neck, which was a favourite of my de- ceased companion.'

The whole behaviour of this venerable person, was so primitive, innocent, sensible, and humane, that I contracted a filial respect for her, and begged her advice with regard to my future conduct, as soon as I was in a condition to act for myself.—She dissuaded me from a design I had formed of travelling to London in hopes of re- trieving my cloaths and pay, by returning to my ship, which by this time, I read in a newspaper, was safely arrived in the river Thames:

'Because (said she) you run the hazard of being treated not only as a deserter, in quitting the sloop, but also as a mutineer in assaulting your commanding officer, to the malice of whose revenge you will moreover be exposed.'—She then promised to recommend me as a servant to a single lady of her acquaintance, who lived in the neighbourhood with her nephew, who was a young fox-hunter of great fortune, where I might be very happy, provided I could bear with the disposition and manners of my mistress, which were somewhat whimsical and particular.—But above all things, she counselled me to conceal my story, the knowledge of which would effectually poison my entertainment; for it was a maxim among most people of condition, that no gentleman in distress ought to be admitted into a family, as a domestick, lest he become proud, lazy, and insolent.— I was fain to embrace this humble proposal, because my affairs were desperate; and in a few days was hired by this lady, to serve in quality of her footman; being represented by my hostess, as a young man, who having been sent to sea by his relations against his inclinations, was shipwrecked and robbed, which had encreased his disgust to that way of life so much, that he rather chose to go to service on shore than enter himself on board of any other ship.— Before I took possession of my new place, she gave me a sketch of my mistress's character, that I might know better how to regulate my conduct. 'Your lady (said she) is a maiden of forty years, not so remarkable for her beauty as her learning and taste, which is famous all over the county.—Indeed she is a perfect female *virtuosi*,[1] and so eager after the pursuit of knowledge, that she neglects her person even to a degree of sluttishness; this negligence, together with her contempt for the male part of the creation, gives her nephew no great concern, as by that means, he will probably keep her fortune, which is considerable, in the family. He therefore permits her to live in her own way, which is something extraordinary, and gratifies her in all her whimsical desires.—Her apartment is at some distance from the other inhabited parts of the house; and consists of a dining-room, bed-chamber and study: She keeps a cook-maid, waiting-woman, and footman of her own, and seldom eats or converses with any of the family, but her niece, who is a very lovely creature, and humours her aunt often to the prejudice of her own health, by sitting up with her whole nights together; for your mistress is too much of a philosopher to be swayed by the customs of the world, and never sleeps or eats as other people do.

——Among other odd notions, she professes the principles of Rosi-crucius,[1] and believes the earth, air, and sea are inhabited by in-visible beings, with whom it is possible for the human species to entertain correspondence and intimacy, on the easy condition of living chaste.—As she hopes one day to be admitted into an ac-quaintance of this kind, she no sooner heard of me and my cat, than she paid me a visit, with a view, as she has since owned, to be intro-duced to my familiar; and was greatly mortified to find herself dis-appointed in her expectation. Being by this visionary turn of mind, abstracted as it were from the world, she cannot advert to the com-mon occurrences of life; and therefore is frequently so absent as to commit very strange mistakes and extravagancies, which you will do well to rectify and repair, as your prudence shall suggest.'

CHAPTER XXXIX

My reception by that lady——I become enamoured of Narcissa ——recount the particulars of my last misfortune——acquire the good opinion of my mistress——an account of the young 'Squire—I am made acquainted with more particulars of Narcissa's situation—conceive a mortal hatred against Sir Timothy—I examine my lady's library and performances— her extravagant behaviour

FRAUGHT with these useful instructions, I repaired to the place of her habitation, and was introduced by the waiting-woman, to the presence of my lady, who had not before seen me.—She sat in her study, with one foot on the ground, and the other upon a high stool at some distance from her seat; her sandy locks hung down in a disorder I cannot call beautiful from her head, which was deprived of its coif, for the benefit of scratching with one hand, while she held the stump of a pen in the other.——Her fore-head was high and wrinkled, her eyes large, grey and prominent; her nose long, sharp and aquiline; her mouth of vast capacity; her visage meagre and freckled, and her chin peeked like a shoemaker's paring-knife: Her upper-lip contained a large quantity of plain Spanish,[2] which by continual falling, had embroidered her neck that was not natur-ally very white, and the breast of her gown, that flowed loose about her with a negligence truly poetic, discovering linen that was very

fine and to all appearance, never *washed but in Castalian streams.*[1]—
Around her lay heaps of books, globes, quadrants, telescopes, and
other learned apparatus: Her snuff-box stood at her right hand, at
her left lay her handkerchief sufficiently used, and a convenience to
spit in appeared on one side of her chair.—Being in a reverie when
we entered, the maid did not think proper to disturb her; so that we
waited some minutes unobserved, during which time, she bit the
quill several times, altered her position, made many wry faces, and
at length, with an air of triumph, repeated aloud:

'Nor dare th' immortal Gods my rage oppose!'

Having committed her success to paper, she turned toward the
door, and perceiving us, cried, 'What's the matter?'—'Here's the
young man (replied my conductress) whom Mrs. Sagely recommended as a footman to your ladyship.' On this information, she
stared in my face a considerable time, and then asked my name,
which I thought proper to conceal under that of John Brown.—
After having surveyed me with a curious eye, she broke out into
'O! ay, thou wa'st shipwrecked I remember.——Whether didst
thou come on shore on the back of a whale or a dolphin?'[2] To this
I answered, I had swam ashore without any assistance.—Then she
demanded to know if I had ever been at the Hellespont, and swam
from Sestos to Abydos.[3] I replied in the negative: Upon which, she
bid the maid order a suit of new livery for me, and instruct me in the
articles of my duty; so saying, she spit in her snuffbox, and wiped
her nose with her cap which lay on the table, instead of a handkerchief.—We returned to the kitchin, where I was regaled by the
maids, who seemed to outvie with one another, in expressing their
regard for me.—From them I understood, that my business consisted in cleaning knives and forks, laying the cloth, waiting at
table, carrying messages, and attending my lady when she went
abroad.—There being a very good suit of livery in the house, which
had belonged to my predecessor deceased, I dressed myself in it,
and found it fitted me exactly, so that there was no occasion for
employing a taylor on my account.—I had not been long equipped
in this manner, when my lady's bell rung; upon which I ran up
stairs, and found her stalking about the room in her shift and under-
petticoat only. I would have immediately retired, as became me,
but she bid me come in, and air a clean shift for her; which having
done with some backwardness, she put it on before me without any

Chapter XXXIX

ceremony, and I verily believe was ignorant of my sex all the time, being quite absorpt in contemplation.—About four o'clock in the afternoon, I was ordered to lay the cloth, and place two covers, which I understood was for my mistress and her niece, whom I had not as yet seen.—Though I was not very dexterous at this operation, I performed it pretty well for a beginner, and when dinner was upon the table, saw my mistress approach accompanied with the young lady, whose name for the present shall be Narcissa.—So much sweetness appeared in the countenance and carriage of this amiable apparition, that my heart was captivated at first sight, and while dinner lasted I gazed upon her without intermission.—Her age seemed to be seventeen, her stature tall, her shape unexceptionable, her hair, that fell down upon her ivory neck in ringlets, black as jet; her arched eyebrows of the same colour; her eyes piercing, yet tender; her lips of the consistence and hue of cherries; her complexion clear, delicate and healthy; her aspect noble, ingen'ous and humane; and the whole so ravishingly delightful, that it was impossible for any creature, endued with sensibility, to see without admiring, and admire without loving her to excess! How often did I curse the servile station, that placed me so infinitely beneath the regard of this idol of my adoration! and how often did I bless my fate, that enabled me to enjoy daily the sight of so much perfection! When she spoke, I listened with pleasure; but when she spoke to me, my soul was thrilled with an exstasy of tumultuous joy! I was even so happy as to be the subject of their conversation: For Narcissa having observed me, said to her aunt, 'I see your new footman is come.' Then addressing herself to me, asked, with ineffable complacency, if I was the person who had been so cruelly used by robbers? When I satisfied her in this, she expressed a desire of knowing the particulars of my fortune both before and since my being shipwrecked: Hereupon (as Mrs. Sagely had counselled me) I told her, that I had been bound apprentice to the master of a ship, contrary to my inclination, which ship had foundered at sea;—that I and four more, who chanced to be on deck when she went down, made shift to swim to the shore, where my companions, after having overpowered me, stript me to the shirt, and left me, as they imagined, dead of the wounds I received in my own defence: Then I related the circumstances of my being found in a barn, with the inhuman treatment I met with from the country people and parson; which I perceived, drew tears from the charming creature's eyes! When I had finished my recital, my mistress said, '*Ma foy! le garçon est bien fait!*' To which opinion Narcissa assented, with a compliment to my understanding in the same language, that flattered my vanity extremely.

The conversation, among other subjects, turned upon the young 'Squire, whom my lady enquired after, under the title of the Savage; and was informed by her niece, that he was still in bed, repairing the fatigue of last night's debauch, and recruiting strength and spirits to undergo a fox-chace to-morrow morning, in company with Sir Timothy Thicket, 'Squire Bumper,[1] and a great many other gentlemen of the same stamp, whom he had invited on that occasion; so that by day-break, the whole house would be in an uproar.—This was a very disagreeable piece of news to the *virtuosi*, who protested she would stuff her ears with cotton when she went to bed, and take a dose of opium to make her sleep the more sound, that she might not be disturbed and distracted by the clamour of the brutes.

When their dinner was over, I and my fellow-servants sat down to ours in the kitchen, where I understood that Sir Timothy Thicket was a wealthy knight in the neighbourhood, between whom and Narcissa a match had been projected by her brother, who proposed at the same time to espouse Sir Timothy's sister; by which means, as their fortunes were pretty equal, the young ladies would be provided for, and their brothers be never the poorer; but that the ladies did not concur in the scheme, each of them entertaining a hearty contempt for the person allotted to her for a husband, by this agreement.—This information begat in me a mortal aversion to Sir Timothy, whom I looked upon as my rival, and cursed in my heart for his presumption.—Next morning by day-break, being awaked by the noise of the hunters and hounds, I got up to view the cavalcade, and had a sight of my competitor, whose accomplishments (the estate excluded) did not seem brilliant enough to give me much uneasiness with respect to Narcissa, who, I flattered myself, was not to be won by such qualifications as he was master of, either as to person or mind.—My mistress, notwithstanding her precaution, was so much disturbed by her nephew's company, that she did not rise till five o'clock in the afternoon: So that I had an opportunity of examining her study at leisure, to which I was strongly prompted by my curiosity.—Here I found a thousand scraps of her own poetry, consisting of three, four, ten, twelve and twenty lines, on an infinity of subjects, which, as whim inspired, she had begun, without constancy or capacity to bring to any degree of composition: But what was very extraordinary in a female poet, there was not the least mention made of love in any of her performances.—I counted fragments of five tragedies, the titles of which were, 'The stern Philosopher.—The double Murder.—The sacrilegious Traitor.—The fall of Lucifer;—And the Last Day.' From whence I gathered, that her disposition was gloomy, and her imagination delighted with objects of horror.—Her library was composed of the best English historians, poets, and philosophers; of all the French criticks and poets, and of a few books in Italian, chiefly poetry, at the head of which were Tasso and Ariosto,[1] pretty much used.—Besides these, translations of the classicks into French, but not one book in Greek or Latin; a circumstance that discovered her ignorance of these languages.—After having taken a full view of this collection, I retired, and at the usual time was preparing to lay the cloth, when I was told by the maid that her mistress was still in bed, and had been so affected with the notes of the hounds in the morning, that she actually believed herself a hare beset with the hunters; and begged a few greens to munch for her breakfast.—When I testified my surprize at this unaccountable imagination,[2] she let me know that her lady was very much subject to whims of this nature; sometimes fancying herself an animal, sometimes a piece of furniture, during which conceited transformations, it was very dangerous to come near her, especially when she represented a beast; for that lately, in the character of a cat, she had flown at her and scratched her face in a terrible manner;—that some months ago, she prophesied the general conflagration was at hand, and nothing would be able to quench it, but her water, which therefore she kept so long that her life was in danger; and she must needs have died of the retention, had they not found an expedient to make her evacuate by kindling a bonfire under her chamber window, and persuading her that the house was in flames; upon which, with great deliberation, she bid them bring all the tubs and vessels they could find, to be filled, for the preservation of the house, into one of which she immediately discharged the cause of her distemper.—I was also informed, that nothing contributed so much to the recovery of her reason, as musick, which was always administered on these occasions by Narcissa, who play'd perfectly well on the harpsicord, and to whom she (the maid) was just then going to intimate her aunt's disorder.—She was no sooner gone, than I was summoned by the bell to my lady's chamber, where I found her sitting squat on her hams, on the floor, in the manner of puss[1] when she listens to the cries of her pursuers.—When I appeared, she started up with an alarmed look, and sprung to the other side of the room to avoid me, whom, without doubt, she mistook for a beagle thirsting after her life.——Perceiving her extreme confusion, I retired, and on the stair-case met the adorable Narcissa coming up, to whom I imparted the situation of my mistress: She said not a word, but smiling with unspeakable grace, went into her aunt's apartment, and in a little time my ears were ravished with the effects of her skill.—She accompanied the instrument with a voice so sweet and melodious, that I did not wonder at the surprizing change it produced on the spirits of my mistress, which were soon composed to peace and sober reflection.

About seven o'clock the hunters arrived, with the skins of two foxes and one badger, carried before them as trophies of their success; and when they were about to sit down to dinner (or supper) Sir Timothy Thicket desired that Narcissa would honour the table with her presence: But this, notwithstanding her brother's threats and intreaties, she refused, on pretence of attending her aunt, who was indisposed; so that I enjoyed the satisfaction of seeing my rival mortified: But this disappointment made no great impression on him, who consoled himself with the bottle, of which the whole company became so enamoured, that after a most horrid uproar of laughing, singing, swearing, dancing, and fighting, they were all carried to bed in a state of utter oblivion.—My duty being altogether detached from the 'Squire and his family, I led a pretty easy and comfortable life, drinking daily intoxicating draughts of love from the charms of Narcissa, which brightened on my contemplation, every day, more and more.—Inglorious as my station was, I became blind to my own unworthiness, and even conceived hopes of one day enjoying this amiable creature, whose affability greatly encouraged these presumptuous thoughts.

CHAPTER XL

She is surprized at my learning——communicates her
performances to me——I impart some of mine to her——am
mortified at her faint praise——Narcissa approves of my
production——I gain an involuntary conquest over the cook-
wench and dairy-maid——their mutual resentment
and insinuations——the jealousy of their lovers

DURING this season of love and tranquillity, my muse, which had lain dormant so long, awoke, and produced several small performances on the subject of my flame: But as it concerned me nearly to remain undiscovered in my real character and sentiments, I was under a necessity of mortifying my desire of praise, by confining my works to my own perusal and applause.—In the mean time I strove to insinuate myself into the good opinion of both ladies; and succeeded so well, by my diligence and dutiful behaviour, that in a little time, I was at least a favourite servant; and frequently enjoyed the pleasure of hearing myself mentioned in French and Italian, with some degree of warmth and surprize, by the dear object of all my wishes, as a person who had so much of the gentleman in my appearance and discourse, that she could not for her soul treat me like a common lacquey.—My prudence and modesty were not long proof against these bewitching compliments. One day, while I waited at dinner, the conversation turned upon a knotty passage of Tasso's Gierusalem, which, it seems, had puzzled them both: After a great many unsatisfactory conjectures, my mistress taking the book out of her pocket, turned up the place in question, and read the sentence over and over without success; at length, despairing of finding the author's meaning, she turned to me, saying, 'Come hither, Bruno,[1] let us see what fortune will do for us; I will interpret to thee what goes before and what follows this obscure paragraph, the particular words of which I will also explain, that thou may'st, by comparing one with another, guess the sense of that which perplexes us.'—I was too vain to let slip this opportunity of displaying my talents, therefore, without hesitation, read and explained the whole of that which had disconcerted them, to the utter astonishment of both.—Narcissa's face and lovely neck

were overspread with blushes, from whence I drew a favourable
omen, while her aunt, after having stared at me a good while with a
look of amazement, exclaimed, 'In the name of heaven! Who art
thou?'—I told her I had picked up a smattering of Italian, during a
voyage up the Straits.¹—At this she shook her head, and observed,
that no smatterer could read as I had done.—She then desired to
know if I understood French, to which I answering in the affirmative: She asked if I was acquainted with the Latin and Greek; I
replied, 'A little.'—'Oho! (continued she) and with philosophy and
mathematicks, I suppose?'—I owned, I knew something of each.—
Whereupon she repeated her stare and interrogation.—I began to
repent my vanity, and in order to repair the fault I had committed,
said, it was not to be wondered at if I had a tolerable education,
because learning was so cheap in my country,² that every peasant
was a scholar; but I hoped her ladyship would think my understanding no exception to my character.—She was pleased to answer,
'No, no, God forbid.'—But during the rest of the time they sat at
table, they behaved with remarkable reserve.

This alteration gave me much uneasiness; and, I passed the night
without sleep, in melancholy reflections on the vanity of young men,
which prompts them to commit so many foolish actions, contrary
to their own sober judgment.—Next day, however, instead of
profiting by this self-condemnation, I yielded still more to the dictates of the principle I had endeavoured to chastize, and if fortune
had not befriended me more than prudence could expect, I should
have been treated with the contempt I deserved.—After breakfast,
my lady, who was a true author, bid me follow her into the study,
where she expressed herself thus: 'Since you are so learned, you
cannot be void of taste; therefore I am to desire your opinion of a
small performance in poetry, which I lately composed.—You must
know, I have planned a tragedy, the subject of which shall be the
murder of a prince before the altar, where he is busy at his de-
votions.—After the deed is perpetrated, the regicide³ will harrangue
the people, with the bloody dagger in his hand; and I have already
composed a speech, which I think will suit the character extremely.
—Here it is.'—Then taking up a scrape of paper, she read with
violent emphasis and gesture, as follows:

> 'Thus have I sent the simple king to hell,
> Without or coffin, shroud, or passing-bell:—

Chapter XL

To me, what are divine and human laws?
I court no sanction but my own applause!
Rapes, robb'ries, treasons yield my soul delight;
And human carnage gratifies my sight:
I drag the parent by the hoary hair,
And toss the sprawling infant on my spear,
While the fond mother's cries regale mine ear.
I fight, I vanquish, murder friends and foes;
Nor dare th'immortal gods my rage oppose.'

Though I did great violence to my understanding in praising this unnatural rhapsody, I nevertheless extolled it as a production that of itself deserved immortal fame; and beseeched her ladyship to bless the world with the fruits of those uncommon talents heaven had bestowed upon her.—She smiled with a look of self-complacency, and encouraged by the incense I had offered, communicated all her poetical works, which I applauded one by one, with as little candour as I had shewn at first.——Satiated with my flattery, which I hope my situation justified, she could not in conscience refuse me an opportunity of shining in my turn; and therefore, after a compliment to my nice discernment and taste, observed, that doubtless I must have produced something in that way myself, which she desired to see.—This was a temptation I could by no means resist.—I owned that while I was at college, I wrote some small detached pieces, at the desire of a friend who was in love; and at her request, repeated the following verses, which indeed my love for Narcissa had inspired.

On Celia playing on the harpsicord and singing[1]

I

When Sapho struck the quiv'ring wire,
The throbbing breast was all on fire:
And when she rais'd the vocal lay,
The captive soul was charm'd away!

II

But had the nymph, possess'd with these
Thy softer, chaster pow'r to please;
Thy beauteous air of sprightly youth,
Thy native smiles of artless truth;

III

The worm of grief, had never prey'd
On the forsaken, love-sick maid:
Nor had she mourn'd an happless flame,
Nor dash'd on rocks her tender frame.

My mistress paid me a cold compliment on the versification, which, she said, was elegant enough, but the subject beneath the pen of a true poet. I was extremely nettled at her indifference, and looked at Narcissa, who by this time had joined us, for her approbation, but she declined giving her opinion, protesting she was no judge of these matters: So that I was forced to retire, very much baulked in my expectation, which was generally a little too sanguine.—In the afternoon, however, the waiting-maid assured me that Narcissa had expressed her approbation of my performance with great warmth, and desired her to procure a copy of it, as for herself, that she (Narcissa) might have an opportunity to peruse it at leisure.—I was elated to an extravagant pitch at this intelligence, and immediately transcribed a fair copy of my Ode, which was carried to the dear charmer, together with another on the same subject, as follows:

I

Thy fatal shafts unerring move,
I bow before thine altar, love!
I feel thy soft, resistless flame
Glide swift through all my vital frame!

II

For while I gaze my bosom glows,
My blood in tides impetuous flows,
Hope, fear and joy alternate roll,
And floods of transports 'whelm my soul!

III

My fault'ring tongue attempts in vain
In soothing murmurs to complain,
My tongue some secret magick ties,
My murmurs sink in broken sighs!

Chapter XL

IV

Condemn'd to nurse eternal care,
And ever drop the silent tear,
Unheard I mourn, unknown I sigh,
Unfriended live, unpitied die!

Whether or not Narcissa discovered my passion, I could not learn from her behaviour, which, though always benevolent to me, was henceforth more reserved and less chearful.—While my thoughts aspired to a sphere so far above me, I had unwittingly made a conquest of the cook-wench and dairy-maid, who became so jealous of one another, that if their sentiments had been refined by education, it is probable one or other of them would have had recourse to poison or steel, to be revenged of her rival; but as their minds were happily adapted to their humble station, their mutual enmity was confined to scolding and fisty-cuffs, in which exercises they were both well skilled.—My good fortune did not long remain a secret; being disclosed by the frequent broils of these heroines, who kept no decorum in their encounters. The coachman and gardiner, who paid their devoirs to my admirers, each to his respective choice, alarmed at my success, laid their heads together, in order to concert a plan of revenge; and the former having been educated at the academy of Tottenham-court, undertook to challenge me to single combat; he accordingly, with many opprobrious invectives, bid me defiance, and offered to box with me for twenty guineas.—I told him, that although I believed myself a match for him, even at that work, I would not descend so far below the dignity of a gentleman, as to fight like a porter; but if he had any thing to say to me, I was his man at blunderbuss, musket, pistol, sword, hatchet, spit, cleaver, fork or needle;—'nay more, that if he gave his tongue any more saucy liberties at my expence, I would crop his ears without any ceremony.—This rhodomontade delivered with a stern countenance, and resolute tone, had the desired effect upon my antagonist, who, with some confusion, sneaked off, and gave his friend an account of his reception.—The story taking air among the servants, procured for me the title of Gentleman John, with which I was sometimes honoured, even by my mistress and Narcissa, who had been informed of the whole affair by the chamber-maid.—In the mean time, the rival queens[1] expressed their passion by all the ways in their power: The cook entertained me with choice bits, the dairy-maid with stroakings;[1] the first would often encourage me to declare myself, by complimenting me upon my courage and learning, and observing, that if she had a husband like me, to maintain order and keep accounts, she could make a great deal of money by setting up an eating-house at London, for gentlemen's servants on board-wages.—The other courted my affection, by shewing her own importance, and telling me, that many a substantial farmer in the neighbourhood would be glad to marry her; but she was resolved to please her eye, if she should plague her heart.—Then she would launch out into the praise of my proper person, and say, she was sure I would make a good husband, for I was very good-natured.—I began to be uneasy at the importunities of these inamoratas, whom at another time, perhaps, I might have pleased without the disagreeable sauce of matrimony; but at present, my whole soul was engrossed by Narcissa, and I could not bear the thoughts of doing any thing derogatory of the passion I entertained for her.

CHAPTER XLI

*Narcissa being in danger from the brutality of Sir Timothy,
is rescued by me, who revenge myself on my rival——I declare
my passion, and retreat to the sea-side——I am surrounded
by smugglers, and carried to Bulloign——I find my uncle
lieutenant Bowling, in great distress, and relieve him——
our conversation*

At certain intervals, my ambition would revive; I would despise myself for my tame resignation to my sordid fate, and revolve an hundred schemes for assuming the character of a gentleman, to which I was intitled by birth and education.—In these fruitless suggestions, time stole away unperceived, and I had already remained eight months in the station of a footman, when an accident happened, that put an end to my servitude, and for the present banished all hopes of succeeding in my love.

Narcissa went one day to visit Miss Thicket, who lived with her brother, within less than a mile of our house, and was persuaded to walk home in the cool of the evening, accompanied by Sir Timothy, who having a good deal of the brute in him, was instigated to use some unbecoming familiarities with her, encouraged by the solitariness of a field through which they passed.—The lovely creature was incensed at his rude behaviour, for which she reproached him in such a manner, that he lost all regard for decency and actually offered violence to this pattern of innocence and beauty.—But heaven would not suffer so much goodness to be violated; and sent me, who passing by accident near the place, was alarmed with her cries, to her succour.—What were the emotions of my soul, when I beheld Narcissa, almost sinking beneath the brutal force of this satyr! I flew like lightening to her rescue, which he perceiving, quitted his prey, and drew his hanger to chastise my presumption. —My indignation was too high to admit one thought of fear, so that rushing upon him, I struck his weapon out of his hand, and used my cudgel so successfully, that he fell to the ground, and lay, to all appearance, without sense.—Then I turned to Narcissa, who had swooned, and sitting down by her, gently raised her head, and supported it on my bosom, while with my hand around her waist, I kept her in that position. My soul was thrilled with tumultuous joy, at feeling the object of my dearest wishes within my arms; and while she lay insensible, I could not refrain from applying my cheek to her's, and ravishing a kiss: In a little time, the blood began to revisit her face, she opened her enchanting eyes, and having recollected her late situation, said, with a look full of tender acknowledgment, 'Dear John, I am eternally obliged to you!' So saying, she made an effort to rise, in which I assisted her, and she proceeded to the house, leaning upon me all the way. I was a thousand times tempted by this opportunity to declare my passion, but the dread of disobliging her, restrained my tongue. We had not got an hundred paces from the scene of her distress, when I perceived Sir Timothy get up and move homeward; a circumstance, which, though it gave me some satisfaction, in as much as I thereby knew I had not killed him, filled me with just apprehension of his resentment, which I found myself in no condition to withstand: especially when I considered his intimacy with our 'Squire, to whom I knew he would easily justify himself for what he had done, by imputing it to his love, and desiring his brother Bruin[1] to take the same liberty with his sister, without any fear of offence.——When we arrived at the house, Narcissa assured me, she would exert all her influence in protecting me from the revenge of Thicket, and likewise engage her aunt in my favour. At the same time, pulling out her purse, offered it as a small consideration for the service I had done her.—But I stood too much upon the punctilios of love to incur the least suspicion of being mercenary, and refused the present, saying, I had merited nothing by barely doing my duty.—She seemed astonished at my disinterestedness, and blushed: I felt the same suffusion, and with a down-cast eye and broken accent, told her, I had one request to make, which if her generosity would grant, I should think myself fully recompensed for an age of misery.—She changed colour at this preamble, and with great confusion, replied, she hoped my good sense would hinder me from asking any thing she was bound in honour to refuse, and therefore bid me signify my desire.—Upon which I kneeled, and begged to kiss her hand. She immediately, with an averted look, stretched it out; I imprinted on it an ardent kiss, and bathing it with my tears, cried, 'Dear Madam, I am an unfortunate gentleman, who loves you to distraction, but would have died a thousand deaths, rather than make this declaration under such a servile appearance, were he not determined to yield to the rigour of his fate, to fly from your bewitching presence, and bury his presumptuous passion in eternal silence.' With these words I rose and went away, before she could recover her spirits so far as to make any reply.—My first care was to go and consult Mrs. Sagely, with whom I had maintained a friendly correspondence ever since I left her house. When she understood my situation, the good woman, with real concern, condoled me on my unhappy fate, and approved of my resolution to leave the country, being perfectly well acquainted with the barbarous disposition of my rival, 'who by this time (said she) has no doubt meditated a scheme of revenge.— Indeed, I cannot see how you will be able to elude his vengeance: being himself in the commission,[1] he will immediately grant warrants for apprehending you; and as almost all the people in this country are dependant on him or his friend, it will be impossible for you to find shelter among them: If you should be apprehended, he will commit you to jail, where you may possibly languish in great misery till the next assizes, and then be transported for assaulting a magistrate.'—While she thus warned me of my danger, we heard a knocking at the door, which threw us both into great consternation, as in all probability, it was occasioned by my pursuers; whereupon this generous old lady, putting two guineas into my hand, with tears in her eyes, bid me, for God's sake, get out at the back door, and consult my safety as providence should direct me.—There was no time for deliberation.—I followed her advice, and escaped by the benefit of a dark night, to the sea-side, where while I ruminated on my next excursion, I was all of a sudden surrounded by armed men, who, having bound my hands and feet, bid me make no noise, on pain of being shot, and carried me on board of a vessel, which I soon perceived to be a smuggling cutter.[1]—This discovery gave me some satisfaction at first, because I concluded myself safe from the resentment of Sir Timothy: But when I found myself in the hands of ruffians, who threatned to execute me for a spy, I would have thought myself happily quit for a year's imprisonment, or even transportation.—It was in vain for me to protest my innocence: I could not persuade them that I had taken a solitary walk to their haunt, at such an hour, merely for my own amusement; and I did not think it my interest to disclose the true cause of my retreat, because I was afraid they would have made their peace with justice by surrendering me to the penalty of the law.—What confirmed their suspicion was, the appearance of a Custom-house yacht, which gave them chace, and had well-nigh made a prize of their vessel; when they were delivered from their fears by a thick fog, which effectually screened them, and favoured their arrival at Buloign.[2]—But before they got out of sight of their pursuer, they held a council of war about me, whom some of the most ferocious among them, would have thrown overboard, as a traitor who had betrayed them to their enemies; but others more considerate, alledged, that if they put me to death, and should afterwards be taken, they could expect no mercy from the legislature, which would never pardon outlawry aggravated by murder.—It was therefore determined by a plurality of votes, that I should be set on shore in France, and left to find my passage back to England, as I should think proper, which would be punishment sufficient for the bare suspicion of a crime in itself not capital.—Although this favourable determination gave me great pleasure, the apprehension of being robbed would not suffer me to be perfectly at ease: To prevent this calamity, as soon as I was untied, in consequence of the foresaid decision, I tore a small hole in one of my stockings, into which I dropped six guineas, reserving half a piece and some silver in my pocket, that finding something, they might not be tempted to make any further inquiry.—This was a very necessary precaution, for when we came within sight of the French shore, one of the smugglers told me, I must pay for my passage.—To this I replied, that my passage was none of my own seeking; therefore they could not expect a reward from me for transporting me into a strange country by force.—'Dam-me! (said the outlaw) none of your palaver; but let me see what money you have got.'—So saying, he thrust his hand into my pocket without any ceremony, and emptied it of the contents: Then casting an eye at my hat and wig, which captivated his fancy, he took them off, and clapping his own on my head, declared, that a fair exchange was no robbery.—I was fain to put up with the bargain, which was by no means favourable to me; and a little while after we went all on shore together.

I resolved to take my leave of these desperadoes, without much ceremony, when one of them cautioned me against appearing to their prejudice if ever I returned to England, unless I had a mind to be murdered; for which service, he assured me, the gang never wanted agents.—I promised to observe his advice, and departed for the Upper Town, where I enquired for a cabaret or publick house, into which I went, with an intention of taking some refreshment.— In the kitchin, five Dutch sailors sat at breakfast, with a large loaf, a firkin of butter, and a cag[1] of brandy on the table, the bung of which they often applied to their mouths with great perseverance and satisfaction.—At some distance from them, I perceived another person in the same garb, sitting in a pensive solitary manner, entertaining himself with a whiff of tobacco, from the stump of a pipe, as black as jet.—The appearance of distress never failed to attract my regard and compassion; I approached this forlorn tar, with a view to offer him my assistance, and notwithstanding the alteration of dress, and disguise of a long beard, I discovered in him my long lost and lamented uncle and benefactor, lieutenant Bowling! Good heaven! what were the agitations of my soul, between the joy of finding again such a valuable friend, and the sorrow of seeing him in such a low condition! The tears gushed down my cheeks, I stood motionless and silent for some time; at length, recovering the use of speech, exclaimed, 'Gracious God! Mr. Bowling!'—My uncle no sooner heard his name mentioned, than he started up, crying with some surprize, 'Holloa!' and after having looked at me stedfastly, without being able to recollect me, said, 'Did you call me, brother?' I told him, I had something extraordinary to communicate, and desired him to give me a few minutes hearing in another room; but he would by no means consent to this proposal, saying, 'Avast there, friend; none of your tricks upon travellers;—if you have any thing to say to me, do it above-board;—you need not be afraid of being over-heard;—here are none who understand our lingo.'— Though I was loath to discover myself before company, I could no longer refrain from telling him, I was his own nephew Roderick Random. On this information, he considered me with great earnest-ness and astonishment, and recalling my features, which though enlarged were not entirely altered since he had seen me, came up and shook me by the hand very cordially, protesting he was glad to see me well. After some pause, he went on thus: 'And yet, my lad, I am sorry to see you under such colours; the more so, as it is not in my power, at present, to change them for the better, times being very hard with me.' With these words I could perceive a tear trickle down his furrowed cheeks, which affected me so much, that I wept bitterly.—Imagining my sorrow was the effect of my own mis-fortunes, he comforted me, by observing, that life was a voyage in which we must expect to meet with all weathers; sometimes it was calm, sometimes rough; that a fair gale often succeeded a storm; that the wind did not always sit one way, and that despair signified nothing; but resolution and skill were better than a stout vessel: For why? Because they require no carpenter, and grow stronger the more labour they undergo. I dried up my tears, which I assured him, were not shed for my own distress, but for his, and begged leave to accompany him into another room, where we could con-verse more at our ease.—There I recounted to him the ungenerous usage I had met with from Potion; at which he started up, stalked across the room three or four times, in a great hurry, and grasping his cudgel, cried, 'I would I were along-side of him—that's all—I would I were along-side of him!'—I then gave him a detail of all my adventures and sufferings, which affected him more than I could have imagined, and concluded with telling him that captain Oakhum was still alive, and that he might return to England when he would, to sollicite his affairs, without danger or molestation.— He was wonderfully pleased at this piece of information, of which however, he said he could not at present avail himself, for want of money to pay for his passage to London. This objection I soon re-moved, by putting five guineas into his hand, and telling him, I thought myself extremely happy in having an opportunity of mani-festing my gratitude to him in his necessity.—But it was with the utmost difficulty I could prevail upon him to accept of two, which he affirmed, were more than sufficient to defray the necessary expence.—After this friendly contest was over, he proposed we should have a mess of something: 'For (said he) it has been banyan day with me a great while.—You must know I was shipwrecked five days ago, near a place called Lisieux,[1] in company with those Dutchmen who are now drinking below; and having but little money when I came ashore, it was soon spent, because I let them have share and share while it lasted.—Howsomever, I should have remembred the old saying, *Every hog his own apple:*[2] For when they found my hold unstowed, they went all hands to shooling[3] and begging; and because I would not take a spell at the same duty, refused to give me the least assistance; so that I have not broke bread these two days.'—I was shocked at the extremity of his distress, and ordered some bread, cheese and wine to be brought immediately, to allay his hunger, until a fricassee of chickens could be prepared.—When he had recruited his spirits with this homely fare, I desired to know the particulars of his peregrination, since the accident at Cape Tiberoon; which were briefly these: The money he had about him being all spent at Port Louis, the civility and hospitality of the French cooled to such a degree, that he was obliged to list on board of one of their king's ships, as a common fore-mastman, to prevent himself from starving on shore.—In this situation, he continued two years, during which time he had acquired some knowledge of their language, and the reputation of a good seaman: The ship he belonged to was ordered home to old France, where she was laid up as unfit for service, and he was received on board of one of monsieur D'Antin's squadron,[4] in quality of quarter-master; which office he performed in a voyage to the West-Indies, where they engaged with our ship, as before related; but his conscience upbraiding him for serving the enemies of his country, he quitted the ship at the same place where he first listed, and got to Currasoa[5] in a Dutch vessel; there he bargained with another skipper, bound to Europe, to work for his passage to Holland, from whence he was in hopes of hearing from his friends in England; but was cast away, as he mentioned before, on the French coast, and must have been reduced to the necessity of travelling on foot to Holland, and begging for his subsistence on the road, or of entering on board of another French man of war, at the hazard of being treated as a deserter, if Providence had not sent me to his succour.——'And now, my lad, (continued he) I think I shall steer my course directly to London,

where I do not doubt of being replaced, and of having the R taken off me[1] by the lords of the admiralty, to whom I intend to write a petition setting forth my case: If I succeed, I will have wherewithal to give you some assistance, because when I left the ship I had two years pay due to me; therefore I desire to know whither you are bound; and beside, perhaps, I may have interest enough to procure a warrant appointing you surgeon's mate of the ship to which I shall belong.—For the beadle of the admiralty is my good friend; and he and one of the under-clerks are sworn brothers, and that under-clerk has a good deal to say with one of the upper-clerks, who is very well known to the under-secretary, who, upon his recommendation, I hope will recommend my affair to the first secretary; and he again, will speak to one of the Lords in my behalf: So that you see, I do not want friends to assist me on occasion.—As for the fellow Crampley, tho'f I know him not, I am sure he is neither seaman nor officer, by what you have told me, or else he could never be so much mistaken in his reckoning, as to run the ship on shore on the coast of Sussex, before he believed himself in soundings; neither, when that accident happened, would he have left the ship until she had been stove to pieces, especially when the tide was making; wherefore, by this time, I do suppose he has been tried by a court-martial and executed for his cowardice and misconduct.'——
I could not help smiling at the description of my uncle's ladder, by which he proposed to clime to the attention of the board of admiralty; and tho' I knew the world too well, to confide in such dependance myself, I would not discourage him with doubts; but asked if he had no friend in London, who would advance a small sum of money to enable him to appear as he ought, and make a small present to the under secretary, who might possibly dispatch his business the sooner on that account.—He scratched his head, and after some recollection, replied, 'Why, yes, I believe Daniel Whipcord the ship-chandler in Wapping would not refuse me such a small matter.—I know I can have what credit I would, for lodging, liquor and cloaths; but as to money, I won't be positive:—Had honest Block been living, I should not have been at a loss.'—I was heartily sorry to find a worthy man so destitute of friends, when he had such need of them; and looked upon my own situation as less miserable than his, because I was better acquainted with the selfishness and roguery of mankind; consequently less liable to disappointment and imposition.

CHAPTER XLII

He takes his passage in a Cutter for Deal—we are accosted by a priest, who proves to be a Scottishman——his professions of friendship——he is affronted by the lieutenant, who afterwards appeases him by submission—my uncle embarks—— I am introduced by the priest to a capuchin, in whose company I set out for Paris——the character of my fellow- traveller——an adventure on the road—I am shocked at his behaviour

WHEN our repast was ended, we walked down to the harbour, where we found a Cutter that was to sail for Deal in the evening, and Mr. Bowling agreed for his passage: In the mean time, we sauntered about the town, to satisfy our curiosity, our conversation turning on the subject of my designs, which were not as yet fixed: Neither can it be supposed, that my mind was at ease, when I found myself reduced almost to extreme poverty, in the midst of foreigners, among whom I had not one acquaintance to advise or befriend me. —My uncle was sensible of my forlorn condition, and pressed me to accompany him to England, where he did not doubt of finding some sort of provision for me: But besides the other reasons I had for avoiding that kingdom, I looked upon it, at this time, as the worst country in the universe for a poor honest man to live in; and therefore determined to remain in France, *coute que coute.*—I was confirmed in this resolution, by a reverend priest, who passing by at this time, and overhearing us speak English, accosted us in the same language, telling us he was our countryman, and wishing it might be in his power to do us any service: We thanked this grave person for his courteous offer, and invited him to drink a glass with us, which he did not think proper to refuse, and we went all to- gether into a tavern of his recommending. After having drank to our healths in a bumper of good Burgundy, he began to enquire into our situation, and asked particularly the place of our nativity, which we no sooner named, than he started up, and wringing our hands with great fervour, shed a flood of tears, crying, 'I come from the same part of the country! perhaps you are my own relations.'— I was on my guard against his caresses, which I suspected very

much, when I remembred the adventure of the money-dropper;
but without any appearance of diffidence, observed, that as he was
born in that part of the country, he must certainly know our
families, which (howsoever mean our present appearance might be)
were none of the most obscure and inconsiderable.—Then I discovered our names, to which I found he was no stranger; he had
known my grandfather personally; and notwithstanding an absence
of fifty years from Scotland, recounted so many particulars of the
families in the neighbourhood, that my scruples were entirely removed, and I thought myself happy in his acquaintance.—In the
course of our conversation, I disclosed my condition without reserve, and displayed my talents to such advantage, that the old
father looked upon me with admiration, and assured me, that if I
stayed in France, and listened to reason, I could not fail of making
my fortune, to which he would contribute all in his power.

My uncle began to be jealous of the priest's insinuation, and very
abruptly declared, that if ever I should renounce my religion, he
would break off all connexion and correspondence with me; for it
was his opinion, that no honest man would swerve from the principles in which he was bred, whether Turkish, Protestant, or
Roman.—The father, affronted at this declaration, with great vehemence, began a long discourse, setting forth the danger of obstinacy, and shutting one's eyes against the light: He said, that
ignorance would be no plea towards justification, when we had
opportunities of being better informed; and that, if the minds of
people had not been open to conviction, the Christian religion
would not have been propagated in the world; and we should now
be in a state of Pagan darkness and barbarity: He endeavoured to
prove, by some texts of scripture, and many quotations from the
fathers, that the Pope was the successor of St. Peter, and vicar of
Jesus Christ; that the church of Rome was the true, holy, catholick
church; and that the protestant faith was an impious heresy, and
damnable schism, by which many millions of souls would suffer
everlasting perdition.—When he had finished his sermon, which I
thought, he pronounced with more zeal than discretion, he addressed himself to my uncle, and desired to know his objections to
what had been said. The lieutenant, whose attention had been
wholly engrossed by his own affairs, took the pipe out of his mouth,
and replied, 'As for me, friend, d'ye see, I have no objection to what
you say, it may be either true or false, for what I know; I meddle

with no body's affairs but my own; the gunner to his linstock,[1] and the steersman to the helm, as the saying is.—I trust to no creed but the compass, and do unto every man as I would be done by; so that I defy the pope, the devil, and the pretender; and hope to be saved as well as another.'—This association of persons gave great offence to the friar, who protested, in a mighty passion, that if Mr. Bowling had not been his countryman, he would have caused him to be imprisoned for his insolence.—I ventured to disapprove of my uncle's rashness, and appeased the old gentleman, by assuring him, there was no offence intended by my kinsman, who by this time, sensible of his error, shook the injured party by the hand, and asked pardon for the freedom he had taken.—Matters being amicably compromised, he invited us to come and see him in the afternoon at the convent to which he belonged, and took his leave for the present; when my uncle recommended it strongly to me to persevere in the religion of my forefathers, whatever advantages I might propose to my self by a change, which could not fail of disgracing myself, and dishonouring my family.—I assured him no consideration should induce me to forfeit his friendship and good opinion, on that score; at which he discovered great satisfaction, and put me in mind of dinner, which we immediately bespoke, and when it was ready eat together.

I imagined my acquaintance with the Scottish Priest, if properly managed, might turn out to my advantage, and therefore resolved to cultivate it as much as I could. With this view we visited him at his convent, according to his invitation, where he treated us with wine and sweet-meats, and shewed us every thing that was remarkable in the monastery.—Having been thus entertained, we took our leave, though not before I had promised to see him next day; and the time fixed for my uncle's embarking being come, I accompanied him to the harbour, and saw him on board.—We parted not without tears, after we had embraced and wished one another all manner of prosperity; and he intreated me to write to him often, directing to lieutenant Thomas Bowling, at the sign of the Union flag, near the Hermitage, London.[2]

I returned to the house in which we had met, where I passed the night in a very solitary manner, reflecting on the severity of my fate, and endeavouring to project some likely scheme of life for the future; but my invention failed me, I saw nothing but unsurmountable difficulties in my way, and was ready to despair at the miserable prospect! That I might not, however, neglect any probable means, I got up in the morning, and went directly to the father, whose advice and assistance I implored.—He received me very kindly, and gave me to understand, that there was one way of life in which a person of my talents could not fail of making a great figure.—I guessed his meaning, and told him once for all, I was fully determined against any alteration in point of religion, therefore if his proposal regarded the church, he might save himself the trouble of explaining it. He shook his head and sighed, saying, 'Ah! son, son, what a glorious prospect is here spoiled, by your stubborn prejudice! Suffer yourself to be persuaded by reason, and consult your temporal welfare, as well as the concerns of your eternal soul.—I can, by my interest, procure your admission as a noviciate into this convent, where I will superintend and direct you with a truly paternal affection.'—Then he launched out into the praises of a monastic life, which no noise disturbs, no cares molest, and no danger invades—where the heart is weaned from carnal attachments, the grosser appetites subdued and chastised, and the soul wafted to the divine regions of philosophy and truth, on the wings of studious contemplation.—But his eloquence was lost upon me, whom two considerations enabled to withstand his temptations; namely, my promise to my uncle, and my aversion to an ecclesiastical life; for as to the difference of religion, I looked upon it as a thing of too small moment to come in competition with a man's fortune.—Finding me immoveable on this head, he told me, he was more sorry than offended at my non-compliance, and still ready to employ his good offices in my behalf.—'The same erroneous maxims (said he) that obstruct your promotion in the church, will infallibly prevent your advancement in the army; but if you can brook the condition of a servant, I am acquainted with some people of rank at Versailles, to whom I can give you letters of recommendation, that you may be entertained by some one of them, in quality of *maitre d' hotel*; and I do not doubt that your qualifications will soon entitle you to a better provision.'—I embraced his offer with great eagerness; and he appointed me to come back in the afternoon, when he would not only give me the letters, but likewise introduce me to a capuchin of his acquaintance, who intended to set out for Paris next morning, in whose company I might travel, without being at the expence of one livre during the whole journey. This piece of good news gave me infinite pleasure; I acknowledged my obligation to the benevolent father, in the most grateful expressions; and he performed his promise to a tittle, in delivering the letters, and making me acquainted with the capuchin, with whom I departed next morning by break of day.

It was not long before I discovered my fellow-traveller to be a merry facetious fellow, who, notwithstanding his profession and appearance of mortification, loved good eating and drinking better than his rosary, and paid more adoration to a pretty girl than to the Virgin Mary, or St. Genevive.[1]—He was a thick brawny young man, with red eye-brows, a hook nose, a face covered with freckles; and his name was Frere Balthazar.[2] His order did not permit him to wear linnen, so that having little occasion to undress himself, he was none of the cleanliest animals in the world; and his constitution was naturally so strong scented, that I always thought it convenient to keep to the windward of him in our march.—As he was perfectly well known on the road, we fared sumptuously without any cost, and the fatigue of our journey was much alleviated by the good humour of my companion, who sung an infinite number of catches on the subjects of love and wine.—We took up our lodging the first night at a peasant's house, not far from Abbe Ville[3] where we were entertained with an excellent ragout, cooked by our landlord's daughters, one of whom was very handsome: After having eat heartily, and drank a sufficient quantity of *vin du Pais*,[4] we were conducted to a barn, where we found a couple of carpets spread upon clean straw for our reception.—We had not lain in this situation above half an hour, when we heard somebody knock softly at the door, upon which Balthazar got up, and let in our host's two daughters, who wanted to have some private conversation with him in the dark; when they had whispered together some time, the capuchin came to me, and asked if I was insensible to love, or so hard-hearted as to refuse a share of my bed to a pretty maid, who had a *tendresse* for me.——I must own, to my shame, that I suffered myself to be overcome by my passion, and with great eagerness seized the occasion, when I understood that the amiable Nanette was to be my bedfellow.—In vain did my reason suggest the respect I owed to my dear mistress Narcissa; the idea of that lovely charmer, rather increased than allayed the ferment of my spirits; and the young Paisanne[5] had no reason to complain of my remembrance.—Early in the morning, the kind creatures left us to our repose, which lasted till eight o'clock, when we got up, and were

treated at breakfast with chocolate and *l'eau de vie*,[1] by our para-
mours, of whom we took a tender leave, after my companion had
confessed and given them absolution.—While we proceeded on our
journey, the conversation turned upon the night's adventure, being
introduced by the capuchin, who asked me how I liked my lodging:
I declared my satisfaction, and talked in raptures of the agreeable
Nanette; at which he shook his head, and smiling said, she was a
morçeau pour la bonne bouche.[2] 'I never valued myself (continued he)
upon any thing so much as the conquest of Nanette; and, vanity
apart, I have been pretty fortunate in my amours.'—This information shocked me not a little, as I was well convinced of his intimacy
with her sister; and though I did not care to tax him with downright
incest, I professed my astonishment at his last night's choice, when,
I supposed, the other was at his devotion.—To this he answered,
that besides his natural complaisance to the sex, he had another
reason to distribute his favours equally between them; namely, to
preserve peace in the family, which could not otherwise be maintained;—that moreover Nanette had conceived an affection for me,
and he loved her too well to baulk her inclination; more especially,
when he had an opportunity of obliging his friend at the same time.
—I thanked him for this instance of his friendship, though I was
extremely disgusted at his want of delicacy, and cursed the occasion
that threw me in his way.—Libertine as I was, I could not bear to
see a man behave so wide of the character he assumed: I looked
upon him as person of very little worth or honesty, and should have
even kept a wary eye upon my pocket, if I had thought he could have
any temptation to steal.—But I could not conceive the use of
money to a capuchin, who is obliged, by the rules of his order, to
appear like a beggar, and enjoys all other necessaries of life *gratis*;
besides, my fellow-traveller seemed to be of a complexion too
careless and sanguine, to give me any apprehension on that score;
so that I proceeded with great confidence, in expectation of being
soon at my journey's end.

CHAPTER XLIII

*We lodge at a house near Amiens, where I am robbed by
the capuchin, who escapes while I am asleep——I go to Noyons
in search of him, but without success——I make my condition
known to several people, but find no relief——I grow
desperate—join a company of soldiers——inlist in the regiment
of Picardy——we are ordered into Germany——I find the
fatigues of the march almost intolerable——quarrel with my
comrade in a dispute upon politicks—he challenges me to
the field, wounds and disarms me*

THE third night of our pilgrimage, we passed at a house near
Amiens,[1] where Balthazar being unknown, we supped upon indifferent fare, and sower wine, and were fain to lie in a garret upon
an old mattrass, which, I believe, had been in the possession of ten
thousand myriads of fleas, time out of mind.—We did not invade
their territory with impunity; in less than a minute we were
attacked with stings innumerable, in spite of which, however, I fell
fast asleep, being excessively fatigued with our day's march, and
did not wake till nine next morning, when, seeing myself alone, I
started up in a terrible fright, and examining my pockets, found my
presaging fear too true! My companion had made free with my
cash, and left me to seek my way to Paris by myself! I run down
stairs immediately; and with a look full of grief and amazement,
enquired for the mendicant, who, they gave me to understand, had
set out four hours before, after having told them, I was a little indisposed, and desired I might not be disturbed, but he informed
when I should wake he had taken the road to Noyons,[2] where he
would wait for my coming, at the Coq D'Or.—I spoke not a word,
but with a heavy heart, directed my course to that place, at which I
arrived in the afternoon, fainting with weariness and hunger; but
learned, to my utter confusion, that no such person had been there!
—It was happy for me that I had a good deal of resentment in my
constitution, which animated me on such occasions, against the
villainy of mankind, and enabled me to bear misfortunes otherwise
intolerable.—Boiling with indignation, I discovered to the host my
deplorable condition, and inveighed with great bitterness against
the treachery of Balthazar; at which he shrugged up his shoulders,

and with a peculiar grimace on his countenance, said, he was sorry for my misfortune; but there was no remedy like patience.—At that instant some guests arrived, to whom he hastened to offer his service, leaving me mortified at his indifference, and fully persuaded that an inn-keeper is the same sordid animal all over the world.— While I stood in the porch, forlorn and undetermined, venting ejaculations of curses against the thief who had robbed me, and the old priest who recommended him to my friendship; a young gentleman richly dressed, attended by a *valet de chambre* and two servants in livery, arrived at the inn. I thought I perceived a good deal of sweetness and good nature in his countenance; therefore, he had no sooner alighted than I accosted him, and in a few words explained my situation: He listened with great politeness, and when I had made an end of my story, said, 'Well, monsieur, what would you have me do?' I was effectually abashed at this interrogation, which I believed no man of common sense or generosity could make, and made no other reply than a low bow: He returned the compliment still lower, and tript into an apartment, while the landlord let me know, that my standing there to interrupt company gave offence, and might do him infinite prejudice.—He had no occasion to repeat his insinuation; I moved from the place immediately; and was so much transported with grief, anger, and disdain, that a torrent of blood gushed from my nostrils.—In this extasy, I quitted Noyons, and betook myself to the fields, where I wandered about like one distracted, till my spirits were quite exhausted, and I was obliged to throw myself down at the root of a tree, to rest my wearied limbs.—Here my rage forsook me, I began to feel the importunate cravings of nature, and relapsed into silent sorrow and melancholy reflection. I revolved all the crimes I had been guilty of, and found them so few and venial, that I could not comprehend the justice of that providence, which after having exposed me to so much wretchedness and danger, left me a prey to famine at last in a foreign country, where I had not one friend or acquaintance to close my eyes, and do the last offices of humanity to my miserable carcase.—A thousand times I wished myself a bear, that I might retreat to woods and desarts, far from the inhospitable haunts of man, where I could live by my own talents independant of treacherous friends, and supercilious scorn.

As I lay in this manner, groaning over my hapless fate, I heard the sound of a violin, and raising my head, perceived a company of men and women dancing on the grass at some distance from me.—I looked upon this to be a favourable season for distress to attract compassion, when every selfish thought is banished, and the heart dilated with mirth and social joy; wherefore I got up and approached those happy people, whom I soon discovered to be a party of soldiers, with their wives and children, unbending and diverting themselves at this rate, after the fatigue of a march.—I had never before seen such a parcel of scare-crows together, neither could I reconcile their meagre gaunt looks, their squalid and ragged attire, and every other external symptom of extreme woe, with this appearance of festivity.—I saluted them however, and was received with great politesse; after which they formed a ring and danced around me.—This jollity had a wonderful effect upon my spirits! I was infected with their gayety, and in spite of my dismal situation forgot my cares, and joined in their extravagance.—When we had recreated ourselves a good while at this diversion, the ladies spread their manteaus on the ground, upon which they emptied their knapsacks of some onions, coarse bread, and a few flasks of poor wine: Being invited to a share of the banquet, I sat down with the rest, and in the whole course of my life never made a more comfortable meal.—When our repast was ended, we got up again to dance; and now that I found myself refreshed, I behaved to the admiration of every body: I was loaded with a thousand compliments, and professions of friendship; the men commended my person and agility, and the women were loud in the praise of my *bonne grace*;[1]—the serjeant in particular, expressed so much regard for me, and described the agreemens of a soldier's life, with so much art, that I began to listen to his proposal of enlisting me in the service; and the more I considered my own condition, the more I was convinced of the necessity I was under to come to a speedy determination.—Having therefore maturely weighed the circumstances *pro* and *con*, I signified my consent, and was admitted into the regiment of Picardy, said to be the oldest corps in Europe.[2]—The company to which this command belonged, was quartered at a village not far off, whither we marched next day, and I was presented to my captain, who seemed very well pleased with my appearance, gave me a crown to drink, and ordered me to be accommodated with cloaths, arms and accoutrements.—Whereupon I sold my livery suit, purchased linnen, and as I was at great pains to learn the exercise in a very short time became a compleat soldier.

It was not long before we received orders to join several more regiments, and march with all expedition into Germany, in order to reinforce Marechal Duc de Noailles,[1] who was then encamped with his army on the side of the river Main, to watch the motions of the English, Austrians, and Hessians, under the command of the earl of Stair.[2] We began our march accordingly, and then I became acquainted with that part of a soldier's life to which I had been a stranger hitherto.—It is impossible to describe the hunger and thirst I sustained, and the fatigue I underwent in a march of so many hundred miles; during which, I was so much chased with the heat and motion of my limbs, that in a very short time the inside of my thighs and legs were deprived of skin, and I proceeded in the utmost torture.—This misfortune I owed to the plumpness of my constitution, which I cursed, and envied the withered condition of my comrades, whose bodies could not spare juice enough to supply a common issue, and were indeed proof against all manner of friction. The continual pain I felt made me fretful, and my peevishness was increased by the mortification of my pride in seeing these miserable wretches, whom a hard gale of wind would have scattered through the air like chaff, bear those toils with alacrity, under which I was ready to sink.

One day while we enjoyed a halt, and the soldiers with their wives had gone out to dance, according to custom, my comrade staid at home with me on pretence of friendship, and insulted me with his pity and consolation! He told me, though I was young and tender at present, I would soon be seasoned to the service; and he did not doubt but I should have the honour to contribute in some measure to the glory of the king.—'Have courage, therefore, my child (said he) and pray to the good God, that you may be as happy as I am, who have had the honour of serving Lewis the Great,[3] and of receiving many wounds in helping to establish his glory.'—When I looked upon the contemptible object that pronounced these words, I was amazed at the infatuation that possessed him; and could not help expressing my astonishment at the absurdity of a rational being, who thinks himself highly honoured in being permitted to encounter abject poverty, oppression, famine, disease, mutilation, and evident death, merely to gratify the vicious ambition of a prince, by whom his sufferings were disregarded, and his name utterly unknown.—I observed, that if his situation was the consequence of compulsion, as having been pressed into the

service, I would praise his patience and fortitude in bearing his lot;
—if he had taken up arms in defence of his injured country, he was
to be applauded for his patriotism;—or if he had fled to this way of
life as a refuge from a greater evil, he was justifiable in his own
conscience, (though I could have no notion of misery more extreme
than that he suffered;) but to put his condition on the footing of
conducing to the glory of his prince, was no more than professing
himself a desperate slave, who voluntarily underwent the utmost
wretchedness and peril, and committed the most flagrant crimes, to
sooth the barbarous pride of a fellow-creature, his superior in
nothing but the power he derived from the submission of such
wretches as he. The soldier was very much affronted at the liberty
I took with his king, which, he said, nothing but my ignorance could
excuse: He affirmed, that the characters of princes were sacred, and
ought not to be profaned by the censure of their subjects, who were
bound by their allegiance to obey their commands, of what nature
soever, without scruple or repining—And advised me to correct
the rebellious principles I had imbibed among the English, who,
for their insolence to their kings, were notorious all over the world,
even to a proverb:

Le roy d'Angleterre,
Est le roy de l'Enfer.[1]

In vindication of my countrymen, I adduced all the arguments
commonly used to prove that every man has a natural right to
liberty; that allegiance and protection are reciprocal; that when the
mutual tie is broken by the tyranny of the king, he is accountable to
the people for his breach of contract, and subject to the penalty of
the law; and that those insurrections of the English, which are
branded with the name of rebellion, by the slaves of arbitrary
power, were no other than glorious efforts to rescue that independance which was their birthright, from the ravenous claws of usurp-
ing ambition.—The Frenchman, provoked at the little deference I
paid to the kingly name, lost all patience, and reproached me in
such a manner, that my temper forsook me, and I clenched my
fist, with an intention to give him a hearty box on the ear.—Perceiving my design, he started back, and demanded a parley; upon
which I checked my indignation, and he gave me to understand that
a Frenchman never forgave a blow; therefore if I was not weary of
my life, I would do well to spare him that mortification, and do him

the honour of measuring his sword with mine, like a gentleman.—
I took his advice and followed him to a field hard by, where indeed
I was ashamed at the pitiful figure of my antagonist, who was a
poor, little, shivering creature decrepid with age, and blind of one
eye.—But I soon found the folly of judging from appearances;
being at the second pass wounded in the sword hand, and immediately disarmed with such a jerk, that I thought the joint was dis-
located.—I was no less confounded than enraged at this event,
especially as my adversary did not bear his success with all the
moderation that might have been expected; for he insisted upon my
asking pardon for my presumption in affronting his king and him.—
This I would by no means comply with, but told him it was a mean
condescension, which no gentleman in his circumstances ought to
propose, nor none in my situation perform;—and that if he persisted in his ungenerous demand, I would in my turn claim satisfaction with my musket, at which weapon we should be more upon
a par than with the sword, of which he seemed so much master.

CHAPTER XLIV

*The gascon does not use his victory with all the moderation
that might have been expected——In order to be revenged I
learn the science of defence.——we join Marechal Duc de
Noailles——are engaged with the allies at Dettingen, and put
to flight——the behaviour of the French soldiers on that
occasion—I industriously seek another combat with the old
gascon, and vanquish him in my turn——our regiment is put
into winter quarters at Rheims,[1] where I find my friend
Strap—our recognition—he supplies me with money, and
procures my discharge——we take a trip to Paris; from
whence we set out for London by the way of Flanders,
where we safely arrive*

HE was disconcerted at this declaration, to which he made no reply,
but repaired to the dancers, among whom he recounted his victory
with many exaggerations and gasconades;[2] while I, taking up my
sword, went to my quarters and examined my wound, which I

found was of no consequence.—The same day, an Irish drummer, having heard my misfortune, visited me, and after having condoled me on the chance of war, gave me to understand, that he was master of his sword, and would in a very short time instruct me so thoroughly in that noble science, that I should be able to chastise the old gascon for his insolent boasting at my expence.—This friendly office he proffered on pretence of the regard he had for his countrymen; but I afterwards learned the true motive was no other than a jealousy he entertained of a correspondence between the Frenchman and his wife, which he did not think proper to resent in person.—Be this as it will, I accepted his offer, and practised his lessons with such application, that I soon believed myself a match for my conqueror.—In the mean time we continued our march, and arrived at the camp of Mareschal Noailles, the night before the battle of Dettingen.[1] Notwithstanding the fatigue we had undergone, our regiment was one of those that were ordered next day to cross the river, under the command of the Duc de Gramont,[2] to take possession of a narrow defile, through which the allies must of necessity have passed at a great disadvantage, or remain where they were, and perish for want of provision, if they would not condescend to surrender at discretion.—How they suffered themselves to be pent up in this manner, it is not my province to relate; I shall only observe, that when we had taken possession of our ground, I heard an old officer in conversation with another, profess a surprise at the conduct of Lord Stair, who had the reputation of a good general.—But it seems, at this time, that nobleman was over-ruled, and only acted in an inferior character; so that no part of the blame could be imputed to him, who declared his disapprobation of the step, in consequence of which the whole army was in the utmost danger; but providence or destiny acted miracles in their behalf, by disposing the Duc de Gramont to quit his advantageous post, pass the defile, and attack the English, who were drawn up in order of battle on the plain, and who handled us so roughly, that after having lost a great number of men, we turned our backs without ceremony, and fled with such precipitation, that many hundreds perished in the river, through pure fear and confusion; for the enemy was so generous, that they did not pursue us one inch of ground; and if our consternation would have permitted, we might have retreated with great order and deliberation.—But not withstanding the royal clemency of the king of Great Britain, who headed the allies in person, and no doubt, put a stop to the carnage, our loss amounted to 5,000 men, among whom were many officers of distinction.—Our miscarriage opened a passage for the foe to Hanau,[1] whither they immediately marched, leaving their sick and wounded to the care of the French, who next day took possession of the field of battle, buried the dead, and treated the living with humanity.—This was a great consolation to us, who thence took occasion to claim the victory; and the genius of the French nation never appeared more conspicuous than now, in the rhodomontades they uttered on the subject of their generosity and courage: Every man, (by his own account) performed feats that would have shamed all the heroes of antiquity.—One compared himself to a lion retiring at leisure from his cowardly pursuers, who keep at a wary distance, and gall him with their darts.—Another likened himself to a bear that retreats with his face to the enemy, who dare not assail him; and a third assumed the character of a desperate stag, that turns upon the hounds and keeps them at bay.——There was not a private soldier engaged, who had not by the prowess of his single arm, demolished a whole platoon, or put a squadron of horse to flight; and among others, the meagre gascon extoled his exploits above those of Hercules or Charlemagne.[2]—As I still retained my resentment for the disgrace I suffered in my last recontre with him, and now that I thought myself qualified, longed for an opportunity to retrieve my honour; I magnified the valour of the English with all the hyperboles I could imagine, and decried the pusilanimity of the French in the same stile, comparing them to hares flying before grey-hounds, or mice pursued by cats; and passed an ironical compliment on the speed he exerted in his flight, which, considering his age and infirmities, I said was surprising.—He was stung to the quick by this sarcasm, and with an air of threatning disdain, bid me know myself better, and remember the correction I had already received from him for my insolence; for he might not be always in the humour of sparing a wretch who abused his goodness. To this inuendo I made no reply but by a kick on the breech, which overturned him in an instant.——He started up with wonderful agility, and drawing his sword, attacked me with great fury: Several people interposed, but when he informed them of its being an affair of honour, they retired and left us to decide the battle by ourselves. I sustained his onset with little damage, having only received a small scratch on my right shoulder, and seeing his breath and vigour almost exhausted, assaulted him in my turn, closed with him, and wrested his sword out of his hand in the struggle.—Having thus acquired the victory, I desired him to beg his life; to which he made no answer, but shrugged up his shoulders to his ears, expanded his hands, elevated the skin of his forehead and eye-brows, and depressed the corners of his mouth, in such a manner, that I could scarce refrain from laughing aloud at his grotesque appearance.—That I might, however, mortify his vanity, which had triumphed without bounds over my misfortune, I thrust his sword up to the hilt in something (it was not a tansy)[1] that lay smoking on the plain, and joined the rest of the soldiers with an air of tranquility and indifference.

There was nothing more of moment attempted by either of the armies during the remaining part of the campaign, which being ended, the English marched back to the Netherlands; part of our army was detached to French Flanders, and our regiment ordered to winter-quarters in Champagne.—It was the fate of the grenadier company, to which I now belonged, to lie at Rheims, where I found myself in the utmost want of every thing: My pay, which amounted to five sols a day, so far from supplying me with necessaries, being scarce sufficient to procure a wretched subsistance, to keep soul and body together; so that I was by hunger and hard duty, brought down to the meagre condition of my fellow-soldiers, and my linen reduced from three tolerable shirts, to two pair of sleeves and necks, the bodies having been long ago converted into spatter-dashes;[2] and after all, I was better provided than any private man in the regiment.—In this urgency of my affairs, I wrote to my uncle in England, though my hopes from that quarter were not at all sanguine, for the reasons I have already explained, and in the mean time had recourse to my old remedy patience, consoling myself with the flattering suggestions of a lively imagination that never abandoned me in my distress.

One day, while I stood centinel at the gate of a general officer, a certain nobleman came to the door, followed by a gentleman in mourning, to whom, at parting, I heard him say, 'You may depend upon my good offices.'—This assurance was answered by a low bow of the person in black, who turning to go away, discovered to me the individual countenance of my old friend and adherent Strap.—I was so much astonished at the sight, that I lost the power of utterance, and before I could recollect myself, he was gone, without taking any notice of me.—Indeed, had he staid, I scarce would have ventured to accost him; because, though I was perfectly well acquainted with the features of his face, I could not be positively certain as to the rest of his person, which was very much altered for the better, since he left me at London; neither could I conjecture by what means he was enabled to appear in the sphere of a gentleman, to which, while I knew him, he had not even the ambition to aspire.—But I was too much concerned in the affair to neglect further information, and therefore took the first opportunity of asking the porter if he knew the gentleman to whom the Marquis spoke. The Swiss told me, his name was Monsieur d'Estrapes, that he had been *valet de chambre* to an English gentleman lately deceased, and that he was very much regarded by the Marquis for his fidelity to his master, between whom and that nobleman a very intimate friendship had subsisted.—Nothing could be more agreeable to me than this piece of intelligence, which banished all doubt of its being my friend, who had found means to frenchify his name as well as his behaviour, since we parted. As soon therefore, as I was relieved, I went to his lodging, according to a direction given me by the Swiss, and had the good fortune to find him at home. That I might surprize him the more, I concealed my name and business, and only desired the servant of the house, to tell Monsieur d'Estrapes, that I begged the honour of half an hour's conversation with him.—He was confounded and dismayed at this message, when he understood it was sent by a soldier, though he was conscious to himself of no crime; all that he had heard of the Bastile appeared to his imagination with aggravated horror, and it was not before I had waited a considerable time, that he had resolution enough to bid the servant shew me up stairs.—When I entered his chamber, he returned my bow with great civility, and endeavoured with forced complaisance, to disguise his fear, which appeared in the paleness of his face, the wildness of his looks, and the shaking of his limbs.—I was diverted at his consternation, which redoubled, when I told him (in French) I had business for his private ear, and demanded a particular audience.—The valet being withdrawn, I asked in the same language, if his name was d'Estrapes, to which he answered, with a faultering tongue, 'The same, at your service.'—'Are you a Frenchman? (said I.)'—'I have not the honour to be a Frenchman born (replied he) but I have an infinite veneration for the country.' —I then desired he would do me the honour to look at me, which he no sooner did, than struck with my appearance, he started back and cried in English, 'O Jesus!—sure it can't!——No, 'tis impossible!'—I smiled at his interjections, saying, 'I suppose you are too much of a gentleman to own your friend in adversity.'—When he heard me pronounce these words in our own language, he leaped upon me in a transport of joy, hung about my neck, kissed me from ear to ear, and blubbered like a great school-boy who has been whipt.——Then observing my dress, he set up his throat, crying, 'O L—d! O L—d! that ever I should live to see my dearest friend reduced to the condition of a foot soldier in the French service! Why did you consent to my leaving you?—But I know the reason —you thought you had got more creditable friends, and grew ashamed of my acquaintance.—Ah! Lord help us! though I was a little short-sighted, I was not altogether blind;—And though I did not complain, I was not the less sensible of your unkindness, which was indeed the only thing that induced me to ramble abroad, the Lord knows whither; but I must own it has been a lucky ramble to me, and so I forgive you, and may God forgive you:—O L—d! O L—d! is it come to this?'—I was nettled at the charge, which, though just, I could not help thinking unseasonable, and told him with some tartness, that whether his suspicions were well or ill-grounded, he might have chosen a more convenient opportunity of introducing them: And that the question now was, whether or no he found himself disposed to lend me any assistance.——'Disposed! (replied he with great emotion) I thought you had known me so well, as to assure yourself, without asking, that I, and all that belongs to me, are at your command.—In the mean time, you shall dine with me, and I will tell you something that, perhaps, will not be displeasing unto you.'——Then wringing my hand, he said, 'It makes my heart bleed to see you in that garb!'—I thanked him for his invitation, which, I observed, could not be unwelcome to a person who had not eaten a comfortable meal these seven months; but I had another request to make, which I begged he would grant before dinner, and that was the loan of a shirt: For although my back had been many weeks a stranger to any comfort of this kind, my skin was not yet quite familiarized to the want of it.—He stared in my face, with a woful countenance, at this declaration, which he would scarce believe, until I explained it, by unbuttoning my coat, and disclosing my naked body; a circumstance that shocked the tender-hearted Strap, who, with tears in his eyes, run to a chest of drawers, and taking out some linen, presented to me a very fine ruffled holland shirt, and cambrick neckcloth, assuring me, he had three dozen of the same kind at my service.—I was ravished at this piece of good news, and having accommodated myself in a moment, hugged my benefactor for his generous offer, saying, I was overjoyed to find him undebauched by prosperity, which seldom fails of corrupting the heart. He bespoke for dinner, some soup and boillé,[1] a couple of pullets roasted, and a dish of sparrowgrass,[2] and in the interim entertained me with biscuit and Burgundy; after which he entreated me to gratify his longing desire of knowing every circumstance of my fortune since his departure from London. —This I complyed with, beginning at the adventure of Gawky, and relating every particular event in which I had been concerned from that day to the present hour. During the recital, my friend was strongly affected, according to the various situations described: He started with surprize, glowed with indignation, gaped with curiosity, smiled with pleasure, trembled with fear, and wept with sorrow, as the vicissitudes of my life inspired these different passions; and when my story was ended, signified his amazement on the whole, by lifting up his eyes and hands, and protesting, that tho' I was a young man, I had suffered more than all the blessed martyrs.

After dinner, I desired, in my turn, to know the particulars of his peregrination, and he satisfied me in a few words, by giving me to understand that he had lived a year at Paris with his master, who in that time, having acquired the language, as well as the fashionable exercises, to perfection, made a tour of France and Holland, during which excursion, he was so unfortunate as to meet with three of his own countrymen on their travels, in whose company he committed such excesses, that his constitution failed, and he fell into a consumption; that by the advice of physicians he went to Montpelier[3] for the benefit of good air, and recovered so well in six weeks, that he returned to Rheims, seemingly in good health, where he had not continued above a month, when he was seized with a looseness,[4] that carried him off in ten days, to the unspeakable sorrow of all who knew him, and especially of Strap, who had been very happy in his service, and given such satisfaction, that his master on his deathbed, recommended him to several persons of distinction, for his diligence, sobriety, and affection, and left him by will, his wearing apparel, gold watch, sword, rings, ready money, and all the moveables he had in France, to the value of three hundred pounds, 'which I now (said he) in the sight of God and man, surrender to your absolute disposal: Here are my keys, take them, I beseech you, and God give you joy of the possession.'——My brain was almost turned with this sudden change of fortune, which I could scarce believe real; however, I positively refused this extravagant proffer of my friend, and put him in mind of my being a soldier; at which he started, crying, 'Odso! that's true—we must procure your discharge—I have some interest with a nobleman who is able to do me that favour.'—We consulted about this affair, and it was determined that Monsieur d'Estrapes, should wait upon the Marquis in the morning, and tell him he had by accident found his brother, whom he had not seen for many years before, a private soldier in the regiment of Picardie, and implore that nobleman's interest for his discharge.—In the mean time, we enjoyed ourselves over a bottle of good Burgundy, and spent the evening in concerting schemes for our future conduct, in case I should be so lucky as to get rid of the army.—The business was to make ourselves easy for life, by means of his legacy, a task very difficult, and, in the usual methods of laying out money, altogether impracticable; so that after much canvasing, we could come to no resolution that night, but when we parted, recommended the matter to the serious attention of each other. As for my own part, I puzzled my imagination to no purpose; when I thought of turning merchant, the smallness of our stock, and the risk of seas, enemies and markets, deterred me from that scheme.—If I should settle as a surgeon in my own country, I would find the business already overstocked; or if I pretended to set up in England, must labour under want of friends and powerful opposition, obstacles unsurmountable by the most shining merit; neither would I succeed in my endeavours to rise in the state, inasmuch as I could neither flatter nor pimp for courtiers, nor prostitute my pen in defence of a wicked and contemptible administration.—Before I could form one feasible project, I fell asleep, and my fancy was blessed with the image of my dear Narcissa, who seemed to smile upon my passion, and offer her hand as a reward for all my toils.

Early in the morning, I went to the lodgings of my friend, whom I found exulting over his happy invention; for I no sooner entered his apartment, than he addressed me in these words, with a smile of self-applause: 'Well, Mr. Random, a lucky thought may come into a fool's head sometimes.—I have hit it—I'll hold you a button my plan is better than yours, for all your learning.—But you shall have the preference in this as in all other things; therefore proceed, and let us know the effects of your meditation,—and then I will impart my own simple excogitations.'——I told him, that not one thought occurred to me which deserved the least notice, and signified my impatience to be acquainted with the fruits of his reflection.— 'As we have not (said he) money sufficient to maintain us during a tedious expectation, it is my opinion, that a bold push must be made; and I see none so likely to succeed as your appearing in the character of a gentleman (which is your due) and making your addresses to some lady of fortune who can render you independant at once.——Nay, don't stare—I affirm that this scheme is both prudent and honourable; for I would not have you throw yourself away upon an old, toothless, wheezing dame, whose breath would stink you into a consumption in less than three months; neither would I advise you to assume the character of a wealthy 'Squire, as your common fortune-hunters do, by which means many a poor lady is cheated into matrimony, and instead of enjoying the pomp and grandeur that was promised, sees her dowry seized by her husband's rapacious creditors, and herself reduced to misery and despair.—No, I know you have a soul that disdains such imposition; and are master of qualifications both of mind and body, which alone entitle you to a match, that will set you above the world.—I have cloaths in my possession, that a Duke need not be ashamed to wear.—I believe they will fit you as they are—if not, there are plenty of taylors in France.—Let us take a short trip to Paris, and provide ourselves in all other necessaries, then set out for England, where I intend to do myself the honour of attending you in quality of valet. —This will save you the expence of a servant, shaving and dressing; and I doubt not but by the blessing of God, we shall bring matters to a speedy and fortunate issue.'——Extravagant as this proposal was, I listened to it with pleasure, because it flattered my vanity, and indulged a ridiculous hope I began to entertain of inspiring Narcissa with a mutual flame.

After breakfast, Monsieur d'Estrapes went to pay his devoirs to the Marquis, and was so successful in his application, that I obtained a discharge in a few days, upon which we set out for Paris.—Here I had time to reflect and congratulate myself upon this sudden transition of fate, which to bear with moderation, required some degree of philosophy and self-denial.—This will be more obvious, if I give a detail of the particulars, to the quiet possession of which I was raised in an instant, from the most abject misery and contempt.—My wardrobe consisted of five fashionable coats full-mounted, two of which were plain, one of cut velvet,[1] one trimed with gold, and another with silver-lace; two frocks, one of white drab[2] with large plate buttons, the other of blue, with gold binding; one waistcoat of gold brocard; one of blue sattin, embroidered with silver; one of green silk, trimmed with broad figured gold lace; one of black silk, with figures; one of white sattin; one of black cloth, and one of scarlet; six pair of cloth breeches; one pair of crimson, and another of black velvet; twelve pair of white silk stockings, as many of black silk, and the same number of fine cotton; one hat, laced with gold *point d'Espagne*,[3] another with silver-lace scolloped, a third with gold binding, and a fourth plain; three dozen of fine ruffled shirts, as many neckcloths; one dozen of cambrick handkerchiefs, and the like number of silk. The other moveables which I possessed by the generosity and friendship of Strap, were, a gold watch with a chased case, two valuable diamond rings, two mourning swords,[4] one with a silver handle, and a fourth cut steel inlaid with gold; a diamond stock-buckle,[5] and a set of stone buckles[6] for the knees and shoes; a pair of silver mounted pistols with rich housings,[7] a gold-headed cane, and a snuff-box of tortoise-shell mounted with gold, having the picture of a lady in the lid.—The gentleman left many other things of value, which my friend had converted into cash before I met with him, so that over and above these particulars, our stock in ready money amounted to something more than two hundred pounds.

Thus equipt, I put on the gentleman of figure, and attended by my honest friend, who was contented with the station of my valet. I visited the Louvre, examined the gallery of Luxemburgh,[8] and appeared at Versailles, where I had the honour of seeing his Most Christian Majesty eat a considerable quantity of olives.—During the month I spent at Paris, I went several times to court, the Italian opera, and play-house, danced at a masquerade, and in short saw every thing remarkable in and about that capital.—After which we set out for England by the way of Flanders, passed through Brussels, Ghent, and Bruges, and took shipping at Ostend, from whence in fourteen hours we arrived at Deal, hired a post-chaise, and in twelve hours more got safe to London; having disposed of our heavy baggage in the waggon.

CHAPTER XLV

I enquire about my uncle, and understand he is gone to sea—
take lodgings at Charing-cross——go to the play, where I
meet with an adventure——I go to an ordinary; the guests
described—become acquainted with Medlar and doctor
Wagtail

As soon as we alighted at the Inn, I dispatched Strap to enquire about my uncle, at the Samson and Lion in Wapping; and he returned in a little time, with an account of Mr. Bowling's having gone to sea, mate of a merchant ship, after a long and unsuccessful application and attendance at the admiralty; where, it seems, the interest he depended upon, was not sufficient to reinstate him, or recover the pay that was due to him when he quitted the Thunder.

Next day I hired very handsome lodgings not far from Charing-cross; and in the evening, dressed myself in a plain suit of the true Paris cut, and appeared in a front box at the play, where I saw a good deal of company, and had vanity enough to make me believe, that I was observed with an uncommon degree of attention and applause. This silly conceit intoxicated me so much, that I was guilty of a thousand ridiculous coquetries;[1] and I dare say, how favourable soever the thoughts of the company might be at my first appearance, they were soon changed by my absurd behaviour, into pity or contempt.—I got up and sat down, covered and uncovered my head twenty times between the acts; pulled out my watch, clapped it to my ear, wound it up, set it, gave it the hearing again;—displayed my snuff-box, affected to take snuff, that I might have an opportunity of shewing my brilliant, and wiped my nose with a perfumed handkerchief;—then dangled my cane, and adjusted my sword-knot, and acted many more fooleries of the same kind, in hopes of obtaining the character of a pretty fellow, in the acquiring of which, I found two considerable obstructions in my disposition; namely, a natural reserve, and jealous sensibility.—Fain would I have entered into conversation with the people around me; but was restrained by the fear of being censured for my assurance, as well as by reflecting that I was more entitled to a compliment of this kind from them than they to such condescension from a stranger like me.

—How often did I redden at the frequent whispers and loud laughter of my fellow beaus, which I imagined were excited by me! and how often did I envy the happy indifference of those choice spirits who beheld the distress of the scene, without discovering the least symptom of approbation or concern! My attention was engaged in spite of myself, and I could not help weeping with the heroine of the stage; though I practised a great many shifts to conceal this impolite piece of weakness.—When the play was ended, I sat waiting for an opportunity of handing some lady to her coach; but every one was attended by such a number of officious gallants, that for a long time I was baulked in my expectation.—At length, however, I perceived a very handsome creature, genteelly dressed, sitting by herself in a box, at some distance from me; upon which I went up to her, and offered my service.—She seemed to be in some confusion, thanked me for my complaisance, and with a tender look declined giving me the trouble; looking at her watch, and testifying her surprize at the negligence of her footman, whom she had ordered to have a chair ready for her at that hour.—I repeated my intreaty with all the eloquence and compliment I was master of; and in the event, she was prevailed upon to accept of a proposal I made, to send my servant for a chair or coach: Accordingly, Strap was detached for that purpose, and returned without success, there being none to be found; by this time the play-house was quite empty, and we were obliged to retire: As I led her through the passage, I observed five or six young fellows of fashion, standing in a corner, one of whom, as I thought, tipt my charmer the wink, and when we were past, I heard them set up the loud laugh.—This arroused my attention, and I was resolved to be fully satisfied of this lady's character, before I should have any nearer connexion with her.—As no convenience appeared, I proposed, that I should conduct her to a tavern, where we might stay a few minutes, until my servant could fetch a coach from the Strand.[1]—She seemed particularly shy of trusting herself in a tavern with a stranger; but at last, yielded to my pathetic remonstrances, rather than endanger her health, by remaining in a cold damp thorough-fare.—Having thus far succeeded, I begged to know what wine she would be pleased to drink a glass of; but she professed the greatest aversion to all sorts of strong liquors; and it was with much difficulty that I could persuade her to eat a jelly.—In the mean time, I endeavoured to alleviate the uneasiness she discovered, by saying all the agreeable things I could think of; at which she would often sigh, and regard me with a languishing look, that seemed too near a-kin to the lewd leer of a courtezan.—This discovery added to my former suspicion, while it put me upon my guard against her arts, divested me of reserve, and enabled me to entertain her with more gaity and freedom.—In the course of our conversation, I pressed her to allow me the honour of waiting upon her next day, at her lodgings, which she, with many apologies, refused, lest it should give umbrage to Sir John, who was of a disposition apt to be fretted with trifles.— This information, by which I was to understand that her husband was a knight, did not check my addresses, which became more and more importunate, and I was even hardy enough to ravish a kiss.— But, O heavens! instead of banqueting on the ambrosial flavour, that her delicacy and complexion promised, I was almost suffocated with the steams of Geneva![1] An exhalation of this kind from a mouth which had just before declared an utter abhorrence of all spirituous liquors, not only changed my doubts into certainty, but my raptures into loathing; and it would have been impossible for me to have preserved common complaisance five minutes longer, when my servant returned with a coach.—I took the advantage of this occasion, and presented my hand to the lady, who put in practice against me the whole artillery of her charms, ogling, languishing, sighing, and squeezing, with so little reserve, that Strap perceived her tenderness, and rubbed his hands with joy as he followed us to the door;—but I was proof against all her endearments, and handed her into the coach with an intention to take my leave immediately. She guessed my design, and invited me to her house, whispering, that now Sir John was gone to bed, she could have the pleasure of my conversation for half an hour without interruption.—I told her, there was no mortification I would not undergo, rather than endanger the repose of her ladyship; and bidding the coachman drive on, wished her a good night.—She lost all temper at my indifference, and stopping the coach at the distance of about twenty yards from me, popped out her head, and bawled with the lungs of a fish-woman, 'D—n you, you dog, won't you pay the coach-hire?' I made no answer: Upon which she held forth against me with an eloquence peculiar to herself; calling me pitiful fellow, scoundrel, and an hundred such appellations; and concluding with an oath, that for all my appearance, she believed I had got no money in my pocket.

Having thus vented her indignation, she ordered the coachman to proceed, and I returned to the tavern, where I bespoke something for supper, very well pleased at the issue of this adventure.—I dispensed with the attendance of the waiter at table, on pretence that my own servant was present, and when we were alone, said to Strap; 'Well, Monsieur d'Estrapes, what d'ye think of this lady?'[1] My friend, who had not opened his mouth since her departure, could make no other reply than the monosyllable 'Think!' which he pronounced with a note of fear and astonishment.—Surprized at this emphasis, I surveyed my valet, and perceiving a wildness in his looks, asked if he had seen his grandfather's ghost?—'Ghost! (said he) I am sure I have seen a devil incarnate! Who would have thought that so much devilish malice and Billingsgate,[2] could lurk under such sweetness of countenance and modesty of behaviour? Ah! God help us! *Fronti nulla fides—nimium ne crede colori*[3]—but we ought to down on our knees and bless God from delivering us from the jaws of that painted sepulchre.'—I was pretty much of Strap's opinion, and though I did not believe myself in any danger from the allurements of that sisterhood, I determined to act with great circumspection for the future, and shun all commerce of that kind, as equally prejudicial to my purse and constitution.

My next care was to introduce myself into a set of good acquaintance; for which purpose, I frequented a certain coffee-house, noted for the resort of good company, English as well as foreigners, where my appearance procured all the civilities and advances I could desire. There being an ordinary in the same house, I went up stairs to dinner with the other guests, and found myself at table with thirteen people, the greatest part of whom were better dressed than myself.—The conversation, which was mostly carried on in French, turned chiefly on politicks; and I soon found the whole company was in the French interest, myself excepted, and a testy old gentleman, who contradicted every thing that was advanced in favour of his Most Christian Majesty, with a surliness truly English.—But this trusty patriot, who had never been out of his own country, and drew all his maxims and notions from prejudice and hearsay, was very unequal to his antagonists, who were superior to him in learning and experience, and often took the liberty of travellers, in asserting things which were not strictly true, because they thought themselves in no danger of being detected by him.—The claim of the queen of Spain[4] to the Austrian dominions in Italy, was fully explained and vindicated, by a person who sat opposite to me, and by the solemnity of his manner, and the richness of his apparel, seemed to be a foreign ambassador.—This dissertation introduced another on the Pragmatic Sanction,[1] handled with great warmth by a young gentleman at my right hand, dressed in a green frock trimmed with gold, who justified the French king for his breach of that contract; and affirmed that he could not have observed it, without injuring his own glory.—Although I was not at all convinced by this gentleman's arguments, I could not help admiring his vivacity, which I imagined must be the effect of his illustrious birth, and noble education, and accordingly rated him in my conjecture as a young prince on his travels.—The discourse was afterwards shifted by an old gentleman of a very martial appearance, to the last campaign, when the battle of Dettingen was fought over again, with so many circumstances to the honour of the French, and disadvantage of the Allies, that I began to entertain some doubts of my having been there in person; and took the liberty to mention some objections to what he advanced.—This introduced a dispute which lasted a good while, to the mortification of all present; and was at last referred to the determination of a grave person, whom they stiled doctor, and who under a shew of great moderation, decided it against me, with so little regard to truth, that I taxed him with partiality in pretty severe terms, to the no small entertainment of the true English politician, who rejoiced at my defence of a cause he had so often espoused without success: My opponent pleased with the victory he had gained, affected a great deal of candour, and told me, he would not have been so positive, if he had not been at great pains to inform himself of each particular—'Indeed, (said he) I am convinced, that, the previous steps considered, things could not happen otherwise; for we generals who have seen service, tho' we may not be on the spot ourselves, know by the least sketch of the disposition, what must be the event.'—He then censured, with great freedom, every circumstance of the conduct of those who commanded the Allies; from thence made a transition to the Ministry, which he honoured with many invectives, for employing people who had neither experience nor capacity, to the prejudice of old officers who had been distinguished for both; dropt many hints of his own importance; and concluded with observing, that the French and Spaniards knew better how to value generals of merit; the good effects of which are seen in the conquests they gain, and the admirable discipline of their troops, which are at the same time better cloathed and paid than any soldiers in the universe. These remarks furnished the green knight with an opportunity of launching out in the praise of French government in general, civil as well as military; on which occasion he made many odious comparisons to the disadvantage of the English: Every body, almost, assented to the observations he made, and the doctor gave his sanction, by saying, the people in France were undoubtedly the happiest subjects in the world.—I was so much astonished and confounded at their infatuation and effrontery, that I had not power to utter one word in opposition to their assertions; but my morose associate could not put up with the indignity that was offered to old England, and therefore with a satirical grin addressed himself to the general in these words: 'Sir, Sir, I have often heard it said, *She's a villainous bird that befouls her own nest.*—As for what those people who are foreigners say, I don't mind it, they know no better; but you who were bred and born, and have got your bread under the English government, should have more regard to gratitude as well as truth, in censuring your native country.—If the ministry have thought fit to lay you aside, I suppose they have their own reasons for so doing; and you ought to remember that you still live on the bounty of this nation.—As for these gentlemen, (meaning the prince and ambassador) who make so free with our constitution, laws and genius of our people, I think they might shew a little more respect for their benefactors, who, I must own, are to blame in harbouring, protecting and encouraging such ungrateful vagrants as they are.' —At these words the chevalier in green started up in a great passion, and laying his hand on the hilt of his hanger, exclaimed, 'Ha! *foutre!*'[1]—The Englishman on the other hand, grasping his cane, cried, 'Don't *foutre* me, sirrah, or by G—d, I'll knock you down.'— The company interposed, the Frenchman sat down again, and his antagonist proceeded—'Lookee, monsieur, you know very well, that had you dared to speak so freely of the administration of your own country in Paris, as you have done of ours in London, you would have been sent to the Bastile without ceremony, where you might have rotted in a dungeon, and never seen the light of the sun again.—Now, Sir, take my word for it, although our constitution screens us from such oppression, we want not laws to chastise the authors of seditious discourse; and if I hear another syllable out of your mouth, in contempt or prejudice of this kingdom, I will give you a convincing proof of what I advance, and have you laid by the heels for your presumption.'—This declaration had an effect on the company, as sudden as surprizing.—The young prince became supple as a spaniel, the ambassador trembled, the general sat silent and abashed, and the doctor, who, it seems, had felt the rod of power, grew pale as death, and assured us all, that he had no intention to affront any person or people.—'Your principles, doctor, (resumed the old gentleman) are no secret—I have nothing to say upon that head; but am very much surprized, that a man who despises us so much, should notwithstanding live among us, when he has no visible motive for so doing.—Why don't you take up your habitation in your beloved France, where you may rail at England without censure?'——To this the doctor thought proper to make no reply; and an unsocial silence ensued; which I perceiving, took notice, that it was pity such idle disputes, maintained very often for whim or diversion, should create any misunderstanding among gentlemen of good sense; and proposed to drink down all animosity in another bottle.—This motion was applauded by the whole company: The wine was brought, and the English champion declaring he had no spleen against any man for differing in opinion from him, any more than for difference of complexion, drank to the good health of all present; the compliment was returned, and the conversation once more became unreserved, though more general than before.—Among other topicks, the subject of war was introduced, on which the general declaimed with great eloquence, recounting many of his own exploits by way of illustration.—In the course of his harrangue he happened to mention the word *epaulement*,[1] upon which the testy gentleman asked the meaning of that term.—'I'll tell you what an epaulement is, (replied he)—I never saw an epaulement but once—and that was at the siege of Namur[2]—in a council of war, monsieur Cohorn,[3] the famous engineer, affirmed that the place could not be taken.'—'Yes, (said the prince of Vaudemont)[4] it may be taken by an epaulement.'—'This was immediately put in execution, and in twenty-four hours Mareschal Boufflers[5] was fain to capitulate.'—Here he made a full stop, and the old gentleman repeated the question, 'But pray what is an epaulement?'——To this the officer made no immediate reply, but rung the bell and called for a bill, which being brought, he threw down his proportion of the reckoning, and telling the company, he would shew them what an epaulement is, when his Majesty thought fit to entrust him with the command of our army abroad, strutted away with great dignity.—I could not imagine why he was so shy of explaining one of the most simple terms of fortification; which I forthwith described as a side-work composed of earth, gabions,[1] or faschins; but I was very much surprized when I afterwards understood that his reserve proceeded from his ignorance.—Having paid our bill, we adjourned to the coffee-room, where my fellow-labourer insisted on treating me with a dish,[2] giving me to understand at the same time, that I had acquired his good opinion, both with respect to my principles and intellects.——I thanked him for his compliment, and professing myself an utter stranger in this part of the world, begged he would have the goodness to inform me of the quality and characters of the people who dined above.—This request was a real favour to one of his disposition, which was no less communicative than curious; he therefore complied with great satisfaction, and let me know, to my extreme astonishment, that the supposed young prince was a dancer at one of the theatres; and the ambassador no other than a fidler belonging to the opera. 'The doctor (said he) is a Roman Catholick priest, who sometimes appears in the character of an officer, and assumes the name of captain; but more generally takes the garb, title and behaviour of a physician, in which capacity he wheedles himself into the confidence of weak-minded people, and by arguments no less specious than false, converts them from their religion and allegiance.—He has been in the hands of justice more than once for such practices; but he is a sly dog, and manages matters with so much craft, that hitherto he has escaped for a short imprisonment.—As for the general, you may see he has owed his promotion more to his interest than his capacity; and now that the eyes of the ministry are opened, his friends dead, or become inconsiderable, he is struck off the list, and obliged to put up with a yearly pension; in consequence of this reduction, he is become malecontent, and enveighs against the government in all companies, with so little discretion, that I am surprised at the lenity of the administration in overlooking his insolence, but the truth of the matter is, he owes his safety to his weakness and want of importance.—He has seen a little, and but a little service, and yet if you will take his word for it, there has not been a great action performed in the field since the revolution, in which he was not principally concerned. When a story is told of any great general, he immediately matches it with one of himself, though he is often unhappy in his invention, and commits such gross blunders in the detail, that every body is in pain for him.—Cæsar, Pompey, and Alexander[1] the Great are continually in his mouth; and as he reads a good deal without any judgment to digest it, his ideas are confused, and his harrangues as unintelligible as infinite; for, once he begins, there is no chance of his leaving off speaking, while one person remains to yield attention; therefore the only expedient I know, of putting a stop to his loquacity, is to lay hold of some incongruity he has uttered, and demand an explanation; or ask the meaning of some difficult term that he knows by name only, this will effectually put him to silence, if not to flight, as it happened when I enquired about an *epaulement*.—Had he been acquainted with the signification of that word, his triumph would have been intolerable, and we must have quitted the field first, or been worried with impertinence.'—Having thus gratified my curiosity, the old gentleman began to discover his own, in questions relating to myself, to which I thought proper to return ambiguous answers.—'I presume, Sir, (said he) you have travelled.'—I answered, 'Yes.'—'I dare say, you would find it very expensive (said he.)'—I replied, 'To be sure, one cannot travel without money.'—'That I know by experience (said he) for I myself take a trip to Bath or Tunbridge[2] every season; and one must pay sauce[3] for what he has on the road as well in other countries as in this.—That's a very pretty stone in your ring,—give me leave, Sir,—the French have attained to a wonderful skill in making compositions of this kind.—Why now, this looks almost as well as a diamond.'—'Almost as well, Sir, (said I) why not altogether?—I'm sure if you understand any thing of jewels, you must perceive at first sight, that this stone is a real diamond, and that of a very fine water.—Take it in your hand, and examine it.'——He did so, with some confusion, and returned it, saying, 'I ask your pardon, I see it is a true brilliant of immense value.'—I imagined his respect for me increased after this inquiry; therefore to captivate his esteem the more, I told him, I would shew him a seal of composition,[4] engraved after a very valuable antique; upon which I pulled out my watch with a rich gold chain, adorned with three seals set in gold, and an opal ring.—He viewed each of them with great eagerness, handled the chain, admired the chased case, and observed that the whole must have cost me a vast sum of money. I affected indifference, and replied in a careless manner, 'Some trifle of sixty or seventy guineas.' Upon which he stared in my face for some time, and then asked if I was an Englishman.—I answered in the negative.—'You are from Ireland then, Sir, I presume, (said he.)' I made the same reply. 'O! perhaps (said he) you was born in one of our settlements abroad.'—I still answered no.—He seemed very much surprized, and said, he was sure I was not a foreigner. I made no reply, but left him upon the tenter-hooks of impatient uncertainty.—He could not contain his anxiety, but asked pardon for the liberties he had taken, and to encourage me the more to disclose my situation, display'd his own without reserve.——'I am (said he) a single man, have a considerable annuity, on which I live according to my own inclination; and make the ends of the year meet very comfortably.—As I have no estate to leave behind me, I am not troubled with the importunate officiousness of relations, or legacy hunters, and I consider the world as made for me, not me for the world: It is my maxim therefore to enjoy it while I can, and let futurity shift for itself.'—While he thus indulged his own talkative vein, and at the same time, no doubt, expected a retaliation from me; a young man entered, dressed in black velvet and an enormous tye-wig, with an air in which natural levity and affected solemnity were so jumbled together, that on the whole, he appeared a burlesque on all decorum. This ridiculous oddity[1] danced up to the table at which we sat, and after a thousand grimaces, asked my friend by the name of Mr. Medlar,[2] if we were not engaged upon business.—My companion put on a surly countenance, and replied, 'No great business, doctor—but however.'—'O! then (cried the physician) I must beg your indulgence a little, pray pardon me, gentlemen.—Sir, (said he, addressing himself to me) your most humble servant, I hope you will forgive me, Sir—I must beg the favour to sit—Sir—Sir—I have something of consequence to impart to my friend Mr. Medlar—Sir, I hope you will excuse my freedom in whispering, Sir.'—Before I had time to give this complaisant person my permission, Mr. Medlar cried, 'I'll have no whispering —if you have any thing to say to me, speak with an audible voice.'— The doctor seemed a little disconcerted at this exclamation, and turning again to me, making a thousand apologies for pretending to make a mystery of any thing, which he said was owing to his ignorance of my connexion with Mr. Medlar; but now he understood I was a friend, he would communicate what he had to say, in my hearing.—He then began, after two or three hems, in this manner: —'You must know Sir, I am just come from dinner at my lady

Chapter XLV

Flareit's,[1] (then addressing himself to me) a lady of quality, Sir, at whose table I have the honour of dining sometimes.—There was lady Stately, and my lady Larum,[2] and Mrs. Dainty, and Miss Biddy Gigler, upon my word, a very good natured young lady, with a very pretty fortune, Sir.—There was also my Lord Straddle, Sir John Shrug, and master Billy Chatter, who is actually a very facetious young gentleman.—So, Sir, her ladyship seeing me excessively fatigued, for she was the last of fifteen patients (people of distinction, Sir) whom I have visited this fore-noon,—insisted upon my staying dinner,—though upon my word, I protest I had no appetite; however, in compliance with her ladyship's request, Sir, I sat down, and the conversation turning on different subjects, among other things, Mr. Chatter asked very earnestly when I saw Mr. Medlar.—I told him I had not had the pleasure of seeing you these nineteen hours and a half; for you may remember, Sir, it was nearly about that time; I won't be positive as to a minute.'—'No! (says he) then I desire you will go to his lodgings immediately after dinner, and see what is the matter with him, for he must certainly be very bad from having eat last night such a vast quantity of raw oysters.'—The crusty gentleman, who from the solemnity of his delivery, expected something extraordinary, no sooner heard his conclusion, than he started up in a testy humour, crying, 'Pshaw, pshaw! d—n your oysters;' and walked away after a short compliment of 'Your servant, Sir,' to me.—The doctor got up also, saying, 'I vow and protest, upon my word, I am actually amazed.'—and followed Mr. Medlar to the bar, which was hard by, where he was paying for the coffee; there he whispered so loud that I could overhear, 'Pray, who is this gentleman?'—His friend replied hastily, 'I might have known that before now, if it had not been for your impertinent intrusion,'—and walked away very much disappointed.——The ceremonious physician returned immediately and sat down by me, asking a thousand pardons for leaving me alone; and giving me to understand that what he had communicated to Mr. Medlar at the bar was an affair of the last importance, that would admit of no delay.—He then called for some coffee, and launched out into the virtues of that berry,[3] which, he said, in cold phlegmatic constitutions, like his, dried up the superfluous moisture, and braced the relaxed nerves.—He let me know, that it was utterly unknown to the ancients; and derived its name from an Arabian word, which I might easily perceive by the sound and termination.—From this topick he transferred his disquisitions to the verb *drink*, which he affirmed, was improperly applied to the taking of coffee, in as much as people did not drink, but sip or sipple that liquor;—that the genuine meaning of drinking is to quench one's thirst, or commit a debauch by swallowing wine;—that the Latin word, which conveyed the same idea, was *bibere* or *potare*, and that of the Greeks *pinein* or *poteein*, though he was apt to believe they were differently used on different occasions: For example; to drink a vast quantity, or, as the vulgar express it, to drink an ocean of liquor, was in Latin *potare*, and in Greek *poteein*; and on the other hand, to use it moderately, was *bibere* and *pinein*;—that this was only a conjecture of his own, which, however, seemed to be supported by the word *bibulous*, which is particularly applied to the pores of the skin, that can only drink a very small quantity of the circumambient moisture, by reason of the smallness of their diameters;——whereas, from the verb *poteein*, is derived the substantive *potamos*, which signifies a river, or vast quantity of liquor.—I could not help smiling at this learned and important investigation; and to recommend myself the more to my new acquaintance, whose disposition I was by this time well informed of, I observed, that what he alledged, did not, to the best of my remembrance, appear in the writings of the ancients; for, Horace uses the words *poto* and *bibo* indifferently for the same purpose, as in the twentieth Ode of his first Book.

> *Vile potabis modicis sabinum cantharis,——*
> *——Et prælo domitam caleno tu bibes uvam.*[1]

That I had never heard of the verb *poteein*, but that *potamos*, *potema*, and *potos*, were derived from *pino*, *poso*, *pepoka*: in consequence of which, the Greek poets never use any other word for festal drinking.—Homer describes Nestor at his cups in these words:

> *Nestora d' ouk elathen jache* pinonta *perempes.*[2]

And Anacreon mentions it on the same occasion almost in every page,

> Pionti *d' oinon hedun*
> Otan pino *ton oinon.*
> Opliz' *ego de* pino.[3]

And in a thousand other places.—The doctor, who, doubtless, in-tended by his criticism, to give me an high idea of his erudition, was infinitely surprized to find himself schooled by one in my appearance; and after a considerable pause, cried, 'Upon my word! you are in the right, Sir.—I find I have not considered this affair with my usual accuracy.'—Then accosting me, in Latin, which he spoke very well, the conversation was maintained full two hours, on a variety of subjects, in that language; and indeed, he spoke so judiciously, that I was convinced, notwithstanding his whimsical appearance, and attention to trifles, of his being a man of extensive knowledge, especially in books; he looked upon me, as I afterwards understood from Mr. Medlar, as a prodigy in learning, and pro-posed that very night, if I was not engaged, to introduce me to several young gentlemen of fortune and fashion, with whom he had an appointment at the Bedford coffee-house.[1]

CHAPTER XLVI

*Wagtail introduces me to a set of fine gentlemen, with whom
I spend the evening at a tavern——our conversation——the
characters of my new companions——the doctor is roasted——
the issue of our debauch*

I ACCEPTED his offer with pleasure, and we went thither in a hackney-coach, where I saw a great number of gay figures fluttering about, most of whom spoke to the doctor with great familiarity. Among the rest, stood a groupe of them around the fire, whom I immediately knew to be the very persons who had the night before, by their laughing, alarmed my suspicion of the lady who had put herself under my protection.—They no sooner perceived me enter with Dr. Wagtail[2] (for that was my companion's name) than they tittered and whispered one to another; and I was not a little sur-prized to find that they were the gentlemen to whose acquaintance he designed to recommend me; for when he observed them together, he told me who they were, and desired to know by what name he should introduce me. I satisfied him in that particular, and he ad-vanced with great gravity, saying, 'Gentlemen, your most obedient —give me leave to introduce my friend Mr. Random, to your

society.' Then turning to me, 'Mr. Random, this is Mr. Bragwell—
Mr. Banter, Sir—Mr. Chatter—my friend Mr. Slyboot, and Mr.
Ranter, Sir.'—I saluted each of them in order, and when I came to
take Mr. Slyboot by the hand, I perceived him thrust his tongue in
his cheek, to the no small entertainment of the company; but I did
not think proper to take any notice of it, on this occasion.—Mr.
Ranter too, (who I afterwards learned was a player) displayed his
talents, by mimicking my air, features and voice, while he returned
my compliment:—This I should not have been so sensible of, had
I not seen him behave in the same manner, to my friend Wagtail,
when he made up to them at first.—But for once I let him enjoy the
fruits of his dexterity without question or controul, resolved however, to chastize his insolence at a more convenient opportunity.—
Mr. Slyboot guessing I was a stranger, asked if I had been lately
in France; and when I answered in the affirmative, enquired if I
had seen the Luxemburg gallery: I told him, I had considered it
more than once, with great attention: Upon this a conversation
ensued, in which I discovered him to be a painter.—While we were
discoursing upon the particular pieces of this famous collection, I
overheard Banter ask Dr. Wagtail, where he had picked up this Mr.
Random.—To which question the physician answered, 'Upon my
word, a mighty pretty sort of a gentleman—a man of fortune, Sir—
he has made the grand tour—and seen the best company in Europe,
Sir.'—'What, he told you so? I suppose, (said the other) I take him
to be neither more nor less than a French *valet de chambre*.'——
'Oh! barbarous, barbarous! (cried the doctor) this is actually, upon
my word, altogether unaccountable.—I know all his family perfectly well, Sir—He's of the Randoms in the north—a very ancient
house, Sir, and a distant relation of mine.'—I was extremely nettled
at the conjecture of Mr. Banter, and began to entertain a very indifferent opinion of my company in general; but as I might possibly,
by their means, acquire a more extensive and agreeable acquaintance, I determined to bear these little mortifications as long as I
could, without injuring the dignity of my character.—After having
talked for some time on the weather, plays, politicks, and other
coffee-house subjects, it was proposed that we should spend the
evening at a noted tavern in the neighbourhood, whither we repaired in a body.—Having taken possession of a room, called for
French wine, and bespoke supper, the glass went about pretty
freely, and the characters of my associates opened upon me more

and more.—It soon appeared that the doctor was entertained as a butt for the painter and player to exercise their wit upon, for the diversion of the company. Mr. Ranter began the game, by asking him what was good for a hoarseness, lowness of spirits and indigestion, he being troubled with all these complaints to a very great degree.—Wagtail immediately undertook to explain the nature of his case, and in a very prolix manner, harrangued upon prognostics, diagnostics, symptomatics, therapeutics, inanition, and repletion; then calculated the force of the stomach and lungs in their respective operations; ascribed the player's malady to a disorder in these organs, proceeding from hard drinking and vociferation, and prescribed a course of stomachics, with abstinence from venery, wine, and loud speaking, laughing, singing, coughing, sneezing or hollowing.——'Pah, pah, (cried Ranter, interrupting him) the remedy is worse than the disease—I wish I knew where to find some tinder-water.'—'Tinder-water! (said the doctor) upon my word I don't apprehend you, Mr. Ranter.'—'Water extracted from tinder (replied the other) an universal specific for all distempers incident to man.—It was invented by a learned German monk, who, for a valuable consideration, imparted the secret to Paracelsus.'[1]— 'Pardon me (cried the painter) it was first used by Solomon, as appears by a Greek manuscript, in his own hand-writing, lately found at the foot of mount Lebanon, by a peasant who was digging for potatoes.'—'Well, (said Wagtail) in all my vast reading, I never met with such a preparation! neither did I know till this minute, that Solomon understood Greek, or that potatoes grew in Palestine.' ——Here Banter interposed, saying, he was surprized that doctor Wagtail should make the least doubt of Solomon's understanding Greek, when he is represented to us as the wisest and best educated prince in the world; and as for potatoes, they were transplanted thither from Ireland, in the time of the Crusades, by some knights of that country.—'I profess (said the doctor) there is nothing more likely—I would actually give a vast sum for a sight of that manuscript, which must be inestimable—and if I understood the process, would set about it immediately.'——The player assured him, the process was very simple—that he must cram a hundred weight of dry tinder into a glass retort, and distilling it by the force of animal heat, it would yield half a scruple[2] of insipid water, one drop of which is a full dose.—'Upon my integrity! (exclaimed the credulous doctor) this is very amazing and extraordinary! that a *caput*

271

mortuum[1] shall yield any water at all—I must own, I have always been an enemy to specifics,[2] which I thought inconsistent with the nature of the animal œconomy; but certainly the authority of Solomon is not to be questioned.—I wonder where I shall find a glass retort large enough to contain such a vast quantity of tinder, the consumption of which must undoubtedly raise the price of paper[3]—or where shall I find animal heat sufficient, even to warm such a mass.'
—Slyboot informed him, that he might have a retort blown for him as big as a church, and that the easiest method of raising the vapour by animal heat, would be to place it in the middle of an infirmary for feverish patients, who might lie upon matrasses around, and in contact with it.—He had no sooner pronounced these words, than Wagtail exclaimed in a rapture, 'An admirable expedient, as I hope to be saved! I will positively put it in practice.'——This simplicity of the physician furnished excellent diversion for the company, who in their turns, sneered at him in ironical compliments, which his vanity swallowed as the genuine sentiments of their hearts.—Mr. Chatter, impatient of so long a silence, now broke out, and entertained us with a catalogue of all the people who danced at the last Hampstead assembly,[4] with a most circumstantial account of the dress and ornaments of each, from the lappets[5] of the ladies to the shoe-buckles of the men; concluding with telling Bragwell, that his mistress Melinda was there and seemed to miss him; and soliciting his company at the next occasion of that kind.——'No, no, damme (said Bragwell) I have something else to mind than dangling after a parcel of giddy-headed girls;—besides, you know my temper is so unruly, that I am apt to involve myself in scrapes, when a woman is concerned.—The last time I was there, I had an affair with Tom Trippet.'[6]——'O! I remember that (cried Banter) you lugged out before the ladies; and I commend you for so doing, because you had an opportunity of shewing your manhood, without running any risk.'—'Risk! (said the other with a fierce countenance) d—n my blood! I fear no risks.—I a'n't afraid of lugging out against any man that wears a head, damme! 'tis well known I have drawn blood more than once, and lost some too; but what does that signify?'—The player begged this champion to employ him as his second the next time he intended to kill, for he wanted to see a man die of a stab, that he might know how to act such a part the more naturally on the stage.——'Die! (replied the hero) No, by G—d! I know better things than to incur the verdict of a Middlesex jury—I should look

upon my fencing-master to be an ignorant son of a b—ch, if he had not taught me to prick any part of my antagonist's body, that I please to disable.'—'Oho! (cried Slyboot) if that be the case, I have a favour to ask: You must know I am employed to paint a Jesus on the cross; and my purpose is to represent him at that point of time, when the spear is thrust into his side.—Now I should be glad you would, in my presence, pink[1] some impertinent fellow into convulsions, without endangering his life, that I may have an opportunity of taking a good clever agony from nature:—The doctor will direct you where to enter, and how far to go; but pray let it be as near the left side as possible.'—Wagtail, who took this proposal seriously, observed, that it would be a very difficult matter to penetrate into the left side of the thorax, without hurting the heart, and of consequence killing the patient; but he believed it was possible for a man of a very nice hand, and exact knowledge of anatomy, to wound the diaphragma somewhere about the skirts,[2] which might induce a singultus,[3] without being attended with death;—that he was ready to demonstrate the insertion of that muscle to Mr. Bragwell; but desired to have no concern with the experiment, which might essentially prejudice his reputation in case of a miscarriage.—Bragwell was as much imposed upon by the painter's waggery as the doctor, and declined engaging in the affair, saying, he had a very great regard for Mr. Slyboot, but had laid it down as a maxim, never to fight except when his honour was engaged.—A thousand jokes of this kind were pass'd; the wine circulated, supper was served in, we eat heartily, returned to the bottle, Bragwell became noisy and troublesome, Banter grew more and more severe, Ranter rehearsed, Slyboot made faces at the whole company, I sung French catches, and Chatter kissed me with great affection; while the doctor with a woful countenance, sat silent like a disciple of Pythagoras.[4]—At length, it was proposed by Bragwell, that we should scour[5] the hundreds, sweat the constable, maul the watch, and then reel soberly to bed.

While we deliberated upon this expedition, the waiter came into the room, and asked for doctor Wagtail; when he understood he was present, he told him, there was a lady below to enquire for him; at which the physician started from his melancholy contemplation, and with a look of extreme confusion, assured the company, he could not possibly be the person wanted, for he had no connexion with any lady whatever; and bid the drawer tell her so.—'For shame! (cried Banter) would you be so impolite as to refuse a lady the hearing? perhaps she comes for a consultation.—It must be some extraordinary affair that brings a lady to a tavern at this time o'night.—Mr. Ranter, pray do the doctor's baise-mains[1] to the lady, and squire her hither.'—The player immediately staggered out, and returned, leading in with much ceremony, a tall strapping wench, whose appearance proclaimed her condition. We received her with the utmost solemnity, and with a good deal of intreaty she was persuaded to sit, when a profound silence ensued, during which she fixed her eyes, with a disconsolate look, upon the doctor, who was utterly confounded at her behaviour, and returned her melancholy four-fold; at length, after a good many piteous sighs, she wiped her eyes, and accosted him thus: 'What! not one word of comfort? Will nothing soften that stony heart of thine? Not all my tears! not all my affliction! Not the inevitable ruin thou hast brought upon me! Where are thy vows, thou faithless perjured man?—Hast thou no honour?—no conscience—no remorse for thy perfidious conduct towards me!—answer me, wilt thou at last do me justice, or must I have recourse to heaven and hell for my revenge!'—If poor Wagtail was amazed before she spoke, what must his confusion be on hearing this address. His natural paleness changed into a ghastly clay colour, his eyes rolled, his lip trembled, and he answered in an accent not to be described;——'Upon my word, honour, and salvation! madam, you are actually mistaken in my person,—I have a most particular veneration for your sex, madam, and am actually incapable of injuring any lady in the smallest degree, madam,—besides, madam, to the best of my recollection, I never had the honour of seeing you before, as I hope to be saved, madam!'—'How, traitor! (cried she) dost thou disown me then?— Mistaken! no,—too well I know that fair bewitching face! too well I know that false enchanting tongue! alas! gentlemen, since the villain compels me, by his unkindness, to expose myself and him, know, that this betrayer, under the specious pretence of honourable addresses, won my heart, and taking advantage of his conquest, robbed me of my virgin treasure, and afterwards abandoned me to my fate!—I am now four months gone with child by him, turned out of doors by my relations, and left a prey to misery and want! Yes, thou Barbarian (said she, turning to Wagtail) thou tiger, thou Succubus! too well thou knowest my situation—but I will tear out thy faithless heart, and deliver the world from such a monster.'—

So saying, she sprung forward at the doctor, who, with incredible agility, jumped over the table and got behind Bragwell, while the rest of us endeavoured to appease the furious heroine—Although every body in the company affected the utmost surprize, I could easily perceive it was a scheme concerted among them, to produce diversion at the doctor's expence; and being under no concern about the consequence, I entered into the confederacy, and enjoy'd the distress of Wagtail, who with tears in his eyes, begged the protection of the company, declaring himself as innocent of the crime laid to his charge, as the fœtus in utero; and hinting at the same time, that nature had not put it in his power to be guilty of such a trespass—'Nature! (cried the lady,) there was no nature in the case—he abused me by the help of charms and spells; else how is it possible, that any woman could have listened to the addresses of such a scarecrow?—Were these owlish eyes made for ogling; that carrion complexion to be admired; or that mouth like a horse-shoe to be kissed? No, no, you owe your success to your philtres, to your drugs and incantations; and not to your natural talents, which are in every respect mean and contemptible'—The doctor now thought he had got an opportunity of vindicating himself effectually; and desired the complainant to compose herself but for half an hour, in which he undertook to prove the absurdity of believing in the power of incantations, which were only idle dreams of ignorance and superstition.—He accordingly pronounced a very learned discourse upon the nature of ideas, the powers and independance of the mind, the properties of stimulating medicines, the difference between a proneness to venery, which many simples[1] would create, and a passion limited to one object, which can only be the result of sense and reflection; and concluded with a pathetic remonstrance, setting forth his unhappiness of being persecuted with the resentment of a lady whom he had never injured, nor even seen before that occasion, and whose faculties were, in all likelihood, so much impaired by her misfortunes, that an innocent person was in danger of being ruined by her disorder.—He had no sooner finished his harrangue, than the forlorn princess began her lamentations afresh, and cautioned the company against his eloquence, which, she said, was able to byass the most impartial bench in christendom.—Banter advised him to espouse her immediately, as the only means to salve his reputation, and offered to accompany him to the Fleet[2] for that purpose; but Slyboot proposed that a father should be purchased for the child, and a comfortable alimony settled on the mother. Ranter promised to adopt the infant *gratis*. Wagtail was ready to worship him for his generosity; and though he persisted in protesting his innocence, condescended to every thing rather than his unblemished character should be called in question. —The lady rejected the expedient, and insisted on matrimony. Bragwell took up the cudgels for the doctor, and undertook to rid him of her importunity, for half a guinea; upon which Wagtail, with great eagerness, pulled out his purse and put it into the hand of his friend, who taking half a piece out of it, gave it to the plaintiff, and bid her thank God for her good fortune. When she had received this bounty, she affected to weep, and begged, since the physician had renounced her, he would at least vouchsafe her a parting kiss; this he was prevailed upon to grant, with great reluctance, and went up, with his usual solemnity, to salute her; she laid hold of his cheek with her teeth and held fast, while he roared with anguish, to the unspeakable diversion of all present. When she thought proper to release him, she dropped a low courtesy to the company, and quitted the room, leaving the doctor in the utmost horror, not so much on account of the pain, as the apprehension of the consequence of the bite; for by this time, he was convinced of her being mad. Banter prescribed the actual cautery, and put the poker in the fire to be heated, in order to sear the place.—The player was of opinion that Bragwell should scoop out the part affected with the point of his sword; but the painter prevented both these dreadful operations, by recommending a balsam he had in his pocket, which never failed to cure the bite of a mad dog: With these words, he pulled out a small bladder of black paint, with which he instantly anointed not only the fore, but the greatest part of the patient's face, and left it in a frightful condition.—In short, the poor creature was so harrassed with fear and vexation, that I pitied him extremely, and sent him home in a chair, contrary to the inclination of every body present.

This freedom of mine, gave umbrage to Bragwell, who testified his displeasure, by swearing a few threats, without making any application; which was no sooner perceived by Slyboot, who sat by me, than with a view of promoting a quarrel, he whispered to me, that he thought Bragwell used me very ill; but every man was the best judge of his own affairs.—I answered aloud, that I would neither suffer Mr. Bragwell nor him to use me ill with impunity;

and that I stood in no need of his counsel in regard to the regulation of my conduct.—He thought proper to ask a thousand pardons, and assure me, he meant no offence; while Bragwell feigned himself asleep, that he might not be obliged to take notice of what passed.— But the player, who had more animal spirits, and less prudence than Slyboot, unwilling to let the affair rest, where he had dropt it, jogged Mr. Bragwell, and told him softly, that I called him names, and threatned to cudgel him.—This I understood by his starting up and crying, 'Blood and wounds! you lie—No man durst treat me so ignominiously,—Mr. Random, did you call me names, and threaten to drub me?' I denied the imputation, and proposed to punish the scoundrel, who endeavoured to foment disturbance in the company; Bragwell signified his approbation, and drew his sword; I did the same, and accosted the actor in these words, 'Lookee, Mr. Ranter, I know you possess all the mimickry and mischievous qualities of an ape, because I have observed you put them in practice more than once to-night, on me and others; now I want to see if you resemble one in nimbleness also; therefore I desire you to leap over this sword without hesitation;' so saying, I held it parallel to the horizon, at the distance of about three feet from the floor, and called, 'Once—twice—thrice, and away;'—but instead of complying with my command, he snatched his hat and hanger, and assuming the looks, swagger, and phrase of Pistol,[1] burst out in the following exclamation, 'Ha! must I then perform inglorious prank, of Sylvan ape in mountain forest caught![2] Death rock me asleep, abridge my doleful days, and lay my hand in fury's lap—Have we not Hiren here?'[3]—This buffoonery did not answer his expectation, for by this time the company was bent on seeing him in a new character. Mr. Banter desired me to hold my sword a foot or two higher, that he might have the better opportunity of exerting himself.—The painter told him, if he performed well, he would recommend him as a vaulter to the proprietors of Sadler's Wells;[4] and Bragwell crying, 'Leap for the king,' applied the point of his sword to the player's posteriors, with such success, that he sprung over in a trice, and finding the door unguarded, vanished in a twinkling; glad, no doubt, of having paid his share of the reckoning so easily.

It being now near two a-clock in the morning, we discharged the bill, and sallied out into the street.—The painter slunk away without taking his leave.—Billy Chatter being unable to speak or stand, was sent to a Bagnio; and Banter and I accompanied Bragwell to Moll King's coffee-house,[1] where after he had kicked half a dozen of hungry whores, we left him asleep on a bench, and directed our course towards Charing-Cross, near which place both he and I lodged.

The natural dryness of my companion being overcome by liquor, he honoured me by the way with many compliments and professions of friendship, for which I made suitable acknowledgments, and told him, I thought myself happy in having, by my behaviour, removed the unfavourable opinion he entertained of me at first sight.—He was surprized at this declaration, and begged me to explain myself: Upon which I mentioned what I had over-heard him say of me to Wagtail, in the coffee-house.—He laughed, and made an apology for his freedom, assuring me, that my appearance had very much prepossessed him in my favour; and what he said, was only intended as a joke on the doctor's solemnity.—I was highly pleased at being undeceived in this particular, and not a little proud of the good opinion of this wit, who shook me by the hand at parting, and promised to meet me next day at the ordinary.

CHAPTER XLVII

Strap communicates to me a conquest he had made on a chandler's widow—finds himself miserably mistaken——I go to the opera——admire Melinda ——am cautioned by Banter ——go to the assembly at Hampstead——dance with that young lady—receive an insolent message from Bragwell, whose mettle is soon cooled——am in favour with my mistress, whom I visit next day; and am bubbled out of eighteen guineas at cards——Strap triumphs at my success, but is astonished at my expence——Banter comes to my lodging, is very sarcastic at my expence, and borrows five guineas from me, as a proof of his friendship

IN the morning before I got up, Strap came into my chamber, and finding me awake, hemmed several times, scratched his head, cast his eyes upon the ground, and with a very foolish kind of a simper on his face, let me know he had something to communicate.—'By your countenance (said I) I expect to hear good tidings.'—'Indifferent (replied he, tittering) that is, thereafter as it shall be.—You must know, I have some thoughts of altering my condition.'—— 'What! (cried I, astonished) a matrimonial scheme? O rare Strap! thou hast got the heels of me at last.'[1]—— 'N'–no less, I'll assure you (said he, bursting into a laugh of self-approbation) a tallow-chandler's widow, that lives hard by, has taken a liking to me.—A fine jolly dame, as plump as a partridge.—She has a well furnished house, a brisk trade, and a good deal of the ready.—I may have her for the asking.—She told a friend of mine, a brother footman, that she would take me out of a stinking clout.—But I refused to give my final answer, till I knew your opinion of the matter.'—I congratulated Monsieur d'Estrapes upon his conquest, and approved of the scheme, provided he could be assured of these circumstances of her fortune; but advised him to do nothing rashly, and give me an opportunity of seeing the lady before matters should be brought to a conclusion.—He assured me he would do nothing without my consent and approbation, and that very morning, while I was at breakfast, introduced his innamorata to my acquaintance.——She was a short thick woman, about the age of thirty-six, and had a particular prominence of belly, which I perceived at first sight, not without some suspicion of foul play.—I desired her, however, to sit, and treated her with a dish of tea; the discourse turning on the good qualities of Strap, whom I represented as a prodigy of sobriety, industry and virtue.—When she took her leave, he followed her to the door, and returned licking his lips, and asking if I did not think she was a luscious creature.—I made no mystery of my apprehension, but declared my sentiments of her without reserve; at which he was not surprized, telling me, he had observed the same symptom, but was informed by his friend that she was only livergrown,[2] and would in a few months be as small in the Waist as ever.—'Yes, (said I) a few weeks, I believe, will do the business.—In short, Strap, it is my opinion, that you are egregiously imposed upon; and that this friend is no other than a rascal who wants to palm his trull upon you for a wife, that he may at once deliver himself from the importunities of the mother, and the expence of her bantling; for which reason I would not have you trust implicitly to the report he makes of her wealth, which is inconsistent with his behaviour; nor run your head precipitately into a noose, that you may afterwards wished exchanged for the hangman's.' He seemed very much startled at my insinuation, and promised to look twice before he leaped; saying, with some heat, 'Odd, if I find his intention is to betray me, we shall see which of us is the better man.'—My prediction was verified in less than a fortnight; her great belly producing an infant, to the unspeakable amazement of Strap, who was, before this happened, inclinable to believe I had refined a little too much in my penetration. His false friend disappeared, and in a few days after, an execution was issued against her goods and household-furniture, which were seized by the creditors.

Mean while I met my friend Banter at the ordinary, and in the evening went to the opera with him and Mr. Chatter, who pointed out Melinda in one of the boxes, and offered to introduce me to her, observing at the same time, that she was a reigning toast worth ten thousand pounds.—This piece of information made my heart bound with joy, and I discovered great eagerness to accept the proposal; upon which he assured me I should dance with her at the next assembly, if he had any influence in that quarter; so saying, he went round, spoke to her some minutes, and, as I imagined, pointed to me, then returning, told me, to my inexpressible pleasure, that I might depend upon what he had promised, for she was now engaged as my partner.—Banter, in a whisper, gave me to understand that she was an incorrigible coquette, who would grant the same favour to any young fellow in England, of a tolerable appearance, meerly to engage him among the herd of her admirers, that she might have the pleasure of seeing them increase daily;—that she was of a cold insensible disposition, dead to every passion but vanity, and so blind to merit, that he would lay any wager, the wealthiest fool should carry her at last. I attributed a good deal of this intelligence to the satirical turn of my friend, or resentment, for having himself suffered a rebuff from the lady in question; and at any rate, trusted so much to my own accomplishments, as to believe no woman could resist the ardour of my addresses.

Full of this confidence, I repaired to Hampstead, in company with Billy Chatter, my Lord Hobble, and doctor Wagtail.—Here I saw a very brilliant assembly, before whom I had the honour to walk a minuet with Melinda, who charmed me with her frank manner of receiving me, and easiness of behaviour.—Before the country dances began, I received a message by a person I did not know, from Bragwell, who was present, importing that no body who knew him, presumed to dance with Melinda, while he was there in person; and that I would do well to relinquish her without noise, because he had a mind to lead up a country dance with her. This extraordinary intimation, which was delivered in the lady's hearing, did not at all discompose me, who by this time was pretty well acquainted with the character of my rival. I therefore, without the least symptom of concern, bid the gentleman tell Mr. Bragwell, that while I was so happy as to obtain the lady's consent, I should not be sollicitous about his; and desired the bearer himself to bring me no such impertinent messages for the future. Melinda affected a sort of confusion, and pretended to wonder that Mr. Bragwell should give himself such liberties with regard to her, who had no manner of connexion with the fellow. I laid hold of this opportunity to display my valour, and offered to call him to account for his insolence, which she absolutely refused, under pretence of consulting my safety; though I could perceive by the sparkling of her eyes, that she would not have thought herself affronted in being the subject of a duel. I was by no means pleased with this discovery of her thoughts, which not only argued the most unjustifiable vanity, but likewise the most barbarous indifference; however, I was allured by her fortune, and resolved to gratify her pride, in making her the occasion of a publick quarrel between me and Bragwell, who, I was pretty certain, would never drive matters to a dangerous extremity.

While we danced together, I observed this formidable rival at one end of the room, encircled with a cluster of beaus, to whom he talked with great vehemence, casting many big looks at me, from time to time: I guessed the subject of his discourse, and as soon as I had handed my partner to her seat, strutted up to the place where he stood, and cocking my hat in his face, demanded aloud, if he had any thing to say to me. He answered with a sullen tone, 'Nothing, at present, Sir,' and turned about upon his heel.—'Well, (said I) you know where I am to be found at any time.'—His companions stared at one another, and I returned to the lady, whose features brightened at my approach, and immediately a whisper run thro' the whole room; after which, so many eyes were turned upon me, that I was ready to sink with confusion.—When the ball broke up, I led her to her coach, and, like a true French gallant, would have got up behind it, in order to protect her from violence on the road; but she absolutely refused my offer, and expressed her concern that there was not an empty seat for me within it.

Next day in the afternoon I waited on her at her lodgings, by permission, in company with Chatter, and was very civilly received by her mother, with whom she lived;—there were a good many fashionable people present, chiefly young fellows, and immediately after tea a couple of card tables were set, at one of which I had the honour to play with Melinda, who in less than three hours made shift to plunder me of eight guineas.—I was well enough content to lose a little money with a good grace, that I might have an opportunity to say soft things in the mean time, which are still most welcome, when attended with good luck; but I was by no means satisfied with her fair play, a circumstance that shocked me not a little, and greatly impaired my opinion of her disinterestedness and delicacy.—However, I was resolved to profit by this behaviour, and treat her in my turn with less ceremony; accordingly, I laid close siege to her, and finding her not at all disgusted with the gross incense I offered, that very night made a declaration of love in plain terms.—She received my addresses with great gaity, and pretended to laugh them off, but at the same time treated me with such particular complacency, that I was persuaded I had made a conquest of her heart, and concluded myself the happiest man alive.—Elevated with these flattering ideas, I sat down again to cards, after supper, and with great chearfulness suffered myself to be cheated of ten guineas more.

It was late before I took my leave, after being favoured with a general invitation; and when I got into bed, the adventures of the day hindered me from sleeping.—Sometimes I pleased myself with the hopes of possessing a fine woman with ten thousand pounds; then I would ruminate on the character I had heard of her from Banter, and compare it with the circumstances of her conduct towards me, which seemed to bear too great a resemblance to the picture he had drawn.—This introduced a melancholy reflection on the expence I had undergone, and the smallness of my funds to support it, which, by the bye, were none of my own.—In short, I found myself involved in doubts and perplexities, that kept me awake the greatest part of the night.

In the morning, Strap, with whom I had not conversed these two days, presented himself with the utensils for shaving me; upon which, I asked his opinion of the lady whom he had seen me conduct to her coach at Hampstead.—'Odd! she's a delicious creature (cried he) and, as I am informed, a great fortune.—I am sorry you did not

insist on going home with her.—I dare say, she would not have
refused your company; for she seems to be a good-humoured soul.'
——'There's a time for all things (said I.) You must know, Strap, I
was in company with her till one o'clock this morning.'—I had no
sooner pronounced these words, than he began to caper about the
room, and snap his fingers, crying in a transport, 'The day's our
own!—the day's our own!' I gave him to understand that his triumph was a little premature, and that I had more difficulties to
surmount than he was aware of; then I recounted to him the intelligence I had received from Banter.—At which he changed colour,
shook his head, and observed there was no faith in woman.—I told
him, I was resolved to make a bold push notwithstanding, although
I foresaw it would lead me into a great expence; and bid him guess
the sum I had lost last night at cards.—He scratched his chin, and
professed his abhorrence of cards, the very name of which being
mentioned made him sweat with vexation, as it recalled the money-
dropper to his remembrance; 'But however (said he) you have to
do with other guess people now.—Why, I suppose, if you had a
bad run last night, you would scarce come off for less than ten or
twelve shillings.'—I was mortified at this piece of simplicity, which
I imagined, at that time, was all affected by way of reprimand for
my folly; and asked with some heat, if he thought I had spent the
evening in a cellar with chairmen and bunters;[1] giving him to
know, at the same time, that my expence amounted to eighteen
guineas.—It would require the pencil of Hogarth[2] to express the
astonishment and concern of Strap, on hearing this piece of news;
the bason in which he was preparing the lather for my chin,
dropped out of his hands, and he remained some time immoveable
in that ludicrous attitude, with his mouth open, and his eyes
thrust forward considerably beyond their station; but remembering
my disposition, which was touchy and impatient of controul, he
smothered his chagrin, and attempted to recollect himself.—With
this view he endeavoured to laugh, but in spite of his teeth,[3] broke
out into a whimper, took up his washball and pewter-pot, scrubbed
my beard with the one, and discharged the other upon my face.—I
took no notice of his confusion, but after he had fully recovered
himself, put him in mind of his right, and assured him of my
readiness to surrender his effects whenever he should think proper
to demand them.—He was nettled at my insinuation, which he
thought proceeded from my distrust of his friendship; and begged

I would never talk to him in that strain again, unless I had a mind to break his heart.

This good creature's unalterable friendship for me affected me with the most grateful sentiments, and acted as a spur to my resolution of acquiring a fortune, that I might have it in my power to manifest my generosity in my turn.—For this purpose, I determined to bring matters to a speedy conclusion with Melinda; well knowing that a few such nights as the last, would effectually incapacitate me from prosecuting that, or any other advantageous amour.

While my meditation was busied in planning out my future conduct, Mr. Banter favoured me with a visit; and after breakfast, asked how I had passed the preceeding evening—I answered, I was very agreeably entertained at a private house.—'Yes, (said he, with a sarcastic smile) you deserved something extraordinary for the price you paid.'—I was surprised at his remark, and pretended ignorance of his meaning.—'Come, come, Random (continued he) you need not make a mystery of it to me, the whole town has it. I wish that foolish affair between you and Bragwell at Hampstead had been less publick—It has set all the busy bodies at work to find out your real character and situation; and you cannot imagine what conjectures have already circulated at your expence: One suspects you to be Jesuit in disguise; another believes you are an agent from the Pretender;[1] a third believes you to be an upstart gamester, because no body knows any thing of your family or fortune; a fourth is of opinion, that you are an Irish fortune-hunter.'—This last hypothesis touched me so near, that, to conceal my confusion, I was fain to interrupt his detail, and damn the world for an envious meddling community, that would not suffer a gentleman to live without molestation. He took no notice of this apostrophe, but went on, 'For my own part, I neither know nor desire to know, who, or what you are; this I am certain of, that few people make a mystery of their origin and situation, who can boast of any thing advantageous in either;—and my own opinion of the matter is, that you have raised yourself by your industry, from nothing to the appearance you now maintain, and which you endeavour to support by some matrimonial scheme.'—Here he fixed his eyes stedfastly upon me, and perceiving my face covered with blushes, told me, now he was confirmed in his opinion;—'Look ye, Random, (said he) I have divined your plan, and am confident it will never succeed—

You are too honest and too ignorant of the town, to practice the necessary cheats of your profession, and detect the conspiracies that will be formed against you—Besides, you are downright bashful—what the devil! set up for a fortune-hunter, before you have conquered the sense of shame!——Perhaps you are entitled by your merit, and I believe you are, to a richer and better wife than Melinda; but take my word for it, she is not to be won at that rate; —or, if you are so lucky as to carry her, between you and me, you may say, as Teague[1] did, *By my soul I have gained a loss!* She would take care to spend her own fortune in a twinkling, and soon make you sick of her extravagance.'—I was alarmed by this discourse, while I resented the freedom of it, and expressed my disgust, by telling him, he was mistaken in my intentions, and desiring he would give me leave to regulate my conduct according to the dictates of my own reason.—He made an apology for the liberty he had taken, and ascribed it to the warmth of his friendship for me; as an uncommon instance of which, he borrowed five guineas, assuring me, there were very few people in the world whom he would so far favour with his confidence.——I gave him the money, and professed myself so well convinced of his sincerity, that he had no occasion to put it to such extraordinary proofs for the future.—'I thought (said he) to have asked five pieces more, but hearing you was bubbled of eighteen last night, I presumed you might be out of cash, and resolved to model my demand accordingly.' I could not help admiring the cavalier behaviour of this spark, of whom I desired to know his reason for saying I was bubbled.—Whereupon he gave me to understand, that before he came to my lodgings, he had beat up[2] Tom Tossle, who having been present, informed him of the particulars, rehearsed all the fine things I said to Melinda, with which he proposed to entertain the town; and among other circumstances, assured him, my mistress cheated with so little art, that no body but a meer novice could have been imposed upon.

The thoughts of becoming a subject of raillery for coxcombs, and losing my money to boot, stung me to the quick; but I made a virtue of my indignation, and swore that no man should with impunity, either asperse the character of Melinda, or turn my behaviour into ridicule. He replied in a dry manner, that I would find it a Herculean task to chastise every body who should laugh at my expence; and as for the character of Melinda, he did not see how it could suffer by what was laid to her charge; for that cheating at cards, so far from being reckoned a blemish among people of fashion, was looked upon as an honourable indication of superior genius and address.—'But let us wave[1] this subject (said he) and go to the coffee-house, in order to make a party for dinner.'

CHAPTER XLVIII

We repair to the coffee-house, where we overhear a curious dispute between Wagtail and Medlar, which is referred to our decision——the doctor gives us an account of his experiment—Medlar is roasted by Banter, at the ordinary —the old gentleman's advice to me

BEING as willing to drop the theme, as he to propose it, I accompanied him thither, where we found Mr. Medlar and doctor Wagtail, disputing upon the word Custard, which the physician affirmed should be spelled with a G, because it was derived from the Latin verb *gustare*, 'to taste.'—But Medlar pleaded custom in behalf of C, observing, that by the doctor's rule, we ought to change pudding into budding, because it is derived from the French word *boudin*; and in that case, why not retain the original orthography and pronounciation of all the foreign words we have adopted; by which means our language would become a dissonant jargon without standard or propriety. The controversy was referred to us; and Banter, notwithstanding his real opinion to the contrary, decided it in favour of Wagtail: Upon which, the peevish annuitant arose, and uttering the monosyllable, *pish!* with great emphasis, removed to another table.

We then enquired of the doctor, what progress he had made in the experiment of distilling tinder-water; and he told us, he had been at all the glass-houses about town, but could find no body who would undertake to blow a retort large enough to hold the third part of the quantity prescribed; but he intended to try the process on as much as would produce five drops, which would be sufficient to prove the specific, and then he would make it a parliamentary affair;—that he had already purchased a considerable weight of rags, in the reducing of which to tinder, he had met with a misfortune which had obliged him to change his lodgings: For he had gathered them in a heap on the floor, and set fire to them with a candle, on the supposition that the boards would sustain no damage, because it is the nature of flame to ascend; but by some very extraordinary accident, the wood was invaded, and began to blaze with great violence, which disordered him so much, that he had not presence of mind enough to call for assistance, and the whole house must have been consumed with him in the midst of it, had not the smoke that rolled out of the windows in clouds alarmed the neighbourhood, and brought people to his succour.—That he had lost a pair of black velvet breeches and a tye-wig in the hurry, besides the expence of the rags, which were rendered useless by the water used to quench the flame, and the damage of the floor, which he was compelled to repair.—That his landlord believing him distracted, had insisted on his quitting his apartment at a minute's warning, which put him to incredible inconvenience; but now he was settled in a very comfortable house, and had the use of a large paved yard for preparing his tinder: So that he hoped in a very short time to reap the fruits of his labour.

After having congratulated the doctor on his prospect, and read the papers, we repaired to an auction of pictures, where we entertained ourselves an hour or two; from thence we adjourned to the Mall,[1] and after two or three turns, went back to dinner, Banter assuring us, that he intended to roast Medlar, at the ordinary; and indeed, we were no sooner set than this Cynic began to execute his purpose by telling the old gentleman, he looked extremely well, considering the little sleep he had enjoyed last night. To this compliment Medlar made no reply, but by a stare, accompanied with a significant grin;—and Banter went on thus: 'I don't know whether most to admire the charity of your mind, or the vigour of your body.—Upon my soul, Mr. Medlar, you do generous things with the best taste of any man I know! You extend your compassion to real objects, and exact only such returns as they are capable of making.—You must know, gentlemen, (said he, turning to the company) I had been up most part of the night with a friend who is bad of a fever, and on my return home this morning, I chanced to pass by a gin-shop still open, whence issued a confused sound of mirth and jollity: Upon which I popped in my head, and perceived Mr. Medlar dancing bare-headed in the midst of ten or twenty ragged Bunters, who rejoiced at his expence. But indeed, Mr. Medlar, you

ought not to sacrifice your constitution to your benevolence.—
Consider you grow old apace; and therefore have a reverend care o
your health, which must certainly be very much impaired by thes
nocturnal expeditions.'—The testy senior could no longer contai
himself, but cried hastily, "Tis well known that your tongue is n
slander.'—'I think (said the other) you might spare that observation
as you are very sensible that my tongue has done you signal servic
on many occasions.—You may remember, that when you mad
your addresses to the fat widow, who kept a publick-house a
Islington,[1] there was a report spread very much to the prejudice o
your manhood; which coming to the ears of your mistress, you wa
discarded immediately; and I brought matters to a reconciliation
by assuring her you had three bastards at nurse in the country: Hov
you ruined your own affair afterwards, it is neither my business no
inclination to relate.'—This anecdote, which had no other founda
tion than in Banter's own invention, afforded a good deal of mirt
to every body present, and provoked Mr. Medlar beyond all suffer
ance; so that he started up in a mighty passion, and forgetting tha
his mouth was full, bespattered those who sat next to him, while h
discharged his indignation in a volly of oaths, and call'd Banter in
significant puppy, impertinent jackanapes, and an hundred suc
appellations; telling the company, he had invented these fals
malicious aspersions, because he would not lend him money t
squander away upon rooks and whores.——'A very likely story
(said Banter) that I should attempt to borrow money of a man wh
is obliged to practice a thousand shifts to make his weekly allowanc
hold out to Saturday's night. Sometimes he sleeps four and twent
hours at a stretch, by which means he saves three meals beside
coffee-house expence.—Sometimes he is fain to put up with brea
and cheese and small beer for dinner; and sometimes he regales o
two pennyworth of ox-cheek in a cellar.'——'You are a lying mis
creant (cried Medlar, in an exstacy of rage) I can always comman
money enough to pay your taylor's bill, which I'm sure is no trifle
and I have a good mind to give you a convincing proof of my cir
cumstances, by prosecuting you for defamation, sirrah.'—By thi
time the violence of his wrath had deprived him of his appetite, an
he sat silent, unable to swallow one mouthful, while his tormento
enjoyed his mortification, and encreased his chagrin, by advisin
him to lay in plentifully for his next day's fast.

Dinner being ended, we came down stairs to the coffee-room, an

Chapter XLVIII

Banter went away to keep an appointment, saying, he supposed he should see Wagtail and me in the evening at the Bedford coffee-house.—He was no sooner gone, than the old gentleman took me aside, and said, he was sorry to see me so intimate with that fellow who was one of the most graceless rakes about town, and had already wasted a good estate and constitution upon harlots;—that he had been the ruin of many a young man, by introducing them into debauched company, and setting a lewd example of all manner of wickedness; and that, unless I was on my guard, he would strip me in a short time, both of my money and reputation. I thanked him for his information, and promised to conduct myself accordingly, wishing however, his caution had been a few hours more early, by which means I might have saved five guineas. Notwithstanding this intelligence, I was inclinable to impute some part of the charge to Medlar's revenge for the liberties taken with him at dinner; and therefore, as soon as I could disengage myself, applied to Wagtail for his opinion of the character in question; resolved to compare their accounts, allowing for the prejudice of each, and form my judgment upon both, without adhering strictly to either.—The doctor assured me that he was a very pretty gentleman, of family and fortune; a scholar, a wit, a critick, and perfectly well acquainted with the town; that his honour and courage were unquestionable, though some extravagancies he had been guilty of, and his talent for satire, had procured him enemies, and made some people shy of his acquaintance.—From these different sketches, I concluded that Banter was a young fellow of some parts, who had spent his fortune, but retained his appetites, and fallen out with the world because he could not enjoy it to his wish.

I went to the Bedford coffee-house in the evening, where I met my friends, from thence proceeded to the play, and afterwards carried them home to my lodgings, where we supped with great harmony and satisfaction.

CHAPTER XLIX

I receive a challenge——the consequences of it——the quarrel being made up, I am put in arrest, by the care and affection of Strap—but immediately released upon explaining my affair——the behaviour of Mr. Oregan and his two friends—— I visit Melinda, whom I divert with an account of the duel——I propose marriage——she refers the matter to her mother, of whom I make a solemn demand of her daughter—— the old lady's behaviour——I am discarded, resent their disdain

W HEN I was ready to go abroad next day, Strap brought me a letter, directed *To Mr. Random, Esq; Those.*[1]——Which, upon opening, I found contained a challenge, couched in these very extraordinary terms:

'S IR ,
W HEREAS , I am informed that you make love to Miss Melinda Goosetrap, This is to let you know, that she is under promise of marriage to me; and that I am at this present writing, at the back of Montague-house,[2] with a pair of good pistols in my hand, and if you will keep your appointment, I will make your tongue confess (after the breath is out of your body) that you do not deserve her as well as
Yours, &c.

Rourk Oregan.

I guessed from the stile and subscription of this billet, that my rival was a true Milesian,[3] and was not a little uneasy at the contents, especially that part, where he asserts his right to my mistress by promise, a circumstance I did not know how to reconcile to her penetration.——However, this was no time for me to decline the invitation, because the success of my addresses might in a great measure depend upon my behaviour in that affair. I therefore immediately loaded my pistols, and betook myself in a hackney-coach to the place appointed, where I found a tall raw-boned man, with a hard featured countenance, and black bushy beard, walking by himself, wrapped up in a shabby great coat, over which his own hair descended in a leathern queue from his head, that was covered with a greasy hat trimmed with a tarnished *pointe d'espagne*. He no sooner perceived me advancing, than without any preamble, he pulled a pistol from his bosom, and presenting at me, snapt it. Alarmed at his rude salutation, I made a stand, and before he could adjust his other piece, fired one of mine at him, without doing any damage. By this time he was ready with his second, that flashed in the pan without going off: Upon which he called, with a true Tipperary[1] cadence, 'Fire away, honey,'—and began to hammer his flint with great deliberation.—But I was resolved to make use of the advantage Fortune had given me; and therefore stept up, without throwing away my fire, desiring him to ask his life, or prepare for another world;—but this stout Hibernian refused to condescend, and complained bitterly of my having quitted my ground before he could return my shot; saying I ought to go back to my station, and let him have an equal chance with me.—I endeavoured to persuade him that I had given him a double chance already; and it was my business to prevent him from enjoying a third;—but now, since I had an opportunity, I demanded a parley, and desired to know his condition, and reason for calling me to the field, who, to the best of my remembrance, so far from having done him any injury, had never before seen him.—He told me, that he was a gentleman of fortune, who had spent all he had, and hearing that Melinda had got ten thousand pounds, he intended to make himself master of that sum by espousing her, and was determined, in an honourable way, to cut the throats of all those who stood between him and his hopes.—I then demanded to know the foundation of his hopes; and now that I had seen him, being more and more astonished at the circumstance of the promise, desired he would explain that mystery: —He gave me to understand, that he trusted entirely to his birth and personal merit; that he had frequently wrote to Melinda, setting forth his claim and pretensions, but she was never kind enough to send an answer, or even to admit him into her presence; and that the promise he mentioned in his letter, was made by his friend Mr. Gaghagan, who assured him, that no woman could resist a man of his appearance.—I could not forbear laughing to excess, at the simplicity of my rival, who did not seem to relish my mirth; but began to be very serious: Upon which I endeavoured to appease him, by giving him my word and honour, that so far from prejudicing his addresses to the lady, I would represent him to her in the most favourable light I could, with any regard to truth; but he must not be surprized if she should remain blind to his deserts, for nothing was more capricious than a woman's mind, and the affection of that sex was seldom purchased with virtue alone.—That my declaration might have the better effect, I took notice of his dishabille, and professing sorrow at seeing a gentleman reduced, slipt two guineas into his hand, at the sight of which, he threw away his pistols, and hugging me in his arms, cried, 'Arrah, by Jesus, now, you are the best friend I have met with these seven long years.'—When I had suffered some minutes in his embrace, he quitted me, and picking up his rusty arms, wished the devil might burn him if ever he should give me any further trouble about woman-kind.

The quarrel being thus amicably composed, I begged leave to look at his pistols, which I found so crazy and so foul, that, I believe, it was happy for him neither of them was discharged, for one of them would certainly have split in the going off, and he would, in all probability, have lost his hand in the explosion; but what gave me a lively idea of the man's character, was to find, upon examination, that one of them had been loaded without being primed, and the other primed without a charge.

While we walked homeward together, I expressed a desire of knowing my new friend's history; and he informed me of his having served in the German army as a volunteer against the Turks; that for his behaviour at the siege of Belgrade,[1] he had been honoured with an ensign's commission, and afterwards promoted to the rank of lieutenant, in which station, it was his misfortune to affront his captain, who challenged him to the field, and was killed in the duel, upon which he was obliged to retreat;—that he had been in England some years solliciting his friends for provision in the British army; but being hitherto unsuccessful, he was desired by Mr. Gaghagan to turn his thoughts to matrimony, and make his fortune by an advantageous match; in consequence of which advice, he had made up to Melinda, and having heard, by means of an Irish footman in the family, that I was her chief favourite, had called me out in hopes of removing by my death, the greatest obstruction to his desires; but now he was convinced of my honour and generosity, he swore by the blessed Virgin, he would think of her no more, if there was not another woman in the world.—As a further proof of his veracity, which I did not at all doubt, he opened an old iron snuff-box, and pulled out his commission in the imperial army, and his captain's challenge, which he preserved as testimonials of his character.—I was so well convinced of this poor man's honesty and courage, that I determined to speak in his behalf to some of my acquaintance, who might recommend his case to the consideration of those who could provide for him; and in the mean time to accommodate him with a few cloaths, by which his appearance would be much mended, and himself enabled to renew his solicitations in person.

As we walked along, conversing socially together, we were met by a file of Musqueteers, and Strap at their head, who no sooner approached, than with a frantick look, he cried, 'Seize them!—in the name of God! seize them'—We were accordingly surrounded, and I put in arrest by the corporal, who was commanding officer; but captain Oregan disengaged himself, and run with such speed towards Tottenham-court-road, that he was out of sight in a moment. When my arms were delivered up, and myself secured, Strap became a little more composed, and asked pardon for the liberty he had taken, which he hoped I would excuse, as it proceeded from his affection: He then told me that, suspecting the letter (which by the bye was brought by the author himself) contained something extraordinary, he had peeped through the key-hole, and seen me load my pistols; upon which he run down to Whitehall,[1] and applied to the officer on guard, for a party to put me in arrest, but before he returned, I was gone in a coach; that he had enquired which way I went, and having often heard, that duels were commonly fought at the back of Montague-house, he conducted the guard to this place, where he thanked God for having found me safe and sound. I let him know, that I forgave his officious concern for once, but cautioned him in pretty severe terms, from making me the subject of idle conversation for the future; then, turning to the corporal, I thanked him for his care, and gave him a crown to drink with his men, assuring him that the rencontre was over long before he came up, and every thing compromised, as he might have observed by our behaviour; as a farther proof of which, he would find upon examination, that one of my pistols had been discharged;—but this civil person, without giving himself or me any further trouble, received the bounty with a thousand bows and acknowledgments, and returning the pistols, released me immediately.

He was not gone an hundred yards, when my friend Oregan came up, in order to rescue me, with two Tatterdemalions whom he had engaged for that purpose, about the purlieus of St. Giles's:[2] One of them was armed with a musket that wanted a lock, and another with a rusty broad-sword; but their dress surpassed all description.—When he understood I was already free, he made an apology for his abrupt departure, and introduced me to his two companions: First, to counsellor Fitz-clabber,[1] who, he told me, was then employed in compiling a history of the kings of Munster, from Irish manuscripts; and then to his friend Mr. Gaghagan, who was a profound philosopher and politician, and had projected many excellent schemes for the good of his country.—But it seems these literati had been very ill rewarded for their ingenious labours; for between them both, there was but one shirt and half a pair of breeches.—I thanked them very kindly for their readiness to assist me, and having offered my service in my turn, wished them a good-morrow, desiring Oregan to accompany me to my lodgings, where he was fitted with decent cloaths from my wardrobe, so much to his satisfaction, that he swore eternal gratitude and friendship to me, and at my request, recounted all the adventures of his life.

In the afternoon, I waited on Melinda, who received me with great kindness and familiarity, and laughed excessively at my adventure with the Irishman, to whose wishes she was no stranger, having more than a dozen letters in her possession, which he had wrote to her on the subject of love, and which, for my entertainment, she submitted to my perusal.—Having made ourselves merry at the expence of this poor admirer, I seized the opportunity of her mother's going out of the room, and introduced my own passion, which I recommended to her with all the ardour and eloquence I was master of.—I flattered, sighed, swore, intreated, and acted a thousand extravagancies, in hopes of making some impression on her heart; but she heard every thing I said without discovering the least emotion; and other company came in, before she would vouchsafe one serious reply.—After tea, the cards were brought in according to custom, and it was my good fortune to have Melinda for my partner; by which means, instead of losing, I came off with five guineas clear gain.

I soon became acquainted with a good many people of fashion, and spent my time in the modish diversions of the town, such as plays, operas, masquerades, drums,[2] assemblies and puppet-shews; chiefly in company with Melinda, whom I cultivated with all the eagerness and address that my prospect could inspire, and my education afford: I spared neither my person nor my purse, to gratify her vanity and pride; my rivals were intimidated, and indeed outshone; and after all, I began to fear that the dear creature had not a heart to lose.—At last, finding myself unable to support the expence of this amour much longer, I was determined to bring the matter to a crisis; and one evening, while we were *tête a tête*, complained of her indifference, described the tortures of suspense to a love-sick mind, and pressed her to disclose her sentiments of matrimony and me, with such earnestness, that she could not with all her art, shift the subject; but was obliged to come to an eclaircissement.——She let me know with a careless air, that she had no objection to my person, and if I could satisfy her mother in other particulars, I should not find her averse to the match; but she was resolved to do nothing in an affair of such moment'ous concern, without the advice and consent of her parent.—This was not a very agreeable declaration to me, whose aim had been to win her inclination first, and then secure my conquest by a private marriage, to which I flattered myself she would express no reluctance.—That I might not, however, desert my cause before it was desperate, I waited on the mother, and with great formality demanded the daughter in marriage: The good lady, who was a very notable woman, behaved with great state and civility; thanked me for the honour I intended her family, and said, she did not doubt that I was in all respects qualified to make a woman happy; but it concerned her as a parent anxious about the welfare of her child, to enquire into the particulars of my fortune, and know what settlement I proposed to make. To this intimation, which would have utterly disconcerted me, if I had not expected it, I replied without hesitation, that though my fortune was very small, I was a gentleman by birth and education, would maintain her daughter in the sphere of a gentlewoman, and settle her own dowry on her and her heirs for ever.—This careful matron did not seem to relish my proposal, but observed with a demure countenance, that there was no necessity for settling that upon her child which was her own already: However, if I pleased, her lawyer should confer with mine upon the matter; and in the mean time, she desired I would favour her with the perusal of my rent-roll.—Notwithstanding the vexation I was under, I could scarce forbear laughing in her face, at the mention of my rent-roll, which was, indeed, a severe piece of satire upon my pretensions. I frankly owned I had no landed estate: and told her, that I could not exactly specify the sum I was master of, until I had regulated my affairs, which were at present in some disorder; but that I would take an opportunity of satisfying her on that head very soon.

It was not long before I took my leave, and returned to my lodgings in a very melancholy mood, persuaded that I had nothing more to expect from that quarter: I was confirmed in this opinion next day, when I went back with a view of explaining myself more fully to the old gentlewoman; and was told by the footman, that his ladies were not at home, although I had seen Melinda through the blinds of a parlour window, as I went up to the door. Incensed at this affront I quitted the door, without saying one word, and as I repassed the parlour, bowed to Miss, who still remained in the same situation, securely screened, as she thought, from my view.

This disappointment gave me more uneasiness on Strap's account, than my own; for I was in no danger of dying for love of Melinda; on the contrary, the remembrance of my charming Narcissa, was a continual check upon my conscience, during the whole course of my addresses; and perhaps contributed to the bad success of my scheme, by controuling my raptures, and condemning my design.

There was a necessity for acquainting my companion with every thing that happened to me, and I performed this piece of duty in an affected passion, swearing I would be his pack-horse no longer, and desiring him to take the management of his affairs into his own hand. This finesse had the desired effect, for instead of grumbling over my miscarriage, Strap was frightened at the passion I feigned, and begged me for the love of God to be appeased; observing, that although we had suffered a great loss, it was not irreparable; and if fortune frowned today, she might perhaps smile to-morrow.—I pretended to acquiesce in his remarks, praise his equanimity, and promise to improve by misfortune.—He, on the other hand, pretended to be perfectly well satisfied with my conduct, and conjured me to follow the dictates of my own reflection; but in spite of all his affectation, I could perceive his inward affliction, and his visage sensibly increased in longitude from that day.

CHAPTER L

I long to be revenged on Melinda——apply to Banter for his assistance——he contrives a scheme for that purpose, which is put in execution with great success——I make an attempt on the heart of Miss Gripewell, but am disappointed——I grow melancholy at my disappointment, and have recourse to the Bottle——receive a billet doux——am ravished with the contents—find myself involved in an intrigue, which I imagined would make my fortune——am counfounded at my mistake, which banishes all thoughts of matrimony

IN the mean time, my attention was wholly engrossed in search of another mistress, and the desire of being revenged on Melinda, in both which schemes I was very much assisted by Billy Chatter, who was such a necessary creature among the ladies, that in all private dances he engaged the men.—To him therefore I applied, desiring he would introduce me to a partner of some figure, at the next private assembly, for the sake of a frolick, the intention of which I would afterwards communicate. Billy, who had heard something of a difference between Melinda and me, immediately smoaked[1] part of my design, and thinking I only wanted to alarm her jealousy a little, promised to gratify my desire, by matching me with a partner worth thirty thousand pounds, whom the ladies of this end of the town, had lately taken into their management and protection.— Upon further inquiry, I found this person's name was Miss Biddy Gripewell,[2] that her father, who had been a pawnbroker, died intestate, by which means all his substance descended to this daughter, who was so little a favourite, that could the old man have prevailed with his own rapacious disposition, to part with as much money as would have paid the expence of a will, she would not have inherited the sixth part of his fortune;—that during his life, so far from being educated in a way suitable to such great expectations, she was obliged to live like a servant wench, and do the most menial offices in the family.—But his funeral was no sooner performed, than she assumed the fine lady, and found so many people of both sexes, to

297

flatter, caress and instruct her, that, for want of discretion and experience, she was grown insufferably vain and arrogant, and pretended to no less than a duke or earl at least, for her husband; that she had the misfortune to be neglected by the English quality, but a certain poor Scottish Lord was then making interest to be introduced to her acquaintance.—In the mean time, she was fallen into the hands of a notable lady, who had already disposed of her to a lieutenant of foot, a distant relation of her ladyship's, though Miss, as yet, knew nothing of the affair; and lastly, that if I proposed to dance with her, I must give him leave to represent me as a knight or foreign count at least.[1]—I was ravished at this piece of information, and contented, for one night, to personate a French Marquis, that I might the easier fulfil my revenge.

Having made the appointment with Chatter, I went to Banter's lodgings, having by this time conceived a great opinion of his penetration and knowledge; and after I had injoined secrecy, told him every circumstance of my disgrace with Melinda, and imparted the plan I had projected to mortify that proud coquette, desiring his advice in improving, and assistance in executing the scheme.—Nothing could be more agreeable to his misanthropical temper, than an account of her behaviour and my resentment: He applauded my resolution, and proposed that I should not only provide myself in a proper partner, but also procure such an one for Miss Goosetrap, as would infallibly intail upon her the ridicule of all her acquaintance: For this purpose he mentioned his barber, who, he said, was an exceeding coxcomb, lately come from Paris, whose absurd affectation and grimace would easily pass upon her, for the sprightly politesse of a gentleman improved by travel.—I hugged him for this hint; and he assured me, it would be no difficult matter to make him believe, that Melinda having seen him by accident, was captivated by his appearance, and longed for his acquaintance.——He actually engaged him on this pretence, and painted his good fortune in such colours, that the poor shaver was quite beside himself with joy,—He was immediately fitted with a tawdry suit of cloaths belonging to Banter, and by him recommended to Chatter, as a very pretty fellow, just returned from his travels.—Master Billy, who acted as gentleman-usher to a great many of the fair sex in and about town undertook, at once, to bespeak Melinda in his behalf; and every thing happened according to my wish.

Chapter L

At the time appointed, I appeared, dressed to the best advantage; and in the character of Marquis, had the honour of opening the ball with the rich heiress, who attracted the eyes of the whole company, by the prodigious number of jewels with which she was adorned.— Among others, I perceived Melinda, who could no more conceal her envy than astonishment at my success: Her curiosity was still more flagrant and tormenting, for she had never seen Miss Gripewell before; and Chatter, who alone could give her any satisfaction on that head, was engaged in conversation at the other end of the room.——I observed her impatience, and exulted in her chagrin; and after my partner was set, took the opportunity of passing by her to make a slight bow without stopping; which compleated my triumph and her indignation. She changed colour, bridled up, assumed an air of disdain, and flirted her fan with such fury, that it went to pieces in a moment, to the no small entertainment of those who sat near and observed her.

At length the metamorphosed barber took her out, and acted his part with such ridiculous extravagance, that the mirth of the whole company was excited at his expence, and his partner so much ashamed, that before the country dances began, she retired in great confusion, under pretence of being taken suddenly ill, and was followed by her gallant, who no doubt, imagined her indisposition was nothing but love; and laid hold of the occasion of conducting her home, to comfort her, with an assurance of his entertaining a reciprocal passion.—They were no sooner gone, than an inquisitive whisper of 'Who is he?' run round the room; and Chatter could give them no other intelligence about him, than that he was a man of fortune, just returned from his travels: I, who alone was acquainted with his real quality, affected ignorance, well knowing that female curiosity would not rest satisfied with such a general account, and that the discovery would proceed with a better grace from any body than me.

Mean while, I was tempted by the richness of the prize, to practise upon Miss Gripewell's heart, but soon found it too well fortified with pride and indifference to yield to any efforts in my own character, and I neither would nor could preserve the title I had borrowed, longer than this night.

As I expected, every thing came to light next day: The barber, in pure simplicity of heart, detected himself to Melinda, and discovered the foundation of his hopes; she sickened at the affront, and was ashamed to shew her face in publick for many weeks after this accident. Poor Chatter found it impossible to justify himself to her satisfaction; was in utter disgrace with Miss Gripewell, for having imposed me upon her as a nobleman; and suffered very much in his character and influence among the ladies in general.

Finding my finances diminished more than one half, and my project as little advanced as on the first day of my arrival in town, I began to despair of my success, and grew melancholy at the prospect of approaching want.—To dispel the horrors of this fiend, I had recourse to the bottle, and kept more company than ever.—I became particularly attached to the play-house, conversed with the actors behind the scenes, got acquainted with a body of templars,[1] and in a short time commenced a professed wit and critick. Indeed I may say without vanity, that I was much better qualified than any one of my companions, who were, generally speaking, of all the creatures I ever conversed with, the most ignorant and assuming.— By means of these avocations I got the better of care, and learned to separate my ideas in such a manner, that whenever I was attacked by a gloomy reflection, I could shove it aside, and call in some agreeable reverie to my assistance.—This was not the case with Strap, who practised a thousand shifts to conceal the sorrow that preyed upon his carcass, and reduced him to the resemblance of a meer skeleton.

While I thus posted, in a thoughtless manner, towards poverty, I one day received, by the penny-post,[2] a letter written in a woman's hand, containing a great many high-flown compliments, warm protestations of love, couched in a very poetical stile, an earnest desire of knowing whether or not my heart was engaged, by leaving an answer at a certain place directed to R. B. and the whole subscribed, 'Your incognita.' I was transported with joy on reading the contents of this billet doux, which I admired as a master-piece of tenderness and elegance, and was already up to the ears in love with the author, whom my imagination represented as a lady of fortune, in the bloom of youth and beauty.—Elevated with this conjecture, I went to work and exhausted my invention in composing an answer suitable to the sublimity of her stile, and the ardour of her sentiments.—I expressed my admiration of her wit, in terms the most hyperbolical, and while I acknowledged myself unworthy of her regard, declared myself enamoured of her understanding; and in the most pathetick manner, implored the honour of an interview.—

Chapter L

Having finished this performance, and communicated it to Strap, who skipped about for joy, I dispatched him with it to the place appointed, which was the house of a milliner not far from Bond-street,[1] and desired him to keep watch near the door for some time, that he might discover the person who would call for it.——In less than an hour he returned, with a joyful countenance, and told me, that soon after he had delivered the letter a chairman was called, to whom it was given, with directions to carry it to the house of a rich gentleman in the neighbourhood, whither he (Strap) followed him, and saw it put into the hands of a waiting-woman, who paid the messenger and shut the door;—That upon inquiry at an ale-house hard by, where he called for a pint of beer, he understood, that the gentleman to whom the house belonged had an only daughter, very handsome, who would inherit his whole estate; and who certainly was the author of the billet I had received.—I was of the same opinion, and hugging myself in the happy prospect, dressed immediately, and passed in great state by the house that contained my unknown admirer.—Nor was my vanity disappointed; for I perceived a beautiful young creature standing at one of the windows of the dining-room, who, I imagined, observed me with more than common curiosity. That I might indulge her view, and at the same time feast my own, I affected to stop, and give orders to Strap, in the street, just opposite to her station, by which means I had an opportunity of seeing her more distinctly, and of congratulating myself on having made a conquest of so much perfection.—In a few moments she retired, and I betook myself to the ordinary, in a rapture of hope, which deprived me of my appetite for that meal, and sent me home in the evening to indulge my contemplation.

Early next day, I was favoured with another epistle from my unknown charmer, signifying her unutterable joy at the receipt of mine, which, while it made a tender of my heart, convinced her of the value of it. Above all things, she professed extreme pleasure in finding me so much attached to her understanding, a circumstance that not only flattered her in the most sensible part, but at the same time argued my own sagacity.—As for the interview I desired, she assured me, that I could not be more eager for such an occasion than she; but she must not only sacrifice a little more to decorum, but be satisfied of my honourable intentions, before she would grant that request: Mean while, she gave me to understand, that although she might owe some deference to the opinion of certain persons, she was resolved, in an affair that so nearly concerned her happiness, to consult her own inclination, preferably to the advice of the whole world; especially, as she was urged to such condescension by no consideration of fortune, what she depended upon, being her own without restriction or controul.——Struck with admiration at the philosophy and self-denial of my mistress, who seemed insensible of the beauty she possessed; and in particular, ravished with that piece of intelligence, by which I learned her fortune was independent, I resumed the pen, launched out into encomiums of the dignity of her sentiments, affected to undervalue the charms of external beauty, pretented to ground my passion on the qualities of her mind; complained of her rigour, in sacrificing my repose to an overscrupulous regard to decorum, and declared the purity of my designs in the most solemn and pathetic vows.—— This performance being sealed and directed, was sent to the place appointed, by Strap, who, that we might be still the more confirmed in our belief, renewed his watch, and in a little time brought back the same information as before, with this addition, that Miss Sparkle, (the name of my supposed correspondent) looking out at the window, no sooner saw the messenger arrive, than she shut the casement in a sort of beautiful confusion, and disappeared; eager, no doubt, to hear from the dear object of her love.

My doubts now vanished, the long expected port appeared, and I looked upon myself as perfectly secure of that happiness I had been in quest of so long.—After dinner, I sauntered in company with doctor Wagtail, to that part of the town in which my inamorata lived; and as he was a meer register, enquired of him into the name, character and fortune of every body who possessed a good house in the streets through which we passed: When it came to his turn to mention Sir John Sparkle, he represented him as a man of an immense estate and narrow disposition, who mewed up his only child, a fine young lady, from the conversation of mankind, under the strict watch and inspection of an old gouvernante, who was either so honest, envious or insatiable, that no body had been, as yet, able to make her a friend, or get access to her charge, though numbers attempted it every day; not so much on account of her expectations from her father, who being a widower, might marry again, and have sons, as for a fortune of twelve thousand pounds left her by an uncle, of which she could not be deprived.—This piece of news exactly tallying with the last part of the letter I had been honoured with in the morning, had such an effect on me, that any man, except Wagtail, might have observed my emotion; but his attention was too much engrossed on the contemplation of his own importance, to be affected with the deportment of any other body, unless it happened to be so particular, that he could not help taking notice of it.

When I had disengaged myself from him, whose conversation grew insipid to me, I went home, and made Strap acquainted with the fruits of my researches.—This faithful Squire was almost choaked with transport, and even wept for joy; but whether on account of himself or me, I shall not pretend to determine.——Next day a third *billet doux* was brought to me, containing many expressions of tenderness, mingled with some affecting doubts about the artifice of man, the inconstancy of youth, and the jealousy often attending the most sincere passion; withal desiring I would excuse her, if she should try me a little longer, before she declared herself beyond the power of retracting.—These interesting scruples added fuel to my flame, and impatience to my hope; I redoubled my complaints of her indifference, and pressed her to an assignation, with such fervid intreaties, that in a few days, she consented to meet me at the house of that milliner, who had forwarded all my letters.— During the interval between the date of her promise, and the hour of appointment, my pride soared beyond all reason and description; I lost all remembrance of the gentle Narcissa, and my thoughts were wholly employed in planning triumphs over the malice and contempt of the world.

At length the happy hour arrived, I flew to the place of rendezvous, and was conducted into an apartment, where I had not waited ten minutes, when I heard the rustling of silk and the sound of feet ascending the stairs: My heart took the alarm, and beat quick, my cheeks glowed, my nerves thrilled, and my knees shook with exstasy! I perceived the door opening, saw a gold brocade petticoat advance, and sprung forward to embrace my charmer.—— Heaven and earth! how shall I paint my situation, when I found Miss Sparkle converted into a wrinkled hag turned of seventy! I was struck dumb with amazement, and petrified with horror! This ancient urganda[1] perceived my disorder, and approaching with a languishing air, seized my hand, asking in a squeaking tone, if I was indisposed.—Her monstrous affectation compleated the disgust

I had conceived for her at her first appearance; and it was a long time before I could command myself so much, as to behave with common civility: At length, however, I recollected myself and pronounced an apology for my behaviour, which, I said, proceeded from a dizziness that seized me all of a sudden.—My hoary Dulcinea, who, no doubt, had been alarmed at my confusion, no sooner learned the cause to which I now ascribed it, than she discovered her joy in a thousand amorous coquettries, and assumed the sprightly arts of a girl of sixteen. One while, she ogled me with her dim eyes, quenched in rheum; then, as if she was ashamed of that freedom, she affected to look down, blush, and play with her fan, then toss her head that I might not perceive a palsy that shook it, ask some childish questions with a lisping accent, giggle and grin with her mouth shut, to conceal the ravages of time upon her teeth, leer upon me again, sigh piteously, fling herself about in her chair to shew her agility, and act a great many more absurdities that youth and beauty can alone excuse.—Shocked as I was at my disappointment, my disposition was incapable of affronting any person who loved me; I therefore endeavoured to put a good face on the matter for the present, resolved to drop the whole affair as soon as I should get clear of her company; with this view, I uttered some civil things, and in particular desired to know the name and condition of the lady who had honoured me so much.——She told me her name was Withers, that she lived with Sir John Sparkle in quality of governess to his only daughter, in which situation she had picked up a comfortable sufficiency to make her easy for life; that she had the pleasure of seeing me at church, where my appearance and deportment made such an impression upon her heart, that she could enjoy no ease until she had inquired into my character, which she found so amiable in all respects, that she yielded to the violence of her inclination, and ventured to declare her passion, with too little regard, perhaps, to the decorum of her sex; but she hoped I would forgive a trespass, of which I myself was, in some measure, the cause, and impute her intrusion to the irresistible dictates of love.—No decayed rake ever swallowed a bolus with more reluctance than I felt in making a reply suitable to the compliment, when instead of the jewel, I found the crazy casket only in my power; and yet my hopes began to revive a little, when I considered, that by carrying on the appearance of an intrigue with the Duenna, I might possibly get access to her charge. Encouraged by this suggestion, my temper grew more serene, my reserve wore off, I talked *en cavalier*, and even made love to this antiquated coquette, who seemed extremely happy in her adorer, and spread all her allurements to make her imagined conquest more secure.——The good woman of the house treated us with tea and sweet-meats, and afterwards withdrew, like a civil experienced matron as she was.—— Left thus to our mutual endearments, Miss Withers (for she was still a maiden) began to talk of matrimony, and expressed so much impatience in all her behaviour, that, had she been fifty years younger, I might possibly have gratified her longing without having recourse to the church; but this my virtue as well as interest forbad. When the inclinations of an old maid settle upon a young fellow, he is persecuted with her addresses; but, should he once grant her the favour, he will never be able to disentangle himself from her importunities and reproaches. It was my business to defer the ceremony as long as possible under the most specious pretences, with a view of becoming acquainted with Miss Sparkle, in the mean time; and I did not despair of success, when I considered, that in the course of our correspondence I would, in all probability, be invited to visit my mistress in her own apartment, and by that means have an opportunity of conversing with her charming ward. Pleased with this prospect, my heart dilated with joy, I talked in raptures to the stale gouvernante, and kissed her shriveled hand with great devotion: She was so much transported with her good fortune, that she could not contain her exstasy, but flew upon me like a tygeress,[1] and pressed her skinny lips to mine; when (as it was no doubt concerted by her evil genius) a dose of garlick[2] she had swallowed that morning, to dispel wind I suppose, began to operate with such a sudden explosion, that human nature, circumstanced as I was, could not endure the shock with any degree of temper.—I lost all patience and reflection, flung away from her in an instant, snatched my hat and cane, and run down stairs as the devil had me in pursuit, and could scarce restrain the convulsion of my bowels, which were grievously offended by the perfume that assaulted me.—Strap, who waited my return with impatience, seeing me arrive in the utmost disorder, stood motionless with apprehension, and durst not enquire into the cause.

After I had washed my mouth more than once, and recruited my spirits with a glass of wine, I recounted to him every particular of what had happened; to which he made no other reply, for some time, than lifting up his eyes, clasping his hands, and uttering a hollow groan.—At length he observed, in a melancholy tone, that it was a thousand pities my organs were so delicate as to be offended with the smell of garlick: 'Ah! God help us (said he) 'tis not the steams of garlick, no, nor of something else, that would give me the least uneasiness—see what it is to be a cobler's son.'—I replied hastily, 'I wish then, you would go and retrieve my miscarriage.'— At this he started, forced a smile, and left the room, shaking his head. Whether the old gentlewoman resented my abrupt departure so much, that her love changed into disdain, or was ashamed to see me on account of her infirmity, I know not, but I was never troubled again with her passion.

CHAPTER LI

I cultivate an acquaintance with two noblemen——am introduced to Earl Strutwell——his kind promise and invitation——the behaviour of his porter and lacquey——he receives me with an appearance of uncommon affection—— undertakes to speak in my behalf to the minister——informs me of his success, and wishes me joy——introduces a conversation about Petronius Arbiter——falls in love with my watch, which I press upon him—I make a present of a diamond ring to lord Straddle——impart my good fortune to Strap and Banter, who disabuses me, to my utter mortification

BAFFLED hitherto in my matrimonial schemes, I began to question my talents for the science of fortune-hunting, and to bend my thoughts towards some employment under the government.—With the view of procuring which, I cultivated the acquaintance of Lords Straddle and Swillpot, whose fathers were men of interest at court. —I found these young noblemen as open to my advances as I could desire: I accompanied them in their midnight rambles, and often dined with them at taverns, where I had the honour of paying the reckoning.

I one day took the opportunity, while I was loaded with pro-

testations of friendship, to disclose my desire of being settled in
some sine-cure; and to solicit their influence in my behalf.——
Swillpot squeezing my hand, said, I might depend upon his service,
by G—d. The other swore that no man would be more proud than
he to run my errands. Encouraged by these declarations I ventured
to express an inclination to be introduced to their fathers, who were
able to do my business at once. Swillpot frankly owned he had not
spoke to his father these three years; and Straddle assured me his
father having lately disobliged the Minister by subscribing his name
to a protest in the house of peers, was thereby rendered incapable of
serving his friends at present; but he undertook to make me acquainted with Earl Strutwell, who was hand and glove with a
certain person that ruled the roast. This offer I embraced with
many acknowledgments, and plied him so closely, in spite of a
thousand evasions, that he found himself under a necessity of
keeping his word, and actually carried me to the levée of this great
man, where he left me in a crowd of fellow-dependants, and was
ushered to a particular closet audience; from whence in a few
minutes, he returned with his lordship, who took me by the hand,
assured me he would do me all the service he could, and desired to
see me often.—I was charmed with my reception, and although I
had heard that a courtier's promise is not to be depended upon, I
thought I discovered so much sweetness of temper and candour in
this Earl's countenance, that I did not doubt of profiting by his protection.—I resolved therefore, to avail myself of his permission, and
waited on him next audience day, when I was favoured with a
particular smile, squeeze of the hand, and a whisper, signifying that
he wanted half an hour's conversation with me *tête a tête*, when he
should be disengaged, and for that purpose desired me to come and
drink a dish of chocolate with him to-morrow morning.—This
invitation, which did not a little flatter my vanity and expectation,
I took care to observe, and went to his lordship's house at the time
appointed. Having rapped at the gate, the porter unbolted and kept
it half open, placing himself in the gap, like soldiers in a breach, to
dispute my passage.—I demanded to know if his lord was stirring?
—He answered with a surly aspect, 'No.'——'At what hour does he
commonly rise? (said I)'—'Sometimes sooner, sometimes later
(said he, closing the door upon me by degrees.)'—I then told him
I was come by his lordship's own appointment; to which this
Cerberus replied, 'I have received no orders about the matter;' and

was upon the point of shutting me out, when I recollected myself
all of a sudden, and slipping a crown into his hand, begged as a
favour that he would enquire and let me know whether or not the
Earl was up. The grim janitor relented at the touch of my money,
which he took with all the indifference of a tax-gatherer, and shewed
me into a parlour, where, he said, I might amuse myself till such
time as his lord should be awake.—I had not sat ten minutes in
this place, when a footman entered, and without speaking, stared at
me; I interpreted this piece of his behaviour into 'Pray Sir, what is
your business?' and asked the same question I had put to the porter,
when I accosted him first. The lacquey made the same reply, and
disappeared before I could get any further intelligence.—In a little
time he returned, on pretence of poking the fire, and looked at me
again with great earnestness; upon which I began to perceive his
meaning, and tipping him with half a crown, desired he would be
so good as to fall upon some method of letting the Earl know that I
was in the house.—He made a low bow, said, 'Yes, Sir,' and vanished.—This bounty was not thrown away, for in an instant he
came back, and conducted me to a chamber, where I was received
with great kindness and familiarity by his lordship, whom I found
just risen, in his morning gown and slippers.—After breakfast, he
entered into a particular conversation with me about my travels, the
remarks I had made abroad, and examined me to the full extent of
my understanding.—My answers seemed to please him very much,
he frequently squeezed my hand, and looking at me with a singular
complacency in his countenance, bid me depend upon his good
offices with the ministry in my behalf. 'Young men of your qualifications (said he) ought to be cherished by every administration—
For my own part, I see so little merit in the world, that I have laid
it down as a maxim, to encourage the least appearance of genius and
virtue, to the utmost of my power—You have a great deal of both;
and will not fail of making a figure one day, if I am not mistaken;
but you must lay your account with mounting by gradual steps to
the summit of your fortune.—*Rome was not built in a day.*—As you
understand the languages perfectly well, how would you like to
cross the sea, as secretary to an embassy?'—I assured his lordship,
with great eagerness, that nothing could be more agreeable to my
inclination: Upon which he bid me make myself easy, my business
was done, for he had a place of that kind in his view.—This piece
of generosity affected me so much, that I was unable for some time

to express my gratitude, which at length broke out in acknowledgments of my own unworthiness, and encomiums on his benevolence. —I could not even help shedding tears, at the goodness of this noble lord, who no sooner perceived them, than he caught me in his arms, hugged and kissed me with a seemingly paternal affection.—Confounded at this uncommon instance of fondness for a stranger, I remained a few moments silent and ashamed, then got up and took my leave, after he had assured me that he would speak to the Minister in my favour, that very day; and desired that I would not for the future give myself the trouble of attending at his levée, but come at the same hour every day, when he was at leisure, which was three times a week.

Though my hopes were now very sanguine, I determined to conceal my prospect from every body, even from Strap, until I should be more certain of success; and in the mean time, give my patron no respite from my sollicitations.—When I renewed my visit, I found the street door opened to me as if by enchantment; but in my passage towards the presence-room, I was met by the *valet de chambre*, who cast some furious looks at me, the meaning of which I could not comprehend. The Earl saluted me at entrance with a tender embrace, and wished me joy of his success with the Premier, who, he said, had preferred his recommendation to that of two other noblemen very urgent in behalf of their respective friends, and absolutely promised that I should go to a certain foreign court in quality of secretary to an embassador and plenipotentiary, who would set out in a few weeks, on an affair of vast importance to the nation. I was thunder-struck with my good fortune, and could make no other reply, than kneel and attempt to kiss my benefactor's hand, which he would not permit, but raising me up, pressed me to his breast with surprizing emotion, and told me he had now taken upon himself the care of making my fortune.—What inhanced the value of the benefit still the more, was his making light of the favour, and shifting the conversation to another subject: Among other topics of discourse, that of the *Belle Lettre* was introduced, upon which his lordship held forth with great taste and erudition, and discovered an intimate knowledge of the authors of antiquity.—'Here's a book (said he, taking one from his bosom) written with great elegance and spirit, and though the subject may give offence to some narrow-minded people, the author will always be held in esteem by every person of sense and learning.' So saying, he put into my hand

Petronius Arbiter,[1] and asked my opinion of his wit and manner.—
I told him, that in my opinion, he wrote with great ease and vivacity,
but was withal so lewd and indecent, that he ought to find no
quarter or protection among people of morals and taste.—'I own
(replied the Earl) that his taste in love is generally decried, and indeed condemned by our laws; but perhaps that may be more owing
to prejudice and misapprehension, than to true reason and deliberation.—The best man among the ancients is said to have entertained
that passion; one of the wisest of their legislators has permitted the
indulgence of it in his commonwealth; the most celebrated poets
have not scrupled to avow it at this day; it prevails not only over all
the east, but in most parts of Europe; in our own country it gains
ground apace,[2] and in all probability will become in a short time a
more fashionable vice than simple fornication.—Indeed there is
something to be said in vindication of it, for notwithstanding the
severity of the law[3] against offenders in this way, it must be confessed that the practice of this passion is unattended with that
curse and burthen upon society, which proceeds from a race of
miserable deserted bastards, who are either murdered by their
parents, deserted to the utmost want and wretchedness, or bred up
to prey upon the commonwealth: And it likewise prevents the debauchery of many a young maiden, and the prostitution of honest
men's wives; not to mention the consideration of health, which is
much less liable to be impaired in the gratification of this appetite,
than in the exercise of common venery, which by ruining the constitutions of our young men, has produced a puny progeny that
degenerates from generation to generation: Nay, I have been told,
that there is another motive perhaps more powerful than all these,
that induces people to cultivate this inclination; namely, the
exquisite pleasure attending its success.'

From this discourse, I began to be apprehensive that his lordship
finding I had travelled, was afraid I might have been infected with
this spurious and sordid desire abroad, and took this method of
sounding my sentiments on the subject.—Fired at this supposed
suspicion, I argued against it with great warmth, as an appetite
unnatural, absurd, and of pernicious consequence; and declared my
utter detestation and abhorrence of it in these lines of the satyrist:[4]

'Eternal infamy the wretch confound
Who planted first, this vice on British ground!

Chapter LI

A vice! that 'spite of sense and nature reigns,
And poisons genial¹ love, and manhood stains!'

The Earl smiled at my indignation, told me he was glad to find
my opinion of the matter so conformable to his own, and that what
he had advanced was only to provoke me to an answer, with which
he professed himself perfectly well pleased.

After I had enjoyed a long audience, I happened to look at my
watch, in order to regulate my motions by it; and his lordship observing the chased case, desired to see the device, and examine the
execution, which he approved with some expressions of admiration.
—Considering the obligations I lay under to his lordship, I thought
there could not be a fitter opportunity than the present to manifest,
in some shape, my gratitude; I therefore begged he would do me
the honour to accept of the watch as a small testimony of the sense
I had of his lordship's generosity; but he refused it in a peremptory
manner, and said he was sorry I should entertain such a mercenary
opinion of him, observing at the same time, that it was the most
beautiful piece of workmanship he had ever seen; and desiring to
know where he could have such another.—I begged a thousand
pardons for the freedom I had taken, which I hoped he would impute to nothing else than the highest veneration for his person—
let him know that as it came to my hand by accident in France, I
could give him no information about the maker, for there was no
name on the inside; and once more humbly entreated that he would
indulge me so far as to use it for my sake.—He was still positive in
refusing it; but was pleased to thank me for my generous offer,
saying, it was a present that no nobleman needed be ashamed of
receiving; though he was resolved to shew his disinterestedness
with regard to me, for whom he had conceived a particular friendship; and insisted (if I was willing to part with the watch) upon
knowing what it cost, that he might at least indemnify me, by refunding the money. On the other hand, I assured his lordship, that
I would look upon it as an uncommon mark of distinction, if he
would take it without further question; and rather than disoblige
me, he was at last persuaded to put it in his pocket, to my no small
satisfaction, who took my leave immediately, after having received
a kind squeeze, and an injunction to depend upon his promise.

Buoyed up with my reception, my heart opened, I gave away a
guinea among the lacqueys, who escorted me to the door, flew to

the lodgings of Lord Straddle, upon whom I forced my diamond ring, as an acknowledgment for the great service he had done me, and from thence hied myself home, with an intent of sharing my happiness with honest Strap.—I determined, however, to heighten his pleasure by depressing his spirits at first, and then bringing in the good news with double relish.—For this purpose, I affected the appearance of disappointment and chagrin, and told him in an abrupt manner, that I had lost the watch and diamond. Poor Hugh, who had been already harrassed into a consumption[1] by intelligence of this sort, no sooner heard these words, than, unable to contain himself, he cried with distraction in his looks, 'God in heaven forbid!'—I could carry on the farce no longer, but laughing in his face, told him every thing that had befallen, as above recited. His features were immediately unbended, and the transition so affecting, that he wept with joy, calling my Lord Strutwell by the appellations of Jewel, Phœnix, *Rara avis*,[2] and praising God, that there was still some virtue left among our nobility.—Our mutual congratulations being over, we gave way to our imagination, and anticipated our happiness by prosecuting my success through the different steps of promotion, till I arrived at the rank of a prime minister, and he to that of my first secretary.

Intoxicated with these ideas I went to the ordinary, where, meeting with Banter, I communicated the whole affair in confidence to him, concluding with an assurance that I would do him all the service in my power.—He heard me to an end with great patience, then regarding me a good while with a look of disdain, pronounced, 'So, your business is done, you think?'——'As good as done, I believe, (said I.)'——'I'll tell you (replied he) what will do it still more effectually—A halter—'Sdeath! if I had been such a gull to two such scoundrels as Strutwell and Straddle, I would without any more ado tuck myself up.' Shocked at this exclamation, I desired him with some confusion to explain himself: Upon which he gave me to understand, that Straddle was a poor contemptible wretch, who lived by borrowing and pimping to his fellow peers; that in consequence of this last capacity, he had, doubtless, introduced me to Strutwell, who was so notorious for a passion for his own sex, that he was amazed his character had never reached my ears; and that so far from being able to obtain for me the post he had promised, his interest at court was so low, that he could scarce provide for a superannuated footman once a year, in Chelsea-hospital;[1]———that it was a common thing for him to amuse strangers whom his jack-calls[2] run down, with such assurances and caresses as he had bestowed on me, until he had stript them of their cash and every thing valuable about them;—very often of their chastity, and then leave them a prey to want and infamy;—that he allowed his servants no other wages than that part of the spoil which they could glean by their industry; and that the whole of his conduct to-wards me was so glaring, that no body who knew any thing of mankind could have been imposed upon by his insinuations.

I leave the reader to judge how I relished this piece of informa-tion, which precipitated me from the most exalted pinnacle of hope to the lowest abyss of despondence; and well nigh determined me to take Banter's advice, and finish my chagrin with a halter.—I had no room to suspect the veracity of my friend, because upon re-collection, I found every circumstance of Strutwell's behaviour, exactly tallying with the character he had described: His hugs, embraces, squeezes and eager looks, were now no longer a mystery; no more than his defence of Petronius, and the jealous frown of his *valet de chambre*, who, it seems, was at present the favourite pathic[3] of his lord.

CHAPTER LII

*I attempt to recover my watch and jewel, but to no purpose
———resolve to revenge myself on Strutwell by my importunity
———am reduced to my last guinea———obliged to inform Strap
of my necessity, who is almost distracted with the news——
but nevertheless obliged to pawn my best sword for present
subsistence———that small supply being exhausted, I am almost
stupified with my misfortunes———go to the gaming table, by
the advice of Banter, and come off with unexpected success
———Strap's exstacy———Mrs. Gawkey waits upon me, professes
remorse for her perfidy, and implores my assistance———I do
myself a piece of justice by her means, and afterwards
reconcile her to her father*

I WAS so confounded that I could make no reply to Banter, who re-proached me with great indignation, for having thrown away upon rascals, that which, had it been converted into ready money, would have supported the rank of a gentleman for some months, and enabled me, at the same time, to oblige my friends.——Stupified as I was, I could easily divine the source of his concern, but sneaked away in a solitary manner, without yielding the least answer to his expostulations; and began to deliberate with myself, in what manner I should attempt to retrieve the moveables I had so foolishly lost.— I would have thought it no robbery to take them again by force, could I have done it without any danger of being detected; but as I could have no such opportunity, I resolved to work by finesse, and go immediately to the lodgings of Straddle, where I was so fortunate as to find him.—'My Lord, (said I) I have just now recollected, that the diamond I had the honour of presenting to you, is loosened a little in the socket, and there is a young fellow just arrived from Paris, who is reckoned the best jeweller in Europe; I knew him in France, and if your lordship will give me leave, will carry the ring to him to be set to rights.'—His lordship was not to be caught in this snare—he thanked me for my offer, and let me know, that having himself observed the defect, he had already sent it to his own jeweller to be mended.—And indeed, by this time, I believe it was in the jeweller's hands, though not in order to be mended, for it stood in need of no alteration.

Baulked in this piece of politicks, I cursed my simplicity; but resolved to play a surer game with the Earl, which I had thus devised.—I did not doubt of being admitted into familiar conversation with him, as before, and hoped by some means, to get the watch into my hand, then on pretence of winding or playing with it, drop it on the floor, which in all probability would disorder the work so as to stop its motion: This event would furnish me with an opportunity of insisting upon carrying it away in order to be repaired; and had this happened, I should have been in no hurry to bring it back.—What pity it was I could not find an occasion of putting this fine scheme in execution! When I went to renew my visit to his lordship, my access to the parlour was as free as ever; but after I had waited some time, the *valet de chambre* came in with his Lord's compliments, and a desire to see me to-morrow at his levée, being at present so much indisposed that he could not see company.—I interpreted this message into a bad omen, and came away muttering curses against his lordship's politeness, and ready to go to logger-heads with myself for being so egregiously duped.—But that I might have some satisfaction for the loss I had sustained, I besieged him closely at his levée, and persecuted him with my solicitations; not without faint hopes indeed, of reaping something more from my industry, than the bare pleasure of making him uneasy; though I could never obtain another private hearing, during the whole course of my attendance; neither had I resolution enough, to un-deceive Strap, whose looks in a little time, were so whetted with impatience, that whenever I came home, his eyes devoured me, as it were, with eagerness of attention.

At length, however, finding myself reduced to my last guinea, I was compelled to disclose my necessity, though I endeavoured to sweeten the discovery by rehearsing to him the daily assurances I received from my patron.—But these promises were not of efficacy sufficient to support the spirits of my friend, who no sooner under-stood the lowness of my finances, than uttering a dreadful groan, he exclaimed, 'In the name of God, what shall we do?'—In order to comfort him, I said that many of my acquaintance, who were in a worse condition than we, supported, notwithstanding, the character and appearance of gentlemen; and advising him to thank God that we had as yet incurred no debt, proposed he should pawn my sword of steel inlaid with gold, and trust to my discretion for the rest. This expedient was wormwood and gall[1] to poor Strap, who, in spite of his invincible affection for me, still retained notions of œconomy and expence suitable to the narrowness of his education; nevertheless he complied with my request, and raised seven pieces[2] on the sword in a twinkling.—This supply, inconsiderable as it was, made me as happy for the present, as if I had had five hundred pounds in bank; for by this time I was so well skilled in procrastinating every troublesome reflection, that the prospect of want seldom affected me very much, let it be ever so near.—And now indeed it was nearer than I imagined; for my landlord having occasion for money, put me in mind of my being indebted to him five guineas in lodging; and telling me he had a sum to make up, begged I would excuse his importunity and discharge the debt. Though I could ill spare so much cash; my pride took the resolution of disbursing it, which I did in a cavalier manner, after he had written a discharge, telling him with an air of scorn and resentment, I saw he was re-solved that I should not be long in his books; while Strap, who stood by, and knew my circumstances, wrung his hands in secret, gnawed his nether lip, and turned yellow with despair.—Whatever appearance of indifference my vanity enabled me to put on, I was thunderstruck with this demand, which I had no sooner satisfied, than I hastened into company, with a view of beguiling my cares with conversation, or of drowning them in wine.

After dinner, a party was accordingly made in the coffee-house, from whence we adjourned to the tavern, where instead of sharing the mirth of the company, I was as much chagrined at their good humour as a damned soul in hell would be at a glimpse of heaven.— In vain did I swallow bumper after bumper! the wine had lost its effect upon me, and so far from raising my dejected spirits, could not even lay me asleep.—Banter, who was the only intimate I had (Strap excepted) perceived my anxiety, and when we broke up, reproached me with pusilanimity, for being cast down at any disappointment that such a rascal as Strutwell could be the occasion of.—I told him I did not at all see how Strutwell's being a rascal alleviated my misfortune; and gave him to understand that my present grief did not so much proceed from that disappointment, as from the low ebb of my fortune, which was sunk to something less than two guineas.—At this declaration, he cried, 'Pshaw! is that all?' and assured me, there were a thousand ways of living in town without fortune, he himself having subsisted many years entirely by his wit.—I expressed an eager desire of being acquainted with some of these methods, and he, without further expostulation, bid me follow him.—He conducted me to a house under the piazzas in Convent Garden, which we entered, and having delivered our swords to a grim fellow who demanded them at the foot of the staircase, ascended to the second story, where I saw multitudes of people standing round two gaming tables, loaded in a manner, with gold and silver.—My conductor let me know that this was the house of a worthy Scotch Lord,[1] who availing himself of the privilege of his peerage, had set up publick gaming tables, from the profits of which he drew a comfortable livelihood.—He then explained the difference between the *sitters* and the *betters*; characterized the first as old rooks, and the last as bubbles; and advised me to try my fortune at the silver table by betting a crown at a time.—Before I would venture any thing, I considered the company more particularly, and there appeared such a groupe of villainous faces, that I was struck with horror and astonishment at the sight! I signified my surprize to Banter, who whispered in my ear, that the bulk of those present were composed of sharpers, highwaymen, and apprentices, who having embezzled their master's cash, made a desperate push in this place, to make up their deficiencies.—This account did not encourage me to hazard any part of my small pittance; but at length being teized by the importunities of my friend, who assured me there was no danger of being ill used, people being hired by the owner to see justice done to every body; I began by risquing one shilling, and in less than an hour, my winning amounted to thirty.— Convinced by this time of the fairness of the game, and animated with success, there was no need of further persuasion to continue the play: I lent Banter (who seldom had any money in his pocket) a guinea, which he carried to the gold table and lost in a moment.— He would have borrowed another, but finding me deaf to his arguments, went away in a pet.—Mean while my gain advanced to six pieces, and my desire of more increased in proportion; so that I moved to the higher table, where I laid half a guinea on every throw, and fortune still favouring me, I became a sitter, in which capacity I remained until it was broad day; when I found myself, after many vicissitudes, one hundred and fifty guineas in pocket.

Thinking it now high time to retire with my booty, I asked if any body would take my place, and made a motion to rise; upon which an old gascon, who sat opposite to me, and of whom I had won a little money, started up with fury in his looks, crying, '*Restez foutre, restez, il faut donner moi mon ravanchio!*'[1] At the same time, a Jew who sat near the other, insinuated that I was more beholden to art than fortune, for what I had got; that he had observed me wipe the table very often, and that some of the divisions seemed to be greasy. This intimation produced a great deal of clamour against me, especially among the losers, who threatned with many oaths and imprecations to take me up by a warrant as a sharper, unless I would compromise the affair by refunding the greatest part of my winning.—Though I was far from being easy under this accusation, I relied upon my innocence, threatned in my turn to prosecute the Jew for defamation, and boldly offered to submit my cause to the examination of any justice in Westminster; but they knew themselves too well to put their characters on that issue, and finding I was not to be intimidated into any concession, dropt their plea, and made way for me to withdraw.—I would not however, stir from the table until the Israelite had retracted what he said to my disadvantage, and asked pardon before the whole assembly.

As I marched out with my prize, I happened to tread upon the toes of a tall raw-boned fellow, with a hooked nose, fierce eyes, black thick eye-brows, a pig-tail wig of the same colour, and a formidable hat pulled over his forehead, who stood gnawing his fingers in the crowd, and no sooner felt the application of my shoe-heel, than he roared out in a tremendous voice, 'Blood and wounds! you son of a whore, what's that for?'—I asked pardon with a great deal of submission, and protested I had no intention of hurting him; but the more I humbled myself the more he stormed, and insisted upon gentlemanly satisfaction, at the same time provoking me with scandalous names that I could not put up with; so that I gave a loose to my passion, returned his Billingsgate, and challenged him to follow me down to the piazzas.—His indignation cooling as mine warmed, he refused my invitation, saying, he would chuse his own time, and returned towards the table muttering threats, which I neither dreaded nor distinctly heard; but descending with great deliberation, received my sword from the door-keeper, whom I gratified with a guinea according to the custom of the place, and went home in a rapture of joy.

My faithful valet, who had sat up all night in the utmost uneasiness on my account, let me in with his face beslubbered with tears, and followed me to my chamber, where he stood silent like a condemned criminal, in expectation of hearing that every shilling was spent.—I guessed the situation of his thoughts, and assuming a sullen look, bid him fetch me some water to wash.—He replied, without lifting his eyes from the ground, 'In my simple conjecture, you have more occasion for rest, not having (I suppose) slept these four and twenty hours.'—'Bring me some water,' (said I in a peremptory tone;) upon which he sneaked away shrugging his shoulders. Before he returned I had spread my whole stock on the table in the most ostentatious manner; so that when it first saluted his view, he stood like one intranced, and having rubbed his eyes more than once, to assure himself of his being awake, broke out into, 'Lord have mercy upon us, what a vast treasure is here!'——''Tis all our own, Strap, (said I) take what is necessary, and redeem the sword immediately.' He advanced towards the table, stopt short by the way, looked at the money and me by turns, and with a wildness in his countenance, produced from joy checked by distrust, cried, 'I dare say, it is honestly come by.' To remove his scruples, I made him acquainted with the whole story of my success, on hearing of which, he danced about the room, in an exstacy, 'God be praised!—a white stone!¹—God be praised!—a white stone!' So that I was afraid the sudden change of fortune had disordered his intellects, and that he was run mad with joy.—Extremely concerned at this event, I attempted to reason him out of his frenzy, but to no purpose; for, without regarding what I said, he continued to frisk up and down, and repeat his rhapsody of 'God be praised! a white stone!' At last, I rose in the utmost consternation, and laying violent hands upon him put a stop to his extravagance, by fixing him down to a settee that was in the room.—This constraint banished his delirium; he started as if just awoke, and terrified at my behaviour, cried, 'What is the matter?' When he learned the cause of my apprehension, he was ashamed of his transports, and told me, that in mentioning the white stone, he alluded to the *Dies fasti* of the Romans, *albo lapide notati*.

Having no inclination to sleep, I secured my cash, dressed, and was just going abroad, when the servant of the house told me, there was a gentlewoman at the door, who wanted to speak with me.—Surprized at this information, I bid Strap shew her up, and in less than a minute saw a young woman of a shabby decayed appearance enter my room. After half a dozen court'sies, she began to sob, and told me her name was Gawkey; upon which I immediately recollected the features of Miss Lavement, who had been the first occasion of my misfortunes.—Though I had all the reason in the world, to resent her treacherous usage of me, I was moved at her distress, and professing my sorrow at seeing her so reduced, desired her to sit, and enquired into the particulars of her situation.—She fell upon her knees, and implored my forgiveness for the injuries she had done me, protesting before God, that she was forced against her inclination, into that hellish conspiracy which had almost deprived me of my life, by the intreaties of her husband, who having been afterwards renounced by his father on account of his marriage with her, and unable to support a family on his pay, left his wife at her father's house, and went with the regiment to Germany, where he was broke for misbehaviour at the battle of Dettingen; since which time she had heard no tidings of him. She then gave me to understand with many symptoms of penitence, that it was her misfortune to bear a child four months after marriage, by which her parents were so incensed, that she was turned out of doors with the infant, that died soon after; and had hitherto subsisted in a miserable indigent manner, on the extorted charity of a few friends, who were now quite tired of giving; that not knowing where or how to support herself one day longer, she had fled for succour even to me, who of all mankind had the least cause to assist her, relying upon the generosity of my disposition, which, she hoped, would be pleased with this opportunity of avenging itself in the noblest manner, on the wretch who had wronged me.—I was very much affected with her discourse, and having no cause to suspect the sincerity of her repentance, raised her up, freely pardoned all she had done against me, and promised to befriend her as much as lay in my power.

Since my last arrival in London, I had made no advances to the apothecary, imagining it would be impossible for me to make my innocence appear, so unhappily was my accusation circumstanced: Strap indeed had laboured to justify me to the schoolmaster; but so far from succeeding in his attempt, Mr. Concordance dropt all correspondence with him, because he refused to quit his connexion with me.—Things being in this situation, I thought a fairer opportunity of vindicating my character could not offer, than that which now presented itself;—therefore stipulated with Mrs. Gawkey, that before I yielded her the least assistance, she should do me the justice to clear my reputation, by explaining upon oath before a Magistrate, the whole of the conspiracy, as it had been executed against me.—When she had given me this satisfaction, I presented her with five guineas, a sum so much above her expectation, that she could scarcely believe the evidence of her senses, and was ready to worship me for my benevolence.—The declaration signed with her own hand, I sent to her father, who, upon recollecting and comparing the circumstances of my charge, was convinced of my integrity, and waited on me next day, in company with his friend the schoolmaster, to whom he had communicated my vindication.— After mutual salutation, Monsieur Lavement began a long apology for the unjust treatment I had received; but I saved him a good deal of breath, by interrupting his harrangue, and assuring him, that so far from entertaining any resentment against him, I thought myself obliged to his lenity, which allowed me to escape, after such strong presumptions of guilt appeared against me. Mr. Concordance thinking it now his turn to speak, observed, that Mr. Random had too much candour and sagacity to be disobliged at their conduct, which, all things considered, could not have been otherwise, with any honesty of intention. 'Indeed (said he) if the plot had been unravelled to us by any supernatural intelligence; if it had been whispered by a genie, communicated by a dream, or revealed by an angel from on high, we should have been to blame in crediting ocular demonstration;—but as we were left in the mist of mortality, it cannot be expected we should be incapable of imposition.—I do assure you, Mr. Random, no man on earth is more pleased than I am at this triumph of your character; and as the news of your misfortune panged me to the very intrails, this manifestation of your innocence makes my midrif quiver with joy.'—I thanked him for his concern, desired them to undeceive those of their acquaintance who judged harshly of me, and having treated them with a glass of wine, represented to Lavement the deplorable condition of his daughter, and pleaded her cause so effectually, that he consented to settle a small annuity on her for life; but could not be persuaded to take her home, because her mother was so much incensed that she would never see her.

CHAPTER LIII

*I purchase new cloaths——reprimand Strutwell and Straddle——Banter proposes another matrimonial scheme—
I accept of his terms——set out for Bath in a stage-coach, with the young lady and her mother—the behaviour of an officer and lawyer, our fellow-travellers, described—a smart dialogue between my mistress and the captain*

HAVING finished this affair to my satisfaction, I found myself perfectly at ease, and looking upon the gaming-table as a certain resource for a gentleman in want, became more gay than ever.— Although my cloaths were almost as good as new, I grew ashamed of wearing them, because I thought every body, by this time, had got an inventory of my wardrobe.—For which reason, I disposed of a good part of my apparel to a salesman in Monmouth-street,[1] for half the value, and bought two new suits with the money. I likewise purchased a plain gold watch, despairing of recovering that which I had so foolishly given to Strutwell, whom, notwithstanding, I still continued to visit at his levée, until the embassador he had mentioned, set out with a secretary of his own chusing.—I thought myself then at liberty to expostulate with his lordship, whom I treated with great freedom in a letter, for amusing me with vain hopes, when he neither had the power nor inclination to provide for me.—Nor was I less reserved with Straddle, whom I in person reproached for misrepresenting to me the character of Strutwell, which I did not scruple to aver was infamous in every respect.— He seemed very much enraged at my freedom, talked a great deal about his quality and honour, and began to make some comparisons which I thought so injurious to mine, that I demanded an explanation with great warmth; and he was mean enough to equivocate, and condescend in such a manner, that I left him with a hearty contempt of his behaviour.

About this time, Banter, who had observed a surprizing and sudden alteration in my appearance and disposition, began to enquire very minutely into the cause; and as I did not think fit to let him know the true state of the affair, lest he might make free with my purse, on the strength of having proposed the scheme that filled it, I told him that I had received a small supply from a relation in the country, who at the same time had promised to use all his interest (which was not small) in solliciting some post for me that would make me easy for life.—'If that be the case (said Banter) perhaps you won't care to mortify yourself a little, in making your fortune another way.—I have a relation who is to set out for Bath next week, with an only daughter, who being sickly and decrepid, intends to drink the waters for the recovery of her health.—Her father, who was a rich Turkey merchant, died about a year ago, and left her with a fortune of twenty thousand pounds, under the sole management of her mother, who is my kinswoman.—I would have put in for the plate myself,[1] but there is a breach at present between the old woman and me.——You must know, that some time ago I borrowed a small sum of her, and promised, it seems, to pay it before a certain time; but being disappointed in my expectation of money from the country, the day elapsed, without my being able to take up my note; upon which she wrote a peremptory letter, threatning to arrest me, if I did not pay the debt immediately: Nettled at this precise behaviour, I sent a damned severe answer, which enraged her so much, that she actually took out a writ against me.— Whereupon, finding the thing grow serious, I got a friend to advance the money for me, discharged the debt, went to her house, and abused her for unfriendly dealing.—She was provoked by my reproaches, and scolded in her turn. The little deformed urchin joined her mother with such virulence and volubility of tongue, that I was fain to make my retreat, after having been honoured with a great many scandalous epithets, which gave me plainly to understand that I had nothing to hope from the esteem of the one, or the affection of the other.—As they are both utter strangers to life, it is a thousand to one that the girl shall be picked up by some scoundrel or other at Bath, if I don't provide for her otherwise.—You are a well-looking fellow, Random, and can behave as demurely as a quaker.—Now if you will give me an obligation for five hundred pounds, to be paid six months after your marriage, I will put you in a method of carrying her in spite of all opposition.'

This proposal was too advantageous for me, to be refused: The writing was immediately drawn and executed; and Banter giving me notice of the time when, and the stage-coach in which they were to set out, I bespoke a place in the same convenience; and having hired a horse for Strap, who was charmed with the project, set out accordingly.

As we embarked before day, I had not the pleasure for some time of seeing Miss Snapper (that was the name of my mistress) nor even of perceiving the number and sex of my fellow-travellers, although I guessed that the coach was full, by the difficulty I found in seating myself.—The first five minutes passed in a general silence, when all of a sudden, the coach heeling to one side, a boisterous voice pronounced, 'To the right and left, cover your flanks, damme!' I easily discovered by the time and matter of this exclamation, that it was uttered by a son of Mars; neither was it hard to conceive the profession of another person, who sat opposite to me, and observed, that we ought to have been well satisfied of the security, before we entered upon the premises,—These two sallies had not the desired effect: We continued a good while as mute as before, till at length, the gentleman of the sword, impatient of longer silence, made a second effort, by swearing, he had got into a meeting of quakers.— 'I believe so too, (said a shrill female voice, at my left hand) for the spirit of folly begins to move.'—'Out with it then, madam,' (replied the soldier.)—'You seem to have no occasion for a midwife,' (cried the lady.)—'D—n my blood! (exclaimed the other) a man can't talk to a woman, but she immediately thinks of a midwife.'—— 'True, Sir, (said she) I long to be delivered.'—'What! of a mouse, madam?' (said he.)—'No, Sir, (said she) of a fool.'—'Are you far gone with fool?' (said he.)[1]—'Little more than two miles,' (said she.)—'By Gad, you're a wit, madam!' (cried the officer)—'I wish I could with any justice return the compliment,' (said the lady.)—'Zounds! I have done,' (said he.)—'Your bolt is soon shot, according to the proverb,' (said she.)—The warrior's powder was quite spent; the lawyer advised him to drop the prosecution, and a grave matron, who sat on the left hand of the victorious wit, told her, she must not let her tongue run so fast among strangers.—This reprimand softened with the appellation of *child*, convinced me that the satyrical lady was no other than Miss Snapper, and resolved to regulate my conduct accordingly. The champion finding himself so smartly handled, changed his battery, and began to expatiate on his own exploits.——'You talk of shot, madam, (said he) damme! I have both given and received some shot in my time——I was wounded in the shoulder by a pistol ball at Dettingen, where—I say nothing —but by G—d! if it had not been for me—all's one for that—I despise boasting, G—d d—me!'—So saying, he whistled one part and hummed another of Black Joke;[2] then addressing himself to the lawyer, went on thus, 'Wouldn't you think it damn'd hard, after having, at the risk of your life, recovered the standard of a regiment, that had been lost, to receive no preferment for your pains! I don't chuse to name no names, sink me! but howsomever, this I will refer, by G—d, and that is this, a musqueteer of the French guards, having taken a standard from a certain cornet of a certain regiment, damme! was retreating with his prize as fast as his horse's heels could carry him, damme! Upon which, I snatched up a firelock that belonged to a dead man, damme! and shot his horse under him, d—n my blood! The fellow got upon his feet and began to repose me, upon which I charged my bayonet breast high, and run him through the body, by G—d!—One of his comrades coming to his assistance, shot me in the shoulder, as I told you before; and another gave me a confusion on the head with the butt end of his carbine; but damme, that did not signify—I killed one, put the other to flight, and taking up the standard carried it off very deliberately—But the best joke of all was, the son of a b—ch of a cornet who had surrendered it in a cowardly manner, seeing it in my possession, demanded it from me, in the front of the line.'—'D—n my blood (says he) where did you find my standard?' (says he)—'D—n my blood (said I) where (said I) did you lose it?' (said I.)—'That's nothing to you (says he) 'tis my standard (says he) and by

G—d I'll have it.' (says he.)—'D—n—ti—n seize me (says I) if you shall (says I) till I have first delivered it to the General (says I;) and accordingly I went to the head quarters, after the battle, and delivered it to my Lord Stair, who promised to do for me, but I am no more than a poor lieutenant still, d—n my blood.'

Having vented this repetition of expletives, the lawyer owned he had not been requited according to his deserts; observed, that the labourer is always worthy of his hire,[1] and asked if the promise was made before witnesses, because in that case the law could compel the General to perform it;—but understanding that the promise was performed during a *tête a tête*, over a bottle, without being restricted to time or terms, he pronounced it not valid in law, proceeded to enquire into the particulars of the battle, and affirmed, that although the English had drawn themselves into a premunire[2] at first, the French managed their cause so lamely in the course of the dispute, that they would have been utterly nonsuited,[3] had they not obtained a noli-prosequi.[4]—In spite of these enlivening touches, the conversation was like to suffer another long interruption; when the lieutenant, unwilling to conceal any of his accomplishments that could be displayed in his present situation, offered to regale the company with a song; and interpreting our silence into a desire of hearing, began to warble a fashionable air, the first stanza of which be pronounced thus:

> 'Would task the moon-ty'd hair,
> To yon flagrant beau repair;
> Where waving with the poppling vow
> The bantling fine will shelter you, &c.'[5]

The sense of the rest he perverted as he went on, with such surprizing facility, that I could not help thinking he had been at some pains to burlesque the performance.—Miss Snapper ascribed it to the true cause, namely ignorance; and when he asked her how she relished his musick, answered, that in her opinion, the musick and the words were much of a piece.—'O! d—n my blood! (said he) I take that as a high compliment; for every body allows the words are damnable fine.'——'They may be so, (replied the lady) for ought I know, but they are above my comprehension.'—'I an't obliged to find you comprehension, madam, curse me!' (cried he.)—'No, nor to speak sense neither,' (said she.)——'D—n my heart (said he) I'll speak what I please.'——Here the lawyer interposed, by telling him

there were some things he must not speak.—And upon being de-
fyed to give an instance, mentioned Treason and Defamation.—'As
for the king, (cried the soldier) God bless him—I eat his bread, and
have lost blood in his cause, therefore I have nothing to say to him
—but by G—d, I dare say any thing to any other man.'—'No, (said
the lawyer) you dare not call me rogue.'—'Damme, for what?' said
the other.—'Because (replied the counsellor) I should have a good
action against you, and recover.'[1]—'Well, well, (cried the officer) if
I dare not call you rogue, I dare think you one, damme!'—This
stroke of wit he accompanied with a loud laugh of self-approbation,
which unluckily did not affect the audience, but effectually silenced
his antagonist, who did not open his mouth for the space of an hour
thereafter, except to clear his pipes with three *hemms*, which, however, produced nothing.

CHAPTER LIV

*Day breaking, I have the pleasure of viewing the person of
Miss Snapper, whom I had not seen before——the soldier is
witty upon me—is offended, talks much of his valour——is
reprimanded by a grave gentlewoman——we are alarmed with
the cry of highwaymen——I get out of the coach, and stand
on my defence——they ride off without having attacked us——
I pursue them——one of them is thrown from his horse and
taken——I return to the coach—am complimented by miss
Snapper——the captain's behaviour on this occasion——the
prude reproaches me in a soliloquy——I upbraid her in the
same manner——the behaviour of Mrs. Snapper at breakfast,
disobliges me——the lawyer is witty upon the officer, who
threatens him*

In the mean time, day breaking in upon us, discovered to one
another, the faces of their fellow-travellers; and I had the good fortune to find my mistress not quite so deformed nor disagreeable as
she had been represented to me.—Her head, indeed, bore some resemblance to a hatchet, the edge being represented by her face;

but she had a certain delicacy in her complexion, and a great deal of vivacity in her eyes, which were very large and black; and though the protuberance of her breast, when considered alone, seemed to drag her forwards, it was easy to perceive an equivalent on her back which balanced the other, and kept her body in equilibrio.—On the whole, I thought I should have great reason to congratulate myself, if it should be my fate to possess twenty thousand pounds encumbered with such a wife.—I began therefore to deliberate about the most probable means of acquiring the conquest, and was so much engrossed by this idea, that I scarce took any notice of the rest of the people in the coach, but revolved my prospect in silence; while the conversation was maintained as before, by the object of my hopes, the son of Mars, and the barrister, who by this time had recollected himself, and talked in terms as much as ever.—At length a dispute happened, which ended in a wager, to be determined by me, who was so much absorpt in contemplation, that I neither heard the reference nor the question which was put to me by each in his turn; affronted at my supposed contempt, the soldier with great vociferation, swore, I was either dumb or deaf, if not both, and that I looked as if I could not say *Boh to a goose*.[1]—Arroused at this observation, I fixed my eyes upon him, and pronounced with emphasis, the interjection *Boh!* Upon which he cocked his hat in a fierce manner and cried, 'Damme, Sir, what d'ye mean by that?'—Had I intended to answer him, which by the bye, was not my design, I should have been anticipated by Miss, who told him, my meaning was to shew, that I could cry boh! to a goose; and laughed very heartily at my laconic reproof.—Her explanation and mirth did not help to appease his wrath, which broke out in several martial insinuations, such as—'I do not understand such freedoms, damme! —D—n my blood! I'm a gentleman, and bear the king's commission.—'Sblood! some people deserve to have their noses pulled for their impertinence.'——I thought to have checked these ejaculations by a frown; because he had talked so much of his valour, that I had long ago rated him an ass with a lion's skin; but so far from answering my expectation, that he took umbrage at the contraction of my brows, swore he did not value my sulky look a fig's end, and protested he feared no man breathing.—Miss Snapper said, she was very glad to find herself in company with a man of so much courage, who she did not doubt, would protect us all from the attempts of highwaymen, during our journey.——'Make yourself perfectly easy on that head, madam, (replied the officer) I have got a pair of pistols (here they are) which I took from a horse officer at the battle of Dettingen—they are double loaded, and if any highwayman in England robbs you of the value of a pin, while I have the honour of being in your company, d—n my heart.'—When he had expressed himself in this manner, a prim gentlewoman, who had sat silent hitherto, opened her mouth, and said, she wondered how any man could be so rude as to pull out such weapons before ladies.—'Damme, madam, (cried the champion) if you are so much afraid at sight of a pistol, how d'ye propose to stand fire if there should be occasion?'— She let him know, that if she thought he could be so unmannerly as to use fire-arms in her presence, whatever might be the occasion, she would get out of the coach immediately, and walk to the next village, where she might procure a convenience to herself.—Before he could make any answer, my Dulcinea interposed, and observed, that so far from being offended at a gentleman's using his arms in his own defence, she thought herself very lucky in being along with one by whose valour she stood a good chance of saving herself from being rifled.—The prude cast a disdainful look at Miss, and said, that people who have but little to lose, are sometimes the most solicitous about preserving it.—The old lady was affronted at this inuendo, and took notice, that people ought to be very well informed before they speak slightingly of other people's fortune, lest they discover their own envy, and make themselves ridiculous.—The daughter declared, that she did not pretend to vie with any body in point of riches; and if the lady who insisted upon non-resistance, would promise to indemnify us all for the loss we should sustain; she should be one of the first to persuade the captain to submission, in case we should be attacked.—To this proposal, reasonable as it was, the reserved lady made no other reply, than a scornful glance and a toss of her head.—I was very well pleased with the spirit of my mistress; and even wished for an opportunity of distinguishing my courage under her eye, which I believed, could not fail of pre-possessing her in my favour; when all of a sudden, Strap rode up to the coach door, and told us in a great fright, that two men on horse-back were crossing the heath (for by this time we had passed Hounslow)[1] and made directly towards us. This piece of information was no sooner delivered, than Mrs. Snapper began scream, her daughter grew pale, the other lady pulled out her purse to be in readiness, the lawyer's teeth chattered, while he pronounced, "'Tis no matter—we'll sue the county and recover.'—The captain gave evident signs of confusion; and I, after having commanded the coachman to stop, opened the door, jumped out, and invited the warrior to follow me.—But finding him backward and astonished, I took his pistols, and giving them to Strap, who had by this time alighted, and trembled very much, I mounted on horse-back; and taking my own, (which I could better depend upon) from the holsters, cocked them both, and faced the robbers, who were now very near us.—Seeing me ready to oppose them on horse-back, and another man armed a foot, they made a halt at some distance to reconnoitre us, and after having rode round us twice, myself still facing about as they rode, went off the same way they came, at a hand gallop.[1]—A gentleman's servant coming up with a horse at the same time, I offered him a crown to assist me in pursuing them, which he no sooner accepted, than I armed him with the officer's pistols, and we galloped after the thieves, who trusting to the swiftness of their horses, stopped till we came within shot of them, and then firing at us, put their nags to the full speed.—We followed them as fast as our beasts could carry us, but not being so well mounted as they, our efforts would have been to little purpose, had not the horse of one of them stumbled and thrown his rider with such violence over his head, that he lay senseless, when we came up, and was taken without the least opposition, while his comrade consulted his own safety in flight, without regarding the distress of his friend. We scarce had time to make ourselves masters of his arms, and tye his hands together, before he recovered his senses; when learning his situation, he affected surprize, demanded to know by what authority we used a gentleman in that manner, and had the impudence to threaten us with a prosecution for robbery.—In the mean time we perceived Strap coming up with a crowd of people, armed with different kinds of weapons; and among the rest a farmer, who no sooner perceived the thief, whom we had secured, than he cried with great emotion, 'There's the fellow who robbed me an hour ago, of twenty pounds, in a canvas bag.'—He was immediately searched, and the money found exactly as it had been described: Upon which, we committed him to the charge of the countryman, who guarded him to the town of Hounslow, which it seems the farmer had alarmed; and having satisfied the footman for his trouble according to promise, returned with Strap to the coach, where I found the captain and lawyer busy in administring smelling

329

bottles and cordials to the grave lady, who had gone into a fit at the noise of the firing.

When I had taken my seat, Miss Snapper, who from the coach had seen every thing that happened, made me a compliment on my behaviour, and said, she was glad to see me returned, without having received any injury; her mother too owned herself obliged to my resolution; and the lawyer told me, that I was intitled by act of parliament to a reward of forty pounds, for having apprehended a highwayman.—The soldier observed, with a countenance in which impudence and shame struggling, produced some disorder, that if I had not been in such a damned hurry to get out of the coach, he would have secured the rogues effectually, without all this bustle and loss of time, by a scheme which my heat and precipitation ruined.—'For my own part, (continued he) I am always extremely cool on these occasions.'——'So it appeared, by your trembling' (said the young lady.)—'Death and damnation (cried he) your sex protects you, madam; if any man on earth durst tell me so much, I'd send him to hell, d—n my heart! in an instant.'—So saying, he fixed his eyes on me, and asked if I had seen him tremble.—I answered without hesitation, 'Yes.'—'Damme, Sir, (said he) d'ye doubt my courage?'—I replied, 'Very much.'—This declaration quite disconcerted him.—He looked blank, and pronounced with a faultering voice, 'O! 'tis very well—d—n my blood! I shall find a time.'—I signified my contempt of him, by thrusting my tongue in my cheek, which humbled him so much, that he scarce swore another oath during the whole journey.

The precise lady, having recruited her spirits by the help of some strong waters, began a soliloquy, in which she wondered that any man, who pretended to maintain the character of a gentleman, could, for the sake of a little paultry coin, throw persons of honour into such quandaries as might endanger their lives; and professed her surprize, that women were not ashamed to commend such brutality. At the same time vowing, that for the future she would never set foot in a stage-coach, if a private convenience could be had for love or money.

Nettled at her remarks, I took the same method of conveying my sentiments, and wondered in my turn, that any woman of common sense, should be so unreasonable as to expect that people who had neither acquaintance nor connexion with her, would tamely allow themselves to be robbed and mal-treated, meerly to indulge her capricious humour. I likewise confessed my astonishment at her insolence and ingratitude in taxing a person with brutality, who deserved her approbation and acknowledgment; and vowed, that if ever we should be assaulted again, I would leave her to the mercy of the spoiler, that she might know the value of my protection.

This person of honour did not think fit to carry on the altercation any further, but seemed to chew the cud of her resentment, with the crest-fallen captain, while I entered into discourse with my charmer, who was the more pleased with my conversation, as she had conceived a very indifferent opinion of my intellects from my former silence. I should have had cause to be equally satisfied with the sprightliness of her genius, could she have curbed her imagination with judgment; but she laboured under such a profusion of talk, that I dreaded her unruly tongue, and felt by anticipation the horrors of an eternal clack! However, when I considered on the other hand, the joys attending the possession of twenty thousand pounds, I forgot her imperfections, seized occasion by the forelock, and endeavoured to insinuate myself into her affection.—The careful mother kept a strict watch over her, and though she could not help behaving civilly to me, took frequent opportunities of discouraging our communication, by reprimanding her for being so free with strangers, and telling her she must learn to speak less, and think more.—Abridged of the use of speech, we conversed with our eyes, and I found the young lady very eloquent in this kind of discourse. In short, I had reason to believe, that she was sick of the old gentlewoman's tuition, and that I should find it no difficult matter to supersede her authority.

When we arrived at the place where we were to breakfast, I alighted and helped my mistress out of the coach, as well as her mother, who called for a private room, to which they withdrew, in order to eat by themselves.—As they retired together, I perceived that Miss had got more twists from nature, than I had before observed, being bent sideways into the figure of an S, so that her progression very much resembled that of a crab.—The prude also chose the captain for her mess-mate, and ordered breakfast for two only to be brought into another separate room; while the lawyer and I, deserted by the rest of the company, were fain to put up with one another. I was a good deal chagrined at the stately reserve of Mrs. Snapper, who I thought did not use me with all the complaisance I deserved; and my companion declared, that he had been a traveller these twenty years, and never knew the stage-coach rules so much infringed before. As for the honourable gentlewoman, I could not conceive the meaning of her attachment to the lieutenant; and asked the lawyer if he knew for which of the soldier's virtues she admired him? The counsellor facetiously replied, 'I suppose the lady knows him to be an able conveyancer,[1] and wants him to make a settlement intail.'—I could not help laughing at the archness of the barrister, who entertained me during breakfast, with a great deal of wit of the same kind, at the expence of our fellow-travellers; and among other things said, he was sorry to find the young lady saddled with such incumbrances.

When we had made an end of our repast, and paid our reckoning, we went into the coach, took our places, and bribed the driver with six-pence, to revenge us on the rest of his fare, by hurrying them away in the midst of their meal.—This he performed to our satisfaction, after he had disturbed their enjoyment with his importunate clamour.—The mother and daughter obeyed the summons first, and coming to the coach-door, were obliged to desire the coachman's assistance to get in because the lawyer and I had agreed to shew our resentment by our neglect.—They were no sooner seated, than the captain appeared as much heated as if he had been pursued a dozen of miles by an enemy; and immediately after him came the lady, not without some marks of disorder.—Having helped her up, he entered himself, growling a few oaths against the coachman for his impertinent interruption; and the lawyer comforted him, by saying, that if he had suffered a *nisi prius* through the obstinacy of the defendant, he would have an opportunity to join issue[2] at the next stage. This last expression gave offence to the grave gentlewoman, who told him, if she was a man, she would make him repent of such obscenity, and thanked God she had never been in such company before.—At this insinuation, the captain thought himself under a necessity of espousing the lady's cause; and accordingly threatned to cut the lawyer's ears out of his head, if he should give his tongue any such liberties for the future.—The poor counsellor begged pardon, and universal silence ensued.

CHAPTER LV

I resolve to ingratiate myself with the mother, and am
favoured by accident—the precise lady finds her husband,
and quits the coach—the captain is disappointed of his
dinner—we arrive at Bath——I accompany Miss Snapper to
the long room, where she is attacked by beau N——h, and
turns the laugh against him——I make love to her, and
receive a check——I squire her to an assembly, where I am
blest with a sight of my dear Narcissa, which discomposes
me so much, that Miss Snapper observing my disorder, is
at pains to discover the cause—is picqued at the occasion,
and in our way home, pays me a sarcastic compliment——I am
met by Miss Williams, who is maid and confidante of
Narcissa——she acquaints me with her lady's regard for me
while under the disguise of a servant, and describes the
transports of Narcissa on seeing me at the assembly, in the
character of a gentleman——I am surprized with an account
of her aunt's marriage, and make an appointment to meet
Miss Williams next day

DURING this unsocial interval, my pride and interest maintained a
severe conflict, on the subject of Miss Snapper, whom the one represented as unworthy of my notice, and the other proposed as the
object of my whole attention: The advantages and disadvantages
attending such a match, were opposed to one another by my
imagination; and at length, my judgment gave it so much in favour
of the first, that I resolved to prosecute my scheme, with all the
address in my power.—I thought I perceived some concern in her
countenance, occasioned by my silence, which she no doubt imputed to my disgust at her mother's behaviour; and as I believed
the old woman could not fail of ascribing my muteness to the same
motive, I determined to continue that sullen conduct towards her,
and fall upon some other method of manifesting my esteem for the
daughter; nor was it difficult for me to make her acquainted with
my sentiments by the expression of my looks, which I modelled

into the characters of humility and love; and which were answered by her with all the sympathy and approbation I could desire. But when I began to consider, that without further opportunities of improving my success, all the progress I had hitherto made could not much avail, and that such opportunities could not be enjoyed without the mother's permission; I concluded it would be requisite to vanquish her coldness and suspicion by my assiduities and respectful behaviour on the road; and she would in all likelihood invite me to visit her at Bath, where I did not fear of being able to cultivate her acquaintance as much as would be necessary to the accomplishment of my purpose.—And indeed accident furnished me with an opportunity of obliging her so much, that she could not with any appearance of good manners, forbear to gratify my inclination.

When we arrived at our dining-place, we found all the eatables in the inn bespoke by a certain nobleman, who had got the start of us; and in all likelihood, my mistress and her mother must have dined with Duke Humphrey,[1] had I not exerted myself in their behalf, and bribed the landlord with a glass of wine to curtail his lordship's entertainment of a couple of fowls and some bacon, which I sent with my compliments to the ladies; they accepted my treat with a great many thanks, and desired I would favour them with my company at dinner, where I amused the old gentlewoman so successfully, by maintaining a seemingly disinterested ease, in the midst of my civility, that she signified a desire of being better acquainted, and hoped I would be so kind as to see her sometimes at Bath.——While I enjoyed myself in this manner, the precise lady had the good fortune to meet with her husband, who was no other than gentleman, or in other words, *valet de chambre* to the very nobleman, whose coach stood at the door. Proud of the interest she had in the house, she affected to shew her power by introducing the captain to her spouse, as a person who had treated her with great civility; upon which he was invited to a share of their dinner; while the poor lawyer, finding himself utterly abandoned, made application to me, and was, through my intercession, admitted into our company.—Having satisfied our appetites, and made ourselves very merry at the expence of the person of honour, the civil captain, and complaisant husband, I did myself the pleasure of discharging the bill by stealth, for which I received a great many apologies and acknowledgments from my guests, and we reimbarked at the first warning.—The officer was obliged, at last, to appease his hunger with a luncheon of bread and cheese, and a pint bottle of brandy, which he dispatched in the coach, cursing the inappetence of his lordship, who had ordered dinner to be put back a whole hour.

Nothing remarkable happened during the remaining part of our journey, which was ended about twelve a-clock, when I waited on the ladies to the house of a relation, in which they intended to lodge, and passing that night at the inn, took lodgings next morning for myself.

The forenoon was spent in visiting every thing that was worth seeing in the place, which I did in company with a gentleman to whom Banter had given me a letter of introduction; and in the afternoon I waited on the ladies, and found Miss a good deal indisposed with the fatigues of the journey.—As they foresaw they would have occasion for a male acquaintance to squire them at all publick places, I was received with great cordiality, and had the mother's permission to conduct them next day to the long room, which we no sooner entered, than the eyes of every body present were turned upon us; and when we had suffered the martyrdom of their looks for some time, a whisper circulated at our expence, which was accompanied with many contemptuous smiles, and tittering observations, to my utter shame and confusion.—I did not so much conduct as follow my charge to a place where she seated her mother and herself with astonishing composure, notwithstanding the unmannerly behaviour of the whole company, which seemed to be assumed meerly to put her out of countenance.—The celebrated Mr. N—h,[1] who commonly attends in this place, as master of the ceremonies, perceiving the disposition of the assembly, took upon himself the task of gratifying their ill-nature still further, by exposing my mistress to the edge of his wit.—With this view he approached us, with many bows and grimaces, and after having welcomed Miss Snapper to the place, asked her, in the hearing of all present, if she could inform him of the name of Tobit's dog.[2]—I was so much incensed at his insolence, that I should certainly have kicked him where he stood, without ceremony, had not the young lady prevented the effects of my indignation, by replying with the utmost vivacity, 'His name was N—sh, and an impudent dog he was.' This repartee, so unexpected and just, raised such an universal laugh at the aggressor, that all his assurance was insufficient to support him under their derision; so that after he had endeavoured to compose himself, by taking snuff, and forcing a smile, he was obliged to sneak off in a very ludicrous attitude; while my Dulcinea was applauded to the skies, for the brilliancy of her wit, and her acquaintance immediately courted by the best people of both sexes in the room.—This event, with which I was infinitely pleased at first, did not fail of alarming me, upon further reflection, when I considered that the more she was caressed by persons of distinction, the more her pride would be inflamed, and consequently, the obstacles to my success multiplied and enlarged.—Nor were my presaging fears untrue.—That very night I perceived her a little intoxicated with the incense she had received, and though she still behaved with a particular civility to me, I foresaw that as soon as her fortune should be known, she would be surrounded with a swarm of admirers, some one of whom might possibly, by excelling me in point of wealth, or in the arts of flattery and scandal, supplant me in her esteem, and find means to make the mother of his party.— I resolved therefore to lose no time, and being invited to spend the evening with them, found an opportunity, in spite of the old gentlewoman's vigilance, to explain the meaning of my glances in the coach, by paying homage to her wit, and professing myself enamoured of her person.——She blushed at my declaration, and in a favourable manner disapproved of the liberty I had taken, putting me in mind of our being strangers to one another, and desiring I would not be the means of interrupting our acquaintance, by any such unseasonable strokes of gallantry for the future.—My ardour was effectually checked by this reprimand, which was, however, delivered in such a gentle manner, that I had no cause to be disobliged; and the arrival of her mother relieved me from a dilemma in which I should not have known how to demean myself a minute longer.—Neither could I resume the easiness of carriage with which I came in, my mistress acted on the reserve, and the conversation beginning to flag, the old lady introduced her kinswoman of the house, and proposed a hand at whist.

While we amused ourselves at this diversion, I understood from the gentlewoman, that there was to be an assembly next night, at which I begged to have the honour of dancing with Miss. She thanked me for the favour I intended her, assured me, she never did dance, but signified a desire of seeing the company; upon which I offered my service, and was accepted; not a little proud of being exempted from appearing with her, in a situation, that, notwithstanding my profession to the contrary, was not at all agreeable to my inclination.

Having supped, and continued the game, till such time as the successive yawns of the mother warned me to begone, I took my leave, and went home, where I made Strap very happy with an account of my progress.—Next day I put on my gayest apparel, and went to drink tea at Mrs. Snapper's, according to appointment, when I found, to my inexpressible satisfaction, that she was laid up with the tooth-ach, and that Miss was to be intrusted to my care.— Accordingly, we set out for the ball-room, pretty early in the evening, and took possession of a commodious place, where we had not sat longer than a quarter of an hour, when a gentleman dressed in a green frock came in, leading a young lady, whom I immediately discovered to be the adorable Narcissa! Good heaven! what were the thrillings of my soul at that instant! my reflection was over- whelmed with a torrent of agitation! my heart throbbed with sur- prizing violence! a sudden mist overspread my eyes! my ears were invaded with a dreadful sound! I panted for want of breath, and in short, was for some moments intranced!—This first tumult sub- siding, a crowd of flattering ideas rushed upon my imagination: Every thing that was soft, sensible, and engaging in the character of that dear creature, recurred to my remembrance, and every favour- able circumstance of my own qualifications appeared in all the aggravation of self-conceit, to heighten my expectation!—Neither was this transport of long duration: The dread of her being already disposed of, intervened, and over-cast my enchanting reverie! My presaging apprehension represented her encircled in the arms of some happy rival, and of consequence for ever lost to me! I was stung with this suggestion, and believing the person who con- ducted her, to be the husband of this amiable young lady, already devoted him to my fury, and stood up to mark him for my ven- geance; when I recollected, to my unspeakable joy, her brother the fox-hunter, in the person of her gallant.—Undeceived so much to my satisfaction in this particular, I gazed in a frenzy of delight, on the irresistible charms of his sister, who no sooner distinguished me in the crowd, than her evident confusion afforded a happy omen to my flame.—At sight of me she started, the roses instantly vanished from her polished cheeks, and returned in a moment with a double glow that over-spread her lovely neck, while her enchanting bosom heaved with strong emotion.—I hailed these favourable symptoms, and lying in wait for her looks, did homage with my eyes.—She seemed to approve my declaration, by the complacency of her aspect; and I was so transported with the discovery, that more than once, I was on the point of making up to her, and disclosing the throbbings of my heart in person, had not that profound veneration which her presence always inspired, restrained the unseasonable impulse.——My whole powers being engrossed in this manner, it may be easily imagined how ill I entertained Miss Snapper, on whom I could not now turn my eyes, without making comparisons very little to her advantage.—It was not even in my power to return distinct answers to the questions she asked from time to time, so that she could not help observing my absence of behaviour; and having a turn, for observation, watched my glances, and tracing them to the divine object, discovered the cause of my disorder.—That she might, however, be convinced of the truth of her conjecture, she began to interrogate me with regard to Narcissa, and notwithstanding all my endeavours to disguise my sentiments, perceived my attachment by my confusion.—Upon which, she assumed a stateliness of behaviour, and sat silent during the remaining part of the entertainment.—At any other time I should have been prodigiously alarmed at her suspicion, but at that instant, I was elevated by my passion above every other consideration. —The mistress of my soul having retired with her brother, I discovered so much uneasiness at my situation, that Miss Snapper proposed to go home; and while I conducted her to a chair, told me she had too great a regard for me to keep me any longer in torment.—I feigned ignorance of her meaning, and having seen her safely at her lodgings, took my leave, and went home in an exstasy; where I disclosed every thing that had happened to my confident and humble servant Strap, who did not relish the accident so well as I expected; and observed, that a bird in hand is worth two in the bush.—'But however (said he) you know best—you know best.'—Next day as I went to the Bath, in hopes of seeing or hearing some tidings of my fair enslaver, I was met by a gentlewoman, who having looked hard at me, cried, 'O Christ! Mr. Random!' Surprized at this exclamation, I examined the countenance of the person who spoke, and immediately recognized my old sweet-heart and fellow-sufferer Miss Williams.

I was mightily pleased to find this unfortunate woman under such a decent appearance, professed my joy at seeing her well, and desired to know where I should have the pleasure of her conversation. She was as heartily rejoiced at the apparent easiness of my fortune, and gave me to know that she, as yet, had no habitation that she could properly call her own; but would wait on me at any place I would please to appoint—Understanding that she was disengaged for the present, I shewed her the way to my own lodgings, where, after a very affectionate salutation, she informed me of her being very happy in the service of a young lady, to whom she was recommended by a former mistress deceased, into whose family she had introduced herself by the honest deceit she had concerted, while she lived with me in the garret at London—She then expressed a vehement desire to be acquainted with the vicissitudes of my life since we parted, and ascribed her curiosity to the concern she had for my interest—I forthwith gratified her request, and when I described my situation in Sussex, perceived her to attend to my story with particular eagerness. She interrupted me when I had finished that period, with 'good God! is it possible,'—and then begged I would be so good as to continue my relation; which I did as briefly as I could, burning with impatience to know the cause of her surprize, about which I had already formed a very interesting conjecture—Having therefore brought my adventures down to the present day, she seemed very much affected with the different circumstances of my fortune; and saying with a smile, she believed my distresses were now at a period, proceeded to inform me, that the lady whom she served was no other than the charming Narcissa, who had honoured her with her confidence for some time,—that in consequence of that trust, she had often repeated the story of John Brown, with great admiration and regard; that she loved to dwell upon the particulars of his character, and did not scruple to own a tender approbation of his flame—I became delirious with this piece of intelligence, strained Miss Williams in my embrace, called her the angel of my happiness, and acted such extravagancies, that she would have been convinced of my sincerity, had not my honour been clear enough to her before—As soon as I was in a condition to yield attention, she described the present situation of her mistress, who had no sooner come home the night before, than she closeted her, and in a rapture of joy, gave her to know that she had seen me at the ball, where I appeared in the character which she always thought my due, with such advantage of transformation, that unless my image had been engraven on her heart, it would have been

impossible to know me for the person who had worn her aunt's livery;
—that by the language of my eyes, she was assured of the continu-
ance of my passion for her, and consequently of my being unengaged to any other; and that though she did not doubt, I would
speedily fall upon some method of being introduced, she was so
impatient to hear of me, that she (Miss Williams) had been sent
abroad this very morning, on purpose to learn tidings of the name
and character I at present bore.—My bosom had been hitherto a
stranger to such a flood of joy as now rushed upon it: My faculties
were over-born by the tide: It was some time, before I could open
my mouth; and much longer 'ere I could utter a coherent sentence
—At length, I fervently requested her to lead me immediately to
the object of my adoration: but she resisted my importunity, and
explained the danger of such premature conduct—'How favourable
soever (said she) my lady's inclination towards you may be, this you
may depend upon, that she will not commit the smallest trespass on
decorum, either in disclosing her own, or in receiving a declaration
of your passion: and altho' the great veneration I have for you, has
prompted me to reveal what she communicated to me in confidence,
I know so well the severity of her sentiments with respect to the
punctilios of her sex, that, if she should learn the least surmise of
it, she would not only dismiss me as a wretch unworthy of her
benevolence, but also for ever shun the efforts of your love'—I
assented to the justness of her remonstrance, and desired she would
assist me with her advice and direction: upon which, it was concerted between us, that for the present, I should be contented with
her telling Narcissa that in the course of her inquiries, she could
only learn my name: and that if in a day or two, I could fall upon
no other method of being made acquainted, she would deliver a
letter from me, on pretence of consulting her happiness; and say
that I met her in the streets, and bribed her to that piece of service.
—Matters being thus adjusted, I kept my old acquaintance to
breakfast, and learned from her conversation, that my rival Sir
Timothy had drunk himself into an apoplexy, of which he died five
months ago, that the savage was still unmarried, and that his aunt
had been seized with a whim which he little expected, and chosen
the school-master of the parish for her lord and husband: but
matrimony not agreeing with her constitution, she had been hec-
tick[1] and dropsical a good while, and was now at Bath in order to
drink the waters for the recovery of her health; that her niece had

accompanied her thither at her request, and attended her with the same affection as before, notwithstanding the *faux pas* she had committed: and that her nephew who had been exasperated at the loss of her fortune, did not give his attendance out of good will, but purely to have an eye on his sister, lest she should likewise throw herself away, without his consent or approbation.—Having enjoyed ourselves in this manner, and made an assignation to meet next day at a certain place, Miss Williams took her leave; and Strap's looks being very inquisitive about the nature of the communication subsisting between us, I made him acquainted with the whole affair, to his great astonishment and satisfaction.

CHAPTER LVI

I become acquainted with Narcissa's brother who invites me to his house—where I am introduced to that adorable creature—after dinner, the squire retires to take his nap— Freeman, guessing the situation of my thoughts, withdraws likewise on pretence of business—I declare my passion for Narcissa—am well received—charmed with her conversation ——the squire detains us to supper—I elude his design by a stratagem, and get home sober

IN the afternoon, I drank tea at the house of Mr. Freeman, to whom I had been recommended by Banter; where I had not sat five minutes 'till the fox-hunter came in, and by his familiar behaviour, appeared to be intimate with my friend—I was, at first, under some concern, lest he should recollect my features; but when I found myself introduced to him as a gentleman from London, without being discovered, I blessed the opportunity that brought me into his company; hoping, that in the course of our acquaintance, he would invite me to his house—nor were my hopes frustrated, for as we spent the evening together, he grew extremely fond of my conversation, asked a great many childish questions about France and foreign parts; and seemed so highly entertained with my answers, that in his cups, he shook me often by the hand, pronounced me an honest fellow, and in fine, desired our company at dinner next day, in his own house.—My imagination was so much employed in anti-cipating the happiness I was to enjoy the next day, that I slept very little that night; but getting up early in the morning, went to the place appointed, where I met my she-friend, and imparted to her my success with the squire—She was very much pleased at the occasion, which (she said) could not fail of being agreeable to Narcissa, who in spite of her passion for me, had mentioned some scruples relating to my true situation and character, which the delicacy of her sentiments suggested, and which she believed I would find it necessary to remove, though she did not know how.—I was a good deal startled at this insinuation, because I foresaw the difficulty I should find in barely doing myself justice; for although it never was my intention to impose myself upon any woman, much less on Narcissa, as a man of fortune, I laid claim to the character of a gentleman, by birth, education and behaviour; and yet (so unlucky had the circumstances of my life fallen out) I should find it a very hard matter to make good my pretensions even to these, especially to the last, which was the most essential—Miss Williams was as sensible as I, of this my dis-advantage; but comforted me with observing, that when once a woman has bestowed her affections on a man, she cannot help judging of him in all respects, with a partiality easily influenced in his favour;—she remarked that altho' some situations of my life had been low, yet none of them had been infamous; that my indigence had been the crime not of me, but of fortune; and that the miseries I had undergone, by improving the faculties both of mind and body, qualified me the more for any dignified station; and would of con-sequence, recommend me to the good graces of any sensible woman; —she therefore advised me to be always open and unreserved to the inquiries of my mistress, without unnecessarily betraying the meanest occurrences of my fate; and trust to the strength of her love and reflection, for the rest.—The sentiments of this sensible young woman on this, as well as on almost every other subject, perfectly agreed with mine; I thanked her for the care she took of my interests, and promising to behave myself according to her direction, we parted, after she had assured me, that I might depend upon her best offices with her mistress, and that she would from time to time, communicate to me such intelligence as she could procure, relating to my flame.—Having dressed myself to the best advantage, I waited for the time of dinner with the most fearful impatience; and as the hour drew nigh, my heart beat with such increased velocity, and my spirits contracted such disorder, that I began to suspect my resolution, and even to wish myself disengaged:—At last Mr. Freeman called at my lodgings, in his way, and I accompanied him to the house where all my happiness was deposited.—We were very kindly received by the squire, who sat smoking his pipe in a parlour, and asked if we chose to drink any thing before dinner; tho' I never had more occasion for a cordial, I was ashamed to accept his offer, which was also refused by my friend. We sat down (however) and entered into conversation, which lasted half an hour, so that I had time to recollect myself; and (so capricious were my thoughts) even to hope that Narcissa would not appear—when all of a sudden, a servant coming in, gave us notice that dinner was upon the table—and my perturbation returned with such violence, that I could scarce conceal it from the company as I ascended the staircase.—When I entered the dining-room, the first object that saluted my ravished eyes, was the divine Narcissa, blushing like Aurora, adorned with all the graces that meekness, innocence and beauty can diffuse! I was seized with a giddiness, my knees tottered, and I scarce had strength enough to perform the ceremony of salutation, when her brother slapping me upon the shoulder, cried 'Measter Randan, that there is my sister.' I approached her with eagerness and fear; but in the moment of our embrace, my soul was agonized with rapture!—It was a lucky circumstance for us both, that my entertainer was not endued with an uncommon stock of penetration; for our mutual confusion was so manifest, that Mr. Freeman perceived it, and as we went home together, congratulated me on my good fortune.—But so far was Bruin from entertaining the least suspicion, that he encouraged me to begin a conversation with my mistress in a language unknown to him, by telling her, that he had brought a gentleman (meaning me) who could jabber with her in French and other foreign lingos, as fast as she pleased: then turning to me, said, 'Odds bobs! I wish you would hold discourse with her, in your French or Italiano; and tell me if she understands it as well as she would be thought to do—there's her aunt and she will chatter together whole days in it, and I can't have a mouthful of English for love or money.' I consulted the looks of my amiable mistress, and found her averse to his proposal, which indeed she declined with a sweetness of denial peculiar to herself, as a piece of disrespect to that part of the company which did not understand the language in question. As I had the happiness of sitting opposite to her, I feasted my eyes much more than my palate, which she tempted in vain with the most delicious bits carved by her fair hand, and recommended by her persuasive tongue;—but all my other appetites were swallowed up in the immensity of my love, which I fed by gazing incessantly on the delightful object.—Dinner was scarce ended, when the squire became very drousy, and after several dreadful yawns, got up, stretched himself, took two or three turns across the room, begg'd we would allow him to take a short nap, and having laid a strong injunction on his sister to detain us 'till his return, went to his repose without any further ceremony.—He had not been gone many minutes, when Freeman guessing the situation of my heart, and thinking he could not do me a greater favour, than to leave me alone with Narcissa, pretended to recollect himself all of a sudden, and starting up, begg'd the lady's pardon for half an hour, having luckily remembered an engagement of some consequence, that he must perform at that instant,—so saying, he went away, promising to be back in time enough for tea; leaving my mistress and me in great confusion.—Now that I enjoyed an opportunity of disclosing the pantings of my soul, I had not power to use it—I studied many pathetic declarations, but when I attempted to give them utterance, my tongue denied its office; and she sat silent, with a downcast look full of anxious alarm, her bosom heaving with expectation of some great event.—At length, I endeavoured to put an end to this solemn pause, and began with 'It is very surprizing, Madam'—here the sound dying away, I made a full stop—while Narcissa starting, blushed, and with a timid accent, answered, 'Sir?'—Confounded at this note of interrogation, I pronounced with the most sheepish bashfulness, 'Madam!' to which she replied, 'I beg pardon—I thought you had spoke to me.'—Another pause ensued—I made another effort, and tho' my voice faultered very much at the beginning, made shift to express myself in this manner:—'I say, Madam, 'tis very surprizing that love should act so inconsistent with itself, as to deprive its votaries of the use of their faculties, when they have most occasion for them. Since the happy occasion of being alone with you presented itself, I have made many unsuccessful attempts to declare a passion for the loveliest of her sex—a passion which took possession of my soul, while my cruel fate compell'd me to wear a servile disguise so unsuitable to my birth, sentiments, and let me add, my deserts; yet favourable in one respect, as it furnished me with opportunities of seeing and adoring your perfections—Yes,

344

Chapter LVI

Madam, it was then your dear idea entered my bosom, where it has lived unimpaired in the midst of numberless cares, and animated me against a thousand dangers and calamities!'——While I spoke thus, she concealed her face with her fan; and when I ceased, recovering herself from the most beautiful confusion, told me, that she thought herself very much obliged by my favourable opinion of her; and that she was very sorry to hear I had been unfortunate—Encouraged by this gentle reply, I proceeded, owned myself sufficiently recompensed by her kind compassion for what I had undergone, and declared that the future happiness of my life depended solely upon her.—'Sir, (said she) I should be very ungrateful, if after the signal protection you once afforded me, I could refuse to contribute towards your happiness, in any reasonable condescension.'—Transported at this acknowledgment, I threw myself at her feet, and begged she would regard my passion with a favourable eye: She was alarmed at my behaviour, intreated me to rise lest her brother should discover me in that posture, and to spare her, for the present, upon a subject for which she was altogether unprepared.—Upon this, I rose, assuring her I would rather die than disobey her; but in the mean time begged her to consider how precious the minutes of this opportunity were, and what restraint I put upon my inclination, in sacrificing them to her desire.—She smiled with unspeakable sweetness, and said, there would be no want of opportunities, provided I could maintain the good opinion her brother had conceived of me; and I, enchanted with her charms, seized her hand, which I well nigh devoured with kisses—But she check'd my boldness with a severity of countenance; and desired I would not so far forget myself or her, as to endanger the esteem she had for me;—she reminded me of our being almost strangers to one another, and of the necessity there was, for her knowing me better, before she could take any resolution in my favour; and, in short, mingled so much good sense and complacency in her reproof, that I became as much enamoured of her understanding, as I had been before of her beauty, and asked pardon for my presumption with the utmost reverence of conviction—She forgave my offence with her usual affability; and sealed my pardon with a look so full of bewitching tenderness, that for some minutes, my senses were lost in exstasy! I afterwards endeavoured to regulate my behaviour according to her desire, and turn the conversation upon a more indifferent subject; but her presence was an unsurmountable obstacle to my design; while I beheld so much

345

excellence, I found it impossible to call my attention from the contemplation of it! I gazed with unutterable fondness! I grew mad with admiration!—'My condition is unsupportable (cried I) I am distracted with passion! why are you so exquisitely fair?—Why are you so enchantingly good?—Why has nature dignified you with charms so much above the standard of woman; and, wretch that I am, how dares my unworthiness aspire to the enjoyment of such perfection!'

She was startled at my ravings, reasoned down my transport, and by her irresistible eloquence, soothed my soul into a state of tranquil felicity; but lest I might suffer a relapse, industriously promoted other subjects to entertain my imagination—she chid me for having omitted to inquire about her aunt, who (she assured me) in the midst of all her absence of temper, and detachment from common affairs, often talked of me with uncommon warmth.—I professed my veneration for the good lady, excused my omission, by imputing it to the violence of my love, which engrossed my whole soul, and desired to know the present situation of her health.—Upon which, the amiable Narcissa repeated what I had heard before, of her marriage, with all the tenderness for her reputation that the subject would admit of; told me, she liv'd with her husband, hard by, and was so much afflicted with a dropsy, and wasted by a consumption, that she had small hopes of her recovery.—Having expressed my sorrow for her distemper, I questioned her about my good friend Mrs. Sagely, who I learned (to my great satisfaction) was still in good health, and by the encomiums she bestowed upon me after I was gone, confirmed the favourable impression, my behaviour at parting had made on Narcissa's heart—This circumstance introduced an inquiry into the conduct of Sir Timothy Thicket, who (she informed me) had found means to incense her brother so much against me, that she found it impossible to undeceive him; but on the contrary, suffered very much in her own character, by his scandalous insinuations—that the whole parish was alarmed, and actually in pursuit of me; so that she had been in the utmost consternation upon my account, well knowing how little my own innocence and her testimony would have weighed with the ignorance, prejudice and brutality of those, who must have judged me, had I been apprehended—that Sir Timothy being seized with a fit of the apoplexy, from which with great difficulty he was recovered, began to be apprehensive of death, and to prepare himself accordingly for that great event; as a step to which, he sent for her brother, owned with great contrition, the brutal design he had upon her, and of consequence acquitted me of the assault, robbery and correspondence with her, which he had laid to my charge, after which confession he lived about a month in a languishing condition, and was carried off by a second assault.

Every word that this dear creature spoke, rivetted the chains with which she held me enslaved! My mischievous fancy began to work, and the tempest of my passion to wake again; when the return of Freeman destroyed the tempting opportunity, and enabled me to quell the rising tumult.—A little while after, the Squire staggered into the room, rubbing his eyes, and called for his tea, which he drank out of a small bowl, qualified with brandy; we sipped some in the ordinary way: Narcissa left us in order to visit her aunt, and when Freeman and I proposed to take our leave, the fox-hunter insisted on our spending the evening at his house with such obstinacy of affection, that we were obliged to comply.—For my own part, I should have been glad of the invitation, by which, in all likelihood, I would be blest with his sister's company, had I not been afraid of risking her esteem, by entering into a debauch of drinking with him, which, from the knowledge of his character, I foresaw would happen; but there was no remedy—I was forced to rely upon the strength of my constitution, which I hoped would resist intoxication longer than the Squire's; and to trust to the good-nature and discretion of my mistress for the rest.

Our entertainer resolving to begin by times,[1] ordered the table to be furnished with liquor and glasses immediately after tea, but we absolutely refused to set in for drinking so soon; and prevailed upon him to pass away an hour or two at whist, in which we engaged as soon as Narcissa returned.—The savage and I happened to be partners at first, and as my thoughts were wholly employed on a more interesting game, I play'd so ill that he lost all patience, swore bitterly, and threatened to call for wine if they would not grant him another associate.—This desire was gratified, and Narcissa and I were of a side; he won for the same reason that made him lose before; I was satisfied, my lovely partner did not repine, and the time slipped away very agreeably, until we were told that supper was served in another room.

The Squire was enraged to find the evening so unprofitably spent, and wrecked his vengeance on the cards, which he tore, and committed to the flames with many execrations; threatning to make us redeem our loss with a large glass and a quick circulation; and indeed we had no sooner supped, and my charmer withdrawn, than he began to put his threats in execution. Three bottles of port (for he drank no other sort of wine) were placed before us, with as many water-glasses, which were immediately filled to the brim, after his example, by each out of his respective allowance, and emptied in a trice, *to the best in christendom.*[1]—Though I swallowed this, and the next as fast as the glass could be replenished, without hesitation or shew of reluctance, I perceived that my brain would not be able to bear many bumpers of this sort; and dreading the perseverance of a champion who began with such vigour, I determined to make up for the deficiency of my strength by a stratagem, which I actually put in practice when the second course of bottles was called for.—The wine being strong and heady, I was already a good deal discomposed by the dispatch we had made, Freeman's eyes began to reel, and Bruin himself was elevated into a song, which he uttered with great vociferation.——When I therefore saw the second round brought in, I assumed a gay air, entertained him with a French catch on the subject of drinking, which, though he did not understand it, delighted him highly, and telling him that your choice spirits at Paris never troubled themselves with glasses, asked if he had not a bowl or cup in the house that would contain a whole quart of wine. —'Odds niggers!'[2] (cried he) I have a silver caudle-cup[3] that holds just the quantity, for all the world—fetch it hither, Numps.'[4]—The vessel being produced, I bid him decant his bottle into it, which having done, I nodded in a very deliberate manner, and said, 'Pledge you.'—He stared at me for some time, and crying, 'What! all at one pull, measter Randan?'—I answered, 'At one pull! Sir, you are no milk-sop—we shall do you justice.'—'Shall you? (said he, shaking me by the hand) odd then, I'll see it out, an't were a mile to the bottom—Here's to our better acquaintance, measter Randan.' So saying, he applied it to his lips, and emptied it in a breath.—I knew the effect of it would be almost instantaneous; therefore, taking the cup, I began to discharge my bottle into it, telling him he was now qualified to drink with the Cham of Tartary.[5]—I had no sooner pronounced these words, than he took umbrage at them, and after several attempts to spit, made shift to stutter out, 'A f—f—t for your Chams of T—Tartary! I am a f—f— free-born Englishman, worth th— three thousand a year, and v— value no man, damme!'—

then dropping his jaw, and fixing his eyes, he hickup'd aloud, and fell upon the floor as mute as a flounder.—Mr. Freeman, heartily rejoiced at his defeat, assisted me in carrying him to bed, where we left him to the care of his servants, and went home to our respective habitations, congratulating one another on our good fortune.

CHAPTER LVII

Miss Williams informs me of Narcissa's approbation of my flame——I appease the Squire—write to my Mistress, am blessed with an answer——beg leave of her brother to dance with her at a ball; obtain his consent and her's——enjoy a private conversation with her—am perplexed with reflections ——have the honour of appearing her partner at the ball—— we are complimented by a certain Nobleman—he discovers some symptoms of passion for Narcissa——I am stung with jealousy——Narcissa alarmed, retires——I observe Melinda in the company——the Squire is captivated by her beauty

I WAS met next morning, at the usual place by Miss Williams, who gave me joy of the progress I had made in the affection of her mistress, and blessed me with an account of that dear creature's conversation with her, after she had retired the night before from our company.——I could scarce believe her information, when she recounted her expressions in my favour, so much more warm and passionate were they than my most sanguine hopes had presaged; and was particularly pleased to hear that she approved of my behaviour to her brother, after she withdrew.—Transported at the news of my happiness, I presented my ring to the messenger, as a testimony of my gratitude and satisfaction; but she was above such mercenary considerations, and refused my compliment with some resentment, saying, she was not a little mortified to see my opinion of her so low and contemptible.—I did myself a piece of justice by explaining my behaviour on this head and to convince her of my esteem, promised to be ruled by her directions in the prosecution of the whole affair, which I had so much at heart, that the repose of my life depended upon the consequence.

As I fervently wished for another interview, where I might pour out the effusions of my love, without danger of being interrupted, and perhaps reap some endearing return from the queen of my desires, I implored her advice and assistance in promoting this event;—but she gave me to understand, that Narcissa would make no precipitate compliances of this kind, and that I would do well to cultivate her brother's acquaintance, in the course of which, I would not want opportunities of removing that reserve, which my mistress thought herself obliged to maintain during the infancy of our correspondence.—In the mean time, she promised to tell her lady that I had endeavoured by presents and persuasions, to prevail upon her, (Miss Williams) to deliver a letter from me, which she had refused to charge herself with, until she should know Narcissa's sentiments of the matter; and said, by these means she did not doubt of being able to open a literary communication between us, which could not fail of introducing more intimate connexions.

I approved of her counsel, and our appointment being renewed for next day, left her with an intent of falling upon some method of being reconciled to the Squire, who, I supposed, would be offended with the trick we had put upon him.—With this view, I consulted Freeman, who from his knowledge of the Fox-hunter's disposition, assured me there was no other method of pacifying him, than that of sacrificing ourselves for one night, to an equal match with him in drinking: This I found myself necessitated to comply with, for the interest of my passion, and therefore determined to commit the debauch at my own lodgings, that I might run no risk of being discovered by Narcissa, in a state of brutal degeneracy.—Mr. Freeman, who was to be of the party, went, at my desire, to the Squire in order to engage him, while I took care to furnish myself for his reception. —My invitation was accepted, my guests honoured me with their company in the evening, when Bruin gave me to understand that he had drank many tuns of wine in his life, but was never served such a trick as I had played upon him the night before. I promised to atone for my trespass, and having ordered to every man his bottle, began the contest with a bumper to the health of Narcissa.—The toasts circulated with great devotion, the liquor began to operate, our mirth grew noisy, and as Freeman and I had the advantage of drinking small French claret, the savage was effectually tamed before our senses were in the least affected, and carried home in a kind of apoplexy of drunkenness.

I was next morning, as usual, favoured with a visit from my kind and punctual confidante, who telling me, she was permitted to receive my letters for her mistress; I took up the pen immediately, and following the first dictates of my passion, wrote as follows:

'DEAR MADAM,

Were it possible for the powers of utterance, to reveal the soft emotions of my soul; the fond anxiety, the glowing hopes, and chilling fears that rule my breast by turns; I should need no other witness than this paper, to evince the purity and ardour of that flame your charms have kindled in my heart. But alas! expression wrongs my love! I am inspired with conceptions that no language can convey! Your beauty fills me with wonder! your understanding with ravishment, and your goodness with adoration! I am transported with desire, distracted with doubts, and tortured with impatience! Suffer me then, lovely arbitress of my fate, to approach you in person, to breathe in soft murmurs my passion to your ear, to offer the sacrifice of a heart overflowing with the most genuine and disinterested love; to gaze with exstasy on the divine object of my wishes, to hear the musick of her enchanting tongue! to rejoice in her smiles of approbation, and banish the most intolerable suspence from the bosom of

Your enraptured

R——R——.

Having finished this effusion, I committed it to the care of my faithful friend, with an injunction to second my intreaty with all her eloquence and influence; and in the mean time went to dress, with an intention of visiting Mrs. Snapper and Miss, whom I had utterly neglected and indeed almost forgot, since my dear Narcissa had resumed the empire of my soul. The old gentlewoman received me very kindly, and Miss affected a frankness and gaiety, which, however, I could easily perceive was forced and dissembled; among other things, she pretended to joke me upon my passion for Narcissa, which she averred was no secret, and asked if I intended to dance with her at the next assembly.—I was a good deal concerned to find myself become the town-talk on this subject, lest the Squire, having notice of my inclinations, should disapprove of them, and by breaking off all correspondence with me, deprive me of the opportunities I now enjoyed.—But I resolved to use the interest I had with him, while it lasted; and that very night, meeting him occasionally, asked his permission to solicit her company at the ball, which he very readily granted, to my inexpressible satisfaction.

Having been kept awake the greatest part of the night, by a thousand delightful reveries that took possession of my fancy, I got up betimes, and flying to the place of rendezvous, had in a little time the pleasure of seeing Miss Williams approach with a smile on her countenance, which I interpreted into a good omen. Neither was I mistaken in my presage: She presented me with a letter from the idol of my soul, which, after having kissed it with great devotion, I opened with the utmost eagerness, and was blessed with her approbation in these terms.

'SIR,

To say I look upon you with indifference, would be a piece of dissimulation which, I think, no decorum requires, and no custom can justify. As my heart never felt an impression that my tongue was ashamed to declare, I will not scruple to own myself pleased with your passion, confident of your integrity, and so well convinced of my own discretion, that I should not hesitate in granting you the interview that you desire, were I not over-awed by the prying curiosity of a malicious world, the censure of which might be fatally prejudicial to the reputation of

Your
NARCISSA.

No Anchorite in the exstasy of devotion, ever adored a relique with more fervour than that with which I kissed this inimitable proof of my charmer's candour, generosity and affection! I read it over a hundred times; was ravished with her confession in the beginning; but the subscription of YOUR NARCISSA, yielded me such delight as I had never felt before! My happiness was still increased by Miss Williams, who blessed me with a repetition of her lady's tender expressions in my favour, when she received and read my letter.— In short, I had all the reason in the world to believe that this gentle creature's bosom was possessed by a passion for me, as warm, though perhaps not so impetuous, as mine for her.

I informed my friend of the Squire's consent, with regard to my dancing with Narcissa at the ball, and desired her to tell her mistress, that I would do myself the honour of visiting her in the afternoon, in consequence of his permission, when I hoped to find her as indulgent as her brother had been complaisant in that particular.— Miss Williams expressed a good deal of joy, at hearing I was so much in favour with the fox-hunter, and ventured to assure me, that my visit would be very agreeable to my mistress, the rather because Bruin was engaged to dine abroad.—This was a circumstance, which I scarce need say, pleased me.—I went immediately to the long-room,[1] where I found him, and affecting to know nothing of his engagement, told him, I would do myself the pleasure to wait upon him in the afternoon and to present his sister with a ticket for the ball.—He shook me by the hand, according to custom, and giving me to understand that he was to dine abroad, desired me to go and drink tea with Narcissa notwithstanding, and promised to prepare her for my visit in the mean time.

Every thing succeeding thus to my wish, I waited with incredible patience for the time, which no sooner arrived, than I hastened to the scene, which my fancy had pre-occupied long before.—I was introduced accordingly, to the dear enchantress, whom I found accompanied by Miss Williams, who, on pretence of ordering tea, retired at my approach.—This favourable accident, which alarmed my whole soul, disordered her also.—I found myself actuated by an irresistible impulse, I advanced to her with eagerness and awe; and profiting by the confusion that prevailed over her, clasped the fair angel in my arms, and imprinted a glowing kiss upon her lips, more soft and fragrant than the dewy rosebud just bursting from the stem! Her face was in an instant covered with blushes, her eyes sparkled with resentment; I threw myself at her feet, and implored her pardon.—Her love became advocate in my cause; her look softened into forgiveness, she raised me up, and chid me with so much sweetness of displeasure, that I was tempted to repeat the offence, had not the coming of a servant with the tea-board, prevented my presumption.—While we were subject to be interrupted or over-heard, we conversed about the approaching ball, at which she promised to grace me as a partner; but when the equipage was removed, and we were left alone, I resumed the more interesting theme, and expressed myself with such transport and agitation, that my mistress, fearing I would commit some extravagance, rung the bell for her maid, whom she detained in the room, as a check upon my vivacity.—I was not sorry for this precaution, because I could unbosom myself without reserve, before Miss Williams, who was the confidante of us both.—I therefore gave a loose to the inspirations of my passion, which operated so successfully upon the tender affections of Narcissa, that she laid aside the restraint she had hitherto wore, and blessed me with the most melting declaration of her mutual flame!—It was impossible for me to forbear taking the advantage of this endearing condescension.—She now gently yielded to my embrace, while I encircling all that I held dear, within my arms, tasted in advance, the joys of that paradise I hoped in a little time wholly to possess!—We spent the afternoon in all the exstacy of hope that the most fervent love exchanged by mutual vows could inspire; and Miss Williams was so much affected with our chaste caresses, which recalled the sad remembrance of what she was, that her eyes were filled with tears.

The evening being pretty far advanced, I forced myself from the dear object of my flame, who indulged me in a tender embrace at parting; and repairing to my lodgings, communicated to my friend Strap every circumstance of my happiness, which filled him with so much pleasure, that it run over at his eyes; and he prayed heartily, that no envious devil might, as formerly, dash the cup of blessing from my lip.—When I reflected on what had happened, and especially on the unreserved protestations of Narcissa's love, I could not help being amazed at her omitting to enquire into the particular circumstances of the life and fortune of one whom she had favoured with her affection, and I began to be a little anxious about the situation of her finances; well knowing that I should do an irreparable injury to the person my soul held most dear, if I should espouse her, without being enabled to support her in the rank which was certainly her due.—I had heard indeed, while I served her aunt, that her father had left her a considerable sum; and that every body believed she would inherit the greatest part of her kinswoman's dowry, but I did not know how far she might be restricted by the old gentleman's will, in the enjoyment of what he left her; and I was too well informed of the virtuosi's late conduct, to think my mistress could have any expectations from that quarter.—I confided, however, in the good sense and delicacy of my charmer, who, I was sure, would not consent to unite her fate with mine, before she had fully considered and provided for the consequence.

The Ball-night being arrived, I dressed myself in a suit I had reserved for some grand occasion; and having drank tea with Narcissa and her brother, conducted my angel to the scene, where she in a moment eclipsed all her female competitors for beauty, and attracted the admiration of the whole assembly.—My heart dilated with pride on this occasion, and my triumph rejected all bounds when, after we had danced together, a certain nobleman, remarkable for his figure and influence in the *beau monde*, came up, and in the hearing of all present, honoured us with a very particular compliment, upon our accomplishments and appearance;—but this transport was soon checked, when I perceived his lordship attach himself with great assiduity to my mistress; and say some warm things, which I thought, favoured too much of passion.—It was then I began to feel the pangs of jealousy—I dreaded the power and address of my rival—I sickened at his discourse; when she opened her lips to answer, my heart died within me—when she smiled, I felt the pains of the damned!—I was enraged at his presumption; I cursed her complaisance! when he quitted her and went to the other side of the room.—Narcissa suspecting nothing of the rage that inflamed me, put some questions to me, as soon as he was gone, to which I made no other reply than a grim look, which too well denoted the agitation of my breast, and surprized her not a little.—She no sooner observed my emotion, than she changed colour, and asked what ailed me; but before I could make answer, her brother pulling me by the sleeve, bid me take notice of a lady who sat fronting us, whom I immediately, to my vast astonishment, distinguished to be Melinda, accompanied by her mother and an elderly gentleman, whom I did not know.—'Wounds! Mr. Randan, (cried the Squire) is she not a delicate piece of stuff?—'Sdeath! I have a good mind—if I thought she was a single person.'—Notwithstanding the perplexity I was in, I had reflection enough to foresee that my passion might suffer greatly by the presence of this lady, who in all probability would revenge herself upon me for having formerly disgraced her, by spreading reports to my prejudice.—I was therefore alarmed at these symptoms of the Squire's admiration; and for some time did not know what reply to make, when he asked my opinion of her beauty: At length I came to a determination, and told him that her name was Melinda, that she had a fortune of ten thousand pounds, and was said to be under promise of marriage to a certain lord, who deferred his nuptials, until he should be of age, which would happen in a few months:—I thought this piece of intelligence, which I had myself invented, would have hindered him effectually from entertaining any further thoughts of her; but I was egregiously mistaken: The fox-hunter had too much self-sufficiency to despair of success with any competitor on earth. He therefore made light of her engagement, saying, with a smile of self-approbation,

'Mayhap she will change her mind——what signifies his being a Lord? Lord?—I think myself as good a man as e'er a Lord in christendom; and I'll see if a commoner worth three thousand a year won't serve her turn.'—This determination startled me not a little; I knew he would soon discover the contrary of what I advanced, and as I believed he would find her ear open to his addresses, did not doubt of meeting with every obstacle in my amour, that her malice could invent, and her influence with him execute.—This reflection increased my chagrin—My vexation was evident—Narcissa insisted on going home immediately; and as I led her to the door, her noble admirer, with a look full of languishment, directed to her a profound bow, which stung me to the soul.—Before she went into the chair, she asked, with an appearance of concern, what was the matter with me? and I could pronounce no more than, 'By heaven! I'm distracted!'

CHAPTER LVIII

*Tortured with jealousy, I go home and abuse Strap——
receive a message from Narcissa, in consequence of which, I
hasten to her apartment, where her endearing assurances
banish all my doubts and apprehensions——in my retreat I
discover somebody in the dark, whom, suspecting to be a spy,
I resolve to kill: but, to my great surprize, am convinced of
his being no other than Strap——Melinda slanders me——
I become acquainted with Lord Quiverwit, who endeavours
to sound me, with regard to Narcissa——the Squire is
introduced to his lordship, and grows cold towards me——I
learn from my confidante, that this nobleman professes
honourable love to my mistress, who continues faithful to me,
notwithstanding the scandalous reports she has heard to my
prejudice——I am mortified with an assurance that her whole
fortune depends upon the pleasure of her brother——
Mr. Freeman condoles me on the decline of my character,
which I vindicate so much to his satisfaction, that he undertakes to combat fame in my behalf*

HAVING uttered this exclamation, at which she sighed, I went home in the condition of a frantic Bedlamite; and finding the fire in my apartment almost extinguished, vented my fury upon poor Strap, whose ear I pinched with such violence, that he roared hideously with pain, and when I quitted my hold looked so foolishly aghast, that no unconcerned spectator could have seen him, without being seized with an immoderate fit of laughter.—It is true, I was soon sensible of the injury I had done, and asked pardon for the outrage I had committed; upon which my faithful valet, shaking his head, said, 'I forgive you, and may God forgive you.'—But he could not help shedding some tears at my unkindness. I felt unspeakable remorse for what I had done, cursed my own ingratitude, and considered his tears as a reproach that my soul, in her present disturbance, could not bear.—It set all my passions into a new ferment, I swore horrible oaths without meaning or application, I foamed at the mouth, kicked the chairs about the room, and play'd abundance of mad pranks that frightened my friend almost out of his senses.—At length my transport subsided, I became melancholy, and wept insensibly.[1]

During this state of dejection, I was surprized with the appearance of Miss Williams, whom Strap, blubbering all the while, had conducted into the chamber without giving me previous notice of her approach:—She was extremely affected with my condition, which she had learned from him, begged me to moderate my passion, suspend my conjectures, and follow her to Narcissa, who desired to see me forthwith.—That dear name operated upon me like a charm! I started up, and without opening my lips, was conducted into her apartment through the garden, which we entered by a private door. —I found the adorable creature in tears! I was melted at the sight— we continued silent for some time—my heart was too full to speak— her snowy bosom heaved with fond resentment; at last she sobbing cried, 'What have I done to disoblige you?'—My heart was pierced with the tender question! I drew near with the utmost reverence of affection! I fell upon my knees before her, and kissing her hand, exclaimed, 'O! thou art all goodness and perfection! I am undone by my want of merit! I am unworthy to possess thy charms, which heaven hath destined for the arms of some more favoured being.'— She guessed the cause of my disquiet, upbraided me gently for my suspicion, and gave me such flattering assurances of her eternal fidelity, that all my doubts and fears forsook me, and peace and satisfaction reigned within my breast.

At midnight I left the kind nymph to her repose, and being let out by Miss Williams, at the garden gate by which I entered, began to explore my way homeward in the dark, when I heard at my back a noise like that of a baboon when he mows and chatters. I turned instantly, and perceiving something black, concluded I was discovered by some spy, employed to watch for that purpose: Arroused at this conjecture, by which the reputation of the virtuous Narcissa appeared in jeopardy, I drew my sword, and would have sacrificed him to her fame, had not the voice of Strap restrained my arm: It was with great difficulty he could pronounce, 'D—d—d—do! mum—um—um—murder me, if you please!' Such an effect had the cold upon his jaws, that his teeth rattled like a pair of castanets—Pleased to be thus undeceived, I laughed at his consternation, and asked what brought him thither? Upon which he gave me to understand that his concern for me had induced him to dodge me to that place, where the same reason had detained him till now; and he frankly owned, that in spite of the esteem he had for Miss Williams, he began to be very uneasy about me, considering the disposition in which I went abroad; and if I had staid much longer, would have certainly alarmed the neighbourhood in my behalf.—The knowledge of this his intention confounded me! I represented to him the mischievous consequences that would have attended such a rash action, and cautioning him severely against any such design for the future, concluded my admonition with an assurance, that in case he should ever act so madly, I would, without hesitation put him to death.—'Have a little patience (cried he, in a lamentable tone) your displeasure will do the business, without your committing murder.' —I was touched with this reproach; and as soon as we got home, made it my business to appease him, by explaining the cause of that transport, during which I had used him so unworthily.

Next day when I went into the long room, I observed several whispers circulate all of a sudden; and did not doubt that Melinda had been busy with my character; but I consoled myself with the love of Narcissa, upon which I rested with the most perfect confidence, and going up to the rowly-powly[1] table, won a few pieces from my suspected rival, who with an easy politeness, entered into conversation with me, and desiring my company to the coffee-house, treated me with tea and chocolate.—I remembered Strutwell, and guarded against his insinuating behaviour; nor was my suspicion wrong placed; he artfully turned the discourse upon Narcissa, and endeavoured, by hinting at an intrigue he pretended to be engaged in elsewhere, to learn what connexion there was between her and me.—But all his finesse was ineffectual; I was convinced of his dissimulation, and gave such general answers to his inquiries, that he was forced to drop the subject and talk of something else.

While we conversed in this manner, the savage came in, with another gentleman, who introduced him to his lordship; and he was received with such peculiar marks of distinction, that I was persuaded the courtier intended to use him in some shape or another; and thence I conceived an unlucky omen.—But I had more cause to be dismayed the following day, when I saw the Squire in company with Melinda and her mother, who honoured me with several disdainful glances; and when I afterwards threw myself in his way, instead of the cordial shake of the hand, returned my salute with a cold repetition of 'Servant, servant,' which he pronounced with such indifference, or rather contempt, that if he had not been Narcissa's brother I should have affronted him in publick.

These occurrences disturbed me not a little, I foresaw the brooding storm, and armed myself with resolution for the occasion; but Narcissa being at stake, I was far from being resigned.—I could have renounced every other comfort of life with some degree of fortitude; but the prospect of losing her, disabled all my philosophy, and tortured my soul into madness.

Miss Williams found me, next morning, full of anxious tumult, which did not abate, when she told me, that my Lord Quiverwit, having professed honourable intentions, had been introduced to my lovely Mistress by her brother, who had at the same time, from the information of Melinda, spoke of me as an Irish fortune-hunter, without either birth or estate to recommend me; who supported myself in the appearance of a gentleman by sharping, and other infamous practices; and who was of such an obscure origin, that I did not even know my own extraction.——Though I expected all this, I could not hear it with temper, especially as truth was so blended with falshood in the assertion, that it would be almost impossible to separate the one from the other in my vindication.— But I said nothing on this head, being impatient to know how Narcissa had been affected with the discovery.—That generous creature, far from believing these imputations, was no sooner withdrawn with her confidante, than she inveighed with great warmth against the malevolence of the world, to which only she ascribed the whole of what had been said to my disadvantage; and calling every circumstance of my behaviour to her, into review before her, found every thing so polite, honourable and disinterested, that she could not harbour the least doubt of my being the gentleman I appeared to be.—'I have indeed (said she) purposely forbore to ask the particulars of his life, lest the recapitulation of some misfortunes, which he has undergone, should give him pain: And as to the article of his fortune, I own myself equally afraid of inquiring into it, and of discovering the situation of my own, lest we should find ourselves both unhappy in the explanation; for alas! my provision is conditional, and depends entirely on my marrying with my brother's consent.'

Thunderstruck with this intelligence, the light forsook my eyes, the colour vanished from my cheeks, and I remained in a state of universal trepidation!—My female friend perceiving my disorder, encouraged me with assurances of Narcissa's constancy, and the hope of some accident favourable to our love; and as a further consolation let me know, that she had acquainted my mistress with the out-lines of my life; and that although she was no stranger to the present low state of my finances, her love and esteem were rather encreased than diminished by the knowledge of my circumstances. —I was greatly comforted by this assurance, which saved me a world of confusion and anxiety: For I must have imparted my situation one day to Narcissa; and this I could not have done without shame and disorder.

As I did not doubt that by this time, the scandalous aspersions of Melinda were diffused all over the town, I resolved to collect my whole strength of assurance, to brow-beat the efforts of her malice, and to publish her adventure with the Frenchified barber, by way of reprisal.—In the mean time, having promised to be at the garden gate about midnight, Miss Williams took her leave, bidding me repose myself entirely on the affection of my dear Narcissa, which was as perfect as inviolable.—Before I went abroad I was visited by Freeman, who came on purpose to acquaint me with the infamous stories, that were raised at my expence; I heard them with great temper, and in my turn informed him of every thing that had happened between Melinda and me; and among other things entertained him with the story of the barber, letting him know what share his friend Banter had in that affair: He was convinced of the injury my reputation had suffered, and no longer doubting the source from whence this deluge of slander had flowed upon me, undertook to undeceive the town in my behalf, and roll the stream back upon its origin; but in the mean time cautioned me from appearing in publick while the prepossession was strong against me, lest I should meet with some affront that might have bad consequences.

CHAPTER LIX

I receive an extraordinary message at the door of the long room, which I however enter, and affront the Squire, who threatens to take the law of me——I rebuke Melinda for her malice——She weeps with vexation——Lord Quiverwit is severe upon me——I retort his sarcasm——am received with the utmost tenderness by Narcissa, who desires to hear the story of my life——we vow eternal constancy to one another——I retire——am waked by a messenger, who brings a challenge from Quiverwit, whom I meet, engage, and vanquish

I THANKED him for his advice, which, however, my pride and resentment would not permit me to follow; for he no sooner left me, in order to do justice to my character among his friends and acquaintance, than I sallied out, and went directly to the long-room. —I was met at the door by a servant, who presented to me a billet without a subscription, importing that my presence was disagreeable to the company, and desiring I would take the hint without further disturbance, and bestow myself elsewhere for the future.— This peremptory message filled me with indignation.—I followed the fellow who delivered it, and seizing him by the collar, in presence of all the company, threatned to put him instantly to death, if he did not discover the scoundrel who had charged him with such an impudent commission, that I might punish him as he deserved.— The messenger, affrighted at my menaces and furious looks, fell upon his knees, and told me, that the gentleman who ordered him to deliver the letter was no other than Narcissa's brother, who at that time stood at the other end of the room, talking to Melinda.—I went up to him immediately, and in the hearing of his inamorata, accosted him in these words: 'Lookee, Squire, was it not for one consideration that protects you from my resentment, I would cane you where you stand, for having had the presumption to send me this scurrilous intimation,' which I tore to pieces and threw in his face; at the same time darting an angry regard at his mistress, and telling her, I was sorry she had put it out of my power to compliment her upon her invention, but at the expence of her good nature and veracity.—Her admirer, whose courage never rose but in proportion to the wine he had swallowed, instead of resenting my address in what is called an honourable way, threatned to prosecute me for an assault, and took witnesses accordingly; while she, piqued at his pusilanimous behaviour, and enraged at the sarcasm I had uttered against her, endeavoured to make her quarrel a publick cause, and wept aloud with spite and vexation.—The tears of a lady could not fail of attracting the notice and concern of the spectators, to whom she complained of my rudeness, with great bitterness, saying, If she was a man I durst not use her so.—The greatest part of the gentlemen, already prejudiced against me, were offended at the liberty I had taken, as appeared from their looks; though none of them signified their disgust any other way, except my Lord Quiverwit, who ventured to say with a sneer, that I was in the right to establish my own character, of which he had now no longer any doubt.—Nettled at this severe *equivoque*, which raised a laugh at my expence, I replied with some warmth, 'I am proud of having in that particular got the start of your lordship.'—He made no answer to my repartee, but with a contemptuous smile, walked off, leaving me in a very disagreeable situation.—In vain did I make up to several people of my acquaintance, whose conversation, I hoped, would banish my confusion; every body shunned me like a person infected, and I should not have been able to bear my disgrace, had not the idea of the ever faithful and fond Narcissa come to my relief.—I quitted the scene of my mortification, and sauntering about the town, happened to wake from my contemplation, when I found myself just opposite to a toy-shop,[1] which I entered, and purchased a ring set with a ruby in the form of a heart, surrounded by diamond sparks,[2] for which I paid ten guineas, intending it for a present to the charmer of my soul.

I was introduced, at the hour appointed, to this divine creature, who, notwithstanding what she had heard to my disadvantage, received me with the utmost confidence and tenderness; and having been informed of the general sketches of my life, by Miss Williams, expressed a desire of knowing the particular circumstances, which I

related with great candour, omitting however, some things which I
concluded altogether improper for her ear, and which the reader's
reflection will easily suggest.—As my story was little else than a recital of misfortunes, the tear of sympathy ceased not to trickle from
her inchanting eyes, during the whole of the narration, which when
I had finished, she recompensed me for my trouble, with the
most endearing protestations of eternal love.——She bewailed her
restricted condition, as it was the means of retarding my happiness;
told me, that Lord Quiverwit, by her brother's permission, had been
to drink tea with her that very afternoon, and actually proposed
marriage; and seeing me extremely affected with this piece of
information, offered to give me a convincing proof of her affection,
by espousing me in private, and leaving the rest to fate.—I was
penetrated with this instance of her regard, but that I might not be
outdone in generosity, resisted the bewitching temptation, in consideration of her honour and interest; at the same time, presented
my ring as a pledge of my inviolable attachment, and on my knees,
implored heaven to shower its curses on my head, if ever my heart
should entertain one thought unworthy of the passion that I then
avowed.—She received my token, gave me in return her picture in
miniature, exquisitely drawn and set in gold; and in the same posture called heaven to witness and to judge her flame.—Our vows
thus reciprocally breathed, a confidence of hope ensued, and our
mutual fondness becoming as intimate as innocence would allow, I
grew insensible of the progress of time, and it was morning before I
could tear myself from this darling of my soul!—My good angel
foresaw what would happen, and prompted me to indulge myself on
this occasion, in consideration of the fatal absence I was doomed to
suffer.

I went to bed immediately on my return to my lodging, and
having slept about two hours, was waked by Strap, who, in great
confusion, told me, there was a footman below with a letter for me,
which he would deliver to no body but myself.—Alarmed at this
piece of news, I desired my friend to shew him up to my chamber,
and received a letter from him, which, he said, required an
immediate answer: Upon which I opened it, and read

'SIR,
When any man injures my honour, let the difference of rank between
us be ever so great, I am contented to wave the privilege of my

quality, and seek reparation from him on equal terms.—The insolence of your reply to me yesterday, in the long-room, I might have overlooked, had not your presumptive emulation in a much more interesting affair, and a discovery which I made this morning, concurred in persuading me to chastise your audacity with my sword.——If you therefore, have spirit enough to support the character you assume, you will not fail to follow the bearer immediately to a convenient place, where you shall be met by

QUIVERWIT.

Whether I was enervated by the love and favour of Narcissa, or awed by the superior station of my antagonist, I know not, but I never had less inclination to fight than at this time: However, finding there was a necesssity for vindicating the reputation of my mistress, as well as for asserting my own honour, I forthwith rose, and dressing in a hurry, put on my sword, bid Strap attend me, and set out with my conductor, cursing my bad fortune all the way, for having been observed in my return from my angel—So I interpreted his lordship's discovery.—When I came within sight of my rival, his lacquey told me, he had orders to stop; upon which, I commanded Strap to halt also, while I walked forward; resolved, if possible, to come to an explanation with my challenger, before we should come to battle.—Nor was an opportunity wanting; for I no sooner approached, than he asked with a stern countenance, what business I had in Mr. Tophall's[1] garden, so early in the morning: 'I don't know, my Lord, (said I) how to answer a question put to me with such a magisterial haughtiness.—If your lordship will please to expostulate calmly, you will have no cause to repent of your condescension—Otherwise, I am not to be intimidated into any confession.'—'There's no room for denial (answered he) I saw you come out with my own eyes.'—'Did any other person see me?' (said I.)—'I neither know nor care (said he) I want no other evidence than that of my own senses.'—Pleased to hear that the suspicion was confined to him alone, I endeavoured to appease his jealousy, by owning an intrigue with the waiting-maid; but he had too much discernment to be so easily imposed upon, and told me there was only one way to convince him of the truth of what I alledged; which was no other than renouncing all claim to Narcissa upon oath, and promising upon honour, never to speak to her for the future.—Exasperated at this proposal, I unsheathed my sword, saying,

'Heavens! what title have you, or any man on earth, to impose such terms on me!' He did the same, and making towards me with a contracted brow, said I was a villain, and had dishonoured Narcissa.— 'He's a scandalous villain (I replied, in a transport of fury) who brands me with that imputation! She is a thousand times more chaste than the mother who bore you; and I will assert her honour with my heart's blood!'—So saying, I rushed upon him with more eagerness than address, and endeavouring to get within his point, received a wound in my neck, which redoubled my rage.—He excelled me in temper as well as in skill, by which means he parried my thrusts with great calmness, until I had almost exhausted my spirits; and when he perceived me beginning to flag, attacked me fiercely in his turn.—Finding himself however better opposed than he expected, he resolved to follow his longe,[1] and close with me; accordingly, his sword entered my waistcoat, on the side of the breast-bone, and running up between my shirt and skin, appeared over my left shoulder: I imagined that his weapon had perforated my lungs, and of consequence, that the wound was mortal; therefore determined not to die unrevenged, I seized his shell, which was close to my breast, before he could disintangle his point, and keeping it fast with my left hand, shortned my own sword with my right, intending to run him through the heart; but he received the thrust in the left arm, which penetrated up to the shoulder-blade.—Disappointed in this expectation, and afraid still that death would frustrate my revenge, I grappled with him, and being much the stronger, threw him upon the ground, where I wrested his sword out of his hand, and so great was my confusion, instead of turning the point upon him, struck out three of his fore-teeth with the hilt. —In the mean time, our servants seeing us fall, run up to separate and assist us; but before their approach, I was upon my feet, and had discovered, that my supposed mortal wound was only a slight scratch. The knowledge of my own safety, disarmed me of a good deal of my resentment, and I began to enquire with some concern into the situation of my antagonist, who remained on the ground bleeding plentifully at his mouth and arm.—I helped his footman to raise him, and having bound up his wound with my handkerchief, assured him it was not dangerous; I likewise restored his sword, and offered to support him to his own house.—He thanked me, with an air of sullen dignity; and whispering to me, that I should hear from him soon, went away, leaning on his servant's shoulder.

I was surprized at this promise, which I construed into a threat, and resolved, if ever he should call me out again, to use whatever advantage fortune might give me over him, in another manner.—In the mean time, I had leisure to take notice of Strap, who seemed quite stupified with horror; and (after having recovered him from his exstasy, with an assurance that I had received no damage) to explain the nature of this affair as we walked homeward.—By that time I had got into my apartment, I found the wound in my neck stiff and uneasy, and a good deal of clotted blood run down upon my shirt: Upon which I pulled off my coat and waistcoat, and unbuttoned my collar, that I might dress it with more ease.—My friend no sooner perceived my shirt quite dyed with blood, than imagining I had got at least twenty dreadful wounds, he cried, 'O Jesus!' and fell flat on the floor.—I stopt the bleeding with a little dry lint, and applying a plaister over it, cleaned myself from the gore, shifted and dressed, while he lay senseless at my feet; so that when he recovered, and saw me perfectly well, he could scarce believe his own eyes.—Now that the danger was past, I was very well pleased with what had happened, which I did not doubt, would soon become known, and consequently dignify my character not a little in this place.—I was also proud of having shewn myself, in some shape, worthy of the love of Narcissa, who, I was persuaded, would not think the worse of me for what I had done.

CHAPTER LX

I am visited by Freeman, with whom I appear in public, and am carressed——I am sent for by Lord Quiverwit, whose presence I quit in a passion——Narcissa is carried off by her brother——I intend to pursue him, and am dissuaded by my friend——I engage in play, and lose all my money——set out for London——try my fortune at the gaming-table, without success——receive a letter from Narcissa——bilk my taylor

WHILE I entertained myself with these reflections, the news of this duel being communicated by some unknown channel, spread all over the town.—I was visited by Freeman, who testified his surprize at finding me, having been told, that Lord Quiverwit being dead of his wounds, I had absconded, in order to avoid the cognizance of the law. I asked if people guessed the occasion of the quarrel; and understanding it was attributed to his lordship's resentment of my reply in the Long-room, confirmed that conjecture, glad to find Narcissa unsuspected.—My friend, after I had assured him that my antagonist was in no danger, wished me joy of the event, than which, he said, nothing could happen more opportunely to support the idea he had given me of my character, to his friends among whom he had been very assiduous in my behalf.

On the strength of this assurance, I went with him to the coffee-house, where I was saluted by a great many of those very persons, who shunned me the preceeding day.—And I found every body making merry with the story of Melinda's French gallant.—While I remained in this place, I received a message from Lord Quiverwit, desiring, if I was not engaged, to see me at his house.

Thither I immediately repaired, and was conducted to an apartment where I was received by his lordship in bed.—Being left by ourselves, he thanked me in very polite terms, for having used the advantage fortune had given me over him, with such moderation; and asked pardon for any offence his resentment might have prompted him to commit.—'I would willingly, (said he) make you my friend; but as it is impossible for me to divest myself of my passion for Narcissa, I am too well convinced of your sentiments, to think we shall ever agree on that subject. I took the liberty, therefore, of sending for you, in order to own candidly, that I cannot help opposing your success with that young lady; though at the same time, I promise to regulate my opposition by the dictates of justice and honour: This, however, I think proper to advertise you of, that she has no independant fortune, and if you should even succeed in your addresses, you would have the mortification to see her reduced to indigence, unless you have wherewithal to support her—And I am credibly informed of your incapacity that way.—Nay, I will confess, that, urged by this consideration, I have actually sent notice to her brother, of the progress I suspect you have made in her affection, and desired him to take his precautions accordingly.'——Alarmed and provoked at this information, I told his lordship, that I did not see how he could reconcile that piece of conduct with his profession of open dealing, and flung away from him in a passion.

As I walked homeward, in hopes of hearing from my mistress as usual by means of Miss Williams, I was surprized with the waving of a handkerchief, from the window of a coach and six that passed by me at full speed; and upon further observation, I saw a servant on horse-back riding after it, who, I knew by his livery, belonged to the Squire.—Thunderstruck with this discovery, the knowledge of my misfortune rushed all at once upon my reflection! I guessed immediately that the signal was made by the dear hand of Narcissa, who being hurried away in consequence of Lord Quiverwit's message to her brother, had no other method of relating her distress, and imploring my assistance.——Frantick with this conjecture, I run to my lodging, snatched my pistols, and ordered Strap to get post-horses, with such incoherence of speech and disorder, that the poor valet, terrified with the suspicion of another duel, instead of providing what I desired, went forthwith to Freeman, who being informed of my behaviour, came streight to my apartment, and conjured me so pathetically to acquaint him with the cause of my uneasiness, that I could not refuse to tell him my happiness was fled with Narcissa, and that I must retrieve her or perish. He represented the madness of such an undertaking, and endeavoured to divert me from it with great strength of friendship and reason: But all his arguments would have been ineffectual, had he not put me in mind of the dependance I ought to have on the love of Narcissa, and attachment to her maid, which could not fail of finding opportunities enow to advertise me of their situation; and at the same time, demonstrated the injury my charmer's reputation must suffer from my precipitate retreat. I was convinced and composed by these considerations: I appeared in publick with an air of tranquility, was well received by the best company in town, and my misfortune taking air, condoled accordingly; while I had the satisfaction of seeing Melinda so universally discountenanced, that she was fain to return to London, in order to avoid the scoffs and censure of the ladies at Bath.—But though the hope of hearing from the darling of my soul supported my spirits a little while, I began to be very uneasy, when at the end of several weeks, I found that expectation disappointed.— In short, melancholy and despondence took possession of my soul; and repining at that providence, which by acting the stepmother towards me, kept me from the fruition of my wishes, I determined, in a fit of despair, to risk all I had at the gaming table, with a view of acquiring a fortune sufficient to render me independant for life; or of plunging myself into such a state of misery, as would effectually crush every ambitious hope that now tortured my imagination.

Actuated by this fatal resolution, I engaged in play, and after some turns of fortune, found myself, at the end of three days, worth a thousand pounds; but it was not my intention to stop there, for which cause I kept Strap ignorant of my success, and continued my career, until I was reduced to five guineas, which I would have hazarded also, had I not been ashamed to fall from a bett of two hundred pounds to such a petty sum.

Having thus executed my scheme, I went home, amazed to find myself so much at ease, and informed my friend Strap of my mischance, with such calmness, that he imagining I joked, affected to receive the tidings with great equanimity.—But both he and I found ourselves mistaken very soon.—I had misinterpreted my own stupidity into deliberate resignation, and he had reason to believe me in earnest, when he saw me next morning agitated with the most violent despair, which he endeavoured to alleviate with all the consolation in his power.

In one of my lucid intervals, however, I charged him to take a place in the stage coach for London; and in the mean time, pay'd my debts in Bath, which amounted to thirty shillings only.—Without taking leave of my friends I embarked, Strap having the good fortune to find a return horse, and arrived in town, without having met with any thing remarkable on the road; save that, while we crossed Bagshot Heath, I was seized with a sort of inclination to retrieve my fortune, by laying passengers under contribution, in some such place.—My thoughts were so circumstanced at this time, that I should have digested the crime of robbery, so righteously had I concerted my plan, and ventured my life in the execution, had I not been deterred by reflecting upon the infamy that attends detection.

The apartment I formerly lived in being unengaged, I took possession of it, and next day went in quest of Banter, who received me with open arms, in expectation of having his bond discharged to his liking: But when he understood what had happened, his countenance changed of a sudden, and he told me, with a dryness of displeasure peculiar to himself, that if he was in my place, he would put it out of fortune's power to play him such another trick, and be avenged of his own indiscretion at once.—When I desired him to explain his meaning, he pointed to his neck, raised himself on his tip-toes, and was going away without any further ceremony, when I put him in mind of my indigence, and demanded the five guineas I had formerly lent him. 'Five guineas! (cried he) Zounds! had you acted with common prudence you might have had twenty thousand in your pocket by this time.—I depended upon five hundred from you, as much as if I had had notes for it in the bank; and by all the rules of equity, you are indebted to me for that sum.'—I was neither pleased nor convinced by this computation, and insisted on my right with such determined obstinacy, that he was fain to alter his tone, and appease my clamour, by assuring me, that he was not master of five shillings.—Society in distress, generally promotes good understanding among people; from being a dun, I descended to be a client, and asked his advice about repairing my losses.—He counselled me to have recourse again to the gaming table, where I had succeeded so well before, and to put myself in a condition, by selling my watch.—I followed his directions, and having accommodated him with a few pieces, went to the place, where I lost every shilling.

I returned to my lodgings full of desperate resolution, and having made Strap acquainted with my fate, ordered him to pawn my sword immediately, that I might be enabled to make another effort. —This affectionate creature no sooner understood my purpose, than seized with insuppressible sorrow at the prospect of my misery, he burst into tears, and asked what I proposed to do after the small sum he could raise on the sword should be spent: 'On my own account (said he) I am quite unconcerned; for while God spares me health and these ten fingers, I can earn a comfortable subsistence any where; but what must become of you, who have less humility to stoop, and more appetites to gratify.'—Here I interrupted him, by saying, with a gloomy aspect, I could never want a resource while I had a loaded pistol in my possession.—Stupified with horror, at this dreadful insinuation, he stood mute for some time, and then broke out into 'God of his infinite mercy enable you to withstand that temptation of the devil!—consider your immortal soul—there's no repentance in the grave!—O Lord! that ever it should come to this—Are we not enjoined to resign ourselves to the will of heaven? —where is your patience?—*Durum patientia frango*[1]—you are but a young man—there may be many good things in store for you— *accidit in puncto, quid non speratur in anno*[2]—remember your uncle, Mr. Bowling; perhaps he is now on his voyage homeward, pleasing himself with the hopes of finding and relieving you—nay, peradventure he is already arrived, the ship was expected about this time.'—A ray of hope shot athwart the darkness of my soul, at this suggestion; I thanked my friend for his seasonable recollection, and after having promised to take no resolution till his return, dismissed him to Wapping for intelligence.

In his absence I was visited by Banter, who being informed of my bad luck at play, told me, that fortune would probably be one day weary of persecuting me, 'In the mean time, (said he) here's a letter for you, which I received just now inclosed in one from Freeman.'— I snatched it with eagerness, and knowing the superscription to be of Narcissa's hand-writing, kissed it with transport, and having opened it, read

'I T is with great difficulty, that I have stolen from the observation of those spies who are set over me, this opportunity of telling you, that I was suddenly carried away from Bath, by my brother, who was informed of our correspondence by Lord Quiverwit, whom, I since understand, you have wounded in a duel on my account.——As I am fully convinced of your honour and love, I hope I shall never hear of such desperate proofs of either for the future.—I am so strictly watched, that it will be impossible for you to see me, until my brother's suspicion shall abate, or heaven contrive some other unforeseen event in our behalf.—In the mean time, you may depend on the constancy and affection of

Your own
NARCISSA.

P.S. Miss Williams, who is my fellow prisoner, desires to be remembered to you—We are both in good health, and only in pain for you, especially, as it will be impracticable for you to convey any message or letter to the place of our confinement——for which reason, pray desist from the attempt, that by miscarrying must prolong our captivity.

N——.

This kind letter afforded me great consolation: I communicated it to Banter, and at the same time, shewed him her picture: He approved her beauty and good sense, and could not help owning, that my neglect of Miss Snapper was excusable, when such a fine creature engrossed my attention.

I began to be reconciled to my fate, and imagined, that if I could contrive means of subsisting until my uncle should arrive, in case he was not already at home, that he would enable me to do something effectual in behalf of my love and fortune——I therefore consulted Banter about a present supply, who no sooner understood that I had credit with a taylor, than he advised me to take off two or three suits of rich cloaths and convert them into cash, by selling them at half price to a salesman in Monmouth-street.—I was a little startled at his proposal, which I thought savoured a little of fraud; but he rendered it palatable, by observing, that in a few months, I might be in a condition to do every body justice; and in the mean time, I was acquitted by the honesty of my intention—I suffered myself to be persuaded by his salvo, by which my necessity, rather than my judgment, was convinced; and when I found there were no accounts of the ship in which my uncle embarked, actually put the scheme in practice, and raised by it, five and twenty guineas, paying him for his advice with the odd five.

CHAPTER LXI

I am arrested—carried to the Marshalsea—find my old acquaintance beau Jackson in that jail—he informs me of his adventures—Strap arrives, and with difficulty is comforted—Jackson introduces me to a poet—I admire his conversation and capacity—am deeply affected with my misfortune—Strap hires himself as a journeyman-barber

BUT this expedient was in a few weeks attended with a consequence I did not foresee: a player having purchased one of the suits which were exposed to sale, appeared in it on the stage one night, while my taylor unfortunately happened to be present.—He knew it immediately, and enquiring minutely into the affair, discovered my whole contrivance: upon which he came to my lodgings, and telling me that he was very much straitened for want of money, presented his bill, which amounted to 50 *l.*—Surprized at this unexpected address, I affected to treat him cavalierly, swore some oaths, asked if he doubted my honour, and, telling him I should take care who I dealt with for the future, bid him come again in three days.—He

obeyed me punctually, demanded his money, and finding himself
amused with bare promises, arrested me that very day in the street.
—I was not much shocked at this adventure, which, indeed,
rescued me from a horrible suspence in which I had lived since his
first visit. I refused to go to a spunging-house,[1] where I had heard
there was nothing but the most flagrant imposition; and a coach
being called, I was carried to the Marshalsea, attended by a bailiff
and his follower, who were very much disappointed and chagrined
at my resolution.

The turnkey guessing, from my appearance, that I had got money
in my pocket, received me with the repetition of the Latin word
depone,[2] and gave me to understand, that I must pay before-hand
for the apartment[3] I should chuse to dwell in.—I desired to see his
conveniences, and hired a small, paultry bed-chamber, for a crown
a week, which, in any other place, would not have let at eighteen-
pence.—Having taken possession of this dismal habitation, I sent for
Strap, and my thoughts were busied in collecting matter of consolation to that faithful squire, when somebody knocked at my door,
which I no sooner opened, than a young fellow entered, in very
shabby cloaths and marvellous foul linnen. After a low bow, he
called me by my name, and asked if I had forgot him. His voice
assisted me in recollecting this person, whom I soon recognized to
be my old acquaintance beau Jackson, of whom mention is made in
the first part of my memoirs.—I saluted him, expressed my satisfaction at finding him alive, and condoled with him on his present
situation; which, however, did not seem to affect him much, for he
laughed very heartily at the occasion of our meeting so unexpectedly
in this place. After our mutual compliments were over, I enquired
about his amour with the lady of fortune, which seem'd to be so
near an happy conclusion when I had the pleasure of seeing him last:
and after an immoderate fit of laughter, he gave me to understand,
that he had been egregiously bit in that affair.—'You must know,
(said he) that a few days after our adventure with the bawd and her
b—ches, I found means to be married to that same fine lady you
speak of, and passed the night with her at her lodgings, so much to
her satisfaction, that early in the morning, after a good deal of
sniveling and sobbing, she owned, that so far from being an heiress
of a great fortune, she was no other than a common woman of the
town, who had decoyed me into matrimony, in order to enjoy the
privilege of a femme couverte;[4] and that, unless I made my escape

immediately, I should be arrested for a debt of her contracting, by bailiffs employed and instructed for that purpose.—Startled at this intimation, I got up in a twinkling, and taking leave of my spouse with several hearty damns, got safe into the verge of the court;[1] where I kept snug, until I was appointed surgeon's mate of a man of war at Portsmouth; for which place I set out on a Sunday, went on board of my ship, in which I sailed to the Straits, where I had the good fortune to be made surgeon of a sloop that came home in a few months after, and was put out of commission: whereupon I came to London, imagining myself forgotten and freed from my wife and her creditors; but had not been in town a week before I was arrested for a debt of her's, amounting to 20 *l.* and brought to this place, where I have been fixed by another action since that time.—However, you know my disposition; I defy care and anxiety; and being on the half-pay list, make shift to live here tolerably easy.'—I congratulated him on his philosophy, and remembering that I was in his debt, repay'd the money he formerly lent me, which, I believe, was far from being unseasonable. I then enquired about the œconomy of the place, which he explained to my satisfaction; and after we had agreed to mess together, he was just going to give orders for dinner when Strap arrived.

I never in my life saw sorrow so extravagantly expressed in any countenance, as in that of my honest friend, which was, indeed, particularly adapted by nature for such impressions.—Being left by ourselves, I communicated to him my disaster, and endeavoured to console him with the same arguments he had formerly used to me, withal representing the fair chance I had of being relieved, in a short time, by Mr. Bowling.—But his grief was unutterable; he seemed to give attention without listening, and wrung his hands in silence; so that I was in a fair way of being infected with his behaviour, when Jackson returned, and perceiving the deference I payed to Strap, altho' in a footman's habit, distributed his crumbs of comfort with such mirth, jollity and unconcern, that the features of the distressed squire relaxed by degrees, he recovered the use of speech, and begun to be a little more reconciled to this lamentable event.—We dined together on boiled beef and greens, brought from a cook's shop in the neighbourhood: and altho' this meal was served up in a manner little corresponding with the sphere of life in which I had lately lived, I made a virtue of necessity, eat with good appetite, and treated my friends with a bottle of wine, which had the desired effect, of increasing the good humour of my fellow-prisoner, and exhilarating the spirits of Strap, who now talked of my misfortune *en Cavalier*.

After dinner Jackson left us to our private affairs; when I desired my friend to pack up all our things, and carry them to some cheap lodging he should chuse for himself in the neighbourhood of the Marshalsea, after he had discharged my lodging, for which I gave him money.—I likewise recommended to him the keeping my misfortune secret, and saying to my landlord, or any other who should enquire for me, that I was gone into the country for a few weeks: at the same time I laid strong injunctions upon him to call every second day upon Banter, in case he should receive any letters for me from Narcissa, by the canal of Freeman; and by all means to leave a direction for himself, at my uncle's lodgings in Wapping, by which I might be found when my kinsman should arrive.

When he departed to execute these orders, (which, by the bye, were punctually perform'd that very night) I found myself so little seasoned to my situation, that I dreaded reflection, and sought shelter from it in the company of the beau, who, promising to regale me with a lecture upon taste, conducted me to the common side,[1] where I saw a number of naked miserable wretches assembled together.—We had not been here many minutes, when a figure appeared, wrapp'd in a dirty rug, tied about his loins with two pieces of list,[2] of different colours, knotted together; having a black bushy beard, and his head covered with a huge mass of brown periwig, which seemed to have been ravished from the crown of some scare crow.—This apparition, stalking in with great solemnity, made a profound bow to the audience, who signified their approbation by a general response of 'How d'ye do, doctor?' He then turned towards us, and honoured Jackson with a particular salutation: upon which my friend, in a formal manner, introduced him to me, by the name of Mr. Melopoyn.[3]—This ceremony being over, he advanced into the middle of the congregation, which crowded around him, and hemming three times, to my utter astonishment, pronounced with great significance of voice and gesture, a very elegant and ingenious discourse upon the difference between genius and taste, illustrating his assertions with apt quotations from the best authors, ancient as well as modern. When he had finished his harangue, which lasted a full hour, he bowed again to the spectators; not one of whom (I was informed) understood so much as a sentence of what he uttered. They manifested, however, their admiration and esteem by voluntary contribution, which, Jackson told me, one week with another, amounted to eighteen pence.—This moderate stipend, together with some small presents that he received for making up differences, and deciding causes amongst the prisoners, just enabled him to breathe and walk about in the grotesque figure I have described.—I understood also, that he was an excellent poet, and had composed a tragedy, which was allowed, by every body who had seen it, to be a performance of great merit; that his learning was infinite, his morals unexceptionable, and his modesty invincible.——Such a character could not fail of attracting my regard; I longed impatiently to be better acquainted with him, and desired Jackson would engage him to spend the evening in my apartment.—My request was granted, he favoured us with his company, and in the course of our conversation, perceiving that I was not illiterate, and that I had a strong passion for the Belle Lettres, acquitted himself so well on that subject, that I expressed a fervent desire of seeing his productions.—In this too he gratified my inclination:—he promised to bring his tragedy to my room next day, and, in the mean time, entertained me with some detach'd pieces, which gave me a very advantageous idea of his poetical talent.—Among other things I was particularly pleased with some elegies, in imitation of Tibullus;[1] one of which I beg leave to submit to the reader, as a specimen of his complexion and capacity.

I.

Where now are all my flatt'ring dreams of joy!
Monimia,[2] give my soul her wonted rest;—
Since first thy beauty fix'd my roving eye,
Heart-gnawing cares corrode my pensive breast!

II.

Let happy lovers fly where pleasures call,
With festive songs beguile the fleeting hour;
Lead beauty thro' the mazes of the ball,
Or press her wanton in love's roseate bow'r.

III.

For me, no more I'll range th' empurpled mead,
Where shepherds pipe, and virgins dance around;
Nor wander thro' the woodbine's fragrant shade,
To hear the music of the grove resound.

IV.

I'll seek some lonely church, or dreary hall,
Where fancy paints the glimm'ring taper blue,
Where damps hang mould'ring on the ivy'd wall,
And sheeted ghosts drink up the midnight dew:

V.

There leagu'd with hopeless anguish and despair,
A-while in silence o'er my fate repine;
Then, with a long farewell to love and care,
To kindred dust my weary limbs consign.

VI.

Wilt thou, Monimia, shed a gracious tear
On the cold grave where all my sorrows rest?
Wilt thou strew flow'rs, applaud my love sincere,
And bid the turf lie light upon my breast!

I was wonderfully affected with this pathetic complaint, which
seem'd so well calculated for my own disappointment in love, that I
could not help attaching the idea of Narcissa to the name of
Monimia, and of forming such melancholy presages of my passion,
that I could not recover my tranquility; and was fain to have
recourse to the bottle, which prepared me for a profound sleep that
I would not otherwise have enjoyed.—Whether these impressions
invited and introduced a train of other melancholy reflections, or my
fortitude was all exhausted in the effort I made against despondence,
the first day of my imprisonment, I cannot determine; but I awaked
in the horrors, and found my imagination haunted with such dismal
apparitions, that I was ready to despair:—and believe the reader will
own, that I had no great cause to congratulate myself, when I considered my situation.—I was interrupted in the midst of these
gloomy apprehensions by the arrival of Strap, who contributed not a
little to the re-establishment of my peace, by letting me know that
he had hired himself as a journeyman-barber; by which means he
would not only save me a considerable expence, but even make shift
to lay up something for my subsistence after my money should be
spent, in case I should not be relieved before.

CHAPTER LXII

*I read Melopoyn's tragedy, and conceive a vast opinion of
his genius——he recounts his adventures*

WHILE we eat our breakfast together, I acquainted him with the
character and condition of the poet, who came in with his play at
that instant, and imagining we were engaged about business, could
not be prevailed upon to sit; but leaving his performance, went
away.—My friend's tender heart was melted at the sight of a gentleman and Christian (for he had a great veneration for both these
epithits) in such misery; and assented with great chearfulness to a
proposal I made of cloathing him with our superfluities; a task with
which he charged himself, and departed immediately to perform it.

He was no sooner gone, than I locked my door and sat down to
the tragedy, which I read to the end with vast pleasure, not a little
amazed at the conduct of the managers who had rejected it.—The
fable, in my opinion was well chosen, and naturally conducted, the
incidents interesting, the characters beautifully contrasted, strongly
marked, and well supported; the diction poetical, spirited and
correct; the unities of the drama maintained with the most scrupulous exactness; the opening gradual and engaging; the *Περιπετεια*[1]
surprizing, and the catastrophe affecting: in short, I judged it by the
laws of Aristotle and Horace, and could find nothing in it exception-
able, but a little too much embellishment in some few places, which
objection he removed to my satisfaction, by a quotation from
Aristotle's Poetics, importing, that the least interesting parts of a
poem ought to be raised and dignified by the charms and energy
of diction.

I revered his genius, and was seized with an eager curiosity to
know the particular events of a fortune so unworthy of his merit.—
At that instant Strap returned with a bundle of cloaths, which I sent
with my compliments to Mr. Melopoyn, as a small token of my
regard, and desired the favour of his company to dinner.—He
accepted my present and invitation, and in less than half an hour
made his appearance in a decent dress, which altered his figure very
much to his advantage.—I perceived by his countenance, that his
heart was big with gratitude, and endeavoured to prevent his

378

acknowledgments, by asking pardon for the liberty I had taken; he made no reply, but with an aspect full of admiration and esteem, bowed to the ground, while the tears gushed from his eyes.— Affected with these symptoms of an ingenuous mind, I shifted the conversation from this subject, and complimented him on his performance, which I assured him, afforded me infinite pleasure.—My approbation made him happy; dinner being served, and Jackson arrived, I begged their permission for Strap to sit at table with us, after having informed them, that he was a person to whom I was extremely obliged; they were kind enough to grant that favour, and we eat together with great harmony and satisfaction.

Our meal being ended, I expressed my wonder at the little regard Mr. Melopoyn had met with from the world; and signified a desire of hearing how he had been treated by the managers of the playhouses, to whom, I understood from Jackson, he had offered his tragedy, without success.[1] 'There is so little entertaining in the incidents of my life (said he) that I am sure the recital will not recompence your attention; but since you discover an inclination to know them, I understand my duty too well to disappoint your desire.

My father, who was a curate in the country, being by the narrowness of his circumstances, hindred from maintaining me at the university, took the charge of my education upon himself, and laboured with such industry and concern in the undertaking, that I had little cause to regret the want of publick matters.—Being at great pains to consult my natural byass, he discovered in me betimes, an inclination for poetry; upon which he recommended to me an intimate acquaintance with the classicks, in the cultivation of which, he assisted me with paternal zeal and uncommon erudition.—When he thought me sufficiently acquainted with the ancients, he directed my studies to the best modern authors, French and Italian as well as English, and laid a particular injunction upon me, to make myself master of my mother tongue.

About the age of eighteen, I grew ambitious of undertaking a work of some consequence; and with my father's approbation, actually planned the tragedy you have read; but before I had finished four acts, that indulgent parent died, and left my mother and me in very indigent circumstances.—A near relation compassionating our distress, took us into his family, where I brought my fable to a conclusion; and soon after, my mother quitted this life.—When my sorrow for this melancholy event had subsided, I told my kinsman, who was a farmer, that having paid my last duty to my parent, I had now no attachment to detain me in the country, and therefore was resolved to set out for London, and offer my play to the stage, where I did not doubt of acquiring a large share of fame as well as fortune; in which case I should not be unmindful of my friends and benefactors.—My cousin was ravished with the prospect of my felicity, and willingly contributed towards the expence of fitting me out for my expedition.

Accordingly, I took a place in the waggon, and arrived in town, where I hired an apartment in a garret, willing to live as frugally as possible, until I should know what I had to expect from the manager, to whom I intended to offer my play.—For though I looked upon myself as perfectly secure of a good reception, imagining that a patentee would be as eager to receive, as I to present my production; I did not know whether or not he might be pre-engaged in favour of another author, which would certainly retard my success.—On this consideration too, I determined to be speedy in my application, and even to wait upon one of the managers, the very next day. For this purpose, I enquired of my landlord, if he knew where either, or both of them lived; and he being curious to know my business, and at the same time, appearing to be a very honest friendly man (a tallow-chandler) I made him acquainted with my design; upon which he told me, that I went the wrong way to work; that I would not find such easy access to a manager as I imagined; and that if I delivered my performance without proper recommendation, it would be as one to a thousand if ever it should be minded.—'Take my advice (said he) and your business is done.—One of the patentees[1] is a good catholick, as I am, and uses the same father who confesses me.—I will make you acquainted with this good priest, who is an excellent scholar, and if he shall approve of your play, his recommendation will go a great way in determining Mr. Supple[2] to bring it on the stage.'—I applauded his expedient, and was introduced to the friar, who having perused the tragedy, was pleased to signify his approbation, and commended me in particular, for having avoided all reflections upon religion.—He promised to use all his influence with his son Supple, in my behalf, and to inform himself that very day, when it would be proper for me to wait upon him with the piece.—He was punctual in performing his engagement, and next morning gave me to understand, that he had mentioned my affair to the manager, and that I had no more to do, than to go to his house any time in the forenoon, and make use of his name, upon which I would find immediate admittance.—I took his advice, put my performance in my bosom, and having received directions, went immediately to the house of Mr. Supple, and knocked at the door, that had a wicket in the middle, faced with a net-work of iron, through which a servant having viewed me some time, demanded to know my business.—I told him, my business was with Mr. Supple, and that I came from Mr. O Varnish.—He examined my appearance once more, then went away, returned in a few minutes, and said his master was busy and could not be seen.—Although I was a little mortified at my disappointment, I was persuaded that my reception was owing to Mr. Supple's ignorance of my errand; and that I might meet with no more obstructions of the same kind, I desired Mr. O Varnish to be my introductor the next time.——He complied with my request, and obtained immediate admittance to the manager, who received me with the utmost civility, and promised to read my play with the first convenience.—By his own appointment I called again in a fortnight, but he was gone out; I returned in a week after, and the poor gentleman was extremely ill; I renewed my visit in a fortnight after that, and he assured me, he had been so much fatigued with business, that he had not been able as yet to read it to an end; but he would take the first opportunity; and in the mean time, observed, that what he had yet seen of it was very entertaining.—I comforted myself with this declaration a few weeks longer, at the end of which I appeared again before his wicket, was let in, and found him laid up with the gout. I no sooner entered his chamber, than looking at me with a languishing eye, he pronounced, 'Mr. Melopoyn, I'm heartily sorry for an accident that has happened during my illness— you must know, that my eldest boy, finding your manuscript upon the table, in the dining-room, where I used to read it, carried it into the kitchin, and leaving it there, a negligent wench of a cook maid, mistaking it for waste-paper, has expended it all but a few leaves in singeing fouls upon the spit—But I hope the misfortune is not irreparable, since, no doubt, you have several copies.'

I protest to you, my good friend Mr. Random, I was extremely shocked at this information! but the good-natured gentleman seemed to be so much affected with my misfortune, that I suppressed my concern, and told him, that altho' I had not another copy, I should be able to retrieve the loss by writing another from my memory, which was very tenacious. You cannot imagine how well pleased Mr. Supple was at this assurance; he begged I would set about it immediately, and carefully revolve and recollect every circumstance, before I pretended to commit it to paper, that it might be the same individual play that he had perused.—Encouraged by this injunction, which plainly demonstrated how much he interested himself in the affair, I tasked my remembrance and industry, and in three weeks produced the exact image of the former, which was conveyed to him by my good friend, father O Varnish,[1] who let me know next day, that Mr. Supple would revise it superficially, in order to judge of its sameness with the other, and then give his final answer.——For this examination I allotted a week; and in full confidence of seeing it acted in a little while, demanded an audience of the manager, when that term was expired.—But alas! the season had slipt away insensibly; he convinced me, that if my play had been put into rehearsal at that time, it could not have been ready for performing, until the end of March, when the benefit nights[2] come on; consequently it would have interfered with the interest of the players, whom it was not my business to disoblige.

I was fain to acquiesce in these reasons, which to be sure were extremely just; and to reserve my performance to the next season, when he hoped I would not be so unlucky.—Although it was a grievous disappointment to me, who by this time, began to want both money and necessaries; having, on the strength of my expectation from the theatre, launched out into some extravagancies, by which the sum I brought to town was already almost consumed.— Indeed, I ought to be ashamed at this circumstance of my conduct: For my finances were sufficient, with good œconomy, to have maintained me comfortably a whole year.—You will perhaps be amazed when I tell you, that in six months, I expended not a farthing less than ten guineas: But when one considers the temptations to which a young man is exposed in this great city, especially if he is addicted to pleasure as I am, the wonder will vanish, or at least abate.—Nor was the cause of my concern limited to my own situation entirely: I had wrote an account of my good reception to my kinsman the farmer, and desired him to depend upon me for the money he had kindly accommodated me with, about the end of February: which promise I now found myself unable to perform.— However, there was no remedy but patience: I applied to my landlord, who was a very good-natured man, candidly owned my distress, and begged his advice in laying down some plan for my subsistence.—He readily promised to consult his confessor on this subject, and in the mean time, told me, I was welcome to lodge and board with him, until fortune should put in it my power to make restitution.

Mr. O Varnish being informed of my necessity, offered to introduce me to the author of a weekly paper, who, he did not doubt, would employ me in that way, provided he should find me duly qualified; but upon enquiry, I understood, that this journal was calculated to foment divisions in the commonwealth, and therefore I desired to be excused from engaging in it.—He then proposed that I should write something in the poetical way, which I might dispose of to a bookseller for a pretty sum of ready money, and perhaps establish my own character into the bargain; this event would infallibly procure friends; and my tragedy would appear next season to the best advantage, by being supported both by interest and reputation. —I was charmed with this prospect, and having heard what friends Mr. Pope[1] acquired by his pastorals, set about a work of that kind, and in less than six weeks, composed as many ecclogues, which I forthwith offered to an eminent bookseller, who desired I would leave them for his perusal, and he would give me an answer in two days.—At the end of that time, I went to him, when he returned the poems, telling me, they would not answer his purpose, and sweetned his refusal, by saying there were some good clever lines in them.— Not a little dejected at his rebuff, which, I learned from Mr. O Varnish, was owing to the opinion of another author, whom this bookseller always consulted on these occasions, I applied to another person of the same profession, who told me, that the town was cloyed with pastorals, and advised me, if I intended to profit by my talents, to write something satirical or luscious,[2] such as the *Button Hole, Shocky and Towzer, the Leaky Vessel*, &c.[3]—and yet this was a man in years, who wore a reverend periwig, looked like a senator, and went regularly to church.—Be that as it will, I scorned to prostitute my pen in the manner he proposed, and carried my papers to a third, who assured me, that poetry was intirely out of his way; and asked, if I had got never a piece of secret history, thrown into a series of letters, or a volume of adventures, such as those of Robinson Crusoe, and Colonel Jack,[4] or a collection of conundrums, where-with to entertain the plantations.—Being quite unfurnished for this dealer, I had recourse to another with as little success, and I verily believe was rejected by the whole trade.

I was afterwards persuaded to offer myself as a translator, and accordingly repaired to a person, who was said to entertain numbers of that class in his pay; he assured me, he had already a great deal of that work on his hands, which he did not know what to do with; observed that translation was a meer drug, that branch of literature being overstocked by an inundation of authors from North-Britain; and asked what I would expect per sheet, for rendering the Latin classicks into English.—That I might not make myself too cheap, I determined to set a high price upon my qualifications, and demanded a guinea for every translated sheet.—'A guinea!' (cried he, staring at me) then paused a little, and said; he had no occasion for my service at present.—I found my error, and resolving to make amends, fell one half in my demand; upon which he stared at me again, and told me his hands were full.—I attempted others, without finding employment, and was actually reduced to a very uncomfortable prospect, when I bethought myself of offering my talents to the printers of halfpenny ballads, and other such occasional essays as are hawked about the streets.—With this view, I applied to one of the most noted and vociferous of this tribe, who directed me to a person whom I found entertaining a whole crowd of them with gin, bread and cheese; he carried me into a little back parlour, very neatly furnished, where I signified my desire of being enrolled among his writers; and was asked, what kind of composition I professed?— Understanding that my inclination leaned towards poetry, he expressed his satisfaction, telling me, one of his poets had lost his senses, and was confined in Bedlam, and the other was become dozed with drinking drams; so that he had not done any thing tolerable these many weeks.—When I proposed, that we should enter into terms of agreement, he gave me to understand, that his bargains were always conditional, and his authors paid in proportion to the sale of their works.

Having therefore settled these conditions, which (I do assure you) were not very advantageous to me, he assigned me a subject for a ballad, which was to be finished in two hours; and I retired to my garret in order to perform his injunction.—As the theme happened to suit my fancy, I compleated a pretty sort of an ode, within the time prescribed, and brought it to him, big with hope of profit and applause. He read it in a twinkling, and to my utter astonishment, told me, it would not do; though indeed, he owned I wrote a good hand, and spelled very well, but my language was too high flown, and of consequence not at all adapted to the capacity and taste of his customers.—I promised to rectify that mistake, and in half an hour humbled my stile to the comprehension of vulgar readers; he approved of the alteration, and gave me some hopes of succeeding in time, though he observed, that my performance was very deficient in that quaintness of expression that pleases the multitude: However, to encourage me, he ventured the expence of printing and paper, and, if I remember a-right, my share of the sale amounted to four pence halfpenny.

From that day, I studied the Grub-street[1] manner with great diligence, and at length became such a proficient, that my works were in great request among the most polite of the chairmen, draymen, hackney-coachmen, footmen and serving maids: Nay, I have enjoyed the pleasure of seeing my productions adorned with cuts, pasted upon the wall as ornaments in beer-cellars and cobler's stalls; and have actually heard them sung in clubs of substantial tradesmen. —But empty praise (you know, my dear friend) will not supply the cravings of nature.—I found myself in danger of starving in the midst of all my fame; for of ten songs I composed, it was well if two had the good fortune to please.——For this reason I turned my thoughts to prose, and during a tract of gloomy weather, published an apparition, on the substance of which I subsisted very comfortably a whole month: I have made many a good meal upon a monster; a rape has often afforded me great satisfaction; but a murder, well-timed, was my never-failing resource. What then? I was a most miserable slave to my employers, who expected to be furnished at a minute's warning with prose and verse, just as they thought the circumstances of the times required, whether the *inclination was absent or present.* Upon my sincerity, Mr. Random, I have been so much pestered and besieged by these children of clamour, that my life became a burden to me.

CHAPTER LXIII

The continuation and conclusion of Mr. Melopoyn's story

I MADE shift, notwithstanding, to maintain myself till the beginning of next winter, when I renewed my addresses to my friend Mr. Supple, and was most graciously received.—'I have been thinking of your affair Mr. Melopoyn, (said he) and am determined to shew how far I have your interest at heart, by introducing you to a young nobleman of my acquaintance, who is remarkable for his fine taste in dramatic writings, and is, beside, a man of such influence, that if once he should approve your play, his patronage will support it against all the efforts of envy and ignorance: For I do assure you, that merit alone will not bring success.—I have already spoken of your performance to Lord Rattle,[1] and if you will call at my house, in a day or two, you shall have a letter of introduction to his lordship.'—I was sensibly touched with this mark of Mr. Supple's friendship, and looking upon my affair as already done, went home and imparted my good fortune to my landlord, who, to render my appearance more acceptable to my patron, procured a suit of new cloaths for me on his own credit.

Not to trouble you with idle particulars, I carried my tragedy to his lordship's lodgings, and sent it up along with Mr. Supple's letter, by one of his servants, who desired me, by his lord's order, to return in a week.—I did so, and was admitted to his lordship, who received me very courteously, told me he had perused my play, which he thought, on the whole, was the best *coup d'essai* he had ever seen; but that he had marked some places in the margin, which he imagined might be altered for the better.—I was transported with this reception, and promised (with many acknowledgments of his lordship's generosity) to be governed solely by his advice and direction.—'Well then (said he) write another fair copy with the alterations I have proposed, and bring it to me as soon as possible, for I am resolved to have it brought on the stage this winter.'—You may be sure I set about this task with alacrity, and although I found his lordship's remarks much more numerous, and of less importance than I expected, I thought it was not my interest to dispute upon trifles with my patron; therefore new-modelled it according to his desire, in less than a month.

Chapter LXIII

When I waited upon him with the manuscript, I found one of the actors[1] at breakfast with his lordship, who immediately introduced him to my acquaintance, and desired him to read a scene of my play.
—This he performed very much to my satisfaction, with regard to emphasis and pronounciation; but he signified his disgust at several words in every page, which I presuming to defend, Lord Rattle told me, with a peremptory look, I must not pretend to dispute with him, who had been a player these twenty years, and understood the œconomy of the stage better than any man living. I was forced to submit, and his lordship proposed the same actor should read the whole play, in the evening, before some gentlemen of his acquaintance, whom he would convene at his lodgings for that purpose.

I was present at the reading; and I protest to you, my dear friend, I never underwent such a severe trial in the whole course of my life, as at that juncture! for although the player might be a very honest man and a good performer, he was excessively illiterate and assuming, and made a thousand frivolous objections, which I was not permitted to answer: However, the piece was very much applauded on the whole; the gentlemen present, who I understood were men of fortune, promised to countenance and support it as much as they could; and Lord Rattle assuring me, that he would act the part of a careful nurse to it, desired me to carry it home and alter it immediately according to their remarks:——I was fain to acquiesce in his determination, and fulfilled his injunctions with all the expedition in my power; but before I could present the new copy, my good friend Mr. Supple had disposed of his property and patent to one Mr. Brayer;[2] so that fresh interest was to be made with the new manager.—This task Lord Rattle undertook, having some acquaintance with him, and recommended my performance so strongly, that it was received.

I looked upon myself now, as upon the eve of reaping the fruits of all my labour: I waited a few days in expectation of its being put into rehearsal, and wondering at the delay, applied to my worthy patron, who excused Mr. Brayer on account of the multiplicity of business in which he was involved; and bid me beware of teizing[3] the patentee.—I treasured up this caution, and exerted my patience three weeks longer; at the end of which, his lordship gave me to understand that Mr. Brayer had read my play, and owned it had undubitable merit; but as he had long been pre-engaged to another author,[4] he could not possibly represent it that season; though if I would reserve it for the next, and in the interim make such alterations as he had proposed by observations on the margin, I might depend upon his compliance.

Thunderstruck at this disappointment, I could not, for some minutes, utter one syllable: At length, however, I complained bitterly of the manager's insincerity in amusing me so long, when he knew from the beginning, that he could not gratify my desire.—But his lordship reprimanded me for my freedom, said Mr. Brayer was a man of honour, and imputed his behaviour with respect to me, to nothing else but forgetfulness.—And indeed I have had some reason since that time, to be convinced of his bad memory; for, in spite of appearances, I will not allow myself to interpret his conduct any other way.—Lord Rattle observing me very much affected with my disappointment, offered his interest to bring on my play at the other house, which I eagerly accepting, he forthwith wrote a letter of recommendation to Mr. Bellower, actor, and prime minister to Mr. Vandal,[1] proprietor of that theatre; and desired me to deliver it with my tragedy, without loss of time.—Accordingly, I hastened to his house, where after having waited a whole hour in a lobby, I was admitted to his presence, and my performance received with great state.—He told me he was extremely busy at present, but he would peruse it as soon as possible; and bid me call again in a week. I took my leave, not a little astonished at the pert and supercilious behaviour of this stage-player, who had not treated me with good manners; and began to think the dignity of a poet greatly impaired since the days of Euripides and Sophocles, but all this was nothing in comparison of what I have since observed.

Well, Mr. Random, I went back at the appointed time, and was told that Mr. Bellower was engaged, and could not see me.—I repeated my visit a few days after, and having waited a considerable time, was favoured with an audience, during which, he said, he had not as yet read my play.—Nettled at this usage, I could contain myself no longer, but telling him, I imagined he would have paid more deference to Lord Rattle's recommendation, demanded my manuscript with some expressions of resentment.——'Ay, (said he, in a theatrical tone) with all my heart.'—Then pulling out a drawer of the bureau at which he sat, he took out a bundle, and threw it upon a table that was near him, pronouncing the word 'There,' with great disdain.—I took it up, and perceiving with some surprize, that it was a comedy, told him, it did not belong to me; upon which

he offered me another, which I also disclaimed—A third was
produced, and rejected for the same reason. At length, he pulled out
a whole handful, and spread them before me, saying, 'There are
seven—take which you please—or take them all.'—I singled out my
own, and went away, struck dumb with admiration[1] at what I had
seen—not so much on account of his insolence, as of the number of
new plays, which from this circumstance, I concluded were yearly
offered to the stage.——You may be sure I did not fail to carry my
complaint to my patron, who did not receive it with all the indignation I expected; but taxed me with precipitation, and told me, I
must lay my account with bearing the humours of the players, if I
intended to write for the stage.—'There is now no other remedy
(said he) but to keep it till the next season for Mr. Brayer, and alter
it at your leisure, in the summer, according to his directions'—I
was now reduced to a terrible alternative, either to quit all hopes of
my tragedy, from which I had all along promised myself a large
share of fortune and reputation, or to encounter eight long months
of adversity in preparing for, and expecting its appearance.—This
last pennance, painful as it was, seemed most eligible to my reflection
at that time, and therefore I resolved to undergo it.

Why should I tire you with particulars of no consequence? I
wrestled with extreme poverty, until the time of my probation was
expired; and went to my Lord Rattle in order to remind him of my
affair, when I understood, to my great concern, that his lordship
was on the point of going abroad, and, which was still more unfortunate for me, Mr. Brayer had gone into the country; so that my
generous patron had it not in his power to introduce me personally,
as he intended: However, he wrote a very strong letter to the
manager in my favour, and put him in mind of the promise he had
made in behalf of my play.

As soon as I was certified of Brayer's return, I went to his house
with this letter, but was told he was gone out.—I called again next
day early in the morning, received the same answer, and was desired
to leave my name and business; I did so, and returned the day after,
when the servant still affirmed that his master was gone abroad;
though I perceived him, as I retired, observing me through a
window.—Incensed at this discovery, I went to a coffee-house hard
by, and inclosing his lordship's letter in one from myself, demanding
a categorical answer, I sent it to his house by a porter, who returned
in a few minutes, and told me Mr. Brayer would be glad to see me

at that instant.—I obeyed the summons, and was received with such profusion of compliments and apologies, that my resentment immediately subsided, and I was even in pain for the concern which this honest man shewed at the mistake of his servant, who, it seems, had been ordered to deny him to every body but me.—He expressed the utmost veneration for his good and noble friend Lord Rattle, whom he should always be proud to serve; promised to peruse the play with all dispatch, and give me a meeting upon it; and as a testimony of his esteem, made me a present of a general order for the season, by which I would be admitted to any part of the theatre.— This was a very agreeable compliment to me, whose greatest pleasure consisted in seeing dramatic performances, and you need not doubt that I often availed myself of my privilege. As I had an opportunity of being behind the scenes when I pleased, I frequently conversed with Mr. Brayer about my play, and asked when he intended to put it into rehearsal, but he had always so much business upon his hands, that it remained with him unopened a considerable while; and I became very uneasy about the season, that wasted apace, when I saw in the papers, another new play advertised, which had been written, offered, accepted and rehearsed in the compass of three months, without my knowledge or suspicion. —You may easily guess how much I was confounded at this event! I own to you, that in the first transports of my anger, I suspected Mr. Brayer of having acted towards me in the most pitiful, perfidious manner; and was actually glad at his disappointment in the success of his favourite piece, which by the strength of art, lingered till the third night,[1] and then died in a deplorable manner. But now that passion has no share in my reflection, I am willing to ascribe his behaviour to his want of memory or want of judgment, which, you know, are natural defects, that are more worthy of compassion than reproach.

About this time, I happened to be in company with a gentlewoman, who having heard of my tragedy, told me, she was acquainted with the wife of a gentleman, who was very well known to a lady, who had great interest with a person who was intimate with Earl Sheerwit,[2] and that if I pleased, she would use her influence in my behalf.—As this nobleman had the character of a Mæcenas[3] in the nation, and could stamp a value upon any work by his sole countenance and approbation, I accepted her offer with eagerness, in full confidence of seeing my reputation established, and my wishes fulfilled in a very short time, provided that I should have the good fortune to please his Lordship's taste. I withdrew the manuscript from the hands of Mr. Brayer, and committed it to the care of this gentlewoman, who laboured so effectually in my interest, that in less than a month it was conveyed to the Earl, and in a few weeks after, I had the satisfaction to hear, that he had read, and approved it very much. Transported with this piece of intelligence, I flattered myself with the hopes of his interesting himself in its favour; but hearing no more of the matter in three whole months, I began (God forgive me) to suspect the veracity of the person who brought me the good tidings, for I thought it impossible, that a man of his rank and character, who knew the difficulty of writing a good tragedy, and understood the dignity of the work, should read and applaud an essay of this kind, without feeling an inclination to befriend the author, whom his countenance alone could raise above dependance. —But it was not long before I found my friends very much wronged by my opinion.

You must know, that the civilities I had received from Lord Rattle, and the desire he manifested to promote the success of my play, encouraged me to write an account of my bad fortune to his Lordship, who condescended so far as to desire, by letter, a young Squire of a great estate, with whom he was intimate, to espouse my cause, and in particular, make me acquainted with one Mr. Marmozet[1] a celebrated player, who had lately appeared on the stage with astonishing eclat, and bore such sway in the house where he acted, that the managers durst not refuse any thing he recommended. The young gentleman whom Lord Rattle had employed for this purpose, being diffident of his own interest with Mr. Marmozet, had recourse to a nobleman of his acquaintance, who, at his sollicitation, was so good as to introduce me to him; and the conversation turning upon my performance, I was not a little surprized as well as pleased to hear, that Earl Sheerwit had spoke very much in its praise, and even sent Mr. Marmozet the copy, with a message expressing a desire that he would act in it next season—Nor was this favourite actor backward in commending the piece, which he mentioned with some expressions of regard, that I do not chuse to repeat; assuring me that he would appear in it, provided he should be engaged to play at all during the ensuing season. In the mean time, he desired I would give him leave to peruse it in the country, whither he intended to remove next day, that he might have leisure to consider and point out such alterations as might, perhaps, be necessary for the *jeu de theatre*; and took my direction, that he might communicate by letter, the observations he should make. Trusting to these assurances and the interest which had been made in my behalf, I hugged myself in the expectation of seeing it, not only acted, but acted to the greatest advantage, which I thought could not fail of recompensing me in an ample manner, for the anxiety and affliction I had undergone. But six weeks being elapsed, I did not know how to reconcile Mr. Marmozet's silence, with his promise of writing to me in ten days after he set out for the country; however, I was at last favoured with a letter, importing that he had made some remarks on my tragedy, which he would freely impart at meeting, and advising me to put it, without loss of time, into the hands of that manager, who had the best company: for he himself was quite uncertain, whether or not he should be engaged that winter.—I was a good deal alarmed at this last part of his letter, and advised about it with a friend, who told me, it was a plain indication of Mr. Marmozet's desire to be rid of his promise: that his pretended uncertainty about acting next winter, was no other than a scandalous evasion; for to his certain knowledge, he was already engaged, or at least, in terms with Mr. Vandal; and that his design was to disappoint me, in favour of a new comedy, which he had purchased of the author, and intended to bring upon the stage for his own advantage.—In short, my dear Sir, this person, who, I must own, is of a very sanguine complexion, handled the moral character of Mr. Marmozet with such severity, that I began to suspect him of some particular prejudice, and put myself upon my guard against his insinuations.—I ought to crave pardon for this tedious narration of trivial circumstances, which, however interesting they may be to me, must certainly be very dry and insipid to the ear of one unconcerned in the affair.—But I understand the meaning of your looks, and will proceed.—Well, Sir, Mr. Marmozet, upon his return to town, treated me with uncommon complaisance, and invited me to his lodgings, where he proposed to communicate his remarks, which I confess were more unfavourable than I expected; but I answered his objections, and, as I thought, brought him over to my opinion; for, on the whole, he signified the highest approbation of the performance.—In the course of our dispute, I was not a little surprized to find this poor gentleman's memory so treacherous as to let him forget what he had said to me, before he went out of town, in regard to Earl Sheerwit's opinion of my play, which he now professed himself ignorant of; and I was extremely mortified at hearing from his own mouth, that his interest with Mr. Vandal was so very low, as to be insufficient of itself, to bring a new piece upon the stage. I then begged his advice, and he counselled me to apply to Earl Sheerwit for a message in my favour to the manager, who would not presume to refuse any thing recommended by so great a man; and he was so kind as to promise to second this message with all his power.—I had immediate recourse to the worthy gentlewoman my friend already mentioned, who opened the channels of her conveyance with such expedition, that in few days, I had a promise of the message, provided I could assure myself of Mr. Vandal's being uningaged to any other; for his Lordship did not chuse to condescend so far, until he should understand that there was a probability (at least) of succeeding; at the same time in which I was blessed with this piece of news, I was startled at another, by the same canal of communication; which was, that Mr. Marmozet, before he advised me to this application, had informed the Earl, that he had read my play, and found it altogether unfit for the stage.—Though I could not doubt the certainty of this intelligence, I believed there was some misapprehension in the case; and without taking any notice of it, told Mr. Marmozet the answer I had been favoured with; upon which, he testified much joy, and promised to ask Mr. Vandal the question proposed.—I waited upon him in a day or two, when he gave me to understand, that Mr. Vandal having professed himself free of all engagements, he had put my play into his hands, and represented it as a piece strongly recommended by Earl Sheerwit, who (he assured him) would honour him with a message in its favour; and he desired me to call for an answer at Mr. Vandal's house, in three days.—I followed his directions, and found the manager, who, being made acquainted with my business, owned, that Mr. Marmozet had given him a manuscript play, but denied that he had mentioned Earl Sheerwit's name.—When I informed him of the circumstances of the affair, he said, he had no engagement with any author; that he would read my tragedy forthwith; and did not believe he should venture to reject it in contradiction to his Lordship's opinion, for which he had the utmost veneration, but put it into rehearsal without loss of time.—I was so much intoxicated with this encouragement, that I overlooked the mysterious conduct of Mr. Marmozet, and attended the manager at the time appointed, when, to my infinite confusion! he pronounced my play improper for the stage, and rejected it accordingly. As soon as I could recollect myself from the disorder into which this unexpected refusal had thrown me, I expressed a desire of hearing his objections, which were so groundless, indistinct and unintelligible, that I persuaded myself he had not at all perused the piece, but had been prompted by somebody whose lessons he had not rightly retained. However, I have been since informed, that the poor man's head, which was not naturally very clear, had been disordered with superstition, and that he laboured under the tyranny of a wife, and the terrors of hell fire at the same time.——Precipitated in this manner, from the highest pinnacle of hope, to the abyss of despondence, I was ready to sink under the burthen of my affliction; and in the bitterness of my anguish, could not help entertaining some doubts of Mr. Marmozet's integrity, when I recollected and compared the circumstances of his conduct towards me. I was encouraged in this suspicion, by being told, that my Lord Sheerwit had spoke of his character with great contempt; and in particular, resented his insolence in opposing his own taste to that of his Lordship, concerning my tragedy.—While I hesitated between different opinions of the matter, that friend, who (as told you before) was a little hot-headed, favoured me with a visit, and having heard a circumstantial account of the whole affair, could not contain his indignation, but affirmed without ceremony, that Marmozet was the sole occasion of my disappointment; that he had acted from first to last with the most perfidious dissimulation, cajoling with insinuating civilities, while he underhand employed all his art and influence to prejudice the ignorant manager against my performance; that nothing could equal his hypocrisy, but his avarice, which ingrossed the faculties of his soul so much, that he scrupled not to be guilty of the meanest practices to gratify that sordid appetite; that in consequence of this disposition, he had prostituted his honour in betraying my in-experience, and in undermining the interest of another author of established reputation, who had also offered a tragedy to the stage, which he thought would interfere with the success of the comedy he had bought, and determined to bring on at all events.

I was shocked at the description of such a monster, which I could not believe existed in the world, bad as it is, and argued against the asseverations of my friend, by demonstrating the bad policy of such behaviour, which could not fail of entailing infamy upon the author;

and the small temptation that a man of Mr. Marmozet's figure and success, could have to consult his interest in such a groveling manner, which must create contempt and abhorrence of him in his patrons, and effectually deprive him of the countenance and protection he now enjoys in such an eminent degree.——He pretended to laugh at my simplicity, and asked if I knew for which of his virtues he was so much caressed by the people of fashion.—— 'It is not (said he) for the qualities of his heart, that this little parasite is invited to the tables of Dukes and Lords, who hire extraordinary cooks for his entertainment: His avarice they see not, his ingratitude they feel not, his hypocrisy accommodates itself to their humours, and is of consequence pleasing; but he is chiefly courted for his buffoonery, and will be admitted into the choicest parties of the quality for his talent of mimicking[1] Punch and his wife Joan, when a poet of the most exquisite genius, is not able to attract the least regard.'—God forbid, Mr. Random, that I should credit assertions that degrade the dignity of our superiors so much, and represent that poor man as the most abject of all beings! No! I looked upon them as the hyperboles of passion; and though that comedy of which he spoke, did actually appear, I dare not doubt the innocence of Mr. Marmozet, who, I am told, is as much as ever in favour with the Earl; a circumstance that, surely, could not happen, unless he had vindicated his character to the satisfaction of his lordship.—Pray forgive this long digression, and give me the hearing a little longer; for, thank heaven! I am now near the goal.

Baffled in all my attempts, I despaired of seeing my play acted, and bethought myself of chusing some employment, that might afford a sure, though mean subsistence; but my landlord, to whom I was by this time considerably indebted, and who had laid his account with having his money paid all in a heap, from the profits of my third night, could not brook his disappointment, therefore made another effort in my behalf, and by dint of interest, procured a message from a lady of fashion,[2] to Mr. Brayer, who had always professed a great veneration for her, desiring that he would set up my play forthwith, and assuring him that she and all her friends would support it in the performance: To strengthen my interest, she engaged his best actors in my cause; and in short, exerted herself so much, that it was again received, and my hopes began to revive.— But Mr. Brayer, honest man, was so much engrossed by business of vast consequence, though to appearance he had nothing at all to do, that he could not find time to read it until the season was pretty far advanced; and read it he must, for notwithstanding his having perused it before, his memory did not retain one circumstance of the matter.

At length he favoured it with his attention, and having proposed certain alterations, sent his duty to the lady who patronized it, and promised on his honour, to bring it on next winter, provided these alterations should be made, and the copy delivered to him before the end of April.—With an aching heart, I submitted to these conditions, and performed them accordingly: But fortune owed me another unforeseen mortification; Mr. Marmozet during the summer, became joint patentee with Mr. Brayer,[1] so that when I claimed performance of articles, I was told, he could do nothing without the consent of his partner, who was pre-engaged to another author.

My condition was rendered desperate by the death of my good friend and landlord, whose executors obtained a judgment against my effects, which they siezed, turning me out into the street naked, friendless, and forlorn; there I was arrested at the suit of my taylor, and thrown into this prison, where I have made shift to live there five weeks on the bounty of my fellow-prisoners, who, I hope, are not the worse for the instruction and good offices, by which I manifest my gratitude; but in spite of all their charitable endeavours, my life was scarce tolerable, until your uncommon benevolence enabled me to enjoy it with comfort.'

CHAPTER LXIV

*I am seized with a deep melancholy, and become a sloven——
I am relieved by my uncle——he prevails upon me to engage
with his owners, as surgeon of the ship which he commands
——he makes me a considerable present—entertains Strap as
his steward——I take my leave of my friends, and go on
board——the ship arrives at the Downs*

I SHALL not make any reflections on this story, in the course of which the reader must perceive how egregiously the simplicity and milky disposition of this worthy man, had been duped and abused by a set of scoundrels, who were so habituated to falshood and equivocation, that I verily believe, they could not utter one syllable of truth, though their lives depended upon their sincerity.—Notwithstanding all I had suffered from the knavery and selfishness of mankind, I was amazed, and incensed at that base indifference which suffered such uncommon merit as he possessed, to languish in obscurity, and struggle with all the miseries of a loathsome jail;—and should have blessed the occasion that secluded me from such a perfidious world, had not the remembrance of the amiable Narcissa, preserved my attachment to that society of which she constituted a part.—The picture of that lovely creature was the constant companion of my solitude: How often did I contemplate the resemblance of those enchanting features that first captivated my heart! How often did I weep over those endearing scenes which her image recalled! and how often did I curse my perfidious fate for having robbed me of the fair original! In vain did my imagination flatter me with schemes of future happiness; surly reason always interposed, and in a moment overthrew the unsubstantial fabrick, by chastising the extravagance of my hope, and representing my unhappy situation in the right point of view: In vain did I fly for refuge to the amusements of the place, and engage in the parties of Jackson, at cards, billiards, nine-pins, and fives; a train of melancholy thoughts took possession of my soul, which even the conversation of Melopoyn could not divert.—I ordered Strap to inquire every day at Banter's lodgings, in expectation of hearing again from my charmer; and my disappointment considerably augmented my chagrin.—My affectionate valet was infected with my sorrow, and often sat with me whole hours without speaking, uttering sigh for sigh, and shedding tear for tear.—This fellowship increased our distemper; he became incapable of business, and was discarded by his master; while I seeing my money melt away, without any certainty of deliverance, and in short, all my hopes frustrated; grew negligent of life, lost all appetite, and degenerated into such a sloven, that during the space of two months, I was neither washed, shifted nor shaved; so that my face rendered meagre with abstinence, was obscured with dirt, and overshadowed with hair, and my whole appearance squalid and even frightful; when, one day, Strap brought me notice, that there was a man below who wanted to speak with me. Roused at this intelligence, and in full hope of receiving a letter from the dear object of my love, I run down stairs with the utmost precipitation, and found, to my infinite surprize, my generous uncle Mr. Bowling! Transported at the sight, I sprung forward to embrace him. Upon which he started aside with great agility, drew his hanger, and put himself upon his guard, crying, 'Avast, brother, avast! sheer off—Yo ho! you turnkey, why don't you keep a better look out? here's one of your crazy prisoners broke from his lashings, I do suppose.'—I could not help laughing heartily at his mistake, which I soon rectified by my voice, which he instantly recollected, and shook me by the hand with great affection, testifying his concern at seeing me in such a miserable condition.

I conducted him to my apartment, where, in presence of Strap, whom I introduced to him as one of my best friends, he let me know, that he was just arrived from the coast of Guinea,[1] after having made a pretty successful voyage, in which he had acted as mate, until the ship was attacked by a French privateer; that the captain being killed during the engagement, he had taken the command, and was so fortunate as to sink the enemy; after which he fell in with a merchant ship from Martinico,[2] laden with sugar, indigo, and some silver; and by virtue of his letter of marque,[3] attacked, took, and brought her safe into Kinsale[4] in Ireland, where she was condemned as a lawful prize; by which means, he had not only got a pretty sum of money, but also acquired the favour of his owners, who had already conferred upon him the command of a large ship, mounted with twenty nine-pounders, ready to sail upon a very advantageous voyage, which he was not at liberty to discover—And he assured me, that it was with the greatest difficulty he had found me, in consequence of a direction left for him at his lodgings in Wapping.

I was rejoiced beyond measure, at this account of his good fortune; and, at his desire, recounted all the adventures that had happened to me since we parted.—When he understood the particulars of Strap's attachment to me, he squeezed his hand very cordially, and promised to make a man of him; and giving me ten guineas for my present occasion, took a direction for the taylor who arrested me, and went away, in order to discharge the debt, telling me at parting, that he would soon fetch up all my lee-way with a wet sail.[5]

I was utterly confounded at this sudden transition, which affected me more than any reverse I had formerly felt; and a crowd of incoherent ideas rushed so impetuously upon my imagination, that my reason could neither separate nor connect them; when Strap, whose joy had manifested itself in a thousand fooleries, came into my room with his shaving utensils, and without any previous intimation, began to lather my beard, whistling with great emotion all the while. —I started from my reverie, and being too well acquainted with Strap, to trust myself in his hands while he was under such agitation, desired to be excused, sent for another barber, and suffered myself to be trimmed.—Having performed the ceremony of ablution, I shifted, and dressing in my gayest apparel, waited for the return of my uncle, who was agreeably surprized at my sudden transformation.

This beneficent kinsman had satisfied my creditor, and obtained an order for my discharge, so that I was no longer a prisoner; but as I had some reluctance to part with my friends and fellows in distress, I prevailed upon Mr. Bowling to favour us with his company, and invited Mr. Melopoyn and Jackson to spend the evening at my apartment, where I regaled them with a supper, good wine, and the news of my release, on which they heartily congratulated me, notwithstanding the loss of my company, which, they were pleased to say, they would severely feel.—As for Jackson, his misfortune made so little impression on himself, and he was altogether so loose, indifferent and indiscreet, that I could scarce pity his situation: But I had conceived a veneration and friendship for the poet, who was in all respects, an object much more worthy of compassion and regard.—When our guests withdrew, and my uncle had retired, with an intention to visit me next morning, I made up a bundle of some linnen, and other necessaries, and bidding Strap carry them to Mr. Melopoyn's lodging, went thither myself, and pressed it upon his acceptance with five guineas, which with much difficulty he received, assuring me at the same time, that he should never have it in his power to make satisfaction. I then asked if I could serve him any other way, to which he answered, 'You have already done too much,' and unable to contain the emotions of his soul any longer, burst into tears, and wept aloud.—Moved at the spectacle, I left him to his repose, and when my uncle returned in the morning, represented his character in such a favourable light, that the honest seaman was affected with his distress, and determined to follow my example, in presenting him with five pieces more: Upon which, that I might save him some confusion, I advised Mr. Bowling to inclose it in a letter to be delivered by Strap, after we should be gone.

This was accordingly done. I took a formal leave of all my acquaintance in the jail, and just as I was about to step into a hackney-coach at the gate, Jackson calling me, I returned, and he asked me in a whisper, if I could lend him a shilling! His demand being so moderate, and in all likelihood, the last he would make upon me, I slipt a guinea into his hand, which he no sooner perceived, than he cried, 'O Jesus! a guinea!' then laying hold of a button of my coat, he broke out into an immoderate fit of laughter; and when his convulsion was ended, told me, I was an honest fellow, and let me go.——The coachman was ordered to drive to Mr. Bowling's lodgings, where, when we arrived, he entered into a serious discourse with me, on the subject of my situation, and proposed that I should sail with him in quality of his Surgeon; in which case, he would put me on a method of getting a fortune in a few years, by my own industry; and assured me, that I might expect to inherit all that he should die possessed of, provided I should survive him.—Though I was penetrated with a sense of his generosity, I was startled at a proposal that offered violence to my love, and signified my sentiments on that head, which he did not seem to relish; but observed that love was the fruit of idleness, that when once I should be employed in business, and my mind engaged in making money, I would be no more troubled with these silly notions, which none but your fair-weather Jacks, who have nothing but their pleasure to mind, ought to entertain.—I was piqued at this insinuation, which I looked upon as a reproach, and without giving myself time to deliberate, accepted his offer.—He was overjoyed at my compliance, carried me immediately to his chief owner, with whom a bargain was struck, so that I could not retract with honour, should I be never so much disposed thereto.—That I might not have time to cool, he bid me draw out a list of medicines for a compliment of five hundred men, adapted to the distempers of hot climates, and sufficient for a voyage of eighteen months; and carry it to a certain wholesale apothecary, who would also provide me in two well-qualified mates.—While I was thus employed, Strap came in, and looked very blank, when he understood my resolution: However, after a pause of some minutes, he insisted upon going along with me; and at my desire was made ship's steward by captain Bowling, who promised to be at the expence of fitting him out, and to lend him two hundred pounds to purchase an adventure.[1]

When I had delivered my list of medicines, chosen a couple of my own countrymen for mates, and bespoke a set of chirurgical instruments, my uncle told me, that by his last voyage, he had cleared almost three thousand pounds, one thousand of which he would immediately make over and put into my hands; that he would procure for me credit to the value of as much more, in such goods as would turn to best account in the country to which we were bound; and that although he looked upon my interest as his own, he would keep the remaining part of his fortune in his own disposal, with a view of preserving his independance, and the power of punishing me, in case I should not make a good use of what he had already bestowed upon me.

Without troubling the reader with an account of the effect which this surprizing generosity had upon my mind, I shall only say, that his promises were instantly performed, and an invoyce of merchandize proper for the voyage presented to me, that I might purchase the goods, and ship them with all expedition.—In the midst of this hurry the remembrance of my charming Narcissa often interposed, and made me the most miserable of all mortals. I was distracted with the thought of being torn from her, perhaps, for ever; and though the hope of seeing her again, might have supported me under the torments of separation, I could not reflect upon the anguish she must feel at parting with me, and the incessant sorrows to which her tender bosom would be exposed during my absence, without being pierced with the deepest affliction! As my imagination was daily and nightly upon the rack to invent some method of mitigating this cruel stroke, or at least of acquitting my love and honour in the opinion of that gentle creature, I at length stumbled upon an expedient, with which the reader will be made acquainted in due time; and in consequence of my determination, became less uneasy and disturbed.

My business being finished, and the ship ready to sail, I resolved to make my last appearance among my acquaintance at the other end of the town, where I had not been seen since my imprisonment; and as I had, by the advice of my uncle, taken off some very rich cloaths for sale, I put on the gayest suit in my possession, and went in a chair to the coffee-house I used to frequent, where I found my friend Banter so confounded at the magnificence of my dress, that when I made up to him, he gazed at me with a look of astonishment, without being able, for some minutes, to open his lips;—then pulling me aside by the sleeve, and fixing his eyes on mine, accosted me in this manner: 'Random, where the devil have you been! eh?— What is the meaning of all this finery?—Oho! I understand you—

You are just arrived from the country! what! the roads are good, eh!—well, Random, you are a bold fellow, and a lucky fellow!—but take care, the pitcher goes often to the well, but is broke at last.' So saying, he pointed to his collar; by which gesture, and the broken hints he had ejaculated, I found he suspected me of having robbed on the highway; and I laughed very heartily at his supposition.— Without explaining myself any farther, I told him he was mistaken in his conjecture; that I had been for some time past with the relation of whom he had frequently heard me speak; and that being to set out next day upon my travels, I had come thither to take my leave of my friends, and to receive of him the money he had borrowed from me, which, now that I was going abroad, I should have occasion for.—He was a little disconcerted at this demand; but recollecting himself in a moment, swore, in an affected passion, that I had used him extremely ill, and he would never forgive me, for having, by this short warning, put it out of his power to free himself of an obligation he could no longer bear.—I could not help smiling at this pretended delicacy, which I commended highly, telling him, he needed not be uneasy on that score, for I would give him a direction to a merchant in the city, with whom I would leave a discharge for the sum, to be delivered upon payment.—He professed much joy at this expedient, and with great eagerness asked the person's name and place of abode, which he forthwith wrote in his pocket-book, assuring me, that he would not be long in my debt. —This affair, which I knew he would never after think of, being settled to his satisfaction, I sent cards to all my friends, desiring the favour of their company at a tavern in the evening, when they honoured my invitation, and I had the pleasure of treating them in a very elegant manner, at which they expressed as much admiration as applause. Having enjoyed ourselves till midnight, I took my leave of them all, being well-nigh stifled with caresses; and next day I set out with Strap in a post-chaise for Gravesend, where we went on board, and the wind serving, weighed anchor in less than twelve hours.—Without meeting with any accident, we got as far as the Downs, where we were obliged to come to an anchor, and wait for an easterly wind to carry us out of the Channel.

CHAPTER LXV

I set out for Sussex—consult Mrs. Sagely—atchieve an interview with Narcissa—return to the ship—we get clear of the Channel—I learn our destination—we are chaced by a large ship—the company are dismayed, and encouraged by the captain's speech—our pursuer happens to be an English man of war—we arrive on the coast of Guinea, purchase 400 negroes, sail for Paraguay, get safe into the river of Plate, and sell our cargo to great advantage

IT was now I put in execution the scheme I had projected at London; and asking leave of the captain, for Strap and me to stay on shore till the wind should become favourable, my request was granted, because he had orders to remain in the Downs until he should receive some dispatches from London, which he did not expect in less than a week.—Having imparted my resolution to my trusty valet, who (tho' he endeavour'd to dissuade me from such a rash undertaking) would not quit me in the enterprize, I hired horses, and set out immediately for that part of Sussex where my charmer was confined, which was not above thirty miles distant from Deal where we mounted:—As I was perfectly well acquainted with the extent of the Squire's estate and influence, I halted within five miles of his house, where we remained 'till the twilight, at which time we set forward, and, by the favour of a dark night, gained a copse about half a mile from the village where Mrs. Sagely lived.— Here we left our horses tied to a tree, and went directly to the house of my old benefactress, Strap trembling all the way, and venting ejaculatory petitions to heaven for our safety. Her habitation being quite solitary, we arrived at the door without being observed, when I ordered my companion to enter by himself, and in case there should be company with her, deliver a letter which I had wrote for the purpose, and say that a friend of hers in London, understanding that he intended to travel this road, had committed it to his care.— He rapped at the door, to which the good old matron coming, told him, that being a lone woman, he must excuse her, if she did not open it, until he had declared his name and business.—He answered, that his name was unknown to her, and that his business was to deliver a letter, which (to free her from all manner of apprehension) he would convey to her through the space between the door and threshold.—This he instantly performed; and she no sooner read the contents, which specified my being present, than she cried, 'If the person who wrote this letter be at hand, let him speak, that I may be assured by his voice whether or not I may safely admit him.'—I forthwith applied my mouth to the key-hole, and pronounced, 'Dear mother, you need not be afraid, it is I, so much indebted to your goodness, who now crave admittance.'—She knew my voice, and opening the door immediately, received me with a truly maternal affection, manifesting by the tears she let fall, her concern lest I should be discovered, for she had been informed of every thing that had happened between Narcissa and me, from the dear captive's own mouth.—When I explained the motive of my journey, which was no other than a desire of seeing the object of my love before I should quit the kingdom, that I might in person convince her of the necessity I was under to leave her, reconcile her to that event, by describing the advantages that in all probability would attend it, repeat my vows of eternal constancy, and enjoy the melancholy pleasure of a tender embrace at parting——I say, when I had thus signified my intention, Mrs. Sagely told me, that Narcissa, upon her return from the Bath, had been so strictly watched, that no body, but one or two of the servants devoted to her brother, was admitted to her presence; that afterwards she had been a little enlarged, and was permitted to see company; during which indulgence, she had been several times at her cottage: but of late she had been betrayed by one of the servants, who discovered to the squire, that he had once carried a letter from her to the post-house directed to me; upon which information, she was now more confined than ever, and that I could have no chance of seeing her, unless I would run the risque of getting into the garden, where she and her maid were every day allowed to take the air, and lie hid until I should have an opportunity of speaking to them—an adventure which would be attended with such danger, that no man in his right wits would attempt it.—This enterprize, hazardous as it was, I resolved to perform, in spite of all the arguments of Mrs. Sagely, who reasoned, chid, and intreated by turns; and the tears and prayers of Strap, who conjured me on his knees, to have more regard to myself as well as to him, than to tempt my own destruction in such a precipitate manner. But I was deaf to every thing, but the suggestions of my love; and ordering him to return immediately with the horses to the inn from whence we set out, and wait for my coming in that place, he at first peremptorily refused to leave me, until I perswaded him, that if our horses should remain where they were 'till day-light, they would certainly be discovered, and the whole county alarmed. On this consideration, he took his leave in a sorrowful plight, kissed my hand, and weeping, cried, 'God knows if ever I shall see you again.' —My kind landlady finding me obstinate, gave me her best advice how to behave in the execution of my project; and after having perswaded me to take a little refreshment, accommodated me with a bed, and left me to my repose.—Early in the morning, I got up, and armed with a couple of loaded pistols and a hanger, went to the back of the Squire's garden, climbed over the wall, and, according to Mrs. Sagely's direction, concealed myself in a thicket, hard by an alcove which terminated a walk at a good distance from the house, which (I was told) my mistress chiefly frequented.—Here I absconded from five a-clock in the morning to six in the evening, without seeing a human creature; at last I perceived two women approaching, whom by my throbbing heart I soon recogniz'd to be the adorable Narcissa and Miss Williams. I felt the strongest agitation of soul at the sight; and guessing that they would repose themselves in the alcove, I stept into it unperceiv'd, and laid upon the stone-table a picture of myself in miniature, for which I had sat in London, purposing to leave it with Narcissa before I should go abroad. I exposed it in this manner, as an introduction to my own appearance, which, without some previous intimation, I was afraid might have an unlucky effect upon the delicate nerves of my fair enslaver; and then withdrew into the thicket, where I could hear their discourse, and suit myself to the circumstances of the occasion. —As they advanced, I observed an air of melancholy in the countenance of Narcissa, blended with such unspeakable sweetness, that I could scarce refrain from flying into her arms, and kissing away the pearly drop that stood collected in each bewitching eye. According to my expectation, she entered the alcove, and perceiving something on the table, took it up. No sooner did she cast her eye upon the features, than she startled, crying, 'Gracious God!' and the roses instantly vanished from her cheeks.—Her confidante, alarm'd at this exclamation, looked at the picture, and, struck with the resemblance, cried, 'O Jesus! the very features of Mr. Random!' Narcissa having recollected herself a little, said, 'Whatever angel brought it hither as a comfort to me in my affliction, I am thankful for the benefit, and will preserve it as the dearest object of my care.' So saying, she kissed it with surprising ardour, shed a flood of tears, and then deposited the lifeless image in her lovely bosom. Transported at these symptoms of her unaltered affection, I was about to throw myself at her feet, when Miss Williams, whose reflection was less engaged than that of her mistress, observed, that the picture could not transport itself hither, and that she could not help thinking I was not far off.—The gentle Narcissa starting at this conjecture, answered, 'Heaven forbid! for although nothing in the universe could yield me satisfaction equal to that of his presence for one poor moment, in a proper place, I would rather forfeit his company—almost for ever, than see him here, where his life would be exposed to so much danger.'—I could no longer restrain the impulse of my passion, but breaking from my concealment, stood before her, when she uttered a fearful shriek, and fainted in the arms of her companion. I flew towards the treasure of my soul, clasped her in my embrace, and with the warmth of my kisses, brought her again to life. O! that I were endowed with the expression of a Raphael, the graces of a Guido, the magick touches of a Titian,[1] that I might represent the fond concern, the chastened rapture, and ingenuous blush that mingled on her beauteous face, when she opened her eyes upon me, and pronounced, 'O heavens! is it you!'

I am afraid I have already encroached upon the reader's patience, with the particulars of this amour, on which (I own) I cannot help being impertinently circumstantial. I shall therefore omit the less material passages of this interview, during which I convinced her reason, tho' I could not appease the sad presages of her love, with regard to the long voyage, and dangers I must undergo.—When we had spent an hour (which was all she could spare from the barbarity of her brother's vigilance) in lamenting over our hard fate, and in repeating our reciprocal vows, Miss Williams reminded us of the necessity there was for our immediate parting; and sure, lovers never parted with such sorrow and reluctance as we. But because my words are incapable of doing justice to this affecting circumstance, I am obliged to draw a veil over it, and observe, that I returned in the dark to the house of Mrs. Sagely, who was overjoy'd to hear of my success, and opposed the tumults of my grief with such strength of reason, that my mind regained in some measure its tranquility;

and that very night, after having forced upon this good gentle-woman a purse of twenty guineas, as a token of my gratitude and esteem, I took my leave of her, set out on foot for the inn, where my arrival freed honest Strap from the horrors of unutterable dread.

We took horse immediately, and alighted early next morning at Deal, where I found my uncle in great concern on account of my absence, because he had received his dispatches, and must have weighed with the first fair wind, whether I had been on board or not. —Next day, a brisk easterly gale springing up, we set sail, and in eight and forty hours got clear of the Channel.

When we were about 200 leagues from the Land's end, the captain taking me apart into the cabbin, told me, that, now he was permitted by his instructions, he would disclose the intent and destination of our voyage: 'The ship, said he, which has been fitted out at a great expence, is bound for the coast of Guinea, where we shall exchange part of our cargo for slaves and gold dust; from thence we will transport our negroes to Buenos-Ayres in New-Spain, where (by virtue of passports obtained from our own court, and that of Madrid)[1] we will dispose of them and the goods that remain on board for silver, by means of our supercargo, who is perfectly well acquainted with the coast, the lingo and inhabitants.' —Being thus let into the secret of our expedition, I borrowed of the supercargo a Spanish grammar, dictionary, and some other books of the same language, which I studied with such application, that before we arrived in New-Spain, I could maintain a conversation with him in that tongue.—Being arrived in the warm latitudes, I ordered (with the captain's consent) the whole ship's company to be blooded and purged,[2] myself undergoing the same evacuation, in order to prevent those dangerous fevers to which northern constitutions are subject in hot climates; and I have reason to believe that this precaution was not unserviceable, for we lost but one sailor during our whole passage to the coast.

One day, when we had been about five weeks at sea, we descried to windward a large ship bearing down upon us with all the sail she could carry. Upon which, my uncle ordered the studding-sails to be hoisted, and the ship to be cleared for engaging; but finding, that (to use the seamen's phrase) we were very much wronged by the ship[3] which had us in chace, and which by this time had hoisted French colours, he commanded the studding-sails to be taken in, the courses to be clewed up, the main-top-sail to be backed, the tompions to be taken out of the guns,[1] and every man to repair to his quarters. While every body was busied in the performance of these orders, Strap came upon the quarter-deck, trembling, and looking aghast, and, with a voice half suppressed by fear, asked if I thought we were a match for the vessel in pursuit of us. Observing his consternation, I said, 'What! are you afraid, Strap?' 'Afraid! (he replied) n-n-no, what should I be afraid of? I thank God I have a clear conscience;—but I believe it will be a bloody battle, and I wish you may not have occasion for another hand to assist you in the cockpit.'—I immediately perceived his drift, and making the captain acquainted with his situation, desired he might be stationed below with me and my mates. My uncle, incensed at his pusilanimity, bid me send him down instantly, that his fear might not infect the ship's company; whereupon I told the poor steward, that I had begg'd him for an assistant, and desired him to go down and help my mates to get ready the instruments and dressings.—Notwithstanding the satisfaction he must have felt at these tidings, he affected a shyness of quitting the upper deck; and said, he hoped I did not imagine he was afraid to do his duty above board, for he believed himself as well prepared for death as any man in the ship, no disparagement to me or the captain.—I was disgusted at this affectation, and in order to punish his hypocrisy, assured him, he might either go down to the cockpit, or stay upon deck during the engagement. Alarmed at this indifference, he replied, 'Well, to oblige you, I'll go down, but remember it is more for your sake than my own.' So saying, he disappeared in a twinkling, without waiting for an answer.—By this time we could observe two tire of guns in the ship which pursued us, and which was now but two short miles astern. This discovery had an evident effect upon the sailors, who did not scruple to say, that we should be tore to pieces, and blown out of the water, and that if in case any of them should lose their precious limbs, they must go a-begging for life, for there was no provision made by the merchants for those poor souls who are maimed in their service. The captain understanding this backwardness, ordered the crew abaft, and spoke to them thus; 'My lads, I am told you hang an a—se.—I have gone to sea thirty years, man and boy, and never saw English sailors afraid before.—Mayhap you think I want to expose you for the lucre of gain.—Whosoever thinks so, thinks a damned lie, for my whole cargo is insured; so that in case I should be taken, my loss will not be great.—The enemy is stronger than we to be sure.—What then? have we not a chance for carrying away one of her masts, and so get clear of her?—If we find her too hard for us, 'tis but striking at last.—If any man is hurt in the engagement, I promise on the word of an honest seaman, to make them a recompence according to his loss.—So now, you that are lazy, lubberly, cowardly dogs, get away, and sculk in the hold, and bread-room; and you that are jolly boys, stand by me, and let us give one broad-side for the honour of old England.' This eloquent harangue was so well adapted to the disposition of his hearers, that one and all of them, pulling off their hats, waved them over their heads, and saluted him with three chears; upon which he sent his boy for two large case-bottles of brandy, and having treated every man with a dram, they repaired to their quarters, and waited impatiently for the word of command.—I must do my uncle the justice to say, that in the whole of his disposition, he behaved with the utmost intrepidity, conduct and deliberation.—The enemy being very near, he ordered me to my station, and was just going to give the word for hoisting the colours, and firing, when the supposed Frenchman, hauled down his white pennant jack and ensign, hoisted English ones, and fired a gun a-head of us: This was a joyful event to captain Bowling, who immediately shewed his colours, and fired a gun to leeward: Upon which the other ship run alongside of him, hailed him, and giving him to know that she was an English man of war of forty guns, ordered him to hoist out his boat and come on board.—This he performed with the more alacrity, because upon enquiry, he found that she was commanded by an old mess-mate of his, who was over-joyed to see him, detained him to dinner, and sent his barge for the supercargo and me, who were very much caressed on his account.— As this commander was destined to cruise upon the French, in the latitude of Martinico, his stem and quarters were adorned with white flowers de lis, and the whole shell of the ship so much disguised, for a decoy to the enemy, that it was no wonder my uncle did not know her, although he had sailed on board of her many years.—We kept company with her four days, during which time the captains were never asunder, and then parted, our course lying different from hers.

In less than a fortnight after, we made the land of Guinea, near the mouth of the river Gambia, and trading along the coast as far to the southward of the Line as Angola and Bengula,[1] in less than six months disposed of the greatest part of our cargo, and purchased four hundred negroes, my adventure having been laid out chiefly in gold dust.

Our compliment being made up, we took our departure from Cape Negro,[1] and arrived in the Rio de la Plata in six weeks, having met with nothing remarkable in our voyage, except an epidemic fever, not unlike the jail distemper,[2] which broke out among our slaves, and carried off a good many of the ship's company; among whom I lost one of my mates, and poor Strap had well nigh given up the ghost.—Having produced our passport to the Spanish governor, we were received with great courtesy, sold our slaves in a very few days, and could have put off five times the number at our own price; being obliged to smuggle the rest of our merchandize, consisting of European bale goods, which however we made shift to dispose of at a great advantage.

CHAPTER LXVI

I am invited to the Villa of a Spanish Don, where we meet with an English gentleman, and make a very interesting discovery——we leave Buenos Ayres, and arrive at Jamaica

Our ship being freed from the disagreeable lading of Negroes, to whom indeed I had been a miserable slave, since our leaving the coast of Guinea, I began to enjoy myself, and breathe with pleasure the pure air of Paraguay, this part of which is reckoned the Montpelier of South America, and has obtained, on account of its climate, the name of Buenos Ayres.—It was in this delicious place, that I gave myself entirely up to the thoughts of my dear Narcissa, whose image still kept full possession of my breast, and whose charms, enhanced by absence, appeared to my imagination, if possible, more engaging than ever! I calculated the profits of my voyage, which even exceeded my expectation; resolved to purchase a handsome sine-cure upon my arrival in England, and if I should find the Squire as averse to me as ever, marry his sister by stealth; and in case our family should encrease, rely upon the generosity of my uncle, who was by this time worth a considerable sum.

While I amused myself with these agreeable projects, and the transporting hopes of enjoying Narcissa, we were very much caressed by the Spanish gentlemen, who frequently formed parties of pleasure for our entertainment, in which we made excursions a good way into the country. Among those who signalized themselves by their civility to us, there was one Don Antonio de Ribera, a very polite young gentleman, with whom I had contracted an intimate friendship, who invited us one day to his country-house, and as a further inducement to our compliance, promised to procure for us the company of an English signor, who had been settled in these parts many years, and acquired the love and esteem of the whole province by his affability, good sense, and honourable behaviour.

We accepted his invitation, and set out for his Villa, where we had not been longer than an hour, when the person arrived, in whose favour I had been so much prepossessed.—He was a tall man, remarkably well shaped, of a fine mein and appearance commanding respect, and seemed to be turned of forty; the features of his face were saddened with a reserve and gravity, which in other countries would have been thought the effect of melancholy; but here, appeared to have been contracted by his commerce with the Spaniards, who are remarkable for that severity of countenance: Understanding from Don Antonio, that we were his countrymen, he saluted us all round very complaisantly, and fixing his eyes attentively on me, uttered a deep sigh.——I had been struck with a profound veneration for him at his first coming into the room; and no sooner observed this expression of his sorrow, directed, as it were, in a particular manner to me, than my heart took part in his grief, I sympathized involuntarily, and sighed in my turn.— Having asked leave of our entertainer, he accosted us in English, professed his satisfaction at seeing so many of his countrymen in such a remote place, and asked the captain, who went by the name of Signor Thoma, from what part of Britain he sailed, and whither he was bound.—My uncle told him that we had sailed from the river Thames, and were bound for the same place, by the way of Jamaica, where we intended to take in a lading of sugar.

Having satisfied himself in these and other particulars about the state of the war, he gave us to understand, that he had a longing desire to revisit his native country, in consequence of which, he had already transmitted to Europe the greatest part of his fortune in neutral bottoms, and would willingly embark the rest of it, with himself, in our ship, provided the captain had no objection to such a passenger.—My uncle very prudently replied, that for his part, he should be glad of his company, if he could procure the consent of the governor, without which he durst not admit him on board, whatever inclination he had to oblige him.—The gentleman approved of his discretion, and telling him, that there would be no difficulty in obtaining the connivance of the governor, who was his good friend, shifted the conversation to another subject.

I was overjoyed to hear his intention, and already interested myself so much in his favour, that had he been disappointed, I should have been very unhappy: In the course of our entertainment, he eyed me with uncommon attachment; I felt a surprizing attraction towards him; when he spoke, I listened with attention and reverence; the dignity of his deportment filled me with affection and awe; and in short, the emotions of my soul, in presence of this stranger, were strong and unaccountable.

Having spent the best part of the day with us, he took his leave, telling captain Thoma, that he would hear from him in a short time: He was no sooner gone, than I asked a thousand questions about him, of Don Antonio, who could give me no other satisfaction, than that his name was Don Rodriguez, that he had lived fifteen or sixteen years in these parts, was reputed rich, and supposed to have been unfortunate in his younger years, because he was observed to nourish a pensive melancholy, even from the time of his first settlement among them; but that no body had ventured to enquire into the cause of his sorrow, in consideration of his peace, which might suffer in the recapitulation of his misfortunes.

I was seized with an irresistible desire of knowing the particulars of his fate, and enjoyed not one hour of repose during the whole night, by reason of the eager conceptions that inspired me, with regard to his story, which I resolved (if possible) to learn.—Next morning, while we were at breakfast, three mules richly caparisoned arrived, with a message from Don Rodriguez, desiring our company, and that of Don Antonio, at his house, which was situated about ten miles further up in the country.—I was pleased with this invitation, in consequence of which we mounted the mules which he had provided for us, and alighted at his house before noon.—Here we were splendidly entertained by the generous stranger, who still seemed to shew a particular regard for me, and after dinner, made me a present of a ring set with a beautiful amethyst, the production of that country, saying at the same time, that he was once blessed with a son, who, had he lived, would have been nearly of my age. This observation, delivered with a profound sigh, made my heart throb with violence; a crowd of confused ideas rushed upon my imagination, which, while I endeavoured to unravel, my uncle perceived my absence of thought, and tapping me on the shoulder, said, 'Oons! are you asleep, Rory!' Before I had time to reply, Don Rodriguez, with an uncommon eagerness of voice and look, pronounced, 'Pray, captain, what is the young gentleman's name?'—'His name (said my uncle) is Roderick Random.'—'Gracious Powers!' (cried the stranger, starting up)—'And his mother's'—'His mother (answered the captain, amazed) was called Charlotte Bowling.'——'O bounteous heaven! (exclaimed Don Rodriguez, springing across the table, and clasping me in his arms) my son! my son! have I found thee again? do I hold thee in my embrace, after having lost and despaired of seeing thee, so long?' So saying, he fell upon my neck and wept aloud with joy; while the power of nature operating strongly in my breast, I was lost in rapture, and while he pressed me to his heart, let fall a shower of tears into his bosom.—His utterance was choaked up a good while, by the agitation of his soul; at length he broke out into 'Mysterious Providence!—O my dear Charlotte! there yet remains a pledge of our love! and such a pledge!—so found! —O infinite goodness! let me adore thy all-wise decrees!' Having thus expressed himself, he kneeled upon the floor, lifted up his eyes and hands to heaven, and remained some minutes in a silent exstacy of devotion: I put myself in the same posture, adored the all good Disposer in a prayer of mental thanksgiving; and when his ejaculation was ended, did homage to my father, and craved his parental blessing. He hugged me again with unutterable fondness, and having implored the protection of heaven upon my head, raised me from the ground, and presented me as his son to the company, who wept in concert over this affecting scene.—Among the rest my uncle did not fail of discovering the goodness and joy of his heart, *albeit unused to the melting mood*;[1] he blubbered with great tenderness, and wringing my father's hand, cry'd, 'Brother Random, I'm rejoiced to see you— God be praised for this happy meeting.'—Don Rodriguez, understanding that he was his brother-in-law, embraced him affectionately, saying, 'Are you my Charlotte's brother?—alas! unhappy Charlotte! —but why should I repine? we shall meet again, never more to part!—Brother, you are truly welcome—Dear son, I am transported with unspeakable joy!—This day is a jubilee—my friends and servants shall share my satisfaction.'

While he dispatched messengers to the gentlemen in the neighbourhood, to announce this event, and gave orders for a grand entertainment, I was so much affected with the tumults of passion, which assailed me on this great, sudden, and unexpected occasion, that I fell sick, fevered, and in less than three hours, became quite delirious; so that the preparations were countermanded, and the joy of the family converted into grief and despair.—Physicians were instantly called, I was plentifully blooded in the foot, my lower extremities were bathed in a decoction of salutiferous[1] herbs; in ten hours after I was taken ill, I enjoyed a critical sweat, and next day, felt no remains of the distemper, but an agreeable lassitude, which did not hinder me from getting up.—During the progress of this fever, which, from the term of its duration, is called *Ephemera*, my father never once quitted my bed-side, but administred the prescriptions of the physicians with the most pious care; while Captain Bowling manifested his concern by the like attendance.— I no sooner found myself delivered from the disease, than I bethought myself of my honest friend Strap; and resolving to make him happy forthwith, in the knowledge of my good fortune, told my father, in general, that I had been infinitely obliged to this faithful adherent; and begged he would indulge me so far as to send for him, without letting him know my happiness, until he could receive an account of it from my own mouth.

My request was instantly complied with, and a messenger with a spare mule detached to the ship, carrying orders from the captain to the mate to send the steward by the bearer.—My health being, in the mean time, re-established, and my mind composed, I began to relish this important turn of my fortune, in reflecting upon the advantages with which it must be attended; and as the idea of my lovely Narcissa always joined itself to every scene of happiness I could imagine, I entertained myself now, with the prospect of possessing her in that distinguished sphere, to which she was intitled by her birth and qualifications.—Having often mentioned her name while I was deprived of my senses, my father guessed that there was an intimate connexion between us, and discovering the picture which hung in my bosom by a ribbon, did not doubt that it was the resemblance of my amiable mistress: In this belief he was confirmed by my uncle, who told him that it was the picture of a young woman to whom I was under promise of marriage.— Alarmed at this piece of information, Don Rodriguez took the first opportunity of questioning me about the circumstances of this affair, which when I had candidly recounted, he approved of my passion, and promised to contribute all in his power towards its success: though I never doubted his generosity, I was transported on this occasion, and throwing myself at his feet, told him, he had now compleated my happiness; for without the possession of Narcissa, I should be miserable among all the pleasures of life.—He raised me with a smile of paternal fondness; said, he knew what it was to be in love; and observed, that if he had been as tenderly beloved by his father, as I was by mine, he would not now, perhaps, have cause——Here he was interrupted by a sigh, the tear stood collected in his eye, he suppressed the dictates of his grief, and the time being opportune, desired me to relate the passages of my life, which my uncle had told him were manifold and surprizing.—I recounted the most material circumstances of my fortune, to which he listened with wonder and attention, manifesting from time to time those different emotions, which my different situations may be supposed to have raised in a parent's breast; and when my detail was ended, blessed God for the adversity I had undergone, which, he said, enlarged the understanding, improved the heart, steeled the constitution, and qualified a young man for all the duties and enjoyments of life, much better than any education which affluence could bestow.

When I had thus satisfied his curiosity, I discovered an inclination to hear the particulars of his story, which he gratified, by beginning with his marriage, and proceeding to the day of his disappearing, as I have related in the first part of my memoirs, 'Careless of life (continued he) and unable to live in a place where every object recalled the memory of my dear Charlotte, whom I had lost through the barbarity of an unnatural parent, I took my leave of you, my child, then an infant, with an heart full of unutterable woe, but little suspecting that my father's unkindness would have descended to my innocent orphan; and setting out alone, at midnight, for the nearest sea-port, early next morning got on board a ship, bound, as I had heard, for France, and bargaining with the master for my passage, bid a long adieu to my native country, and put to sea with the first fair wind. The place of our destination was Granville,[1] but we had the misfortune to run upon a ridge of rocks near the island of Alderney called the Gaskets,[2] where the sea running high, the ship went to pieces, the boat sunk along-side, and every soul on board perished, except myself, who by the assistance of a grating, got ashore on the coast of Normandy: I went directly to Caen,[1] where I was so lucky as to meet with a Count, whom I had formerly known in my travels: With this gentleman, I set out for Paris, where I was recommended by him and other friends, as a tutor to a young nobleman, whom I accompanied to the court of Spain.— There we remained a whole year, at the end of which my pupil being recalled by his father, I quitted my office and staid behind, by the advice of a certain Spanish grandee who took me into his protection, and introduced me to another nobleman, who was afterwards created Viceroy of Peru.—He insisted on my attending him to his government in the Indies, where, however, by reason of my religion, it was not in his power to make my fortune any other way than by encouraging me to trade, which I had not long prosecuted when my patron died, and I found myself in the midst of strangers, without one friend to support or protect me; urged by this consideration, I sold my effects and removed to this country, the governour of which having been appointed by the Vice-roy, was my intimate acquaintance.—Here has heaven prospered my endeavours, during a residence of sixteen years, in which my tranquillity was never invaded, but by the remembrance of your mother, whose death I have in secret mourned without ceasing; and the reflection of you, whose fate I could never learn, notwithstanding all my inquiries, by means of my friends in France, who, after the most strict examination, could give me no other account, than that you went abroad six years ago, and was never after heard of.—I could not rest satisfied with this imperfect information, and though my hope of finding you was but languid, resolved to go in quest of you in person; for which purpose, I have remitted to Holland the value of twenty thousand pound, and am in possession of fifteen thousand more, with which I intended to embark myself on board of captain Bowling, before I discovered this amazing stroke of providence, which you my be sure has not altered my intention.

My father having entertained us with this agreeable sketch of his life, withdrew in order to relieve Don Antonio, who in his absence, had done the honours of his house; and I was just dressed for my appearance among the guests, when Strap arrived from the ship.

He no sooner entered the grand apartment, in which I was, and saw the magnificence of my apparel, than his speech was lost in amazement, and he gaped in silence at the objects that surrounded

416

him.—I took him by the hand, observed that I had sent for him to be a witness and sharer of my happiness, and told him I had found a father.—At these words he started, and after having continued some minutes with his mouth and eyes wide open, cried, 'Aha!—odd, I know what! go thy ways, poor Narcissa, and go thy ways somebody else—well—Lord, what a thing is love?—God help us! are all our mad pranks and protestations come to this? what! and you have fixed your habitation in this distant land! God prosper you —I find we must part at last—for I would not leave my poor carcass so far from my native home, for all the wealth of the universe!' With these ejaculations, he began to sob and make wry faces; upon which I assured him of his mistake, both in regard to Narcissa, and my staying in Paraguay, and informed him as briefly as I could, of the great event which had happened.—Never was rapture more ludicrously expressed, than in the behaviour of this worthy creature, who cried, laughed, whistled, sung and danced, all in a breath; his transport was scarce over, when my father entered, who no sooner understood that this was Strap, than he took him by the hand, saying, 'Is this the honest man, who befriended you so much in your distress? you are welcome to my house, and I shall soon put it in the power of my son to reward you for your good offices in his behalf; in the mean time, go with us and partake of the repast that is provided.' Strap, wild as he was with joy, would by no means accept of the profered honour, crying, 'God forbid! I know my distance—your worship shall excuse me.' And Don Rodriguez finding his modesty invincible, recommended him to his Major Domo, to be treated with the utmost respect; while he carried me into a large saloon, where I was presented to a numerous company, who loaded me with compliments and caresses, and congratulated my father in terms not proper for me to repeat.

Without specifying the particulars of our entertainment, let it suffice to say, it was at the same time elegant and sumptuous, and the rejoicing lasted two days: After which, Don Rodriguez settled his affairs, converted his effects into silver and gold, visited and took leave of all his friends, who were grieved at his departure, and honoured me with considerable presents; and coming on board of my uncle's ship, with the first favourable wind we sailed from the Rio de la Plata, and in two months came safe to an anchor in the harbour of Kingston in the island of Jamaica.

CHAPTER LXVII

*I visit my old friend Thomson——we set sail for Europe,
meet with an odd adventure—arrive in England——I ride
across the country from Portsmouth to Sussex——converse
with Mrs. Sagely, who informs me of Narcissa's being in
London—in consequence of this intelligence, I proceed to
Canterbury—meet with my old friend Morgan——arrive at
London—visit Narcissa——introduce my father to her—he is
charmed with her good sense and beauty——we come to a
determination of demanding her brother's consent to our
marriage*

I ENQUIRED, as soon as I got ashore, about my generous companion
Mr. Thomson; and hearing that he lived in a flourishing condition,
upon the estate left to him by his wife's father, who had been dead
some years, I took horse immediately, with the consent of Don
Rodriguez, who had heard me mention him with great regard, and
in a few hours reached the place of his habitation.

I should much wrong the delicacy of Mr. Thomson's sentiments,
to say barely he was glad to see me: He felt all that the most sensible
and disinterested friendship could feel on this occasion, introduced
me to his wife, a very amiable young lady, who had already blessed
him with two fine children; and being as yet ignorant of my circumstances, frankly offered me the assistance of his purse and interest.
I thanked him for his generous intention, and made him acquainted
with my situation, on which he congratulated me with great joy,
and after I had staid with him a whole day and night, accompanied
me back to Kingston to wait upon my father, whom he invited to
his house: Don Rodriguez complied with his request, and having
been handsomely entertained during the space of a week, returned
extremely well satisfied with the behaviour of my friend and his
lady, to whom at parting, he presented a valuable diamond ring, as
a token of his esteem. During the course of my conversation with
Mr. Thomson, he let me know, that his and my old commander
captain Oakhum was dead some months, and that immediately after
his death, a discovery had been made of some valuable effects that
he had feloniously secreted out of a prize, by the assistance of Dr.

Mackshane, who was now actually in prison on that account, and being destitute of friends, subsisted solely on the charity of my friend, whose bounty he had implored in the most abject manner, after having been the barbarous occasion of driving him to that terrible extremity on board of the Thunder, which we have formerly related.—Whatsoever this wretch might have been guilty of, I applauded Mr. Thomson's generosity towards him in his distress, which wrought so much upon me also, that I sent him ten pistoles, in such a private manner, that he could never know his benefactor.

While my father and I were caressed among the gentlemen on shore, captain Bowling had wrote to his owners, by the packet, which sailed a few days after our arrival, signifying his prosperous voyage hitherto, and desiring them to ensure his ship and cargo homeward bound; after which he applied himself so heartily to the loading his ship, that with the assistance of Mr. Thomson, she was full in less than six weeks. This kind gentleman likewise procured for Don Rodriguez, bills upon London for the greatest part of his gold and silver, by which means it was secured against the risk of the seas and the enemy; and before we sailed, supplied us with such large quantities of all kinds of stock, that not only we, but the whole ships company, fared sumptuously during the voyage.

Every thing being ready, we took our leave of our kind entertainers, and going on board at Port Royal, set sail for England on the first day of June.—We beat up to windward, with fine easy weather; and one night, believing ourselves near Cape Tiberoon, lay to, with an intention to wood and water next morning in the bay: While we remained in this situation, a sailor having drank more new rum than he could carry, staggered over-board, and notwithstanding all the means that could be used to preserve him, went to the bottom and disappeared. About two hours after this melancholy accident happened, as I enjoyed a cool air on the quarter-deck, I heard a voice rising, as it were, out of the sea, and calling, 'Ho, the ship, a hoy!' Upon which one of the men upon the forecastle cried, 'I'll be d—n'd, if that an't Jack Marlinspike, who went over-board!' Not a little surprized at this event, I jumped into the boat that lay along-side, with the second mate and four men, and rowing towards the place, from whence the voice (which repeated the hail) seemed to proceed, we perceived something floating upon the water; when we had rowed a little farther, we discerned it to be a man riding upon a hencoop, who seeing us approach, pronounced with a hoarse voice,

'D—n your bloods! why did you not answer when I hailed?' Our mate, who was a veritable seaman, hearing this salute, said, 'By G—d, my lads, this is none of our man—This is the devil—pull away for the ship.' The fellows obeyed his command, without question, and were already some fathoms on our return, when I insisted on their taking up the poor creature, and prevailed upon them to go back to the wreck, which when we came near the second time, and signified our intention, we received an answer of, 'Avast, avast—what ship, brother?' Being satisfied in this particular, he cried, 'D—n the ship, I was in hopes it had been my own—where are you bound?' We gratified his curiosity in this too; upon which he suffered himself to be taken on board, and after being comforted with a dram, told us, he belonged to the Vesuvio man of war, upon a cruize off the island of Hispaniola; that he had fallen over-board about four and twenty hours ago, and the ship being under sail, they did not chuse to bring to, but tossed a hen-coop over-board for his convenience, upon which he was in good hopes of reaching the Cape next morning; howsomever, he was as well content to be aboard us, because he did not doubt that we should meet his ship; and if he had gone ashore in the bay, he might have been taken prisoner by the French.—My uncle and father were very much diverted with the account of this fellow's unconcerned behaviour; and in two days, meeting with the Vesuvio, as he expected, sent him on board of her according to his desire.

Having beat up successfully the windward passage, we stretched to the northward, and falling in with a westerly wind, in eight weeks arrived in soundings, and in two days after made the Lizzard.—It is impossible to express the joy I felt at sight of English ground! Don Rodriguez was not unmoved, and Strap shed tears of gladness. —The sailors profited by our satisfaction; the shoe that was nailed to the mast, being quite filled with our liberality.—My uncle resolved to run up into the Downs at once, but the wind shifting when we were a-breast of the isle of Wight, he was obliged to turn in to St. Helens, and come to an anchor at Spithead, to the great mortification of the crew, thirty of whom were immediately pressed on board of a man of war.[1]

My father and I went a shore immediately to Portsmouth, leaving Strap with the captain to go round with the ship and take care of our effects; and I discovered so much impatience to see my charming Narcissa, that my father permitted me to ride across the country to her brother's house; while he should hire a post-chaise for London, where he would wait for me at a place to which I directed him.

Fired with all the eagerness of passion, I took post that very night, and in the morning reached an inn, about three miles from the Squire's habitation; here I remained till next evening, allaying the torture of my impatience with the rapturous hope of seeing that divine creature, after an absence of eighteen months, which so far from impairing, had raised my love to the most exalted pitch! Neither were my reflections free from apprehension, that sometimes intervened in spite of all my hope, and represented her as having yielded to the importunity of her brother, and blessed the arms of an unhappy rival.——My thoughts were even maddened with the fear of her death; and when I arrived in the dark at the house of Mrs. Sagely, I had not for some time courage to desire admittance, lest my soul should be shocked with dismal tidings. At length, however, I knocked, and no sooner certified the good gentlewoman of my voice than she opened the door, and received me with a most affectionate embrace, that brought tears into her aged eyes: 'For heaven's sake! dear mother (cried I) tell me, how is Narcissa? is she the same that I left her?' She blessed my ears with saying, 'She is as beautiful, in as good health, and as much yours as ever.'—Transported at this assurance, I begged to know if I could not see her that very night; when this sage matron gave me to understand that my mistress was in London, and that things were strangely altered in the Squire's house since my departure; that he had been married a whole year to Melinda, who at first found means to wean his attention so much from Narcissa, that he became quite careless of that lovely sister, comforting himself with the clause in his father's will, by which she would forfeit her fortune, if she should marry without his consent;—that my mistress being but indifferently treated by her sister-in-law, had made use of her freedom some months ago, and gone to town, where she was lodged with Miss Williams, in expectation of my arrival; and had been pestered with the addresses of Lord Quiverwit, who finding her heart engaged, had fallen upon a great many shifts, to perswade her that I was dead: but finding all his artifices unsuccessful, and despairing of gaining her affection, he had consoled himself for her indifference, by marrying another lady some weeks ago, who had already left him on account of some family uneasiness.—Besides this interesting information, she told me, that there was not a great deal of harmony between

Melinda and the Squire, who was so much disgusted at the number of gallants who continued to hover about her even after marriage, that he hurried her down into the country much against her inclination, where their mutual animosities had risen to such a height, that they preserved no decency before company or servants, but abused one another in the grossest terms.

This good old gentlewoman, to give me a convincing proof of my dear Narcissa's unalterable love, gratified me with a sight of the last letter she had favoured her with, in which I was mentioned with so much honour, tenderness and concern, that my soul was fired with impatience, and I determined to ride all night, that I might have it the sooner in my power to make her happy.—Mrs. Sagely perceiving my eagerness, and her maternal affection being equally divided between Narcissa and me, begged leave to remind me of the sentiments with which I went abroad, that would not permit me for any selfish gratification to prejudice the fortune of that amiable young lady, who must entirely depend upon me, after having bestowed herself in marriage. I thanked her for her kind concern, and as briefly as possible described my flourishing situation, which afforded this humane person infinite wonder and satisfaction. I told her, that now I had an opportunity to manifest my gratitude for the obligations I owed, I would endeavour to make her old age comfortable and easy; as a step to which, I proposed she should come and live with Narcissa and me.—This venerable gentlewoman was so much affected with my words, that the tears run down her ancient cheeks; she thanked heaven that I had not belied the presages she had made, on her first acquaintance with me; acknowledging my generosity, as she called it, in the most elegant and pathetick expressions; but declined my proposal, on account of her attachment to the dear melancholy cottage where she had so peacefully consumed her solitary widowhood. Finding her immoveable on this subject, I insisted on her accepting a present of thirty guineas, and took my leave, resolving to accommodate her with the same sum annually, for the more comfortable support of the infirmities of age.

Having rode all night, I found myself at Canterbury in the morning, where I alighted to procure fresh horses; and as I walked into the inn, perceived an apothecary's shop on the other side of the street, with the name of Morgan over the door: Alarm'd at this discovery, I could not help thinking that my old mess-mate had settled in this place; and upon enquiry, found my conjecture true, and that he was married lately to a widow of that city, by whom he had got three thousand pounds. Rejoiced at this intelligence, I went to his shop as soon as it was open, and found my friend behind the counter, busy in preparing a glyster. I saluted him at entrance, with 'Your servant, Mr. Morgan.'—Upon which he looked at me, and replying, 'Your most humble servant, goot Sir;' rubbed his ingredients in the mortar, without any emotion. 'What! (said I) Morgan, have you forgot your old mess-mate?' At these words, he looked up again, and starting, cried, 'As Got is my—sure it cannot—yes by my salfation, I pelieve it is my tear frient Mr. Rantom.'— He was no sooner convinced of my identity, than he threw down the pestle, overset the mortar, and jumping over the board, swept up the contents with his cloaths, flew about my neck, hugged me affectionately, and daubed me all over with turpentine and the yolks of eggs, which he had been mixing when I came in.—Our mutual congratulations being over, he told me, that he found himself a widower upon his return from the West Indies; that he had got interest to be appointed surgeon of a man of war, in which capacity he had served some years, until he married an apothecary's widow, with whom he now enjoyed a pretty good sum of money, peace and quiet, and an indifferent good trade.—He was very desirous of hearing my adventures, which I assured him I had not time to relate, but told him in general, my circumstances were very good, and that I hoped to see him when I should not be in such a hurry as at present.—He insisted however on my staying breakfast, and introduced me to his wife, who seemed to be a decent sensible woman, pretty well stricken in years. In the course of our conversation, he shewed the sleeve-buttons I had exchanged with him at our parting in the West Indies, and was not a little proud to see that I had preserved his with the same care. When I informed him of Mackshane's condition, he seem'd at first to exult over his distress; but after a little recollection, he said, 'Well, he has paid for his malice, I forgife him, and may Got forgife him likewise.' He expressed great concern for the soul of captain Oakhum, which he believed was now gnashing its teeth: but it was some time before I could convince him of Thomson's being alive, at whose good fortune nevertheless he was extremely glad.

Having renewed our protestations of friendship, I bid the honest Welchman and his spouse farewell, and taking post horses, arrived at London that same night, where I found my father in good health, to whom I imparted what I had learned of Narcissa.—This indulgent parent approved of my intention of marrying her, even without a fortune, provided her brother's consent could not be obtained; promised to make over to me in a few days a sufficiency to maintain her in a fashionable manner, and expressed a desire of seeing this amiable creature, who had captivated me so much.—As I had not slept the night before, and was besides fatigued with my journey, I found myself under a necessity of taking some repose, and went to bed accordingly: next morning about ten a-clock, I took a chair, and, according to Mrs. Sagely's directions, went to my charmer's lodgings, and enquired for Miss Williams.—I had not waited in a parlour longer than a minute, when this young woman entered, and no sooner perceived me, than she shrieked and run backward; I got between her and the door, and clasping her in my arms, brought her to herself by an embrace. 'Good heaven (cried she) Mr. Random is it you indeed! my mistress will run distracted with joy.'—I told her, it was from an apprehension that my sudden appearance would have some bad effect on my dear Narcissa, that I had desired to see her first, in order to concert some method of acquainting her mistress gradually with my arrival. She approved of my conduct, and after having yielded to the suggestions of her own friendship, in asking if my voyage had been successful, charged herself with that office, and left me glowing with desire of seeing and embracing the object of my love. In a very little time I heard some body coming down stairs in haste, and the voice of my angel pronounce, with an eager tone, 'O heaven! is it possible! where is he?' How were my faculties arroused at this well-known sound! and how was my soul transported, when she broke in upon my view, in all the bloom of ripened beauty! *Grace was in all her steps, heaven in her eye, in every gesture dignity and love!*[1]—You whose souls are susceptible of the most delicate impressions, whose tender bosoms have felt the affecting vicissitudes of love, who have suffered an absence of eighteen long months from the dear object of your hope, and found at your return the melting fair, as kind and constant as your heart could wish; do me justice on this occasion, and conceive what unutterable rapture possessed us both, while we flew into one anothers arms! This was no time for speech,—locked in a mutual embrace, we continued some minutes in a silent trance of joy!—When I thus encircled all that my soul held dear,—while I hung over her beauties,—beheld her eyes sparkle, and every feature flush with virtuous fondness; when I saw her enchanting bosom heave with undissembled rapture, and knew myself the happy cause—Heavens! what was my situation!—I am tempted to commit my paper to the flames, and to renounce my pen for ever, because its most ardent and lucky expression so poorly describes the emotions of my soul. O adorable Narcissa! (cried I) O miracle of beauty, love and truth! I at last fold thee in my arms! I at last can call thee mine! no jealous brother shall thwart our happiness again; fortune hath at length recompenced me for all my sufferings, and enabled me to do justice to my love.—The dear creature smiled ineffably charming, and with a look of bewitching tenderness, said, 'And shall we never part again?' 'Never! (I replied) thou wonderous pattern of all earthly perfection! never, until death shall divide us! by this ambrosial kiss, a thousand times more fragrant than the breeze that sweeps the orange grove, I never more will leave thee!'

As my first transport abated, my passion grew turbulent and unruly. I was giddy with standing on the brink of bliss, and all my virtue and philosophy were scarce sufficient to restrain the inordinate sallies of desire.—Narcissa perceived the conflict within me, and with her usual dignity of prudence, called off my imagination from the object in view, and with eager expressions of interested curiosity, desired to know the particulars of my voyage.—In this I gratified her inclination, bringing my story down to the present hour. She was infinitely surprized at the circumstances of my finding my father, which brought tears into her lovely eyes. She was transported at hearing that he approved my flame, discovered a longing desire of being introduced to him, congratulated herself and me upon my good fortune, and observed that this great and unexpected stroke of fate seemed to have been brought about by the immediate direction of providence.—Having entertained ourselves some hours with the genuine effusions of our souls, I obtained her consent to compleat my happiness as soon as my father should judge it proper; and applying with my own hands a valuable necklace, composed of diamonds and amethysts set alternately, which an old Spanish lady at Paraguay presented me with, I took my leave, promising to return in the afternoon with Don Rodriguez. —When I went home, this generous parent enquired very affectionately about the health of my dear Narcissa, to whom that I might be the more agreeable, he put into my hand a deed, by which I found myself in possession of fifteen thousand pounds, exclusive of the profits of my own merchandize, which amounted to three thousand more.—After dinner I accompanied him to the lodging of my mistress, who being dressed for the occasion, made a most dazzling appearance. I could perceive him struck with her figure, which I really think was the most beautiful that ever was created under the sun. He embraced her tenderly, and told her, he was proud of having a son who had spirit to attempt, and qualifications to engage, the affections of such a fine lady.—She blushed at this compliment, and with eyes full of the softest languishment turned upon me, said, she would have been unworthy of Mr. Random's attention, had she been blind to his extraordinary merit.—I made no other answer than a low bow. My father sighing, pronounced, 'Such once was my Charlotte!' while the tear rushed into his eye, and the tender heart of Narcissa manifested itself in two precious drops of sympathy, which, but for his presence, I would have kissed away. Without repeating the particulars of our conversation, I shall only observe, that Don Rodriguez was as much charmed with her good-sense as with her appearance; and she was no less pleased with his understanding and polite address.—It was determined that he should write to the Squire signifying his approbation of my passion for his sister, and offering a settlement which he should have no reason to reject; and that, if he should refuse the proposal, we would crown our mutual wishes without any farther regard to his will.

CHAPTER LXVIII

My father makes a present to Narcissa—the letter is dispatched to her brother—I appear among my acquaintance —Banter's behaviour—the Squire refuses his consent—my uncle comes to town——approves of my choice—I am married ——we meet the Squire and his lady at the play—our acquaintance is courted

AFTER having spent the evening to the satisfaction of all present, my father addressed himself thus to Narcissa, 'Madam, give me leave to consider you hereafter as my daughter, in which capacity I insist upon your accepting this first instance of my paternal duty

and affection.' With these words, he put into her hand a bank-note
for 500 *l.* which she no sooner examined, than with a low curtesy she
replied, 'Dear Sir, tho' I have not the least occasion for this supply,
I have too great a veneration for you, to refuse this proof of your
generosity and esteem, which I the more freely receive, because I
already look upon Mr. Random's interest as inseparably connected
with mine.' He was extremely well pleased at her frank and ingenuous reply, upon which we saluted, and wished her good night.
—The letter, at my request, was dispatched to Sussex by an express,
and in the mean time, Don Rodriguez, to grace my nuptials, hired a
ready-furnished house, and set up a very handsom equipage.

Though I passed the greatest part of the day with the darling of
my soul, I found leisure sometimes to be among my former
acquaintance, who were astonished at the magnificence of my
appearance: Banter in particular was confounded at the strange
vicissitudes of my fortune, the causes of which he endeavoured in
vain to discover, until I thought fit to disclose the whole secret of my
last voyage, partly in consideration of our former intimacy, and
partly to prevent unfavourable conjectures which he and others, in
all probability, would have made in regard to my circumstances.
He professed great satisfaction at this piece of news, and I had no
cause to believe him insincere, when I considered that he would now
look upon himself as acquitted of the debt he owed me, and at the
same time flatter himself with hopes of borrowing more.—I carried
him home to dinner with me, and my father liked his conversation
so much, that upon hearing his difficulties, he desired me to
accommodate him for the present, and enquire if he would accept
of a commission in the army, towards the purchase of which he
would willingly lend him money. Accordingly, I gave my friend an
opportunity of being alone with me, when, as I expected, he told
me that he was just on the point of being reconciled to an old rich
uncle, whose heir he was, but wanted a few pieces for immediate
expence, which he desired I would lend him, and take his bond for
the whole. His demand was limited to ten guineas; and when I put
twenty into his hand, he stared at me for some moments, then
putting it into his purse, said, 'Ay, 'tis all one,—you'll have the
whole in a very short time.' When I had taken his note, to save the
expence of a bond, I expressed some surprize that a fellow of his
spirit should loiter away his time in idleness, and asked why he did
not choose to make his fortune in the army.—'What! (said he)

throw away money upon a subaltern's commission, to be under the command of a parcel of scoundrels who have raised themselves above me by the most infamous practices! no, I love independency too well to sacrifice my life, health and pleasure for such a pitiful consideration.'——Finding him averse to this way of life, I chang'd the subject, and return'd to Don Rodriguez, who had just received the following epistle from the Squire.

SIR,

'Concerning a letter which I received, subscrib'd R. Random, this is the answer.—As for you, I know nothing of you.—Your son, or pretended son, I have seen;—if he marries my sister, at his peril be it; I do declare, that he shall not have one farthing of her fortune, which becomes my property, if she takes a husband without my consent.—Your settlement, I do believe, is all a sham, and yourself no better than you should be; but if you had all the wealth of the Indies, your son shall never match in our family, with the consent of

Orson[1] Topehall.

My father was not much surprised at this polite letter, after having heard the character of the author: and as for me, I was even pleased at his refusal, because I now had an opportunity of shewing my disinterested love. By his permission I waited on my charmer; and having imparted the contents of her brother's letter, at which she wept bitterly, in spite of all my consolation and caresses, the time of our marriage was fixed at the distance of two days.—During this interval, in which my soul was wound up to the last stretch of rapturous expectation, Narcissa endeavoured to reconcile some of her relations in town to her marriage with me; but finding them all deaf to her remonstrances, either out of envy or prejudice; she told me with the most enchanting sweetness, while the tears bedewed her lovely cheeks, 'Sure the world will no longer question your generosity, when you take a poor forlorn beggar to your arms.' Affected with her sorrow, I pressed the fair mourner to my breast, and swore that she was more dear and welcome on that account, because she had sacrificed her friends and fortune to her love for me. —My uncle, for whose character she had a great veneration, being by this time come to town, I introduced him to my bride; and although he was not very much subject to refined sensations, he was struck dumb with admiration at her beauty. After having kissed and gazed at her for some time, he turned to me, saying, 'Odds bobs,

Rory! here's a notable prize indeed, finely built and gloriously rigged, I'faith! if she an't well manned when you have the command of her, sirrah, you deserve to go to sea in a cockle-shell.—No offence, I hope, niece; you must not mind what I say, being (as the saying is) a plain sea-faring man, thof mayhap I have as much regard for you as another.'—She received him with great civility, told him she had longed a great while to see a person to whom she was so much indebted for his generosity to Mr. Random, that she looked upon him as her uncle, by which name she begged leave to call him for the future, and that she was very sure he could say nothing that could give her the least offence. The honest captain was transported at her courteous behaviour, and insisted upon *giving her away* at the ceremony, swearing that he loved her as well as if she was his own child, and that he would give two thousand guineas to the first fruit of our love, as soon as it could squeak.—Every thing being prepared for the solemnization of our nuptials, which were to be performed privately at my father's house, the auspicious hour arrived, when Don Rodriguez and my uncle went in the coach to fetch the bride and Miss Williams; leaving me with a parson, Banter and Strap, neither of whom had as yet seen my charming mistress.—My faithful valet, who was on the rack of impatience to behold a lady of whom he had heard so much, no sooner understood that the coach was returned, than he placed himself at a window to have a peep at her as she alighted; and when he saw her, he clapped his hands together, turned up the white of his eyes, and with his mouth wide open, remained in a sort of extasy, which broke out into, '*O Dea certe!*[1]—*qualis in Eurotæ ripis, aut per juga Cynthi exercet Diana choros!*[2]—The doctor and Banter were supriz'd to hear my man speak Latin, but when my father led Narcissa into the room, the object of their admiration was soon changed, as appear'd in the countenances of both.—Indeed they must have been the most insensible of all beings, could they have beheld without emotion the divine creature that approached! She was dressed in a sack of white sattin, embroidered on the breast with gold; the crown of her head was covered with a small French cap, from whence descended her beautiful hair in ringlets that waved upon her snowy neck, which dignified the necklace I had given her; her looks glowed with modesty and love; and her bosom, thro' the veil of gauze that shaded it, afforded a prospect of Elyzium!—I received this inestimable gift of providence as became me; and in a little time the clergyman did his office, my uncle, at his own earnest request, acting the part of a father to my dear Narcissa, who trembled very much, and had scarce spirits sufficient to support her under this great change of situation. —Soon as she was mine by the laws of heaven and earth, I printed a burning kiss upon her lips, my father embraced her tenderly, my uncle hugged her with great affection, and I presented her to my friend Banter, who saluted her in a very polite manner; Miss Williams hung round her neck, and wept plentifully; while Strap fell upon his knees, and begged to kiss his lady's hand, which she presented with great affability.—I shall not pretend to describe my own feelings at this juncture; let it suffice to say, that after having supped and entertained ourselves 'till ten a-clock, I cautioned my Narcissa against exposing her health by sitting up too late, and she was prevailed upon to withdraw with her maid to an apartment destin'd for us. When she left the room, her face was overspread with a blush that set all my blood in a state of fermentation, and made every pulse beat with tenfold vigour! She was so cruel as to let me remain in this condition a full half hour; when, no longer able to restrain my impatience, I broke from the company, burst into her chamber, pushed out her confidante, locked the door, and found her——O heav'n and earth! a feast, a thousand times more delicious than my most sanguine hope presaged!—But let me not profane the chaste mysteries of hymen—I was the happiest of men!

In the morning I was awaked by three or four drums, which Banter had placed under the window; upon which I withdrew the curtain, and enjoyed the unspeakable satisfaction of contemplating those angelic charms, which were now in my possession! *Beauty! which whether sleeping or awake, shot forth peculiar graces!*[1]—The light darting upon my Narcissa's eyes, she awoke also, and re-collecting her situation, hid her blushes in my bosom.—I was distracted with joy! I could not believe the evidence of my senses, and looked upon all that had happened, as the fictions of a dream! In the mean time my uncle knocked at the door, and bid me turn out, for I had had a long spell.—I got up accordingly, and sent Miss Williams to her mistress, myself receiving the congratulation of captain Bowling, who rallied me in his sea phrase, with great success.—In less than an hour, Don Rodriguez led my wife in to breakfast, where she received the compliments of the company on her looks, which, they said, if possible, were improved by matrimony.——As her delicate ears were offended with none of those indecent ambiguities, which are too often spoke on such occasions, she behaved with dignity, unaffected modesty, and ease; and as a testimony of my affection and esteem, I presented her, in presence of them all, with a deed, by which I settled the whole fortune I was possessed of, on her and her heirs for ever.—She accepted it with a glance of most tender acknowledgement, observed, that she could not be surprized at any thing of this kind I should do, and desired my father to take the trouble of keeping it, saying, 'Next to my own Mr. Random, you are the person in whom I ought to have the greatest confidence.' Charm'd with her prudent and ingenuous manner of proceeding, he took the paper, and assured her that it should not lose its value while in his custody.

As we had not many visits to give and receive; the little time we stayed in town was spent in going to publick diversions, where I have the vanity to think Narcissa seldom was eclipsed.—One night in particular, we had sent our footman to keep one of the stage-boxes,[1] which we no sooner entered, than we perceived in the opposite box the Squire and his lady, who seem'd not a little surprised at seeing us. I was pleased at this opportunity of confronting them; the more, because Melinda was robbed of all her admirers by my wife, who happened that night to outshine her sister both in beauty and dress.—She was piqued at Narcissa's victory, tossed her head a thousand different ways, flirted her fan, looked at us with disdain, then whispered to her husband, and broke out into an affected giggle; but all her arts proved ineffectual, either to discompose Mrs. Random, or to conceal her own mortification, which at length forced her away long before the play was done.—The news of our marriage being spread, with many circumstances to our disadvantage, by the industry of this malignant creature, a certain set of persons, fond of scandal, began to enquire into the particulars of my fortune, which they no sooner understood to be independant, than the tables were turned, and our acquaintance was courted as much as it had been despised before: But Narcissa had too much dignity of pride, to encourage this change of conduct, especially in her relations, whom she could never be prevailed upon to see, after the malicious reports they had raised to her prejudice.

CHAPTER LXIX

My father intends to revisit the place of his nativity—we propose to accompany him—my uncle renews his will in my favour, determining to go to sea again——we set out for Scotland——arrive at Edinburgh—purchase our paternal estate——proceed to it——halt at the town where I was educated——take up my bond to Crab——the behaviour of Potion and his wife, and one of my female cousins——our reception at the estate——Strap marries Miss Williams, and is settled by my father to his own satisfaction——I am more and more happy

M Y father intending to revisit his native country, and pay the tribute of a few tears at my mother's grave, Narcissa and I resolved to accompany him in the execution of this pious office, and accordingly prepared for the journey; in which, however, my uncle would not engage, being resolved to try his fortune once more at sea. In the mean time, he renewed his will in favour of my wife and me, and deposited it in the hands of his brother-in-law: While I (that I might not be wanting to my own interest) summoned the Squire to produce his father's will at Doctor's Commons,[1] and employed a proctor to manage the affair in my absence.

Every thing being thus settled, we took leave of all our friends in London, and set out for Scotland, Don Rodriguez, Narcissa, Miss Williams, and I in the coach, and Strap with two men in livery on horse-back: As we made easy stages, my charmer held it out very well, till we arrived at Edinburgh, where we proposed to rest ourselves some weeks. People of our figure could not fail of attracting the notice of such a small place,[2] where, as soon as our family was known, we were loaded with caresses, and Narcissa was so much pleased with the civilities she received, that she protested she would never desire to live in any other part of the world.

Here Don Rodriguez having intelligence that his nephew the fox-hunter had spent his estate, which was to be exposed to sale by publick auction, he determined to make a purchase of the spot where he was born, and actually bought the whole of his father's lands.

In a few days after this bargain was made, we left Edinburgh, in order to go and take possession; and by the way, halted one night in that town where I was educated.[1]—Upon inquiry, I found that Mr. Crab was dead; whereupon I sent for his executor, paid the sum I owed, with interest, and took up my bond. Mr. Potion and his wife hearing of our arrival, had the assurance to come to the inn where we lodged, and send up their names, with a desire of being permitted to pay their respects to my father and me: But their sordid behaviour towards me, when I was an orphan, had made too deep an impression on my mind, to be effaced by this mean mercenary piece of condescension; I therefore rejected their message with disdain, and bid Strap tell them, that my father and I desired to have no communication with such low-minded wretches as they were.

They had not been gone half an hour, when a woman without any ceremony, opened the door of the room where we sat, and making towards my father, accosted him with, 'Uncle, your servant—I am glad to see you.'—This was no other than one of my female cousins, mentioned in the first part of my memoirs, to whom Don Rodriguez replied, 'Pray, who are you, madam?'——'O! (cried she) my cousin Rory there, knows me very well—Don't you remember me, Rory?'——'Yes, madam, (said I) for my own part, I shall never forget you.—Sir, this is one of the young ladies, who (as I have formerly told you) treated me so humanely in my childhood!' When I pronounced these words, my father's resentment glowed in his visage, and he ordered her to be gone, with such a commanding aspect, that she retired in a fright, muttering curses as she went down stairs: We afterwards learned that she was married to an ensign, who had already spent all her fortune; and that her sister had bore a child to her mother's footman, who is now her husband, and keeps a petty ale-house in the country.

The fame of our flourishing condition having arrived at this place before us, we got notice that the magistrates intended next day to compliment us with the freedom of their town; upon which my father, considering their complaisance in the right point of view, ordered the horses to the coach early in the morning, when we proceeded to our estate, which lay about a dozen miles from this place.

When we came within half a league of the house, we were met by a prodigious number of poor tenants, men, women and children, who testified their joy by loud acclamations, and accompanied our

coach to the gate.—As there is no part of the world, in which the peasants are more attached to their Lords, than in Scotland, we were almost devoured by their affection,[1] in getting out of the coach: My father had always been their favourite, and now that he appeared their master, after being thought dead so long, their joy broke out into a thousand extravagancies: When we got into the court-yard, we were surrounded by a vast number, who crowded together so closely to see us, that several were in danger of being squeezed to death; those who were near Don Rodriguez fell upon their knees, and kissed his hand, or the hem of his garment, praying aloud for long life and prosperity to him; others approached Narcissa and me in the same manner; while the rest clapped their hands at a distance, and invoked heaven to shower its choicest blessings on our heads!
——In short, the whole scene, though rude, was so affecting, that the gentle partner of my heart wept over it, and my father himself could not refrain from dropping a tear.

Having welcomed his daughter and me to his house, he ordered some bullocks to be killed, and some hogsheads of ale to be brought from the neighbouring village, to regale those honest people, who had not enjoyed such a holiday for many years before.

Next day we were visited by the gentlemen in the neighbourhood, most of them our relations, one of whom brought along with him my cousin, the fox-hunter, who had staid at his house, since he was obliged to leave his own: My father was generous enough to receive him kindly, and even promise to purchase for him a commission in the army, at which he expressed great thankfulness and joy.

My charming Narcissa was universally admired and loved for her beauty, affability and good sense; and so well pleased with the situation of the place, and the company around, that she has not, as yet, discovered the least desire of changing her habitation.

We had not been many days settled, when I prevailed upon my father to pay a visit to the village where I had been at school. Here we were received by the principal inhabitants, who entertained us in the church, where Mr. Syntax the schoolmaster (my tyrant being dead) pronounced a Latin speech in honour of our family: And none exerted themselves more than Strap's father and relations, who looked upon the honest valet as the first gentleman of their race, and honoured his benefactors accordingly.—Having received the homage of this place, we retired, leaving forty pounds for the benefit of the poor of the parish; and that very night, Strap being a little elevated with the regard that had been shewn to him, and to me on his account, ventured to tell me, that he had a sneaking kindness for Miss Williams, and that if his lady and I would use our interest in his behalf, he did not doubt that she would listen to his addresses. Surprized at this proposal, I asked if he knew the story of that unfortunate young gentlewoman: Upon which, he replied, 'Yes, yes, I know what you mean—she has been unhappy, I grant you— but what of that? I am convinced of her reformation; or else you and my good lady would not treat her with such respect.—As for the censure of the world, I value it not a fig's end—besides, the world knows nothing of the matter.' I commended his philosophy, and interested Narcissa in his cause; who interceded so effectually, that in a little time, Miss Williams, yielded her consent, and they were married with the approbation of Don Rodriguez, who gave him five hundred pounds to stock a farm, and made him overseer of his estate. My generous bedfellow gave her maid the same sum; so that they live in great peace and plenty within half a mile of us, and daily put up prayers for our preservation.

If there be such a thing as true happiness on earth, I enjoy it.— The impetuous transports of my passion are now settled and mellowed into endearing fondness and tranquillity of love, rooted by that intimate connexion and interchange of hearts, which nought but virtuous wedlock can produce.—Fortune seems determined to make ample amends for her former cruelty; for my proctor writes, that notwithstanding the clause in my father-in-law's will, on which the Squire founds his claim, I shall certainly recover my wife's fortune, in consequence of a codicil annexed, which explains that clause, and limits her restriction to the age of nineteen, after which she was at her own disposal.—I would have set out for London immediately after receiving this piece of intelligence,[1] but my dear angel has been qualmish of late, and begins to grow remarkably round in the waist; so that I cannot leave her in such an interesting situation, which I hope will produce something to crown my felicity.

NOTES

ABBREVIATIONS

I SMOLLETT'S WORKS

RR	*Roderick Random* (1748)
PP	*Peregrine Pickle* (1751) Edited with an Introduction by James L. Clifford, Oxford English Novels, 1964
FCF	*Ferdinand Count Fathom* (1753) Edited with an Introduction by Damian Grant, Oxford English Novels, 1971
LG	*Launcelot Greaves* (1760–1) Edited with an Introduction by David Evans, Oxford English Novels, 1973
HC	*Humphry Clinker* (1771) Edited with an Introduction by Lewis M. Knapp, Oxford English Novels, 1966

II GENERAL WORKS (in alphabetical order)

Boucé	P.-G. Boucé, *The Novels of Tobias Smollett* (1976)
Buck	H. S. Buck, *A Study in Smollett, Chiefly 'Peregrine Pickle'* (1925)
Falconer	William Falconer, *Marine Dictionary* (1st edn. 1769; 1970 reprint of 1780 edn.)
Jacob	Giles Jacob, *A New Law-Dictionary* (6th edn. 1750)
James	Robert James, *Pharmacopoeia Universalis or, a New Universal English Dispensatory* (1747)
Kahrl	G. M. Kahrl, *Tobias Smollett, Traveler-Novelist* (1945)
Kemp	*The Oxford Companion to Ships and the Sea* (1976), ed. Peter Kemp
Knapp	L. M. Knapp, *Tobias Smollett, Doctor of Men and Manners* (1949)
Letters	*The Letters of Tobias Smollett* (1970), edited by L. M. Knapp
Maitland	William Maitland, *The History of London from its Foundation to the Present Time* (2nd edn. 1756)
Phillips	Hugh Phillips, *Mid-Georgian London* (1964)
Quincy	John Quincy, *Lexicon Physico-Medicum : Or, A New Medicinal Dictionary* (5th edn. 1736)

Unless otherwise stated, all books referred to in the Notes were published in London.

Notes

Title-page. On the title-page of the first edition there was a line from Horace, *Satires,* II. v.:

> *Et genus & virtus, nisi cum re, vilior alga est.*
>
> [And yet birth and worth, without substance,
> are more paltry than seaweed.]

Preface

Page xliv. (1) Xenophon, Athenian writer, born *c.*430 B.C. His *Cyropaedia,* or *Education of Cyrus,* is a moralistic narrative of the career of Cyrus the Great.

(2) *Don Quixote* (pt. I, 1605; pt. II, 1615), which Smollett was already busy translating in 1748. His translation was published in 1755. On the influence of Cervantes on Smollett, see Boucé, pp. 71–4 and *passim.*

(3) The French novelist Alain-René Lesage (1668–1747) published his *Gil Blas* 1715–35. Smollett's translation was published in October 1748, some nine months after *RR.* On the influence of Lesage on Smollett, see Boucé, pp. 71–8, 81–3, 85–90.

Page xlv. (1) This statement should be compared with Smollett's letter to Alexander Carlyle (London, 7 June 1748) disclaiming any autobiographical character for *RR* (*Letters,* pp. 7–9). On the complex relationship between autobiographical elements and Smollett's fictive creation, see Boucé, pp. 40–67, 'Autobiography and the Novels'.

Page 1. (1) Cf. Webster's *The Duchess of Malfi,* v. iv. 64–5: 'We are merely the stars' tennis-balls, struck and bandied / Which way please them.'

Page 2. (1) An allusion to Daniel 6: 8: unalterable laws

Page 3. (1) Wool or cotton refuse and torn rags were used to stuff mattresses of poor quality.

Page 6. (1) An allusion to the proverbial phrase 'Old as Methuselah', referring to the oldest man mentioned in the Bible (Genesis 5: 27): he died at the age of 969.

Page 7. (1) 'Roderick' was used in Scotland to render the Gaelic name 'Ruaidhri', meaning, most appositely, 'the red', the Irish equivalent being 'Rory'. The erratic connotation of 'Random' is obvious enough.

(2) In Greek mythology the hunter Actaeon incurred the displeasure of the goddess Artemis, who changed him into a stag; he was torn to pieces by his own hounds.

Page 9. (1) The gilded scroll work and carvings decorating the stern and quarters of large ships from the fifteenth to eighteenth centuries: gingerbread was often gilded in the eighteenth century. Hence, 'gaudy and tasteless decorations' (*OED*).

(2) Or swabber, originally a ship's sweeper, used as a term of contempt for a useless seaman.

(3) These two slang phrases are synonymous, and mean 'to give a good beating'.

Page 10. (1) The lieutenant's name may refer either to a ship 'bowling along', or to a rope used to keep the sail taut and steady. See Kemp, s.v. *bowline*. For a discussion of Tom Bowling's literary forebears, see Kahrl, pp. 14–15.

Page 11. (1) An indirect allusion to the proverb 'Nine tailors make a man'. See also *HC*, p. 212.

(2) Colloquial or slang for a sixpence.

Page 12. (1) Stopped the vessel, brought the ship to anchor.

(2) Said of an anchor when raised perpendicularly from the ground.

(3) In the eighteenth century *porpus* was the prevalent form of *porpoise*.

(4) 'The position of the anchor when the bows of the ship have been drawn directly above it during weighing, just before it is broken out of the ground', Kemp, s.v. *apeak*.

Page 13. (1) Athwart.

(2) The spritsail was a small square sail attached to a yard hanging under the bowsprit.

Page 14. (1) Possibly an oblique reference to the 'Hunting Adventure' in *Joseph Andrews* (1742), bk. III, ch. 6.

Page 15. (1) J. C. Pepusch (1667–1752) arranged the tunes of *Perseus and Andromeda*, an entertainment written by Roger and John Weaver, dancing-masters, performed in 1717. Bowling is whistling 'The Sailor's Ballad'— later known as the 'Sailor's Rant'—from this entertainment. The lines quoted here are from the chorus: 'Then why whould we quarrel for riches / Or any such glittering toy? / A light heart and a thin pair of breeches / Goes thorough the world brave boy.'

(2) A set phrase meaning 'make haste', 'hurry up'.

(3) 'To bring a sailing vessel to a stop with her sails still set', Kemp, s.v. *Bring-to*.

(4) Glasgow, where Smollett himself attended the university, without graduating. See Knapp, pp. 10–23.

Page 16. (1) A name denoting physical awkwardness and mental imbecility. On possible identifications of Gawky and Strap (*infra*), see Knapp, pp. 101–2, 325–6, 328–30.

(2) The surname 'Strap' is relevant to both the young man's origins—a poor cobbler's son—and to his future trade, 'strap' being a dialectal form of 'strop'.

Page 17. (1) A phrase denoting an intention to attack, used again by Smollett in *The Reprisal* (1757), II. 9.

Page 22. (1) Tiberoon, or Tiburon on the south-west tip of Haiti.

(2) Hispaniola, or St Domingo as it was also called in the eighteenth century, the second largest of the Caribbean islands, now divided into the Republic of Haiti (West) and the Dominican Republic (East).

(3) The substance obtained from condemned ropes when they are unpicked, used for caulking the seams. Unpicking oakum was often the labour of workhouse inmates, and a traditional naval punishment.

(4) Seaport of East Kent, formerly of great importance to the Navy because of the proximity of the twenty miles' safe anchorage of the Downs.

Page 26. (1) Another grotesque surname, referring either to the surgeon's *crabbed* disposition (cf. the misanthrope Cadwallader Crabtree in *PP*), his shape and complexion resembling a crustacean's or to the materia medica, crab's eyes. For the original of Crab, see Knapp, p. 101.

Page 29. (1) See 1 Sam. 25: 2–39: the rich man who refused any gifts to David, hence a churlish miser.

Page 30. (1) The so-called War of Jenkins's Ear, declared on 19 October 1739.

Page 31. (1) As Smollett himself was careful to stress (see *Letters*, p. 8), this should not be read as autobiography. On Smollett's status in 1738–9, see Knapp, pp. 23–6.

(2) Richard Wiseman (1622?–1676), serjeant-surgeon to Charles II; one of the first truly great surgeons, an excellent clinical observer, whose *Several Chirurgicall Treatises* (1676) were reprinted as *Eight Chirurgical Treatises* (1734), probably the edition in Roderick's possession.

(3) The legal rate fixed by the statute 12 Anne, c. 16, called 'the statute against Excessive Usury'. Compare with the extortionate rate demanded by Isaac Rapine, p. 49. See Jacob, s.v. *Usury*.

Page 32. (1) Low flat-bottomed river vessels used especially on the river Tyne to convey coal from Newcastle in order to load the colliers.

Page 34. (1) Another instance of occupational onomastics, from the verb *rifle*, i.e. to plunder or rob someone after a thorough search.

Page 35. (1) He drank the bottle.

(2) The name of Don Quixote's beloved; hence a mistress or sweetheart.

Page 36. (1) A minced form of 'God's blood'.

(2) An illiterate variant of *obstreperous*, i.e. noisy, turbulent, again used in *LG*, p. 133.

Page 39. (1) Restive.

Page 40. (1) An incomplete reference to the proverb 'I wot well how the world wags, he is best loved that hath most bags'.

(2) By statute (13 Anne, c. 11) curates were to receive a stipend not exceeding £50 a year nor less than £20 a year. At the age of fifty, Fielding's Parson Adams 'was provided with a handsome Income of twenty-three Pounds a year' in *Joseph Andrews*, bk. I, ch. 3.

Page 41. (1) The name denotes not only the manipulation of cards but also a *trick*.

(2) Excise, a duty laid on numerous commodities, from spirituous liquors to salt, soap, glass, or wire, was highly unpopular in the eighteenth century. Excisemen who had the right to search any premises were both detested and feared. Dr Johnson in his *Dictionary* (1755) defined excise as a 'hateful tax levied upon commodities', and excisemen as 'wretches hired by those to whom excise is paid'. See the 'Adventure with the Exciseman' in *PP*, ch. xvi.

Page 42. (1) In strict confidence; a rendering of the Latin phrase *sub rosa*, the rose having become the emblem of silence.

(2) A generic name currently applied to innkeepers in the eighteenth century, for instance in Farquhar's *The Beaux' Stratagem* (1707).

Page 44. (1) From the Spanish phrase *en cuerpo*, without a cloak, hence in a state of undress.

(2) Identified by Knapp, p. 102, as Richard Cooper, living 'some thirty miles south of Newcastle on the main London highway'.

(3) 'Welcome boys! Come in.'

(4) Horace, *Odes*, I. ix. 5–6. 'Dispel the chill by piling high the wood upon the fire.'

(5) 'Dearest son! whence do you come? from above, unless I am mistaken.' The schoolmaster probably intends a joke: *a superis* may refer either to heaven or to some higher regions, i.e. Scotland.

Page 45. (1) Horace, *Odes*, I. ix. 7–8. 'Bring forth in Sabine jar the wine four winters old, O Thaliarchus.'

(2) Horace, *Odes*, I. xi. 1–2, 8. 'Ask not (it is forbidden to know), what end the gods have set for me, for thee—Reap the harvest of today, and put as little trust as possible in tomorrow.'

(3) Horace, *Odes*, I. ix. 9. A slightly altered quotation for 'permitte . . .': 'leave to the gods everything else'.

Page 46. (1) Horace, *Odes*, III. xvi. 17. 'As money grows, care follows after.'

(2) Horace, *Satires*, II. ii, 110. 'content with little'.

(3) Horace, *Odes*, III. xvi. 37. 'importuna tamen abest pauperies': 'yet distressing poverty is absent'.

Page 47. (1) Horace, *Epistles*, I. ii. 56. 'The covetous is always in want.'

(2) Horace, *Epistles*, I. ii. 62–3. 'Rule your passion, for unless it obeys, it gives orders.'

Page 48. (1) See Numbers 13: 22, 33: Anak was the ancestor of the Anakims (Deut. 2: 10–11), a race of giants.

Page 49. (1) French for a fast stage-coach, hence the arch irony here.

(2) A hundred for every hundred, or the interest equals the principal.

(3) A possible allusion to 'The Old Fumbler', a broadside song with music, set by Henry Purcell, *c*.1695, where a rich old man who has 'wedded a Juicy brisk Girl of the Town' proves impotent. Jenny knows many songs (see p. 56). See *Merry Songs and Ballads*, ed. John S. Farmer (privately printed, n. p., 1897), vol. I, p. 167.

Page 50. (1) Mumbled: the obsolete meaning, 'grinned' is not impossible either.

(2) There is no mention of Ancient Pistol's hat in the plays where he appears, *2 Henry IV*, *The Merry Wives of Windsor* and *Henry V*, but the part came to be strongly identified at the time with the actor Theophilus Cibber (1703–58), who was not unlike Weazel (see *DNB*). The allusion to Pistol is all the more apposite as Falstaff's ensign in *2 Henry IV* is called an 'Irregular Humorist' and a 'swaggerer'. Cf. also p. 277 *infra*.

(3) This dehumanizing absurdity may be an oblique reference to Locke's well-known concepts of extension and substance in his *Essay Concerning Human Understanding* (1690). See Peter H. Nidditch's edn. (Clarendon Press, 1975), II, xiii, §11–25, pp. 171–9, and also II, xxiii, 'Of our Complex Ideas of Substances', pp. 295–318.

(4) Plutarch, *Moralia: Sayings of Spartans*, § 233A, where 'A man plucked a nightingale and finding almost no meat, said, "It's all voice ye are, and nought else." ' (Loeb Classical Library, *Moralia*, III, p. 399). But Plutarch was only using the well-known Latin phrase *Vox et praeterea nihil*, sometimes attributed to Seneca.

(5) 'A shaggy kind of woollen cloth used for overcoats' (*OED*).

Page 51. (1) Fielding's 'A Modern Glossary' (*Covent-Garden Journal*, 14 January 1752) defines the term as 'A Quality Expression of low Contempt, properly confined to the Mouths of Ladies who are Right Honourable.'

(2) One that couples with noblemen. The noun reappears as a surname in ch. xxv, meaning a bawd or madam.

(3) Flay.

Page 52. (1) A person of dwarfish size.

(2) Of slender frame.

Page 53. (1) See Isaiah 11:8; 14:29; 59:5: originally an adder, identified with the basilisk; in the first half of the eighteenth century: a whore.

Page 54. (1) Another minced variant of 'God's blood'.

Page 55. (1) In allusion to Sextus, son of Tarquinius Superbus, who ravished the chaste Lucretia.

(2) Jenny may refer either to the Great Minories, 'a broad and spacious street [between Aldgate and the Tower] which is very well inhabited by considerable Tradesmen in most Branches, but chiefly noted for the Gunsmiths' (Maitland, ii, 1009), or more probably to the less affluent Little Minories nearby, one of the Tower Liberties.

Page 56. (1) The name suggests voracious greed; it appears again in *LG*, ch. xi, as a rapacious judge's.

(2) Small birds, the garden buntings, highly esteemed by gourmets.

(3) In the context, the surname probably denotes futile trifling and time-wasting.

Page 57. (1) Suggests bold and wanton horse-play. See *OED*, s.v. verb *ramp*[1].

Page 60. (1) Laid under legal obligation to keep the peace and to be of good behaviour.

Page 62. (1) See Farquhar's *The Beaux' Stratagem* (1707), where Scrub is Mr Sullen's servant and man-of-all-work in Lady Bountiful's household.

(2) 'Eh? What did you say?'

Page 63. (1) A double swipe at the Scots, oats being jocularly supposed—even by Dr Johnson in his *Dictionary*—to be their staple food, whereas *brimstone* refers to Presbyterian 'fire and brimstone' sermons.

(2) For contemporary evidence of keen interest in boxing see Paul Whitehead's *The Gymnasiad or Boxing Match* (1744), and Captain John Godfrey's *A Treatise upon the Useful Science of Defence* (1747). Pierce Egan in his *Boxiana* (1812) reproduces the rules set up by Broughton 'for the better regulation of the Amphitheatre, 10 August 1743', pp. 51–2. Rule 7 provides 'That no person is to hit his adversary when he is down', a rule obviously not familiar to the Scotsman Roderick. Boxing and cudgelling were banned from 'Southwark Fair' in 1749.

Page 64. (1) An obsequious, fawning person.

(2) A current periphrasis for footmen wearing livery.

(3) Probably St Martin's-le-Grand, in Aldersgate ward, with a sanctuary on both sides and many tradesmen in the vicinity. See Maitland, ii, 774–5.

Page 67. (1) Lay near The Hay Market and disappeared when Regent Street was built; was noted chiefly for its butchers' stalls.

Notes

Page 68. (1) *Caul*: 'The net foundation of silk or other suitable material to which wig hair is secured.' J. Stevens Cox, *An Illustrated Dictionary of Hairdressing and Wigmaking* (1966), p. 30.

(2) Cadaver hair, used in the manufacture of wigs.

(3) 'A man's 17/18th cent. periwig with the bottom hair turned up into short curls or bobs.' Ibid., p. 22.

Page 69. (1) A well-known trick, described as 'guinea-dropping' or 'sweetning' in a pamphlet, *The Tricks of the Town Laid Open* (1747), letter xiii. See Boucé, pp. 265–6.

(2) Hot beer with gin, to which ginger and sugar were sometimes added; a morning draught.

(3) Egg-nog, a mixture of hot beer, cider, wine, with the white and yolk of eggs.

Page 70. (1) Indulged in drinking.

Page 72. (1) See Proverbs 27: 22.

(2) Pliny, *Natural History*, VII. xl. 131. An incomplete quotation 'Nemo mortalium . . .' 'Nobody is wise all the time.' Also used by Partridge, in very similar circumstances, *Tom Jones*, bk. XII, ch. 13.

Page 73. (1) A Scots pun on two homonyms, the first referring to 'a mean contemptible person', literally 'a squirt'; the second referring to a cobbler: 'Cobblers are termed *scouts* being always on the prowl' (*The Scottish National Dictionary*).

Page 74. (1) In Aldgate Ward, with its main entrance from Crutched Friars. It was removed in 1788. Described by Maitland, ii, 787 as 'a large modern Building, very commodious for Business; . . . This Office has another Entrance into Seething Lane, and another by Tower-hill.'

Page 75. (1) Stay binding, used by tailors; also meant a tailor in eighteenth-century slang.

(2) 'A kind of man's wig (1742). From the family name Spencer and probably after Charles Spencer, Third Earl of Sunderland (1674–1722).' J. Stevens Cox, *Illustrated Dictionary of Hairdressing and Wigmaking* (1966), p. 141.

(3) Variegated with dark veins; cf. Pope's description of the beau, Sir Plume, in *The Rape of the Lock* (1714), iv, 123–4.

Page 76. (1) In Broadstreet Ward, where the Pay-Office was situated. 'Here are made all Payments for the Service of the royal Navy', Maitland, ii, 852.

(2) In Monkwell Street, Cripplegate. See Maitland, ii, 911. After the Barber-Surgeons' Company was dissolved in 1745, the Surgeons 'built a new Theatre in the *Old Bailey*' (ibid.).

Notes

(3) One of the six divisions into which men-of-war were grouped, according to the number of guns they mounted, and the proportion of men to man them. The *Chichester*, on which Smollett served, was a third rate, mounting eighty guns, with a complement of 600–650 men. See John Chamberlayne, *The Present State of Great-Britain* (1748), pt. II, bk. iii, 'A List of His Majesty's Ships . . . Oct. 10th, 1747', p. 165.

Page 78. (1) In Cornhill, the Royal Exchange was a thriving business-centre and a fashionable gathering-place. For a detailed description, see Maitland, ii, 898–902.

Page 79. (1) On the Middlesex side of the River Thames, chiefly frequented by seafaring men and tradesmen in Smollett's time. This locality was Captain Crowe's favourite district: see *LG*, pp. 62, 161–2. See also Maitland, ii, 1366.

Page 80. (1) See Proverbs 23: 5.

(2) Horace, *Epistles*, I. ii. 47–9. 'No house or estate, no heap of bronze or gold, has ever expelled fevers from the owner's sick body, or cares from his mind.'

Page 81. (1) One of the most popular London playhouses, in St Giles's parish, an area where prostitution was rife: see Hogarth's *Harlot's Progress*, and Phillips, pp. 154 and 279.

(2) Vinegar Yard, properly Vine Garden Yard, or Vineyard, referred to by Gay in *The Beggar's Opera* and by later eighteenth-century authors, as a most disreputable purlieu. See also *The Spectator*, no. 53, Tuesday 1 May 1711.

(3) This is Smollett's first extensive piece of comic polysemy, brilliantly displayed in the letters or speech of illiterate characters, such as Mrs Hornbeck in *PP* (p. 219), Justice Gobble in *LG*, pp. 93–6, the unforgettable Tabitha Bramble and her maid Win Jenkins in *HC*. Smollett revised the letter in the next three editions: see the relevant 1970 article by O. M. Brack, jr., and James B. Davis cited in the Select Bibliography.

Page 82. (1) Seaport in Kent, adjoining to Rochester, on the river Medway; one of the principal stations of the Royal Navy in the eighteenth century.

Page 84. (1) A mild oath, a variant of *Egad, Egod*.

(2) Cast amorous looks.

(3) A mill where cloth was thickened by beating and cleansed from its oil or grease with fuller's earth. See *Don Quixote* (in Smollett's 1755 translation), pt. I, bk. iii, ch. 6, where the sound of six fulling-hammers bemuses Don Quixote and Sancho a whole night.

(4) 'Not a bad presage.'

Notes

Page 85. (1) Roderick is punning on the Scots dialectal meaning of *shaver*: a cunning fellow, joker or wag.

Page 86. (1) Smollett actually passed his examination at Barber-Surgeons' Hall in Monkwell Street on 4 Dec. 1739, and qualified as second mate of a third rate. From the records of the Company of Barber-Surgeons, it appears that his examiners were William Petty (1673–1753), Master of the Company; James Ferne (d. 1740); Claudius Amyand (d. 1740), and the eminent William Cheselden (1688–1752). The first examiner was probably W. Petty; the second—'a plump gentleman'—probably W. Cheselden. See Jessie Dobson's little-known article (1957), listed in the Select Bibliography.

(2) See Exodus 10: 12–15.

(3) A surgical instrument used for boring holes in the skull.

Page 87. (1) The adjective was applied to people suffering from an over-supply of blood or of the humours, hence to a florid complexion, or circulatory disturbances.

(2) Horace, *Epistles*, 1. i. 14. Incomplete quotation from 'nullius *addictus jurare* in verba *magistri*': 'I do not feel bound to swear as any master dictates.'

(3) Independent.

Page 88. (1) 'A man's wig with a tied queue which came into fashion early in the 18th cent. during the reign of George I.' J. Stevens Cox (see *supra* note (1) to p. 68), p. 156. *Smoaked*: having the colour of smoke.

(2) 'On the North Bank of the River Thames, near the East Extremity of *Fleet-Street*', Maitland, ii, 979: a house of correction where petty criminals were 'forced to beat Hemp in publick View, with due Correction of whipping according to their Offence' (ibid., p. 981). See also Hogarth's *Harlot's Progress* (1732), plate iv, showing women at their hemp blocks.

Page 89. (1) An alcoholic hot drink flavoured with liquor distilled from rice and sugar, fermented with coconut juice.

Page 90. (1) Formerly a place of temporary detention.

(2) A prison at the north-west extremity of Faringdon Ward within, at the corner of Newgate Street, and extending down the East side of the Old Bailey; notorious for its foul living conditions and promiscuous over-crowding; burnt down during the Gordon Riots in 1780.

(3) 'Old Bailey Sessions House' or 'Central Criminal Court', for crimes committed in London, Westminster, and the county of Middlesex. See Maitland, ii, 989.

Page 91. (1) Formerly part of the Convent Garden of the Abbey of Westminster. For a systematic description of its architecture and riotous night-life, see Phillips, pp. 137–51.

(2) 'A decayed strumpet' (Johnson).

(3) An offender returning from transportation 'before the end of his term shall be liable to be punished as a person attainted of felony', R. Burn, *The Justice of the Peace and Parish Officer* (1755), i, 475. Surgeons bought the bodies of hanged criminals for dissection.

(4) Too cunning or clever, a somewhat cruel pun.

(5) Here 'a Precept in Writing, under the Hand and Seal of a Justice of Peace, directed to the Gaoler, for the Receiving and safe Keeping of an Offender, until he is delivered by Law' (Jacob, s.v. *Mittimus*).

Page 93. (1) Shared, divided.

(2) See *supra* note (1) to p. 78 on 'Change'; Scotch-walk was situated on the left-hand side of the Threadneedle Street entrance. See Maitland's diagram, ii, 901.

Page 94. (1) The celebrated gallows permanently set near the present site of Marble Arch between 1571 and 1759. See also Maitland, ii, 1373.

Page 95. (1) A penny loaf of bread.

(2) The correct French phrase is 'Coûte que coûte', i.e. at whatever cost.

(3) 'To err is human': a current Latin proverbial phrase, used by several authors with slight variations. In English see Pope, *Essay on Criticism*, l. 525, 'To err is human; to forgive, divine'.

Page 96. (1) A meaningless imprecation.

(2) The translation is given by Strap. No classical source has been found, apart from an attribution to Archimedes in Nicholas Ling's *Wits Commonwealth* (1722 edn.), p. 137, of what looks like a translation of the same aphorism: 'There is nothing more troublesome than doubtful thoughts.' Ling's work, often attributed, but wrongly so, to John Bodenham, was first published in 1597, went through numerous editions as it was meant 'for the Use of Schools'.

(3) The inner part of a building, a sanctuary, especially those of the Penates.

Page 97. (1) Cacus was a semi-human monster living in a cave on the Aventine: see Virgil, *Aeneid*, viii, 185–280. For 'sanctum sanctorum' see the Vulgate Exodus 26: 34: the holy of holies was the innermost apartment of the Tabernacle and of the Temple; hence a private apartment.

(2) French for clyster or enema.

(3) Spanish for the cheek-pouches of a baboon.

(4) Lavement's ludicrous Frenglish idiolect is a typical phonetic and syntactic rendering of the broken English spoken by French people in the eighteenth century. See also M. de Champignon in Smollett's play *The Reprisal* (1757).

(5) 'Faith! He's a fine, lusty lad!'

Page 98. (1) Mrs Lavement rules the roast, or 'wears the breeches'. See G. L. Apperson, *English Proverbs* (1929), p. 274, for the origin of the phrase.

Page 100. (1) A minced oath, also used by Champignon in *The Reprisal* (1757); a variant of *Mère Dieu*, i.e. 'by the mother of God'.

(2) Huguenot refugees who had fled from France at various times before and after the repeal of the Edict of Nantes (1685). Many lived in St Martin's parish, Westminster, or in the vicinity.

(3) Defined by John Quincy in his *Lexicon Physico-Medicum*, 5th edn. (1736) as 'anything substituted in the room of another' (p. 436). The charge of fraudulent adulteration of drugs was a frequent one, going back at least to mid-sixteenth century.

(4) Little stones found in the stomach of crawfish, 'often prescribed in nephritic Pains, Pleurisies, Asthma's [*sic*] and Colics; they are also proper for cleansing the Teeth' (James, p. 485).

(5) Made chiefly from balsam of Tolu, considered as an excellent pectoral medicine.

(6) Water of cinnamon, either with or without wine. Cinnamon was 'classed among the stomachic and uterine Medicines', and was considered an excellent cordial: James, p. 292.

(7) Turpentine or *Terebinthina* was used internally 'to heal the Lungs and in Gonorrheas' (James, p. 452), and externally as an ingredient in many plasters. Capivi (copahu or copaiba), a resinous juice of Brazilian origin, used mostly in the cure of venereal and urinary diseases. See James, p. 248.

(8) A scarlet dye made from the dried bodies of insects native to Mexico, principally employed in giving a crimson colour to tinctures.

(9) Quack remedies, or, as here, a special remedy of a secret composition, jealously guarded by its inventor; from Latin *nostrum*, neuter form of *noster*: 'our own'.

(10) A current cure of venereal disease, using mercury to evacuate humours by an excessive flow of saliva. Salivation was not always successful; it could take up to five or six weeks in confinement and be rather painful.

(11) A possible allusion to George Cheyne's *The English Malady* (1733), in which the celebrated physician advocated a diet of milk and vegetables, which would have cooled 'the natural warmth' of Mrs Lavement's constitution.

Page 101. (1) Literally 'By the death of my life', an oath used for instance by the Dauphin in *Henry V*, IV. v. also by the Duke of Bourbon, III. v.

(2) See Hogarth's *A Chorus of Singers* (1732), where the head of the string instrument is carved into a grotesque figure, then a fairly common practice.

(3) Traitor, deceiver.

(4) A minced oath for *Ventre de Dieu*, i.e. literally 'By God's belly'.

(5) 'Your servant, Captain, you are a gallant man—my wife feels most obliged', to which as a *sotto voce* innuendo, Lavement adds 'And, doubtless, damn obliging too.'

Page 102. (1) In Surrey, on the River Thames, about a dozen miles from London in Smollett's time.

Page 104. Now part of the London Borough of Kensington and Chelsea but still a village in Smollett's time. The author of *Roderick Random* resided there from 1750 to 1763, in what is now Lawrence Street.

Page 106. (1) In Surrey, three miles south of Ascot, over twenty-five miles from London. The adjacent Bagshot Heath was notorious for highwaymen in the eighteenth century.

Page 107. (1) Flayed.

Page 108. (1) Outer layer of the skin, or epidermis.

Page 110. (1) A title that could be applied, or flatteringly misapplied, to an officer of any rank, a practice most virulently denounced by Doll Tearsheet (*2 Henry IV*, II. iv.) when Pistol is addressed as 'Captain Pistol'.

(2) The adjective applied to any soothing remedies, anodynes, that could assuage pain. Paregoric elixir is a camphorated tincture of opium, invented in the early eighteenth century.

Page 111. (1) 'A coward, by God!'

(2) Smollett here alludes to the runaway marriages of the Gretna Green type, performed by unscrupulous clergymen within the Liberty of the Fleet, comprising the north side of Ludgate Hill and the Old Bailey up to Fleet Lane. Lord Hardwicke's Marriage Act of 1753 put an end to the scandal.

(3) Bagnios were originally public bathing-houses, which soon turned into brothels or assignation houses, although some remained respectable.

Page 114. (1) 'Scoundrel!'

Page 115. (1) An oblique, but apt, reference to Daniel's wisdom and love of truth, as exemplified in the Apocrypha, 'The History of Susannah'.

(2) (1683–1725) A notorious thief and chief of a crime syndicate. See Defoe's *The True and Genuine Account . . . of the Late Jonathan Wild* (1725), and Fielding's *Jonathan Wild* (1743).

(3) Women 'whose trade is to rake in heaps of ashes for cinders' (Johnson, *Dictionary*).

(4) The area round the church of St Giles-in-the-Fields had become notorious for its thieving, prostitution, drunkenness and general wretchedness. See Hogarth's *Gin Lane* (Feb. 1750/1) which is set there.

Notes

Page 117. (1) Third Earl of Shaftesbury (1671–1713), moral philosopher, author of *Characteristicks* (1711); his benevolent and optimistic view of Man opposed Hobbes's theories, and Locke's.

(2) Matthew Tindal (1657–1733), deist philosopher, his *Christianity as Old as the Creation* (1730) appealed to reason.

(3) Thomas Hobbes (1588–1679), man of letters and philosopher; his materialism and determinism in *The Leviathan* (1651) resulted in his pessimistic assessment of man and society. In some copies of the first edition, John Locke (1632–1704) heads the list of the 'freethinking' philosophers.

Page 119. (1) The chivalrous hero of a ten-volume French romance, *Cassandra* (1642–5) by La Calprenède (1609?–1663). Translated into English in 1676 and again in 1705, it was well known in eighteenth-century England. Aimwell refers to Oroondates as 'all that Romance can in a Lover paint' in Act III of *The Beaux' Stratagem* (1707); *Cassandra* and another of La Calprenède's romances, *Cleopatra* (first published in 1647) figure in the 'Lady's Library' described in *The Spectator*, no. 37, 12 April 1711.

Page 122. (1) The name, often preceded by *gay*, denotes a rake or a libertine, as in Davenant's *The Cruel Brother* (1630) and Rowe's *The Fair Penitent* (1703).

Page 123. (1) Bethlehem Hospital for lunatics in Moorfields. See Hogarth's *Rake's Progress* (1735), plate viii, and Maitland, ii, 1290.

Page 125. (1) Another character from Rowe's *The Fair Penitent* (1703) who discovers the heroine Calista's affair with Lothario.

Page 126. (1) One of the four Inns of Court situated on the north side of High Holborn. See Maitland, ii, 1279.

Page 127. (1) 'Now the *Bailiff*'s Name and Office is grown into Contempt, they being, generally Officers to serve Writs, etc. within their Liberties.' They could not arrest a man without a warrant from the sheriff of the county, 'and shall be punished for malicious Distresses, by Fine and treble Damages'. See Jacob, s.v. *bailiff*.

Page 128. (1) Originally an inferior bailiff, from medieval Latin *Cacepollus*, literally a 'chase-fowl'. Here, taken derisively.

(2) See note (1) to p. 373 *infra* on 'spunging-houses'.

(3) The phrase 'Myrmydons of the law, of Justice' was often applied contemptuously in the eighteenth century to a 'bailiff or other inferior administrative officer of the law' (*OED*).

(4) A prison, mostly for debtors, in Southwark, adjoining the King's Bench.

Page 129. (1) Ran parallel to Drury Lane between Russell Street and the Strand.

Page 130. (1) Fined.

(2) At the junction of the Strand, Whitehall, and Cockspur Street.

Page 131. (1) Posset is a hot drink composed of milk curdled with ale, wine, or any other liquor, with sugar and spices often added. Formerly regarded as a delicacy and a remedy for colds.

Page 132. (1) The hundreds were administrative subdivisions, of obscure origin, referring perhaps to a group of a hundred families of freeholders; here it means 'area, district'. Although *OED* defines *hundred* exclusively in relation to counties or shires, the phrase 'the hundreds of Drury' seems to have been quite current: see for instance the *Grub-Street Journal* of 6 Aug. 1730 and 24 Sept. 1730, and Fielding's *Journey from this World to the Next* (1743), bk. I, ch. 3.

Page 133. (1) Infected with venereal disease.

Page 134. (1) Apart from the obvious nautical meaning—'an old vessel filled with combustible materials, and fitted with grappling-irons to hook, and set fire to, the enemies' ships' (Falconer)—the wit intends a pun on the slang meaning of the word, already known to Wycherley: a diseased whore.

(2) Be clapped in irons this time. Bilboes—taking their name from the steel made at Bilbao—were long padlocked bars with sliding iron shackles in which the ankles of prisoners were confined on board ship. The sailors called them 'iron-garters'.

(3) Sea-wit again. Literally, a ship was 'hove down' on one side, or 'careened', in order to cleanse her bottom of any filth adhering to it.

(4) West of Grosvenor Square, in a most fashionable area. See Phillips, p. 258.

Page 136. (1) A commercial phrase of nautical origin—cf. the proverb 'Venture not all in one bottom'—denoting independence.

(2) From St Paul's Cathedral, probably down Ludgate Hill, Fleet Street, and the Strand.

(3) Here, a man picked up by a prostitute.

Page 137. (1) A well-known manifestation of tertiary syphilis was the ulceration of the nose, leading ultimately to its total mutilation. Hence noses were not only a bawdy topic in the eighteenth century but also a very touchy one. The Parisian procuress in *FCF*, ch. xxiii, has also 'lost her nose in the course of her ministration' (p. 93).

Page 138. (1) This is most probably reminiscent of Moll Hackabout's arrival from the country in plate i of Hogarth's *Harlot's Progress* (1732).

Page 139. (1) In front of the Tower, in the vicinity of Tower Hill and of the Navy Office, a favourite hunting ground for press-gangs. See Boucé, p. 263.

(2) A small vessel used to convey impressed men to receiving ships.

Page 140. (1) One of the sailors' favourite drinks, made of beer mixed with spirit and sugar, heated with a red-hot iron. 'Flip' is the name of a commodore of the old school in Charles Shadwell's *Fair Quaker of Deal* (1710). See Boucé, pp. 267–8.

(2) Midshipmen in the East Indian service, but more generally a term of contempt, used again by Trunnion in *PP*, p. 9: 'I was none of your guinea-pigs.'

(3) For *taut*, i.e. stiff.

(4) *Ratlines* or *ratlings* were small horizontal lines traversing the shrouds, and thus forming rope ladders to the mastheads.

Page 141. (1) In a sailing ship, *block* is the name given to a variety of pullies, or systems of pullies, usually made of elm. One of the sailor-characters in Smollett's *The Reprisal* (1757) is also called Ben Block.

(2) 'To hand the sails' meant to furl them. 'To reef' is to reduce the surface of a sail exposed to the wind. The same phrase is used by Ben Block in the last scene of *The Reprisal*.

(3) A nautical set phrase. The 'small bower anchor' and 'the best bower anchor', slightly different in size, were both carried on the bows of the ship.

(4) It will bring the ship to a standstill.

(5) A tag associated with nautical speech.

(6) No other example of the phrase has been traced: the implicit meaning seems to be haughtiness.

(7) 'An apartment without the great cabin of a ship, from which it is separated by a thin partition' (Falconer).

(8) Back and forth, in Jack's nautical parlance.

(9) A ship's boat, resembling a barge, but smaller, rowed with eight oars.

(10) Smaller and broader than a barge or a pinnace, a cutter was used to carry stores, provisions, or passengers to and from the ship. Technically the captain's boat was the barge—see *PP*, p. 393—and lieutenants were accommodated in the pinnace.

Page 142. (1) According to nautical regulations, the captain placed the letter 'R' (for 'run') next to the name of any man or officer who was reputed to have deserted. See *Regulations and Instructions Relating to His Majesty's Service at Sea* (1734, 2nd edn.), p. 28. See also note (1) to p. 235 *infra*.

(2) A naval anchorage, taking its name from a sandbank lying off the entrance to the River Medway. It was the scene in 1797 of a great naval mutiny.

(3) A narrow platform made of planks, connecting the quarter deck to the forecastle, usually referred to as 'gangway'. (See Falconer.)

(4) To pay (same family as *pitch*) means to smear the bottom and sides of a ship with such substances as tar, turpentine, or resin, in order to protect them from the injuries of the water and the weather.

(5) This is a reference to man-ropes, often covered with red baize, on either side of the officers' gangway. Ben Block in *The Reprisal*, last scene, uses the same image to describe Champignon's queue with red ribbons: 'the red ropes hanging over his stern'. W. N. Glascock in his *Naval Sketch Book*, 2nd series, i (1834) objects to Smollett's nautical phrase which he corrects thus: ' "Red ropes are *shipped* to your bows" instead of to your side' (p. 125).

(6) Situated near the after hatchway, under the lower gun-deck, it was the space allotted to the surgeon and his mates as living quarters, and operating theatre in action.

(7) A tough pliant stick, a rattan, often used by officers to inflict a summary mode of punishment known as 'starting', never sanctioned in the service by law, only by custom.

(8) A warrant officer responsible for disciplinary matters on board. (See Falconer.)

Page 143. (1) That part of the upper deck between the mainmast and the stern, traditionally reserved for the exclusive use of the captain and the officers. Warrant officers and ratings were summoned there to receive orders, and when detailed for specific duties.

Page 144. (1) Again, accurate, doubly so. The 1734 *Regulations* provided that condemned provisions were not to be thrown overboard, except cheese, in certain conditions (see pp. 118–19). Butter was *never* to be thrown overboard but returned to the victualling agent or supplied to the boatswain for the ship's use. Moreover, according to the manuscript journal kept by Robert Watkins, a lieutenant in Smollett's *Chichester*, a survey of provisions was carried out on 22 Dec. 1740 and 'Eighteen Hundred and Ninety five pounds of cheese' were condemned (see Knapp, p. 32).

(2) On the orlop deck, where the cables are stowed.

(3) A vaguer term in the eighteenth century than nowadays, for the west coast of Africa. Thus, the Navy surgeon John Atkins, in his *Voyage to Guinea, Brasil, and the West Indies* (1737, 2nd edn.): 'By Guinea here, I mean all *Negro-land*, from about the river *Senega* Northward to within a few Degrees of *Cape Bon Esperance*' (p. 38).

(4) 'A large rowing boat having a tilt or awning, formerly used on the Thames, esp. as a passenger boat between London and Gravesend' (*OED*).

(5) Gravesend: riverport in Kent on the south bank of the Thames,

about 24 miles from London. Rochester: a town in Kent on the south bank of the River Medway, about 30 miles south-east by east of London.

Page 145. (1) 'Formerly the title of officers of control appointed in the royal ports and dockyards' (*OED*).

(2) Variously spelt 'Monachdeny', 'Monuchdenny', 'Mounth-Denny' on seventeenth- and eighteenth-century maps of Wales. James Brome in his *Travels Over England, Scotland and Wales* (1700), p. 22, locates it three miles from Brecon. Professors Cecil Price, R. H. Greenwood, D. E. Evans (Swansea) and D. Thomas (Lampeter) identify it with the modern Pen-y-Fan, the main peak of the Brecon Beacons (2906 feet). We have been unable so far, to trace any legend about Mounchdenny and the devil, but James Brome (op. cit., p. 21) marvels at the mountains in Wales 'of so unconceivable a Height, and so steep an Ascent, that they seem, as it were, Nature's Stair-Cases, by which we may climb up to some higher Regions, and have an Entercourse and Correspondence with the Inhabitants of the Moon, or converse more frequently and familiarly with the Aereal Daemons'. Brome (ibid.) does mention a legend according to which nothing, except 'stones, or the like' could fall from the top of Mounchdenny, but would be blown up again, a strange tale traced back to John Speed's (1552?–1629) description of Brecknockshire (1627) by Mr T. Roberts (Bangor). In *PP*, p. 183, Morgan asserts that 'there was not a mountain in Wales, which had not been in his memory the scene of necromancy and witchcraft'.

Page 146. (1) Smollett may have known the name and works of the naval surgeon John Atkins (1685–1757): *The Navy Surgeon* (1734) and *A Voyage to Guinea* (1735). But Atkins stopped sailing after 1723. The name of the *Chichester*'s surgeon, while Smollett was on board, was Atkinson (see Knapp, p. 33).

(2) A typical Welshman, reminiscent of Shakespeare's Fluellen in *Henry V*: '... valiant / And touch'd with choler, hot as gunpowder / And quickly will return an injury' (IV. vii). Smollett was obviously fond of the character, who reappears briefly in *PP*, ch. xxxviii. Bramble refers to 'Morgan's widow' in the opening letter of *HC*: she may be the late first mate's widow as Morgan in *PP* (p. 185) had already decided to retire to his beloved Glamorganshire.

Page 147. (1) 'All Liquors are so called, which are us'd as Dissolvents, or to extract the Virtues or Ingredients by Infusion, Decoction etc.', Quincy, p. 278.

(2) Caradoc, King of the Britons, who after putting up an energetic resistance to the Romans for nearly nine years, was vanquished in A.D. 50, and sent to Rome, where he was spared by the Roman Emperor Claudius Caesar (A.D. 41–54). The fondness of the Welsh for tracing genealogical descents was well known.

Page 148. (1) Two ships were 'yard arm and yard arm' when during an action they were fighting at such close quarters that their yard-arms nearly touched; the 'glasses' here may have been hour-glasses, or more probably half-hour glasses.

(2) A latinate phrase for *Welshman* (*Cambria*: Wales).

(3) To lower or strike the flag as a token of surrender to a victorious enemy.

(4) Various places of retreat on deck where, behind strong barriers of wood (called 'close quarters') especially fitted with loopholes, the crew of a merchant ship could defend themselves against boarding parties.

(5) A traditional warning cry in the Navy when hot food, especially soup, is being carried from the galley.

(6) An earthen pot used by apothecaries for various ointments and medicines.

Page 149. (1) A meatless day, on which fish, or cheese only, was issued. Smollett's etymological explanation is correct, the Banians being a Hindu sect abstaining from eating flesh.

(2) The regulation space in which to sling a hammock.

Page 151. (1) Probably 'Shitten luck is good luck'. See *Oxford Dictionary of English Proverbs*, s.v. *shitten*.

Page 154. (1) *Loblolly* is an obsolete word for a ship-doctor's medicines. Hence, a *loblolly boy* was an attendant assisting a ship's surgeon and his mates in their various duties.

Page 155. (1) Hockley in the Hole was a popular place of public diversion near Clerkenwell Green, complete with bear and bull baitings, and other trials of skill and strength such as boxing. It is referred to by Gay's Mrs Peachum in *The Beggar's Opera*, as a school of valour.

(2) Tottenham Court Road was also associated with boxing: see Phillips, pp. 223–9.

(3) 'A peculiar throw over the hip made use of in wrestling and formerly in pugilism' (*OED*).

(4) A thrusting blow, with a straight arm.

Page 156. (1) A dislocation of the upper arm.

Page 157. (1) A minced oath for 'Christ's blood and wounds'.

(2) A Turkish variant of *pasha*, denoting here a petty tyrant. Fielding in *A Voyage to Lisbon* (1755) uses the word several times to describe the tyrannical sway of a ship's commander.

Page 158. (1) 'An intermitting Fever, where the Fit returns every third Day, the two sick Days being reckoned, and the two intermitting ones making four', Quincy, p. 396.

Notes

(2) An acute pain in the side caused by pleurisy. Quincy recommends 'Evacuation, Suppuration, or Expectoration, or all together' (p. 369), but not exercise.

Page 159. (1) One of the kinds of dropsy, due to a collection of fluid in the peritoneal cavity. 'Tapping' the fluid was the usual (painful) remedy. See *HC*, pp. 18–19.

(2) Not quite clear. It was the boatswain's mate who usually inflicted all punishments under the direction of the ship's commander. 'Driver' may be derived from the verb 'to drive' (*OED*, 11 (b)) meaning 'to aim (a blow); to strike (a person) with a thrust of the arm'.

(3) Now usually 'futtock shrouds', supporting the top on a lower mast. See Falconer, s.v. *shrouds*, and Kemp, diagram, p. 332.

Page 160. (1) In Rosemary Lane (now Royal Mint Street), a squalid place of evil reputation where frippery was sold.

Page 161. (1) Sir Chaloner Ogle (1681 ?–1750), knighted in 1723, Rear-Admiral of the Blue in 1739, commanded the reinforcement fleet sent to Vice-Admiral Vernon; Admiral and Commander-in-Chief in 1749.

(2) A convenient naval anchorage off Deal on the east coast of England, lying inside the Goodwin Sands and between the North and South Foreland.

(3) Generally the fore part of a ship, including the bows on each side, but here 'in a confined sense, also signifies that part on each side of the stem, which is appropriated to the private use of the sailors' (W. Burney, *A New and Universal Dictionary of the Marine* (1830), s.v. *head*, p. 189).

Page 162. (1) A traditional anchorage and assembly point in the east Solent between Portsmouth and Ryde, Isle of Wight.

(2) A bay on the east coast of the Isle of Wight, often used as a rendezvous point by the Royal Navy in the eighteenth century.

(3) Cartagena is now the capital of the province of Bolivar, in Columbia. Smollett, as a surgeon's second mate on board the *Chichester*, sailed for Jamaica with Sir Chaloner Ogle's fleet (26 October 1740), which joined Admiral Vernon's squadron there on 9 January 1741. By February 1741 this large expeditionary force numbered 124 sail, some 15,000 sailors, and 12,000 soldiers under the command of Brigadier-General Wentworth (see note (1) to p. 187 *infra*). The various abortive attacks and the siege of Cartagena were over by 7 May 1741. Smollett analysed the lamentable fiasco twice in his 'Account of the Expedition against Carthagene', published anonymously in *The Compendium of Authentic and Entertaining Voyages* (1756), v, 312–42, reprinted in W. E. Henley's edition of Smollett's *Works*, xii, 187–221, and secondly in his *Complete History of England* (1757–8), iv. 600, 107–10. *A Journal of the Expedition to Carthagena* (1744), a pamphlet in defence of Wentworth's land forces, has sometimes

been attributed to him, but with little certainty. Most biographies or critical studies listed in the Select Bibliography deal at variable length with this pivotal experience in Smollett's life and fiction. The most complete study is L. L. Martz's 1941 article listed in the Select Bibliography. See also Kahrl, pp. 1–27, and Boucé, pp. 8–12, 48–50. The phrase 'the ever memorable expedition of Carthagena' recurs verbatim in the 'Account', xii, 221 of W. E. Henley's edition.

(4) *League* here means precisely three nautical miles; *The Lizard* is the southernmost promontory of England.

(5) The speaking trumpets used to convey orders especially in tempestuous weather.

(6) A long vertical chain, equipped with a number of valves, working on a sprocket wheel, by which the water is pumped out of the ship's hold.

(7) Changed to 'I rose' in fourth edn., 1755.

(8) Not to be confused with the top of the mast: 'topmast' is the name of the *middle* section of a three-piece mast, the lowest being the 'lower mast' and the highest the 'top-gallant-mast'.

Page 164. (1) Amputated.

(2) Roadstead, anchorage.

(3) Any remnants or pieces of old, frayed, cable.

Page 165. (1) A current medical tag meaning 'according to the rules of the art'. On the treatment, see Boucé, p. 275.

Page 170. (1) Shuttlecock.

Page 171. (1) Sir Edward Coke (1552–1634)—very often pronounced and spelled *Cooke* in his own day and afterwards—the author of the so-called *Institutes of the Laws in England* in four parts (*First Part*, 1628), which were a commentary on Sir Thomas Littleton's (1422–1481) *Treatise on Tenures. Coke upon Littleton*, repeatedly reprinted throughout the eighteenth century, is still occasionally quoted as an authority on the law of real property. Oakhum's garbled reference to it points to his crass ignorance in legal matters.

Page 172. (1) The name given by Europeans to the ruler of the Mohammedan-Tartar empire in India, which disintegrated after the death of Aurungzebe in 1707, and disappeared in 1857.

Page 173. (1) *The Book of Common Prayer* (article xxv) recognizes only the sacraments of Roman Baptism and the Supper of the Lord. Catholics recognize five other sacraments: Orders, Confirmation, Penance, Extreme Unction, and Matrimony.

(2) See article xxviii, 'Of the Lord's Supper', where this Roman Catholic doctrine of 'the change of the substance of Bread and Wine' is condemned.

Notes

Page 175. (1) Tackled 'one who unexpectedly proves to be too formidable' (*OED*), probably from the ferocious reputation of Tartars.

(2) Does not appear to be a specific nautical term, but denotes a paltry room or apartment immediately under the ridge of the roof, to which access is usually gained by a ladder.

Page 176. (1) The brothers Hengist and Horsa were the legendary leaders of the first Anglo-Saxon settlers, who came to Britain about A.D. 450.

Page 178. (1) See Eccles. 3: 5, formerly ascribed to 'the wise man' (Solomon).

Page 179. (1) A small island, Ile à Vache, off the southern coast of Haiti.

Page 180. (1) Fascines were faggots of small wood, between two or three feet in thickness, four feet in length, loaded with earth, or covered with raw hides to prevent their being destroyed by fire. Here they are used for protecting the battery.

(2) Small mortars, named after the Dutch military engineer who invented them, Baron Coehorn (1641–1704).

Page 181. (1) Technically Mackshane was right, since he could avail himself of the instructions to surgeons in the 1734 *Regulations and Instructions*. See Boucé, p. 274.

(2) A rope from the ship's stern attached to the anchor cable when a ship lies at anchor. This device was used to bring the ship's broadside battery to bear on another ship, or on a fortress, as is the case here.

Page 184. (1) To let the cable run quite out, usually in an emergency, when there is no time to weigh anchor, which is not the case here; to 'sheer off' is to move off to a greater distance.

Page 185. (1) A quart short in measure; pursers, whose duty on board was to distribute the provisions to officers and crew, were notorious thieves. Again referred to by Smollett in his 'Account of the Expedition against Carthagene' (1756) and estimated as 'about three half-pints'.

Page 186. (1) A reference to Admiral Vernon's famous order of 21 August 1740, Port Royal, instituting what later came to be known as 'grog'; after the Admiral's nickname 'Old Grogram' derived from his grogram cloak. The 'tot', as the daily rum issue was called in the Navy, was suppressed on 31 July 1970.

(2) This is no polemical exaggeration, but harsh facts. By May 1741, only 1,500 soldiers out of General Wentworth's force of 8,000 were fit to fight; in July 2,260 men died in three weeks. See C. Lloyd and J. L. S. Coulter, *Medicine and the Navy: 1200–1900* (1961), pp. 104–6, and Boucé, pp. 275–6.

Notes

(3) A simile taken from *Henry V*, III. vii.

Page 187. (1) Brigadier-General Wentworth, who assumed command of the troops on Lord Cathcart's death (20 Dec. 1740). For a balanced appraisal of Wentworth's and Vernon's responsibilities in the Cartagena expedition, see J. W. Fortescue, *A History of the British Army*, ii (1899), 59–79.

(2) Admiral Edward Vernon (1684–1757), the celebrated inventor of 'grog'—see *supra*—to whom Smollett, either out of personal bias or ignorance, is most probably unfair.

(3) Caesar (102?–44 B.C.) and Pompey (106–48 B.C.) both famous Roman generals, contended for power in 49–48 B.C. This is a verbatim translation of Lucan, *De Bello Civili*, i, 125–6: 'Nec quemquam iam ferre potest Caesarve priorem / Pompeiusve parem.'

(4) Here, not so much 'to hang back' or 'hesitate' as 'to grumble'.

(5) A joint-stool was made by a joiner, as distinguished from an ordinary stool; the word was often used allusively to convey ridicule or disparagement. A close-stool enclosed a chamber-pot in a stool or box.

(6) A well-known and most controversial episode: the Spanish admiral's ship, the *Galicia*, was used as a floating battery to cannonade the town; but being moored too far from the walls, according to Smollett and the detractors of the Navy, could do little or no damage. After this final abortive attempt (16 April 1741) the siege of Cartagena was virtually over.

Page 188. (1) See *Don Quixote*, pt. I. bk. 1, ch. viii in Smollett's translation (1755).

Page 189. (1) The yellow fever also described by Smollett in *A Compendium of Authentic and Entertaining Voyages* (1756), v, 342, and in his *Present State of All Nations* (1768–9), viii, 382.

Page 190. (1) It was a commonly held belief then that stenches, caused by heat, filth, and overcrowding—in prisons and on board ships—propagated illness. See J. Atkins, *The Navy Surgeon* (1742 edn.), p. 358. Hence also the efforts of such inventors as Stephen Hales and Samuel Sutton in order to ventilate ships properly. On this important issue see C. Lloyd and J. L. S. Coulter, op. cit. note (2) to p. 186 *supra*, pp. 72–7; Boucé, pp. 272–3.

Page 191. (1) Which Roderick was probably wise to do, but which Smollett did not do himself, since according to P.R.O. Ad. 33/410, he ran up a hospital bill of 10s. 8d., which meant a considerable amount of money out of his monthly wages of about £2 0s. 0d. See Knapp, pp. 32 and 35.

(2) A *bolus* was any medicine of spherical shape, larger than an ordinary pill, yet not too large to be swallowed. *Diaphoretic*: having the property of producing perspiration.

Notes

Page 192. (1) The Test Act (1673) required that all civil and military officers, with a few minor exceptions, or persons receiving pay from the Crown, should take the oath of allegiance and supremacy, declare against transubstantiation, and receive the sacrament according to the rites of the Church of England. Although directed against the Roman Catholic Recusants, the Test Act was equally crippling for Protestant Dissenters. It was not repealed until 1828. The Toleration Act (1689) made religious practice easier for the Dissenters, and opened up municipal and other offices to them, but not to the Roman Catholics, who were excluded from its benefits. Dissenters still had to take the oaths of allegiance and supremacy, and subscribe a declaration against transubstantiation. The provision in the Test Act that all persons in office, or receiving pay from the Crown, should receive the sacrament according to the usage of the Church of England remained valid. Hence, the (feigned?) surprise of the chaplain who is in fact deviously trying to find out whether Roderick is a fellow crypto-Roman Catholic.

Page 193. (1) An exclamation of sorrow, originally Scots, but also to be heard in Wales.

Page 195. (1) *right*: 'true, genuine'; *mechlin*: lace produced at Mechlin, a town now in Belgium.

(2) Morocco leather.

(3) See *The Rape of the Lock* (1714), i, 101 and G. Tillotson's note on sword-knots worn by beaux (Twickenham edition).

(4) Tassel.

(5) The name connotes fickleness and trifling insignificance. Whiffle's most direct literary forebear—without any implication of homosexuality— is the 'finical sea fop' Mizen, in Charles Shadwell's *The Fair Quaker of Deal* (1710): see Boucé, pp. 267–8. Smollett had already attacked homosexuality in his poem *Advice* (1746), ll. 91–114. Strutwell, another homosexual, appears in ch. li of *RR*. An Italian Marquis and a German Baron are chastised for their unnatural practices in *PP*, ch. xlix.

(6) The Ancients commonly divided Arabia into three parts: Arabia Felix, or *happy*; Petraea, or *stony*; Deserta, or *desert*. See Pliny, *Natural History*, bk. v, xii, § 65. Arabia Felix was famous for its wealth and perfumes.

Page 196. (1) Foppish pronunciation for 'Zounds', noted as early as Farquhar's *Love and a Bottle* (1699), ii. 2.

(2) A distilled water made from rosemary flowers infused in rectified spirit of wine, used chiefly to perfume linen.

(3) The River Tawe rising in the western part of the Brecon Beacons near Cray, and entering the Bristol Channel at Swansea. Compare with Fluellen to King Henry in *Henry V*, IV. vii: 'All the water in Wye cannot wash your Majesty's Welsh plood out of your pody.'

459

Notes

(4) Pertaining to the head, and more precisely here, having the property of curing any distempers of the head.

Page 197. (1) French for a brush or clothes whisk, but also a sly pun on the sexual meaning of 'verge': a small penis.

Page 198. (1) *Castor*: an oily substance extracted from the anal glands of the beaver, usually prescribed as a stimulant in nervous disorders, and reputed to correct 'the virulence of Opium' (Quincy, pp. 498–9). *Laudanum* is a tincture of opium.

(2) Hot milk curdled with Spanish white wine, with sugar and spices, formerly much used as a restorative.

Page 200. (1) Surgeon's first mates received £2. 10s. monthly wages, irrespective of their ships' rates. A sloop received sixth rate's pay. See J. Entick, *A New Naval History* (1757), p. xlvi.

(2) It was the captain's duty to deliver a duly signed ticket, or pay-warrant, to any man discharged from his books. The cause of the discharge had to be stated on the ticket, which could be delivered to none but the party or an attorney. But the ticket was often sold to a money-lender at a discount.

(3) For disabled or superannuated seamen of the Navy, until 1873. For a detailed account of its organization, see J. Chamberlayne, *The Present State of Great-Britain* (1748), pt. II, bk. iii, pp. 186–90.

Page 201. (1) Or *barca-longa*, a large Spanish fishing-boat, with two or three masts.

(2) Near the eastern tip of Jamaica.

(3) The outer harbour of Kingston, on the south coast of Jamaica.

(4) Brails were ropes used to gather in sails temporarily before furling.

Page 204. (1) A Spanish gold coin worth somewhat less than a pound, from 16s. 6d. to 18s.

Page 205. (1) Bad feeling, lack of cordiality.

Page 206. (1) Spanish gold coins, originally worth two pistoles.

(2) A public auction.

(3) A game at dice.

(4) William III (1650–1702), King of England from 1689.

(5) In order to scrape off all the accretions hindering the ship's penetration into the water, and hence her speed.

Page 207. (1) A disease of the urinary tract, the formation and passage of many small concretions.

Page 208. (1) The hand lead line, of about 20 fathoms in length, was used to measure the depth in shallow waters, near coasts. The gunner

Notes

rightly thinks that the ship is drawing near the land, where the depth of water may be reckoned by means of the sounding lead.

(2) The Scilly islands are a cluster of islands, islets, and rocks lying 25 to 30 miles off Land's End in Cornwall. The light, described by William Borlase in his *Observations on the Ancient and Present State of the Islands of Scilly* (Oxford, 1756), pp. 37–9, stood on St Agnes island.

Page 209. (1) As pointed out first by H. F. Watson, *The Sailor in English Fiction and Drama 1550–1800* (New York, 1931), pp. 166–8, the episode of the sloop's wreck on the coast of Sussex is taken directly from the story of the *Wager*, one of Anson's ships, wrecked on the coast of Chile on 14 May 1741. Two survivors, the gunner John Bulkeley, and the carpenter John Cummins, published their *Voyage to the South Seas* in 1743 (see pp. 13–15 on the looting of the wreck by the crew, and drunkenness). Smollett may also have known another survivor's account, Alexander Campbell's *The Sequel to Bulkeley and Cummins's Voyage to the South Seas* (1747), which confirms (pp. 14–16) his predecessors' observations. Smollett may also have heard the story from Captain Cheap, who commanded the *Wager*: see Kahrl, pp. 15–16. See also Boucé, pp. 269–70.

(2) Or Jonah, a bearer of ill-luck, an allusion to the Book of Jonah.

Page 212. (1) For an analysis of the Sussex peasants' dialect, see T. K. Pratt's 1975 Ph.D. thesis (Select Bibliography), pp. 350–6.

(2) A portmanteau word conflating *Christian* and *chrisom*, the white robe used for a child's baptism, and also for burial, as a shroud, if the child died within a month from baptism. See also *Henry V*, II. iii, where the hostess describes Falstaff's death 'an it had been any christom child'.

Page 213. (1) A traditional and condescending name for a rustic, an abbreviated and altered form of *Roger*.

(2) See Luke 10: 30–7.

Page 214. (1) Pestered.

Page 215. (1) As many battles during the Flanders campaigns took place in or near woods, which made concealment of movements possible, the identification of the battle cannot be absolutely certain. Brigadier Peter Young, in a private letter, suggests Wynendael, 28 Sept. 1708, where the action took place, for a large part, inside a wood: see J. W. Fortescue's description in his *History of the British Army* (1899), i, 507, and also Thackeray's *Esmond* (1852), bk. II, ch. 15. Malplaquet, 11 Sept. 1709, the bloodiest battle in the eighteenth century, was also fought partly in adjoining woods, but, strictly speaking, the village is not situated in Flanders, but in French Hainaut.

Page 216. (1) More correctly 'virtuosa', (Italian fem. of *virtuoso*): here an amateur or dilettante dabbling in arts or sciences.

Notes

Page 217. (1) The 'Rosicrucian Philosophy', briefly summed up here by Mrs Sagely, was well known to eighteenth-century readers since Pope had taken his 'machinery' from it in *The Rape of the Lock* (1714). The Rosicrucian society, or order, had been supposedly founded by Christian Rosenkreuz in 1484, but was not mentioned until 1614. See the Twickenham edition of Pope's *Poems*, ii, ed. G. Tillotson, Appendix B, 'The Sylphs'.

(2) Snuff.

Page 218. (1) Castalia was the name of a spring on Mount Parnassus, held sacred to Apollo and the Muses. This quotation, otherwise untraced, may be an ironic reference to Horace, *Odes*, III. iv. 61–2, where Apollo 'rore puro Castaliae lavit / crines solutos' i.e. 'laves his flowing locks in Castalia's pure dew'.

(2) A reference to Arion, a semi-mythical poet of Lesbos, who after being thrown overboard by rapacious sailors, was carried to land by a dolphin. Narcissa's aunt may also be thinking of Jonas who 'was three days and three nights in the whale's *belly*' (Matt. 12: 40), a word a polite lady might be loth to pronounce then.

(3) The Hellespont, now known as the Dardanelles, the narrows separating Europe from Asia Minor. According to legend, Leander, a youth of Abydos, used at night to swim across to Sestos on the opposite shore, where Hero, the beautiful priestess of Aphrodite, waited for him with a lighted torch. See Marlowe's *Hero and Leander* (1598).

Page 220. (1) Derogatory labels, rather than names, to qualify these boorish squires. 'Bumper': 'a cup or glass filled to the brim, esp. for a toast' (*OED*) implies an all too frequent proclivity to drink.

Page 221. (1) Torquato Tasso (1544–95) the greatest Italian poet of the late Renaissance whose *Gerusalemme Liberata* (1581) reflects the rather romantically morbid feelings of his melancholy soul. In eighteenth-century Europe he became the emblem of misunderstood and persecuted genius which must have been highly congenial to Narcissa's aunt. Ludovico Ariosto (1474–1533) author of *Orlando Furioso* (1516, 1521, 1532).

(2) See F. McCombie's 1971 article and J. W. Sena's article (1977) cited in the Select Bibliography. For similar delusions, see the Cave of Spleen passage in canto iv of *The Rape of the Lock* (1714), esp. ll. 47–54.

Page 222. (1) Here, a hare.

Page 223. (1) Roderick's assumed name, John Brown, playfully translated into Italian.

Page 224. (1) Of Gibraltar.

(2) 'In every Parish there is a *School* set up by Act of Parliament . . .

whose Master has a Salary from the Publick, and the Scholars allow them some small matter Quarterly. In *Country Schools* they teach *Writing* and *Arithmetick*, and Reading *English*, and in some *Latin*. In the Royal Burghs they teach *Latin* and *Greek*, and have tolerable Salaries: besides that each Scholar gives 2*s*. or 2*s*. 6*d*. a Quarter; and in these Schools they teach nothing else, having *English* and *Writing-Schools* in all Places where they have *Grammar-Schools*.' J. Chamberlayne, *The Present State of Great-Britain* (1748), pt. II, bk. iii, p. 419.

(3) An oblique, and possibly—but not certainly so—humorous reference to Smollett's own ill-fated tragedy, *The Regicide*, finally published in 1749.

Page 225. (1) This is a slightly modified version of Smollett's (probably) earliest publication 'A New Song', which first appeared in John Newbery's *Universal Harmony* (1745), p. 86, with music by James Oswald. See Knapp, pp. 44–5, 195.

Page 227. (1) Possibly a humorous allusion to Nathaniel Lee's tragedy *The Rival Queens* (1667) often revived in the eighteenth century.

Page 228. (1) Also known as 'afterings' locally, the last milk drawn from a cow, thought to be the richest.

Page 229. (1) From the name of the bear in *Reynard the Fox*, hence an uncouth boor.

Page 230. (1) 'The warrant or Letters Patent, which all Men exercising Jurisdiction either ordinary or extraordinary, have to authorize them to hear or determine any Cause or Action.' (Jacob).

Page 231. (1) Smuggling, especially with Ireland, France, and Holland was rife throughout the eighteenth century. Tea, sugar, spirits, tobacco, wool, and lace, were among the smugglers' favourite commodities. By the statute 19 Geo. 2, c. 34, smugglers were outlawed.

(2) A phonetic rendering of *Boulogne*, a large seaport on the coast of Picardy, 17 miles south of Calais.

Page 232. (1) Keg.

Page 234. (1) In Upper Normandy, a dozen miles from the sea.

(2) This proverb, advocating independence, not to say downright selfishness, is recorded in several modern dictionaries of proverbs, e.g. W. C. Hazlitt's (1907) and B. Stevenson's (1948), but no earlier source than *RR* is given.

(3) A cant term: to go begging or sponging.

(4) Marquis Antoine-François d'Antin (1709–41), Vice-Admiral in 1739.

(5) Curaçao, the largest of the Dutch West Indies, in the Caribbean, about 60 miles from Venezuela.

Notes

Page 235. (1) So that he would no longer be considered as a deserter.

Page 238. (1) A staff about three feet long with a forked head to hold a lighted match, ready for firing the guns in an engagement. This seems to be the first recorded use of the proverb. A variant is 'The cobbler to his last, the gunner to his linstock.'

(2) In St Katharine's, Wapping, the Hermitage being a dock there. The 'Union flag' refers to the Union between Scotland and England (1707). In chap. xlv, Bowling's address is given as 'the Samson and Lion', but this was made consistent with the reference above in later editions.

Page 240. (1) Geneviève (426–512), chief patroness of Paris, where she exerted great influence at the time of a threatened attack by Attila.

(2) See Daniel 5 for the story of King Belshazzar's feast and the writing on the wall; but the monk's name may also refer, ironically, to one of the three Magi, who brought myrrh to the infant Saviour. The name means 'the possessor of treasures'. The greedy and bawdy monk was an anti-Papist stock figure.

(3) Abbeville in Lower Picardy, 20 miles north-west of Amiens, and 90 miles north of Paris.

(4) In modern French 'Vin du Pays', local wine.

(5) A peasant-girl.

Page 241. (1) Any kind of distilled spirits.

(2) A tit-bit or choice morsel.

Page 242. (1) The capital of Picardy, 75 miles north of Paris.

(2) In Ile-de-France, some 60 miles north by east of Paris.

Page 244. (1) Handsome looks.

(2) One of the four oldest French regiments of foot officially formed in the 1560s from bands of irregulars existing since 1480. It was also one of the largest, counting up to 120 companies, i.e. 6,000 men.

Page 245. (1) Adrien-Maurice de Noailles (1678–1766), Marshal in 1734, politician and diplomatist.

(2) John Dalrymple, second Earl of Stair (1673–1747), general and diplomatist, created a field-marshal in 1742.

(3) Louis XIV (1638–1715), King of France from 1643, the longest reign in French history.

Page 246. (1) An old saying, attributed to the German Emperor Maximilian by Fleury de Bellingen in *L'Etymologie ou Explication des Proverbes François* (La Haye, 1656), p. 13; also referred to by Nathaniel Ward in *The Simple Cobler of Aggawam in America* (1647): 'There is a quadrobulary saying, which passes current in the Westerne world, that the Emperour is King of Kings, the Spaniard, King of Men, the French,

King of Asses, the King of *England*, King of Devills.' The proverb was deleted from the fourth and later editions, probably because Smollett feared it might be misinterpreted out of its proper context.

Page 247. (1) An ancient cathedral town in Champagne 85 miles north-east of Paris.

(2) Vainglorious bragging.

Page 248. (1) In Germany, 9 miles east of Hanau, on 27 June 1743, where the British and their Austrian allies won a rather inconclusive victory over the French. This was the last battle in which a reigning king of England, George II, actually commanded his forces in person.

(2) Louis-Antoine de Gramont (1689–1745), lieutenant-general in 1738. His disregard of the Duke of Noailles's standing orders was the chief cause of the French defeat at Dettingen.

Page 249. (1) Then the capital of Hanau county, now a port on the right bank of the Main, about 10 miles east of Frankfurt, West Germany.

(2) (742?–814), King of the Franks (768), Emperor of the West (800), conquered practically the whole of Europe, except for Asturias in Spain, southern Italy, and the British Isles.

Page 250. (1) A strongly aromatic plant, and also a cake, pudding, or omelette flavoured with its juice. Lismahago's sword in *HC*, p. 283, is 'passed through a close-stool', a similar indignity.

(2) Long gaiters or leggings of cloth or leather.

Page 253. (1) *Bouilli* in modern French, boiled beef.

(2) A corruption of *asparagus*.

(3) Montpellier, one of the handsomest towns of Languedoc, with a celebrated school of medicine in the eighteenth century and a popular resort then for consumptives. Smollett stayed there for his health in October–November 1763: see his *Travels through France and Italy* (1766), letters ix–xi, and Knapp, pp. 252–4.

(4) Diarrhoea.

Page 256. (1) 'Velvet having the pile cut so as to form patterns' (*OED*).

(2) A sort of woollen cloth.

(3) A kind of lace.

(4) Black swords and buckles were worn for court mourning.

(5) The stock, or neckcloth, wound closely round the neck, was buckled behind.

(6) May refer either to knee or shoe buckles, which could be diamond-studded.

(7) Coverings of cloth, or possibly, leather.

(8) In the 'Palais du Luxembourg', then famous for its paintings by Rubens (1577–1640).

Notes

Page 257. (1) For closely similar foppish behaviour at the theatre see *The Spectator*, no. 240, Wednesday 5 December 1711.

Page 258. (1) In the eighteenth century technically only from Charing Cross to Essex Street, a busy artery, lined almost exclusively with shops. For a detailed study of the Strand see Phillips, pp. 119–84.

Page 259. (1) Gin (for the confusion with the Swiss town, see *OED*).

Page 260. (1) A common woman of the town, plying her trade at the theatre, as is fully documented in *The Tricks of the Town* (1747), letter vii.

(2) Foul language deriving its name from the vituperative rhetoric of the fishwomen in that market, a little below London Bridge.

(3) (a) Juvenal, *Satires*, ii. 8: 'Men's faces should not be trusted.' (b) Virgil, *Eclogues*, ii. 17; the shepherd Corydon advises the fair Alexis: 'Trust not too much to your beautiful complexion.' Here the quotation is fraught with contextual irony, since it is Roderick who should not judge a lady by her appearance alone.

(4) Isabella Farnese (1692–1766), second wife of King Philip V, who throughout her reign (1714–46) strove to secure lands in Italy for her sons.

Page 261. (1) A pronouncement (19 April 1713) made by the Holy Roman Emperor Charles VI (1685–1740) whereby the Habsburg lands should remain undivided and pass to his female heirs in the absence of male progeny. This enabled his daughter Maria Theresa (1717–80) to succeed him in 1740. The invasion of Habsburg Silesia by Frederick II the Great of Prussia stimulated France to take the head of a coalition against Austria, thus causing the war of Austrian Succession (1741–8).

Page 262. (1) Obscene then, 'to fuck': hence Katharine's (apparently) horrified reaction at 'De foot et de coun' in *Henry V*, III. v.

Page 263. (1) Roderick's definition on p. 264 is correct.

(2) At the confluence of the Rivers Sambre and Meuse, one of the strongest fortified cities in Flanders, first taken by Louis XIV and Vauban in 1692, then retaken by King William III and Cohorn in 1695.

(3) A famous military engineer (1641–1704) often referred to as the 'Dutch Vauban'. He built the fortifications of Namur.

(4) Charles-Henri de Lorraine, Prince de Vaudémont (1649–1723).

(5) Louis-François, Duke of Boufflers (1644–1711), Marshal of France in 1694, was forced to capitulate at Namur in Sept. 1695 after a most heroic defence.

Page 264. (1) Great wicker baskets 5 or 6 feet high, about 4 feet in diameter, filled with earth for protection against enemy fire.

(2) A cup.

Notes

Page 265. (1) King of Macedon in 336 B.C., conquered Persia, Syria, and Egypt, died in 323 B.C. aged 32.

(2) Bath, in Somerset, on the River Avon, a little over 100 miles west of London; Tunbridge Wells in Kent, about 30 miles south-east of London: both of these cities being fashionable watering-places in the eighteenth century.

(3) Dearly.

(4) An ornamental trinket formerly often appended to the watch-chain, made of different kinds of stones, or even of coloured glass imitating such a composition.

Page 266. (1) Identified by Professor R. A. Day, in an article kindly communicated before publication, as Dr Thomas Thompson (*c.* 1700–63) an eccentric society doctor but no mere quack. Smollett had already attacked him in *Reproof* (1747) as 'A medling, prating, blund'ring, busy dunce!' (l. 188).

(2) A busybody, a *medler* in other people's affairs. The proverbial simile 'rotten as a medlar' does not seem to be implied here.

Page 267. (1) The name denotes gaudy flashiness.

(2) Aphetic form of *alarum*; here denotes incessant and noisy talk.

(3) 'Coffee in general, seems more proper for Persons of phlegmatic Constitutions, than for Patients of choleric Habits' (James, p. 297). Coffee drinking was popularly supposed to produce effeminacy and impotence.

Page 268. (1) (a) Horace, *Odes*, I. xx: 'thou shalt drink cheap Sabine out of common tankards'. (b) Ibid., 'then thou shalt drink the juice of grapes crushed by Cales' presses'.

(2) Homer, *Iliad*, xiv. 1: 'Nestor heard the cry of battle, though he was drinking.'

(3) A sixth-century B.C. Greek lyric poet, whose verse celebrates mostly the pleasures of love and conviviality. (a) *Anacreontea*, 36, 13: should read *Pinonti*: 'to a drinker of sweet wine'. (b) should read *pio*: 'whenever I drink the wine', ibid., 45, 1. (c) 'Prepare for war, but I go on drinking', ibid., 48, 7. (Loeb Classical Library, *Elegy and Iambus*, ii, *Anacreontea*).

Page 269. (1) A famous coffee-house in Covent Garden, under the Piazza, every night crowded with wits, writers, actors, and fops. See Phillips, pp. 146–7, and *passim*.

(2) The name is rich in ironic possibilities. It may mean either an obsequious person, a harlot, or a dissolute man, which last connotation would be cruelly antiphrastic, since Dr Wagtail's impotence is broadly hinted at in the chapter.

Page 271. (1) Physician and alchemist (1493–1541), vagrant scholar having studied at numerous German and Italian universities, one of the most extraordinary figures of the Renaissance, part 'magician', part chemical and medical genius, he contributed largely to the rise of modern medicine.

(2) 'A medicinal Weight consisting of 20 grains, and making the third of a Dram' (Quincy, p. 413).

Page 272. (1) 'Dead head, is the *Residuum* after Distillation, of any kind whatsoever; or Earth, when all the other Principles are separated from it', ibid., p. 66.

(2) 'Specific medicines' was a phrase 'much in use for such whose Operation could not be accounted for' (Quincy, p. 424).

(3) Tinder, as appears from ch. xlviii, was commonly made from rags, which were also used to make paper.

(4) Hampstead, about 4 miles north-west of the City, formerly a village where elegant crowds flocked to drink the waters of its chalybeate springs. The Long Room of Weatherall House was famous for its dances and assemblies.

(5) Ribbons or streamers depending from a lady's head-dress.

(6) The name suggests a nimble dancing gait: cf. Trippit *supra* p. 59 from the archaic phrase 'To trip it' meaning 'to dance'.

Page 273. (1) To prick or pierce with a pointed instrument or weapon.

(2) Diaphragm or midriff.

(3) 'The Hiccup, is a convulsive Motion of the Stomach, and Parts adjacent, particularly the Diaphragm.' (Quincy, p. 416).

(4) The Greek philosopher Pythagoras (sixth century B.C.) enforced the rules of silence and sexual purity among his disciples.

(5) In eighteenth-century slang, to roam about the town roisterously, and indulge in fashionable pranks such as breaking windows or beating the watch. For *hundreds*, see *supra*, note (1) to p. 132.

Page 274. (1) French for a kiss of the hand, hence formal respects.

Page 275. (1) Medicines composed of a single constituent, especially of one medicinal herb or plant.

(2) See *supra*, note (2) to p. 111.

Page 277. (1) See *supra*, note 2 to p. 50. Again, the histrionic attitude struck by Ranter suggests an oblique reference to the actor Theophilus Cibber's most popular part as Pistol. An excellent engraving of Theo. Cibber 'in the Character of Ancient Pistol', complete with huge cocked hat and swaggering looks, may be seen in his pantomime, *The Harlot's Progress* (1733).

(2) No source has been found.

(3) A burlesque patchwork of quotations taken from *2 Henry IV*, ii. iv. and v. iii, which Ranter deliberately misquotes, since Shakespeare's line

reads: 'Then, Pistol, lay *thy head* in Furies' lap'. The substitution is obviously not devoid of sexual innuendo. For *Hiren*, see *OED*, and Knapp's note in *Letters*, p. 17.

(4) A famous place of public amusement in Islington, about two and a half miles from St Paul's. As Win Jenkins discovered, with awed surprise, the chief entertainments were tumbling, wire-walking, and rope-dancing: see *HC*, p. 108.

Page 278. (1) In Covent Garden, opposite St Paul's Church, a disorderly house frequented by a great variety of patrons, noblemen and beaux included. See Hogarth's *Morning* (1738) where a fight is taking place in Moll King's.

Page 279. (1) Literally, to outrun: Strap seems to have won the marriage race.

(2) Suffering from hypertrophy of the liver.

Page 283. (1) 'A cant word for a woman who picks up rags about the street; and used by way of contempt, for any low vulgar woman' (Johnson, *Dictionary*).

(2) William Hogarth (1697–1764), painter and the most talented and popular engraver in the eighteenth century.

(3) A proverbial phrase meaning 'despite one's original purpose or settled resolution'.

Page 284. (1) A Jacobite agent working for James Francis Edward Stuart (1688–1766) known as the Old Pretender, or his son Charles Edward (1720–88), the Young Pretender.

Page 285. (1) An English nickname for an Irishman. Teague's saying is a typical 'Irish bull', as in Oregan's letter, *infra* p. 290.

(2) Paid a casual visit.

Page 286. (1) Often so spelt formerly for *waive*.

Page 287. (1) In St James's Park, by mid-eighteenth century the most fashionable walk in London. See Phillips, p. 45.

Page 288. (1) See *supra*, note (4) to p. 277.

Page 290. (1) The superscription is trebly incorrect: *Mr.* and *Esq.* should not be used together; Roderick has no right to be styled 'Esq.'; *Those* is illiterate for *These* (i.e. words).

(2) The finest building in Great Russell Street and the mansion which housed the first British Museum in 1753. At its back were gardens where duels were often fought, and where troops camped during the Gordon Riots in 1780. See Phillips, pp. 213–14.

(3) From the two sons of King Milesius, who, according to the legend,

Notes

conquered Ireland about 1300 B.C., and repeopled it after exterminating the aborigines: hence, an Irishman.

Page 291. (1) A county and town in Munster province, Ireland.

Page 292. (1) A strong town of Turkey, in Europe in the eighteenth century, at the confluence of the Danube and Sava rivers, now the capital of Yugoslavia. It was besieged and captured from the Turks on 18 August 1717 by Prince Eugene's Imperial Army.

Page 293. (1) In Westminster; for the description and history of the palace and of the thoroughfare bearing the same name, see Phillips, pp. 30–6.

(2) St Giles-in-the-Fields, at the east end of Oxford Street, one of the worst rookeries or crime quarters in London. See Hogarth's *Gin Lane* (Feb. 1750/1) setting forth the evils of gin-drinking among the poor of St Giles. Many Irishmen had settled in the area. See Phillips, pp. 217–20.

Page 294. (1) *Fitz* is a current Irish onomastic prefix; *clabber*, a dialectal word of Gaelic origin means 'mud'. Smollett uses the name O'Clabber in his *Reprisal* (1757). *Counsellor*, now archaic in English use, still means a barrister or advocate in Ireland (*OED*).

(2) Defined by Smollett in a note to *Advice* (1746). l. 30, as 'a riotous assembly of fashionable people, of both sexes, at a private house, consisting of some hundreds; not unaptly styled a drum from the noise and emptiness of the entertainment'.

Page 297. (1) Suspected.

(2) In slang, *Gripe(s)* meant a covetous person, a usurer. The name over the pawnbroker's door in Hogarth's *Gin Lane* (Feb. 1750/1) is 'S. Gripe'.

Page 298. (1) The title assumed by the eponymous hero of Smollett's *Ferdinand Count Fathom* (1753).

Page 300. (1) Law-students or young barristers in the Inner or Middle Temple, notoriously more interested in fashionable life, especially the theatre, than in the laws of the land. See Steele's characterization of the Templar in *The Spectator*, no. 2, Friday 2 March 1711.

(2) 'Whereby, for one Penny, any Letter or Parcel not exceeding sixteen Ounces Weight, or ten Pounds Value, is most speedily and safely conveyed to and from all Parts within the Bills of Mortality to most Towns within seven Miles round *London*, not conveniently served by the General Post', J. Chamberlayne, *The Present State of Great-Britain* (1748), pt. I, bk. iii, p. 259.

Page 301. (1) Old Bond Street and New Bond Street, joining Piccadilly to Oxford Street. New Bond Street already contained luxury shops, while Old Bond Street was the aristocratic end.

Notes

Page 303. (1) Urganda was an enchantress appearing in the romances of chivalry, *Amadis de Gaula* and *Palmeirim de Inglaterra*. She was famous for her frequent metamorphoses. Smollett again refers to her in *FCF*, ch. xxiii, p. 93, to describe a Parisian procuress.

Page 305. (1) The same simile is used by Fielding in *Joseph Andrews* (1742), bk. I, ch. 6, to describe Mrs Slipslop in very similar amorous circumstances.

(2) Garlic was prescribed to dispel flatulence. See James, pp. 216–19.

Page 310. (1) Latin satirist, who died about A.D. 65, chosen by Nero as 'arbiter elegantiae' i.e. arbiter of taste, author of the *Satyricon*, where the two rogues Encolpius and Ascyltos and their serving boy Giton occasionally indulge in homosexual activities.

(2) See *supra*, note (5) to p. 195 on homosexuality. The reputed spread of homosexuality among the upper classes was a fashionable theme then of moral fulmination. See for instance the anonymous pamphlet *Satan's Harvest Home* (1749) in the British Library (1093. i. 12), pp. 45–62, 'Reasons for the Growth of Sodomy'. See also L. Stone, *The Family, Sex and Marriage in England 1500–1800* (1977), pp. 541–2.

(3) The crime of buggery, or sodomy, was punishable with burning, or burying alive in the sixteenth century, but it is difficult to determine how often the law was enforced. According to Giles Jacob's *A New Law Dictionary* (5th edn. 1745), for many years no exemplary punishment had been inflicted 'till *Anno 12 Geo. 1.* a great Number of these Wretches were convicted of the most abominable Practices, and three of them put to Death; which seasonable Justice seems to have given a Check to the before growing Evil'. According to L. Stone, op. cit. *supra*, p. 541: 'The normal punishment for attempted sodomy was the pillory, but in more than one case this was the equivalent of the death penalty', because of savage mob-violence.

(4) Smollett is here indulging in a piece of what Sheridan called 'puff direct': he is complacently quoting from his *Advice* (1746), ll. 91–4, in slightly altered form.

Page 311. (1) Matrimonial, nuptial, generative. Cf. the phrase 'genial bed' (Latin *lectus genialis*).

Page 312. (1) A wasting away of the body here, not pulmonary consumption.

(2) From Juvenal, *Satires*, vi. 165 'rara avis in terris nigroque simillima cycgno': 'a rare bird on earth very much like a black swan', i.e. a prodigy. This worn out tag assumes a modicum of retrospective irony if the reader bears in mind that Juvenal here is referring to a perfect *wife*.

Page 313. (1) A Royal Hospital for old and disabled soldiers: admitting

Notes

a superannuated footman there would therefore be regarded as a favour. See J. Chamberlayne, *The Present State of Great-Britain* (1748), pt. I, bk. iii, pp. 244–6.

(2) Jackals.

(3) A man or boy who submits to sodomy.

Page 315. (1) A bitter mortification. See Deut. 29: 18.

(2) Guineas.

Page 316. (1) An ironical allusion, possibly not very accurate, to the bigamous George Douglas, fourth Baron Mordington, who occupied the last private house—formerly Sir James Thornhill's—on the north side of Covent Garden, from 1734 to his death in 1741. Lord Mordington was reported to have kept a gaming-house there in 1738. At the time the scene is supposedly taking place (after the battle of Dettingen in 1743) the gaming-table was held by Lord Mordington's long deserted widow, Mary, who is referred to in a presentment of Gaming Houses and other disorderly places by the Middlesex Grand Jury in 1744 (see Maitland, i, 638–9; *Complete Peerage* (1936), ix, 207, 'Her claim, in Jan. 1744/5 as a peeress of Great Britain to keep a gaming-house in the great Piazza, Covent Garden, was disallowed 29 Apr. following by the House of Lords.' For an apt contemporary illustration of this gambling scene, see the reproduction of James Hulett's 'The Covent Garden Gaming Table' in Phillips, p. 143.

Page 317. (1) Rather garbled French supposedly made more readily understandable to foreigners: 'Stay on, fuck it, you must give me my revenge.' *Ravanchio* appears to be a clumsy Gasconization of French *revanche*.

Page 319. (1) An allusion to the Roman custom of marking lucky days with a white stone. See for instance Catullus, *Poems*, ode lxviii, 148; Horace, *Odes*, i. xxvi, 10.

Page 321. (1) In St Giles's, often referred to—by Prior, Gay, and Pope—for its numerous shops dealing in second-hand clothes.

Page 322. (1) Competed for the prize myself: a horse-racing metaphor, the plate being the gold or silver cup awarded to the winner.

Page 324. (1) The captain is punning on the phrase 'To go with child' meaning 'to be pregnant' and 'to go with foal'—a form of which is given as 'fool' in *OED*. There is an oblique allusion to a 'fool' again in Miss Snapper's final retort 'your bolt is soon shot': 'A fool's bolt is soon shot' is another proverbial phrase.

(2) 'A popular tune to a song, having for the burden, "Her black joke and belly so white": figuratively the black joke signifies the monosyllable', F. Grose, *A Classical Dictionary of the Vulgar Tongue* (1963 edn.), s.v.

Notes

black joke. Pope alludes to the tune in his *First Epistle of the Second Book of Horace* (1737), l. 309, where 'The many headed Monster of the Pit' (l. 305) 'Call for the Farce, the Bear or the Black-joke'. See John Butt's note in the Twickenham edn. The song is dated 1730(?) in the British Library Music Catalogue: G.315(99) and G.316.e(99).

Page 325. (1) See Luke 10: 7.

(2) Technically either 'a Writ so called, from the words therein *Praemunire facias*, or *Praemonere facias*, etc. signifying to forewarn or bid the Offender take heed; or it is the Offence on which the Writ is granted'. (Jacob, s.v. *praemunire*). 'The offence of *praemunire* is introducing a foreign power into the land, and creating *imperium in imperio*, by paying that obedience to alien process which constitutionally belongs to the sovereign alone' (Earl Jowitt, *The Dictionary of English Law* (1959), p. 1381). The lawyer is also punning on the non-technical sense of the word: a scrape, or predicament.

(3) 'Where a Man brings a personal Action, and doth not prosecute it with Effect, or if upon the Trial, he refuses to stand a Verdict; then he becomes non-suited.' (Jacob, s.v. *Nonsuit*).

(4) *Nolle prosequi* 'used in the Law, where a Plaintiff in any Action will proceed no further, and may be before or after a Verdict; though it is usually before: And it is stronger against the Plaintiff than a Nonsuit . . .; this is a voluntary Acknowledgement that he hath no Cause of Action'. (Jacob, s.v. *Nolle Prosequi*).

(5) This is a burlesque rendering of John Dalton's highly popular adaptation of Milton's *Comus* (published in 1738, London, and reprinted at least a dozen times in the eighteenth century). The music was composed by Henry Lawes. The song 'By a Woman in a Pastoral Habit' occurs in Act II, p. 34 of the 1738 edition. The first stanza, fravestied here, runs thus: 'Would you taste the noontide Air? / To yon fragrant Bower repair,/ Where woven with the poplar Bough / The mantling Vine will shelter you.' See L. M. Knapp's 1931 article (Select Bibliography).

Page 326. (1) 'To get back or gain by judgement in a court of law; to obtain possession of, or a right to, by legal process.' Also 'to have (a judgement or verdict) given in one's favour' (*OED*).

Page 327. (1) A proverbial phrase meaning here that Roderick looks too much of a simpleton to be able to speak out for himself. The witty repartee is nearly as old as the proverb itself. See *Swift's Polite Conversation*, 1738 (ed. E. Partridge, 1963), p. 109. Ben Jonson is reported to have used it (see *Joe Miller's Jests* (1739, no. 45, p. 13).

Page 328. (1) About fifteen miles south-west of London, in Middlesex. The heath was much larger than nowadays, extending for five miles, and was notorious for its highwaymen in the eighteenth century.

473

Page 329. (1) An easy gallop.

Page 332. (1) The barrister indulges in a series of bawdy innuendoes, very much in the fashion of lawyer Tom Clarke and Ferret in *LG* (pp. 5–6, 9). A conveyancer is a lawyer who deals with the transmission of property. A settlement is 'the act of settling property upon a person or persons' (*OED*). *In tail* (O.F. *taillié*) implies that the property thus settled is 'limited and regulated as to its tenure and inheritance by conditions fixed by the donor' (*OED*). For similar bawdy double entendre by a lawyer in a coach, see *Joseph Andrews* (1742), bk. I, ch. 12.

(2) *Nisi Prius*: 'A writ directed to a sheriff commanding him to provide a jury at the Court of Westminster on a certain day, unless the judges of assize previously come to the county' (*OED*). See also Jacob, s.v. *Nisi Prius*. *To join issue* (of the parties): 'To submit an issue [i.e. the point in controversy] jointly for decision; also, of one party, to accept the issue tendered by the opposite party' (*OED*). Again, the lawyer's bawdy is obvious enough. 'If he had been unable to make love to the lady before, he would have another chance at the next stage.'

Page 334. (1) To go dinnerless. For the explanation of the phrase, see Brewer's *Dictionary of Phrase and Fable*, s.v. *Humphrey*.

Page 335. (1) Richard Nash, known as Beau Nash (1674–1761), wit, gambler, and autocratic master of ceremonies at Bath from 1705 to the mid-1740s, after which his popularity and splendour gradually declined.

(2) This famous quip is repeated almost verbatim by Goldsmith in his *Life of Richard Nash* (1762), pp. 155–6, and in the anonymous *Jests of Beau Nash* (1763), pp. 67–8. The overt allusion is to Tobit's dog in the Apocrypha, 'Tobit', 5 : 16, and 11 : 4. The dog was in fact Tobias's, the son of Tobit, and bears no name. But the joke, quite in character with Nash's cruel habit of ridiculing natural defects, especially deformity, most probably implies a covert allusion to Toby, the dog in 'Punch and Judy', and hence to the hump on Punch's back: it is attested that Nash was fond of the puppet-show drama. 'Toby' also meant 'the buttocks' and the 'female pudenda'.

Page 340. (1) The symptoms of hectic fever were flushed cheeks and hot dry skin, indicating a consumptive state.

Page 347. (1) Betimes, in a short time, speedily.

Page 348. (1) Formerly a very popular toast, 'To the best cunt in Christendom', used again in *HC* pp. 227 and 282.

(2) *Niggers*, in this minced and meaningless oath, is the dialectal variant of *niggard*.

(3) *Caudle*: 'A warm drink consisting of thin gruel, mixed with wine or

ale, sweetened and spiced, given chiefly to sick people, esp. women in childbed; also to their visitors' (*OED*).

(4) A stupid person.

(5) An obsolete form of *Khan*, the sovereign prince of Tartary. It was Smollett who dubbed Dr Johnson 'that great Cham of Literature' in a letter to John Wilkes, 16 March 1759: see *Letters*, p. 75.

Page 353. (1) In one of the two Lower Assembly Rooms, opened in 1730 by Humphrey Thayer, and later known as 'Wiltshire's Rooms'. It was 86 feet long and 30 feet wide. Ball-night was on Fridays. Beau Nash's full-length picture hung there between the busts of Pope and Newton. It is also mentioned in *PP*, ch. lxxv, p. 372.

Page 357. (1) Probably in the obsolete sense of *stupidly, irrationally*.

Page 358. (1) Defined by Dr Johnson as 'A sort of game in which, when a ball rolls into a certain place, it wins.' The chief game of chance at Bath between 1740–5.

Page 362. (1) Where trinkets and knick-knacks were sold. See *HC*, p. 41.
(2) Small diamonds.

Page 364. (1) A most appropriate tag-name. *Top(e)hall*: a country-seat where habitual and copious drinking (cf. *to tope*) takes place, which refers to the squire's bibulous proclivities.

Page 365. (1) Lunge.

Page 370. (1) 'I alleviate hardship by patience.' Unidentified source, but reminiscent of Horace, *Carmina*, i. 24, 19–20 and Virgil, *Aeneid*, v. 710.

(2) 'Something happens in a moment, which you would not have expected in a year's time'; cf. the proverb: 'It chanceth (happens) in an hour, that happeneth not in seven years.' *Quid* should be *quod*. The Latin saying is recorded in Hans Walther, *Proverbia Sententiaeque Latinitatis Medii Aevi* (Göttingen, 1963), I, p. 30, no. 42.

Page 373. (1) In his *State of the Prisons in England & Wales* (1777), the philanthropist J. Howard complains that the bailiffs still 'detain in their houses (properly enough denominated *spunging-houses*) at an enormous expense, prisoners who have money', p. 10.

(2) 'Deposit your money', i.e. 'cash down, please'.

(3) J. Howard advocated the abolition or reduction of fees, including 'the Chamber—Rents for Master-side Debtors' (p. 57). Master-side prisoners could be turned over to the common-side for non-payment of their chamber-rent and for demanding garnish. Howard found that there were 'above forty rooms for Men on the Master's side' in the Marshalsea, while there were only six left for common-side debtors: see J. Howard, op. cit., p. 206.

(4) Or 'feme covert', a married woman, as opposed to a 'feme sole'.

475

Notes

Page 374. (1) 'No person can be arrested within the Verge of his Majesty's Court, without Leave from the Board of *Green Cloth*', G. Miege, *The Present State of Great Britain and Ireland* (1738 edn.), pt. i, 136—but the verge of the court also meant a much larger area, 'privileged from arrests by ordinary officers of the law, and retained its rights till all privileges of sanctuary were abolished' (H. B. Wheatley and P. Cunningham, *London Past and Present* (1891) iii, 432). For the topographical definition of the verge of the court, see John Trusler, *London Adviser and Guide* (1786), pp. 157–8: 'that ground about White-hall and St James's which belongs to the crown . . . Charing Cross . . . Scotland Yard . . . Whitehall . . . and Privy-garden . . . all the parks, St James's, Cleveland-court, and all Hyde-Park, except the mere crossing from the Green-park to Hyde-Park. Most houses in the Verge let lodgings. The Tower is also a privileged place'. See also Paul Whitehead's poem, *The Green-Cloth: Or the Verge of the Court* (1739), which describes the purlieus the debtor is self-confined to.

Page 375. (1) As opposed to the Master-side of the prison: the common offenders were kept there and had to depend largely on charity for their food.

(2) A strip of woven material used to border cloth.

(3) A name of Greek origin, which may be rendered as 'maker of lyrics'.

Page 376. (1) A Roman elegiac poet (*c.* 60–19 B.C.). Melopoyn's elegy is a rather loose imitation.

(2) The name appears in Otway's *The Orphan* (1680) and means 'the lonely girl' in Greek. Smollett used it again as the name of the melancholy heroine in his *FCF* (1753).

Page 378. (1) *Peripeteia*: here used in its proper technical meaning: a sudden change of fortune in a tragedy.

Page 379. (1) Although Melopoyn's story should certainly not be read as straight autobiography, it is nevertheless true that it offers definite parallels with Smollett's vain and bitter struggle to have his tragedy *The Regicide* (finally published in 1749) produced when he first came to London in 1739. For the whole complex eight-year history (1739–47) of *The Regicide*, the preface to the play should be read first; see also Buck (1925), pp. 53–112, whose identifications are adopted here; L. M. Knapp, pp. 49–57, who affords a good factual summary, and P. G. Boucé, pp. 42, 47, 53, 57, on autobiographical elements in Smollett's fictive creation.

Page 380. (1) Drury Lane and Covent Garden operated under Letters Patent granted by Charles II in 1662, a monopoly reinforced by the Licensing Act of 1737, forbidding the acting of 'legitimate' drama elsewhere. The monopoly disappeared in 1843.

476

Notes

(2) Charles Fleetwood (d. 1747) became manager of Drury Lane in 1734, sold his patent in 1744, a gambler and a spendthrift by temperament, well known for his charm. See *The London Stage*, pt. III, 1729–47, ed. A. H. Scouten (Carbondale, 1961), pp. xcii–xcvi. In his preface to *The Regicide* (1749), Smollett refers to him as 'a late Patentee, of courteous Memory, who (rest his Soul!) found Means to amuse me a whole Season', which must have been the theatrical year 1742–3. See Buck (1925), pp. 62–4 on Fleetwood, whose affable duplicity was well known.

Page 382. (1) Unidentified Catholic friend of Smollett, apparently Irish.

(2) Certain performances, fixed long in advance, 'of which the financial proceeds, after deduction of expenses, were given to one—or at the most two—members of the company'. (*The Oxford Companion to the Theatre*, ed. P. Hartnoll (1967), p. 101. See also A. H. Scouten, op. cit., pp. lx–lxvi.

Page 383. (1) Pope's *Pastorals*, written at the age of sixteen in 1704, published in 1709, were first circulated in manuscript among a group of influential literati: Wycherley, Walsh, Congreve, Dr Garth, Sir William Trumbull, and others. As a result, Jacob Tonson was *offering* to print them as early as April 1706.

(2) Lascivious.

(3) The first, *Button, and Button-Hole* (1723) is a bawdy poem replete with sartorial double entendres; the second is unidentified; the third (1721) is also a bawdy tale of lust and drink.

(4) Defoe's popular novels, *Robinson Crusoe* (1719) and *Colonel Jack* (1723).

Page 385. (1) *Grub-street*, in the vicinity of St Giles's, Cripplegate, is best defined by Dr Johnson in his *Dictionary* (1755): 'Originally the name of a street in Moorfields in London, much inhabited by writers of small histories, dictionaries and temporary poems; whence any mean production is called *grubstreet*.' Associated with hack writers from the middle of the seventeenth century.

Page 386. (1) According to Buck (1925), p. 56, 'a composite of all patrons except Chesterfield and the "lady of quality" [Lady Vane]'. Lord Rattle is thus a fictional conflation of the four unnamed patrons mentioned by Smollett in his preface to *The Regicide* (1749).

Page 387. (1) James Quin (1693–1766), a well-known adherent of the old school of acting, a declaimer with a sonorous voice, rather than an actor: he appears again as 'Bellower' in Melopoyn's story. His last years on the stage were eclipsed by the rising star of his young rival, David Garrick. He retired to Bath in 1751. Smollett attacked Quin virulently in the first edition of *PP* (1751) in chapters lv and cii, pp. 274–5. Quin—with whom Smollett had become reconciled—reappears as one of Matt Bramble's

Notes

favourite old friends at Bath in *HC* (1771): see pp. 50–6, 59–60. See also Buck (1925), pp. 65–81.

(2) James Lacy (1698?–1774), a former member of Fielding's company, the first individual to challenge the Licensing Act in the winter of 1737–8, assumed the co-management of Drury Lane with Garrick in April 1747. Basically a theatrical entrepreneur, he is described by Thomas Davies in his *Memoirs of the Life of David Garrick* (1780), i. 93 as 'liberal in his sentiments, though rough and sometimes boisterous in his language', which may perhaps account for his being dubbed 'Brayer' by Smollett. See also Buck (1925), pp. 64–5, 97–9.

(3) Harassing, tormenting.

(4) Smollett's fellow Scotsman, James Thomson (1700–48), whose tragedy *Tancred and Sigismunda* was performed at Drury Lane on 18 March 1745.

Page 388. (1) John Rich (1682?–1761), a famous pantomimist and theatrical manager, produced Gay's *Beggar's Opera* in 1728, and opened his Covent Garden Theatre in Dec. 1732. According to *DNB*, his second wife became a zealous convert to methodism and seems to have terrified him with fire-and-brimstone rant, which explains Smollett's uncharitable allusion to the poor man's head being 'disordered with superstition'. He was quite illiterate and affected never to recall a name. Thomas Davies (op. cit., note (2) to p. 387), i. 325, notices that 'though his understanding was good, his language was vulgar and ungrammatical: he was a perfect male Slip-slop'. This may explain the unflattering nickname, 'Vandal'. Rich had rejected *The Regicide* in the autumn of 1746. Smollett promptly retaliated in *Reproof* (Jan. 1747) where Rich appears 'Fraught with the spirit of a Gothic monk, / . . . with dulness and devotion drunk'. (ll. 167–172). See Buck (1925), pp. 95–7.

Page 389. (1) Astonishment.

Page 390. (1) The playwright's first benefit performance came on the third night, then on the sixth and ninth nights, but the pattern varied with the size of the theatres. The play alluded to is the actor Charles Macklin's *Henry VII* given at Drury Lane on 18 January 1746, which ran for three nights only. The fiasco is also alluded to in the preface to *The Regicide* (1749).

(2) Lord Chesterfield (1694–1773), statesman, diplomatist, and wit, best remembered for his *Letters* to his natural son Philip Stanhope, first published in 1774. He is satirized in *PP* (1751), ch. cii (pp. 646–8). In the preface to *The Regicide* (1749), Smollett calls him 'an eminent Wit'. See Buck (1925), pp. 81–6.

(3) The friend and benefactor of Virgil and Horace, famous for his patronage of the arts; hence, a patron of literature and art.

Notes

Page 391. (1) David Garrick (1717–79), the most celebrated actor of the eighteenth century after his brilliant début in the part of Richard III in London on 19 October 1741, the first actor to attain European fame, manager of Drury Lane (1747–76), and playwright. Smollett attacked him venomously again in the first edition of *PP* (1751) in ch. lv, pp. 273–4, and ch. cii, pp. 651–2. But a reconciliation was effected about 1756, shortly before Garrick produced Smollett's farce at Drury Lane in January 1757. The offending passages were expunged from the second edition of *PP* (1758), and Smollett paid handsome tribute to Garrick in his *Continuation of the Complete History of England*, iv (1761), 126. See Buck (1925), pp. 86–94, 154–6.

Page 395. (1) A talent mentioned by several contemporaries of Garrick, for instance Boswell, who in his *Life of Johnson* (1791) notes his 'admirable talent of mimicry' (Oxford Standard Authors, 1965, pp. 599, 707).

(2) Identified as Lady Vane (*c.* 1715–88) in Buck (1925), pp. 26–7. Her lengthy, and at the time somewhat scandalous 'Memoirs of a Lady of Quality' appeared in *PP* (1751), ch. lxxxviii, pp. 432–539.

Page 396. (1) On 9 April 1747, with Lacy.

Page 398. (1) For a detailed contemporary account of such a trading venture with Guinea, see John Atkins, *A Voyage to Guinea, Brasil, and the West Indies* (1737), pp. 149–80, especially on the proper care to be taken of slaves while on board.

(2) Martinique, one of the French Lesser Antilles islands in the eastern Caribbean.

(3) A commission granted by the Admiralty to the commander of a merchant-ship, or privateer, to cruise in search of enemy merchant vessels. Privateering was abolished in 1856.

(4) A seaport 14 miles south of Cork.

(5) Wetting the sails made them more efficacious, so that a vessel could increase her speed. Technically, 'leeway' means the lateral drift to leeward, or distance between the course steered and the course actually run. In common parlance, the phrase 'to fetch up, make up, catch up leeway' implies that one has fallen behind in something and strives to catch up. Here, Bowling promises to pay quickly Roderick's entire debts.

Page 400. (1) To invest £200 in a commercial venture.

Page 406. (1) Raphael (1483–1520); Titian (*c.* 1490–1576); Guido Reni (1575–1642), early Baroque painter and engraver of Bologna. These three painters are often referred to admiringly by Smollett in his *Travels in France and Italy* (*passim*, letters xxviii, xxxi).

Page 407. (1) During the 1739 war, 'register-ships' were licensed to trade with the Spanish colonies, but forbidden to trade with Spain in Europe.

Notes

See R. Pares, *War and Trade in the West Indies 1739-1763* (1963), pp. 111–127.

(2) A current precaution, or even cure, in the Tropics. See, for instance, John Atkins, *The Navy Surgeon* (1742), p. 359. But T. Aubrey, in his *Sea-Surgeon, or the Guinea Man's Vade Mecum* (1739), already thought this treatment of fever in Negroes ignorant and lethal nonsense (pp. 107–8).

(3) The supposedly French ship outsails Bowling's.

Page 408. (1) The principal sails were made ready for furling; the main topsail is to be set in such a way that it will receive the wind on its forward side, a manoeuvre 'necessary in a naval engagement, to bring a ship back, so as to lie opposite her adversary, when she is too far advanced in the line' (Falconer); tampions were protective plugs of cork or wood fitting into the muzzle of a gun. In other words, the ship was being slowed up or stopped, and prepared for action.

Page 409. (1) Benguela, an Atlantic seaport south of Luanda, now in western Angola.

Page 410. (1) Near Porto Alexandre in Angola 'the most southerly country to which the Europeans usually resort to purchase slaves', R. Brookes, *The General Gazetteer* (1778), 4th edn., s.v. *Negro-Cape*.

(2) Probably a form of typhus, variously called gaol fever, famine fever, Irish ague.

Page 413. (1) *Othello*, v. ii. 349.

Page 414. (1) Conducive to recovery or health.

Page 415. (1) Small seaport on the west coast of Cotentin, Lower Normandy.

(2) Or Caskets, dangerous rocks about 8 miles west of Alderney in the English Channel.

Page 416 (1) The capital of Lower Normandy, a handsome town in the eighteenth century with a celebrated university.

Page 420. (1) A common practice, sometimes not carried out without recourse to violence on both sides. See Boucé, p. 278.

Page 424. (1) *Paradise Lost*, viii. 488–9, Adam's description of bridal Eve to Raphael.

Page 428. (1) Latin *ursus*, a bear: Roderick often refers to the squire as 'Bruin'.

Page 429. (1) Virgil, *Aeneid*, i. 328. 'Oh, a goddess, surely!'

(2) Virgil, *Aeneid*, i. 498–9. 'Even as on the banks of Eurotas, or along the heights of Cynthus, Diana guides her dancing bands!'

Notes

Page 430. (1) *Paradise Lost*, v. 14–15; should read 'whether waking or asleep', again a description of Eve, still asleep, by Adam on awakening.

Page 431. (1) 'Formerly they ran right round the pit, and could hold up to twenty people each' (*Oxford Companion to the Theatre*, p. 123). It was a current practice to send a footman to reserve these fashionably expensive seats and thus show off the family livery.

Page 432. (1) St Bennet's Hill, near St Paul's Churchyard, where the buildings stood until 1867. Defined by W. Maitland, ii, 871 as 'a college for such as study and practise the *Civil Law*, and decide Causes within their own Walls; and the addition of *Commons* is taken from the Manner in which the *Civilians* live here, *Commoning* together, as practised in Colleges'. There were five courts in Doctors' Commons: the Prerogative Court dealt with wills and any contentions arising from them. In these courts the practisers were of two sorts: advocates and proctors, or procurators, the latter being 'they that exhibit their Proxies for their Clients, and make themselves Parties for them' (W. Maitland, ii, 873).

(2) G. Miege in *The Present State of Scotland* (1738) remarks that Edinburgh 'is accounted as populous, if not more so than any city in *Europe* for its bounds', p. 60. But Edinburgh in the eighteenth century was topographically a small place, where, according to W. Maitland, *The History of Edinburgh* (Edinburgh, 1753), pp. 219–24, 9,064 houses were crowded, with a population computed by the author from the accounts of burials at 50,120 inhabitants about 1747, which still made Edinburgh the second most populous city in Great Britain after London (Bristol was the most populous city in *England* next to London).

Page 433. (1) Glasgow, where Smollett also attended the university for some time. See Knapp, pp. 10–23.

Page 434. (1) Cf. *HC*, pp. 242, 254–5.

Page 435. (1) In *PP*, ch. xxxviii, p. 185, the reader is informed that Roderick has 'gained his lawsuit with Mr. Topehall, who was obliged to pay Narcissa's fortune'.